A War
Through Destiny

Sarah Lindsay Peterson

***

ISBN: 979-8-9990589-0-4

Library of Congress Registration 2025

DEDICATION

This book's dedication serves to honor the memory of my two biggest supporters:

My grandmother: Joann N. Iandimarino Forgac.
For being my first listener, but hopefully not my last.

And for my dog, Snoopy, who was right next to me for nearly every word of this book.

CONTENTS

A War Through Destiny

The Path of Purpose Shall Be Fulfilled:
Grace. Love. Purpose. Honor

Author: Sarah Peterson

Cover Illustrator: Amanda Huk

Character Illustrator: Elijah Coker

CHAPTER 1

THE PLAN

Snow swirled around the entrance to the enclave in a dance of jubilant wisdom. Spiraling around as though they were welcoming those who passed through the arch of crystalized ice. Radiant gleams of sunlight seemed to reveal the centuries old markings in historic realism. It was pure, archaic bliss in the one spot that evil never dared lurk.

A centuries old secluded shelter proved to be the best spot for Shaman to gather, though their meeting would not exactly take place in the dwelling. In the beginning, it was distant enough to give them quiet and isolated enough to connect them with the Spirits. In recent years, it was quiet and isolated enough to keep them from being targets of the next vicious battle.

The war had brought with it much change that Dukhovians were not bred for, that the land itself did not know how to become accustomed to. Ancient ice sculptures blown to bits, historic architecture burned to the ground, and once prosperous farmland that grew barely more than a weed.

A gust of wind containing inimitable flakes blew through the opening. The newcomers found their way towards the center—an area surrounded by sculptures which had been there for centuries. Sculptures that always seemed to see more and learn more than those whom dared enter its dwelling.

As they entered, they formed a circle around the statues, seeming to all face one small, stone stoop which appeared to have a hexagonal outline cut from the center. It was only when all eight men, cloaked in dark, hooded wear, gathered silently around this spot, that one man placed a red orb in the center. An orangish-reddish glow illuminated from the orb, encompassing not only the men, but the entire cave.

"Welcome, my friends." It was the man in the center, whom placed the orb, that spoke. "It is always a pleasure to see everyone doing well."

"Alive and well appear to be synonymous these days," remarked the man directly across from the first.

The men were no longer in a cave, but in an area free of anything besides blindingly brilliant light and dense, thick fog. It was now revealed that each cloak bore its own unique color, held together by a similarly unique clasp. The first man who spoke wore green while his responder, a dark burgundy.

"Ah, Serafim, it is important to remember to celebrate the victories we find ourselves able to recognize in these times."

CHAPTER ONE

"I agree with you, Sasha," Serafim replied, while the others nodded in agreement.

Sasha nodded once. "As for recent news, I am afraid I will not have anything which surprises you gentlemen. The most recent battle in this war has ceased and I am hopeful we are on the horizon of peace."

"We are always hopeful," agreed a man called Irenei, a twinkling in his eyes that mirrored his light blue robes.

The room fell silent after that.

"Let us begin the sacred prayer."

In one, smooth motion, each man revealed what appeared to be an exact replica of the statues inside the cave they had once occupied. The objects were placed in front of each man as the prayer began, each taking turns reciting a portion. And then, like a never-ending circle, the prayer turned into a sort of chant, a summons...

"Spirits, we come to you now for guidance, for reassurance. A great battle between our people has ceased, but far greater battles continue to wage. Our people perish; our people suffer. How are we to keep them safe in these times? How are we to keep their faith alive? How might we guide our leader?"

A musical echo encompassed them from all ends. The angelic sound seemed vocal, though rang brilliantly as though instrumental. The stone relics which had previously been placed in front of their holders now rattled about on the stone top, rearranging themselves.

"The Spirits speak of a prosperous time, a time of great harmony," Sasha revealed.

"They speak of a calm to the storm," Irenei added.

"A richness in wealth and an abundance of goods," Grigori spoke it as though it was a command, certain it would come to fruition.

"A day will come of love, where all are one," Aramazd spoke as though he was searching for more behind the words.

"It will come by way of leadership." Artyom was hopeful.

Serafim stared at the relics before him as they shuddered and rearranged, there was a noticeable shift as the energy in the room became chilling, grim. "It will come by way of violence and fear."

"A new heir has been born...?" Anatolii said the words with question. Rarely did the Spirits speak directly to them about the next heir, typically it was announced during the baby's reading at birth.

The Shaman all looked expectantly towards Mitya, awaiting his revelation. His eyes widened and his body began to shake.

The musical echo grew louder and the room seemed to shudder only for a moment before an enchanting voice with piercing words called out around them.

"A joyous event as the Spirit of New Life has bestowed upon us two new lives. The first born to Grace Marie Lin Grayson and Rodney Willard. Here in the country, though banished, she already faces grave danger and danger will continue to follow her as she will be the greatest and strongest heir Dukhovia will ever know. Their relocation will be their greatest strength. The second, born to Nicholas and Annecka Andrews, ensure his past shall be forgiven in order to reserve him a future. The two must grow independently while apart in order to bring great peace and great destruction.

"Though with each new life there comes a purpose, the strength of these young ones will cause great turmoil in our country. There will be war, there will be death. Arrogance will rise once more and the country will be tested like never before. Though to follow them will bring international disdain, to deny them will be a death sentence. And while fear and pain will plague the country ten-fold before a resolution is successful, they are our only hope.

"The war that will unravel as a result of betrayal will be a new beginning or an end to all of Dukhovia. History shall be your greatest guidance, use it as a weapon for peace."

The shining light seemed to fade in and out as the musical voices became ruptured by what could be thought of as wind. Great darkness and silence passed over the men as an array of visions swirled around them…

A boy with dusty blond hair yielding a faux sword in the comfort of his family room.

A field once decorated with ice thistles, blooming once more.

A clock with a hexagonal shape, ticking at lightning speed.

More and more visions of the passing of time flew by until finally silence occupied their space.

Eight pair of eyes made exchanges, penetrating the next or avoiding them altogether in absolute bitter silence.

Another moment of silence passed.

And then another.

Silence echoed into the night all around the howling wind of the enclave.

"Sasha—what can this mean?" Serafim's voice was thick with emotion.

He did not reply. Sasha could not only find his ability to swallow the lump growing larger in his throat, he could not even bear to make eye contact with his comrades or hush the continued wave of swirling thoughts and images in his mind.

"Two new heirs are a blessing…but a Grayson…surely…Sasha?"

Anatolli managed to get the slightest head shake from the shaman.

Another moment of silence passed.

"I think the consequences of these choices are clear, yet perhaps they also might reap benefits," Artyom proclaimed.

"Benefits?" Serafim protested. "Surely the Spirits mean for us to logically decide what to do with this matter. To have an heir from a banished family when tensions are already so high between traditionalists and non-traditionalists…how can it bring anything but devastation?"

"Perhaps that is what the Spirits intend," Artyom spoke wisely and confidently, though his ruffled brow suggested he was still convincing himself of his words. "If our people found fault in a system with no faults, perhaps it will be the thing they fear the most that brings them to a solution."

"It is also imperative to remember that a great number of families were unjustly banished," Grigori said pointedly.

"While none of our family should have been separated for their beliefs, the Grayson family were not amongst the innocent," Mitya proclaimed.

"Where did the family relocate when they were banished, Mitya?" Grigori questioned.

Silence fell around the room as they awaited the response with clenched nerves. "America."

The sound of uneven, gasping breaths and unwavering silence that followed the statement was more conversation than the men had so far. It contained more protest, more agreement, more question, and more response than anything previously uttered.

"We do not know whether this American heir will grow to be traditionalist or non," Aramazd offered uncertainly.

"But from *America*!" He said the name of the country as if to say it were as forbidden as the celebration of its customs.

"Let us not forget that a location does not determine our beliefs," Artyom instructed with diligence.

"Of course. I only mean to look at all points of concern over this matter. Is there any hope of swaying or guiding her upbringing?" Serafim reasoned.

"It will lie in her family's decisions," Mitya said with a shake of his head. "If she could be raised here…Perhaps, if we explain, Arkady would allow the family to move back…"

"The Czar would never allow it." For the first time, Sasha broke from a daze of absolute shock and spoke in a rigid voice. "Two *drastic* decisions have been made here today. To choose an heir whose family has not only been banished, but that has relocated to a country whose common practices are those which would rip our world to shreds…"

Silence fell again for a time until Irenei's voice echoed around in a hollow chill.

"Great destruction and great peace."

Sasha nodded once. "So long as the Spirit's orders are obeyed, this will lead to great peace. Perhaps only after destruction. We must remember that our responsibility is to protect the prediction of the Spirits and never to determine them wise or unwise."

"And the other heir? The Andrews child?"

Sasha winced. "Another grave choice. To choose someone banished due to their family aligning with rebel ideals is dangerous, but to choose an heir whose very ancestry reaps responsibility for creating that divide is a death sentence to this nation."

"The Spirits are tired of war and they are now challenging our citizens to think. I believe that while these choices might be the destruction of Dukhovia, they might also be its savior."

Sasha did not explain further, but this fact would be something he would ruminate over for years to come. After all, it was his job to believe the Spirits and there was no telling from which side the great destruction would come.

"History...shall be a weapon."

Sasha looked down, not answering now, only nodding.

"Why keep them separate?" Serafim questioned. "It seems as though their training must be swayed."

Sasha shook his head. "No. They must be kept separate. They must reach their own paths and beliefs. We must have no factor in who they come to be. In any event, if it is what the Spirits determined, it is her best method of protection."

The others watched Sasha, knowing more was going through his mind on the matter, but they did not push it. Then, suddenly, fiercely, Sasha lifted his eyes to them one final time.

"We must obey the command given to us. We must ensure their protection. Irenei, Serafim, Mitya, and Aramazd, warn the Grayson family and lead them out of the country immediately. Speak to no one else. Let no one else know until the announcing of the new heirs at dawn.

"Anatolii, Grigori, Artyom—we must ensure the safety of the boy. He will not yet be told. This will be best for him. The sooner a protection shield can be cast, the better. Everyone move quickly and discreetly! The Spirits have spoken and so we have a duty to listen and a duty to protect!"

Wide-eyed and still dazed from the events of the evening, the Shaman all moved out, riding horseback through the night, through the winds of the tantalizingly, bitter cold, to complete their missions. Each of them had their own thoughts, their own opinions as to the state of the country, but one thought was universal: this was only the beginning.

In the days, months, and years that would come, the Shaman would come to realize that their most extreme thoughts in the beginning held nothing compared to what would come. From the moment the morning sun rose that next fateful day and the identities of the heirs were divulged, turmoil and disparity began to separate the country. With each passing day, Dukhovians watched as the country they once knew to reign with joy and togetherness, became marred with fear and a rapid increase in emigration. At times, the people were almost certain the state of things could not worsen, but then fate pulled in to prove them wrong. Things could get worse—and they did.

And while the words of the Spirits prediction continued to haunt each and every Shaman for the following days, none struck as painfully, as prominently, as the words uttered to Sasha by Aramazd only moments before leaving the cave...

"Sasha, mind your brother. I fear the moment he finds out, these grave circumstances we are facing will begin."

CHAPTER 2

DECISION OF A LIFETIME

*T*he laughter of Stacy Grace Matthews rang out, calling all stillness to falter and all those weary to transform into jubilance. The gloved hand of the toddler flew into the air and then crashed along with the rest of her body on a snowy bank. It was a relentless business. Her and her mother had been out in the snow patched yard for at least two hours—no—the sun had begun to set, surely it had been longer, but they came out just after lunch time, it could not have been that long...

"Mommy! Mommy!" The voice cried out again and again as she dashed around the mounds of fluff, hiding, and laughing once more as she was discovered. Slowly the aforementioned glove began to move as the protected hand began to wiggle and tear from its chains. More wetness saturated the material, making it even more of an unnecessary nuisance than it already was.

So, she tore it off and wiggled her fingers in front of her mother.

Her mother stood, staring back in defeated, humored awe. "You better get that little glove back on, little missy." Her mother called in a sing-song voice—it was a losing battle and she knew it.

"O-or?" The toddler's voice cooed.

"Or you'll turn into a popsicle and I'll have no choice but to eat you." Her mother grabbed her from behind and pretended to bite at her stomach.

The biggest laughs of all escaped Stacy's mouth. Then she tore off the other glove, her coat, and her hat, and threw herself into the snow where a perfect snow angel was born.

"Feeling better?" Her mother asked.

"F-feel-i-ing be-et-et-etter." The stutter was an addition to her personality at this point. Perhaps due to confusion of learning two languages at once. Perhaps due to confusion over which to use. Perhaps a delay in her processing. It mattered not. It was simply a goal to work towards—and goals were no burden at the Matthews house. They were never without goals.

Stacy's eyelashes blinked flakes away and her green eyes rested on her brother in the window—he had been inside since shortly after lunch—claiming that the cold was hurting his fingers.

"M-mama, w-w-why Dan doesn't l-li-iike the snow?"

Grace looked from the two, a small, meaningful smile on her face. "He does, some people can just handle being colder for longer than others."

"I-it never hu-urts me."

CHAPTER TWO

Grace breathed and smiled. "I know," she said. It was what she would always say.

Until two years later, when she was older and curiosity and confusion began to grow. Then the answer went something more like "because you are from the country of Dukhovia and the cold is in our veins." That led to more questions about the unspoken country of their ancestry—the one they were banished from long ago. What was it like there? Who was there? Why did they leave? Always more questions, always more interest in the country and the feel of the bitter cold...

The answer changed again, after another three years, when there was more puzzlement on her face than there had ever been. The heels of the girl skidded around the ice rink, swinging in her mother's arms. She never even wore a coat now. She had not even owned one in at least four or five years.

"There's something on your mind?" Her mother asked.

Stacy nodded. "It's not the same as everyone else. People can't go out in the cold. I can. I can be out here all day and nothing happens, none of the bad stuff we learn about in school—why?"

Grace breathed in deeply, her famous smile always transfixed on her face. "You are from the glorious land of Dukhovia."

Stacy smiled, ready to soak up another story about the beautiful, wintry country she came from. She always loved the stories, especially as they became scarce—the more her mother divulged, the less she had to offer. She did not live there long and did not have the chance to fully submerge herself when she did.

"But so is Dan. So are you. So is dad and grandpa and Uncle Richey and grandma..."

Grace nodded. "But just like different people are able to handle the cold differently, different people have different purposes in Dukhovia and sometimes this allows people certain...abilities."

"Is that why Rachael can move things without touching them when she's mad?" She asked, pointing out her best friend's ability to make a landslide take place after one screaming match.

"Rachael's traits are more...inherited. They're passed down from her parents. But the country of Dukhovia was built on the foundation that we were all meant for one purpose and that while we might have different strengths and different weaknesses, we'll never fail at where we are meant to be."

She could not explain it, even as time passed and she began to get older. But suddenly all the unasked questions in her head were silenced, the ones that were there but she could never form. Suddenly, they made sense. They made perfect and total sense until she continued to grow and things changed and her friends and peers began to question their own paths in life and the dreaded "what do you want to be when you grew up" question began to surface. It became Stacy's nightmare.

The question never made any sense to her—she would not determine her purpose. She would not simply "choose". She would be called and she would answer. Yet nothing ever rang. And the less it rang and the more questions began to pile up as the pressure was on to answer, the more anxious she became to leave the country and fly home...

...

Stacy yawned setting down yet another pamphlet on a list of criteria to become something that did not seem to need that much criteria. When did she start using the word criteria? Was it before she walked in the gym this morning? Was she becoming college bound by simply being near the tables?

Ugh.

Her eyes watched the clock. Fifteen minutes. Just *fifteen* more minutes of dealing with this place and then she was home bound. The world was her oyster or whatever the phrase was. She could practice with the band, write a new song...She could do anything other than being at school on the absolute worst day of the year.

Career day.

It was the most dreaded day to anyone let alone a high school sophomore. Let alone Stacy. She watched as students stressed themselves out, gathering multiple packets that did not even seems to relate: medical school because dad says that is the only way, entrepreneur because mom says it is the only way to make a lot of money and money equals success, and maybe, just maybe, sneak in beauty school because your passion is telling you to do nails.

Blah.

She tried to at least understand it from her peer's perspective before her own, but failed—they had another three years of experiences that would shape them and possibly alter whatever career choice they chose now—what was the point? What was the point in choosing something and starting out on it just to be swayed completely away from it? Alright, maybe she was being critical. Maybe it was to give them ideas and spell it out so they could make an educated decision. It made total sense. Maybe she simply hated the idea because she had absolutely no idea what career she would choose.

She had considered the question, sure, but never felt passionate towards anything. Nothing specific and nothing completely. She loved music, of course. She loved playing with *The Rockers,* an internationally famous band that she started playing in at just ten-years-old with her four closest friends: Rachael, Cody, Jade, and Miranda. But the idea of doing it as more than just a hobby seemed laughable at best.

The fact was, not only did she not know what she wanted to do or was supposed to do, she also did not think it was her job to necessarily choose.

Okay, so her expectation was not that someone was going to appear before her and whisper that she was meant to be a rocket scientist—that was the last thing she was going to be with her perfect record of D's in advanced science—a class she was only in because the school was waiting for her "family talent" to be realized. Her mother, brother, father, and even her grandparents were the scientists—she was just Stacy.

No, she knew that would not happen. BUT...she did expect that when she stumbled across her big whatever, it would flag her down and deem itself worthy of her. It would not be something she questioned or thought about. It would not be something she would toss to the side simply because the *criteria* were too extreme or not extreme enough—or the pay.

She tried to not be naïve. She did not know if this all-powerful purpose would be something glorious and awe-inspiring. Heck, she was fully prepared to ring someone's groceries up for them one day and be hit with the insight that she was meant to work at the store. All jobs were necessary and that made all jobs important. It might not be flashy, but it would be hers.

"Okay, but in less mystical sounding phrasing and in more words—what does that mean?"

"I will tell you all I know, I promise you that, darling," Grace had laughed. Then her face fell. "But you have to be careful. We aren't supposed to talk about Dukhovia or practice any part of it. We could get in trouble."

"But I thought we were banished—how would they know?"

Grace had shaken her head and confirmed the most difficult part of Stacy's journey—her one and only way of uncovering the country was a locked door. It was not Dukhovia who prohibited them from speaking of the country—it was The United States.

"The reason that your grandfather did all those things in the past..." Grace's voice began to trail off as she unlocked a memory that she never wanted to unhinge. "It was because of Dukhovian herbal remedies blended together to create something that altered his ability to make his own decisions. As part of our punishment, we were banned from anything having to do with Dukhovia."

Stacy's face had fallen too. *"Is that why they don't want to talk when I bring up Dukhovia?"* She felt a singe of guilt now.

Grace nodded, solemnly. *"Yes. They love Dukhovia and know that it isn't right. It makes them very sad...But I know this. The Spirits placed these purposes inside us so if the Winter Spirit gave you your purpose, you might be able to handle the cold better. But, if the Summer Spirit gave me mine, I might be able to better handle the heat. I think they will tell us in their own way, when the time is right..."*

"When's the time going to be right?"

Grace leaned forward and kissed her forehead. *"When you learn patience probably."* She pushed off and skated away into a race.

And so, Stacy never asked her grandparents anything related to Dukhovia. Her mother never offered much more, but at least let her talk about things. She refused to ignore the unfair sting that they were banished from one country just to move to a country that thought Dukhovia was evil. The United States took their entire culture, their entire identity, and she would not accept it. But her only form of rebellion was asking and talking about Dukhovia with at least her mother and convincing her to take her on at least one, secret, forbidden trip. It was two years ago now, but she remembered it like it was yesterday.

Especially since the dream that began that faithful trip continued to come to her.

Another large yawn escaped from her and she caught the eye of her best friend, Rachael. She knew the most about Dukhovia and the dream. Not only was she her very best friend, but the world's best secret keeper—unless it was something related to giving a gift or a surprise—Rachael was a safety net to talk with about Dukhovia and Rachael was the best at getting her to think differently.

She was floating around the education tables. Unlike Stacy, Rachael felt her call and passion surface about a year or two ago, when she volunteered at an after-school program helping first graders learn how to read. She loved children already and being able to help them grow closer to achieving their dreams set her in her spot. It was their foundation; she would always tell them. So, no matter where they went after school, the skills she would start them with would help them find success.

Giver. Lover. That was the entire personality of Rachael Cassidy Leighton: very outgoing, very confident, and very beautiful. Rachael's confidence emanated her ability to ace every test she came into contact with, talk to every boy that flirted with her (which was a high number), and reason her way out of any situation—whether with peer or teacher. Rachael was sure of herself. When a flaw presented itself, she would laugh and soak it up, knowing it was all part of humanity. More knowledgeable in the area than Stacy, Rachael knew she would not be good at everything, but she would be good at what mattered.

Even when her dark side poked out. The weird, genetic condition that Stacy had asked her mother about when trying to understand Dukhovia. Rachael hated it. Ran from it. It was her one and only downfall.

The condition would activate anytime Rachael failed to control her emotions—usually when she was angry or upset. Objects around her would shatter, shake, crash—you name it. Rachael did everything in her power to control it and hide it—sometimes Stacy wondered if her positivity was a façade to keep the condition at bay. But Rachael glowed with happiness to anyone who walked her way, making it easy for people to seemingly forget about the minor issue. Even if it was responsible for the school having several broken doors and several different colors of brick as they had to replace time and time again.

Rachael was laughing with one of the workers of the booth—flipping back her long, soft, golden blonde hair as it flowed down her back in perfection and ease. She dropped the bright red headband that called her brilliant blue eyes to full attention—as if the shine from her magnificent, wide smile needed the help.

She winked at Stacy as she came back up with the headband, taking the moment away from the conversation to narrow her eyes in Stacy's direction. She knew Stacy was thinking about the dream. And she knew what she was trying to convey to her...

Just ask.

That was the confidence of Rachael. Never mind the risk of death and banishment from a second country—just ask your grandparents about the dream. They will have answers. And perhaps they would. But aside from the fact they were not allowed, Stacy saw and felt the sadness that Dukhovia gave them and she refused to be responsible for the reminder.

So, she would continue to think in her own mind, picking apart the dream piece by piece, dissecting each replaying moment: the crash of color, the flash of light, the beckoning of words...

It's coming. They're coming.

The dream first came to her in Dukhovia. She had it each and every night. It grew less frequent as they arrived home and, until recently, was rare. Now, it was picking up pace again. It was always the same things, the same scene, the same words, but more vivid, *louder,* if that made sense for a dream. Like pretty soon the dream would be screaming her awake—as if she ever slept anymore.

The more vivid the dream became, the harder time she had falling back asleep. She would sit for at least an hour thinking about it: what it could mean and who was talking to her—what if it was The Spirit of Winter trying to tell her something? But the land she always viewed was tropical. It never made sense.

And so, sense she did not try to make of it for long before bouncing back to thoughts and questions and then just simply existing...Which was usually when someone approached her.

"Are you okay?" Her cousin and best friend, Cody Robert Grayson, asked as more of a judgment through squinted eyes. Although he was typically hovering close to Rachael, he too heard his calling and was racking up endless information on professional sports. A seemingly needless task as college scouts were already eyeing him.

"Am I okay? I'm at career fair, I'm living the dream, cuz," Stacy joked, ruffling the same jet-black hair all the Grayson's had. He beamed back at her with the matching, Grayson-green eyes.

He shrugged it off as the three went to the front of the gym to meet up with Jade and Miranda.

Jade Cara Corner's arms were full of music programs—she most definitely saw singing as more than just a hobby, even if she would never admit a deep passion with her negative demeanor and lack of pep for virtually anything.

And then there was Miranda Megan Jones. Miranda was the shy sheep of the flock—but powerfully confident when it came to her strengths in computer engineering. Stacy was at least sixty-seven percent positive that was what it was called.

Stacy smiled as she stood with her best friends at the front of the gym. Maybe no one would come speak a job into her brain today, but she had time to figure it out. There was time for her hobbies, time for her friends, and even time for mistakes. Nothing ever seemed clear to her after these stupid, day-long prison sentences. But, today one thing was clear, something that her mother had told her years ago: everything will happen when the time is right.

CHAPTER 3

THE DUKHOVIAN GLORY

There once was a time when peace reigned in Dukhovia. Comradery and a feeling of safe haven was the country's crowning glory. At least, that is what Nicholas had always been told. He had never seen it for himself nor had anyone alive today for that matter.

No, Dukhovia meant something different to him. He noticed himself focusing on his breathing to keep it even as he thought about what those things were. It meant training from birth in every form of martial arts he could master. It was leading a platoon at twelve-years-old, with fire and smoke as his only guide and a trail of blood all he left behind. It was deceit and control. It was intense loneliness. It was shame.

His head began to spin and his vision went rigid as the memories flooded back. Not that they had ever left. They always attempted to consume his every thought, battling one another for a spot at the forefront. The source of power and control within himself nearly perfectly mirrored his external experiences.

There was no comradery. There was no sense of loyalty and safety by those he called ally. Any sense of safety shortly spiraled into intense panic for sheer sport. Dukhovia. The idea that this country was founded on support and patriotism was sheerly laughable. No, Dukhovia to him was something much different, something much more chilling.

He would be lying to himself, however, if he did not admit how, over the years, he had come to feel that he was more like the leaders that had led Dukhovia to its downfall than he was different. Several times he held his head high while carrying out deeds he had been asked to complete. It had not mattered what they were: leading boys younger than himself into battle, setting traps for men he knew were innocent—but it was what he was called to do. He had to get them done one way or another. He had done them with ease and he had done them with honor.

Honor. His eyes grazed the ancient Dukhovian writing on the blade of his sword as he considered the word. That is what this journey, his life, was all about. Redeeming the honor his family had long ago lost. Disdain. Shame. Isolation...

His eyes locked in on the dusty windows fixated on the barn he was standing in. He had been born in this barn. It was all that was left of his childhood memories after his home and the rest of their fields were scorched to the ground. It was here, on the dirt floor, that he was prayed over when a group of Shaman rushed in to explain his fate: that he was an heir, or potential ruler of Dukhovia. Not only did he have potential, he was destined to be the second strongest heir that there had ever been.

This news brought great honor and excitement to his family. For centuries, the family that had to wear the badge of dishonor would finally have a chance at redeeming themselves. Nicholas scoffed thinking of what his training had entailed so far. Yet he ran his hand over the signature on the frame of the barn.

Demitona

It was a name no one knew his family by for several decades. It was a name stripped of them when they were falsely accused of attempting to overthrow the ruler and disrespect the Spirits. Did he miss the double standard? No.

Perhaps that was what Dukhovia was to him—disrespect.

Andrews was the new name given to them. An American name with no meaning and no purpose. The title of such had been given to them unjustly. His family had always been as traditional as a Dukhovian could come and held all the qualities of humble, devote, and hardworking. He had been told there was a time they were sought after as a type of mentor. Again, he had never seen it.

The family he grew up with looked much different. His father, brute and volatile, had always encouraged him to be the best that he could be. No, perhaps encouraged was not the right word...forced. Hm. Perhaps those were not the right words at all. His father had always forced him to obey his every command and reach every skill he was capable of measuring and beyond or suffer the consequences. There. That felt more fitting.

But that was not the fate Nicholas was now faced with—no. He was *second* strongest. Second strongest meant second in line. Shall anything happen to the strongest, he would rule. Shall the strongest lose their ability to rule, he would rule. But until either or those things took place, he would be second. Second was not good enough—not for his family, not for the current ruler, and not for Nicholas.

It seemed almost as if even the Spirits were mocking him now. The chance to finally regain honor for his family was staring him in the face—but not without a blockade as deep as the ocean blocking his ability to access it.

He pressed his hands evenly onto the frame of the window, staring out at the open, snow-covered fields before him, outlined by a thick, humbling forest in the far along distance. Thoughts were infiltrating his mind again and he attempted every strategy he was taught to block them out. Nonetheless, he barely made it through the first breath on his deep-breathing before he stamped his foot angrily onto the hay-covered barn floor.

Second. Could he ever hope for first if he constantly questioned whether he even deserved to be the runner up? His eyes closed and his breathing became uneven as the same images that he saw before bed every night and woke up to in the morning flashed across his memory. The enemies he had forgiven, the friends he had betrayed...

He had walked away with a cold and callous heart in situations that would beg his understanding. He had abandoned those thought to be friends. He had walked away when life and death were on the line, all for the greater of Dukhovia, all for a purpose. He had been responsible for destruction and doom, responsible for loss and chaos. He had been responsible for murder.

Murder.

He sighed. That. That was the fate that now faced him. It was not ruling. It was not regaining his family's honor—well, not exactly anyway. It was the capture and the killing of the one who put him in second place—the strongest heir that Dukhovia had ever predicted to rule.

He was only a child when he was told of his mission to destroy the heir, so it only made sense that the idea would frighten him at that time. Still, even now as he prepared to leave the country and travel to this heir, his heart and mind were at war with each other. The overthrowing of the heir, going against Dukhovian Spirits, was the very thing his family was accused of and disgraced for. Now he was being told it was that very thing that would regain it—he shuddered at the thoughts.

There were differences, though, he was told. It was these differences that led him to agreeing and these differences that compelled him to believe that what he was doing was, in fact, the right thing to do. The heir, though born in Dukhovia, was banished, and consequently brought up in the most traditional country on Earth—The United States of America.

Nicholas had been told a lot of things about Dukhovia—the way it used to be and the way it currently was. He had been told even more about America. Some referred to it as a hellish type place on Earth. Others prayed in its direction as if it were hell itself, hoping to prevent its fire from spreading. Nicholas had heard stories of those from other parts of the world that travelled to America with intent on it being a safe haven—only to find years later that it would turn into quite the opposite.

No matter the story, he knew for certain that Americans were traditionalists. They did not practice the harmonious and simplistic lifestyle that made Dukhovia what it...was supposed to be. Inventions made out of sheer laziness would mock their simplistic way of life. Idol worship of other humans would dishonor even the idea of their Spirits. It was for that very reason that if this heir came to power at a time when Dukhovia's feud over traditionalism and non-traditionalism was at its height, it would mean destruction for any piece of harmony that Dukhovia possibly still held onto.

Going against the Spirits was never a calling. Then again, having two heirs that were greater than any others had ever been called to be was also never the calling. What if this was how he became number one? Through showing the Spirits that he was not afraid to go to any lengths to save his country.

Sometimes the thought made him feel confident in his path, other times it caused the knot in his stomach to grow until it reached his heart and his mind. It made him think of his father. He imagined that the angry and violent demeanor he took on was for the same reason Nicholas adapted his—honor.

Ever since their family became publicly disgraced, it became the new repute of the Demitona name. Or rather, Andrews. They would go to any mountain, cross any river, in order to find what was once theirs. Nevertheless, his father never found that honor before his untimely death, thus making it even more imperative that Nicholas, the last living member of his family, be the one to do so.

And that was why he now had to take on any task assigned to him by his mentors—to regain honor, to save the country from further doom, and because quite honestly…any other option failed to exist. Because anytime he had ever tried to run, he quickly learned through beatings and other various forms of torture that he belonged to anyone but himself. So, he accepted the situation with pride and he accepted it with honor.

Dukhovia. Perhaps it did not mean comradeship to him. Perhaps it did not mean loyalty or patriotism. Perhaps it meant anger. Dukhovia was infuriating.

The sound of horses in the distance brought Nicholas to attention. He continued to stare out the space between the wooden planks of the barn while listening and waiting. The loose plank had always been good for that. When he was growing up, he would stare out it every night awaiting his father's return from town while his mother began dinner. In the beginning he would sit on a stool holding one of his favorite animals from the farm. In the last days, he would be sharpening his knife. He let his thoughts wander only for a moment before sighing heavily once then taking one last glance around.

This barn—it was home. It had always felt that way. From the floor he had been born on nearly sixteen years prior, to the last positive memory of his parents, to this moment: the final time he would stand on this farm without the honor his family rightfully deserved.

He breathed in once, composed himself, and stood at attention as the barn doors swung open and three men walked in as if the farm were just as much their home as his—but a home they found distasteful.

Czar Arkady brought his foot back down on the ground after kicking the door open, managing not even the slightest wrinkle in his neatly pressed, deep blue suit. Nicholas's eyes went straight to his top left breast—as they always had. The area was decorated with badges he had earned and was able to bestow so that the world knew they owed him respect. Nicholas had never been closer to earning his own.

Two men flanked him, both in similar suits, though, Alexander, the Admiral, wore a light blue decorated uniform. He had been in charge of the war at sea for several years and spent most of his time away for this purpose. The number of badges across his front explained that rather well, but it did not give hint as to whether or not these were positive wins for Dukhovia.

The last man, Albert, he was different. If he had to pick one of the three to claim a closeness to, it might have been him. At least, in the beginning. Now he had taken on a certain distaste for the man whose chest only bore two badges that may as well have been as insignificant as the deep green color of his uniform. The same uniform that Nicholas found himself in—until today.

Czar Arkady entered the room in as short-tempered a mood as he was always in, quickly throwing a sack to Nicholas that he was to assume held his clothing and anything else he might need on his travels.

Nicholas's face remained unchanged, as a tribute of respect. It had become all too easy for him now, after all of his training. The years of isolation and discipline he faced after having to leave his family were meant to leave him detached and glacial. Never to shudder in times of sadness, never to blink in times of fear. As if those emotions even existed anymore. Though there was a time when they weighed heavy on his heart, he knew his path and was more inclined now than ever to serve his country.

"Well, Nicholas, your day to become a man has finally come. How do you fair?" It was asked more like he was reading from a script then of genuine concern, still, Nicholas answered on the mark.

"Fine, sir."

"And your skills?"

Without warning, the Czar unhinged a sword from his belt and shot it up in the direction of Nicholas, slicing down on the air where he stood. Nicholas was quicker, after all these years, he immediately dodged the would-be attempt on his life and used his weapon to block the Czar's sword from acting on the offensive any further. With a turn of his blade and a flick of his wrist, he sent the opposing weapon clanking into the dust-filled planks beneath them.

Nicholas could not help but allow a small hint of a smile to take form on his lips.

"Very good, very good indeed," the Czar muttered, again, sounding unimpressed. Nicholas had learned by now that the Czar's agenda was of upmost importance while everyone else's was of upmost inconvenience. However, he was surprised that this attitude would carry over even on this most important of days.

"It appears I have taught you well, Sir Nicholas," The Czar commented, never missing a chance to brag on his skills.

"Yes, sir, you have," Nicholas commented, remaining glacial.

The Czar scoffed and began circling Nicholas, looking him up and down like he was examining a kill brought back by the dining staff, determining if it were good enough to consume. "Then show me." In that same breath, he lifted his leg to kick a loose plank, causing it and the few boards around it to snap out of place and fall directly down towards Nicholas's head.

In a flash quicker than light, Nicholas lifted his elbow, stopping the plank. He then rounded his body, lifting his leg to trick his opponent, only to come back and use the board to capture him and hold it close to his neck.

"Impressive."

Nicholas knew the comment was more a pat on his own back and remained silent.

"At ease, Nicholas…Albert."

The man came forward, opening a map of the world before Nicholas's eyes. The Czar took the map from his hands and made his way over to the back of the barn where a small, frail desk sat. Throwing the contents shattering to the floor with one even swipe, The Czar placed the map down and stuck his finger in a line from Dukhovia to The United States. It was the longest span of time he had ever laid eyes on the map without it being ripped away from him, assuming his memory was photogenic and absorbed all the information he needed to know. He attempted to tune into this undiscovered skill now and memorize as much of the map as possible before this too suffered the same fate.

"Just before sunrise an aircraft will land on our premise to take you as far as the center of Spain…"

"An aircraft?" Nicholas was bewildered. He had never flown before or even seen an aircraft for that matter. He assumed he would be travelling by water and his plan—as much of it as he was able to work out without having much information—was dependent on such. He quickly started recalculating in his mind.

"Which will take you to a station where you will fly with common people. This will take you directly into America."

Nicholas tried to let more information absorb, but his head was spinning already. What did he mean fly with common people? Non-military? Where were they going? Was it for simple leisure? He tried to form a nod, but was almost certain something that more closely resembled a circular motion was put forth.

"Now. The heir you seek will be somewhere in this area." He circled much of the Northeastern region with his finger. Nicholas compared the scale size with that of Dukhovia and the maps key, causing his eyes to bulge.

"You do not know where the heir is?!" He asked frantically.

The Czar slammed his fist down, nearly tearing the frail map. "Nicholas, if you would like to tell me how to do my job, then perhaps you shall do as I say and receive that job. Until then, I suggest you refrain from acting like an insensible, imbecilic child and be grateful that you have survived to even see the last fifteen years and have not starved, not gone without shelter, and have, for all intents and purposes, had a fair life!" His words leaked more venom the longer he drawled on.

Nicholas might have been more frightened, fearing the lashes he had become all too accustomed to, had his mind not immediately burst into laughter. Not starving in and of itself was a joke. Nicholas was barely given enough to be kept alive when he first came to Arkady. The more he did as he was told, the more he was rewarded. But then a moment's hesitation could send all he earned spiraling backward. If he had kept tally, he knew for a fact he would come up with more days locked in a dark cellar than he did sitting in the formal dining rooms.

He looked at the map closer, studying The United States up closely for the first time. It appeared to be separated into fifty different states. What did he need to know about those states? Their customs? Were they ruled under different laws? He was beginning to feel ill with the lack of preparations.

He closed his eyes for a moment. Trying to focus in on what he had been taught. English for one—losing his accent. He had been told that in order for his mission to be successful, he would have to blend. He was not meant to arrive as a Dukhovian, doing so would frighten the heir, due to their banishment. Instead, he was meant to earn their trust, befriend them even, and somehow convince them to return to their native country.

He was versed in some of their practices—things important to Americans, their holidays, and some of their daily functions. He knew that they used electricity for everything, whereas Dukhovia used it sparingly. There were some spots of Dukhovia that even had a computer, but it was reserved for medical doctors, even those were thought to be too traditional over healers.

Nicholas let his mind wander over to his plan to get the heir back to Dukhovia. It took some planning; Nicholas had only ever had one friendship and that did not last very long. Any of the other children in his age group he was quick to threaten a death sentence to any time they hit a nerve—that did not lead to an accumulation of an overabundance of allies. However, he reasoned he would become familiar with the heir's understanding of the country, vaguely engaging conversation around the idea of travel, then recommending it as an act of bravery and honor to the nation. If they had any Dukhovian morals at all, it was a surefire way to yield a positive result.

That was assuming he managed to find the heir.

"Well, what *do* you know, sir?" He asked, tacking on the end as a point of finesse to attempt at receiving an answer rather than another shouting match.

Arkady was not so naïve, but he huffed angrily and answered pointedly. "The heir is the second born to Rachael Grayson. The family was last known to have lived here…" He pointed towards the edge of the map, on a state called New York. "…but they could have travelled anytime in the last 15 years."

The relationship between Arkady and Nicholas was quite unique. Arkady ruled his kingdom and those closest to him under the sharpest sword. He had been known to execute anyone who even slightly appeared "off" in the presence of the Czar. However, Nicholas had learned over the years (though he wished he learned it sooner) that at the end of the day—Arkady needed him and that gave him the upper hand.

"So, you have had fifteen years to find out. What were you doing, sir, picking ice thistles?" The Czar lifted his elbow high in the air, forming a fist that aimed and rounded directly for Nicholas's eye. Nicholas felt the edge of The Czar's sleeve swipe across his face and then nothing. The edges of his mouth turned up into the faintest smile. A black eye would look suspicious. For the first time in his life, Arkady could not touch him.

"Might as I like to have the time to do ANYTHING I might find interest in, I have been raising and training an ungrateful, disrespectful, absolute..."

The Admiral cleared his throat, allowing The Czar to catch himself in the raising of the leather rope he favored in beating Nicholas with.

"How then am I expected to begin my search?"

"I suggest you use your training, Nicholas III. Align your channels to be led to the girl. Shall I travel there for you too? Will you be able to find the rest quarters and empty your bladder independently? The family is also apparently well-known in the country, I suggest you use that as a point of reference as well."

Nicholas's interest peaked. "Well known? In a constructive manner?"

Another sound of pity sounded from Arkady's mouth. "I would highly doubt it, Sir Nicholas, something about the heir playing musical instruments or this or that..."

Instrumentalist. New York. Youngest of Rachael Grayson. Well, he had something to go off of after all—and more to use to get on the heir's good side. Though, Nicholas did not play any instruments himself. However, he would have taken the time to learn— had he been told this information prior to his departure date.

"Now then. Sonjay will arrive any moment to take you to Spain. Are there any other interrogations I should subject myself to?"

"Just one," Nicholas remarked. "Is the heir male or female?"

To his surprise, Arkady burst into what could only be described as laughter.

"Surely you do not think a woman could run a country. They are built for trivial tasks—caring for the home, cleaning the meat."

"So, then, I am to assume the heir is female?" Nicholas retorted, a coy smile on his lips.

Arkady dropped his lax demeanor. He began shouting and screaming at Nicholas, ignoring any attempts from the other men to calm him. Nicholas, however, was already on the defensive. He moved almost gracefully, blocking Arkady's attempts to whip him until Nicholas finally pulled his sword out and held it at the Czar's neck.

CHAPTER THREE

"It appears you have taught me too well," Nicholas grinned.

The Czar hesitated, seeming unsure whether to round the sword on the child himself and develop a new plan entirely, or breathe. Anger rising, he ducked away from the blade, his rage flailing at no target directly. His leg swung up into a roundhouse kick, knocking out the wooden pieces that created Nicholas's peek-hole. Almost simultaneously, his fist rounded into the furthest wall and sent that falling, leaving a cloud of dust and the sign bearing the Demitona name in its wake.

Nicholas only had a moment to glance down at the name, perfectly intact on the ruined floor. In the next moment, a buzzing sounded all around them, distracting every former thought almost entirely. The barn rattled and shook, sending several remaining pieces of roof falling. Had Nicholas's ears not been better trained, he would swear it was an attack. Instead, following the Czar and his men as they marched out of the barn, Nicholas found himself face to face with his very first aircraft. Every piece of former confidence left an empty hole in his stomach. His fingers switched and breathing became uneven.

Sonjay did not waste time with greetings. He touched down just long enough to board Nicholas and launch himself back up, the screeching sound of scraping, broken metal peeling at Nicholas's ears the entire way.

Nicholas looked down as he was flown away. He was not sure what type of send-off he was expecting. It was nothing grand, certainly. But somehow, the image of Arkady and the Admiral glaring at him and the perhaps half wave that Albert gave did not fit the bill.

He sat back in the seat provided for him, clutching the map that Arkady thrust into his hand before he ran off, and considered everything he knew once more.

Youngest of Rachael Grayson.

Possibly living in New York.

Musician.

Absolutely female.

And for Dukhovia? As he relaxed at the thought of being away from The Czar, yet the pit in his stomach only grew, he finally realized what Dukhovia was to him. Loss. Confusion. Brokenness. Pain.

Dukhovia to him was isolation.

CHAPTER 4

A LEAP IN THE PATH OF FAITH

S tacy threw the few packets she picked up from the career fair on her bed, not entirely convinced that she would ever look at any of them again.

There was a music school in New York—completely out of question even if she were to consider staying in the music field. Stacy's family used to live in New York and did not exactly leave the grandest impression—it was one of two states they were not allowed to travel to when the band toured. They were told it was too dangerous for anyone in the family.

Yet another restriction, she mentally noted. No Dukhovia in Dukhovia. No Dukhovia in America. No New York. No Montana—but that was another story.

Teaching was an option she only half considered. The only benefit would be working alongside her best friend, which completely shut down her desire to do something unique and purposeful.

Psychology and Philosophy. Being able to understand the mind of others as well as persuade it always seemed interesting to her. Not to mention a deep call that she could not explain to philosophical understandings. She was never a very spiritual person, at least she had never acted on it.

It was simply one of the few things she knew about Dukhovia—the Winter Spirit was strong in her. Whatever the heck that meant. She never felt cold. Nix that, she felt cold. She felt the numbing of her arm. She felt the chill against her skin. But she loved every moment of it and so did the parts of her body that fought off frostbite and succeeded...or the parts of her Spirit?

Then, for some ungodly reason, she stopped at a government and politics table when it was the only one she was able to get near. She did not have even the slightest bit of interest in keeping the packet let alone actually pursuing a career in politics—the thought alone put her to sleep.

She considered the military a little more strongly than she had anything else. But she found it hard to consider fighting for any cause in the country she presently lived in, when there was another country she loved...

Dukhovia. Stacy's eyes wandered above her dresser, where a flag of the nation loyally hung ever since she was young. A sense of longing filled her. Aside from the two erratic years of back and forth that she spent in Dukhovia after birth while her mother was in a coma, she had only been there once—a few years ago. Her mother decided that it was time she see where she was from.

Thus it was that she fell even more in love with the ice and everything it brought, such as skating. Thus it was she fell even more in love with the water and all it brought, such as swimming. And thus it was she fell even more in love with the snow—submerging herself in it every winter until the chill encapsulated her body enough to get her to feeling as close to Dukhovia as physically possible.

She closed her eyes, allowing her memory to submerge itself in the far-away land. She was a still figure beneath a moonlit path of ice and snow, overlooking frozen lakes and waterways that stood to encompass elegant ice sculptures. Where the water did not freeze, pathways of travel existed in the form of open ocean and straights, right through the heart of the city.

Her heart leapt at the thought of returning to the simplistic markets, built within contrasts of intricate architecture: bridges, stone statues, temples, and shrines. All of these things were encased in the surrounding mountains and pine tree.

The darkness. The cool breeze. It was a law that nothing more than the smallest flame in the street lamps should be ignited at night, so that the moon could shine its strongest and provide as much guidance as possible. It was the Dukhovian belief that fire—and inadvertently electricity—blocked the Moon Spirit from being in its full earthly potential. When the moon shined its brightest, the country was protected.

The scent of wood-burned fire lined every street, while stews and soups simmered in most homes. Scents of finely chopped vegetables and scare amounts of meat fought for rights, then intertwined. Meals were more of a cultural practice than a simple fulfillment of belly growls, as was Stacy's familiarity.

Then there was the water. Of everything Stacy knew about Dukhovia (or the lack thereof) the water meant most to her. It was the one thing that always brought the calmness of Dukhovia. She could not explain it, she did not know why, but a connection and a peacefulness that only existed in the water overtook her. In the rain, in a pool, any time, any place…

She had always been drawn to it—not seeming bothered when rain trickled down her face, picking up swimming as if it were another form of breathing… The waters seemed to wrap themselves around her and protect her, she felt safe even if turbulent seas came through.

Even in the coldest of waters, she felt herself right at home. The winters that she had experienced did not even bring the slightest shiver to her spine let alone bring cause to "bundle up" as was the go-to for others. She only wore a hat, coat, and gloves out of the necessity to avoid illness—but she did not even seem to need that.

Throughout her whole life, Stacy Grace Matthews never so much as had a headache, runny nose, or a cold. She never felt an upset stomach, spent a week in bed, or felt the unnecessary comfort of chicken noodle soup. Her friends laughed and called her the luckiest girl in the world. Wherever Stacy went, good nature seemed to follow.

It was not just with her health she was incredibly lucky: Stacy always seemed to be good at anything she tried. When she failed a test, it did not seem to matter, something always happened that got that grade disregarded or so the bad grade just did not make a difference. When it was basketball, track, or volleyball season, she shined like a star.

But it was never enough. Did she have fun? Absolutely. But compared to the peace, compared to the sure feeling of absolute perfection, she felt…isolated. She also was not sure her connection to the water made sense with her connection to the winter—were they the same Spirit? Different? Cousins?

Stacy was not totally naïve. She was happy to see as she grew that her family did not follow the law of avoiding Dukhovia nearly as strictly as she originally thought—but also not as loosely. They spoke the language—but the main language was Russian. She supposed that was easy enough to cover up as being non-Dukhovian. Though, they did occasionally speak ancient Dukhovian—a language Stacy struggled to learn after struggling to learn Russian and English at the same time as it was.

Still, Dukhovian practices were scarce and inconsistent. Tom and Terra would engage in the telling of a story, but with discretion that seemed to quickly trickle towards nothingness. And so instead of answered questions, Stacy's mind began to pile more and more with them.

Stacy cocked her head to the side as memories of her short journey to Dukhovia flooded her. She did not have many things to remind her of her travels besides the pale blue flag displaying the Dukhovian coat of arms in white at the center: two wolves holding an orb and scepter over the ocean, the moon peaking up from behind. Ancient symbols representing generosity, loyalty, and courage stood between symbols Stacy was not sure what they meant.

Aside from the flag, she had only two other pieces of memorabilia: a necklace given to her by the one and only jerk they spoke to while there, and a stone or a gem or a some type of shiny and deep purple stone. None of them ever helped her feel what she felt when she was in Dukhovia—closeness, peace, purpose…and none of them ever helped with the dream.

The only other Dukhovian prized-possession she held was a half thought-out journal where she began to write down everything her grandparents did tell her about the country. There were never complete sentences, but she could make out the ideas, which was more than she could say for any of her school work.

Vodva—Capital

St. Karsburg—largest city. Palace.

Ugh. Two of the most beautiful cities that she had ever been to. Simple villages spilling into cobblestone streets lined with cottages and shops. The teal blue and faded brick palace. No signs of cars—they did not exist in Dukhovia. No *worldly possessions*. That was the term used by the boy that had shown them around. Everything that existed served a purpose and if it did not serve a positive purpose, it did not exist.

That was where Stacy's struggles came in. She loved Dukhovia. She loved everything that meant being a Dukhovian. But she also loved her style of music that was as taboo to Dukhovia as her own two feet. She loved her guitar pick collection as much as Rachael loved her shoe collection. What would happen if she were to move there? Would she give those things up? Not that she even knew she wanted to move there, but she wanted *something*.

More to it, she felt like this dream was telling her she *had* to find and do that something. She felt a burning inside of her screaming at her to find the answers, find a way. The racing of her heart that usually picked up when these thoughts came was becoming an uneasy expectation at this point. It was not meant to be ignored, yet, what options did she have?

Ask her grandparents. Okay, fair enough. They were extremely knowledgeable about the Spirits and she knew it—more so than her mother and father. But every time she considered this, she pictured their faces—Terra's would be lost, her eyes searching whatever she may have been doing in front of her aimlessly as her thoughts were lost in the past. And Tom—feelings of shame and guilt creeping inside of him, although he would never act on them. They would answer her, sure, but they would be miserable.

And so here she was, doing the only thing she could think to do—nothing. Well, it was either she does nothing or she wait around for years to come for a random Dukhovian stranger to find her on the streets and tell her life's purpose. Ha.

Food in markets. Sold out of homes. Bananas?

Relics only sort of "extras". You know—things that we the people deem necessary that they the people say are irrelevant. Irrelavent? One of those is probably right.

Many other items lie in the locked keepsake box that she stored her most valued belongings in. Some of them she had since she was a baby and looked at them so frequently, she could have sworn they were an everyday part of her life. A torn scrap of a baby blanket was something she revisited often—a reminder of the dangerous escape from the country that resulted in Kevin getting shot in the leg.

She laughed a scornful, pitiful sound as she lifted a silver, heart-shaped necklace out of the box, dangling it from the chain for only a moment. It was given to her by Samuel Beningfield: the one person she met, began falling in love with, and was heartbroken by all during her one and only trip to Dukhovia.

Pained and disgusted by the memories it brought, Stacy dropped it back in her keepsake and locked it up. Horrible memories, but beautiful carvings, handmade in Dukhovia.

"Stacy Grace."

The joyful voice of Stacy's loving and erratic mother infiltrated her thoughts and caused her to fall off track completely. She had ways of charmingly and yet spontaneously bursting in that gave tribute to her name—Grace. Although, that was not her birth name. Her parents had named her Rachael, but, when she lost her Aunt Grace at a very young age, she made the name switch.

Stacy laughed quietly and rolled her eyes; she could not help but smile anytime her mother was nearby. She was always in a good mood, cheering her up even when she did not even know she needed it. Her mother was as go-lucky and easygoing as one could get, while still maintaining total communistic control over remaining a tight knit family.

It was a blessing and a curse. Stacy's family and the life she had in America were the things making it impossible to imagine fulfilling any type of life in Dukhovia. They might travel with her, but she could never ask them to make that sacrifice. It was too much. Not only would they be giving up their country and homes, they would be giving up the lifestyles they were suited to. She cringed trying to imagine Rachael in a country without a mall, Cody in a place without football, and any one of them in a place without the band…

"Grace Marie Lin," Stacy sang back.

Grace Matthews appeared in the doorway, smiling brightly. "That's mother to you." She came into the bedroom and stood next to Stacy expectantly.

"How was career day?" Grace asked with a slight hint of remorse, knowing about Stacy's internal battle.

Stacy looked at her mother with agitated eyes and groaned.

"That good, huh?" Grace smiled, leaning her head against Stacy's dresser, her eyes full of support and adoration as she waited patiently for Stacy to continue.

"I just don't feel like any of that stuff is meant for me," Stacy searched her thoughts for the right words, but they would not come. She could never explain to anyone, even herself, the devotion she felt to fulfilling her life's purpose without knowing what it was. "It's like I'm in a box surrounded by all this stuff that is being forced on me and I'm supposed to break out or give in."

"Maybe you should just focus on the desires you have instead of how exactly you will accomplish them. If you like music, play music and see where it takes you. Don't necessarily plan on a music career. Volunteer at the airport and if you like that, keep doing that and see what speaks to you."

Stacy nodded solemnly. It did make sense, in theory. But as she imagined it, she felt the box closing in tighter and together around her. "I'm not even sure I know what my desires are," Stacy sighed, bending one knee to lean against the dresser in shame.

"But," Grace began optimistically. "You know the things you love."

Without hesitation, Stacy straightened up and reached for the flag beside her. Her mother's eyes followed her, knowingly. Stacy caressed the wolves, stroking the symbols with extra care and ease. The flag was more than a symbol of her nation, though that held a lot of merit—it was a reminder of who she was and who she should be.

"Dukhovia," she whispered. "When we were there, I felt like I belonged. I felt protective and when we left, I felt like I was abandoning everyone there." The box did not feel like it existed.

"When you told me that it was my home," Stacy went on, "there was no question about it. I could be there every day and never feel the isolation I feel here. I feel like…almost like I have to be there." Her voice became a mere whisper as she started speaking only to herself.

Feeling defeated, Stacy wandered over to her vanity table and sat down, staring at her reflection in the mirror as if something would magically change and she would have everything figured out.

"Then you'll find it," Grace replied, taking her daughter's hair into her hand and brushing it soothingly. "Your willingness to end your search is what will make it matter most. People search for many years with desires to bring about change without any idea how to do it and so nothing ever happens. Listen to every smaller call you hear, and it will lead you to your destiny."

Stacy glanced off into the distance, not entirely convinced.

"Do you remember what else I told you?" Grace mused, whisking her daughter's hair into her hand once more.

Stacy closed her eyes and nodded. How could she forget? The sound of the cool waves hugging each other in the Dukhovian waters entered her ears. She felt the breeze of the freezing winds as her mother's words echoed into her mind.

"You are not meant to fit into the world, you will hear your call and the world will open for you."

Stacy gulped, a new fear bubbling in her body at the thought of finally finding what she was meant to do. "What if I fail?"

To her surprise, Grace chuckled casually, as if there were some hidden joke. "Oh darling, the only way you could possibly fail at what you were born to do, is if you don't try. At least, that's what the rumor is, what do I know?" She shrugged.

A smile spread over Stacy's face. The plunge of guilt and confusion ate away at her, but her mother's positivity knew how to turn her pessimism to optimism—perhaps it was her purpose.

And though that lump in the pit of her stomach continued to hang out, her brain could no longer argue. She believed in fate and she believed what her mother was saying.

Honk! Honk!

"Come on, Stacy! We're on a tight schedule!"

"No, no, take your time, we totally have all day!"

"Don't encourage her!"

Grace and Stacy turned their attention to the front of the house.

"Sounds like your brother and cousin are ready for you."

"It's just a small performance, I don't know what the big deal is," Stacy said with a smile and roll of her eyes. She leapt up and dashed over to her dresser, quickly pulling things from inside, leaving shirt sleeves and pant legs hanging out as she slammed the drawers and went again.

"You know your brother," Grace offered.

"The biggest perfectionist and greatest manager in the whole wide world!" Stacy shouted, racing down the steps. She threw the door open, smiling as she spotted her father's '97 Oldsmobile—Dan's for the day while her father, Kevin, was at work and Dan worked on building his 'new' car. Inventions were a favorite for Dan, and that made him the best band manager anyone could ever hope to find.

"Glad you could join us," Rachael winked from next to her. Her hands were busily sewing a red, sparkling dress— no doubt her arrival dress for the performance tonight. The band had matching outfits for when they were on stage, but Rachael was well known for making iconic entrances by always coming out of the bus in some new, flashy, and self-designed outfit. Her fans always looked forward to it with much anticipation.

"Happy to be here," Stacy joked back.

Miranda smiled and waved from next to Rachael, Jade sat unmoved behind the passenger's seat which held Cody.

"Oh, like it's so funny. You guys know it's coming down to crunch time before the show, and we still have to stop for Miss Priss back there to get whatever she needs that's so important."

"It's called fashion, Daniel," Rachael spoke delicately. "Tell me, would you rather have an ordinary band or an extraordinary band that takes the world by storm by appearance alone." Rachael's eyes glowed as she looked off into the distance to imagine it.

Dan ignored her, grunting under his breath as he made each turn slowly and carefully…and slowly. As soon as he got the chance to stop, he rested his head on the steering wheel, running his hands through his spiked, black hair. It nearly mirrored Cody's, save for Dan's shorter length.

"Hurry up, we only have…"

"Three hours before we're expected to perform—be quick and be agile, grasshopper, time is *clearly* of the essence."

With Stacy's words of wisdom in her thoughts, Rachael hopped out of the car, returning as soon as Dan drove once around the parking lot, now carrying a bag containing a single orange flower and a few other items.

"Oh my gosh, wait till you hear what just happened to me…" Rachael pushed a beautiful piece of blonde hair out of her eyes as she quickly crawled over Stacy to take her seat in the car waiting for her.

"Only you could go into the store for thirty seconds and come back out with a story," Cody said with a smirk, his eyes peeking into the mirror from the passenger seat. He met Rachael's gaze for a split second before they both blushed and glanced away.

"It was very traumatizing," she reasoned.

"I just can't believe we stopped at a store for anything twenty minutes before we're expected to arrive." Dan's voice was cross, his face focused, as he looked both ways across the street three times and pulled back onto the one-way street.

"Twenty minutes," Rachael's eyes widened. "I better get busy." Rachael quickly forgot her trauma and bent down in front of her to pick up her large suitcase from the floor of the car. She snapped open the locks revealing all the necessities of a sewing kit.

"What does it even need, Rachael? It looks beautiful already," Cody remarked, turning slightly to turn the dress over in his hands.

"Why thank you, Cody, but it isn't quite perfect. Right now, it's just a normal dress—ravishingly stunning, of course, but too ordinary." Rachael ripped the sleeve on one of the arms of her dress.

"Destruction, that's exactly what it needed," Jade remarked monotonously.

"I'm going to dress up a big, orange flower, it'll be just the touch it needs to draw in everyone's attention." Rachael held the dress up against herself smiling adorningly as she imagined her debut once more.

"That'll be perfect, Rache," Cody smiled.

"Oh, come on, Romeo, just ask her to marry you already," Stacy called out, rolling her eyes at how the two interacted.

"It's called a compliment, cuz, try it sometime," Cody shot back.

Rachael smiled at the exchange, but made no comment as her hands began busily sewing orange ribbon onto the flower and covering it in glitter. Once complete, she planned to sew it onto the shoulder that she had ripped.

Dan's reaction to the bickering was not so low key. He grabbed his steering wheel hard and exhaled a deep breath, honking his horn at the driver in front of him for doing something perfectly safe and legal.

"Oh, lighten up, Danny boy, we'd get there in plenty of time if you didn't stop for green lights," Stacy smiled from the seat directly behind her brother.

"You can't trust anyone, Stacy. It's my job to take care of you guys and I intend to do as good of a job as I can with that," Dan seemed to have a hint of pride in himself, although he was mostly still filled with frustration.

"Actually, I believe your job is to manage us," Stacy reminded him.

"Do our light shows and other electric-y things," Rachael went on.

"Tell us when we sound good and when we sound like crap," Jade offered.

"Fix the bus with your mechanical and inventor skills," Miranda smiled. That was probably one of the greatest things about Dan. The fact that he was an inventor and basically good at anything that they needed him to be for the band made him the ideal manager. Aside from just being able to build cars, Dan was constantly inventing things that made their shows bigger and louder and put himself on the map for making everyday life easier for others as well. Being a pushover and organization freak was definitely an overwhelming trait of Dan's, but he always made sure he took care of his band.

"As band manager, yes. But as a brother, cousin, and friend, I'm sworn to protect you."

"Well, we are very thankful for you accepting your mission, sacrifice noted," Stacy formed her left hand into a fist and held it against the palm of her hand, bowing the way anyone should bow to an honorable Dukhovian.

The band arrived at the remote destination Dan deemed safe enough to keep their band bus. The bus held their instruments: Stacy's red electric guitar and Rachael's drums. It also held the microphones for Cody: lead singer, and Jade and Miranda: backup singers.

The bus was always looked for with anticipation whenever they were touring, though it was hard to miss. Not only was it a large, bright red bus, it was not easily mistaken for anything else as it had each member of the band painted on the side. Cody was in the middle holding a microphone, with Stacy at his right-hand side with her guitar, and Rachael at his left, crossing her arms and holding drumsticks. Jade was next to her holding a microphone in one hand with Miranda next to Stacy in the same pose. Aside from that, whenever it was in motion, the bus played their music out of speakers located on the top of the bus—a very special one of Dan's inventions.

The six got out of Kevin's tiny car and stretched their legs for a brief moment before being shoveled onto the bus.

"I just want us to get all the practice in we can before the big show. Can we all agree to practice every day after school for the next three days leading up to it?" He asked, looking out at them from the front of the bus.

"I'm down as soon as practice is over," Cody smiled wearily, anticipating Dan's reaction.

"Cody, how much are we going to be able to practice if the band leader isn't even there?" Dan demanded, outrage becoming his entire body language.

"Yeah, who made you band leader anyway?" Stacy joked.

"Everyone, when we took a vote," Cody retorted. "It's over at five, Danny, we'll have plenty of time."

"Fine," Dan accepted his defeat, realizing that arguing was not something he had planned into their agenda. "Can everyone do five?"

"Actually," Rachael admitted shyly, slightly raising her hand as guilt spread across her face, "I promised Tom and Terra I would help out at the airport once this week."

"What? Why? Why this week when you know we have a show coming up?"

CHAPTER FOUR

Rachael shrugged, sheepishly crossing her arms and growing quiet. As outgoing as she was, she did not like being yelled at, she tended to avoid any type of confrontation.

"Maybe because we know we're ready, man," Cody, unsurprisingly, interjected. "We've been doing this for years, just because the world hasn't seen us go big in a while doesn't mean we're any less the band we were."

"Yeah, manager," Jade chimed in. "We get that you wanted us to come out even bigger by laying low for a bit, but mission accomplished—we haven't lost any of our style." She flashed him a rare smile.

For the first time that day, they saw Dan take a deep breath and let his body relax. "Okay, guys...I trust you."

CHAPTER 5

THE HUNT

$\mathcal{N}$icholas stayed sitting in his seat even though it had been announced that he could leave. He did not know if the reason lay in him already being exposed to more than he could handle or being too afraid to be exposed to more. From the moment the small air craft's wheels took off the ground, he knew he was entering a world he had never before experienced and landing in Spain confirmed that.

Spain was a non-traditional country. They had everything that Dukhovia did not have, but still also offered a look on traditionalism that he could respect and find comfort in. That ended once he got on the flight.

Being brought directly to the airport was beneficial in shielding him from much of the tourism—but this new plane was nothing he could have imagined. Its exterior vastness alone made the pit in his stomach grow— and then he had to board it. He had spent much time touching the soft, cool material of the seats—leather, he heard someone say. Each row of seats had a light above it and other features that he could not even begin to describe—a screen which featured moving pictures with voice over? It was as though a play had been put onto this screen device.

Carpet lined the center of the aisle, making it look almost more like a cathedral than a type of transportation. He checked the ticket that he had decided would remain glued to his hand and confirmed the flight was only a few short hours—were such accommodations necessary?

Then there were the striking differences to the people on the flight. He had met with Spanish and Russian military before and knew how other countries sometimes viewed the world—primarily Dukhovia—and their views, but this was not the Spanish or Russian military.

His first incident came from a traveling pair of Romanians. They asked the American...ehm, stewardess...how to pronounce a world in English. The stewardess—and many English-speaking folk on the plane—were more than willing to jump and help. Then as soon as heads were turned, they spoke negatively of the Romanians for not knowing. Nicholas wondered how many languages they spoke fluently out of the womb.

Still, it made him aware of himself and he found himself whispering words over and over to check for his own accent.

Over and over, he heard new words and objects that he could not place. Over and over, he heard the mimicking of others, the ridiculing of other practices and the outright disrespect of any person—looks or otherwise—who dared be different. Nicholas's hands wrapped tightly around the arm rests, the sweat on his palms and the paper in his hand being the only thing to cause them to slide off and falter. When this happened, he felt himself digging his fingers deeper into the leather.

His new wardrobe did not help with his lack of comfort. Nicholas continuously tugged at the tight feeling around his neck. He wore what was referred to as a "t-shirt"—baggy, cloth material that wrinkled easily. It tightened from his chest up, making it look almost like part of his skin in that area, then fell loosely around his stomach.

On his lower half he wore "denim jeans"—or so the tag deemed them. They were the most restrictive and uncomfortable material he ever wore and could not imagine why anyone would invent them let alone what would make them America's most popular look. Still, such must have been the case, as he wore the outfit from Spain to America and not a single person looked his way—least of all not in the familiarly terrifying way they did when he was in his military uniform. He cringed. He knew his military uniform would not surpass, but now he doubted even his farming clothing would be deemed acceptable.

Anger and frustration riveted through him when he first looked at the public people and compared their attire to his. His eyes had flickered only for a moment from the helicopter around the Spanish airport before he crumpled back into the seat, cursing. Swallowing what Nicholas's mission meant for him over the last few years was difficult. Tasked not only with redeeming his family honor and determining whether he should listen to the Spirits or Arkady's warnings, he also had his own completely personal, albeit minimalistic, reasons for not wanting to travel to America.

Nicholas was a traditionalist through and through. Though there was much he and Arkady disagreed on, the sheer disgust the thought of traditionalism brought was one shared. He recalled Arkady coaching him through what schooling in America looked like. He often noted it was why they were so simple-minded and naïve. Nicholas had to argue that this seemed logical. It was moments such as these that made him think Arkady must be accurate in his fears of the heir.

Still, he wondered. Arkady could be completely and entirely correct... This heir could be as modernized as they come. Even so, did everything have to go as planned? Was there any chance at changing and reshaping the heir, especially once submerged in Dukhovia?

Nicholas could only ponder it for so long before he had to make his move onto the next plane. With an angry sigh, he shoved his hand into the armor belt beneath his tunic and withdrew his sword, wondering why Arkady even suggested he bring it if it was such a feared weapon that he could not even bring it into the airport. Everyone carried swords everywhere in Dukhovia. What was happening in other countries of the world that they had to regulate so strictly? Did they just run into public places, slashing others when enraged?

In the end, he handed his sword to Sonjay for safe keeping, shaking his head as he half-criticized the people for their lack of appropriate wardrobe, and half criticized himself for thinking there was ever a way around this.

Nicholas caught back up to reality. The plane he now sat on in America had emptied and no one was left aboard. No one coming to assure he would get off, no one ushering him to his next stop. Nicholas used this moment to recognize he could breathe—and then he realized what all that meant.

For the first time in his life, he was moving at his own pace. True, Arkady had given him a deadline, but if he wanted to sit in this chair for an extra minute rather than observing Arkady's rule that "resting is a man's blind spot and makes them open to attack"—he could. If he wanted to end training early and eat a large meal—he could. If he wanted to sleep in tomorrow and begin his hunt at midafternoon—he could. He could do anything he wanted to and the freedom was exhilarating.

Imagine he did not return to Dukhovia—what would come of him? The thought was fleeting, not even there long enough for him to grasp any image of what that life might lead to. He had to return. Dukhovia needed a proper heir. His family needed avenged. And Arkady would never dream of letting him off with something as simple as a runaway—he had scars as deep as his bones that reminded him of that.

Thus it was that Nicholas decided to stand up—slowly and carefully. He did not have much freedom, but he was going to use what he did have to his advantage. He only had one small bag—he would need to buy American clothing here in the country.

He shut his eyes. Back home, Nicholas was known for his calm demeanor—some called it negligence. But he simply acted justly as best as he was taught (albeit, by varying definitions of just) and accepted the country's teachings that all stress was meant to be poured into a metaphorical cup and released to the Spirits. If it was worth worrying about—they could solve it, therefore, making the worry null. He utilized this image now and waited as the thick tension growing at the base of his skull loosened and his mind was free as he stepped off the plane and into the airport.

"Ah!"

Nicholas's hands flew to his ears. He assumed he had just screamed, but could not hear it over everything that was encapsulating him. A noise so obnoxiously loud he could not think filtered through his eardrums. He heard a buzzing, a rattling, a beeping. What sounded like scrapes on pavement rattled his brain, covered only by the obscene sounds of whispers, shouts, laughter, and bellowing.

He breathed in several times as he attempted to sort out everything happening.

The planes landing.
The people talking.
The engines starting.
Music playing…*loudly.*
The people laughing.
The people screaming.
The people…

He uncovered his ears and managed to glance around. There were women walking around, carrying their own bags while men lagged behind. There were men who rushed by in such an angry hurry they did not seem to even have the dedication needed for whatever they were rushing off to pursue. Women held their heads up high and mighty as though they were too good for mannerisms.

He watched as an American flag was dropped to the ground, trampled on by a few feet, and then hung back up on the pole as if everything it stood for was not just shamed. People rushing by, hitting people with their shoulders, slamming doors in each other's faces as they rushed to answer an obviously important phone call. They seemed to not have a care in the world—would that mean they also would not care about having a murderer on their land?

His observations took him around the airport as he glanced at each individual person, memorized their speaking patterns and gaits. They stared right back— laughing, gossiping, and shuddering away from him as he continued to consider whether this country's people truly had any morals at all.

Arkady had taught Nicholas everything he knew about Americans. He was half expecting what he was now looking at. He had heard the country was large on women holding their own, but he was always taught to make anyone intentionally struggle was rude (despite Arkady's beliefs). In that same token, he did not expect their ability to hold their own to shape them into beings that took aid as disrespect.

Then the flag—in Dukhovia, though they did not believe in items holding endearment or value, they believed everything that stood for something Spiritual was sacred. According to Akrady, Americans held similar sacred beliefs regarding their flag. Why then was it being disgraced as such? Was everyone taught these values or only royalty or military?

He was back to holding his aching head, trying to remind himself that he could not possibly have anything to fear or fret over if he was doing right by the Spirits. Still, convincing someone to want to come rule—or even show interest in— another country might be harder than he thought. Surely, they would not have interest in another country when they had no respect for their own. What sort of blatant barbarian had the Spirits chosen?

"They are a most disrespectful people, Nicholas." Arkady's words filled the back of Nicholas's mind. *"They lack any example of culture, they are a hateful, simple-minded people. The world's simplest problems are a challenge for them*

because they are such selfish, prideful, ignorant followers. They work not to better their nation, but to better themselves. Their sense of individuality is bleak..."

Nicholas shook his head and clung to his ticket, exiting the terminal a little less confident and a lot more disgusted than he had entered. He felt as though he would have to do a little more planning than he previously intended, but the more he saw, the more intent he became on fulfilling his mission. The importance of his purpose here was staring him in the face, and there was no time for cowardliness.

Through everything he observed, Nicholas was certain of one thing: anyone who grew up with this kind of upbringing was not suitable to rule Dukhovia. He was not even certain he wanted to keep any of her family members alive—what a disgrace to the country it would be. Beside the point, it might as well become his duty to ensure no more heirs were born of this family. Their banishment made clear and complete sense.

Nicholas glanced around the airport one last time—he could not breathe one more ounce of this air and hope to successfully complete his mission. Ducking around walls and wondering with vague curiosity why the Americans were looking at him and screaming, Nicholas exited the terminal hoping his trip would be short lived.

He braced himself this time, covering his ears and gradually taking them away as he took in the new surroundings.

He was immediately drawn to quickly travelling forms of transportation, weaving in and around each other with carelessness. Cars. He had heard of them, of course. He had even seen them when he travelled on rare occasion to Spain. But he had never seen them in motion. He had never heard the wailing cries of the engine. How fast could they possibly go? What regulations were there, if any?

He shook his head and—keeping his ears covered—headed for a thick covering of trees across the way. Eyes wide in horror for a majority of the walk, Nicholas felt his heart scream that he was not safe as he climbed over a cement bridge and watched as miles and miles of cars honked, zoomed, and slammed their way through a long stretch of road.

"Ah."

Mind over matter, he told himself, managing to push across the billowing vehicles and into the vegetation. He fell to his knees on the forest ground, soaking in the feel of the dirt on his legs and finger tips. The smell of morning dew on the leaves was different than it was back in Dukhovia, but it was a comfort all the same.

Was comfort the word?

Nicholas breathed in and out, grounding himself, settling his booming heart back to a more tamed stage.

His eyes opened and flashed around the forest. His ears peaked and radiated out the surrounding miles—he was alone.

CHAPTER FIVE

Confident in that fact, Nicholas rummaged into his back pocket and drew out the map from Arkady. He closed his eyes and pressed his fingers onto the spot of the map naming his current location.

Power and warmth filled Nicholas, igniting a rising intensity within him. Strength cascaded down his body, relinquishing him unstoppable—he was close, closer than he had ever been before.

Nicholas crossed his legs, folded his hands on his lap, and sat in silence.

In complete, uninterruptable silence.

And sat.

His Spirit open, his mind closed off to any distractions. He searched for the heir, for the source of connection that he knew he felt.

He exhaled.

It is of no use. You will never connect to her here in this miserable country.

Nicholas shook the negativity out of his head. It was a voice he had heard in his mind a hundred times over the years. He had named it Erlik. It seemed fitting enough.

"There is hope," he murmured back.

Hope to succeed in fulfilling a plot that will surely destroy Dukhovia, or hope to find your own path?

Nicholas shook his head, whether out of annoyance or an inability to answer the question honestly.

"She comes from a famous family." The thought entered his head as he drew closer to the feeling of connection.

"This way!"

"What was that?" Nicholas was on his feet in a heartbeat, whipping his head side to side to look for the source of the noises. He heard the murmur of voices, but footsteps had silenced themselves.

Hunters!

Nicholas saw the orange out of the corner of his eye and looked down at his own camouflage appearance—they would never be able to spot him.

"There!"

The sound of gun shots filled his ears before he saw them: bullets swiping one after another, hitting trees, knocking loose bark and falling leaves.

They did not care if he was an animal or not. They heard noises, saw no man, and were firing aimlessly into the woods. Either they were seriously ill-trained or American hunters lacked any basic skills—primarily patience—period.

"Fire!"

Nicholas was surrounded and he knew it, but he had been in this type of arena before. He closed his eyes, breathing in, and tuned out every other sense, keying in only to his sense of sound. It was a skill Arkady taught him. A survival skill.

THE HUNT

If he heard the sound of the weapon clicking back, he never needed to worry about having keen eye sight or reflexes quick enough to dodge a bullet—he would already know what was coming.

Breathing out, Nicholas heard the clicking back of the trigger, metal trickling against metal all around him. Keeping his eyes closed tight, he walked forward.

The trigger was released; he heard the whizzing of bullets through trees on all sides of him.

He ducked down.

"How could we miss?" Someone shouted.

Nicholas kept walking as he heard the sound of them reloading. He was not trying to keep his footsteps whispers; he did not care if they knew his exact location. The training exercise would only prove itself.

Closer and closer Nicholas grew. The closer he became, the more he could hear the panting of the American hunters, the beating of their irregular hearts.

"What the...?"

Nicholas opened his eyes, he was staring a large, dirty man directly into his tiny, murky green eyes. The man lowered his rifle onto his rather large, shelf-like stomach and peered into Nicholas's eyes with shock.

"What are you doing in the woods alone, son?" The man asked.

Nicholas's own heart escalated at the term. He cracked his neck and glanced up into the tree line, once the man was distracted, Nicholas snatched the weapon right out of the man's hand.

"Lesson number one," he breathed. "Never shoot at your prey, without seeing your prey." He looked from each of the men, their mouths gaping. "Only scares it off."

With that, Nicholas dug his feet out of the sinking mud and trailed off further into the deep, dark wood, where humans would be too inconvenienced to journey and animals would be too at home to anticipate disturbance.

That was at least one thing he was good at. While heirs generally shared their spirit with that of the Water and its related Spirits, Nicholas was rather attuned with the Nature Spirit as well. Animals seemed to trust and listen to him, even when he gave no direction.

His strides took him down a narrow path of dirt that disappeared about two miles into his walk. He glanced up as the sun was setting and the moon began to rise—perfect.

Darkness and howling filled the forest. Soon, the lack of sunlight in the sky as well as the lack of ability to be leaked through covering tree tops, warranted the forest almost completely black.

Nicholas looked from the dirt beneath him to a trail now made of moss—rock must be near. Nicholas followed the moss, leading himself to a small, open cave, surrounded by wolves, foxes, and the like.

CHAPTER FIVE

The danger that the animals could impose alone would stop any other man from coming this way. The fact that he was in the middle of the forest, in the complete dark, and the eerie feel of the place only maximized his finding.

Nicholas sat on top the rock and the wolf lifted its head, peering into his eyes. Nicholas looked back.

You are making a mistake, the voice in his head told him.

Nicholas shook his head. "Shut up."

He lifted his hand and allowed the wolf the ability to assess him. The wolf sniffed his arm and then nudged its nose into his side—along one of his worst scars. The wolf looked up and howled into the night.

"I was not the enemy in the fight," he assured the wolf. He lifted his hand and the wolf allowed him to pet its head.

Nicholas glanced around the forest and took in the lack of light. It may help him connect to his spirit, but it would never help him find a place on the map he could not see.

Eyeing the trees, he searched for the perfect setting of branches and climbed to the very top, knocking as few out of the way as he could before returning to the rock, a gleam of moonlight lighting his map.

He folded his legs once more and took in his surroundings: the wolves perched, curiously watching him, pressuring him. The moonlight washed his anxiety completely away. The trees, the rock... For the first time since he left Dukhovia, he was able to breathe. He was able to believe what he kept muttering to himself: that he was doing the right thing and the Spirits would guide him.

There was so much to sort through, so many feelings tearing him in different directions, but out here, in the night, he felt the focus on one thing in particular and he was confident that one thing would lead him to clarity on the rest.

He felt a ball of flame stir in his stomach, then surge out into the night. It was stronger than ever before. He turned, eyes shut, focusing his compass in whatever direction he felt the pull strongest.

West.

He knew it.

But how much further west? Surely not as far as Arkady had suggested—the heir could not be all the way in Kansas. He would not feel this strong.

Though not as strong as he or the heir he now sought, Nicholas had been around other heirs before. Obviously, Arkady, and another. He knew he could not feel this powerful if the heir were on the opposite side of the country.

"Spirit's guide me. Guide me to where I am meant to be."

Nicholas knew he was still sitting on the rock, knew that he could still hear, see, and smell the forest if he wanted to. But he allowed his senses to be overrun, let himself see the flashing images that isolated his mind.

Dukhovia. Years ago, and a rush of men chasing him.

He heard an unfamiliar, young voice speak quick, angry Russian words.

Then he was travelling in a car. He swallowed his own nausea. *Then unboxing. Hands linked, laughter.*

A school. Ugh. What was the name of it? *A shape...the shape of a state.*

He quickly scanned the map and pointed his finger down.

Kansas.

Peace, comfort, assurance.

That was it. The heir lived in Kansas. He felt it was something he knew for years. But, as Arkady had said, a state is large. Where in Kansas was the heir? How very quickly could he find transportation?

"I am going to have to go into town, yes?"

Nicholas looked at the wolf, asking no one in particular. But he felt the wolf look at him with solemn, pleading eyes.

Or back to Dukhovia. One or the other.

"I am not going back to Dukhovia. I have come far."

Distance wise, yes.

Where in Kansas was his next stop? Nicholas felt drawn to the center of Kansas, then a tad further west, but he had no map of the state as a whole. He had tried to obtain those maps and came up short. He knew that if he travelled to Kansas, he could tune in his Spirit again and get even closer, but he had to get close enough that he would be able to access her through other forms of transportation rather than flight after flight.

In the end, Nicholas circled the area he felt called to as best he could, packed up his things, threw his tunic on over the ridiculous clothes, and headed towards town, positive his experience with Americans could not possibly get any worse.

CHAPTER 6

DOUBLE-EDGED SWORD

Trees blew haphazardly in the wind, without being haphazard at all. They had meaning. They had intent. They had purpose.

Leaves and fallen branches ricocheted across the ground.

The scene changed back and forth quickly.

"It's coming."

Lightning crackled in the sky. Then a stream.

"They're coming."

Then faster—then more scenes.

"The heir...it's time."

A man holding hands with a small child.

Another child leaping into the lap of his mother and father.

"Protect them."

And then a face...a face she could not quite make out, but she knew to be the enemy. The face would creep forward, extending a hand to her—or was it a weapon? Her legs failed to move, her body freezing as if to move would cause her pain. Then she was gone, running faster than she would ever think possible for a human. Her body shifted, glancing around for the enemy, being thrown into walls and falling to her knees when she found herself off guard.

Then the enemy was before her. Standing over her with a villainous smile, but such a great smile at the same time...a smile she found almost enchanting.

Then...

Stacy shot up in a pool of sweat and panic, glancing around her room quickly as if to assure herself she was truly there. She pat the bed around her and breathed in, collapsing back down into the pillow.

She did this every time she awoke from this dream. She could not explain the feeling she woke up with. It was not just a scary dream. It was not just panic or sweat from a hard night. It was as if she had physically been present in the moment of her dream. Her body ached in the places she fell in the dream. Her fear, experiences, and flashbacks were so real they were more like live memories than they were a dream that would pass with every given moment...

And the details never did pass. She not only remembered, but thought of them constantly every passing day, thinking, knowing that this dream had to mean something. Each and every piece of it.

CHAPTER SIX

She knew from the first time she had the dream where she was and what she was looking at—Dukhovia. Only, she had never seen it so…dark. Storms serving to sever ties and cause statues to fall, rather than to encourage life and peace.

It's coming…they're coming.

That part she never got any closer on solving—who was coming?

Protect them. Protect them. No matter how many times Stacy had the dream, it was always these words that stuck with her minutes, hours, days, weeks, even months after the dream had passed. The words would find her at any given moment—cornering her as she was leaving the restroom, rendering her dazed during family dinner…But never any closer.

Stacy's thoughts began to drift as they did when these days happened. She was never well rested, she was never able to make it through her day, and then she would shut her eyes and drift back…drift back to the dream.

Stacy was awoken again, but this time not by the dream. This time, she had found that the dream passed and she was in some "normal" type of disarray. Her and her best friends laughing as they plummeted miniature donuts in each other's mouths. It was a strange dream to have after such an…impactful one. But it fit with her lifestyle, so she could not argue with it much.

Her eyes drifted open slowly, but her body refused to move. She glanced over at her closet as clothes were flying out of it, seemingly on their own.

"Ugh—nothing! Nothing! Nothing!"

She already knew it was Rachael before she heard her voice.

"Different isn't nothing, it's just different," Stacy called over, without moving.

Rachael poked her head out of Stacy's closet and looked her up and down. "The dream again?" She asked with a coy look.

Stacy rubbed her eyes and then her arms and nodded. "Really intense this time. I'm surprised I'm not covered in bruises."

"Maybe it's some sort of…weird Dukhovian thing," Rachael offered, back to sifting through Stacy's closet with distaste. "You should try talking with Tom and Terra about it."

Stacy shrugged. Although her grandparents had never specifically told her not to ask about Dukhovia and she did not necessarily feel inclined to follow the rule that they were to not to mention their homeland, she feared upsetting them too much to test the waters. Even with the dream intensifying.

But it was a struggle. If there was someone skilled in Dukhovia's uniqueness, it was her grandparents. Apparently, the mixture of certain herbal remedies Tom had brought from Dukhovia caused some…personality changes and a lack of control which resulted in a lot of damage for the country. In a huge court case that Grace's cousin, Terra Carter, fought on Tom's behalf, they found Tom not guilty, given two things: the family would no longer bring any of these substances into the country or practice anything related to them and Tom would wear a clear wire-like tube on the outside of his head.

The tube was an invention of his wife, Terra. After there was too much skepticism over whether or not they could be certain he was himself once more, she devised a way for them to see the differences in his biochemical make-up or some type of science-y words that Stacy did not bother herself with comprehending. She was quite certain chemicals were involved.

Through her studies, Terra was able to show that when the mixture caused these changes in his brain, black smoke expelled from the tube, but it ran a vibrant blue when he was himself. The court argued that they could not wait on a test to prove to them whether or not they were walking around a maniac, so Terra invented the tube which was transfixed inside Tom's brain and routed to the outside. It needed to be visible at all times. Easy to see equals easy to gun down at a moment's notice. Perfect harmony.

Thus, Stacy did not often think to ask them about Dukhovia. But they were never closed off about the topic. They continued to celebrate holidays best they could—although courts and people argued that one for a while, so they never really looked how they were supposed to—or so Stacy was told. They openly told stories and spoke the language. They now ran the largest airport and hospital in the area and slowly worked their way up to being trusted and well-respected people again. But only as Americans.

The entire thing made Stacy sick to think about—so she often chose not to. Here they were, from a country that prided itself on being unique and non-traditional—forced to either conform or travel back to their country and face death. It was hard to feel confident in one decision or the next. But, while Stacy had an attitude that was fiercer than anything, she was never much of a problem solver.

"Anyway," Rachael sang, throwing the last of Stacy's shirts to the side and grabbing the bag next to her with a smile. "You've already slept through half our sleepover plans which—in case you forgot—is not how a sleepover works."

"Sure it does," Stacy argued. "I was preparing myself for tonight."

Rachael ignored her, instead dumping the contents of her bag out onto the floor. A series of make-up, nail polish, junk food, and music surrounded them.

"I've missed bad decision nights," Stacy grinned.

Rachael laughed in response. Although the two lived right next door to each other, it had been difficult getting one-on-one time with things with the band picking back up.

"Okay, so you already slept through make-up madness," Rachael declared, as if going down an invisible agenda.

Stacy snapped her fingers. "That's too bad."

Rachael side-eyed. Their one dissolution as best friends: Rachael needed fashion and Stacy rolled out of bed and hoped for the best.

"But we can combine mani/pedi power hour with chip-dip testing!" She clapped her hands as she unlocked the lids off some containers and the aromas of spices and meat filled the room.

"My favorite type of testing!" Stacy celebrated, tearing open the bag of chips and choosing which dip she would sample first.

"And the one you're best at. Now, mom says that each one is new this time, so we have to be very careful when deciding a favorite."

"What if I have multiple favorites?" Stacy asked, mouth full of chips as she mixed several of the dips together.

"You're cheating on chip-dip testing!" Rachael laughed, pushing her friend.

"I'm being innovative! Kenny and Ellen would beam with pride!"

"There's more three bean in the wild buffalo than there is wild buffalo—unfair advantage!"

"For who?"

The girls laughed, doing their best to separate and fairly judge the dips in order to report back to Rachael's mom and dad, Ellen and Kenny. Ellen and Kenny were like every high school's power couple—the ones people could not wait to finally get together. They did everything together and loved every minute of it. They were each other's biggest fans and spent each moment of their time together submerged in their shared hobbies—usually cooking. They owned a restaurant in town famous for their random concoctions.

By the time they had the dips sorted and were now eating for sport, Rachael had set up all of her nail supplies and had Stacy's toes in front of her for painting. She chose her favorite color—a pale blue with sparkles. Music was playing and they had started sorting through different sounds for new song ideas.

"Okay, I loooove this sound and it would sound so harmonious with Cody's voice!"

Stacy smiled playfully. "Harmonious would it, Juliette?"

Rachael blushed. "Stop it!"

"Listen, I'm no Cara. I never saw myself as a match maker, but your love is clearer than your parents."

Rachael bit her lip and stuttered over her response.

"But..." Stacy pressed.

"Cody is a good friend. Our best friend. I couldn't forgive myself if something changed that."

Stacy smiled and watched her friend work her magic as she flawlessly finished her pinky toe. "What's that phrase my mom always says? As long as we're doing the right thing, nothing bad can happen?" She said the words as if she did not spend half the day repeating them to herself.

Rachael smiled again, her face bright red. Her thoughts were now getting the better of her and she could tell. "I do like Cody. He's so gentle and kind." She laughed quietly to herself. "He's dedicated. I know it doesn't seem like it sometimes, but he juggles a lot with the band and sports."

"While completely disregarding school," Stacy joked then pushed it to the side. "He focuses on what's important. That does make him quite the choice in boyfriend material."

Rachael nodded her head slowly and then shrugged. "So, then who do we set you up with? Cara has to have someone picked out."

Cara. Their incredible best friend who would do anything for anybody—except for herself. Well, not entirely. Cara had come a long way since they met. She was setting more boundaries and making herself a priority, but ensuring her friends happiness always came before her own. She would go to the ends of the earth to ensure their happiness before her own.

And she was everything Stacy lacked in the hair and make-up and match-maker department. She was Rachael's shopping partner in crime as well as someone to talk romance with. But Cara and her twin brother, Dylan, had their own dark history too. Although the details were sparse timeline wise, Cara and Dylan had been horrifically abused by their parents on and off for years. Anytime the authorities tried to step in, Cara and Dylan were separated and ran back home to each other until the intervening simply...stopped.

That's when Stacy's family stepped in as an "unofficial" caregiver. Unofficial because Dylan, somehow, someway, developed a sense of integrity that would not allow the Grayson family to care for he and Cara. He respected them and did not want their lives to be inconvenienced simply because his parents...lacked. Thus, he found himself working midnights on occasion to support he and Cara while still attending school and playing on the football team.

"No boys for me," Stacy laughed, her head returning to the conversation.

"You can't be a hermit forever, Stace." Rachael smiled coyly.

"I'm fifteen," Stacy said flatly. But she knew what she meant. "It just doesn't seem important right now..."

Rachael shrugged. "But it could be." In the same breath, Rachael readjusted herself, finishing Stacy's last toe and screwing her nail polish shut. "Anyway! It's getting late. It's time for movies and junk. My parents have given us TWO popcorn seasonings to choose from. Caramel drizzle and butter explosion."

"Okay, I'm going to fix your wording for you. They gave us TWO popcorn seasonings—period. We shall not be choosing just one."

The girls kicked back in Stacy's bed, turning the TV on and letting their favorite movie play out. Rachael and Stacy were always the best at staying up late when it came to sleepovers, but Rachael turned her head every so often to see Stacy struggling to keep her lids open and afloat.

Rachael yawned wide and loud at one point, shutting of the TV as she stretched out. "Well, I'm exhausted, we better hit the hay."

Stacy smiled, knowingly, but was too exhausted to fight it. She shut her eyes and lay her head back fully on the pillow.

They're coming. The time is now. Protect them.

Stacy's eyes flew open. She was not even sure she had fallen asleep yet, and yet the voices that filled her slumber encompassed her mind. It was different than normal, it was as though Rachael could have said the words.

She glanced over at her friend who was half pretend sleeping and half looking at Stacy through her now clumped eye lashes, thick with mascara, tears from laughter, and an abnormal amount of rubbing at them. She was adamant about washing it off before bed, but sleepover nights did not usually schedule in planned sleep time. If any at all.

Stacy spent the next several minutes fading in and out, hearing the voices, seeing the visions, and then giving up completely.

"Dukhovia?" She asked it as if she already knew the answer.

Stacy nodded. "I don't understand what it can mean. I'm seeing Dukhovia—at least, I think. Half of it looks the same as when we were there and then the other half is like…like what it's supposed to be." A wave washed over Stacy as soon as she said it. It was like a warmth encompassed her, *reassured* her.

"And the protection—maybe the Spirits want you to protect the traditional part of Dukhovia and they're showing you the former to remind you."

Stacy thought it over for a moment. It seemed to fit, but it did not fit the full picture. "Or this heir…Nothing I have on Dukhovia says anything about an heir."

Rachael's expression shifted. "Gee, something on Dukhovia we don't understand—it's a shame we don't have an entire family from there we could ask. Oh wait."

Stacy nudged her and laughed. "I don't want to cause any issues for them—and what if this is bad news *from* them or involving them? I don't want to stress them out."

Rachael leaned her head into Stacy's and Stacy leaned back into hers as they supported each other. She sighed heavily. "Regardless, we know the Spirits are communicating with you and we know they want you to protect…something. Whether it be this heir or Dukhovia. The question is, what will you do if you're banished?"

Stacy sifted with the thought for a moment. She ran it over and over in her mind with the same options as always, always coming up with the same answer. "I don't know."

"But you will," Rachael yawned, actually tired now. "That's what your mom would say. And you know I'll be here and we'll figure it out together."

"Always," Stacy agreed with a squeeze of her hand before falling off into the mystery.

CHAPTER 7

DESTINATION

$\mathcal{N}$icholas stood tall, feet apart in a library. At least, what was deemed one on the front of the building. To be fair, when he did finally find the books past all the glamour, he was not as disappointed as he was prepared to be.

He sat at a small, rounded table across from a large, stain-glass window in a separated room. Instinctively, he poured himself over maps of the state, crossing places off as he sifted through them in other books. He researched the towns and crossed them off based on Dukhovian belief—that an heir would never choose to live in a place that specialized in industry. However, that was the entire issue—this heir would not meet Dukhovian standards.

Then he was back to square one, considering every city he had once crossed off his list.

His eyes shifted around the library, watching one librarian trickle down the steps away from him.

He breathed in and shut his eyes.

Dayton.

London.

Union.

He truly was not narrowing it down at all. He felt his spirit continue to pull him west, but it was fading more so than it had in the forest.

"May I help you?"

Nicholas looked up. A woman suddenly appeared, leaning closely over Nicholas, a warm smile hanging confidently on her lips.

"No, Marisa, he doesn't want your help. You're not a librarian. Look at him. Say no—you don't want her help. Trust me."

"Shove it, Derek." The woman claimed, taking a seat next to Nicholas.

Nicholas noted that he did draw away from her, then noticed he was still staring at her as she sat. He could not help it. Her head would have hit the floor moments ago if this were Dukhovia. No one approached him so suddenly and survived. And yet he was intrigued—this was the first person to approach him in America.

"Are you new to the area?" She asked, taking in all the maps as he drew out how to get to Kansas from his current location and then over to…wherever.

Nicholas glanced at the man she had appeared with. He was shaking his head, leaning against a bookshelf built into the tattered, white walls as he scanned the titles with his thumb and index finger. He held a notecard in his other hand.

CHAPTER SEVEN

He could kill them both with no feat. Arkady had mentioned that America used security cameras. He would have to find them all or simply destroy the tape at the base. It was a tedious task he did not have time for.

Then there was the less brutal way he often used on women—his looks. His icy blue eyes had been given the nickname "killer blues", accused of being so bright and chilling that harm—or at the very least, blindness—would come to anyone who dare look his way. Well, perhaps there was another habit of his that earned them that nickname as well...

"We have been in the country for a few years now. Travelers." A British accent hung when she said the word.

The idea intensified Nicholas's already surfacing anger. He wanted to be left alone to focus on his task. What help could they provide? What knowledge could they possible have if they would be so dim as to leave Europe and travel America?

"Are you travelling or here to stay?"

Nicholas breathed heavily in and out clanking up from the table. Arkady had told him to shed no blood, but how on Earth was that going to be possible when people asked him questions as if he was just an average man?

He breathed. *No.* Killing was Arkady's resolution to every problem. It was not his. It would not become his. He packed the map he came with in a messy hurry, clenching it in his fist, and head for the exit.

The man—Derek—turned and looked at his maps. "Oh God, not another fan, are you? America is so dreadfully transparent. Full of idol worshipping ninnies."

Nicholas froze at the door and turned back around. "Idol worshipping?"

Marisa gave Derek a solemn look, then glanced back up at Nicholas. "The area you have circled..." she moved her hand and traced his circle with her finger. "It is the general area where *The Rockers* are from. They're a band. A lot of people come through this area on the way to see them."

Derek rolled his eyes. "They track them down just to scream and shout at their feet. Disgusting, really."

"Truly," Nicholas muttered. He paused, rubbing his chin. "Then, the members of this band, they live in this direction? I should avoid it at all costs."

"Shawnee county," Derek said, plainly. "That's all I know. Marisa could probably help you more."

Marisa shot him a warning glance, reaching her hands over Nicholas's work to grab a pen and scrap piece of paper. Then, she paused and took Nicholas in. "Are you a cosplayer?"

Nicholas's mind searched his classes on American culture for the term, but came up blank. But he was bad at thinking once his anger started to rise. Thankfully, Marisa moved past her question.

"They live here. They're very open. Just avoid that area at all costs and you will have a very pleasant stay. Where are you from?"

DESTINATION

Nicholas glanced from Marisa to Derek in deciding whether to expunge the truth. They did not seem all too diabolical. He sincerely doubted they had the ability to thwart his efforts.

Marisa looked on at him curiously, Derek peeked over at him one more time, but had resumed to scanning the row of books.

"Russia," Nicholas decided. "I am visiting family."

Derek made a sneering noise.

Nicholas rose his head in his direction. "Which book are you searching for?"

Derek continued scanning for a moment, then realized Nicholas was talking to him and looked back. "Oh. It is nothing we can't find."

Nicholas tore the paper from his hands before Derek had time to react. His eyes scanned the shelf below where Derek was looking and quickly grabbed the book.

"Khoroshego dnya," he told them with a bow of his head. "Spasibo."

Nicholas reached back and grabbed his maps. Once away from Marisa and Derek, he lay the map of Kansas on the table beneath him and closed his eyes. It took much longer than it did in the forest, but he shut off each sense one at a time.

No vision.

Not a single sound penetrated his ears.

He lifted his hands, ignored the feeling of pressure under his aching feet.

He breathed, letting any scents he picked up drift away.

And then he was a lone figure, hovering over a state, in a town…

A rush of people.

Crowds shouting.

Toristh Hill High…

Home of Shawnee County's best rock band…

A sea of hands coming together.

Laughter.

Sadness.

Nicholas fell out of his connection before he was ready, stumped by what he had felt. A warmth that was similar to happiness, but there was more with it… Security, perhaps?

All the way from Topeka, Kansas, please welcome!

And then he snapped back, in full awareness and consciousness.

Topeka, Kansas. That was where he was headed. That was his destination. After all of these years and all of this time preparing, he was coming close to fulfilling his life's purpose. Anxiety and excitement fought each other for attention, his heart accelerated.

It was a feeling he never experienced before and something he was not quite sure of now. While he was proud of his skill set and ability to find the heir, he continued to struggle with whether what he was doing was the right thing for Dukhovia, for the Spirits, or for his family. He did not know. He may never know.

CHAPTER SEVEN

But one thing he was certain: this was the path he was dealt, and following it would lead him to an answer. Of that, his Spirit assured him.

CHAPTER 8

HEROINE

What on Earth are you doing?"

Rachael's cynical voice leaked into Stacy's ears, interrupting her daydream. Stacy glanced back at her only for a second, seeing her head cocked to the side out of the corner of her left eye. She shrugged, turning back to the front.

"It's a conversation with your grandparents, not a tooth extraction."

Stacy grimaced, thinking she would rather have the latter.

"I could get it if they were mean people, but Tom and Terra are God's gift to Earth. What could possibly go wrong?"

"I upset them, they hate me, I feel guilty, their sad feelings cause them to tamper with forbidden Dukhovian artifacts and the world explodes into a shield of chaos."

"Let's process that, shall we?" Rachael said in a chipper voice, her head appearing around Stacy's side as she grabbed her shoulders and looked her square in the eye. "Tom and Terra know what is on and off limits and they know why— to protect their family. They are smarter and more caring than to just up and risk blowing up the world simply because their curious granddaughter asked them a few questions.

"Next, they love you, they love your mom, they even love their next-door neighbor, Genevieve…"

"Gertrude," Stacy corrected in a faraway voice.

"Gertrude. They don't have an agenda of love that's going to expire the moment you mention your home which is natural to be curious about. I'm also fairly confident your mom grabbed some pointers before our trip there and they maintained their sanity and the world."

Stacy nodded, fully taking in all the words. The thing was, she *did* want to talk with her grandparents. She wanted Rachael's words to work and make sense…and they did. "You're right," she agreed. "Let's do this."

"Thank you!" Rachael said, throwing up her hands. "Now let's go. I'm not used to this you shutting down when it comes to anything Dukhovian related thing. I can't keep being the ring leader here."

Stacy laughed and allowed herself to be pulled into her grandparent's backyard where she knew Tom and Terra would be tending their garden—well, their greenhouse. You can take the farmer out of Dukhovia, but you can't take the farmer out of the Dukhovian—or something like that.

"Girls!" Terra celebrated as soon as they came around the corner. She set down her watering can and opened the greenhouse door. They poured in quickly. Tom smiled and waved from the other side of the greenhouse, lifting whatever tool he had in his hand at the time in a sign of hello.

"Hi Tom and Terra!"

"Hi grams and gramps."

Terra rolled her eyes. Most of the family just called Tom and Terra their names due to never finding a "grandparent" name they thought suit them. It also had a lot to deal with them being gone for so long, it helped with the time lapse, to a degree.

"We thought you might be too busy for a visit with the show coming up—are you all ready?"

"According to Dan, we'll never be," Stacy answered, her fingers toying with a leaf hanging over the table next to them. "But I don't think I've forgotten how to play the guitar."

"You better not have," Tom chuckled. "These old fingers need to turn the teaching skills to someone new."

Stacy laughed, remembering her first lesson with Tom and Cody. It was before they were "allowed" to be friends while their parents were in a huge fight—resulting in many not-so-secret lessons.

"And I am fully prepared even with picking up the shift at the airport," Rachael promised. "Although Dan did yell at me." She hid smally, trying to make a joke of it, knowing it was anything but. Upset meant mood destabilizing and that meant anything from a shaking window to a blown-up car. A useful gift, they were sure, if she figured out how to control it. But Rachael had no desire in controlling, she only wanted it to end.

They shook their heads at Dan's behavior and Terra handed Stacy and Rachael each a spray bottle to spritz at the leaves.

"Anyway," Rachael went on. "You always have such beautiful plants—what's your secret?"

"Love," Terra answered.

"And lots of patience," Tom added.

"It was a gift brought over from Dukhovia," Terra began, almost dreamily. "A permitted one," she said reluctantly. "Most of Dukhovia is comprised of farmers—we are a self-sufficient country. Learning the proper way to grow is the difference between death and survival."

"Very interesting," Rachael replied, eyeing Stacy as if to say *look they spoke of Dukhovia and no one is dead yet.*

Stacy replied with a warning glance. "So Dukhovia has a lot of plant growth—forests and stuff too, even with the temperatures?"

Terra and Tom exchanged a glance and then Terra nodded. "Correct. The Spirits sort of dictate for us where the temperatures change and how much so. The outer parts of the country are warmer and allow for more growth—plus these in the use of green houses." She smiled, holding an arm-full of vegetables. "You'll find hearty soups and stews are most common with the food we have. But they are very different than Americans. Food is part of the culture in a sense, but it is also very minimalist. We eat to survive and celebrate more so than to over enjoy ourselves."

"She could talk about this for hours, don't get her started," Tom laughed. He had just finished picking his last…onion? Scallion? Anyway, he joined them near the front of the greenhouse, hovering over some tall, bushy plants.

"Too late," Terra laughed.

"What about warm temperatures, like tropical? Has any spot in Dukhovia ever been known to be like that?"

Terra thought about this, then looked up at Tom.

"It's highly unlikely, but not impossible," Tom decided. "Our entire country is meant to thrive on the Spirits which keep it cold. That is just our culture. But the Summer Spirit does have a hand in things. Then again, I hear things are quite opposite in the Spirit Realm."

"What's it like there?" Rachael pressed. Neither of the girl's hands were pretending to work anymore, they were both eagerly listening, absorbing any drop for answers.

"I cannot say for certain," Tom mused, "I've never been there. But it's rumored to be the opposite of our climate—tropical. We thrive on balance, so I suppose it makes sense. Though there is controversy that this holds true, proclaiming that if the Spirits wanted our land cool, they would have the same environment."

It's coming. They're coming. Protect the heir.

Stacy opened her mouth to speak, but as soon as she did, the voice hit her like a bag or two of bricks, nearly winding her. It left her feeling almost trapped in a brick wall, but that it was her wall to choose whether to build up or tear down. She wanted to ask about the heir…but the brick wall told her to hold off.

"What other types of things do the Spirits decide?" Stacy wondered—would it be people's thoughts and questions? Their dreams?

"It's different per person," Tom said. "Depending on their purpose. Most humans do not have a close connection with them—only Shaman. Shaman can speak and hear the Spirits directly."

The girls exchanged a look.

"Will they know their purpose? Or if they're a Shaman?"

Tom shifted, as if trying to decide the right way to present the information. "Each person is told their purpose at birth. Shaman are notified and then there is a reveal at the birth of the child."

Stacy's heart sank. "But probably not if you're whisked away in the night to escape certain death from banishment—or if you're banished in general."

Tom and Terra sat for a moment with those words, Stacy started to feel her guilt creep in, but the loss of information kept it from increasing.

"Banishments are from petty, human rivalries," Tom finally said. "They do not determine whether or not the Spirits have a purpose for you, Stacy Grace."

"And I can assure you that you have a most promising purpose," Terra whispered into her ear, holding her close and kissing her cheek.

Stacy felt ignited when they said the words, as if the Spirits had spoken to her through them and confirmed it. Yet, she knew her dreams were telling her more. Perhaps the tropical land she was seeing was a part of Dukhovia or the Spirit Realm. Perhaps the voices were the Spirits or even Shaman. But why her? And why was it such a warning?

Stacy felt her heart beating wildly against her chest, the growing palpitations in her heart warning her to choose her next words carefully.

"Stace?" Rachael prompted her, gazing into the far-off look in her eye.

She did not quite snap out of it, instead, she repeatedly stroked a leaf higher and higher until her eyes met everyone else's. "Are there...bad people in Dukhovia?" She felt stupid and childish but had no idea what she was really asking. Of course, there were bad people in Dukhovia. Kind people rarely chase you out of the country with weapons, banished or not.

"I don't know that good and bad have a border," Terra answered. "Although in Dukhovia—there is supposed to be one."

Stacy shook the response off. "What I mean is...do you think Dukhovia is in trouble?"

Again, Tom and Terra's eyes met each other, this time they seemed to tell a story, speaking in a secret language. Both of their throats were welling up; she could almost see the words jumbling up in them.

Terra smiled as if she was going to speak, then glanced away and found an excuse to leave the green house.

"I think Dukhovia has a lot of demons," Tom finally responded before bidding his own farewell. "But they have even more heroes."

CHAPTER 9

THE WAY FORWARD

*N*icholas closed his eyes and lifted his chin towards the sky. Warmth filled his limbs and a strange sense of ease encapsulated him.

Now, at any point, it might occur to you that this plan is completely idiotic, barbaric, and a double standard. That is the common sense talking. Listen to it.

He shrugged his shoulders back, lifted his one carry-on, and moved down the line of eager Americans in a calm, collected state. They were all anticipant: frantically waving their arms at people who responded with foolhardiness, shouting indecent words and exposing themselves in crude ways. He breathed and attempted to show grace, remaining neutral and focused, the way he always had.

This airport was much smaller than the large one he initially arrived in. There were fewer people rushing and the space was much smaller and simplistic. Whereas the other airport had elaborate, cascading waterfalls and shops as plentiful as the eye could see, this station was limited to one large room of chairs that he poured into as soon as he entered from the terminal. The walls had nothing more than red paint and a few miscellaneous pictures of sorts.

Towards his right were the restrooms and then straight ahead, a large meeting room and the check-in station. All were as modest as a table and chair along with the boards dictating where each flight was going. He almost smiled, the simplicity easing him.

He eyed the door to the exit for a long moment before he found himself stumbling over towards the waiting area chairs, recognizing his need to further plan. Where would he stay? His hand went down to his pocket where Akrady had thrusted several thousand American dollars. "Be resourceful" he was told—and those were the only directions given.

The back wall caught his eye. He noticed several pamphlets. In Dukhovia, pamphlets usually had information about the surrounding area. He hoped and was thankful to find out America was run the same way.

He picked up one depicting a large, castle type building. It stated "hotels and lodging" on the front. Inside, he found information regarding rooms to board. Only, the rooms were rather…lavish.

He considered the inns he had stayed in back in Dukhovia while travelling. They were typically single bedrooms, occasionally accompanied with attached toiletry, though rarely. He would get fair sleep in the straw beds—as fair as one could get travelling with Arkady. Not to mention the loudness coming from below his feet. The bottom of these inns were often home to taverns. Nicholas and Arkady or those he was leading on his own would stop for a bowl of stew before getting the minimal amount of rest required to continue their journeys.

These rooms looked much different. They had elegant and elaborate bathrooms connected to their rooms. Rooms were furnished with televisions and refrigerators. Most of the pamphlets identified even more luxurious items such as swimming pools and recreational rooms.

Nicholas began to feel his heart thudding in his chest and his palms grow sweaty. Nerves. He knew them all too well.

He decided he would not be staying in the so-called hotel and would continue his search elsewhere. His eyes continued to scan the pamphlets for any other useful information.

Dining.

He supposed he would have to eat. He grabbed a pamphlet and tore it open, beginning to feel light-headed as he did so. Looking at the restaurant options, he supposed he prepared himself for the updated atmosphere the pictures indicated, though he was not familiar with American food. Arkady did not seem to be either, to no one's surprise.

His eyes closed. He began to feel his breathing labor and was not sure if the sickness from the flight's harsh landing was catching up with him.

Failure.

Hero.

The words bombarded him and nearly took him off his feet. It was then he knew what was happening. His head began to spin, he grabbed it in an attempt to ground himself, but was acutely aware of whispers surrounding him, causing him to open his eyes.

Murderer.

Idiots. Stupid Americans…

Nicholas's eyes darted around the building, looking for sanctuary. His breathing becoming more difficult, his ability to see straight gone. Eyes seemed to look back at him with judgement, with fear, with ridicule. He grasped even harder at his head, feeling a surge of pain jolt through the side and around his temples. The heaviness in his chest combined with the rigidness in his legs brought him to his knees.

He exhaled in and out deeply trying to bring himself out of the episode. Eyes continued to watch him, whispers continued to surround him, passersby only passed by—but he had to focus. He knew this routine all too well. It happened every time Arkady broke their connection. It was his greatest weakness and one he swore up and down he needed to perfect before leaving—but Arkady's persistence was greater. It was always so much greater.

CHAPTER NINE

But surely this insolent who may not even be aware of their heirship would not know how to recognize they were connected to another let alone fight it off?

Nicholas grabbed his temples and shut his eyes. No use. His mind and body were catching up with each other now as they realized what this meant, the setback.

Setback.

Yes. He breathed in and out. That was all this was and all this would be. A minor setback. In and out again. He would secure his Spirit. He knew he was meant to be here. Whatever he would be brought towards, wherever his final destination—America had to be his stepping stone. In and...

"Hi. Are you okay?"

Nicholas looked up at the sound of the sing-song voice. It sounded like the goddess of beauty herself had entered the airport to speak with him in his time of need.

He turned in half-hesitation to meet her baby blue eyes, identical to his. The brilliantly shining smile of the employee sitting next to him took his breath away only for a moment.

He recognized her almost immediately. The red of her apron matched the red shade she wore on her lips almost perfectly. His eyes travelled down to see the plane surrounded in clouds centered on her chest. She was the one waving people off the terminal; friendly, welcoming, clearly in tune with her job with little care for distraction, even if those she so warmly greeted ignored or disrespected her.

Nicholas stood to his feet the moment he made eye contact with the woman and bowed to her, arching his back until he could have been staring at the ground. Then he took her hand in his light grasp and pressed his lips to the back of her hand.

"Apologies, my lady, it is not at all gentlemen like to display such an imbalance of emotion in the presence of someone such as yourself."

The girl blinked, her face seeming to be attempting to hold back a comical and almost cynical smile. "You should be free to express yourself however you want, whenever you want, dear sir." Then the face vanished and she became one of complete pleasantry. The cynical smile was replaced by one so brilliant, so brightly shining, the angels themselves would have fallen to their knees.

"I'm Rachael. Rachael Leighton."

"Sir Nicholas the Third. It is a pleasure." Nicholas stood and bowed again. Though he was not sure it was a pleasure. He did not have time to pause and make conversation—the longer he took, the more Dukhovia was at risk. Yet he felt compelled to stay in this conversation. Whether it was due to her looks or a spiritual draw, he did not know.

Nicholas never had much time for women in Dukhovia. A few times Arkady suggested he date as a way to distract him when he had no current use for him.

Albert and Alexander spent more time coaching him on how to win women over. Still, he was not sure any of the advice he earned from them would get him far.

Aside from that fact, Nicholas never found himself interested in the world of love. He had too much purpose and promise to fulfill and that took focus. He could not, even for a moment, risk that fading.

The girl named Rachael waved it off with a smile as she began glancing around the airport. "The pleasure is mine, Sir Nicholas." She glanced at his baggage or rather lack of and her eyes became crossed. "You look like you've had a long journey—would you like to sit somewhere a little more private?"

Nicholas looked into her trusting eyes and found himself agreeing to follow her without much argument. She was right, after all, the past fifteen years had been long and hard. What she did not realize was that he was still on his journey and as far as he could tell, there was no end in sight.

He followed her into the room that was behind a closed door and fogged windows. It looked like one of the rooms he and Arkady would sit in to discuss strategy with other leaders around the country—with much less weaponry. Several long tables filled the room, tucked in place with red chairs on either side. In place of the table that held battle axes, hammers, and daggers, was a small, nearly empty table, holding nothing more than a very small refrigerator and a coffee pot. It was this table that Rachael walked over to, after offering him a chair next to the door, in the center of the first table.

"Would you like some?" She asked, offering up the coffee pot.

Nicholas grimaced, remembering the one and only time he tried coffee and how it resulted in Arkady pouring it on his face.

She read his face and sat it back down.

"Thank you," Nicholas told her.

Rachael nodded and took a seat across from him after putting a few ice cubes in her own drink. "So, where are you travelling from, Nicholas?"

Nicholas felt his entire body clench up; nerves kicked into gear and the shutting down he felt just moments ago spread to his entire body. It was like a switch had been flicked at the ending of her question. *Where was he from?* What information would the truth reveal? What difficulties and short comings came with a lie? It was a question they never fully prepared for. It was a story he never meant to reveal.

If you tell the heir or have any hint of an accent, they will dismiss you before you even have a chance to ask them their favorite color. Arkady's words came pouring back to him. *But introduce yourself as American from the beginning and Dukhovian later on and you lose much ground as trustworthy—yes?*

There was, of course, never really an answer. He had to figure that out for himself. And, over time, he did. He concluded he would take bits and pieces of his advice—lose his accent, come off as American, have a very plain and basic backstory, and no questions would ever be asked. Only later would be make the connection with the heir, after he had their trust.

You are in an airport, genius, you have to be coming from somewhere.

Erlik was always right at the times Nicholas hated to admit it most, but that did not change the automatic shield that went up in Nicholas and with his shield came his strongest defense mechanism—anger and frustration.

Rachael nodded her head, sensing he did not want to answer that either. "I get it," she told him. "I get not being able to tell everyone everything or maybe not even understanding it yourself."

And she did. For the first time, Nicholas felt like he was talking with someone who understood his internal struggle, or, at the very least, someone who understood struggle. Perhaps that was not entirely fair—living in Dukhovia had been a struggle for most of the country. However, a majority of them were black and white. Traditionalist or non. Stop the heir or let them rule. No one was like Nicholas. No one had a world of gray. At least not in those areas. At least not anyone he had ever met.

She continued on, her speech not complete after that statement. "The world isn't always kind to us or make a lot of sense, but I've found fighting fire with love goes a long way in putting out flames."

Nicholas looked up into her eyes now. She was looking away, appearing lost, only for a moment, then she came to meet his eyes, two sets of blue, brilliant pair penetrating the next for several moments.

"This is something you have experience with?" He pondered.

Rachael nodded her head gently. "My actions don't always reflect my thoughts or ideals, I guess you could say."

She seemed like her voice would break if she went on, so Nicholas did not press. Instead, he searched in awe, wondering if others in America could relate so closely to him. He also pondered this edge he had with her—it was not one with which he had experience. Typically, he used force and control, fear to get what he wanted. Rachael was...gentle. She did not want to manipulate or harm him and so neither would he.

"I appreciate your kindness, Rachael Leighton. You are the light in a very dark tunnel, I will tell you that."

Rachael smiled, then she rocked back in the chair, everything in her persona completely changing from calm and reassuring to eager and bubbly. "It's what I do," she claimed, with a grin. "Okay, so no coming from—what about where you're going? I have to know something about you, *Sir* Nicholas," she emphasized, "I feel like I'm in the presence of royalty."

Nicholas felt as though he had to shake himself back to reality before processing the question asked to him, but once he did, he realized he was more than eager to answer this new one. He adjusted himself, regained grounding, and brought out confidence.

Next, he dipped his hand into his pockets and withdrew the poster of *The Rockers* he had uncovered at the library. He lay it before her, seizing the opportunity to gain more knowledge. She must live nearby and was around the same age—who better to know about them? "I am a fan—huge fan—of the band, *The Rockers*. Are you familiar with them?"

The girl took the folded poster from his hand and glanced from it to him and back again...multiple times. So many times, in fact, Nicholas's nerves kicked into high gear, his heart working overtime to control its beating.

"Please tell me you did not travel all the way here to see them," she finally said.

Nicholas's heart immediately fell into his stomach. "Why? Are they not around here?" They had to be, he was certain of it. He was *beyond* certain of it. All of his work to connect to her Spirit, his conversation in the library—did they lie to him? Did their false trail throw off his ability to properly connect?

But just as his stomach began to grow uneasy, Rachael answered casually. "No, they're definitely...around...*here.*" She looked like she was trying carefully to choose her words. "I'm just not so sure they're worth a long journey."

"Believe me," Nicholas said, heart rate returning to its normal chaos. "They are worth it."

Rachael smiled and nodded. Her tone of voice seemed almost comical, the look on her face read something Nicholas could not figure out, given the conversation—flatter? Confusion? "And why's that?"

"Well..." he rapped his fingers at the table as his brain fought into overdrive, reminding himself over and over what he already knew. "There is the music, of course. Hearing the way the instruments synthesize with the lyrics shows true emotion no human could deny. Then there is the fact that, given their age, they have achieved much success. Far more than I have at the very same age."

Rachael nodded and her lips curled in as if she were hiding a smile. "I am quite familiar with them. You're in town for the concert, then?"

Nicholas swallowed hard. "Yes, the concert."

"It's going to be so amazing!" Rachael celebrated, her personality seeming to jump out of her body and radiate her over-jubilance to everyone around her. "What's your favorite song?" She waited for a moment, staring into Nicholas's blank face before giving it a second try. "Who is your favorite member?"

Nicholas jumped at that chance, hoping to quickly recover from his obvious shortcoming. "They are all so wonderfully orchestrated, however, I would have to say the one who jumps out most to me...I believe Grayson is the last name." His mind was running together now, why in this final so important moment did his brain refuse to work?

"Cody?"

"Cody?" He asked surprised, that did not seem fitting. "Is that the child of Rachael Grayson?"

"Oh no," Rachael retracted, her face still oddly...stern? Puzzled? No...more like she was the one putting the puzzle together. "That's Stacy."

"Stacy." He repeated the name, thought about it. It felt right on his tongue and sat comfortably in his mind. It was not that it just sat comfortably—it ignited him. It was as though he had long ago burnt out and this was his flame, a divide in him was now bridged. Hearing her name... *her* name.

"There are five band members," Rachael said after nodding her head. "Stacy, Cody, Miranda, Jade..."

She trailed off but Nicholas was still eagerly listening, awaiting the final name. She laughed and drew herself back again, rocking on the back of the chair. "But Stacy is the one you like most." She grinned and appeared to be laughing at a joke Nicholas did not know, then quickly carried on before Nicholas had time to insert anything else into the conversation. "So, you're fifteen? Did your parents not travel with you, then?"

"No, they are not here." It came out hostile and he knew it. It was abrasive, it was abrupt, it was rude...it was completely and utterly uncontrolled. He could swear that the room itself shook with his fury.

His parents. It was another trigger; however, this was not one he could think about long enough to even falsely believe he would overcome. He did not speak of his parents—not to anyone, for any reason, ever. He had his reasons and they would remain his. No questions asked.

But now he was trapped in an explanation and he had put himself there. America had different standards than Dukhovia—he knew that. Americans did not begin their individual lives until 18-years-old and their parents held absolute control. Most Dukhovians were well on their individual paths by that point.

To confirm he travelled alone was to confirm he was from Dukhovia. Well, it confirmed he was from *somewhere*. Which, as Erlik pointed out, was obvious from him being in an airport. He was not even entirely convinced he wanted to keep it a secret. The truth, initially, of course, but to not reveal anything certainly came off as odd and not at all trusting.

Perhaps he did not need to earn the trust of this girl over the heir, but he did need to win over the American people. That may not have been Arkady's agenda, but it was his own. And he truly did not want to be his typical conniving self around Rachael. But then again, he refused to explain the absence of his parents.

"I apologize," Nicholas finally decided. "That was very rude of me. It has become a means of frustration in navigating the understanding of others— explaining their absence. It is something I will never become accustomed to."

"Understandable," Rachael accepted. "Are you staying with anyone, then? Or know where you are staying?"

Nicholas sighed. "That is something I still need to figure out."

"Well," Rachael began, grabbing a few of the pamphlets that he was standing next to. "Depending on how long you're staying, there are a few good hotels with some weekly rates."

"I am intending to stay for a while," Nicholas said matter-of-factly, he provided no further explanation.

"You might be more comfortable in an apartment, then."

Yes, apartment, that word felt like something he may have heard back in Dukhovia in reference to America. Though he did not know much about them.

"What can you tell me about them?" He felt the strangeness in the phrasing, but knew it had to be said just so. He could not act completely unaware of the country's way of working; he could not act like he lacked an edge. It was a trick he used often back home: he simply had to act like there was additional information and he would not let it be known what information he did or did not have. If Rachael noticed, she did not make a show of it.

"An apartment is sort of like a hotel, but a bit larger and you pay a monthly rate. They're usually pretty affordable. I can't really help you much with the process, but I can point you in the direction of someone who can."

Nicholas recoiled at the idea of involving anyone else.

"Okay, okay, no questions," Rachael laughed. "There are quite a few apartments in the area." She withdrew a paper and pen and marked up one of the pamphlets with numbers and words—addresses. After a few addresses were listed, she slid it over to him. She pointed to a number at the very bottom. "That's my phone number at the bottom; in case you get lost. It's my home phone, so my parents may answer, but they are extremely helpful, especially to kids in need."

Kids. Was Nicholas truly considered a child in this country? The thought made him feel as though he were on a different planet.

"A few months is quite a while for a concert," Rachael remarked. Her facial expression revealed she was seeking information. "Although the rumor is there will be more." She chuckled to herself again.

"I suppose it's a bit more than a one-time concert," Nicholas quickly retorted. He licked his lips and rubbed his hands together, piecing together as much of his story as he could reveal. "I am sort of…on a mission, one might say…to find my purpose, my sense of self. You see, I feel called in one direction and yet pushed into another by…by those who raised me." Nicholas delivered the words with perfect eloquence, but inside, he felt his veins screaming. He felt his body pulsating: a warning sign that he developed whenever the foreign nerves dared to peek through, telling him to get it together or his punishment would be most unforgiving.

When he looked up to see Rachael's puzzled look, he searched his memory for what brought up the subject and quickly added, "Music helps answer this call and

I thought if I were to follow my muse, I may discover my answer and my true purpose."

"And so here you are," Rachael contemplated. She was back to being her cheerful, go-lucky, and seemingly careless self, a coy smile etched on her lips.

"And so here I am," Nicholas agreed. "And that is why it is crucial I learn everything there is to know of them."

"Well, while you're here visiting your favorite band, I suppose you'll be enrolling in school?"

Nicholas nodded his head. "Yes, I will enroll and attend school while here, to remain up on my studies and absorb new information."

Rachael's cheeks puffed out and a snorting sound escaped her lips. "Well, if you have no destination in mind, we could get you enrolled at my school."

She sat seemingly poised, anticipating a reaction he was not quite sure he could deliver on. "Yes. Fantastic." He supposed it was not much of a lie, having an ally would definitely help him blend in.

She leaned over the table and added the school's address to his growing list.

1134 Daverwood

Then she looked back up, her eyes boring into his, shining brilliantly and expectantly for an uncomfortably long amount of time.

"Thank you, I will very much appreciate entering school with an alliance. Tell me, the members of the band, do they also attend school?"

Rachael's face spread into a smile. She looked down at the ground and then back up as if she could not hold her laughter in any longer. "You're not too big of a fan, are you?" She finally asked.

"I am new, I will admit," Nicholas said, feeling taken aback and wondering where he faltered. Should he have been making more a scene? Should he have brought more copies for an autograph? What else would Americans do? Pledge his allegiance to them? Kiss the poster?

Rachael only raised an eyebrow before extending her hand out towards him. After a moment of confusion, Nicholas handed the poster back towards her. Flattening the poster against the table and pointing to the far, right corner, she spoke, looking directly at him. "I'm the drummer. Rachael—Rachael Leighton." She said it slower this time as if that should have synthesized with him more. He supposed it should have—if he were truly a fan.

Nicholas's heart rate abandoned all hope of slowing down, his eyes bulging from his skull. He grabbed forward and pulled the poster from her hands, glancing back and forth. There was no way out of this lie and so he did what he was trained to do when caught: avoid. "Then you are familiar with all the members?"

She nodded her head firmly, once. "I would say so. They are my very best friends and I like to think I know a lot about my very best friends."

"Stacy," Nicholas began. Her name seemed familiar and comforting on his lips. "What is she like?"

"Horribly difficult and unflatteringly bad at make-up," Rachael decided after looking up to the sky as she decided her words. "But she's also kind…and abrasive…easy going…but also rather direct. But she loves Dukhovia more than her will to breathe—I expect you'll have that in common."

Rachael did not flinch as she delivered the words.

Nicholas looked up at her, his insides fully aflame with panic and fear. Everything, *everything* he worked years for completely thrown away—how? By what? What did he do now, *lie?* No, he already knew that.

Outwardly, he sat still. For all she knew, he simply came from a difficult time and feared opening up, he had no reason to hide where he was from. Except for that he did.

"You don't have to worry," Rachael said, interrupting his thought. "People around here aren't as afraid of Dukhovians as they are in other places. What with the whole gang of them living right in the neighborhood."

Rachael gestured her hand upward. Nicholas quickly followed it up a dully painted wall to a plaque, manifesting the ancient Dukhovian language in a delicate script.

The language was old and virtually extinct after the natives became friendlier with their sister countries and picked up Russian. However, Nicholas still knew the language perfectly.

All who come shall be welcomed,
No matter the distance traveled.
All who come shall be loved,
No matter the place they've come from.
All who come shall be seen as noble,
No matter the lives they once lived.
Heart of America Airport:
Owned by The Grayson and Matthews Family.
Residents of Topeka, Kansas Est. 2004

Nicholas took a moment to process and rebound off that deposit of knowledge. He did not lie; he did not hide—and he did not need to. Arkady had told him that if they knew he was from another country, that they would treat him differently, unjustly, and yet, here they were, having an entire plaque, an entire outlook based on Dukhovian ideals.

He almost felt comforted in the idea, until the screeching of plane wheels brought him back to reality. But they were still living in America, they were still running a very modernized mode of transportation.

Then again, if he and they were so different, then how did Rachael know he was Dukhovian?

"How did you…?"

"There's only one other person I hear boring purpose and life fulfillment into my ear every minute of their life and that's Ms. Stacy. And no one else speaks with such eloquence and grace than Tom and Terra—occasionally. When they let it slip."

When they let it slip. So, they did not practice Dukhovian ideals all the time. That stumped him for a moment. That and her previous comment... "You say Stacy...she loves Dukhovia?"

Rachael's eyes were glimmering more than they should be if she knew she was setting her friend up for a death sentence. It nearly made Nicholas want to stop, yet he could not. He had a duty to Dukhovia before he had a duty to Rachael.

"If a word existed stronger than love, that would be Stacy. She wants to live and breathe Dukhovia every minute of every day."

"And yet she is in the band?" Nicholas questioned.

Rachael shrugged. It was clear to see where her Dukhovian ideals lacked. "I guess she's a good mix of here and there. I could introduce you to her at the concert tomorrow, you can see for yourself. I think you guys will get along amazing."

Tomorrow. Nicholas's heart elevated, thoughts battling each other at a mile a minute. So many years, so much training, so much questioning...and yet tomorrow would be the night that he made his first move. Tomorrow would be the night that he would move forward and save Dukhovia.

CHAPTER 10

A PLOT OF FATE

*H*ard thudding along with the steady trickle of water met Nicholas's ears as he travelled down the long, stony corridor. Sweat dripped from his brow, no matter how many times he wiped it, reminding him *that his hands shook with unsteady tremors. The anxious pounding of his heart against his chest screamed for him to retrace his steps, to stop, to do anything but keep going forward.*

"Come on."

Nicholas's always confident friend, Vuel, led the way, his eyes darting around the narrow hallways as he moved quickly and snake-like.

"What if we are caught? I do not think we should go. There is no reason."

Vuel sneered. Nicholas was not taken aback, in truth, he expected it more so than the alternative. "He is not telling us everything, I promise you. I am telling you what I heard and they will say it in this meeting; I am certain of that."

Nicholas chanced the pouring rain blinding his vision as he looked up at the building he faced and then back down at the addresses Rachael had written out for him. It was the last on his list of area apartments to look into. None of the others felt fitting. They were too modern, too many people, too in-his-face, too many questions...

He now stood outside of a tall, brick apartment building. It was nothing fancy, in fact, it was the furthest thing from it. It was every bit as run down as the shops in the town and the majority of the houses Nicholas passed on his way. The door itself gave away the age of the building, the railing withering away was simply an added (and rather unnecessary) determiner.

Without further contemplation, he heaved the door open and glanced around inside for someone to speak to—a difficult task, to his gratitude. Nicholas shook his head the moment he opened the door—he was expecting the yellow, stained, and severely outdated carpets. Torn so bad from years—albeit, decades—of people trampling over it, one could barely tell carpet was even there anymore—it went straight down to the floor boards.

Nicholas felt his hand pad the thick stack of money in his pocket—he doubted he would need even a fraction of it.

Knock! Knock!

Nicholas felt something in his stomach sink, a lump formed in his throat, and his body became rigid—nerves.

"What?"

Nicholas entered the dingy, dark and completely disordered room to find a man of about fifty or sixty years of age, balding, and obese in physical description. Mentally, he gave off an unpleasing and unwelcoming demeanor. He did not look up when Nicholas opened the door or even when he shut it tight. He moved around the room full of papers in a hurry, lifting things and setting them back down again in a haste, as if he were looking for something.

"Ahem," Nicholas cleared his throat in an attempt to gain the man's attention. There was no response.

"Excuse me," Nicholas's voice demanded attention.

This took the man off guard, but he quickly resumed his business after a half-glance at Nicholas. Perhaps it was a little more than a half-glance, as he too was taken aback by Nicholas's stature and wardrobe choice.

He had abandoned the too-small t-shirt and threw his tunic back on. Apartment hunting was taking much longer than he thought and he knew he would dress in the unfamiliar clothing at the concert; he wanted to use whatever time he had to feel himself. Whatever that felt like.

"Do I look busy? What do you need?" He barked.

"I would like to rent out an apartment. I won't need it for long, a few months at the most."

The man wrinkled his eyebrow. "That's not how this works," he muttered in a low growl. "You have to apply, have a background check, it's a long process."

"I assure you my record is perfectly clean." Having to assure the man of anything twisted Nicholas's insides. He wanted to kill the man in an instant, or at least put some sense into him. He put his hands behind his back and fidgeted with his fingers to distract them before they found their way to the man's neck.

"Get out of here, kid. I don't have time for this."

Better cool it. Erlik.

Nicholas tapped his foot impatiently. His eyes wandered over to a calendar outlined in a hideous sea green that matched the man's sweater vest. He spotted the date and saw that he had marked his daughter's birthday. Almost instantly, Nicholas's eyes found a pink envelope with a female's name on it. He took it in his hand and held it behind his back.

"I have the money. Everything that you are worried about will be taken care of."

The man shook his head again, clearly irritated and offended. "Are you even old enough for an apartment? Should I call the police to bring you back to your parents?" He spat.

Nicholas huffed and tapped his foot harder. He held up the envelope for the man to see.

The man stopped in his tracks and fully looked Nicholas in the eye.

Nicholas now looked at him with piercing eyes and a straight face. His voice was no longer polite, but hostile and grueling, no sign of entreating was traceable.

CHAPTER TEN

"I said I have the money," Nicholas threw five-thousand dollars on the table. The man's eyes grew. "Now it appears as though we are both very busy men—regardless of age or importance," he waved the envelope. "So, I suggest that you turn around, grab a key for an empty apartment, place it in my hand, and we will both be on our ways. Or do we need to make this difficult?"

The man was still not convinced. Though fear was visible across his face from a mile away, he tried to outsmart Nicholas—a deadly mistake in Dukhovia. The man's fat, unsteady hand reached over for the phone and dialed a 9, only to have fear cause him to drop the phone and fall onto the soft cushioning of his bottom.

Nicholas walked up closer to the L-shaped desk and peered down to look at the man. "Unfortunately for you, the police will not be able to help you much, were you to go in that direction. They might have weaponry, even numbers on me," Nicholas drew a small, pointed knife from his pocket. "But do they have the training to kill twenty men in thirty seconds, wait, no…I do believe my record is thirty men in twenty seconds' flat. Have they ever taken down an entire fleet of men from the greatest military in the world?"

Fear was etched on the face of the bulbous man as he reached a ham-like arm up and placed the phone back on the receiver. His arm dropped without any sense of control.

"Now, I believe that I have made my desires quite clear. Key, please?" Nicholas held out his hand.

The man made several attempts to rise to his feet and find the old, brown keys in the back of his office. A shaking hand made its way over to Nicholas's.

"M-may I have a name to put in the records?"

"Do not worry about it," Nicholas said flatly. He threw the birthday card on the desk in front of the man. "And wish Cassandra a very happy birthday from me."

Nicholas was already half way out the door. He was already beyond frustrated with this country and his mission had barely begun. It was no wonder Arkady and everyone else feared an American ruling Dukhovia. They were unable to even stand on their own two feet when met with adversity. Would they even fight to protect their beliefs?

Nicholas was more than prepared to fight the man, but fear alone made him cave. In Dukhovia, fear was his strongest weapon, especially when he did not want to use force. However, he never met a man that did not at least attempt to stand his ground. Hm. He supposed it was for the best.

He continued to march up the creaking steps, running his hand along the dusty hand rail that threatened to fall to the floor with even an ounce more of pressure. The key told him that apartment 38B would be his new (short lived) home. He thrust the key into the hole and pried it open after much suffering.

Nicholas smirked as he viewed the room that the man had chosen for him—it was fully furnished. To his right was a decent sized kitchen, though there was not much counter space. Something he had only become accustomed to since his time living in the palace.

His fridge was in the furthest corner to the left, against the back wall. There was a small square of white counter space, then his sink. There was approximately double the amount of counter space and then the counter looped to provide the oven. These would be somewhat new to him. They did have a fridge at the palace, though he rarely used it. They never had one at home nor did most Dukhovian families.

Each home had a well either nearby or in their kitchen area which gave them water they would pump out. Stoves were exceedingly rare. Again, the palace did have one, but Nicholas did not prefer to use it most of the time. Other Dukhovian families made fires or cooked over pots in their fireplaces, therefore, Nicholas did too.

He glanced around at the last curious part of his kitchen: the height of the brown cupboards. Those above the refrigerator and across the counter and sink area made him wonder what size of people the designers were building this apartment for. They were no problem for him, but an average sized person would never be able to reach them, let alone a person in a wheel chair. There were no lower cupboards besides the one just below the sink.

He shrugged it off, finding it more difficult to form coherent thoughts anyway. Dukhovia offered accessibility for different types of people in all homes, perhaps America did so in a different manner.

Nicholas glanced around the rest of his apartment, taking in the view of the living area directly across from his kitchen. Two blue and red threaded couches cornered a television with some strange electronic box deemed an X box. Nicholas looked at the CD's next to it, piecing together that it was one of the gaming systems that Arkady had said were rather popular. Once or twice, Arkady had attempted to teach Nicholas how they worked so that, when he arrived in America, he could practice playing it, putting on the front that he had been playing for years. Nicholas refused the very idea…until he no longer could.

He shuddered away the memory, pushing it under a cloak the way he always had. No vision, no memory. No thoughts, no memory. No memory, no past.

He did have to admit how impressed he was by the date on the games. It was probably the newest thing in the room at seven years of age.

The remainder of the apartment was not too noteworthy. A hallway entrance directly across from the front door led to a less noteworthy bedroom. The left end of the hall held a closet while the right, a bathroom, leaving the bedroom in the center. He glanced at everything expectantly, as if either anticipating it to vanish or have some type of trap.

CHAPTER TEN

Nicholas examined the apartment top to bottom looking for hidden devices, weapons, explosives, etc. He came up blank. He examined the likelihood that there was nothing. The man downstairs was arrogant and ignorant, no doubt, however, he did not seem prepared to kill anyone. Nicholas had lived with a killer before, Nicholas lived as a killer, he knew how they functioned.

He also knew he was, in some ways, free. No matter how much power Arkady had, he did not know where Nicholas was staying. He could not send anyone in advance to sabotage this room. It was safe. It was…safe.

For some reason that realization made his heart beat faster. Could that really be true? Had no one followed him into America? Had no one been sent to watch his every move and ensure he was following through on the plan? Of course they would not have. Nicholas had to sell that he was here to complete his mission to Arkady as well as he had to sell it to himself.

And he was here to complete his mission.

He just hoped that mission would somehow…change.

A strange noise coming from the kitchen entered his ears and seemed to reverberate throughout the house. He stood still, listening for a moment. It did not come closer or get louder, signaling that it was not man made.

He walked in closer, following the sound until he ended up staring directly at the fridge. He listened to it and felt immediately like an idiot. It was a motor.

He stayed at the fridge, opening it and closing it with distaste and curiosity. The top part was much cooler—a freezer. He started to shut it then paused, feeling the cool lash against his face. The feeling hit him with incredulousness. For a moment, angst fell over him. He felt the need to glance over his shoulder as his heart plummeted into his stomach. Then, in the next second, he felt calm, comforted by the chill.

He placed his hand in the freezer, touching the bottom for one second, then another. He soon stood, two hands, and his face looming at the entrance of the freezer, breathing in the coolness and familiarity that it offered—until he could no longer stand that familiarity.

He put his hands to his spinning head and sat down on the couch, pressing his fingers into his overworked mind. He had spent just over a day in America and his thoughts were battling each other more than ever before.

Had he been successful thus far? He had managed to find Rachael and receive an invitation to meet Stacy—the heir, the *female* heir. Nicholas needed the chuckle that realization brought to him. He could not wait to see the look on Arkady's face. He needed the slap it would bring.

But it also brought confusion. Nicholas did not particularly agree with the demeaning view of women Arkady seemed to have, but he was a man of tradition. Tradition and his mother had always taught him to protect women, to defend them, to be their breadwinners. The amount of protection Stacy would need as ruler of a country constantly at war would be astronomical.

Perhaps that would be his role in Dukhovia, if he were to somehow find a new one. Men were taught to be sacrificial for women, being biologically more inclined to do so. Because be it judgment or fact, women *were* biologically weaker.

So then there *were* Arkady's fears to consider. Women are weak. Whether due to oppression or natural selection did not matter. Women were never trained in the levels of fighting, knowledge, and history that were required of rulers. Whether they were chosen to rule or not, they would still be expected to follow all the typical functions of the country. Her being American alone would destroy that.

How weak would Stacy be? Stacy. What a common name. There was absolutely no historical or spiritual context behind it that he was aware of. Then again, it did derive from the name of a very famous princess, and that is what she was, after all. At least, that is what she was supposed to be—she would be dead before she even had a chance to envision herself on the throne.

Nicholas hated that way of thinking—one moment hopeful, the next falling right into Arkady's plot. Nicholas would be lying, however, if he did not admit that sometimes he did want to follow through with his mission. As if he could hurry and pull the plug and spend a lifetime making it up to the Spirits. He would rather spend a lifetime at their feet than Arkady's.

Stacy. Female. Heir to the Dukhovian throne. Living in Topeka, Kansas. America. Best friend Rachael Leighton. Musician. Family banished.

He had learned more and already made connections. He supposed he was succeeding after all.

He looked at the bed now, as night began to fall in the Thursday sky. A wave of indigo and orange swirling together for victory over the other. Tranquil, peaceful…

Rest. For the very first time in his life, the idea of rest seemed so very appealing and so very needed. Despite the rather unnatural feel Nicholas was exposed to when climbing into the surprisingly soft and comfortable bed, he was able to adjust rather quickly. No fear, no weapons, no tricks. He was simply getting rest.

He shut his eyes, drifting into a place, a place far away from his journey…

Nicholas's heart did not stop the entire time he and Vuel stood outside the entrance to the meeting. He was nearly certain the pounding would echo around the entire enclave and give away their hiding spot.

"As for the children?"

Arkady took a long sip of tea, smacking his lips with the flavor and bringing the cup down to chest level. He seemed as comfortable and calm as could be as he pondered his response to Alexander.

"They are both strong beyond words. I have no doubt that one of them will be able to succeed."

"What exactly is your plan, your Highness?"

CHAPTER TEN

Another long sip of tea. "It is not my plan, but the Spirits, Sasha. Is that not something you should know? Whether they kill each other intentionally or unintentionally, it is of no concern of mine. So long as one of them sits on the throne instead of the American."

Besides feeling as comfortable as he could expect in his circumstances, Nicholas did not sleep. His eyes remained stuck on the ceiling as he thought about everything that was happening. His stomach once again was an empty pit quickly filling with tension.

You are making a mistake.

"Then why is everything aligning so perfectly?" Nicholas shot back.

All is not going well. You have no idea what to say when asked where you are from and the girl closest to the heir has likely already told her you are Dukhovian.

"But Arkady was wrong. She was not judgmental."

The friend *was not judgmental. The heir very well may be.*

Nicholas stared over his bed and out the window. To that he had no rebuttal. And that led him back to the debate he had been having with himself for years: to tell the truth immediately or not?

In the end, all that mattered was that he had the trust of the heir. She knew he was, at a very minimum, of Dukhovian descent. He could keep up the ruse. He could pretend he had little care for Dukhovia—or that he had much care. He had learned over the years that he had no way of knowing someone's true thoughts, thus honesty should be maintained.

But she supposedly *loves* Dukhovia.

Consider that alternative then. What if she is as traditional and respectful as if she were brought up in Dukhovia. What is your plan, then?

Nicholas swallowed hard, struck with the factualization that Arkady had already been wrong once. And if he was wrong about one thing, what else was he wrong about? He did not answer Erlik, but he knew his sworn enemy already knew the answer.

CHAPTER 11

EVERYTHING WILL CHANGE

Goooood morning, folks! It is a beautiful, sunny December first day and the world is ready to be swept off their feet!" Stacy threw open Dan's curtains at five o' clock in the morning. It was the first time anyone had ever seen her awake before Dan...or awake before anyone, for that matter. While Dan was a 'wake up three hours before necessary' kind of guy, Stacy was the type of girl that you could not get out of bed if you dumped cold water on her...not that the temperature really mattered.

Dan rose out of bed quickly and glanced out the window. "Stacy, it's a blizzard out there, in what world is that sunny?"

"My world," she smiled, throwing his clothes at him. She felt the corner of her mouth twitch. Anytime people discussed Stacy's reaction to the cold, they discussed Dukhovia. With her visions at night getting more vivid and the reminders during the day happening more frequently, she decided to try to block Dukhovia from as much as today as possible. It failed to help that she felt a growing frustration every time she played when her thoughts kept taking her to the other side of the world.

"The sun always shines in the spot light of frost bite. And the spot light that'll be shining on us, tonight, as the world sees that *The Rockers* have returned and we are better than ever!" Stacy got down on one knee and played an invisible electric guitar.

"The show isn't till tonight, rockstar, we still have school."

The enthusiasm on Stacy's face fell. "School? Really, Dan, school? You're going to let all this practice time go to waste on something as insignificant as school?"

"Some of us have colleges scouting us out and skipping school does not look good on your record," Dan reasoned with her, putting notebook after notebook into his book bag.

"So, I'll punch you in the face and break your nose—you'll have a valid excuse not to show."

Dan looked at his sister sternly. "You know what, you're right. The band should practice as much as possible, so if you all of you would like to run the show while I'm getting an education, be my guest. I'll see you at one-thirty."

Stacy's face lit up. She danced up and down happily. "Oh, thank you, thank you, thank you, master," she got on her knees and bowed to him. "We have certainly chosen wisely with you, Oh Great One."

Dan rolled his eyes and sneered, but he could not hide the smile that broke over his face as he swung his backpack strap over his shoulder and headed down to breakfast. As annoyed as he pretended to be, he quite enjoyed his sister's antics and their relationship would not be the same without them.

The two were complete opposites when it came to their personal lives, but they clicked the way any brother sister duo would when it came to being there for each other. Ultimately, they were best friends with extremely different interests.

Besides, it was *actual* crunch time for Dan. While Stacy still had what seemed to be all the time in the world to allow her future to find her, Dan was graduating this year and had every promise of becoming the world renown inventor that he dreamt of.

When they arrived downstairs, Grace was in the kitchen preparing breakfast—as always. Although she possessed the cooking skills that would have any restaurant shut down within an hour, Grace prided herself on having a close family that did everything together, knew everything about each other, and never missed a single chance to allow memories to be made.

Waking up to eat an early breakfast together was one of the ways this could be accomplished. Due to the difficulty of Kevin's work schedule at his overbearing and unfathomably exhausting job (six am to ten pm five days a week), breakfast was the only time they could be together as a whole family. Especially with the band beginning to play on the weekends—his days off.

Stacy slid down the railing, happily skipping past Dan and making it into the kitchen just a moment before he did.

"There's my rockstar," Grace smiled, setting a pan of scrambled eggs on the island counter. "Are you ready to show the world what they've been missing?"

"Don't encourage her," Dan mumbled, rubbing his face as he slid into the seat next to his sister.

Grace cocked her head and glanced at Stacy, confused. "Is he ill?"

"Shall we call the doctor?" Stacy retorted.

"The doctor's already set to arrive in mere moments, the question is: will he make it?"

"Very funny," Dan countered, rolling his eyes. "I have a big test today. I was up all night between studying and working on the sounds for the stage."

"You know, no one expects you to be a perfect know-it-all who never requires sleep," Stacy said in a motherly voice, reprimanding his behavior.

"No, but the amount of work I expect myself to do requires it," he noted. Dan slowly filled his plate with eggs, bacon, and toast before taking out a notebook, flipping to the near back of it, and reading notes only he could comprehend.

The sound of Kevin's thudding footsteps echoed around the house as he flew into the kitchen, wrapping his arm around his wife and kissing her cheek passionately. He had a briefcase in hand which he sat on top the blue, marble counter top, only to receive a glance from Grace telling him that it was not appropriate breakfast table décor.

"Good morning, champions," Kevin announced, receiving a groan from Dan. "Daniel, how helpful are you going to be in class or tonight if you're falling asleep already?"

"I'll be good, dad. I'm just stressed."

"Well that's new," Stacy laughed, jumping off the stool as she wiped her mouth and brought a plate which was once stacked full of food over to the sink. After washing her plate, she took out her phone and began dialing.

"Who do you think is going to be awake this early?" Dan asked, astonished.

"Rachael," Stacy smirked, holding the phone up to her ear.

"Doubtful," Dan retorted, raising his eyebrow to display the immense amount of doubt he felt.

Stacy ignored him and put the phone on speaker, holding it out. Within the same second, an excited scream echoed out from the other side. Stacy answered with the same scream, energy radiating as she jumped up and down.

Dan rolled his eyes yet again. Grace and Kevin smiled while not looking up from their plates, sensing that with the mood Dan was in, the day was only going to be full of bitter instructions and a lot of tension.

"Mr. Happy Pants gave us permission to stay home from school to practice," Stacy reported after the screaming ceased. "Be over here with Cody within the hour. I'll call Jade and Miranda."

"I know you don't think we're *that* unprepared," Rachael said with sass in her voice. "We're already crossing the yard."

Stacy heard Rachael click her phone shut and the sound of the door open and close. The perks of her and Cody living right next door to each other were seamlessly never ending. Whenever they needed help with homework or to borrow something, they were right there. Whenever they wanted to sneak out to hang out, they did not have to travel very far to find one another.

Although, sneaking was not something they could really do much of with their parents. Their parents frequently noted that in their youth, they turned their past traumas into a skill, leading them to be a famous group whom helped find runaway or missing children. They knew all the tricks and even if they did manage to escape, they would be found in a heartbeat.

Along with being able to track better than a well-seasoned hunter, Grace and Kevin were also trained to be able to detect the slightest movement, anticipate surprise attacks, and expect anything. Sneaking up on one of them or trying to surprise them was an impossible task.

"Good morning, my lovely band manager," Rachael sang, walking in with a smile as bright as her flashy, red shirt and skirt. "Band manager's parents, best friend." She nodded to each one individually and waved.

The others poured in behind her.

"Good morning and good luck," Kevin replied, kissing his immediate family members and bidding the rest farewell.

"I've been up all night practicing, I'm so ready for this," Cody exclaimed.

"I'll be the one to determine if you're ready," Dan intervened, closing his notebooks and re-stuffing his bag.

"Didn't you already?" Jade asked, shifting her weight to one foot. "You know, when you 'okay'd' us as decent enough to present ourselves to the world again?"

"Decent enough?" He spat. "Please don't use that word around record labels. I don't want people thinking I would produce anything that was *decent,* only perfection."

"Of course, your majesty," Jade stated with a bow.

"I'm going to school," Dan told them, throwing his bag over his shoulder.

"An hour and a half early, you're practically already late," Jade called out after him as he slammed the door.

"Come on, let's head down to the basement and start practicing," Stacy said through fits of laughter.

"Your wish is my command," Rachael complied, happily skipping over to the basement door. "Also, I have some very exciting news for you after first break!"

While Dan bustled off to school and Grace finished cleaning and getting ready for work herself, the five remaining went to the basement to get their instruments set up and start practicing.

Although they felt rather prepared, there was nothing like the practice before the show. It was both nerve-wracking and exhilarating, orderly and rushed. They felt they knew everything and absolutely nothing. There was so much excitement to look forward to, especially seeing the fans and feeling their adoring energy.

The rush of endorphins, the blaring of the lights, the sound of metal hitting gravel as their instruments were carried in...Then, there was the illustrious moment when they came out on stage, giving them that feeling of euphoria and wholeness for the entire night.

Today, Stacy found, there was an added feeling to her normal jitters. Normally when Rachael had news it was something they likely could care very little about. But ever since their sleepover and the visit to Tom and Terra's, her and Rachael had talked mainly about Dukhovia. Okay, they talked *only* about Dukhovia.

Not only had the dream been in full force, Stacy had been having flashbacks to it constantly throughout the day. Even with the show approaching, they scarcely talked about it. When they did discuss the show, it was usually interrupted by one of Stacy's visions and the conversation of what it meant. So today, she was confident Rachael had something to tell her related to the visions. But, then again, it could be that there is a huge sale on make-up bags and mini-skirts and Stacy "absolutely must" update her wardrobe.

When the Spirits deem it necessary, she thought.

CHAPTER ELEVEN

The other members of the band had picked up Stacy's changes as well. Dan seemed worried—surprising. Jade and Miranda seemed concerned but unmoved and purely concerned without prying, respectively. But Cody knew the most.

Cody had been there with Rachael and his best friend, Dylan, on the one and only trip to Dukhovia. He never quite showed interest in his roots. He lived and breathed the American way of life, but he honored his family the way any Dukhovian would.

Stacy often thought back to when she first told both Cody and Rachael that she was having the dream, several months ago. They had gathered together in a remote part of town, the way they often did. The area was surrounded by thick evergreens and rolling hills. The trees seemed to cave in and form a circle around the land before turning into the unsettled, winding forest. The center of their small town was close, but just out of ear and eye shot.

It was their spot. An almost sacred place that held the history of their friendship. They first stumbled upon the spot when they were trying to reunite their parents as friends. Cody had staged running away and made it seem he were in danger. In the process, however, he had tripped and fallen over a small cliffside. When their parents found them in absolute, real danger, he was dangling over the side, yelling for help.

Cody was saved and the plan worked. Their parents had laughed together, thanked each other, and just *spoke* for the first time in at least ten years. After that, they returned to the spot often, but no one else ever seemed to be there, making it seem magically made only for them.

"Stace, you look like you either saw a ghost or haven't experienced sleep in the better part of six months—which is it?" Rachael had said.

"Possibly both?" Stacy had said through heavy lids. Then, she began to describe the dream. "It doesn't really make any sense because Dukhovia is cold and this place is tropical—maybe it's what's coming? Maybe it's how Dukhovia is supposed to be? But that wouldn't make any sense. I don't know, maybe it doesn't mean anything."

"Remember what Aunt Terra always says," Cody had commented. "The Spirits don't speak unless they have something to say."

That comment had stayed with Stacy. The Spirits were speaking and their voices were getting louder and louder—but why could she not figure out what they were trying to say?

"How are you feeling today?" Cody asked her, the look in his eye sensing more than his words persisted with.

"I'm great," Stacy lied. "It's just that little internal debate of feeling excited to go on stage but with these persistent little thoughts telling me I'm supposed to be doing something else. Just the usual, no big deal."

"You can do both, you know," Rachael sang. "Love Dukhovia and be in the band. I know, I know, it's not the Dukhovian way."

Stacy smiled. "It's not quite that. They have music in Dukhovia, it's not a prison. But I don't think these visions are telling me to go to Dukhovia and live the life I have here. I feel like they're telling me to go to Dukhovia and do...." Her voice trailed, because no matter how much time passed or how often she thought about everything, the end of that sentence never became clear.

"Well of course they don't want you to have the life you have here," Rachael scorned. "You wouldn't even be able to take a hot shower."

Stacy rolled her eyes, knowing Rachael was only...half joking.

The band went to work setting up their instruments and completing sound check. Jade and Miranda plugged their microphones into the stereo speaker system, checking the sound level and functionality several times. The process took much longer than it should have as Dan had a million wires running over the ones they needed. Of course, to him it would have only taken a second to figure out: all the wires were color coded and in just the perfect spot. The rest of the band just saw a mess.

Stacy quickly fastened her guitar into a slot and began tuning it appropriately for their opening song. A song by Cody called 'Gravity'. It was a love song that the band did not lose any sleep over trying to guess where the inspiration came from.

Cody left his mic for last, first assisting Rachael in connecting her drums while she read over the words to a few of her songs. He spent more time than was necessary tightening and shining the drum set, but Rachael liked it to gleam a certain amount in some spots and he did not want her to have any issues.

All the while, Stacy tried to clear her head. She read and reread her music, but her mind continued to wonder, especially leading up to first break...

"So, I met a guy at the airport last night, Stace..." Rachael began in a sing-song voice.

"What guy?" Cody interrupted, shooting up fixing a loose piece on her drum set, hitting his head on one of the drums in the process.

The other girls snickered.

"Sorry, Code, when did you change your name to Stacy?" Jade asked, receiving no response.

Stacy waited with anticipation, but she lost interest the more Rachael talked. So, it was typical Rachael stuff after all—trying to set her up with yet another guy.

"His name was Nick," she went on, much to the disappointment of Cody who was now packing his tools for Rachael's drums away haphazardly. "He was extremely well-spoken, polite, kind..."

"Sounds like a real charmer," Stacy giggled as her cousin panicked and shot her a glaring look. "Did you get his number?"

"What's the relevance?" Jade interrupted, sparing a fight between the cousins.

CHAPTER ELEVEN

Rachael sashayed her skirt and smiled the same coy smile she always did when she was giving information sparingly for a purpose. "For starters, he'll be coming to our school starting next week and I think we can always expand our friend group."

"Maybe," Stacy made a face where she pretended to puke. "We seem to all be forgetting the danger of new students." Her words held merit, but her voice was sarcastic and her face careless as she continued to not lose focus from her guitar.

The other four rolled their eyes. For some reason or the next, Stacy was hell bent on the belief that new students meant a disruption in the status quo and a reason for all others to fear. Something about how they did not know the unspoken relationships already set in and could easily disrupt the imminent love bound to happen between certain people...

"Anyway, I invited him to the concert tonight and afterwards I'm going to find him to introduce him to everyone. I think that will help his first day of school tremendously." She smiled, always impressed with her plans.

Stacy raised her eyebrow and Rachael continued to smile the smile until Stacy looked away. She had never gone so far as to introduce Stacy to a guy before. Surely, he must be her soulmate.

"I don't know, Rache, we shouldn't let just *anyone* come to our shows." Cody tried to appear unattached to the conversation, but screwing in the same screw on his microphone only took so long before it came across as questionable.

"Oh, so we should start screening the random people who order tickets, Romeo?" Stacy asked with a smile.

"Not necessarily," Cody hissed, dropping his microphone to the ground with a loud thud which echoed throughout the basement, running the acoustics test for them. "But being close to us is different."

Stacy rolled her eyes at the holes in his logic.

"I think it's a great idea," Miranda agreed with a smile. She was busily adjusting her microphone to her short level. "What a perfect way for him to make some friends before coming to a totally new school."

The other girls nodded and agreed, except for Jade who had no opinion in the matter or care to listen to the conversation.

"I think he's practically an adult and can make friends on his own," Cody argued. "Are we ready?" Cody grabbed his microphone and stood impatiently in the center of their faux stage.

Although the band was rather high in demand, they did not like to exert their resources unless deemed completely necessary. Dan usually ran up the bill in the electronics department. He wanted them to have the best equipment so that their sound was the best and their shows looked the best. But apparently what they had to practice with did not matter.

All was well, though, because it did not matter to them either. They preferred to keep things the way they were. It made them feel closer to their music and closer to each other, rather than like a band that had long forgotten who they were and where they came from. They wanted the band to be a part of them, not for themselves to be part of (or consumed by) the band.

"My drums aren't even hooked up to the speakers," Rachael said in a sad voice, holding up a wire that ran from her drums to nowhere.

"And my acoustic guitar isn't even out of the case, yet, speed demon," Stacy added, bending down to unlock her treasure from its case.

"I'm sorry, Rache," Cody said remorsefully, ignoring his cousin and heading over to her drum set to finish helping her.

"I forgive you," she said, kissing his cheek lightly.

"So, tell us more about your new boyfriend," Jade egged Rachael on, receiving a dirty look from Cody.

"Yeah, like tell us what's so wrong with him that he needs his hand held on the first day of school," Cody retorted.

"Well for starters, Cody Robert, he's new to the country."

Stacy's interest was back in the game. "What do you mean?"

"Well, I might be assuming," Rachael corrected herself. "I don't actually know how recently he got here, but he was at some point born and lived in Dukhovia."

Stacy shot up, facing Rachael. "He's from Dukhovia?" Stacy felt a sense of hope that she could not explain, a fulfilling urge that at this very moment should only come from music.

Rachael nodded.

"Maybe lead with that next time," Stacy chastised.

Rachael rolled her eyes. "Like I said, I don't know his whole story, but he didn't seem like someone who had been to public school or around a lot of Americans before. But he did seem deeply troubled. He was having a really hard time, so I would really like to do anything possible to help him."

Cody looked sideways at her, locking eyes on each other. He sighed. "I will, Rache. I promise." He sealed the deal with a kiss to her cheek.

"I wonder why he was troubled?"

Protect them.

Stacy's heart was on fire, her dream flashing through her mind at rapid speed. Dukhovian, seeming troubled, arriving just when her dream was starting to pick up...this had to have been what the Spirits were telling her about.

"A lot of him was confusing," Rachael said. "He says he flew in for the concert and was a big fan, but he didn't recognize me."

"That's because not everything is about you, princess," Jade joked, patting Rachael on the head.

"Of course," Rachael sighed. "But he acted like he was our biggest fan, followed us for years, so you'd think he'd know..."

"Maybe he just wasn't expecting to find you working in an airport?" Miranda offered.

"The airport run by the family of the band?" Cody said crossly. "Unlikely. He sounds suspicious."

"I don't know, it's possible." Rachael winked at Stacy. "Anyway, he was very proper and seemed to follow Dukhovian practices very closely."

"What would someone from Dukhovia possibly be doing in America?" Cody spat, he was now grasping his microphone tightly, but was significantly calmer with the mic between his fingers than he previously had been. His voice came across now as mere pungent curiosity.

The others took their places at their instruments and mics. "Scenery change? Grocery stores? Electricity?" Rachael listed off the things in her mind with a coy smile.

Stacy stored away each detail Rachael spoke and knew there would be more to divulge when Cody's cynicism was no longer around. Though, he did seem to lighten up when he realized Rachael was match making and not falling in love.

A true Dukhovian who lived the way a Dukhovian lived was exactly who Stacy needed to talk to about her dream and about her life in Dukhovia—if it was possible it even existed.

Stacy found herself obsessing over her own differences from living in America. What if this guy would not even talk to her? Stacy was never eloquently spoken. She knew little about their traditions and stories aside from the holidays her family celebrated, and she bet those were Americanized.

Her head hurt from thinking about everything she lacked, but perhaps this person was supposed to help her find her path. Perhaps she was the one who needed this protection to return to Dukhovia and find her true purpose.

But, as far as she knew, she was no heir.

Then again, there was Cody's last question to ponder—why was this guy in Dukhovia? And for how long? What if he was banished too and also did not want to talk about anything Dukhovian related? Stacy sighed. Even a Dukhovian being handed to her on a silver platter could not make things easy.

The others laughed and rolled their eyes, suddenly everyone's mood seemed to shift and brighten as Stacy played a few notes on her guitar and Cody began to hum. Rachael's soft thuds on her drums were the signal for Jade and Miranda to enter in with their background vocals. Once the beat was set, Cody began his song.

Everything that they were previously feeling seemed to nearly wash away. Their minds were off of the new kid at school, off of the pressure of the concert, and anything else that possibly restrained them. They carried on strong growing more powerful, livelier, and positively harmonic.

"Give me a push,
oh,
give me a pull,

EVERYTHING WILL CHANGE

Gravity your power is overruled.
No force stronger than our love,
no force stronger except from that above. "

Stacy's mind seemed to wander after Cody sang the words. She had heard the song and played it a million times before—just in one day when Dan was around—but they never affected her like they did in that moment. She fell into a daze as she thought of the power love had over Cody and how strongly she desired to find something that pulled her as powerfully. For the first time in their lives, she envied Cody.

Cody was singing the chorus again and Rachael was increasing the melody on her drums. Jade and Miranda were producing the echo to Cody's last few words stronger than they had in a long time.

A smile crossed Stacy's face as she thought about how music brought her friends together—music and magic. In the strangest of ways, it seemed. But it was a part of them now. It was part of who they were.

Stacy's fingers danced across the strings of her guitar, they knew where to go by memory, but she enjoyed the focus of closing her eyes and feeling that sense of belonging. She held the guitar close to her body, cradling it with as much adoration as possible. The vibrations from her guitar ceased, telling her one song had ended.

"We're going to do Rule the World next," Cody announced, and the sound of flipping music became soothing to their ears.

Again, Stacy got into the same position and drew up her guitar as the words poured out from Cody.

"Follow me, right now.
I'll show you how we do it in my town.
Follow this route, let me show you
next stop is out of my control,
baby
this is how we Rule the World.
They couldn't keep me anchored for too long,
baby,
I had to break free, of these hard chains,
so,
now you see me throwing command after command,
knowing one day I knew I would be called
to this infamous land
and
This is how we Rule the World
They couldn't keep me anchored for too long,
Baby,

CHAPTER ELEVEN

I had to break free of these hard chains,
So,
Now here I am
Standing alone and broken
Wandering how I got where I am
This life's a cryptic cyclone
Yet, here I stand
And I'm wandering...

....

....

who would ever wanna Rule the World."

The music break before the last line always hit them all the most—and the crowd.

Practice continued for a few hours. They took breaks for drinks, discussion, and eventually lunch, and by the time Dan got home they ran the first half of the show twice and the second half once. Being that the concert would last two hours and they had six hours to practice before he made his entry, he was not completely disappointed in the use of their time.

"You seem to have done very well giving each other feedback." He announced as he found his seat at his desk which held a large computer responsible for operating the sound of all the instruments and lights if necessary. His face was already buried in some type of notetaking, a pen cap stuck in his mouth for added effect, making his words muffled.

"Of course, my liege," Jade stated with a bow. "Only the best practice for the world's best performance."

"I like the optimism," Dan retorted, pointing his pen in Jade's direction as he chose to ignore the clear and utter sarcasm in her tone. "What songs did you do?"

"Gravity, Mysterious Wonder, Misfit Hero, Change in Direction, and Rule the World, Stacy did My Way, Hold Me Steady, and Find Me, Jade did Breathe in Me and Blast This Place on Fire, Manda did Rescue Mission and Lover's Tale, and Rachael did Stay, Small Town Love Story, and her new one...the *whole* show, Daniel. Trust us?" Cody listed the songs off the top of his head confirming that he knew them better than the back of his own hand.

"Okay, great. Rache, let's just run your songs one more time, then hit the road. The show starts at seven."

Although a 'does it really?' comment was floating around and dripping with sarcasm from probably every mouth, the band simply smiled and did as they were told. No matter how Dan could seem, they did have dedication and wanted to be prepared and focused.

"If I ask you to stay,
will you say forevermore?
If I beg you to stay with me answer me:

forevermore... "

As Rachael's angelic voice began to encapsulate them all, Cody picked up the drums. Stacy found the beat on her guitar and met the hollow and melancholy sound of Rachael's voice. Rachael loved the drums more than anything and rarely sang, but when she did, the audience was always left in almost a state of shock. The way her voice radiated around everyone—including the band—left them with an almost tingling in their very souls.

The crowd went wild for her and always begged for more—while she never shot down the attention, she knew when to step down. She was very modest...when necessary.

After singing Rachael's songs more times than was necessary, the band packed up the bus that Dan stopped by to retrieve after school, and headed to the site of their show before the streets started getting blocked with traffic of their own cause.

The instruments were piled in and secured first, then Dan's equipment, and finally the band itself. Dan always drove, mainly because he was the only one with a driver's license, but the five of them doubted much would change that in a few weeks when the others were old enough to get their licenses as well.

Richard's police car usually led the procession, along with Grace in her truck. Next, came the bus, then the several cars of their security team which consisted of their close friends and family.

The bus pulled over to the side of a building that was about twenty minutes out of town to unload their instruments. The band went inside to get everything into position. Every time they performed somewhere new, the owners were taken by surprise to see them set up their own set—but they wanted to be as involved in their shows as possible. They did not want people doing things for them—not that Dan would trust anyone to do anything for him.

Stacy hopped out and began helping everyone unpack the bus. Her heart felt tight in her chest as she looked from the venue to the van and back again. She could not deny the excitement of getting on stage for the first time in what felt like forever. When the music left her fingers, she slipped away into a different world. The problem was, she was not sure if that was the world she belonged to.

Rachael came up next to her with a smile, clasping her drum sticks over one shoulder as she heaved part of her drum set over another. Her face held certainty— like she knew it would be a magical night.

"I just feel like this is it," Stacy told her. "If we come back, I can't just slip away and decide to become a Dukhovian wild woman who storms back into the country wearing my banishment on my face."

"To quote the famous Grace Matthews: 'That's the funny thing about life, isn't it? You get to decide what you do and when you do it'."

"Darn that woman and her wisdom." Stacy decided.

CHAPTER ELEVEN

The two joined the rest of the band in looking up expectantly at the building they were about to enter.

"We could get signed tonight," Miranda's voice was shaky as she looked up at the sky, distantly. Her arms were dropped to her sides, heavy under the weight of two microphone stands. "We could get signed and tour in the summer and have shows every weekend and hear our songs nonstop on the radio..."

"We already hear our songs nonstop of the radio," Rachael smirked.

Miranda was quiet. "We could record new songs," she finally said after weighing the difference in what really changed since they broke their contract with the last record label they signed on with.

They had been with that company for six years, but Dan felt they were not being marketed enough and that they were treated like another money mine instead of an individual, gifted band. He wanted whoever they signed with to recognize and respect the potential the band had. While the band mentioned that they should not break their contract until they got signed by someone else, Dan told them that they would become much higher in demand if they disappeared off the radar for a while and came back with all new songs and a brand-new sound. Also, legal logistics or whatever.

From what they heard, he was right. Record labels from all over the world were coming to their show tonight and the fans themselves had caused the show to sell out within just two days of ticket sales. One late night, the band found themselves surfing eBay and came across two of their tickets selling for 3200 apiece. They could not decide if they were mesmerized due to happiness or disgust.

Stacy led the procession of happy musicians onto the stage where they dropped their equipment and everyone got into place. She seemed to dance across the stage as she helped Rachael and Cody set up Rachael's drums on the far left of the stage—right for the crowd. Then she swayed back over to the right to install her guitar and begin tuning it. Jade and Miranda were plugging their microphones in: Miranda next to Stacy and Jade next to Rachael with enough space in between to appear as though they were in the middle between either Stacy or Rachael and their lead singer: Cody, who took center position at the front of the stage.

"Should we run our dances one more time?" Stacy asked with a wide grin as she began spinning with Cody until she got dizzy.

"I think we should run ourselves over to the food table," Cody said, eyeing a large plate of muffins with precision.

"You're the boss," Stacy saluted him and moved on to watch the others get ready.

Their security team went to work, standing by all the doors of the building, manning the metal detector at the front entrance, and hanging back behind stage for optimal security. This position was given to the most trustworthy and strongest people they knew: Cody and Stacy's grandfather: Tom, Cody's best friend: Dylan

Mayue, and Cody's dad: Richard. Richard was Chief of Police and brought with him a number of his force. On occasion, Stacy and Cody's cousin Jimmy Grayson came backstage along with another cousin of Stacy and Cody and Rachael by marriage: Joey Leighton.

"High volume or extremely high volume?" Tom asked with a raised eyebrow, holding up two different colored wires: a lime green and a yellow. He waited for Dan to determine how he wanted the speakers to project.

"High, for now," he stated, sweat dripping from every inch of his body. "Then we'll adjust it as necessary. The venue said they have smoke machines; how many do they have?"

"Three," Tom pointed to the corner where Dylan stood talking with Cody.

"Three? An odd number? Whose bright idea was that? So, we can have either lopsided smoke or barely any?"

Stacy rolled her eyes and exited earshot of their conversation before it got messy. She met Cody and Dylan over at the food table, shoving her own face full of cookies and pies.

"If you ever decide to give more thought to joining the band, feel free…" Cody was saying in a persuasive manner as his friend shoved his hands into his pockets and leaned back.

"I don't sing," Dylan replied with a smirk. He flipped a long, ear-length black hair out of his tan face. When it was possible to see it, his Spanish features and mesmerizing brown eyes daunted anyone brave enough to look his way.

"Dude, you know I've seen you sing. You're incredible," Cody argued. His attempts to get Dylan to join his band of all girls never seemed thwarted. Not that Cody minded, these girls were his best friends, but there was so much more he knew they could accomplish with another male vocalist.

"I sing for my sister," Dylan corrected, still smirking. "That's it."

"At least I still have you on my team. You coming over to watch the game tomorrow night?"

"Wouldn't miss it!" Dylan said, reaching an inhumanly muscular arm up to meet Cody's high-five.

"That's sound check! Who's ready to roll!" The call came from Rachael precisely the moment the last item was in place and Dan finished securing everything.

"Let's do this!" Stacy jumped into the air, jumping into the arms of Jade and Miranda who picked her up and carried her out the door on top their shoulders.

"Ooo and remember—if Nick comes, send him right on in!" Rachael called back to the security team, just before she was out of earshot.

Stacy tried to not let that thought shake her.

The bus doors swung open to greet them in the most nostalgic way—it could potentially be the last time they boarded before their lives returned to the hectic, borderline irresponsible lifestyle of fandom it once was. It could be one of the...resurrected... very first times that the bus took its celebrated circle around the building and dropped off the band at the red carpet that would lead them backstage.

"Alright guys, you can do this!" Dan began as the bus came to a halting stop and he stood before them. "Remember, even if we don't get signed right away, you guys work hard everyday. You got yourselves here and have every right to feel proud and honored."

The band beamed up at their manager as they let his words of encouragement flow through them. The words moved through them like a flame, igniting a spark that gave each of them energy, eagerness, and enthusiastic bodies ready to break free.

The bus door opened and Dan stepped down. The crowd surrounding them erupted into a sea of applause and shouts. Signs flew up in the air deeming their love for the band, for its members. People were jumping up and down, making the sea look like waves that crashed haphazardly back and forth against the hold of the red ropes bound together with golden stakes in front of them.

Cody and Stacy stepped out, eagerly waving, shaking hands with their fans, and reaching their arms up high to meet the waves of people in the back rows. Stacy climbed up on Cody's shoulders so that the people who stretched as far as a mile could catch a glimpse.

Jade and Miranda followed in suite as Dan was already at the front of the building, smiling and answering questions from the media.

Then came Rachael. She stepped out slowly and all attention seemed to turn on her with the slightest hush from the crowd. At first, just a red, glittering heel appeared. The shoe encompassed her entire foot and was secured with a strap. Next, she took a step out, then another, until her flowing red ensemble was visible.

The noise from the crowd raged harder than ever, booming out towards the bus and escalating as they all faced Rachael, flailing their arms out to her. She stepped up to one girl and began answering questions about where she gets her inspiration for each outfit. She plucked at the shimmering flow of her sparkling, blue dress, pointing up to the straps to indicate all her added work.

The band joined together, hugged, and laughed. They joined hands just as they did at the end of every show, in a particular order: Cody on the audiences far right, Stacy, Rachael, Jade, and then Miranda on the far left. The two on the ends lifted their free hand in the air: one in a fist pumping formation, the other in a flexed hand. They took a bow facing one side of the cheering fans, then the other, and once back towards the bus. Then, together, they entered the building that they could only hope would change their futures.

They pushed down a long, dimly lit corridor decorated with framed pictures of every band that had ever played at the arena. They admired the pictures and the familiarity of the bands: everyone had to start small. That was one of the things they enjoyed most about the band: in order to succeed, it took dedication. They knew that they would have to push, climb, and work for everything that they accomplished—and it would not feel like an accomplishment unless they broke a sweat or two in the process.

Dan now closed in on his band in a huddle just before the curtain rose and they ran out, full of stamina and excitement. "Remember guys," he whispered. "No matter what, everything changes tonight."

CHAPTER 12

LOST

"*V*uel! We should not be here."

"*Shh... Aloyoshenka, listen.*" Nicholas responded to his Russian middle name on command. He and Vuel each called each other by their middle names in public to reduce the number of heads in their direction—when they could. They seemed to be naturals at drawing very negative or very positive attention.

"*Suppose neither of the boys sit on the throne.*" A heavy, deep voice sounded as a new man entered the room. Neither Nicholas nor Vuel were familiar with this man. As they glanced around the room, it became clear that this was the entrance of no ordinary meeting. They were meeting with a leader from the opposing army.

Both of them took in a sharp breath that they seemed to hold onto. Remembering to breathe, they took in the dark red uniform, decorated in badges of dishonor.

"*A non-traditionalist,*" Vuel breathed.

Nicholas barely nodded, listening as closely as he could over the thudding of his own heart. "*Spag.*" It was the Dukhovian derogatory term for a non-traditionalist. A low-life, a traitor, a nobody...

"*Viktor, welcome,*" Arkady said through a clenched jaw, not a sign of welcome in his voice. "*That information is not for you to concern yourself with. Take a seat.*"

Viktor held onto the edge of the seat, as if examining it for traps before choosing to remain standing. Arkady and Alexander did the same.

"*It seems as though the ruler of our nation is in the best interest of all of Dukhovia, or is disregarding the greater good of Dukhovia a trait passed down to you from your father?*"

Nicholas watched as Arkady's entire body responded with anger in ways he did not know existed. He clenched his fists, formed his face into a fierce growl, moved forward threateningly... and then let it all go. Nicholas blinked, perplexed.

"*It seems your fear of a traditionalist ruling the country has finally broke you,*" Viktor said with a smug smile.

"*I do everything I do for the greater good of Dukhovia, just as my father before me. That is why I will ensure a non-traditionalist never sits on this throne and tradition is never broken from this land.*"

Viktor seemed to laugh one, solid laugh. "*Then I suppose today's negotiations are mute.*"

LOST

Arkady stood to his feet and walked over to the end of the dark, stone tunnel. There he stopped, hands behind his back, as he stared at a map of Dukhovia for one long moment, then another. "You have formed a resistance around both West End and East Valley, blocking trade from circling to North Bridge and South Gate, the parts of our nation that produce the most food. As a result, our people are starving and we cannot supply enough aid from United Nations to support them..."

"Your aid would be much more plentiful if you were to modernize. No one wants to help a, nation failing from its own poor decisions."

Arkady dropped his hands to his side. He walked over to a steaming kettle of tea and poured himself a cup, drinking slowly.

"History has proven otherwise," Alexander retorted. "History has shown that when we allow the influence of other countries, it is our practices that suffer, not the other way around."

"Then the practices are not too strong, are they? If we had stronger weapons, we would have been able to stand up against those countries and actually make a difference for the refugees we brought in. Instead, they suffered a death more gruesome than had they stayed in the country they came from."

"What do you suggest, Viktor?" Arkady asked, still staring at the map.

"We strengthen our alliances by sitting down with heads of state and remapping our plans for the country. We show them that we will hold elections for a ruler and increase the modernization of our weaponry. Then we rebuild."

"Rebuild what the rebels broke," Arkady said it as a correction. "That seems to be the key part you are missing, Captain. The country is not in this shape due to the lack of resources. Dukhovia has thrived for centuries functioning exactly as it is now. When there is no greed and rebellion coming from the people, we seem to exist exactly as we were meant to."

"You misspeak, Your Eminence," Viktor said, standing to his feet. "And that is General now."

Arkady's hands returned to his tea kettle. "My deepest apologies. I was unaware of your further disloyalty. As it stands, I do not find sense in any of the recommendations your men make. To traditionalize is to throw away everything we and the Spirits have fought hard to achieve. It is to curse our people. We have no further business."

Viktor seemed to chuckle. "I should have known rationalizing with you was a waste of a journey. I suppose I shall wait then, until a non-traditionalist, someone with sense sits on the throne. Then Dukhovia will be saved."

Nicholas and Vuel scarcely had time to react before they heard the tea kettle placed gently back down on the stove. In a moment, Arkady was toppling over the General, forcing him back into his seat. The cup of tea bounced out and forward with a flick of Arkady's wrist.

CHAPTER TWELVE

Alexander took only a moment to react before he was forcefully holding The General down.

A half second later, three other men burst through the door, weapons up.

Arkady looked perplexed, exchanging a look with Alexander, but he did not flutter for long. Just as quickly as the men approached, Arkady and Alexander, a flash of body parts became the only clear image. Swords were drawn, arms were waving, legs were kicking high into the air...

Alexander hit the arm of one of the rebels, knocking his gun to the floor in an instant. Nicholas took the opportunity to stare at it as it fell just steps from his feet. He had only seen a gun one other time. Arkady had showed it to him. He had it kept locked in a case in the dungeons. "I have only used it once," he had said. "The death that I oh so wished was dragged out and painful ended in the blink of an eye. I will not use it rashly again, when our methods of torture are so much more...practical and effective. However, I will keep this on hand, for the case I do need a life to end suddenly and quickly."

Nicholas took the words as a threat and noted the exact placement of the weapon with the intent to return to it and destroy it. He had access to almost everything Arkady did. However, the closer he got, the more he understood when he too might be able to use the weapon...

Nicholas saw Vuel grind his teeth back and gathered his attention back to the scene. The four men had been tied and were badly beaten, blood pouring from unknown places. Hardly conscious, Akrady and Alexander had forced them to their knees, their eyes glaring down at them as if they were vermin.

"Now you listen here, spag," Arkady muttered. "This country will sooner break into two than it modernizes. I am currently training two of the strongest heirs this country has ever seen. They will rise up, they will take the throne, they will maintain Dukhovia for your children and your grandchildren to enjoy in peace long after this day—the day that you and your men will perish."

"And yet there is an heir even stronger in America. He will not only restore peace, but bring in a country stronger than has ever existed before."

"Oh, but General, the American cannot be stronger, if the American does not exist freely—or if he does not exist at all."

Victor's composure began to fade, the glare in his eyes lost in the thin line that appeared on his lips. "To what do you suggest?" He asked through a cracking voice.

"Anything necessary to preserve this nation."

With that, Arkady grabbed his sword, held it high, and sliced across each rebel until the very last head fell.

Nicholas glared at himself in the mirror. He had rifled through the rest of the American clothes packed for him in search of something more flattering, comfortable, appropriate, *anything*. There was nothing even remotely close to his Dukhovian clothing.

He pressed the back of his hand to his forehead, forcing a bead of sweat into his hairline. Currently, he was dressed in another pair of dark jeans and a hooded sweatshirt featuring a red ram on it—the mascot of the school. He had found it in the abandoned section of the laundry room and felt it would make him fit in more. Hopefully it at least did that, as far as comfort goes, he would feel more comfortable naked.

Exhaling deeply, Nicholas strode over to the door. He tugged firmly on the door knob and then let go, dropping his arm to his side. Sighing in some mixture of frustration and nervousness, he retreated towards his bedroom and back again.

This had been his behavior for the last hour as he attempted to decide the next steps of his fate. His readiness. His *willingness*. What if his desire to do the right thing led him to blurting out his intentions the moment he met the girl—what then did that mean for Dukhovia? For his life?

He closed his eyes. He also was not sure he was so ready to interact with Americans again quite yet. Especially at the concert—something he had no idea what to expect from.

But he was not doing this for himself, he never was.

Perhaps this is a sign this is not where you are meant to be.

"My destiny is to destroy the girl."

Then why is it so complicated?

"The moment I exited the plane I ran into her best friend—she is practically boarding the flight with me as we speak," he reiterated.

Silence.

Perhaps you are not meant to destroy her, but to bring her prosperity.

Nicholas made a sound of half humor and half wonderment.

Think about it. Why are you doing this?

"For Dukhovia," Nicholas muttered, straight faced as he ripped the door open and finally exited the apartment.

The cool rush of snow on his face felt familiar and nerve-wracking. He used it as ammunition to keep him going strong, fiercer, more motivated than ever before. Motivated to find her, motivated to bring her to Arkady, motivated to turn things around. He did not understand fully, but he felt his fate pulling him where he needed to be.

He glanced down at the directions Rachael had written out for him, however, there was no need. He quickly ran into a line of cars and blocked off streets that quickly told him he was walking in the right direction. He followed them all the way up to a sea of flashing lights, gates, police, and fire trucks. One would have thought the biggest disaster had just taken place. Nicholas prayed one would not come.

Beyond the lights were people—screaming, cheering. Nicholas felt even more inappropriately dressed when he took them in. Most were wearing tight fitting, black clothing with painted faces. Others wore shirts that were too small, revealing more skin than he had ever seen on a woman. He was clearly out of place.

He huddled into his sweatshirt and darted around the side of the building. Rachael had told him to go around back, though, he had arrived much later than she instructed and he suspected that route was now inaccessible.

The back was much quieter. There were a few men standing around the entrance, talking casually and joking. They both looked rather large—and they both looked Dukhovian.

Nicholas swallowed a lump in his throat and decided to take his chances at the front door. He was not so certain he was ready to meet the heir let alone family members of hers.

"Hello, I am here to view the concert."

The woman was behind a type of box made of glass. Some of the more modern buildings in Dukhovia had ticket booths, but none had this type of encasing. He quickly jogged his memory for everything he knew about America to come up with an explanation for why it was there. Was it a protection of sorts?

Their medical practices are highly underdeveloped; I would be surprised if the country is even populated

That could not possibly be correct. The handing of the tickets and money would transfer any germs.

Surprise, surprise—modern country gets weapons and modern country does not know how to use weapons. They slaughter each other the moment they feel power.

Gun violence. That made sense. Arkady did say the country had a massive issue with gun violence—violence in general, he supposed.

"Do you have your ticket?" She spat.

"No, I am a close friend of the band."

"I bet. No ticket, no entry. The show is almost over anyway."

"Then why would I be so desperate to get in as to lie if it is almost over?"

"You tell me."

Nicholas stared eye-to-eye with the woman for a moment, quickly racking his brain as he sorted through any use of threats that would have been his next move in Dukhovia. But he still had the power of persuasion.

"Look," Nicholas began, soaking his icy blues deep into her soul. He stood with his elbow propped on the ticket booth, leaning in towards her as if to block off the rest of the world. "I promise I do not mean any harm. You may pat me down personally." He looked her up and down as he said the words, his voice throaty. "I understand and envy your job; I am not looking to jeopardize."

"Be that as it may," the woman said, sounding softer. "I cannot let you in. Security!"

Nicholas's eyes grew. He could not have a negative entry to the heir or her family. Acting quickly, he darted towards the back of the building.

It was even less active than it previously had been—looking completely vacated. He approached stealthily, looking and listening for signs of people. They were not far along, but they were not near the door.

He chose to remain outside, standing to the side so that he could just glance part of the right side of the stage, but not much else. The sound filling his ears was as calm and soothing as the voice singing the lyrics that he could scarcely make out. But he could hear meaning, he could *feel* the meaning.

Nicholas was never one for music in Dukhovia. He avoided it intentionally in order to smother a long-ago buried memory. He supposed that was another reason for avoiding the concert.

He let the sound fill his ears now, he imagined what it would be like to see the instruments…to hold them…

"Nicholas! Nicholas, daddy is home!"

"I will grab your lyra!"

***

"Mommy, will you sing me one more song?"

Her warm smile as she reached back for her instrument…

Nicholas pushed down his anger forcefully, swallowing the pain, swallowing the memory. It was not the first time he had thought of his mother. He never stopped.

Nicholas's mother was his best friend, his hero, his…everything a mother should be. Dukhovian tradition teaches that perfect does not exist and that beings of the Spirit Realm no longer walk on Earth, but Nicholas could not pin a single fault in his mother. Perhaps her kindness. Perhaps if her heart were not so forgiving, so loving, she would have left his father in Dukhovia when he was born and they could both be living happily somewhere now.

He tried to think of her less these days because he did not know what she would say about his fate—or perhaps it was that he knew exactly what she would say and it put avenging his family in a completely different parallel.

Suddenly, the music broke and a somehow loud, yet soft voice called out into the audience. "Stacy Matthews everybody! She had been working on that song for the better part of her life—let's give her one more round of applause!"

Nicholas felt himself shift on the dirt. Round of applause, Stacy Matthews. Round of applause. He already felt himself fading and he had not even made it inside.

CHAPTER 13

FORMALITIES

Stacy cocked her head to the side, feeling foolish. Rather, she was feeling exactly how Rachael wanted her to feel, but not exactly in the ways she intended. Butterflies in her stomach were whispering desires into her brain—desires that the promised Dukhovian would arrive at the concert at *some point*.

It was the end of the concert and she had just performed the last song. The way Rachael explained things, she had expected this Sir Whatever to show up early for the show, on time for the show, during the show—literally at any point where they would have time to so much as make eye contact. Yet here they were, packing up their equipment, ready to head out, and not a Dukhovian soul in sight.

Rachael kept singing "just wait" any time Stacy or the other members made a comment about his absence, but she could tell the anticipation was growing weary in Rachael's eyes as well.

"Any minute now!" Rachael said in a cheerful voice as she saw Stacy look over her shoulder. She winked as she walked towards the back door.

Stacy rolled her eyes. She hated Rachael catching her and she knew she could not hide the intent of her glimpses. But, although an impossible concept for Rachael to grasp, her glimpses had little to do with wanting to be wooed into marriage at fifteen and everything to do with wanting to meet a Dukhovian.

She attributed the butterflies to her nerves. While she was excited to meet this person, she was also nervous. What if he was unable to answer her questions after all? What if he came to America because he hated the Dukhovian way of life? The thought put the butterflies into straight knots.

Stacy glanced around, noticing Rachael was nowhere in sight. She made way over to the exit door and froze....

Rachael was talking to someone.

A male someone.

A young male someone...with black hair and brilliant blue eyes that could blind a neighborhood. He looked awkward and out of place—he tugged at his collar an awful lot and did the same thing with the legs of his jeans. Maybe they were new. Maybe he was new to wearing them because he normally wore Dukhovian clothing.

He was quite large, towering over Rachael even though she was even taller than Stacy by at least six or seven inches.

She continued to watch with austerity, examining his every move, watching every breath for signs of Dukhovia in him. Other than the clothing, there was nothing she could place or…really knew what there would be to place him as Dukhovian born and raised versus Dukhovian born or descended. Well, nothing except the feeling she got looking at him…

Her eyes darted from his eyes down to the rest of his body and back up again. She watched as he seemed so lost and could not help but feel a tug in his direction. More than a tug, it felt like she needed to be not only near him, but *with* him. Maybe she was just lost in his breath-taking physical features. She could not say she so much as ever had a crush on a boy before, so maybe this was what Rachael told her she would feel.

But it seemed like so much more. She was drawn to him. It seemed so natural to just go up to him, give him a high-five, and ask him what he thought of the show. She was the puzzle and he was the missing piece. He had always been the missing piece.

The more she watched, the harder her heart seemed to be beating away without her. She was so distracted in her thoughts, she almost failed to notice Rachael's waving hand.

She stood, frozen. So comfortable and sure in essence, but her follow-through was lacking as her brain reminded her she actually did not know this man and this was her one moment to meet someone from Dukhovia, to get her answers—where did she stand if he did not meet her expectations? What if he was not even really from Dukhovia? What if Rachael was wrong? What then? Did she even want to talk to this handsome stranger?

Then she saw the look on his face—a mixture of longing and…angst? As though he were just as nervous to meet her. There was another emotion with it that she could not quite place, but it was not positive. All at once, she began to feel sorry for whatever that emotion was and found herself walking closer and closer towards him.

As she walked, she continued to stare at him, their eyes sometimes locking, sometimes both darting away, looking towards Rachael for safety until they were forced to meet head on.

"The lovely Stacy Grace, meet Sir Nicholas Tyler Andrews the Third. He comes to us from places unknown," Rachael said this with a heavy wink, "in order to meet the greatest band of all time and find out if he has a place in the musical world. Sir Nicholas, this is Stacy Grace—music extraordinaire, yes, but also lover of all things Dukhovian, including their charming men."

"Rachael!" Stacy's eyes grew, from the corner of her eye, she saw a small smirk on Nicholas's face that quickly faded.

"Disagree? I'll let you two figure it out. Farewell!" And with that she tore away.

Stacy blinked after her for a moment, then shifted when she recognized how absolutely still Nicholas was beside her. Her eyes followed from the awkwardness of his perfectly white, new shoes up to those icy blue eyes. He looked as though he was either holding in vomit or about to run away. There may have been a third option, but those two seemed most probable to Stacy.

"So, Sir Nicholas the Third, is it?"

"You may call me Nicholas," he said the words quickly in a velvety voice that begged to be understood.

"Nicholas," Stacy nodded once. "What about Nick?"

Nicholas made a disgruntled face. "I suppose if that is what you wish."

Stacy smiled. "I am rather used to my wishes being granted."

Nicholas did not respond, but the disgruntled look on his face grew.

"Nicholas it is," Stacy decided. "I have a cousin named Nick anyway, it would get too confusing." Even though her cousin was half her age and also her cousin.

Nicholas nodded. "And you are Stacy Grace Matthews, daughter of Grace and Kevin."

Stacy made an awkward face, but nodded. "That much is true, although I feel guilty, I didn't brush up on your family tree."

"Nicholas Tyler Andrews," he said confidently, after making another type of facial expression she could not unpuzzle. "Son of Nicholas and Anecka." He held his hand in front of his stomach and took a bow, then made a face, sort of stumbled as if he was going to redo the motion, then just stopped altogether.

Stacy made the proper Dukhovian gesture in return.

"It is lovely to meet you."

Stacy felt her cheeks burn in response. She looked around quickly for an exit or Rachael or something. She had never felt her heart race the way it was now and it only made matters worse when she looked at the perfect bone structure of his face.

But, no, *Dukhovia.*

"Do you wanna walk up the path? Most people should be cleared out by now so it shouldn't be a huge distraction."

Nicholas seemed to glance up to where she pointed and reluctantly nodded.

Stacy led the way, taking her steps in giant leaps, spinning on her heels and walking backwards half the time. It was second nature to her. "So, are you really interested in playing an instrument or did Rachael make that up?"

For the first time, Stacy saw a full smile spread across Nicholas's face. She almost wished he could take it back. As if his eyes and face were not enough…

"I suppose she made it up, however, she may be very good at guessing."

Stacy grinned, pretend clapping. "Ohh okaaay, so we have an award winner on our hands."

Nicholas sneered, playfully. "I assure you that I have won no awards. My mother used to play the lyra. She would teach me…when she could." His voice became more distant as he spoke. That off emotion was back, now traceable in his eyes.

"What's the lyra?" Stacy asked curiously.

Nicholas eyed her for a moment before answering. "A lyra is an instrument popular in Dukhovian. A string instrument."

"Well, I play guitar, we'll make a good duo."

Nicholas seemed to freeze, but continued onward.

"Rachael says you love Dukhovia," Nicholas began. "Is that truthful?"

Stacy looked to the ground then up at him and smiled—then she ran away.

In an instant, she was climbing on top a rail that overlooked a smog-ridden river. The lights from the city across the way made it difficult to look without being blind-sided, never mind the lack of appeal from the stench erupting from its crevice. The brown color surely had something to do with the amount of trash piling along the sides of the bank.

"This is one of my favorite spots to come because it reminds me of Dukhovia."

Nicholas blinked hard. Stacy watched as his fingers clenched and unclenched against the railing, going from balled fists into palms so flat, he began to push his fingers backwards just to keep them occupied.

"I know, I know," Stacy said casually. "It's not *quite* as pristine as Dukhovia, but the water moves the same. That's one thing that can't be taken away—the way it moves and the way it feels and sounds. It's a little bit of calm to the storm."

"You do not like it here in America?" Nicholas asked the question carefully, as if he were adding this to a list rather than asking out of curiosity.

Stacy shrugged in response. "Well, that's the confusing part. This is home—it always has been. My friends are here, my family, my...everything. But it's like I'm cut in two and part of me is there too."

He was quiet, waiting.

"Dukhovia has every part of my heart," she said, her voice seeming almost poetic as she looked over the water, seemingly absentmindedly. "My full interest, my full passion, my full devotion." She grew quiet. "Yet, unreachable. Like a dream that will never come true." She flinched at the word. "It's all I think about. When I consider my future, it's not the flashing lights and loud music I see, but the calm waves of a peaceful ocean, the open fields, the warm cottages.

"Every part of me longs to be there, but stopped by a foolish, backwards decision that I have no control over. Does that make sense?"

"Yes," Nicholas nearly whispered the word.

And he desperately wished he could add his whole life story to follow.

CHAPTER 14

CONTROL

*P*atience and determination. Patience and determination. Nicholas had been uttering the phrase to himself since he first laid eyes on the black-haired, bright green-eyed girl that bounded toward him as if she were still dancing on stage. She immediately had his heart dipping into his stomach and he was not necessarily sure it was just for the anticipated reasons.

She was not breath-takingly beautiful, at least, as far as other women he could compare to or as far as other American women were made out to be with their make-up and hair styles. She was very…simple and plain and Nicholas supposed that was what drew him to her. That and her Spirit.

Then there was the way she spoke with such confidence. It was both remarkable and unnerving. Annoying when she spoke of her unwavering American customs, yet comforting when she spoke of Dukhovia. Thus, patience and determination. He had to make sure he remained goal focused and did not make any decisions or conceptions with haste.

But that became difficult when she spoke of Dukhovia. The passion that flared inside of her, the motivation to tackle any problem and solve any slight suspicion. She did not fully meet the bland, herd-following American he was expecting, yet she was not quite fully Dukhovian either. It was exactly as was her situation: a Dukhovian soul with aspects of American culture thrown in.

And that made his job that much more difficult. Especially as the more she spoke, the more he found out not only that she did in fact love Dukhovia, but her limitations towards accessing Dukhovia strangely paralleled his own feelings on the subject. Of course.

The more she spoke on the subject, the more irritable he found himself. Confused. Ill-prepared. And it was only their first time meeting. Where he felt stuck in his ambition to earn the honor of his family and protect Dukhovia, yet restricted in the freedom to accomplish this in a way that was honorable to the Spirits, she felt restricted to find out anything about her true purpose due to elements outside her control.

He desired to share his feelings in return, but he could not. No matter what he felt, no matter what type of person Stacy truly was, he had a mission to fulfill. The risk to Dukhovia was too great and the chance to prove his family too prevalent.

The two had continued to stay overlooking the bridge that protected them from standing in likely toxic water. Steam seemed to surface off of it every so often, stemming from swirls of unknown debris. He wondered if he should be holding his breath or wearing a mask of some type.

"I would say I do love Dukhovia, then," she said with a smile, circling their conversation back to his original question. "Rachael told the truth about that one so the sooner we get you belting out classic tunes on the guitar, the better."

"I would not say I'm opposed," Nicholas joked. Force. The only way to not focus on the similarities between this heir and himself would be to force everything that came out of him—including motivation.

"Speaking of, there is much controversy as far as where you hail from, Mr. Andrews. Are you from Dukhovia?"

He thought about the question deeply. "My family is from Dukhovia, yes."

"Right. But what about you? Were you born here or in Dukhovia?"

Nicholas swallowed. "I was born in Dukhovia."

"Me too," Stacy said casually. She skipped a rock as she walked and watched its fate until its final roll. "And then chased out in the dark of the night only to flee to this promising sanctuary." She looked at the sky as if it might throw something back at her. "And you?" She prompted, when he did not respond.

"I was not chased out of the country," he said with a hint of humor, but his blood was beginning to boil, palms beginning to sweat.

"No, but how long have you been in America? And don't give me some 'not long', 'long enough' answer—I want an exact timeframe down to the exact hour." She turned and walked backwards, watching his facial expressions.

Nicholas thought about it, looking at the sky the same way she had. He breathed, considering his options closely. Anything that was not the direct truth was a lie and would eventually elicit distrust. Arkady truly did not have this figured out. "Approximately noon Wednesday," he replied.

Stacy stopped on her heals. "A whole two days? I wish I would have known a celebration was in order."

"I do not know about that," Nicholas grunted.

"Why don't you have an accent?" She asked. "Your English is beyond perfect. I couldn't speak this darn language straight for more than ten years." She seemed to stop her sentence short and blush, Nicholas pretended not to notice, caught in his own problems at the moment.

"Um." He stumbled a bit more with that one. He supposed any number of explanations could have been logical: they spoke English often in Dukhovia and so he lost it, he did business with English speaking countries...Yet, for some reason or the next, he found himself revealing the truth. "I was told to lose it or the Americans would not take me seriously."

Stacy surprised him by barking out a laugh. "That's probably true had you landed with anyone other than Rachael. We're all pretty diverse in this group, but most people are more judgmental than they are accepting. It's quite the double-edged sword here. No one chasing me out with a pitch fork and torch, but also not exactly welcoming me with open arms either."

That sat with Nicholas for a time, the information pulsating in his head like a method of torture rather than just casual conversation. He had already seen so much wrong that Arkady told him, so much that he did not prepare him for, and so much that his stubbornness blew out of proportion. Now here he was, talking with the girl he expected to be the walking definition of all these things he feared, that Dukhovia feared, and he was being faced with the opposite. What did this mean for Dukhovia? For him?

Patience and determination.

It was too soon to tell.

"What is your favorite thing about Dukhovia?"

Stacy smiled looking over the murky waters as she thought. "The feeling," she decided on. "The feeling of calm, the feeling of peace. I know I was only there once and being there as a banished person, calm is probably the last feeling I should have felt...but everything was so...simple. I didn't have to think, I didn't have to solve. I just had to live. I don't feel that here." She paused, then added, "at least, not unless I'm thinking about Dukhovia."

Nicholas found a lump in his throat prevented him from responding. He stared at the girl, processing, storing information. When he finally found his voice, he nodded in agreement. "Peaceful Dukhovia—I am not sure I have ever witnessed such an event."

Stacy's eyes fell, deeper than he would have expected, her mind seeming to drift further away. "Because of the war." It was almost a question, almost a statement.

Nicholas nodded. "It has always controlled the better parts of my life."

"I'm sorry," Stacy said remorsefully. "Is that why you're here now? Why you're really here?"

Nicholas shrugged. He supposed he could not keep the direct questions from coming. "In a way, yes. How much do you know of the war?"

Stacy bit her lip. "Not a lot. My family doesn't like to talk about Dukhovia, so I don't like to ask. My mom is the only one who tries to answer my questions and all she ever told me was we're banished and the people live in fear because of the war. I don't know why, I don't know if there's a way out of it..."

Nicholas nodded understanding, looking for a way to end the conversation, to back out and run. "It seems to be at a standstill now. Things are...not as bad as they have been in the past. At least, nothing new has happened." It was as true as he could muster, as much solace as he could offer.

Stacy looked up, a million thoughts seemed etched on her face and reflected in her eyes, yet she mostly stared at him, as if that would give her the answers, or as if she was afraid to ask him too whatever it was she held back from asking her family. Rightfully so, she had no idea his intentions. Her family was known as an enemy across the world for decades, it would be only natural for her to assume the worst of him.

Finally, after several moments of irritating silence, her voice became as frail as he had heard her, showing a girl so quiet and reserved, he scarcely recognized her. "I just need to know… are the people safe?"

Nicholas offered a slight smile, annoyingly pleased that she would even have the thought. *Americans are all self-centered. Do you truly believe they have the capability to care for even a comrade, even a significant other, let alone a nation of people?* Strike one, Arkady. Strike one.

Then, he focused on the question. Safety in Dukhovia—were they? Really? Well, he supposed, at least some of them were. He nodded hesitantly. "For now."

Her face was immediately tense. "But there's a threat to that?"

He shrugged. "That is war," he remarked. "There are always threats, especially in times of peace."

The next facial expression that appeared on her face, Nicholas found difficult to describe, yet, he understood it completely. The look of apprehension, of fear. Inquisitive. Concerned. A look that beheld a mind that dared to plot and maintain expectation and yet…confinement.

"But people are fighting, Stacy," he added fervently. "They are always fighting—and always will. Dukhovia does not have many of us who would not give our all for our land."

"Yourself included?" She asked with a smile.

Nicholas nodded. *Just a small amount of information*, he told himself. Revealing a small amount would be acceptable, expected even. She could not trust someone she did not know. Thus, he responded… "Without a doubt. I have served Dukhovia my entire life in some form or the next—when the choice was mine."

The way that her head whipped towards him told him immediately that he had chosen the wrong words. Condemning words. Words that, to her, spoke maliciousness.

"Why would the choice not be yours?"

A small amount, he reminded himself, knowing if he went any further, he would not only be unable to stop, but would be caught in too many truths to decipher his lies and figure out who he was portraying—the deceiver here to steal her away, or the lost victim. He was not even certain which one he really was, if either.

He went for an ominous, but true answer. "Dukhovia is a very difficult place."

The inquisitor returned, this time puzzling over pieces he wished she would forget.

"Well," Nicholas began the words slowly, lightening his voice and the mood. "Dukhovia does seem to be in your heart, after all. We shall trust Rachael."

"Maybe," Stacy said with great force, seeming to push her solemn attitude and thoughts aside for the time and exchange it back to her former peppy one. "We won't know that for sure until you prove your undying loyalty to the band."

Nicholas opened his arms. "Give me an instrument and put me on stage."

"Done!" With that, she suddenly vanished. No indication, no exit. If this was the way of her behavior, he was going to have a much more difficult time keeping track of her than he imagined.

He could not say he was not grateful for the moment to breathe that her absence provided. The conversation was going well, certainly. They had met. They were connecting—it was everything he could ever hope for—which is where the problem lied.

Before he had time to focus on the issue too long, Stacy was back—this time carrying a brown, shining guitar.

Nicholas looked at the piece with envy. He had seen them before; they used to frequently be played in pubs until people started to sell their instruments for the money. Others attempted to use their gifts to earn money while maintaining their treasures, but few were lucky enough and an even greater number felt too ashamed to use their music in that manner.

Stacy turned her back to the deadly water base and fell to the ground, cradling the guitar close to her. "Have a seat," she offered.

Nicholas obeyed.

She strummed a few strings on her guitar, looking gleeful, then solemn, then joyous once more.

"How long have you been playing?" Nicholas asked her.

"My grandfather taught Cody and I when we were nine," she answered without removing her eyes from the strings. "I picked up quicker though." She smirked as if there were some type of hidden joke in the statement that Nicholas did not care enough to push further into.

"That is astounding." He started to feel his heart expand in his chest. He was heading for dangerous territory and he knew it. He had to back down.

"He taught us to sing too—all our lives. I suppose it started with just bedtime lullabies and grew. When they were together—my family—they were always singing. The world knew them as singers and the greatest family in the world." Stacy's face suddenly fell, becoming somewhat crossed more so than upset. He supposed she was used to this narrative. "Until they started to know them for something else—I assume you know that story."

"I know what I have heard," Nicholas answered, his eyes locked deeply on hers.

Stacy poured back into his, it seemed her head was swimming of thoughts, her eyes searching his as if looking for where to land. "My grandparents were healers in Dukhovia. When they first came here, they brought the herbs and whatever to make medicines for their patients. People were healed, people loved them. But they never taught my mom and uncles what not to do and didn't keep them out of their reach. So, one day, my mom got mad at my brother, mixed a bunch together, and created a potentially fatal mixture.

"It created a smoke that they ran from, but my grandfather breathed in. It changed something in his brain. He described it as like being in prison. He knew what was going on, he had his own thoughts, sometimes he could even break through, but there was a darkness, keeping him dormant. His body would commit crimes he would never imagine. So many people died, so much destruction."

Nicholas took it in. "I never heard the story quite that way before."

Stacy smiled softly. "So, you could understand why I don't like to press them on issues related to Dukhovia. Once they started the trial, my mom said people went from hating him to fearing Dukhovia and everything related to it. I think they became ashamed. Not of Dukhovia, of course, but that a negative name was created for it."

Before Nicholas could react to the tale while simultaneously hiding his shaking limbs, Stacy had her guitar in her arms and was strumming at the chords. "But I have been working on a song about Dukhovia—wanna heart it?"

The last thing he wanted to do was listen to the song. "Absolutely."

And so her song started—low and soft. The tune was solemn with melancholy hints. Stacy seemed to transform when she was focused. Her impulsive, lax self had disappeared and was replaced by someone who could not be shaken.

"Ice and snow your winds they whisper to my aching heart.
Ice and snow beneath the mountains hear the child's cry.
Place of wonder, place of home
Safety deep inside.

I remember, still I hear, the moment
You wished me ill.
I remember, still I hear,
The moments as they slip away.

Confusion and a whole new world
Soundlessly on replay.
Confusion and a whole new world
Memory seems to fade."

She did not turn to him expectantly, instead she seemed lost in her world. Of this, Nicholas was grateful as he could feel his insides burning. A strange desire to jump into the poisonous lake ran through him, causing him to shuffle uncomfortably next to her. The longer he sat, the more serious the feeling of perspiring became before he was also shaking, short of breath, and seeing stars.

"There you are!"

CHAPTER FOURTEEN

Nicholas and Stacy turned to see Rachael bouncing towards them, licking her fingers on one hand whilst carefully balancing something in her other.

Nicholas could not decide if he felt more comforted or frustrated seeing her come forward in this moment.

Stacy cocked her head. "Tell me you didn't have dessert hour without me?"

Rachael gave her a look of distaste. "What kind of monster do you think I am? Of course, we would never. Mom and dad just brought over a new recipe for us to try." She handed Stacy a chip from her occupied hand and offered another to Nicholas.

"Chip?" She asked.

Nicholas grabbed his stomach as he realized he had not yet eaten since arriving in America. "What exactly is it?"

Stacy and Rachael exchanged a glance. "It's a potato chip dipped in casserole. Okay, now that I said that out loud, that does sound revolting."

"Quite repulsive," Stacy agreed, downing her bit in one bite.

"Thank you, anyway," Nicholas declined.

"So, how are things going over here? Are you in love yet? Are you disappearing into the Dukhovian sunset together?"

"No one is disappearing into any sunsets," Stacy retorted. "We were just finding out if Nicholas truly has music in his heart."

"And?" Rachael pressed.

"And you rudely interrupted."

Rachael raised her eyebrows. "Well, if I hadn't, then Cody would be in there cutting the cake without you in 3, 2..."

"That's my que to go," Stacy started towards the building, stopping to look at Nicholas. "You should come in and try some. It's delicious." Then she was off once again.

"Sooo? How are you two?"

Nicholas was not sure how to answer. The clattering of his brain, her voice, the background sounds...it was all too much. "It was great. She's great." Was she great? Was her being great a good thing or bad thing? How were those things even measured in his situation?

"Come on and eat with us." She waved her hand towards the building, beginning to walk backward. It was more of a command than an invitation and that made Nicholas's blood pressure rise.

"No, thank you, I must go."

"Go? Come on, you still need to meet everyone else."

Nicholas felt his numbers getting even higher at the thought. He looked around, body failing, vision beginning to blur. "I must go, Rachael. I thank you. I cannot stay."

Rachael reached forward, grabbing his arm and pulling him forward. "You won't regret it! Let's..."

Nicholas could hear the laughing, he could see the embraces, he could *hear the music...*

Then there was nothing.

"RACHAEL I AM NOT COMING. DO YOU NOT UNDERSTAND? I AM NOT READY FOR THIS! I AM NOT READY FOR ANY OF THIS. I AM LEAVING NOW." He panted, grabbing his hair. "HAVE I MADE MYSELF CLEAR?"

Rachael stopped, her smile falling along with the hand that grasped him. Her own chest began to rise and fall in a panic. "Yeah," she choked. "Way past crystal."

Nicholas froze in his steps, huffing as the fumes boiled off his body like rising blisters from a wildly growing fire. He felt the fire spreading to everybody around him.

Deep hatred and betrayal penetrated his mind. Angst and failure crippled his body. Hatred at Rachael for not giving up. Betrayal and an even bitterer sense of hatred for Arkady—who left him so vulnerable, so unprepared, so *scarred.*

Everything that Arkady did never prepared him, it made his chances so much worse. He would have had more luck if he never underwent any training and Arkady just found him last week and sent him on his way. He might even be more willing to actually succeed in the mission.

Nicholas turned and fled the area. Racing away from the scene, away from his thoughts, and if he could manage it…away from the mission.

CHAPTER 15

THE PAST IS WRONG

$\mathcal{N}$icholas kicked the wall hard with his foot and instantly fell to the ground, knowing he broke at least three toes. Wall debris landed around him, silent over his scream. He needed to leave. He needed to leave the country, leave this mission. He. Needed. Out.

"AGH!" His fists slammed down onto the floor once, twice, then again, seeming to pound harder to drown out the protest from his neighbor below him. He fell to the floor in defeat, letting tears of frustration well into his eyes only for a moment.

He had ruined everything and he knew it. His relationship with Rachael was crucial and his time with the heir even more so. Everything had been going so perfectly and then his temper…it was always his temper. It always got the better of him, it always led to him making rash decisions that someone usually had to save him from…

There was no one saving him this time. In fact, he might as well run off and change his identity. There was no way he could convince Rachael to trust him again and no way he could gain the heir's trust. That. That was his main frustration and he knew it. Perhaps he could explain his rash, out of control temper and make amends with Rachael. He knew he could…but the heir.

Stacy. He grabbed his hair and flung himself over onto the floor. He lay on his back, looking at the ceiling, but seeing nothing at all. He clenched up, trying to kick out the sense of the walls coming down on him as the lump in his throat grew and grew.

He let his eyes close just for a moment, replaying the events of the night. It seemed to be true. Stacy did have Dukhovia in her heart. She was very clearly American too, but her attachment to the country and its ideals were not as cut and dry as he had been led to believe they would be. His biggest fear had come true.

He knew this was possible and probably knew that, with his luck, it was most likely to happen, but he always feared it because he knew that at the end of the day—he had no choice. He still had to complete the mission. Whether he learned that Stacy was a proper fit for the throne or not, his mission was straight forward—bring her back or *else*. So much had already been taken from him with that *else* already.

But Stacy. Her view of the world and of Dukhovia was simplistic at best. Her mannerisms disgustingly barbaric and on the verge of escaping basic human decency. But she had one thing that was most sought after now—a passionate, traditional Dukhovian heart.

He supposed he was not certain that her heart was fully traditional. Perhaps she would hold rock concerts in the capital every night and make crude jokes during meetings of state. He needed to find out more. He should have found out more. He lost his chance to…all because of the music. He knew better than to attend because of the music…it was all the stupid, stupid music…

Great peace or great destruction. That was what he had been told had been predicted out of the next heir. Overtime, they deduced the meaning: there were two heirs predicted to be stronger than any heir; greater Spiritual connection, greater purpose, one would lead the country to end the war and the other would bring the country to ruins. Find out which.

Nicholas was not so certain. Perhaps it meant that the same heir could be meant for great success, but cause great destruction. It was why he should stay out of it. It was why he should pack his belongings and refuse to have purpose here.

His arms flashed up and pressed onto his temples in an attempt to silence the thoughts. He squeezed shut his eyes. And then he was on his feet—pacing back and forth around the room in a final attempt to silence the anger.

Nicholas knew his anger raged for a multitude of reasons, but mostly, he was angry because meeting the heir meant he was fulfilling his destiny—that the prospect of ever having a choice had abruptly vanished irrevocably.

And that was it. A seemingly new vase found itself smashed against the wall it looked opposite of. An ancient cabinet was brought down to blistering pieces against the thin, blue rug. The damned gaming system met its demise out the window. Nothing was safe, no matter how innocent…

Everything in the room was innocent…

Nicholas stood in the middle of the room, breathing heavily as he dropped his throwing arm and allowed his next victim to land safely on the floor beneath him.

You are not…

"I am."

Nicholas moved slowly and carefully, stepping over the bits of glass and miscellaneous jagged edges that lay in his wake. It was not until he collapsed back onto the ground that he noticed the blood dripping down his arms and the shards of his belongings imbedded into the bottoms of his feet.

There was no choice in the matter. Not anymore. He was an enemy and feared ally of Dukhovia. He had made a deal with the devil and now had honor and his word to uphold. He would have to accomplish what he came to America to do. That need be all that exists on his mind now. And yet he continued to search for another way…

There was only one other time he considered leaving as strongly as he was considering it now. He had packed anything of value—which was not much—and headed east. He was not sure where he would stop or what led him in that direction, but he went for as long as he could. Again, that was not long. Arkady had men find him within a matter of days.

"You experienced some time outside of the country, what did you think?" It was a test that he let him get that far. A test to show him that he needed Arkady, needed Dukhovia, and that he had no clue how to function outside of this destiny. He was beaten past recognition, his body so severely damaged that he had to learn how to walk again—twice. Once after the initial beating, and once when Arkady became frustrated that he was not healing fast enough.

"I can find you. You may run, perhaps it is good training. However, part of our Spirit gift is that we all have a guide that leads us to one another. It will be most helpful for you to learn to use. In the meantime, were you to run again, you could travel to the lowest point of the earth and I would have a trail on you the moment you made the decision."

He gulped, recognizing for about the ten thousandth time that choice evaded him.

He closed his eyes and Stacy's lyrics flooded his mind, then a glimpse of a lyra. He blocked it, tried so hard to block it, just as he tried to block it back with Stacy and Rachael and failed. Just like he always failed...

"Come my precious light."

It was a call he was conditioned into recognizing each and every night, a phrase that filled him with joy and ease. 3-year-old Nicholas III climbed into his mother's lap, hearing the familiar creak of the well-loved rocking chair as he did so. He loved padding up her dress and resting his head on the bundle. Instinctively, her arm wrapped around him and he was safe. He was warm. He was loved.

"Will you play my favorite, mama?" He had asked.

"Always, my little light."

And so she had. Her fingers stroked and drew back the strings with such focus, yet such passion. So gentle she looked, doing something that took such knowledge and skill while also being something she loved dearly.

Nicholas hummed along to the tune as she sang the song to him once, then another time, then another... Music was their secret language, it always had been. When the orchestra was playing, Nicholas and his mother always went. No matter the plans, no matter what his father had said, she would scoop him up and the world would stand still as he listened to the music and held his mother's hand.

Nicholas reached his hand forward now, as if he could touch his mother's soothing hands—rough from all the work around the farm, yet somehow so very gentle. The last ten years that was all he had—memories and imagination. The outstretch of his hand never resulted in a returned hand, it never would again.

Nicholas often thought of what his mother would tell him to do with his situation. That was something he did not need his imagination for. Her confident and reassuring voice constantly echoed around the house, bouncing off anything willing to reflect the sound: *You are who you are. You are your past, present, and future.* You. You and you alone.

He was well aware of his mother and father's history. They fell in love due to her ability to get him out of his lowest point of shame, always brought on by the family's history. He wore the thought of disgrace in every move he made. His mother's words had saved his father, until they were not enough.

Now they were like the twist of a rusted blade in his side. He did not want to be like his father. He did not want the shame of an uncertain past to control his present and certainly not his future.

The best choice is always the right choice, Nicholas, always.

Those were his mother's last words to him. He knew they had to be true. He knew they had to mean that he did have a choice. He could run and everything would fall into place. He could run and nothing could follow him—neither his nor his ancestor's past...

"Long, ago, it was the year 1917, and your great grandfather, Nicholas the First, was sent by the armies to regain control over Dukhovia..."

Six great masses of tall wooden doors stood, all lined and decorated identical with a pale, teal exterior and white for all trimming. A strong and courageous man walked with dignity through the fourth door into a long dark, room filled with a long, dark table where several men in uniform filled the chairs.

Some men were matching, their dark blue uniforms decorated with an even alignment of differently shaded blue and white badges, with white patches on their arms, hidden beneath epaulettes. Others stood out, with different colored uniforms, sashes, and badges across both breasts.

Their eyes seemed to match the stone walls which surrounded them, their personas seeming small next to the tall beams.

The man at the head of the table had on the only light blue uniform in the room, three patches of white decorating his upper arm, and a sash of gold, blue, and white across his double badged chest.

The group assembled were of the strongest portion of Dukhovia's newly formed military. After the attack on their land which cost them half their population and nearly all of their farmland, every able-bodied man, regardless of age, was sent to train in methods of martial arts—the only fighting Dukhovians would use.

They were instructed to teach every member of their family the skills that they learned; in that present time and for generations to come. They would never be asked to join the army, to pick a side—but they would be instructed with absolute austerity to learn how to fight.

The harder they fought, the more the advances from the enemy nation seemed to push back. Although, the majority of the country believed that it was because they saw Dukhovia was no logical threat.

CHAPTER FIFTEEN

However, they were left in fear and with a broken society. Russia offered military aid, a gift for accepting their refugees, but was in no position to offer economic assistance to rebuild. Soon, Russia broke into an entirely separate war, becoming less and less able to assist Dukhovia in anything.

Boleslav Mikhailov, the current Dukhovian ruler, stood by his duty as czar and ordered his land to proceed with the intention of peace: never fighting with more than the methods they were trained to use. Nothing more than self-protection and self-preservation...

Lost and desperately thinking of ways to rebuild, the group of men met now to proceed with the planning phase of the only logical execution...

Nicholas I walked in and nodded his head at everyone, keeping his eyes narrow as a proper soldier should. He was serious and collected.

"Afternoon, men," he said, looking at no one individual.

"Nicholas—have a seat," the man at the head of the table gestured to the seat to his right, his voice echoing about the hollow room.

The man sat, listened.

"Nicholas joins us after receiving report from the refugee camp and the Russian army. Nicholas?"

Nicholas breathed in and out deeply. "Our numbers are lower than expected. Nearly all the refugees were murdered and only twenty-five percent of the south and west end of the country remain. Garmoniya was completely destroyed. However, the outside threat seems low at the present moment. Czar Nicholas reports hearing no intent to invade or attack Dukhovia. The Allied Powers will not provide any protection at this time, but will discuss sending aid."

The room was silent for a moment as they all sat with the information.

"You are well aware of the abdicating of Russian Czar, Nicholas Romanov?" He lowered his head. "Yes."

"And the newly reformed reign we should have thought to be superior has failed us miserably. I dare say we were better off with Czar Nicholas, however, with the proper guidance. Not that we are any better under Mikhailov."

"The Spirits chose a new ruler due to the drastic change in our state; the next will be strong enough to protect us. That is how this process works. They say the Great Spirit spoke to Mikhailov directly and told him to choose Yuriy."

"Why yes, of course, and choosing to listen to the ruler our Spirits chose this time around has proved quite innocuous."

"To what do you suggest?" Nicholas asked through gritted teeth. "The Spirits have chosen a brave, worthy man to govern and protect our country, once he is prepared, which shall be soon. Until then, shall we not simply wait? The Spirits will know what to do for our nation."

General Poval grew angry, clutching a fist, but settled formally. "You suggest we wait, but Dukhovia has never seen graver times. To wait would be to invite the enemy back onto our land with open arms. What we need is a plan, a strong military, and a leader with strong military background who can take control."

"To do what you suggest is treason, General," Nicholas argued, the other men fell stiff as boards at the use of the word. "Dukhovia has always followed the word of the Spirits and we have always remained safe and on our rightful path."

"Until today," the general corrected. "And so, something must change."

There was a rumble of hesitant agreement around the room.

"What happened to our nation happened because the world around us is changing and we must learn to adapt and grow..."

"All the more reason to make the changes," Poval went on, pulling out a folder of tattered paper. "We must strengthen and train our military utilizing the latest technology in weaponry. I suggest a different unit to master each since this will be new to each of us. For example, an explosives unit..."

Nicholas shook his head, muttering to himself. He felt detached from the conversation, surprised, and lost that these words could even be spoken inside Dukhovian walls. He was not the only one who disagreed, other men lazily offered rebuttals, but they were afraid, and craved safety. Nicholas knew that. He knew he was starting a losing argument.

"There will also be the matter of a ruler. Since this will be the first time we elect a ruler all our own, I would suggest it be someone with strong leadership qualities, someone with knowledge on military tactics, someone with experience making quick but careful decisions..."

Nicholas's eyes widened in horror. "You suggest yourself!" He stood to his feet, the terror and angst written on his face and in the beads of sweat that penetrated his neckline, threatening to ruin his perfectly lined suit.

He read the room and gathered himself, reclaiming his righthand-man seat. "The time for change is now, but not so soon and not so drastic. We must not cast aside the Spirits before even hearing their plan."

"Their plan?" A man further down the table finally spoke up. "Their plan is silence—to have us figure it out. So, we are."

"Perhaps we are to figure it out, but with their ideals still in place. The ice is already melting. If we sway much further, we will not have a Dukhovia left to save."

They all looked down at the table for a moment, all avoiding Nicholas's gaze. His heart sank more and more, sending a feeling of unease into his stomach. Saving Dukhovia was never the plan.

"It was only a matter of time before we joined the rest of the world, Sir Nicholas. We can only think about saving lives in this moment."

Nicholas fell silent, his mind replaying how exactly they got here, any possible avenue for how to prevent it...

CHAPTER FIFTEEN

Fear was etched in the eyes of every man in the room, but no one made a sound, no one objected.

"Now, there are a handful of troops that have had moderate training. They will be led to overthrow the castle prior to the newly chosen heir's takeover. Nicholas, you are well suited to lead this mission."

"They will never..."

"They already trust you. Do not forget who led the victory when the enemy tried to seize Vodva."

It was true. Dukhovia never had any need for a formal military as their entire culture was centered on peace. However, the more the world began to change, the more they trained in small numbers in self-defense. The attack Poval spoke of now was dismal compared to what they were now faced with. A desperate country attempting to seize their resources, quickly agreeing to a treaty. There was no chance of any agreement now.

He nodded and listened closer. Poval was trying to read Nicholas, to figure him out. Nicholas had only been in Poval's close guard for a short period of time. When the divide in those wanting to modernize first began, Nicholas joined a small group called Traditsiya's, or traditionalists. They were part of the already formed, small military and distanced themselves when talk of revolution began to grow. Nicholas was chosen as leader and then volunteered to serve as spy on Poval's military—the Revoly, or non-traditionalists/rebels.

General Poval continued. "Once you are inside the castle walls, you will call for back-up, insisting that Mikhailov is under attack. My men will come in," he gestured to some gruff looking men at the end of the table, "and plant explosives. You will hold the control to detonate once you are able to ensure Mikhailov is unable to escape."

Demitona went over it in his mind, scratching his chin, playing every scene in his head, the lump in his stomach growing bigger and bigger. He fought: "Sir, that makes no sense at all, unless..."

The General's eyes narrowed.

Growing large in their sockets, Nicholas's eyes were ready to burst. "No! No! It is one thing to discuss murder of a ruler, but to kill all those innocent men! For what?"

The General simply shrugged. "To save our people. To save those we have left and to save our future from an idiotic, outdated ritual."

Nicholas breathed in once. He knew his next move was deadly, but he played it. "I refuse," he said defensively. "If you wish to establish change, then do so peacefully. Form treaties and establish new laws." He stood to his feet, then paused, hand on the door. "Dukhovia needs to come together and fight for the greater good of all of us, not how one of us gets portrayed in history books."

With his last word final, Nicholas stood up and walked out.

THE PAST IS WRONG

Nicholas III knew that Nicholas I made the best decision he was able to come up with. Nicholas III's strong suit was making heavy decisions in a quick moment. Although he soaked up the honor and pride in his ancestry, he could not help but consider what he would have done differently.

Separating himself from the revolution and attempting to protect Mikhailov's life was the honorable thing to do and he supposed it kept Nicholas completely innocent. Ha. Nicholas III, however, saw it as a wasted opportunity. He was already in. Had Nicholas III been in his shoes, he would have infiltrated the plan from the inside and made sure it was destroyed. How different would his past look then? Where would Nicholas be then? If Dukhovia only knew the truth...

It was midnight. In his small cottage, Nicholas fed the small child of his with a smile and his beautiful wife, Allona, held on to his strong shoulders ruffling his brown, buzzed hair. Pride and support beamed around the home like a ray of hope.

Then there was a knock. Laughable Nicholas wiped his hands readying to answer, but before he could move, the Revoly thrust open the door and made their way into the kitchen with large weapons, folding out a piece of paper immediately.

"We knocked, you refused to answer, we immediately dispatched authorities, and permission was granted to enter your estate," General Poval spoke quickly, still holding out the paper.

Nicholas smiled slowly, standing before them. He knew his place in the history books, whether they would tell of it or not...

"And all this in the matter of a second? I had not heard of the time machine completing."

General Poval narrowed his head, two men chuckled, more locked eyes and exchanged an approving nod, and the other three readied their weapons. Poval held his hand not to shoot, but did not instruct them to lower their weapons.

"I see you are already bringing change and destruction into our nation," Nicholas spoke strongly, eyeing the weapons. He tried as hard as he could to ignore the whimpers of his wife as she shielded their child.

"No use using your humor, now, Demitona," Poval spat, dangling the paper before him. "This is an order to destroy the man plotting to overthrow the throne."

"Is that so?" He laughed, pacing his area once. "Curious as I went just this afternoon and spoke with the Castle Command, informing them of a potential plan. I could have sworn I saw the carriage go by an hour ago."

"Of course, with our men in tow," Poval stated quickly. "Our men are not well trusted in the Command, but we are master negotiators. It was quite simple to inform them that the very man who would lead the raid would tell him exactly where to hide. It only makes sense, no?"

Nicholas's mouth formed a thin line, attempting to see the truth or lie in Poval's eyes. His mouth went dry and his heart rate accelerated. Mikhailov trusted him more than anyone—but fear in these unforeseen times could certainly alter that...

The General could not wipe the smirk from his face as he unfolded a fresh piece of paper with a map sketched on it. At the bottom was a note explaining the overthrow and signed with Nicholas's name.

"Especially with solid evidence."

"Solid evidence," Nicholas made a half-laugh, half choking noise as he eyed his wife and child quickly, stalling the inevitable outcome. "Answer me this, Poval, before you murder even more innocent people. Why even bother with the plan? With your weaponry, surely you can simply storm the palace and have the country bowing to your feet by dawn. You know that."

"It is as you said, Sir Nicholas," he scoffed at the name. "I know whom I want to be remembered as. And shall it be a tyrant killing machine? No, no, those are never well liked. Those are never learned from. I am trying to leave a lasting impression. Therefore, my choice was simple. I thank you for aiding me in that discovery."

"Then let me aid you further into a path all of Dukhovia can agree on. Imagine how great of a man, how great of a ruler, if you were the one to stop the revolution."

"Oh, but Nicholas, this time is different. This time I already decided and not even a Traditsiyan spy can stop me."

That was the moment Nicholas knew his heart would leap for the last time. He knew the rifles would fire before they were ever lifted up, before they ever sounded their click to prepare, or shot their fire.

He quicky turned, flinging his body in a dismal attempt to shield his family. His body fell over top of his child, but his wife scrambled to her feet to save them both and was shot beyond recognition.

Nicholas's chest was hollow as he recounted the details. He remembered playing with the bullet-hole lined floor boards as a child. His father always tried to stop him, but, even when area rugs covered the spots, Nicholas found himself mesmerized by the historical evidence.

Perhaps Nicholas I should have allowed the updating of the county. In the end, being able to match his weaponry might have been his only chance at survival.

Nicholas I's downfall was one story Arkady often cited when training Nicholas. If he would have been stronger, he would have been able to take down the six men with no problem. But Nicholas was weak. Nicholas had to train harder and be more agile. Nicholas had to detach himself further and not fret over what stood behind him—protecting them, loving them, having hope in returning to them...

Nicholas I went down as a hero, yet history still remembered him as the enemy. In the coming weeks, Nicholas was told, General Heroie Poval would attempt to overthrow the castle, fail, and meet his own untimely death. Though not before he ensured Nicholas I's name was brought down with him. He was told how one of the men meant to shoot, one whom held his gunfire when he witnessed the atrocity, returned to the home, found David Christopher alive, and raised him to know the true history of his father. Instilling in him faith, courage, purpose, and honor…

And so, Nicholas must do what he needed to do in order to restore that family honor. If he rebelled against Arkady, his rebellion died with him. He had no son. Yet, if he could at least change the history books, that might make every amount of shame his family endured worthwhile…

Nicholas's hand fell against the carpet once more. He watched it move in and out, up and down, a twirl of his fingers so mindless, yet so intentional. He could almost imagine long, frail fingers reaching back, securing into him, and whispering to him each answer he sought, telling him it was okay, telling him what to decide and how to make it possible. But the prophecy had been spoken, and the decision and path were already clear. Besides, he had to follow this path. What the world thought of his family was everything.

CHAPTER 16

UNCERTAIN CIRCUMSTANCES

Stacy's fists hammered at the door of the Leighton house bright and early the next morning. She had not seen Rachael since she ran back into the stadium for dessert. Neither her nor Nicholas ever came back in. She had gone out shortly after to look for her and found her sitting next to the bridge in a heavy breathing fit—the waters behind her splashing up and down. She knew better than to interfere in that moment.

Indifferent mitosis. It was sort of a joke name that the scientifical people in her family coined Rachael's condition as. Something about cells dividing into identical pieces. However, in Rachael's case, it was indifferent. It was neither predictable nor unpredictable—sometimes a pattern existed and sometimes it did not. All they knew was that when Rachael lost control, it was time to look out.

Her parents first noticed it in infancy, though typical doctors were not much help. These types of "powers" were feared and not well understood in the country after Stacy's grandfather. They wanted Rachael confined. So, Tom, Terra, Kevin, and eventually Grace agreed to monitor and learn about the condition. They determined it was due to the unique genetic make-up of Rachael's parents. Her father—an experimented-on individual who gained inhumane strength—and her mother—a loving and passionate woman who experimented in witchcraft and other symbolic magics that Stacy did not quite understand. Of course.

It was not something Rachael could control and use to her advantage either— at least as far as they knew. Rachael hated the condition and everything about it, so she would never focus on using it intentionally. Thus, when it came up, Rachael needed to find her own way to calm down because any intervention could make it worse or put anyone at risk.

Rachael signaled needing her space and they obligated. Though it was certainly not always easy. Especially in a situation like today where Stacy didn't even know what happened. Of course, there had been guesses...

"She needs her time, I know it," Stacy admitted dryly. *"But what upset her? Everything went great!"*

"It was probably the high pitch you hit when it was supposed to be low pitch," Dan replied, there was a hint of a smile on his face—he knew it went well.

"The high pitch sounded better," Stacy retorted.

"Not when the rest of your band plays in low pitch."

She suppressed a yawn as she waited. It was after midnight before she accepted that Rachael was taking time to calm down and would not be coming over to tell her what made her run away on such a great night. Even despite her brother's suggestion, Stacy knew that for her friend to not only not talk to her about it, but have it impact such a huge night, it had to be something more prominent than her high pitch. Still, she lost an exceptional amount of sleep staring out her bedroom window waiting for any sign that Rachael was on her way over to talk things over. Well, she lost about eighty percent of her sleep doing that—the rest was the dream.

Vivid, extraordinary, and more *real* than she had ever experienced. It had to have been meeting Nicholas that caused it and she knew it. Being so close to another Dukhovian triggered something in her and that solidified her internal argument more and more that she had a life she was meant to live in Dukhovia.

But what made her family different? They were biologically related? They were around each other a lot and she was used to them? She could not fathom the reason, but she also was not vain enough to fail to admit that she was not exactly the most well versed in all of the practices of Dukhovia. She understood Rachael's magic or whatever it was called, she did not understand Dukhovia's...not fully.

She expected there was a second reason the dream was so...intense. Talk of the war. Stacy had always known there was war in Dukhovia. She had grown up with the understanding that they were banished because of it. But she supposed she never really put much thought into it past the initial frustration over the injustice. War was simply a word in the history books.

Until her conversation with Nicholas.

Seeing the grim look on his face, the way the light drained from those brilliant eyes. War was not just a word in a book. It was not random men fighting with guns over stuff she did not understand. War was not being able to live in your own home. War was your father sustaining a lifelong injury escaping the country. War was the boy, no older than yourself, who said his whole life was forever altered. The boy who, just thinking of the very idea, seemed to lose himself.

And maybe his choices.

Stacy was not exactly sure why, but that stuck with her. Nicholas had said that he served Dukhovia in some form when the choice was his. What exactly did he mean by that? Did he serve positively or negatively? Serve in the military or another way? Those were just the curiosity questions. Mostly, she wanted to know why the choice would not be his. Who was controlling his choices and who else were they controlling?

She reasoned that he could have just been speaking vaguely of his parents. Stacy knew that people joined the military in Dukhovia much younger than they did in America. She was not exactly sure what the rules surrounding that were, but she had met a boy there on their one trip who said he was a solider—and they were only twelve at the time.

Perhaps Nicholas only meant that his parents did not approve of whatever way he was serving and it needed to change. Perhaps they were not some controlling monsters, but rather he was just...stuck. Stuck in figuring out who he was and what to do with himself if could not do the thing he felt called to do—sort of like her.

Her breath drew in and out quickly, hardly able to catch it. She felt like she was living in a movie or that the wish she made when she blew out her birthday candles every year finally came true. Meeting Nicholas meant exploring everything about herself and Dukhovia that puzzled her—before she even knew him. Now that she met him and knew the similarities they struggled with—she was hooked.

Whatever his reasons were for how he felt about his life—she could not wait to find out.

Stacy rapped on the Leighton front door for the third time before it finally crept open and Ellen's face appeared, a tired smile on her lips. "Good morning, Stacy. Rachael's upstairs."

Stacy looked at her face for hints of the night, but it revealed little other than this night was one of the more difficult. Her eyes darted around the living room and kitchen which were both in organized disarray—a half-hearted attempt to clean before Stacy entered.

She walked towards the stairs, but did not make it to Rachael's room before she appeared in the hallway with a solemn look, a broom, and a dust pan.

"I'm guessing you're not upset about the drum solo?" Stacy prompted.

Rachael smiled faintly. "The drum solo carried that show."

The two girls walked casually into Rachael's room. Stacy could tell she had just finished rearranging it—the hammer and nails were still out that had been used to piece her dresser back together.

"It was nothing, really—a stupid overreaction and I'm mad at myself for reacting the way I did."

"You feel how you feel," Stacy told her. "You're allowed to do that."

The words were not so easy for Rachael to sit with, but she nodded.

"An overreaction to what?"

She breathed in deeply, mulling over likely rehearsed words. "It was just a disagreement with Nicholas."

"What kind of a disagreement?" Stacy asked casually. Just as much as she wanted to know what was wrong with Rachael, she wanted to tell her the impact she believed Nicholas had on her dream and a deep desire to see him again. But that was something that would totally change if...

Rachael shrugged. "I was just trying to be friendly to get him to meet everyone. He didn't want to. So, we just...disagreed."

Stacy's stomach tightened. "Well, we have disagreed before on what color to paint the van—your house didn't look like an explosion afterward."

"We disagree about design flaws daily," Rachael tried to laugh, but dug her own hole.

Stacy's eyes pressed her on.

"I may have pushed him too much and he snapped. He couldn't have known. It's not his fault."

Her heart was fire in her chest. "What do you mean by snapping?"

"He yelled. Screamed really." Behind Rachael, the windows shuddered, then she smiled and pushed Stacy's hair behind her ears. "Let's get your ears pierced before school Monday."

Stacy grabbed her hand abruptly. "He *yelled* at you?! Yelled? Ugh!" Stacy grabbed her own head in frustration. It was exactly what she thought. Rachael's biggest trigger—being yelled at. She was quick to throw things back in some situations, but when someone belittled or put her in an awkward spot, she caved. Throw in the fact that you were attempting to hide this situation from your best friend because you know how crucial this friendship is and it's the perfect storm for emotional unbalance.

"Well, it's settled," Stacy went on, close to her own tears. "We aren't going to talk to him anymore—no big deal."

"But it is a big deal, Stacy! He can tell you so much about Dukhovia! He can teach you so much."

"I have grandparents," Stacy quickly threw back.

Rachael narrowed her eyes at her.

"I only have two years and a few more weeks until I'm 18—I can travel."

"To a country you're banished from?"

Stacy stared blankly, out of rebuttals and out of the ability to talk about the situation without the room spinning. "Listen, it doesn't matter, Rache. We're not going to hang around a guy who thinks he can yell at you for being friendly."

"But Stacy, seriously. I mean, consider his viewpoint—he's so new here and totally alone and lost and probably just wants to be left alone and I invite him out to this thing and then try to introduce him to everyone. How overwhelming."

"Isn't he here to meet us in the first place?" Stacy taunted.

Rachael threw her arms up. "I don't buy that but I don't know another explanation. Did he seem interested in the band or our music?"

"Not in the least," Stacy said simply, her brain now replaying everything in a different light. Everything that seemed so innocent and exciting a moment ago was now being analyzed as suspicious and criminal. "In fact, he seemed kind of annoyed when I showed him my song about Dukhovia. What exactly did he say about meeting us?"

"Oh Stacy, I can't remember specifics," Rachael sighed, tossing a shirt into a laundry basket next to her bed. "He said that he was really interested in meeting us because of how much we accomplished at a young age. He admitted to being a new fan and he was totally alone and didn't really want to talk about why. He wasn't rude, didn't refuse to tell me anything, he just seemed…scared."

Stacy processed that. It made sense to a degree. He wants to do one thing; his parents tell him to do another. He is completely lost in who he is, but hears about a rather successful band of people around the same age as him so he comes to help himself figure things out. Pretty cut and dry.

Except...

"He's from Dukhovia. They don't have radio, they don't have T.V.s. How did he just suddenly hear about us and come?"

Rachael's heart seemed to stop at the same moment as Stacy's. Her words came out as a stammer. "I-I'm sure he heard of us previously and just now decided to look? Y-your family is infamous and banished."

"Yeah exactly," Stacy said with danger written on her face and a coldness to her words. "A guy with anger issues from Dukhovia comes poking around asking about a band with banished Grayson's in it? I don't like that."

Rachael tried to break the tension, but there was still something unsettling to her tone. "Oh, Stacy, please, he came off totally normal and just frightened. Not a single serial killer red flag."

Stacy considered it for a moment. The likelihood of reasons. Why would someone from Dukhovia come looking for her family after all this time? At a time when things were as calm as they had ever been. She admitted, the idea seemed far-fetched.

When I had the choice. Getting an order to go see a banished family in a country most Dukhovian's strongly dislike certainly seemed like something that someone may not want to do. Again, she admitted a low likelihood, but...

"I don't know, but the fact is, it's my choice whether I determine Mr. Anger Problems to be the all-knowing Dukhovian or not."

Rachael let it drop. "Whatever you say. How did the show go? Did Dan hear anything?"

Now was Stacy's turn to pretend to deflect. "Oh, nothing major. Just a call from STAN SIMMONS!"

Rachael screamed. "STAN SIMMONS! THE STAN SIMMONS!"

"The one and only!" Stacy declared. "He wants us to come to his studio and Dan is ironing out a potential contract with his label now."

"Oh my gosh! Oh my gosh!"

Adding Sir Nicholas to their hit list did not make a reappearance in the conversation after that. But it did continue to filter into Stacy's thoughts in and out. It was not so much their decision—if he was going to yell at Rachael, case closed, he was out. It was more so the reason of why he was in America—alone—and asking around the band. Asking around her family...

It did not make sense for it to be anything related to their banishment. They were in America, far away from Dukhovia or anything that remotely had to do with Dukhovia. Why then did something in her gut seamlessly convince her that his reason for being here had everything to do with their banishment?

CHAPTER 17

SEEDS OF DEFEAT

Nicholas took a deep breath and let his footsteps bring him forward. He stood before a tall, nearly grand building, had it not been for the seemingly impossible to open door. He had been watching several students for the past five minutes—each one had to heave the door open with an intense amount of pressure and pin it to the wall while other students pushed through. They would only be able to hold it for so long before it shut tight on the student. This happened time and time again until an adult walked up, stuck something in the door, then another something, and kept it open for at least another three students before it too slammed shut and shattered the door next over.

His eyes searched the rest of the grounds—tables of chattering teenagers littered the way. Most of them in groups, though there were a few others alone like himself allowing him to not stick out too much. He had a mission, however, and was looking for only one group, one girl that he had to make amends with.

"Rachael..."

He heard her name escape his lips before he truly decided on what to say. He had been going over it again and again all night, of course, yet a decision was scarce. He considered for a moment the fact she was walking alone. Perhaps Stacy did not yet know.

She turned with a smile on her face that quickly faded when she saw him. Her eyes started to dart around, looking for an escape, but he called after her.

"Rachael, please. I only wish to apologize for last night. It was very rash and rude of me. Rachael! Please!"

She pushed passed him and another group of male students that Nicholas did not make much note of before disappearing from view.

Nicholas stopped, sighing. He had higher hopes for their conversation. He certainly did not expect her to turn away. However, perhaps she simply needed more time and did not wrestle with the argument as long as he had. Fearfully, his thoughts entered the worst-case scenario: that she had thought about it plenty and decided her generosity towards him had ended.

Nicholas glanced back up to the sound of cheering and hollering. It was the group of students that Rachael had shoved through. Apparently, she only disappeared to the other side of their huddle and was now being cornered around them.

"What somewhere to be?" One was saying. "And I expect we just have to clear the way for you because you're so great and wonderful?" He had a vicious look on his face that might have frightened Nicholas had he not been faced with much worse. No, to him these were just simple, untrained moronic Americans.

"Oh no, crying?" Another said. "Don't get her too upset—she'll knock the school down."

"Well in that case…"

That was it. Nicholas saw the hands of the tallest one move towards Rachael as she was huddled on the ground with her hands over her teal ear muffs, eyes shut, forcing the scene out.

Why does she not just walk away, part of Nicholas thought, but the scene changed before his thought even surfaced. The tall one put his hands on Rachael's chest and pushed her forward. The next moment was strange, bricks around the school started to suddenly fall and Nicholas wondered if the door was shut too hard again. The boys laughing as if they expected it seemed to conclude his theory—except that they tried again to push Rachael.

Bricks continued to fall and crumble. The sidewalk around them cracked and opened in slight places. Just as the tall one withdrew his first push and went in for a second, Nicholas had him by the collar, high in the air.

"Leave her alone," he muttered, and threw the boy out of sight.

"Who do you think you are?" Another exclaimed, coming toward him.

"Looks like she hired a body guard."

Nicholas threw the other two boys off of himself with ease. Then another came. Then more. Nicholas could not tell if the bricks ceased falling or if his attention was too focused on the influx of boys that began to swarm him. They were easy enough to take down—again, they had no training and barely knew how to throw a proper punch, let alone block. But the more that came, the more distracted Nicholas's mind became.

This was not what he came here to do. This was not who he wanted to be. Sweat fell from his hairline; anger intensified from inside of him. He slipped and one of the boys was able to hit his back—it was over. Suddenly, he saw a sea of red and moved from boy to boy, sight to sound.

His reactions were quick. He threw two boys off, then he felt another hand touch his shoulder, he immediately dropped the two boys he picked off and threw them to the ground. With force, he reached to his back and grabbed the wrist of the hand that touched him.

He heard a loud crunching, then the face of the person made his heart stop and his reality come back together.

Rachael.

"AH!" She screamed out in pain, holding her wrist.

There was a flash of black, and someone was on top of Nicholas, choking him. "STAY AWAY FROM HER!"

Those were the words Nicholas thought he heard, but his eyes were locked onto Rachael. Her face was beat red, panicked, chest heaving.

And there was Stacy. At Rachael's side. Comforting her. Holding her. Right there. Watching everything.

Nicholas jumped to his feet, shoving Cody without much effort.

"I said away!" Cody was quickly next to Nicholas, attempting to stop him in his tracks.

Nicholas lifted a hand to push Cody away, but Cody latched onto the hand, attempting to bend it back. Mistake. Instantly, Nicholas slammed his elbow into Cody's nose and blood began to spurt.

"Cody!" Rachael shouted.

Her shouts brought him back to reality even further. Cody. Cody Grayson. This was another person important to the heir. Important to Stacy.

No. No. No. Calm down, calm down! Now his own breathing was matching Rachael's. He did not know where or how to move. He had lost so much control in such little time.

"I'll take her to the nurse—get my mom," Stacy was saying. She threw Nicholas a grave look before turning away, holding Rachael around her shoulders as she shuttered and shook, her sad eyes looking from Nicholas to Cody and back again.

Her mother was here too?

Nicholas's breath evaded him. Stomach tightening, he felt ready to lose the half piece of bread he picked at this morning.

"Please," he called out.

Stacy's steps came to a halt and she rounded back.

He held his breath, hopeful yet anxious at the way she was steaming towards him.

Then she was before him, her face violent, her words sculpted cruelly as they came out through gritted teeth. "I don't know what's the matter with you but don't you ever come near me or my family ever again, got it? I don't know why you're here and I don't care, but you will leave us out of it."

"But, I just…"

"I said enough!" Stacy screamed—then her eyes darted left and she rolled them.

Nicholas followed her line of vision to a tall, very orderly figure with dark, balding hair upon a very fixated face. Fixated on him. The school grounds seemed to fall silent and the only sound that could be heard was the clapping of this man's shoes as he approached Stacy and Nicholas, tugging at his perfectly pressed suit as he approached them.

"Well, Ms. Matthews, I could see your cousin screaming at the new boy on his first day of school, but you?" His mouth made an unfavorable clicking sound that sentenced dismay.

"No, I was involved too, Santifini, don't worry," Cody called over from where he had taken Stacy's place holding Rachael, simultaneously cradling his own nose.

"I had no doubt," Santfini whispered, not taking his glance from Stacy and Nicholas.

Stacy's face seemed transfixed into a grimace as she stared at the ground. "I didn't do anything," she snarled. "It was all *him*."

It was the first time her deadly eyes locked completely on his. He knew she was seeing far past their beauty, perhaps only into their icy depths. Never having been in an argument that could not be easily won with slaughter, Nicholas remained silent and their stares waged a war with each other.

"So quick to judge and yet we've scarcely been introduced to the poor boy. Nicholas Andrews, I presume?"

"Yes," Nicholas agreed through his own begrudging attitude.

"I am Principal Santifini, it is an honor. And you are visiting us from Dukhovia—a country of strict pleasantries and peace, as it's told, yes?"

Nicholas pushed out another sigh of agreement, as if his name was not enough, rubbing the disaster that was Dukhovia in his face made Nicholas hate the man automatically.

"I don't believe I had the honor to meet your parents. Did they drop you off this morning?" He asked, looking around cluelessly.

Nicholas whipped his head toward the man, looking him up and down only for a moment. "No," he hissed the word through barred teeth. His eyes locked back onto Stacy's, whose daggers had not faltered. "They were murdered in front of me when I was six."

And then the daggers were gone. He observed her as the rest of her features began to falter with them. First her eyes becoming, not gentle, not necessarily unguarded, but inquisitive, puzzled. Then her arms dropped, her body falling more into a stance of...what? Alertness? Awareness? Dare he think—comfort?

"Oh ho," Santifini released the sound, not seeming to know how to react. "That doesn't really fit the script, now then, does it? Of course, you've met Ms. Matthews and Mr. Grayson...Ms. Leighton, how exactly do you fit into all this?" The principal asked, seeming to take in her appearance and remember there was a fight he was interrupting.

"The fault is mine entirely," Nicholas said, eyes still locked on figuring out the heir before him. "I was trying to protect Rachael from those imbeciles..." he pointed to his left, not breaking eye contact. "However, I lost my temper and did not see Rachael attempting to stop me. Her friends were simply trying to protect her. It is my fault and mine alone."

"Hm." Santifini seemed to be glanced around, eyeing the situation. "I am very moved by your ability to own up to your mistakes, Sir Nicholas. Still, a land cannot function without consequences. I am afraid I will have to assign you to detention..."

He rattled on some more about dates and something or other, but Nicholas was lost in watching Stacy's persona change even further. He was not sure if she listened to his speech of him selling himself out, or if her thoughts were playing off what the principal had said regarding the peace of Dukhovia turning into a slaughter house, but she now eyed him openly, up and down as she not so vaguely took in his posture, his persona, and made her own assumptions.

How different she would feel, he thought, if she knew just how common that onslaught was. If she knew that it was more the norm than it was not for him to run into another soldier his age whom had their parents murdered. If she knew that it was this bond that he and his former best friend built their friendship on.

Something The Principal said broke Stacy's train of thought and she was looking up at him, perplexed, frustration returning. "What do you mean detention? I didn't do anything."

"A land cannot function without consequences, Ms. Matthews. That includes consequences for all types of violence and inciting violence."

"I didn't incite any violence!" She argued. "You heard him—he did it!"

"A land cannot function if its strongest powers are torn, Ms. Matthews."

And with that he placed his hands behind his back and strolled away as casually as he arrived.

"What does that even mean!" Stacy shouted after him. She rounded on Nicholas again. She was her new, intrigued self, but frustration remained steady as she scolded him once more and then bounded off towards her friends to accompany them to the nurse's station.

CHAPTER 18

CONSEQUENCES

"Oh, you have *got* to be kidding me."

Stacy watched as Nicholas strode into yet another one of her classes and took a seat. It was fourth period math. If you were in fourth period math, you were certainly in fifth period English and after that options for separation were slim. You either had gym or study hall last period and archery or swimming sixth. Nicholas certainly did not get his muscles sitting in study hall, but she was willing to bet he would rather strengthen his shot at attacking students than join her in swimming class. At least that would be her solace.

It was almost as if Santifini wanted her and Nicholas to fight at this point. *A land divided blah blah blah* whatever he had said. This was not a land—this was a school. They were not plagued enemies destined to be best friends, he wanted to antagonize innocent people and she was a normal person. Point blank.

She supposed she needed to stop looking at herself as the victim. She was not—Rachael was. And Rachael was in all advanced classes—not her classes. Well, not all of her classes, anyway. They forced her into advanced science because they wanted to "uncrack the shell" stopping her from being a science prodigy like the rest of her family. She was certain she had her mother to blame for not failing her in eighth grade science when she had the chance. Trader.

At least that comforted her—knowing that Sir Nicholas was just as stupid as she was. Guess they failed to send the children to slaughter for failing their standardized tests in Dukhovia.

Ugh. Did they even have tests in Dukhovia? Now she would never know. She bit her lip as she watched him breeze through the paper that was put in front of them twenty minutes ago—the paper she had not yet even glanced at. More than once, she caught him turning to look at her too.

What was his angle? He came here from Dukhovia looking for them, but not related to their music. So, what then? He was sixteen, he was not some hired assassin. Or maybe he was. Maybe Dukhovia reconvened on their banishment and decided their whole family and all acquaintances were better off dead.

Now Rachael's outburst that brought down half the school's entryway with it only confirmed the need for annihilation. Fair enough, the brick was getting harder to replace and she was the reason it differed so drastically in color. But they could never lose her and her precious test scores right alongside.

Stacy looked at the door. She knew Rachael *should* not return to school that day, but knew she likely would. She made it through half of science before the pain in her arm became too excruciating and they decided she should go to a hospital and not just be given an ice pack and a pain killer. Cody went with her, of course.

The look on Nicholas's precious face when she left was…ugh. It was remorseful. He looked actually, fully, one-hundred and ten percent apologetic and that killed her. It was accidental. Him yelling really was not that big of a deal. But he was a ticking time bomb and that told her to stay away. But the pain in his eyes told her another…

His parents. She kept replaying the moment he let the information slip in her mind. There was pain somewhere deep inside him, she knew it—yet he revealed nothing. He was like stone. His words and face expressionless as he delivered the blow—they were dead. Not only were they dead—they were murdered, *murdered.* In front of him. At age six. It got worse and worse as she kept piecing it apart and tacking it all together.

She thought of her own life multiple times and kept pushing it out. She could not even fathom the idea of something happening to her parents, yet Nicholas not only went through the experience, but continues to live with it and deliver the news with a straight face. What did that say about him? She did not doubt that Dukhovian assassins lacked emotion. Did any assassin get sad?

She supposed it made sense from what she learned about her mother and her own anger and mistakes along the way after she lived without her parents for so long. *Sadness blocks good decision making*, she would say. So, Nicholas watches his parents get murdered, develops an anger problem, and is quick to recover and prove his wrongdoing. Still made him risky. It still meant he was likely set out to end her family. But it made her want to talk to him.

More than that, she wondered more about him. Had anyone ever talked to him about his parent's deaths? Had he talked to them? He was still here alone, so, was it just swept under the rug and now he has been out doing whatever.

She thought on that for a moment. *Choice. When the choice was mine…* So, he did not have a disagreement with his parents and leave. If they were not alive, they were not controlling him at all. *In front of me.* She winced, hardly able to think about it let alone form a rational thought around how someone would feel if it happened to them—and if it happened to them while their country was also at war and tumbling down around them.

But she bet he felt out of control having to watch them be taken, having to watch his world. Was that all he meant? That things were limited now that he was without his parents? Or was he placed with an evil relative following? If that was the case, who were his parents? She expected that would make them gentle, kind, hopeful…and she would expect anger to flow from him if those were the people who were taken from him.

Ugh! She stomped her foot to the ground and impatiently stared up at the clock.

CONSEQUENCES

I don't know, she told herself, answering questions related to what the hell Nicholas's problem could possibly be. *I don't know, I don't know, I don't know.* The answer she was always stuck with when it related to anything even remotely close to Dukhovia. The answer she would now, it seemed, be permanently stuck with. Lost. Stuck. Out of control.

And it made her angry.

She felt her mind traveling down a path of understanding as she envisioned his life: perfect beyond measure, every choice his to make, then taken from him, now stuck, controlled... She shrugged her shoulders as she felt her own blockades stopping the understanding.

Her family.

He may have lost his, but that did not mean that he was innocent and was not potentially harmful to her own. Then that brought her back to the continuous circle of understanding Nicholas, of contemplating why he was really in America. Not only for fear of her family, but for fear of Dukhovia. Because if Dukhovians were choosing to come to America to start over...what did that say about the state of Dukhovia?

She felt like she was going to vomit. Flashes of condescending light and tropical views flashed in her mind, fighting against those of smoke and fire, of soft, wintery flakes dancing against fresh pines, of homes burnt to the ground with her parent's bodies inside...

She closed her eyes, willing the thoughts at bay. Then, she opened them, gluing them to the back of Nicholas's head.

She thought briefly of a time in their lives when the Grayson family was not feared, but adored for being such a close and loving family. Was it family that had him asking about them? Was that what he travelled to America for? It was a daring trip for sure and a lot to go to, but if Stacy did not have the wonderful family that she did, she would certainly travel to the ends of the earth to find it, let alone America. Even if she feared that country, if there was promise of finding the one thing she cared most for in the world...

But that depended on who Nicholas was. Was love for their family even a commonality between them? Did his family mean to him what Stacy's meant to her?

In that moment, the door to the classroom swung open. Rachael entered the room, Cody with an aggressive look on his face behind her. Stacy smiled at them and then glanced down at Rachael's wrist—it had a bright pink cast.

Her heart sank. No matter if Nicholas was a victim or not, he was a danger to her friends and they needed to come first. Perhaps he had been through hell and back, but she had her fair share of those moments too. She had been banished from a country she loved, banned from certain states, ridiculed, threatened, and attacked in the streets for the actions of her family members—and she still left innocent people alone.

Cody glanced around the room and paused when he caught sight of Nicholas. "Oh no. Oh no."

Rachael halted him with a touch of her arm.

"You've got to be kidding me. How is he *still* allowed in school? Why isn't he in some type of prison?"

Stacy looked at Nicholas and watched his body collapse into itself when he saw Rachael's arm. Remorse.

Cody kept firing off, shooting more and more rage off in Nicholas's direction. Nicholas sat, seemingly lost, everything bouncing off of him.

"Did you call your dad and ask?" Stacy joked. She walked to the front of the room and grabbed Rachael's books from her. Setting the books on the teacher's desk, Stacy took her friend's arm into her hands.

"It's just a fracture," Rachael admitted shyly.

Stacy raised her eyebrow. *Just.*

"It'll be healed in a month or two."

"So, not only do we have a one-armed drummer, but we're also missing practice time for me to sit in detention to think about what I didn't do."

"All seems a very small price to pay," Rachael mused, nudging her eyes in Nicholas's direction. He was now looking at the ground, kicking his feet with anticipation.

The bell for lunch rang and the trio hurried out of the room to find their seats in the cafeteria. The school had been buzzing the entire day about the situation. The bricks outside the school had already been replaced and that was old news, but, finding out that the new student injured the school's sweetheart, Rachael, made him public enemy number one. It was no wonder, then, that when he entered the cafeteria, students were either running from him or giving him the cold shoulder. Everyone except Rachael.

"I think we should invite him to sit with us."

"Did he give you a concussion too?" Jade asked, lazily sipping her chocolate milk from the container.

"Seriously," Cody agreed. "Look what he did to you, Rache. He's lucky I let him live to see sixth period."

Rachael narrowed her eyes at him. "You heard what he told Principal Santifini, though. About his parents...could you imagine?"

"With pleasure," Cody grudgingly remarked.

"Ditto," Dylan sided, raising his milk to Cody's in a type of toast.

While Dylan and Cara's abuse from their parents was more known and focused on, Cody's relationship with his mother seemed almost...ignored. Yasana's erratic history dated back to before she and Richard dated. They were thought to be the perfect couple amongst newspapers everywhere when they first started making headlines related to Tom's issues. Yasana was quick to anger and would lash out on Richard often, yet he would always forgive her due to her rough past. Stacy was quick to make the connection.

Now that Cody was getting older, her anger was becoming harder and harder to ignore. Instead of "your mother is having a moment" excuses, Cody was beginning to see the obvious at face value. And with Cody's struggles, came Richard's own downfall.

Rachael and Stacy's eyes locked as they made the same comparison. "Not a bed I want to make for myself," Stacy commented.

Rachael sighed, but seemed to agree. Still, her eyes looked towards Nicholas who was standing alone, looking solemnly out at the crowd. Then she rose to her feet and began to walk towards him.

"She's insane, isn't she?" Jade asked, blinking after her.

"She's dead is what she is—Rachael!" Cody was on his feet in a second tailing after her.

"It's probably a good moment for a lover's quarrel, but I'm gonna go too," Stacy said and trailed behind them just a few steps.

"Nicholas!" Rachael was calling and waving with her broken arm.

Nicholas turned to her, half in a daze, as if he thought this could be some type of dream.

Cody quickly grabbed her upper arm and held her back. "Rachael, please. He could easily hurt you again. You saw him this morning. You know this behavior. Please be smart."

"I am, Cody Robert. But I need you to trust me. I just had a feeling when I met him—he needs us."

Trust. The word was strong enough to cause Cody to pause and think, but he knew letting go meant more than trust. "I do trust you, Rachael. But I also want to keep you safe."

She reached behind her and tried to squeeze his fingers with her casted ones. "Then let's show him the same kindness and maybe we'll gain a friend."

Cody was the furthest thing from being on board, he let her walk towards Nicholas, but kept a close tail on Rachael, making sure Nicholas knew he was not his friend.

"Rachael," Nicholas's voice was still surprised, but eager all the same. "Rachael, I am so very sorry. I know I can only beg your forgiveness…"

"You have it," Rachael smiled—then she went in for a hug.

Cody reacted quickly to stop her, but knew the moment his and Nicholas's bodies touched it would be war. She slid through Cody's fingers and wrapped her arms around Nicholas's neck. Nicholas stood frozen, seeming paralyzed by what to do. He did not return the hug; he only stood in confusion.

"I'm so sorry for everything. We want you to know you're not alone. You have us." Rachael shifted to reveal Cody and Stacy who looked the furthest thing from welcoming. "Cody and I will sit with you," Rachael began, making her way to a nearby table. "I believe Stacy had something to say to you."

"You believe what?" Stacy argued, but Nicholas was strolling now all-too eagerly toward her.

"Stacy, I have no excuse for my behavior...."

"No, you really don't."

"I know I cannot make amends to you easily, but I would like to try. Please."

"Why's it matter so much?" She asked vaguely, not expecting the answer she really wanted.

Nicholas searched his mind for an answer. "I simply want you to know the true me. Please allow me the chance to earn your trust."

They were murdered in front of me at age six.

"My trust?" Stacy laughed, a coy and devilish sound that seemed to rescind below them. She glanced from his pleading eyes—which made her want to vomit—over to Rachael's discerning pair. Then, she made her gravest mistake and let thoughts wander...

His parents. *Her* support.

Sighing, Stacy turned her cold gaze back up to meet Nicholas's desperately searching eyes. "Fine. I'll let you try. But I wouldn't bet on succeeding."

CHAPTER 19

CHAINS

A blistering whirl of frigid ice swept the thin, red hat from his small, fragile scalp. Fear and a harsh chill ran through the child's body instinctively—it was too cold out to be without complete coverage. He had never been so cold as he was when his mother woke him from his bed and threw him onto his favorite horse—Tanvy.

Without another thought, a larger, softer yet brittle hand reached forward and secured the hat back onto his head. The child's fear disappeared entirely. He returned his face to the comfort of his mother's chest, fully enclosed in the thick, wool blanket she wore to conceal him.

She wore the wool for two reasons, the bitter cold being the least of their concerns.

The horse rode with fierceness, galloping through blocked roads after blocked roads, swerving away from busy streets full of shouting men. The child sensed his mother's panic, surely, but she knew what she was doing. She always did. He would be safe. He would be comfortable.

"No!" Her hiss was barely a whisper, but Nicholas felt the arch in her back change as she tensed and tried to pull him closer to her body.

He turned his head so one ear was revealed, just faintly picking up the sound of additional hooves clopping behind him.

"Ma'am! Ma'am please halt!"

She looked from side to side wildly, her eyes would hide the flooded feeling of panic and pain. Then, she pulled her horse off, obeying.

Two men descended from their horses, looking around at his mother and their horse, taking in the scene before approaching her. They circled her a few times, looking her up and then down.

"So sorry to disturb you on your ride. We are looking for a kidnapped child."

"A kidnapped child?" She sweat, enclosing the wool further.

"Aye. It seems to be happening a lot as of late. The Czar has sent us to find the child. He is small, four or five years, black hair, and bright blue eyes."

His mother's eyes fell.

"Ma'am?"

"I apologize," she said, breaking into tears. "Only, I lost my son of a very similar description years ago. To the war."

CHAPTER NINETEEN

The men looked at each other and paused. They did not necessarily hold a stance of warning or pressure, but it was clear that they were reading each other's thoughts on how to proceed. "Where are you journeying now?"

"Saurahi," she said after a brief pause, causing the men to exchange another look. Saurahi was the closest country over the sea, to the left of Dubishia. It was the country new refugees would leave for.

"I understand," spoke the first man and the other nodded. "Is there anything we can do to aid you?"

Nicholas felt his mother's chest fall as she sighed in relief, then she tensed again. "I only require safe passage."

The men exchanged a look with each other and nodded. "We can trail you as far as West Gate, if needed."

"Oh, I could never ask of such a thing. Especially as you are already heavily occupied. I would hate to take from finding a missing child." Nicholas felt one cool tear roll down his mother's cheek and onto his own.

"As you wish, Ma'am."

The two men began to walk back to their horses when a third set of hooves was heard approaching. "You! Men, have you found the child?"

"She has no child. She is a refugee."

The new arrival spat in disgust. "Fleeing the country is for traitors. She should be taken and tried for treason if that is her explanation. Our country was built on a foundation of obedience and loyalty, not fear."

"I have family in Saurahi."

"You dare speak, woman?" The man charged forward on his horse and stopped close to her. "Was she searched?"

"Nay. There was no need."

The man sneered again, dismantling his horse. In a haste, he kicked over the bag Anecka had packed. He watched it crash to the ground without interest. He licked sweat away from his lips, anger and malice etched in his every being. "Off the horse."

She did not move.

He stared intently into her eyes, waiting one, two, three...

In a rapid succession, before she even had time to think, the man was yanking at the cloak. Her arm instinctively pulled it back around Nicholas and kicked the horse into gear, heading for the cover of the forest up ahead. She heard the pounding hooves following behind her, but she kept her eyes straight ahead.

Nicholas could feel each crashing bump as they raced through the forest, his mother's arms in full work: one tightened securely around him, the other flailing to urge the horse onward. They were getting closer, Nicholas could tell. He heard his mother's unusually even breath began to falter, then the moment he would recount as the scariest moment of his life took place...she let out a piercing scream.

Up ahead, the man jumped out of the covering and in front of her horse, Anecka pulled the horse with all her might towards the left, dodging him narrowly. Nicholas slid from the comfort of her chest down the side of the horse. Anecka slid her own body down the side of the horse to secure him, but she could not hold him and climb back on.

Behind them, they heard metal scrape metal as a sword was withdrawn, making their enemies reach more at ease. Nicholas closed his eyes and began to count, he began to think of the animals at the farm, he began to think of his mother playing him the lyra on her lap in the rickety chair in his bedroom...

Suddenly he had the sensation that he was flying. He clenched closer onto his mother and looked down. They were sailing over a wide gap in the mountain—a fierce river directly below them. His heart pounded but his mind looked on with interest and wonder. Down below, his eye caught sight of two horses falling below—the men that had been chasing them falling along with them.

Crash!

Nicholas and his mother were thrown forward as their horse's foot caught the edge of the cliff side and fell onto its side. Anecka's arms flew protectively around Nicholas, around his body, around his head, and they rolled together forward into the forest.

Quickly, she stood to her feet and disrobed the wool cape. She attempted to lift Nicholas, but her right arm appeared to give out. Lifting him with only her left, she huddled him near a tree and threw the wool around him, rushing back to check on the horse.

Nicholas watched his mother speak Dukhovian words to the horse, stroking its long neck. She assessed all his hooves, then returned to one that Nicholas knew was the problem. He felt confused. He felt cold and hungry. He remembered feeling so many things—but fear was not one. Fear was never one. Neither for himself or for the horse—she was in good hands.

"What is it, mama?" Nicholas called over.

She glanced back, thinking for a moment, and then ushered him forward. "It is his hoof, Nickolai. He has hurt it quite bad. He will not be able to carry us, but if we can find a way to strengthen and secure it, we can get him to a shelter for the night.

Nicholas nodded. They spent the next few hours searching the woods for the herbs and supplies they would need to stabilize the horse and then make its remedy. Slowly, he watched as his mother made a thick paste that went on the horse's leg, fed the remainder to the horse, and then secured sticks and leaves around the sore hoof. Finally, after a long while, she rose the horse upward. He let out a painful yelp, but he was able to walk.

Slowly, she hoisted Nicholas back into her arms and continued forward.

CHAPTER NINETEEN

It was a few short miles before they seemed out of the eye of the town and his mother ceased looking over her shoulder. The horse's pace slowed to a steady stroll and his mother reached forward, rewarding the mare with a rare sugar cube. Then, her arm returned around the child, bringing him in close, her lips touching the fraying end of his cap.

He shut his eyes, being lulled by the motion, by her soft, secure arms.

"Shh. Nicholas. When you wake, we will be safe."

He knew he would be. So, he allowed himself to drift away and dream. He dreamt of a warm cottage where he and his mother laughed as they played music and cooked stew. He dreamt of racing around on horses until the sunset, telling them dinner was complete.

His eyes blinked open a little while later. He was being lowered onto a straw mattress and covered with the thick, wool blanket. He caught sight of his mother lighting candles and hiding them around the room. He blinked again and was asleep.

He was awoken the next morning in a haste. His mother rushing about the room, blowing candles out, and packing up the small bag.

"It's time to go, Nicholas." She pushed a small bowl of porridge towards him. It was the only bowl and she had eaten one or two small spoonfuls before handing the rest to him. "Tanvy cannot travel; she will stay in boarding here. We will head straight for the sea and remain on the sea until we reach America. I have enough crackers to last us. Are you ready, my child?"

He nodded, sleepily climbing into his mother's arms.

She secured him inside the blanket and they were off. Before he knew it, they were trudging through a muddy pass, wind whipping harshly at their faces. The boat was small and offered no shelter from the elements, but they would be safe once they were on it. He was always safe. He never felt scared.

Nicholas felt his mother settle herself down into the boat and push off—but they were stopped. He did not know what happened next. He only heard the gasping of his mother, the thud of the oar, and the intense pounding of his racing heart...

***

Nicholas opened his eyes hours later. He was in a dark cave. Water seeped around them. He was in a corner, tied to a stone pillar. There was nothing around him. Nothing except stone and emptiness. And his mother.

His eyes flailed open. He attempted to get up, attempted to reach the woman whom hung upside down mere feet away, but he was too constricted. "Mommy! Mommy!" He tried to scream but found he had no voice. "Mama!" Tears suddenly streaked his face uncontrollably. Panic flooded his mind as he looked around, panting wildly, searching for a way to help.

"Nicholas..." Her voice was slow, quiet, barely more than a scratchy whisper. *"Nicholas you must breathe."*

He could not. He rapidly took in deep breaths but fear replaced what was meant to be air. *"Mama, mama, I'm scared. I'm scared."*

"There is nothing to be afraid of, my darling. You are safe. You are safe."

"I am...I am..." he tried, tried so hard to repeat the words. Then, footsteps took over his sound—slow, meaningful footsteps. Closer...closer...

"Tsk. Tsk. Anecka. What type of repayment is this?" The voice of The Czar filled Nicholas's ears before he saw the man, petrifying him even more. His breathing became more rigid as he watched the black of his steel boot come into view, followed by his perfectly pressed light blue uniform, then finally his face: darker than normal, malevolence lurking in every twist of his body.

"I take your child, a child whose gifts you can only imagine, teach him to use them to save this country and you what—break into my palace, steal the child, and send me and my men across the country to find him when we have a war going on? Do you understand how many men had to leave their posts to search for you? How many people were left unprotected? How many villages I had to burn when information was refused to me?"

Nicholas's mother choked and a pool of vomit emitted below her.

He sighed, heavily. *"Though we were able to rid the country of several traitors."* He walked around her, the echo of his heavy boots surrounding them. *"For that, I will allow you to live."* Arkady paused just next to his mother. He stood next to her, arms behind his back.

Nicholas closed his eyes as his mother's screams filled the cave. The Czar lifted his fists and shoved them directly into her stomach. *"Yes, we certainly owe you thanks."* His fists came down on her stomach again, his spiked boots lifting to make contact with her mouth, her nose, her eyes...

Nicholas closed his eyes tighter and tighter, trying to block out the image of her spinning around and around, spitting up blood, throwing up, and singing, singing ever so softly to him.

"STOP!" Nicholas screamed, holding his hands to his ears.

Arkady walked slowly over to the wall of the cave, lifting a long, metal rod into his hands. He sized it up in his hand carefully, then, at an instant, he beat Anecka's body over and over until consciousness had nearly evaded her...

Nicholas's felt a vibration in his throat, a piercing unlike anything he ever felt before. His hands continued to press firmly on his ears, squeezing with all his might. He opened his eyes only for a moment to watch his mother's body cut down. Arkady grabbed her by the hair; she was circling attempting to stay upright.

Arkady knelt only slightly, bringing his mother up so that her ear was right next to Arkady's mouth. *"Remember this. You can run. You can run as often as you would like. It will be good practice for my tracking and for teaching your son.*

CHAPTER NINETEEN

But as long as our hearts are both beating, I will be able to find him. I will always find him. As long as this country requires him, he is mine."

CHAPTER 20

A PROMISING FOUNDATION

A whistle blew, snapping Nicholas back to reality. His thoughts vanished and, in their place, came the vision of a large, colorful pit, filled with water and lined with rope. A swimming pool.

They had one in the palace. Though he mostly only swam in the ocean, it was nice to have when he could not leave the palace. It was meant to be a magical place that allowed them to feel closer to their Spirit. Smooth stone had been carved and filled with water purified by Spirit Gifts. The only light was that which bounced off the walls from the flame in the chandeliers. Somehow, Nicholas imagined it would be much more difficult to reach his Spirit in this body of water.

The brightness of 10,000 fluorescent lights, the roar of some type of machine to cleanse the water (never mind the toxic smell), the blowing of the incessant whistle, the screaming and laughing of children throughout—yes, it would be much more difficult.

He had come unprepared for class—or so he was told. Despite stating on his schedule that no materials were required, bathing wear was apparently required of him. He had none in America and certainly nothing anywhere like that of what his classmates now wore. It was no matter, they had spares, and so he stood in the same faded black shorts that many before him had worn—and perhaps were able to find some dignity after they got past the sloshing of the wear around his knees.

The day had not gone as he had planned. Of course. His temper. He came in fully prepared to make amends with Rachael and was so quick to lose control. He shut his eyes, breathing in slowly once and then again. Always so quick to lose control. It was his anger. It was his lack of control. It was his indecision. It was everything.

He had gotten through until lunch time purely on the thought of how Stacy's eyes transfixed upon his when she heard about his parent's deaths. Something in them brought him…comfort? Perhaps it was too fierce of a word for a girl intent on hating him, and yet solace did seem to be what overwhelmed him when he thought of this moment. Perhaps a rare yet fatal flaw in her mapping—empathy. The sorrow she felt for him allowed him the ability to still have a fighting chance.

And then there was Rachael. She had returned to school with her arm in a cast. During lunch, he learned that she fractured five bones. The realization sent his own healed fractures throbbing, yet he felt overwhelmed with a feeling he never experienced when he fought back in Dukhovia—guilt.

Rachael was a good and kind and generous person. He did not want to utilize her trust for wrongdoing—yet what choice did he have? She was so willing to restore her faith in him—why? Because *"everyone makes mistakes"*, she had said. *"I think losing control can happen easier than a lot of people think."*

The bricks falling. The water moving when he yelled at her. It was rare, but he had heard legends of people with telekinetic-like powers. From his understanding, they used their emotions to control what happened. But how would such a thing come to impact Rachael? How much did she know of it? How often did she lose control? Did she feel similar to him when she did?

He had not pressed her. Not in front of Cody, anyway. The look of anger and distaste throughout lunch told him to keep the conversation light. Not that he could not snap his neck before his body even processed what was happening…. No, he easily could. But he would not.

Then there was the heir herself. She had not spoken a word to him during lunch after her agreement to earn his trust—not a single word. It was as though she was taking back the promise the moment it was made. She sat and scolded. He sat and watched. He and Rachael spoke and every so often she received some half-response or a grunt out of Cody. Nothing more, nothing less.

Every moment of this day had been difficult to process, yet he credited himself for being able to make it through the day and into lunch—earning back a chance at succeeding in his mission. Only, as always, he was not sure if what he felt was necessarily positive. Would he rather return to Dukhovia and say that things were much more difficult than they had anticipated, that they pegged Americans all wrong and he could not earn their trust? Or, would he return and convey that the American was fit to rule? The turn of his stomach told him that it did not matter to his fierce leader the personality of the girl—she was American. She was banished. And so, she would be dead before she even had the chance to sleep beneath a Dukhovian starlit sky.

Besides, he questioned now whether he had pegged the heir right at all—perhaps she was just as American as Arkady had warned. He did not know—and finding out required getting her to speak to him without screaming.

"Oh, come on!"

The enraged words startled him. He turned to his left and saw Stacy standing next to him in a black, one-piece suit. Her hands were poised aggressively on her hips, a look of perpetual hatred pasted onto her face where one might expect a smile or least of all neutrality. After all, had she not promised to give him a chance?

"What are *you* doing here?" She said the words like she could not wait to spit them out and be done with them.

Nicholas gestured to the pool, lazily, neutrally. "Swimming class."

"Huh." Stacy turned her eyes toward the pool. "I would have pegged you for someone more interested in archery. Much more violent."

Nicholas allowed the insult to slide off of him. This was an improvement from the silence of lunch. "I am already a perfect shot in archery."

Stacy rolled her eyes, laughing dismally. "Of course, you are. Not a skilled swimmer?"

Nicholas shrugged. "The Ocean Spirit is strong in me. Swimming allows some familiarity to home."

Yep. That got her. Stacy tore her eyes from the pool and back at Nicholas. She had not quite the same, sympathetic eyes on as before, they were... sadder. They were longing.

Rachael was right—she does love Dukhovia.

"The Ocean Spirit?"

Nicholas nodded once, firmly. "Correct."

"What does..."

A whistle blew and a tall teacher came out. He too, was in black, unflattering swimwear.

He could not run. He could not escape. He could only follow the rest of the students into the same line and stand at attention, waiting for further instruction.

"Okay! Today we are going to run a few relays. It appears as though we have a new student and according to his paperwork, he can outswim even Ms. Matthews..."

He rattled on more about putting this to the test, but Nicholas was only focused on the new set of daggers boring into his side—great. He had found another way to make her mad and all he did was write down how fast he could swim.

"I can't believe this," Stacy said, a whistle had blown and she was beginning to stretch her legs. "You're in all my classes, you break my best friend's arm, and now you're stealing my title in swim class? Ugh!"

"If it comforts you, they are discussing moving my class schedule around. Something along the lines of 'advanced classes'," he quoted the unfamiliar term.

Stacy paused, throwing her arms down. "Is there anything you can't do, Mr. Perfect?"

Nicholas shrugged, unable to come up with an answer she wanted. He was trained in everything because he had to be. It was not a choice.

"You know, no one believes you're here to learn about music and meet us," Stacy shot.

Nicholas started stretching now too—flexing his arms up as high as he could and then across his body. The t-shirt that clung to him was becoming an unnecessary barrier to his comfort. Not that that was not something he was used to—but not when he swam. Correction, not when he swam freely. Perhaps this was just another prison.

"Well, I did not come to pacify you," Nicholas returned with the same energy. He looked off, disinterested.

"According to you, you did," she fired back immediately.

She had him there. Although he did also mention that it was the war that brought him to America—did she simply forget that? No. If she was trying to figure out what it was he was doing here, she had stored away each detail he spoke and was pulling them out as needed—piece by piece.

He stopped and pushed on his temples. How? How did he prepare all his life for this moment and she could fill his plot holes better than he could? He should be the pro at his story.

Passion, perhaps.

Yes, perhaps so. Stacy was passionate about protecting her friends, passionate about defending herself...he was passionate about protecting his family in the same way, but he had less clarity on how to do that. Besides that, he had zero passion in succeeding in his mission. He closed his eyes for a moment, processing, thinking, pushing everything down...

He did not need to figure out a story, he needed to figure out what the hell he was doing. Each moment he had messed up so far because he was so intent on sticking to a story, sticking to a timeline. Perhaps his story—which was already shot to hell anyway—was not as important as each decision he made. He froze. He could not and would not figure out what his right move was overall, what he would do if Stacy was good or Stacy was bad for Dukhovia...but he could figure out each step piece by piece and that would lead him to his answer. That would allow the Spirits time to speak to him and direct him.

In this moment, he did not know what he needed to do for Dukhovia or for Stacy or for himself, but he knew fighting with her was not what he wanted regardless of any decision.

So, he poised himself to face her. He waited until she stopped scowling at no one as she leaned down to one side to touch her toes on an outstretched leg. Then, he met her eyes gently, slowly. "I am sorry for stealing your...title," he said the words slowly.

She glanced at him with confusion, back to the angry scowl, back to confusion, back to that look from this morning...the comfort. She turned back towards the direction of the pool, still in her same pose, and shrugged. "I don't really care about the stupid title anyway—it just gets me the only locker that actually locks and a free water bottle."

"Then I am forgiven?" He pressed.

Stacy stood up, looked him in the eye and cocked her head to the side. "I don't know. There sure is a lot of forgiveness going around for someone I just met."

Nicholas gulped—she could be intimidating. Of course, not in the way he was used to. Not at all in the way he was used to. But in terms of someday ruling...

"Then allow me to earn it," Nicholas probed her. "Race me."

Her face contorted into a type of confusion. "A race?"

"Yes." It was a common enough practice in Dukhovia. Perhaps not necessarily with swimming, but in other physical elements. He always won.

"I don't really use swimming for sport," Stacy responded, looking away again. "No?"

Stacy shook her head, then looked away with a cockiness. "You know…Ocean Spirit and all that."

"Well, often times, in Dukhovia, we use our swimming abilities as a way to prove ourselves." It was true. It was mostly for royalty, which, unbeknownst to her, they both were, so they would not technically be doing anything extreme. "Those whom can withstand the turbulent seas the strongest are said to hold more power, that the Ocean Spirit is strong in them."

She was hooked again, watching him up and down, eyeing him with a mixture of interest and suspicion the moment he mentioned Dukhovia.

"Hm," she finally answered. "I guess we'll just see as class goes on." Then she started to walk away.

Nicholas rolled his eyes at himself, shaking off frustration. "Oh, Stacy, come on."

She turned, flabbergasted.

"You promised you would give me a chance to earn your trust—so give it to me."

She eyed him once more and turned, walking slowly towards him. "I gave you my forgiveness and so you have it, but my trust? My trust is a whole other playing field and it's going to take a lot more than a little apology and some nice words to get my guard down. Got it?"

"Understood. But how am I ever to prove it to you if you are so stubbornly intent on shutting me out?"

It did not last long, but he finally saw it—a coy smile crept upon her lips just for a moment. Then, she glanced down, and walked until she was just inches from his face. "Fine. One race? But my terms."

"Of course."

"We do the cold-water race—it's in a non-heated pool, usually kept at around 70 degrees, but they sometimes freeze it for the figure skaters and I think it might still have some ice chunks in it today."

"Sounds perfect."

The smile was back, but this time it stayed. She did not know what she was betting—or perhaps she did, perhaps that was her angle. Either way, he was getting what he wanted.

"Care to make the stakes a bit more interesting?" Nicholas pressed, letting the intimidation rush off.

She raised an eyebrow in response.

"You win and we do things your way—I can earn your trust as fast or slow as you deem fit. But I win and you allow me to take you to dinner and prove what a gentleman I can be."

To his surprise, she laughed. "You're on...Coach Crawley! We're doing the cold-water race!"

"What? No, Ms. Matthews, it's far too cold. It's still defrosting from the figure skaters. You'll get sick."

She turned and gave him a sly look, betting illness to find her. Nicholas followed her, giving the teacher no mind as he yelled after them.

"On my count," she said.

The other students and the coach now circled them. The coach still tried to move them along, but seeing their lack of intent to listen, he withdrew his pocket watch and lifted a hand in the air.

"3, 2..." Stacy drifted off as the coach put his hand down—signaling their time to go.

Both of them darted into the water—it was exhilarating. Although a strange, chemical smell omitted from it, it was the most comfortable and at home Nicholas felt in days or longer. He almost forgot he was racing, wanting to soak in the chill of the water. But the stakes were too high. He needed to win.

He turned his body. He was fast in any position, but he opted to do a combination, moving through the water not only with speed, but to feel and take in each push and pull of the water, each crashing wave-like motion. He wished he could soak it in, soak it all in forever.

His head shot up and he was on the other side of the pool. He wiped water from his eyes and glanced towards where Stacy should be—where she was, gaping, wide-mouthed.

"It's a tie!" Coach shouted.

Stacy's gape turned into a smile. She lifted herself out of the pool and moved over to reach a hand out towards Nicholas. "Too bad, I really wanted to see this gentleman side of you."

Nicholas let out a heavy sigh. Great. Now what? "Best two out of three?"

Stacy smiled, but the coach was blowing the whistle and her attention was swayed. "Tying with me is almost a win. Usually, people in the cold-water swim turn back around and get out. Maybe next time."

Nicholas nodded solemnly, lifting himself the rest of the way out of the water. He started to trail behind her. "Stacy."

She turned.

"I truly am sorry about Rachael. I never meant to harm her and I would never. Rachael is good and kind and deserves to see that. I cannot excuse my actions, but I do vow to you that I will spend every day praying that the Spirits help me better control my temper. Onla's word."

CHAPTER TWENTY

She stared back at him. Her mind was processing a million things at once, he could tell. Yet she responded with a nod. Not a sneer, not ignoring him—but with a nod.

And suddenly he no longer felt so trapped.

CHAPTER 21

UNALIKE WORLDS

S tacy walked home alone in the sharp breeze of the winter's day, snowflakes batting viciously against the protection of her wide-open windbreaker. She broke into an almost skip, pure joy in the perfect weather.

Normally, Rachael and Cody would at least offer to walk with her, despite her always telling them to go ahead and take the car. Today, however, Rachael and Cody apparently left school early during Stacy's swimming class when Rachael realized she was in too much pain to focus on geometry and physics or whatever classes they were in.

The events of the day certainly did not go as planned, but they were tantalizing none the less. Her discussion with the strange Dukhovian in swim class only left her further confused. She recapped her thoughts for the hundredth time that day, trying to figure out how she should move forward. He was a menace and therefore he was too dangerous to be around. Yet, he had watched his parents die and perhaps that made up for his reasons to be a menace. But Stacy had watched her Uncle Richey suffer for years trying to fix someone who had been broken, to no fault of their own. But…Nicholas had apologized. He apologized in a heartfelt way. He looked remorseful. He was making an effort to change…those things…well, none of those things were things she had ever seen her aunt do.

Yasana was a mess and she always had been. Her parents were incessantly controlling, as the story goes, but beyond caring control. They wanted her get good marks on everything and learn everything there was to learn—but there were harsh repercussions if she failed. They had her life planned out for her and when she ran—she planned to leave everything behind her. There was more, she knew, but the kids have been told they did not need the details. Cody never meeting those grandparents told him enough.

She met Richard and he was hurting from his own situation and estrangement from his parents. But she had picked up certain things that her parents had taught her—some she knew were wrong and changed, others she did not think were wrong, others were a defense mechanism, others were cultural, others were her way of remaining in control…

She had not hurt Cody—Uncle Richey would never stay if so. But she was in and out, hot and cold, and doing things that were strange and oftentimes dangerous…

Nicholas did not remind her of Yasana. Not really. She could see the commonalities, sure. Nicholas had his own issues that perhaps caused his anger to be what it was, but it was something that happened to him—it was not *him.*

She replayed the morning in her head, but this time she tried to think about it from his point of view. He messed up at the concert with Rachael. Anxious to talk to her, he meant to defend her. But that anger, the anger he promised to work on, got the best of him. He did not think he was hurting Rachael, he thought he was defending her. He snapped out of it the moment he saw he hurt someone else—someone innocent, someone whom he noted was so very undeserving of the pain...

But that still begged the question of why—why was he so anxious to earn Rachael's trust back? To get on her good side? Why was he really in America? And was he a true, honorable Dukhovian?

He spoke eloquently. He was passionate towards the Spirits. So much had happened in the pool today that made Stacy want to get closer to Nicholas, to ask him more. For one, it was the simple confirmation that he knew about the Spirits. He was the perfect person to talk to. If he knew how The Ocean Spirit impacted him, would he know about dreams? About if Spirits visited in your dreams?

Then there was how little she knew. He had made her a promise, he swore on Onla—a Spirit, she could assume. But which? What did his promise truly mean? There was so little that she knew and for whatever reason that ate her alive. But not nearly as much as the realization that she only had two choices regarding her predicament...

One, ignore Nicholas completely. This would keep her friends and family safe, but would cut off any chance she had of learning anything about Dukhovia.

Two, talk to him. Learn more about Dukhovia. She could do this without risking the safety of others, right? She could set boundaries and rules. She could ask questions without revealing anything damning about herself.

It would be easy.

The wind blew and wrapped her hair around her face; snow rose up in a cyclone motion and spun around her. Passing cars slowed down to gawk at her, probably questioning her sanity, probably wondering if she needed a ride, but never offering to help. She did not feel she fit the stranger danger category they were probably fearing, but after meeting Nicholas, she was not so sure she could determine that look either now. Was the world good and bad? Was Nicholas? Or was it grey?

She laughed and beat her tangling hair away. People always mocked the way she obsessed over the cold weather. The time she spent outside and in water were a certain hypothermia sentence—but not for her. Never for the girl who never so much as received a case of the "sniffles" from being outdoors too long.

Stacy's walk dawned to a close as she opened the door to her house. It was Monday, which meant the majority of her family would be over for dinner. Every

Monday, her aunts, uncles, cousins, and grandparents ate dinner together to make up for the time lost over the years. She opened the door to Uncle Richard, Aunt Yasana, and Cody already there, along with her mother and Dan.

"Hello everyone," she called as she found her way back to them in the kitchen. "Nice face, cuz."

Cody's face was badly bruised just above his eye, a series of red cuts and other discolorations below, threatening to cross his nose line. It was worse than it was at lunchtime, and Stacy wondered if something happened between he and Nicholas at the end of the day. He gave her a dirty look in response to her comment, but did not speak.

"Seems like I'm going to have to teach both of you self-defense," her Uncle Richard said, embracing her in a one-arm hug, brushing back his tall, black hair. He was identical to Cody, but obviously older and slightly taller with a more muscular build. Every once in a while, he was caught with a thin beard crossing his cheeks, mocking Cody's inability to grow facial hair. Not that he would keep it if he had it, he was adamant about shaving the single hair that did approach...perhaps it was part of his front not to care.

"How's Rachael?" Stacy asked, beginning to rummage through the fridge.

"He fractured her wrist," Cody said through clenched teeth, balling his fists. He said it as if it was something he had been chanting all afternoon...and he probably was. He made eye contact with his father who gave him an understanding, but warning look. He did not want Cody seeking vengeance. "I'm going over there tonight to see her if you want to come."

"I'll let the lovebirds have their time, I'll catch up with her tomorrow," Stacy waved it off simply. She knew that if she saw Rachael, she would ask about Nicholas. She did not want to get into that in front of Cody, she would wait until she could get her alone at school. "You probably have your ways of helping her heal." She winked at him.

"I for one am simply proud that she jumped in," Grace interjected. She cut a browning part of a potato, eyed it suspiciously in comparison to the others, shrugged, and decided to toss it in the pan. "No child of mine gonna sit back and hold off on a little karate chop where it's well deserved." She brought the knife down hard on a potato to show her point, sending potatoes flying across the kitchen.

Richard laughed and joined in assisting his sister, as he always did. Cooking the meal together was part of the fun. Stacy grabbed a roll and stood with Cody near the entry way, waiting for their other cousins before beginning their portion of the meal.

"Well, I'll be the parent here and say I'm very disappointed," Dan chimed in—of course.

The others remained quiet, some smirked, others rolled their eyes.

"Neither one of you can be provoking fights. What are you going to do if you break a finger? Play guitar with your mind?"

"I did want to learn mind control, but now that you mention it, keeping me in a bubble my whole life might be easier," Stacy rested her hand on her chin and looked off, thoughtfully.

"Ugh," Dan rolled his eyes. "How are we going to explain your face to the public, Cody?"

"I don't know, maybe tell them I was in a fight?" He offered sarcastically. "Let 'em know even rock stars live like the other half." He smiled at his suggestion, laughing with Stacy.

"Knock, knock!" Terra Grayson's warm voice filled the house. Her and Tom's tall figures filled the kitchen, welcoming smiles on their faces, lighting up their brilliant, hazel-green eyes. She shook snowflakes out of her shoulder-length black hair and set down numerous gift bags, orange with pink Hawaiian flowers. "I brought gifts."

"Of course, you brought gifts," Grace commented, rolling her eyes, but a smile crossed her face. She glanced up at her father who matched her grin and winked. Her mother was the definition of the grandmother who spoiled her grandchildren—even if she was not a fan of the 'grandmother' term. Due to spending most of their time away from their children and missing out on parenthood, they did not prefer labels which made them feel old, thus their grandchildren mostly referred to them by their first names. Though, their youngest grandchildren, usually just called them grandma and grandpa.

"My grandchildren deserve to be spoiled," she beamed.

"Every week, extravagantly," Tom smiled, kissing his wife on her cheek.

Terra laughed. "Speaking of, Stacy, I heard you were in a fight today."

Stacy spit out a piece of her roll, causing Cody to make a disgusted face and move away from her. "How on Earth did you hear...ugh, Santifini."

Terra grinned. "I'm subbing for Mrs. Chartreuse tomorrow."

"Darn social studies," Stacy cursed. Darn her grandmother for working every job known to man. As if the hospital and airport were not enough, she had to substitute at the school every so often. How she managed to get all these degrees Stacy was unsure. Perhaps she too was unclear on her path.

"Ruslan called this morning. He told me you got into a fight with a new student."

"How did *I* get into a fight with a new student? Why am I secluded? What about Cody? What about Rachael?" Stacy asked in shock, frustration rising inside her at the reminder of detention. "What about Sir Nicholas in general for not being able to control his temper and getting us both detention?"

Suddenly Dan shut his computer and jumped up. "You got DETENTION?!"

"Why do you think I'm so angry about it?" She asked, planting herself into a chair. "*Two days* of missed practice?"

"*Two days*?" Dan repeated, heat rising in his face as his fists balled up. He grabbed his phone, more than likely ready to call Santifini. He spent more time than necessary with the principal, filling out college applications and asking him fifty questions a minute—they were best friends.

Terra walked over and pat his hand. "A break is good once in a while, darling." She turned to face Stacy and Cody. "I'll speak with Ruslan tomorrow about meeting with the boy and his parents. Where is he from?"

"He doesn't have parents," Stacy commented. She leaned her head into her hand, perched up on her elbow, and absentmindedly traced circles into the table. "And he's from Dukhovia."

Terra and Tom looked perplexed. "What do you mean he doesn't have parents?" Tom inquired with concern. Tom was well humored; it took a lot for him to be genuinely concerned over a situation.

"He said they were murdered in front of him when he was six," Stacy glanced off, unable to explain the complexity of emotion rising inside of her. Concern, compassion, frustration, anger— but not at Nicholas? At who? "He claimed he came to learn about our music, but didn't seem all that interested in it and didn't know who Rachael was. He ran into her at the airport then showed up at the concert."

She paused after seeing the worried expressions on Tom and Terra's faces, wanting to take it back—she had no reason to believe this type of thing happened often in Dukhovia, but she knew neither Terra or Tom had their parents growing up and she knew she had mentioned Dukhovia.

She quickly tore into a new roll in an attempt to distract the conversation.

"We got a security alert that someone was claiming to know us and get into the concert," Dan said, alarm in his voice.

Terra and Tom exchanged a look. "What's his last name?" Tom asked.

Stacy swallowed a bite. She wondered what the information would reveal. "Andrews," Stacy said, her mouth full.

"Andrews?" Dan repeated, writing it down in his notepad for further investigation.

"Not very Dukhovian, I know. Probably why they evicted him." Stacy's words and expression were careless as she was completely lost in analyzing her roll, biting it off in order of crunchiest to softest.

"Hello!" Fred, Grace's younger brother, entered the kitchen with his wife Jennifer and their two children, Jimmy and Jamie. Jennifer had red hair resulting in two children who were the only Grayson's without black hair. They still had the family green eyes, but their brown hair stood out amongst the black of the others.

In a similar fashion to their distinctions, Jamie also kept her hair relatively short. It was just above her shoulders, shorter than Terra's. She usually kept it back with a single barrette. Jimmy kept his hair down, rather than spiked, it split at his part and went down to about his ears. Both twins had rather frizzy, untamable hair, but it did not seem to make a difference to any of the others.

"Hi Freddy, you're just in time to see mom and dad drill Stacy and Cody about the fight they had at school today," Richard laughed as he mixed a bowl of unknown contents. Tom was the best cook of the family, but it was probably his own personal joke to stand by and let his culinary-challenged children lead the charade.

"We are not drilling, we're parenting," Terra offered, adoringly placing an arm around Cody and then fussing over his eye.

"Parent your own children," Grace offered. "By teaching them how to cook...is this supposed to be smoking?"

Her parents both laughed and wondered over to the stove to help, just as Sara and her four children walked in. They were the youngest of the cousins, as Sara was the youngest of the children. Katie and Fred were only four while Nicholas and Garrett were two and one, respectively.

The family seemed to let talk of the fight and the mysterious boy drop for the moment. No one else brought it up unless it was to make fun of the moment or explain the swollen bruises on Cody's eye to Aunt Sara and their cousins. Instead, they got to work making dinner and making memories in the process.

***

Nicholas put his hood up around his face, the wind whipping at his face gave him a slight chill, but he was in perfect, comfortable bliss otherwise. Well, physically, anyway. Mentally, he was battling thoughts of suicide as he replayed the events of the morning in his head, trying to keep from going insane as he tried to figure out why he did not feel more upset. He was angry and disgusted beyond belief, but he did not feel the sense of tension that normally existed 24/7 within his body. Instead, he felt...calm, comforted.

He could not grasp the reasoning. Everything had gone so wrong and the race—how could he mess up the race? He should have known it would be a close competition. He had only raced one other heir before and he was much weaker than he. Stacy was stronger—the strongest there had ever been. Of course she would be a good swimmer. Idiot!

But she did not hate him. Perhaps that is where this feeling arose from. She came off angry and bitter and towards the end she was at the very least indifferent. He replayed their conversation and what she had said about trust. Perhaps she did not verbally give him all too much to feel confident with, but she had held out her hand.

He dashed quickly behind a building— a car of the heir's friends was going by. They seemed to be laughing and joking around as if the events of the day did not just unwind. Perhaps the others had not yet heard. Surely, they had not. They would be angry or at least anxious—yes, definitely fearful. If they were anything like the strongest heir, that is.

The car passed slowly, the driver clearly being unseasoned to driving on slippery roads. Or perhaps he was just extra cautious. The second it passed, Nicholas went back to the sidewalk, following the only other footsteps that dared tread through the snow—the heir.

He was tracking her. Well, trying to anyway. It was a skill he was supposed to have perfected prior to leaving Dukhovia, but Arkady moved when Arkady wanted to move, thus here he was—in America with barely a forty percent success rate at the skill.

Fine, he could admit it.

He had never connected even once. Nothing besides the minor skills he used to get where he currently was, but his skills were supposed to be ten times that. Arkady was always able to find him immediately, to track him to his very location.

It was all about connecting to her Spirit. Willing his own to exist outside of his body and find its severed piece. It was Arkady's greatest accomplishment. He was the most skilled tracker anyone had ever heard of. There was nothing anyone could do and nowhere one could go that he would not be able to find their Spirit. Perhaps his inability to do so showed what a failure he was, or showed that the Spirits did not want him to succeed.

Nicholas pushed the thought away, breathing in deeply.

He waited until she was a good distance ahead, then started implementing every physical skill he had learned to find her—spirit aside. Her tracks, his sensitized sense of smell and hearing. It would be easier once he got to know her, he would know the types of landmarks that would likely be from her—a kicked over snowman, a puddle that had been danced in, a left behind hair clip…

"Well look at me now."

Yes, have a look at you.

He ignored the inner voice and refocused himself.

Arkady. He wondered what he was doing now. If he was not so seasoned at connecting with Nicholas, he would likely think him dead by now. He was not certain what all he was capable of when he connected, whether he could just sense him being alive or if there was more to it. But Nicholas did know for a fact that Arkady had bets placed on him failing his mission, on him disappearing or dying (whether by his own hand or that of another) before he even entered the country.

He scoffed at the thought. Nicholas would be lying, however, if he did not think often about the freedom death would bring. He would be out of this mess. He would be with his mother. But the Demitona name would die out in shame. He could not allow that to happen.

He closed his eyes, feeling his own Spirit. Arkady always said that their two Spirits, his and Stacy's that is, were one in the same, that they would naturally bond to one another and that should make it all the easier. Nicholas had other theories, as did those who studied the Spirits more closely. They believed that the two halves were, instead, at war with each other, begging for independence, causing the split.

Now that Nicholas had met Stacy, he believed the theory all the more. Not that she did not have a right to hate him, after what he did, but she seemed more intent to stay angry with him than even Rachael. Only an angry Spirit could be behind that. Unless, of course, the evil Spirit lived in him.

He imagined his Spirit reaching out for hers and hers latching on—nothing happened. Of course nothing happened.

He sighed angrily and looked up ahead. He had caught up to her now. She was looking both ways before dancing across the street, a smile stuck on her face. Was she really so naïve? Could she not sense the danger within him simply from their first interaction? Did her intuition, her Spirit, really tell her to be no more than standoffish? Not petrified? Not in some method of planning to protect herself and those around her? He could not even begin to consider what was on her mind making her happy after the day she had.

He tried to think of her as the heir—as the ruler of Dukhovia. She was stubborn, yet that could be good in negotiations. She was protective of her friends, loyal... She had passion for the country. Yet, she was conceited. She was immature and uneducated. And that fatal flaw.

Empathy.

Twice he had seen her go from protective as a cement wall to crumbling at his feet when all he did was show an ounce of remorse. Not that his remorse was not genuine—it was—but what did she know of his true intentions? What if the enemy told her a sob story? Arkady had one, sure, would she crumble at his feet as well?

Pathetic.

Pathetic, yet the thought led him to potentially identifying why it was he felt calmer than he should. The remorse she gave him, the pity, the...kindness. He yearned for it. Especially around his parent's deaths.

When they died, Arkady told him to 'toughen up'. He told him it was just the type of devastation he needed to learn how to become immune to tragedy... mission way past accomplished. Now Nicholas scarcely even tried to make friends let alone grow close enough to care over losing them. It was simply the way of the world to him. Beginning and end. Death and rebirth. Why bother?

Perhaps she held some form of sympathy, a concern over the wellbeing of others. Nicholas must have detected one positive thing about the woman which could potentially account for her heirship and deescalate the level of doom she was predisposed to. That had to be the explanation for this false sense of comfort that had overwhelmed him.

He emptied his mind of his thoughts, focusing on the scene before him. He had made it to her home. A large, white, two-story house very similar to the remainder in the neighborhood, with slight differences in build. The inside was filled with soft furnishings, some that seemed to exist simply for the sake of existing.

He sat just close enough that he could peer into the living room window and read lips, but just far enough that even the most skilled of her family could not detect him. He was positioned behind a tall pine, entirely out of their view. Not that they had much of a chance, anyway. He knew the instincts of humans: their body posture before they turned to look somewhere, the things that might make them want to look this way…Plus, he would close his mind to anything on the outside and focus only on these people. He would block out any senses that were no use to him now, strengthening the ones that were. This was a large and very different group than what he was used to, but he knew their type…Americans were very predictable.

They were talking about the fight…there would probably be defiance from the heir—a sort of frustration towards her family for being overprotective and overbearing…spoiled.

The heir rolled her eyes in frustration at the assumption that she was responsible for the fight, but her family merely laughed off the drama. That was rather strange for Americans. Did they not care or were they so advanced they realized how to effectively handle problems? He continued to watch and she seemed, for the most part… calm. Other than every so often, her mind would seem to drift away and her foot would tap on and on and on…

Time rolled on and Nicholas was in utter shock, not only at how the family seemed to respond to the news, but by the fact that as time progressed, the heir's entire family began to arrive.

A tan car slowly made its way up the road. Nicholas pushed his body flat against the house and scaled the back until the car was in the driveway. Then, he peeked around the front and watched as two older people entered the home, hands full of bags.

The man was very tall—probably seven feet. The woman he was with was also tall for a woman, perhaps nearing six feet.

It was a clear and nonnegotiable sign, he decided. The Spirits wanted him to succeed. He memorized the faces of all her family members, making a mental note of their cars and where they said they worked in case he needed to take hostages.

"How are things with your parents?" The heir whispered the phrase, but the secret was no match for his lip reading.

Cody shrugged and glanced over his shoulder at what Nicholas presumed to be his mother. She was a young, Japanese woman. She sat in what seemed to be annoyance at the table, looking as though she might burst with anger any moment.

Nicholas glanced from her to Cody trying to make a comparison, but he appeared to inherit all of his looks from his father. Nothing about him reflected the Japanese side of his genes.

CHAPTER TWENTY-ONE

"She yells at him a lot, he's not happy."

Nicholas laughed a disgruntled sound. So, the family was not all sunshine.

"Do you think he'll…?"

"No," Cody cut her off, he became rather absorbed with stirring whatever was in his bowl. "He'd never leave me without a mother. Not that I have much of one now."

Nicholas observed that statement for a little while. It was true. His mother never so much as got up to speak to him. Whereas his grandmother was concerned with his eye, his mother did not glance up at the sight. She seemed angry at the fact that the fight happened, but made no comments.

She ate in silence, refusing help from everyone, even though they persisted with kindness.

Cody's father seemed strange around her. He did not try to communicate with her and when she did speak to him, he was very careful about his word choice, hoping not to set her off, though this was impossible. Everything he did agitated her and caused him to become upset.

He did not stay around her long—no one did.

His heart plummeted into his stomach, the knots strengthening and intertwining when she mentioned his last name. Her grandparents had asked and puzzlement over his reason for being in the country crossed each of their minds—but then it was brushed under the table as quickly as it started.

The family was laughing and cooking together now, the heir had a bright smile as she shoved cloves into a ham with her cousins. Nicholas's stomach felt a twist and he began to feel almost dizzy as he watched the family. He could not determine what the feeling was, but the more he thought of them as a family working together rather than a unit, the worse the feeling grew.

Hunger. He thought of the word as he watched the heir and her cousin…Cody…put the large ham in the oven. Now that he thought about it, he had still not eaten since he arrived in America on Thursday. It would have bothered him sooner had it not been for him training to go without.

Time passed in tranquil slowness. Nicholas was sitting in the snow, leaning against the house, listening to the laughter, the compassion. He moved his fingers absent-mindedly after a while, watching keenly as his thumb rose then fell, his index finger rose, then fell, and so on…

He rested his head against the softness of the pine and closed his eyes, drifting into a different time…

"Nicholas, Nicholas, alloy-a!" It is time.

A boy no older than five or six ran to the front door of his house in excitement. His mother was pulling his favorite dinner out of the oven: honey glazed turkey, roasted potatoes, and sautéed carrots. It was his going away meal.

He threw his arms around her waist, a smile taking over his face. She wrapped her free arms around his back and laughed with joy.

"Oh, my little Nicholas. You will make this family so proud."

The glow in his eyes made it a promise. "Is it done?" He pressed, he stood on his tip-toes, nose high in the sky to attempt to get any sort of sensation from the meal.

His mother laughed and began to answer, but the front door swung open and slammed shut, causing the tiny cottage to rattle.

"Alloy-a," his father grunted, heading for Nicholas.

The boy hid behind his mother, fearfully, she put up a hand on him to defend him. "Nicholas, he has not even eaten yet."

"He will survive," he grumbled, grabbing the little boy by the arm. "Come, boy! We will not keep the Czar waiting."

Nicholas was afraid, but he did not protest out loud. He dragged his feet as his father dragged him by the arm toward the front door.

"Wait! Wait!" His mother shouted. "I did not even get to tell my baby good bye!"

"Enough, woman!" His father put up his hand, smacking his mother's face as she fell to the ground.

"WAIT!" Her screams cried. "NO!"

Nicholas glanced back, his mother lay on the floor, crying, watching her only son go, tears and blood streaming down her face.

It was the last time he saw his mother.

"Dinner's done!"

The call smacked him back into reality. He peeked up in the window again.

"Is it done?" Cody asked for clarification.

The heir poked and prodded the ham gingerly, sticking it with a knife and letting the juices run. "It's not *done*," she began. "But it's not *not done* enough that it will kill you." She smiled and lifted the ham, ready to deliver it to the table.

Nicholas blinked hard. If he just left this girl alone long enough, she would end up killing herself and save the Czar and himself the trouble.

Gathered around the table, they came off as a normal and happy family. The protective bonds they seemed to put around each other were stronger than anything, threatening to defeat the world if anyone tried to break them.

But they were doomed.

Or else all of Dukhovia would be.

CHAPTER 22

FORGIVENESS

Stacy arose bright and early the next day. Well, not too bright and not too early. Definitely later than she had awoken for the concert, significantly later than the previous day, but at somewhat a responsible time. She was brighter than usual, though.

She was not certain what drove her out of bed and over to her closet, rifling for something somewhat more presentable than normal. She threw on black, silky sweat pants with a white sweatshirt and headed into her bathroom. She ran the comb through her hair meticulously, yanking at knots that could not have possibly appeared overnight. She always thought she was such a sound sleeper.

She already had her phone ringing on speaker phone, ready to talk to Rachael in a Cody-less, private moment. It only rang once before she was on the other end.

"Wellll?"

"Well what?" Stacy asked, taken aback. As if she did not know. As if she did not call specifically to dish exactly what Rachael wanted.

"He wasn't in archery sixth period so he had to be in swimming," her voice sang, expectantly.

"How do you know he wasn't in archery? Do you have spies on him?"

"I very well should," Rachael said in confidence, Stacy guessed she was examining her arm. "But no, I asked Principal Santifini. It seemed an innocent enough question. Is the guy who beat me up allowed to train to become more violent—yes or no? It was a no."

Stacy rolled her eyes. "You have that whole school wrapped around your finger."

"Something like that," Rachael shrugged it off. "Soooo."

So, Stacy told her the whole story…the pool, her feelings. All of the things that she could and could not explain. "So, basically, I don't know what I'm supposed to do. I don't know if I tread lightly, I don't know if I forgive and forget. I don't know, I don't know, I don't know!"

Rachael was thoughtful for a moment. "I think you should just talk to him— take things slow, but normal…. I know, I know," Rachael added the words after an unheard of pause on Stacy's end. "…Yes, it's still me telling you to take it slow. But you're right. We don't know what truly brought him here, if he lied, *why* he lied if so, or just how often this snapping happens. But we know it was an accident and we know he feels remorse. So, just talk to him like a friend and see what happens. If he's a monster, no harm no foul, if he can help you…"

"But what about his parents?" Stacy interjected, her stomach in knots at the very thought.

"Let him, lead, Stacy," she said calmly. "The same thing I think you should do with Tom and Terra. If they show signs of exploding, stop. But if they're okay…they're okay." Her voice got quiet. "I think he would appreciate someone to talk to. He seemed open during lunch. I think having a listening ear would help and usually conversations are two-sided."

Stacy agreed reluctantly. She could not place why she was so ready to be understanding, she was ready to burn him at the stake yesterday. It was like she was seeking a reason to deem him acceptable. Maybe she was.

That basically ended the topic of Sir Nicholas. They moved onto Rachael's arm and if it would clash with her outfits. Fortunately, Rachael seemed to be in a rather uplifting mood and commented on how her cast could become an accessory to almost any outfit—Stacy had guessed Cody had a long talk with her before she felt this way.

She told Stacy rather positively that the doctor told her she would be healed in a matter of weeks and that the least restrictive casting method should not affect her drumming.

Stacy finished getting ready and slid down the railing into the kitchen, feeling a bit more excited to enter the school doors.

"Morning princess," her mother called, kissing her on the cheek.

"Hi mom," Stacy responded, quickly pouring cereal into a bowl and sitting next to her father and brother at the table. She shoved the food into her mouth so fast her father had to blink to believe what he was seeing.

"We're excited for school this morning," he commented questionably, looking at his wife who shot back a confused look.

"Born excited," she mouthed quickly, milk spilling from her mouth.

"You do realize that it starts the same time, no matter how quick you get there," Dan chuckled.

Stacy took that into consideration and slowed down. Normal. Her and Rachael talked about being normal. Sir Nicholas could very well still be a huge red flag. Regardless, he probably did not plan to show up to school an hour early. She did not want to get there before him and be surrounded by…books. Maybe be forced by a teacher to…study. The thought repulsed her.

"Tell that to yourself, brother," she advised, patting him on the back.

Dan chose to ignore her comment. "So, I ordered you new guitar picks and Rachael's been complaining about her uniform not doing anything for her figure so I'm ordering them in different material…do you want anything else?"

"Just the love and support of my big brother up on stage in two weeks," she grinned and lifted her bowl to her face to drink the milk.

"You'll have that," he smiled, now envisioning the small show they were set to play. "Stan wants us to send some of our newest songs and then go down to meet with him in the next couple months."

"The next couple months?" Stacy wiped milk from her mouth, surprise inflicted on her face. "I thought he wanted to sign us now?"

"He does," Dan answered, pulling up file after file on his computer. He had so much pulled up Stacy wasn't sure how he was focusing on anything. "But I explained to him the priority of school and he was very understanding. Willing to wait until we're able."

"School?" Stacy jumped up, angry. "Why do we have to wait for school? Ugh."

"Stacy, you know I can't miss anything. I told him we'll come to California on an extended weekend. We have one in February…"

"And what about WINTER BREAK!" She shouted it as if it was the simplest solution and he was an idiot for overlooking it.

"I have that convention in New Jersey over Winter Break," Dan replied. He shut his lap top and shoved it into his bag.

Grace and Kevin silently rose and began washing the dishes.

Stacy rolled her eyes, but then she began to weigh the advantages of having no Dan during winter break. No Dan meant free time—actual free time. And if she wanted to both have that free time and prepare enough for Stan, she should probably use all of their after-school practice time…which meant getting out of detention.

"We're doing a recording this weekend to send to him," Dan continued, rising from his seat.

"Can we send him the one with my guitar solo?" She asked innocently, smiling from above her clutched books.

"Yes," he sighed with a grin. "As long as you don't take over when we get to the bridge."

"Who, me? Why, I'd never." She hopped up to kiss his cheek. "Ready, mama?" Stacy asked in a cheerful tone, checking her watch to verify it was, in fact, an appropriate time to leave for school.

The three kissed Kevin, climbed in Grace's truck, and rode to school with *The Rocker's* music blaring out of the speakers, causing supportive car honks to fill the streets the whole two-mile drive.

Stacy hopped out of the truck, taking a bow for the imaginary audience she perceived in her mind. They went wild, demanding she replay her guitar solo again and again. She was on her knees in a heartbeat, strumming at the same figurative red, electric guitar that Tom bought and taught her to play ten years ago.

"Let's go, Rockstar," Grace smiled, leading her children up to the school.

"No guitar solo if you pull that," Dan grinned. "No one likes a show off."

"I'm not here to be liked," Stacy said with a flip of her hair. "I'm here to be adored."

"Regardless," he began, holding the broken door to the school open for her while she pushed open the other. It was a trick a majority of the student body knew about: in order to not get the first door slammed in to you, the second had to be opened first. "Where are you going?"

Stacy veered right as Dan went left towards his senior classes. "Office to try and get out of detention," she smiled, walking backward. "I'll petition for a lunch detention, suspension, community service..." She pivoted around. "I'll do anything!" She shouted in mock desperation.

Dan shook his head, a smile spreading up his face until he disappeared up the stairs where he met up with his two best friends: Matt and Rob.

The morning was in perfect swing, but the closer she got to the office and her thoughts allowed themselves to infiltrate her mind, the closer she began to analyze everything over and over again. She did it off and on at dinner, but having her family to distract her helped, then her call with Rachael—another reason she put talk of Nicholas on the back burner. But it turned out, being alone with her thoughts was becoming a rather dangerous place to be.

She went back and forth analyzing his behavior, his motives, the fact that he was a ticking time bomb and a danger to both her and her friends. Not even a perceived danger, an actual danger whom had already struck once and they would be stupid to give him the chance to strike again.

Yet he knew so much. Yet, the afterthought of her and Rachael's conversation plagued her mind...

Did he even want to talk about Dukhovia? His parents. The more Stacy thought about it, the more she was able to think about things from his side and not just her selfish intent. Maybe that was the reason he came to America—to just get away from Dukhovia. She doubted that if he watched his family murdered in front of him that he had very fond memories.

Stacy pushed the door to the office open with a fast heave, nearly smacking Nicholas in the back of the head.

"Oh!" She exclaimed in a cheerful voice, not at all apologetic. "That was a close one. Almost got even with you, there." She walked up next to him and set her books on the office counter.

He gave her a sideways glance. "I shall forgive you this once, but my eye will be on you for certain."

"An honor and entirely understandable," she noted, pinching the ends of an invisible gown and curtsying towards him, not at all disheveled by his strangely, personable tone. "What brings you to mingle with the commoners in the office? Another fight?"

He held a piece of paper up for her to observe. "Schedule alterations, remember?"

"Ah, of course," she recalled. She grabbed the paper and scanned it in .2 seconds, shoving it back towards him almost the instant it was in her hand. "But if you're not in my classes…"

"Then I will be in Rachael's classes and there seems to lie the dilemma." Nicholas shook his head and seemed to be restraining himself as if he thought the idea utterly ridiculous. He would not be wrong.

"Well, if Santifini is anything, it's a brilliant, wise, diligent man of character and if he can't figure out this conundrum, no one can."

He only had time to respond with an eyebrow raise before the bubbling secretary bounced forward with what she presumed to be yet another schedule. "Here you are, Mr. Andrews. If you need any help, I would be more than happy to help you as I'm sure Ms. Matthews would. She is one of our best students." She winked at Stacy.

Stacy doubled back in confusion while Nicholas gave her an expectant side glance.

"I'm what now?" She looked into Nicholas's eyes and decided not to get into how her grades resembled more of the third and fourth letters of the alphabet than they should. "Actually, Ms. Frieda, I highly suspect that Santifini is trying to keep us away from each other. Hence the schedule change. That and rumor has it that he's a super genius that belongs in all advanced classes."

"Oh," she seemed embarrassed. She drew back his schedule and then realized she had no reason for doing so other than confusion and handed it back to him. "I was unaware. Ms. Matthews, what can I help you with?"

Stacy laughed at how quickly she became a menace. "I need to convince my old friend Santifini to let me out of detention."

Ms. Frieda laughed. "I'm sure many have tried that before to no avail, Ms. Matthews."

"Right, but I'll do anything," Stacy had her hands together in a pleading form. "Scrub the toilets, free manual labor, I'll wash your car, Ms. Frito Lay."

The secretary rolled her eyes at the nickname, but could not suppress a laugh. She had probably been told not to allow the children to make fun of her, but was too well humored by it herself to give it much concern.

"I will serve extra time if it would help," Nicholas interjected. His voice held the same soft, polite, gentleness that it did when he was apologizing on Rachael's behalf after their race the day prior. There was almost a hint of pleading.

Ms. Frieda shook her head. "You both committed the crime, you must both do the time," she giggled at her lame, but oddly satisfying joke.

"Oh, come on," Stacy let on. She smacked her hands on the office counter and rolled her eyes with as much exaggeration as possible, staring up into the sky for assistance. "I can't miss practice. We just got signed and we have to record this weekend…"

"I'll tell you what," Ms. Frieda began. "I know *Mr.* Santifini is a fan of your music. I will speak with him and let you know what I can do."

"Thank you, Lord," Stacy looked up into the sky dramatically again.

"Now, get to class you two," Ms. Frieda instructed with another not-so-threatening smile.

Nicholas lowered his head in a bow to her as he exited. Stacy raised her hand and dropped it back to her side quickly as a sign of goodbye, already halfway out the door.

"Are you that desperate to not spend detention with me?" Nicholas asked once they were outside. He smiled playfully, flashing his perfectly crystal blue eyes and dazzling pearls at her tauntingly.

Stacy stared into them for a moment, then grinned back. "Hardly, Mr. Self-centered," Stacy scoffed. "I just want to be able to get as much playing time in as possible. There's a lot riding on this for the band."

"For the band?" Nicholas was staring at her deliberately, expectantly, as if he was trying to get her to confess a crime or hypnotize her into saying something.

"Right," Stacy nodded once, firmly. She was not looking at him anymore. She had started walking and was keeping her vision anywhere other than his face.

Nicholas stopped walking and lightly reached over to touch Stacy's right forearm. "And what about for you?" His voice was that calm, sweet tone again. It almost started a warmth inside of her, but she would not admit that.

She looked into his eyes and laughed shyly. *Of course I want the same things,* she wanted to tell him. But, the look on those concerning, questioning eyes pulled her towards something else—answers. That was what she wanted him for. Why not open up about this miniscule aspect of her life? Of her desires? What harm was there in saying *something*? Not as a Dukhovian, but as Rachael suggested, as a friend. Small steps.

"You tap your foot a lot—when you are anxious," he said, seemingly answering her unspoken thoughts. "And you seemed to at the concert and when your friends spoke of it at lunch…It is simply an observation, I did not mean any judgment."

She bit her lip, considering her words. "The band means a lot to me too. It's just…I've had a lot of thoughts lately about the future and I'm not really sure what I want."

"Is it to be in your band?" He pressed, meaningfully.

Stacy shrugged, her face turning into a grimace. Her cheeks filled with warmth. "Yes," she answered after a brief pause. "Right now, anyway. But, I'm not so sure there's a place for the band in my future and I don't know how to move away from it or when if that's the case."

"Hence the anxiousness," Nicholas noted as he observed her tapping her foot and biting her lip until it nearly bled.

Stacy looked from him down and stopped, causing the slightest chuckle. "Hence the anxiousness," she whispered. She took the realization as a sign to start walking—she was supposed to be going to class, after all.

Nicholas trailed after her. "What do you suppose might be in your future?"

Ring! Ring! Ring!

The bell for first period startled Stacy out of her trance. She glanced from the books she had clutched to her chest to Nicholas and back again. "See you later?" Stacy said, lifting her books. She never thought she would be the one to hurry off to class before being late—late was her middle name. She shook her head not sure what she was even doing. Would she see him again? She did not even ask to see his schedule.

She ran around the corner towards science class, her heart pounding the entire time. The conversation had barely gotten her anywhere, yet the feeling that invaded every part of her told her it held promise. Her body felt calm, her mind clear, her soul comforted. Nicholas had interest in her debacle—to some degree anyway. He did not have to respond, right? And so maybe she could talk to him without fearing traumatization.

She managed an awkward smile as she took her seat next to Rachael and Cody in first period science, attempting to bury the thoughts before Rachael read them from her soul and sent Cody into cardiac arrest. The two were in a cluster of three desks, the last one empty, knowingly reserved for her.

Cody and Rachael had their heads inclined towards each other, one of his arms was around the back of her seat, the other resting lightly on her pink, casted wrist. His fingers were delicately stroking the area back and forth.

"Hey," she breathed, taking her seat.

"Hey," the two replied in unison. Rachael's voice was as bright as her smile, Cody's was welcoming, but he quickly drew back his hands. Rachael seemed to study Stacy's face for a moment, boring an unspoken promise to gossip later.

It was moments like those when her and Rachael could read each other like the book Stacy would never in her life open. She knew she had everything she would ever need in Rachael and the feeling brought her comfort even when her insides were screaming at her from all directions.

"You guys ready to study some cells?" Stacy groaned, flipping open her textbook.

Cody raised his eyebrow and leaned back in his chair, arms folded behind his head. "I only come to school ready to do two things: play football and sleep."

"Ditto." Dylan had appeared, pushing on Cody's back so that he lost balance in his chair and nearly fell had it not been for his excellent reflexes. The two laughed and knocked each other's fists up and down before touching once in the middle.

CHAPTER TWENTY-TWO

"Welcome! To the world of life and death. Of sickness and health…"

"Is this marriage class or biology?" Cody joked.

"If it is the former, I'd start taking lots of notes," Stacy winked at him.

Rachael laughed softly but Cody reached over and shoved his cousin when Rachael was not paying attention.

"Today, we are diving into the magnificent world of dissection. We are going to be studying a *human* cell," the animated science teacher rubbed his hands together, hardly able to contain his bubbling excitement as he began passing out microscopes and worksheets. "Courtesy of *Heart of America* Hospital."

"Thanks grandma and grandpa," Stacy sighed, zero trace of thankfulness in her tone. She pulled the microscope in front of her, slowly. Rachael leapt to pull the worksheet in front of her. She pushed it between her and Cody and gave him an eager smile, trying to prompt interest out of him.

He gave a meager smile.

"Work through the steps on your worksheet to see what types of cells you have. Ready?" The scientist held up his black and white checkered flag with a smile of anticipation on his face. "Go!" He brought the flag down in one quick swoosh.

Some of the students started chattering quickly, moving things about fast and knocking them over in the process—it was not a race. There was no prize other than Mr. Galley's excitement over the person who got done first. Aside from his next lecture over disappointment that Stacy and Cody—the daughter and nephew of a great scientist—did not get finished first.

Their nearly failing grades in the class should be enough to tell him that they were never going to be first done…and that they never would get done at all without Rachael. They did not belong in advanced science by a long shot…but someone did.

Nicholas. Stacy imagined the true intentions of his class rearrangement were to get him out of either hers or Rachael's classes, but Nicholas had mentioned advanced level classes. This would put him in Rachael's classes, another problem, but he was not in advanced science today. So where was he? And where was he going next? There was only one advanced class per day per subject and Rachael was in all of them.

She supposed there was a line between remedial and advanced, but she was in most of those classes. So, where the heck was he going? And why the heck did she care so much?

"Okay, we have to figure out if we have mostly red blood cells or white blood cells…Stace?" Rachael grabbed the pen and looked over at her friend, hopeful.

Stacy looked down. "We have purple blood cells," she noted, peering into the glass.

"Those are white blood cells, they leave a purple stain," Rachael said with a smile. She started writing in perfectly scripted handwriting.

"Someone's been paying attention to Mr. Dread's exhilarating lectures," Cody joked.

Rachael shrugged. "I listen and do my homework, Mr. Grayson, it would work wonders for you if you ever gave it a shot." She smiled at him flirtatiously.

Cody made a face as if she asked him to eat a dead rodent. "Where exactly does football come into play in all that?" He asked, reassuming his dangerous position with his chair.

"Mr. Grayson, unless you want your entire body to match that eye of yours, I suggest you lower your chair," Mr. Galley instructed from across the room. He was still beaming with pleasure.

Cody sat down on all fours just until Mr. Galley looked away, then he was back in his previous form. Mr. Galley glanced back over and shook his head.

"You know what else we need to figure out?" Stacy pressed. She had her eye glued to the microscope, trying to find the fascination that her mother and grandparents found in science. She was drawing a blank. "What we're singing for Stan this weekend."

"Oh, I'm sure our manager has more than dictated that based on what we 'know best'," Cody replied, forming air quotes around the last two words of his statement.

"What about one by Jade and one by Stacy? Jade and Miranda just started taking lead, we need to exploit them more and show our fans their sound. But having an old timer won't make them feel completely lost," Rachael smiled at this well thought out procedure. It was a good idea.

"Love it...and I can't say I'm disappointed at being called an old timer in the slightest. Cody, what's the next question?"

"Cody?" Rachael pushed the paper closer to him.

Cody sighed but read the next question. "If you have a white blood cell, what kind?"

"The overmultiplying kind," Stacy commented examining the cells with newfound interest. She and Rachael both looked back and forth from their sample to the sheet with pictures of basophils, neutrophils, eosinophils, monocytes, and lymphocytes.

"Definitely monocytes and neutrophils," Rachael wrote cheerfully. "But I'm not sure why there are so many compared to the picture he gave us?"

"I can't find anything in my book," Stacy said, skimming through the pages quickly.

"Pass me the microscope," Rachael requested of Stacy, reaching out her hand. "They seem to be rapidly growing compared to the video we watched. And they're oddly shaped."

"We're onto something now," Cody said sarcastically, rolling his eyes. "Someone call in Mr. Corners, we need a detective on this case."

Rachael shoved Cody with her elbow, smiling playfully.

"The nucleus should be smaller, I thought," Rachael looked up at Stacy and Cody for input, but neither faltered.

"The mystery continues," Cody laughed, receiving a gentle smack on the head from Rachael's book. "Ah," he rubbed the back of his head. "Maybe someone should go ask?"

Cody and Stacy both eyed Rachael.

"He actually likes you," Cody offered, his voice holding some type of charm.

"He likes all of us equally...but I'll go ask," Rachael volunteered, jumping up and sashaying over to the teacher's desk in the most graceful of manners. Her skirt did not even wrinkle as she stood.

The teacher looked thrilled as she placed the paper in front of him and began asking questions. Mr. Galley was already in full explanation mode.

"Such a goody-goody," Stacy smiled, looking after her friend.

"She's amazing," Cody said, not taking his eyes off Rachael for a moment before he turned back to face Stacy. He raised an eyebrow suspiciously. "I noticed your boyfriend isn't in class today."

"Fiancé," Stacy corrected, looking around as if she had just noticed. "Maybe you finally got through to Santifini. This is the beginning of a beautiful friendship for you two."

"Ha-ha," Cody rolled his eyes. "Listen, Stace, I get feeling bad for the guy, I think anyone in our family would, but that still doesn't stop the fact that he's dangerous."

Stacy looked back at him, choosing her words slowly. "Do you think I don't know that, cuz? I'm just as hesitant as you, it's just...I don't know. It feels like I'm supposed to talk to him and he's supposed to help me sort out this Dukhovia stuff. I know that sounds insane and I know that evidence stands to emotion and all that, but I don't feel like he's dangerous."

Stacy could tell Cody was reeling in his seat, but he tried to swallow his opposition. "Maybe he is—or was. But you can't risk yourself and look what already happened to Rachael—twice."

"I won't put myself at risk—I'll play this smart. Feel him out, but keep my distance. I just want to give him a chance, knowing everything about him," Stacy promised.

"Again, we gave him a chance, and he blew it—twice."

Stacy sighed in defeat, keeping her voice at a whisper as Rachael looked up and her and the teacher began heading their way. "I know, but I think knowing more about him helps us—and protects us."

"You appear to have cells from a leukemia patient, my friends!" Mr. Galley was back over with Rachael smiling behind him. He grabbed their microscope and looked at it for confirmation. "These cells do not behave like normal cells. Instead, white blood cells are more common and will be disformed. Look for varying sizes and shapes, a larger nucleus, and many divisions in wild arrays.

"Students! Everyone take a look at these cells and compare them to your own! How exciting! Thank your grandparents, will you?" Mr. Galley did not wait for a reply, he considered the request done and trailed away, collecting their paper and bringing their cells around for the others to compare. The last table was still looking when the bell rang.

"That's gym class, I'll see you guys at lunch." Cody was out the door in a heartbeat, running down the hall with Dylan, football in hand.

Rachael and Stacy started walking down the hall to art together. Rachael grabbed a magnificent painting of a landscape from her locker while Stacy grabbed something that most people assumed was abstract art.

"Ms. Matthews."

Stacy turned around, hitting several students with her painting in the process. "Santifini. I mean, Mr. Santifini, sir."

The tall, sophisticated principal was in his normal wear of a suit too fancy for a royal ball let alone a day in the life of high school. He stood with his hands poised behind his back, assertively and purposefully. He ignored Stacy's stumbling and averted his eyes towards Rachael. "Ms. Leighton, how are you?"

Rachael smiled and shook the principal's hand. "I'm well. And you?"

"Wonderful. I hear there are great things happening with your band?" He addressed both girls now, eyes narrowed.

"Yes, we're recording a song this weekend to send to our new record label," Stacy commented, looking to Rachael for her supportive head nod. "Dan says it's very important we get lots of practice…" She made sure to throw her brother's wishes in there.

"Yes, I spoke with him last night, he says it is very important that you practice your guitar solo."

Stacy snarled a little, she was not sure if she should be angry or grateful for the excuse. "It's true. I'm absolutely awful." She looked down, ashamed.

Rachael nudged her. "Oh, she's being modest, she's wonderful!"

Stacy gave her a look of disagreement, but Rachael shrugged it off.

"Well, then I suppose you do not have any time for detention…"

The girls were on their toes in anticipation.

"We honor and respect whatever Stacy needs to do to make up what happened," Rachael began. "Following rules is what makes you such a great leader. But if there's any way you could help us out, we would definitely be grateful." Rachael beat her eyelashes, pleadingly.

"Agreed, I was so horrible for doing whatever it is I did and also a land can't function without its leaders or something—those are words I won't soon forget."

Mr. Santifini smiled and nodded his head, eyeing Stacy with suspicion, his face as unreadable as always. "I suppose we could move detention, pending moves with your band. I would not want to hinder progress. Would that buy you some time?"

"Oh yes! Yes, yes, yes! That would be perfect!" Rachael celebrated. She hugged the principal and then Stacy.

"Works for me," Stacy smiled, shaking the principal's hand, awkwardly.

"Good. Good luck with your record, girls. I cannot wait to hear it." Then he nodded to Stacy, staring piercingly into her soul. "I will see you in due time." He turned and began to walk off, but turned on his heel. "Keep your cousin out of trouble, Ms. Matthews," he added.

"Will do!" She shouted back.

The girls turned to each other and squealed in delight.

"You totally had that thought through," Stacy accused, giving her friend an approving look.

"Of course," Rachael said with a fluff of her hair. "I'm always prepared to bust my friends out of crimes."

"One of your many talents and the reason we keep you around," Stacy told her, patting her on the back.

Rachael laughed and snatched Stacy's arm into a loop with hers. Then, in typical Rachael and Stacy fashion, they practiced singing on the way to their next class, shoving through a sea of applause and eyerolls.

"*Sweet as victory*," Rachael sang.

"*Honey we're home free*," Stacy replied.

"*Can we take this beckoned call*," both girls sang at the top of their lungs, smiling with enthusiasm. "*Become like the legends after a-a-all*."

CHAPTER 23

EXPOSED

Rachael and Stacy glided through their next couple classes together in a fit of happiness. They were told to hush more than once…a period…and when Jade and Miranda happened to be in a class with them, the joy only increased. The focus was back on the record and getting the band's new sound out there—they were unstoppable.

The bell signaling lunch finally rang, reuniting all of the friends at their long lunch table, shoved along the back wall of the cafeteria. Stacy and Rachael bounced down in a fit of happiness, bringing a smile to an unhappy Cody who was holding his head over a history test decorated with a bright red 'D' at the top of it.

"D's get degrees," Stacy beckoned, pointing to the top. "At least, I'm like ninety-nine percent sure that's passing, right? Not passing well, but passing?"

"He needs to maintain a C grade point average to stay on the team," Rachael said in a hushed voice, as she tried to comfort Cody.

"Ugh!" Cody threw his head down, frustrated with himself. "There's just so much to learn in every class and the band and the team…I can't do it all."

"It's a plateful," Rachael said softly, squeezing his shoulders. The pun was not missed by Stacy, who laughed quietly. "Why don't you come over tonight after practice? I'll help you study."

Cody lifted his face, a small smile crossing his lips. "Okay."

"Welp, crisis averted, time for me to eat," Stacy jumped away from the table over to the lunch line. Luckily for her, most people got in the salad line or packed, choosing to stay away from the artery clogging grease pits that were school lunches.

The school, of course, had to go around state regulations and provide a protein, grain, fruit, dairy, and vegetable at every meal, but it was a processed protein, canned fruit surrounded in high fructose corn syrup, canned vegetables swimming in sodium, and white bread with a choice of enriched wheat bread: white bread that was brown.

Of course, milk was always provided, but the school ordered more chocolate than white and always ran out—it was cheaper. Regardless of the fact, the state was more worried about obesity than proper vitamin efficiency, so it was either the more processed one percent milk or nothing at all.

Stacy loaded her tray up anyway, unable to determine what the protein was for the day (some type of ground meat in gravy?) or the side (corn bread mashed potatoes? Mashed potatoes with cheese? Just regular mashed potatoes? Why were they brown?). She grabbed two mixed fruit cups and her chocolate milk before glancing around the cafeteria for teachers and pushing half her peas into the trash.

The further she walked from her friends, the more her brain fog seemed to clear, reminding her of what had preoccupied her thoughts all day when they failed to be distracted by the happiness of the band. No matter the joy that singing brought her and the cheers that encouraged her onward, she still found herself glancing around each classroom in an attempt to find where the new and mysterious boy could possibly be.

But, as the lunch bell rang and more and more people began to quickly fill the cafeteria, her questioning stopped. She found him quickly—sitting alone with a tray of unknown substances before him. Smiling to herself, she immediately bounded towards him, setting her own tray of unknowns beside his.

"So, you didn't get kicked out after all?" Stacy asked him, folding her arms in front of her.

He immediately looked up at her, a calm look on his face. A look that told her he was a friend, a look she felt sucked into—as if she could trust him by the look alone. "Not quite," he started, slipping his schedule into her hand. "Although the way I hear it, the principal is far too excited about a certain band recording new songs to enforce any type of changes."

Stacy smiled, folding the schedule into her hand and taking the bait. "That might be true, sad as it is, having to leave you to suffer this evening alone in bitter silence. But with all due respect, the situation was entirely your fault and you deserve to suffer alone."

"As I live alone, I assure you I will suffer in the same silence as every other night," Nicholas said, matching her sarcastic tone with a coy smile.

Stacy paused and looked up at him. "You mean he moved your detention too?" She asked, puzzled. She looked down at the table, her mind racing. "Why on earth would he do that?"

Nicholas tried to find her eyes and read her expression, but she was too difficult to decipher. In any matter, he was usually wrong when he guessed her reactions anyway. He would not have pegged her first insulting statement, but she delivered it with full force, ready for whatever negative repercussions it brought her.

"Maybe he wants me to get in trouble, he wants us to fight. Maybe he wants me to get in trouble to provoke Cody so he can finally expel him…"

He was right. Stacy surprised him yet again. Not only was she actually trying to formulate reasons for the detention sentencing, she was actually coming up with logical explanations.

"That would explain me, but why you?" She continued to babble on, not really speaking to him, but to her mystery lunch. "Why would he want to get a new student in trouble?" She ran through their first interaction in her mind and remembered Nicholas's words when Santifini asked about his parents.

"Perhaps the origin of the reasoning is not so simplistic," Nicholas suggested, a coy smile remaining on his face, despite obvious frustration lines creasing his forehead. "Maybe he simply wants us to work out our troubles on our own?" He looked in her eyes, reaching forward to push her hair out of her eyes and behind her ear.

Stacy bore into his eyes while he spoke, his unique words captivating her every time he spoke. She shook her head the moment he pushed her hair back—she liked it in her face.

"Then I suppose I'll just have to keep on starting fights until then," Stacy reasoned. Then her thoughts drifted, sifting over what Nicholas had said earlier. "Wait, did you say you're here completely alone? No aunt? Uncle? Grandpa Jim?"

"No, Grandpa Jim does not travel well," he joked. "It is not such a strange concept in Dukhovia. We typically start our independent lives much younger than Americans."

Stacy sifted over the words, over his delivery, looking for the hidden meaning. He not only travelled alone, but was staying here alone. She thought he may at least have been staying with someone once he arrived. "Why come here, then?" Stacy automatically started. "I mean…most Dukhovians hate America."

Nicholas shrugged, but his eyes were penetrating hers, seeming to look for some hidden meaning of his own.

That was it. He did not elaborate, made no move to get up, to run, to change the subject—nothing. She figured even an assassin would have a back story, so did that mean he just did not want to talk about Dukhovia? Just like her family?

She responded with the same silence, hoping the awkwardness would at least break him if she failed to figure out her next words.

Thankfully, he did break. "Dukhovia never quite gave me the peace I had hoped for, my mother always said that there was hope in America, so I decided to do a bit of research."

Stacy slammed her eyes shut, recoiling as images of Dukhovia flashed through her mind—images she knew to be true, images her dreams convinced her to be true, and ideas of what her idea of the war plagued Dukhovia with. Fire. Screams. Melted ice and snow leaking into a pool of lava…

Stacy steadied herself, meeting Nicholas's either concerned or intrigued eyes. "Where exactly does the band fit in with that?" She asked, referencing his apparent reason for being here as he told Rachael.

Nicholas knew exactly what she meant, but again, had not rehearsed a story. Still, he never broke that trance that perhaps if she was not so cocky and protective would have broken her. Instead, she just stared right back into those full, demeaning, inquisitive eyes.

Then, his eyes flashed down to whatever it was he was eating and he began talking quickly. "Your family in Dukhovia is as famous as the band is here. The idea of finding you intrigued me—for the sake of the war. I thought I might observe one of the most well-known, banished families, see how they truly behave and if the actions of Dukhovia were justified, in any sense."

Her blood ran cold, but she pressed forward. Now, getting information was dire. "So, you came looking for my family specifically?"

Penetrating eyes again, and then, in a sharp, but tender voice, "I want to understand, Stacy. My family was taken from me because of the fear of our world. Because we fear variance, we fear what we cannot control." He paused a moment, then his voice became less like a plea to understand and more casual, storytelling. "It was shortly after my parent's deaths that I learned of the band, but I had always known the stories of your family, of how they went from being known as brave, all-knowing, and kind to a level of evil so dark that the world did not have enough fear to even comprehend."

Stacy felt every breath rise and fall in her chest as he spoke, her brain going from contemplating how to surprise a Dukhovian assassin, to a blur of absolute nothingness.

"Yet, the world was split in half when it came to your family. Even having witnessed directly the atrocities that unfolded, they still were able to find innocence and goodness."

Stacy's fists balled up. She was ready to stand and either walk away or punch him when his eyes sized her up, read her body language, and added his next words quickly, yet casually...

"It reminded me of my own family."

Stacy calmed herself, her facial features giving away her curiosity along with her sympathetic heart.

Murdered in front of me at age six...

"Your family?"

He nodded slowly. "My family shares similar...disregard. In Dukhovia."

"Why?" Her words flew out of her mouth without a thought.

"Lies." It was all he gave by way of explanation. "Lies that forever altered how Dukhovia saw us. The idea has tormented me for the majority of my life. Thus, I became curious. Curious why your family was banished, but not mine if mine was hated more. Curious if what was said of your family was entirely true, knowing that my own history was not.

"Then that prompted an idea that I thought could perhaps aid in at least turning the tides of the war. If we were fighting over modernization and banishing anyone who might possibly agree with it, but I could somehow prove the banished families were traditionalist, would that prompt our people to have an open mind? To not label and assume traditionalism is black and white."

His thoughts seemed to be taking him somewhere else, but Stacy waited for him to return, intrigued and yet petrified by every word he spoke.

He shrugged. "A dream, perhaps. Thus, once I gained an ability to travel, I thought it best to come here. So, no, I am not truly a fan of the band, but I am more than willing to learn to be."

Stacy stared at him. Her eyes penetrating his, uncaring what message that conveyed, be it obsession or strangeness. Then her body started to catch up with the millions of thoughts that pummeled her mind, piling up and fighting one another for attention. Her heart began to race, sweat dripped down her brow, her foot began to tap...

"You're a solider, aren't you?" She asked carefully.

His body did not move. "In the past."

Stacy's breathing stopped. What was she to do with that information? Did all of the soldier's uphold the law of Dukhovia? Was that even the role of a solider? Had it changed? Did it matter whether he was traditional or not?

Her heart thud in her chest, a caged lion ready to erupt. Was her family really safe? Was this all some elaborate story to get closer to them and she was falling right into it? Was it better to talk to her family and make them upset or talk to Nicholas and get them killed/imprisoned? Whatever.

Her foot was tapping a million miles a minute and now that she was aware of its occurrence, it was all she thought about. Until the reality of what he was saying entered her mind and she realized—she had an answer to her questions. At least, she had partial answers to some of her questions. The "why he was here", but also if he cared for his family the same way she did. Not only that, but the connection that both their families wore unnecessary blame.

She wondered what his family did to earn theirs, but knew that was a question for another time. She knew how she felt about divulging her own past, and tabled that for next time. Still, along with the imminent fear she felt for her family, she felt more of a connection to Nicholas, more of a...peace, a calm. And she yearned for a closeness with someone so similar to hers, so desperately much that it hurt.

She never really thought about if other families in Dukhovia were treated with the same unjust banishment. She assumed that it was only because of the actions of her family members that resulted in the action.

Stacy forced her thoughts forward as the visions of fire and blood now coupled with thousands and millions of people packing up their homes, wandering the streets, fighting for their lives to escape on a tiny boat, in a huge ocean, minutes from death...

Here he sat before her. This person so knowledgeable about Dukhovia, so connected to her. Ridiculed family, wrongly accused, and it altered his entire life...just like this did hers. Just like this limited her ability to be in Dukhovia finding out whatever the heck this dream was supposed to tell her.

Either the Spirits were ready for her to find out or.... there was a catch.

She breathed, attempting to poise herself comfortably enough to formulate coherent words. "And if the banished families are open minded? Then what?"

"Then there would be hope," he answered, simply. "There would be hope that I could get Dukhovia to realize that all this time arguing over right and wrong, good and evil has turned us all into the enemy."

Stacy's stomach was in knots. The tang of blood nearly coated her nose as the images rushed by, but remained all too clear: blood, fire, death, families fleeing, Nicholas at war...

She swallowed a lump in her throat, holding onto the table with sweat-drenched hands for support. The words he spoke seemed so promising, so similar to hers that she so desperately wanted to believe his innocence. So much more she needed to know, so many new questions pounding her head, and yet...

Her eyes tore up at the ticking clock getting eerily closer to the end of lunch and eerily closer to wherever the heck it was he would go next.

Where *was* he going next?

She rubbed her hands together, surprised by the realization she still held his schedule in hand. She tore it open.

"Your schedule is exactly the same," she said, flabbergasted.

"Exactly the same," he confirmed with poise. His eyes still reflected heavy emotion, but he seemed to match her and push it back, his own hands clenching and unclenching.

She stared from him to the schedule, the confusion only adding to what she previously felt. "Then where were you today?"

Nicholas rolled his eyes. "The principal's office," he offered. "Mr. Santifini felt I needed one-on-one time to find where I would best fit."

Stacy stared at him. She felt like she had entered some weird third dimension where nothing made any type of sense. "And?" She pressed.

"Inconclusive as far as I understand it."

Stacy started to speak again, but the sound of the bell declaring the end of lunch signaled before her. It felt like a gunshot wound to her stomach.

Nicholas stood, slowly and patiently grabbing his things. "Until we meet again, my princess." He ducked his head into a bow and trailed away, leaving Stacy staring after him.

"What was that all about?" Cody asked the moment Nicholas was out of ear shot. Rachael had a pleased look on her face and a reassuring smile, but the rest of her friends looked at her just as skeptically as Cody.

"He was just wishing us luck with the recording, that's all," Stacy said still in a daze, exchanging a knowing look with Rachael that she would have more to divulge later. "His detention got moved too."

"What?" Cody shouted with irritated surprise. "Why would they want you to serve it together? That's a small, cramped room that you'll be together in for hours. Santifini doesn't even usually stay in the room."

"You'd know the set up best, huh, cuz?" Stacy laughed, clapping him on the back and beginning to move towards the hall for their lockers.

"Did you ever think maybe he was just having a bad day and he's a perfectly sensible human being?" Rachael asked Cody as they walked.

Cody rounded on her. "You're *still* in on this? Even after what he did?" Cody gestured to Rachael's pink cast. "Even after finding out you need surgery?" She looked down at it and shrugged with a smile.

"Surgery?" Stacy asked with surprise.

"Surgery," Cody confirmed.

"Non-invasive, totally routine surgery," Rachael emphasized in good spirits.

"They're drilling a hole in your arm and putting metal into it, it's hardly non-invasive," Jade commented in a dry voice.

Stacy now stopped in the hall to face her friend, her eyes wide.

"Doesn't change a thing," she told her with a wink.

Stacy nodded her head. The debate continued into the following periods, with Stacy feeling confident in her resolution by the time swim class rolled around. It was fact: Rachael was right. The fact that she needed surgery did not negate the conversations they already had, the in-depth look they did into Nicholas's personality and story, and the fact that she was dying to continue on with their conversation.

The second the bell rang for sixth period, Stacy was out the door, having gathered her books and stood just seconds before the sound. She ignored the comments from her friends—whether they be positive or mostly negative—and found her way to the principal's office.

She approached the door slowly and stealthily, it was around the back end of the office, where she was not technically supposed to be—oops. Her eyes darted around the corners, waiting for Ms. Frito Lay to go in the back and meet with Ms. M. After they gossiped for fifteen minutes, Ms. M was due out front to give Ms. Frito Lay a break.

The minute Ms. F disappeared, Stacy darted across to the door. The door was slightly opened, so she started to just walk in, but paused as she heard a very demeaning voice—Nicholas's voice. He was speaking with a tone far from respect to the big man in charge.

"It's very unbecoming..." Santifini's words trailed off.

Stacy heard the noise of Nicholas's chair being pushed back as he stood. "Unbecoming, is it? I shall keep that in mind the next time I make the unanimous decision to come to this God-forsaken country."

The footsteps of another teacher coming back to use the copy room alerted Stacy away from the conversation. She shot across the hall into the nurse's office, her heart pounding. Once the coast was clear, she leaned her head out from the entrance as close to Santifini's office as she could.

CHAPTER TWENTY-THREE

"...If I were you, I might take that into consideration the next time you decide to force me to say something that you already know. The task is simple: help me do what I came here to do and perhaps we can both have a chance at returning to Dukhovia."

CHAPTER 24

COMPANION IN THE DARKNESS

*K*ill the heir? You intend to train us to kill the heir? A sacred person to Dukhovia?" Nicholas felt himself falling forward into the room, unable to control himself. Vuel was there at an instant, bounding forward ready to defend anything Nicholas said or did.

"What do you think you are doing spying?" Arkady stood to his feet, eyeing the boys.

Nicholas's demeanor did not change. His heart and mind were racing at full force, trying to piece together everything he just heard.

"We are meant to follow the predications made by the Spirits. If the Spirits say the American heir will rule, then it is so! I will not go against the Spirits. The Demitona's stand with Su Ana and Su Ata and their decisions."

Arkady looked at the boys, preparing to fight back with force the way he always did. They would receive their lashes, be reminded of their place, and sent back to their chambers as always. However, this time was different. Instead, Arkady strolled over to his tea kettle again and poured a cup. He took another cup and then sat himself back in his chair, setting the cups down in front of himself without drinking.

"Sir Nicholas, what do you know of America?"

Nicholas stumbled for a moment, keeping his focus on the issue at hand, maintaining deep eye contact with Arkady before glancing to Vuel whom was still stone-faced. Nicholas turned back, his face blank.

"You have been to Spain, yes? What do you know of Spain?"

"They are non-traditional," Nicholas said the words slowly after pondering their purpose for a moment. "But cultured."

Arkady nodded once. "Non-traditional, but cultured. They have adapted much more than we have, they have no connection to the Spirits, however, they do have unique purpose and honor their ancestors by maintaining some traditions."

The boys remained silent. Vuel appeared to be getting on edge as he stood, feet apart in a fighting stance.

Arkady moved his cups, still not sipping from them. "And Moragon? What do you know of Moragon?"

Nicholas squinted. Moragon was a country to the east of Asia that they dealt with often during the first World War for information on their safety. In exchange, Dukhovia failed to mention any alliance with Moragon.

CHAPTER TWENTY-FOUR

"*Moragon is moderately traditional. They will use traditional equipment if available or donated, however, they live nearly as modestly as we do with ancestry and culture prized most high.*" *He recited the knowledge he and Vuel had drilled into their heads over the last several years.*

"*Yes, Sir Nicholas. Now let me paint you a picture of America. Ancestry, culture, and tradition are not minimal, they are non-existent. Once thought to be the "melting pot" of accepting and endorsing all cultures, America seems to instead wipe the slate clean, forcing their customs of non-practice amongst those who enter it. Names are stripped away, titles...*"

"*The forms of transport utilized in Spain? Not only are they utilized as the norm, they are utilized for dangerous sport. Purpose is insignificant, they chase only monetary value. The dead are thought to be abandoned and forgotten the moment their corpses hit the cold, cold ground.*"

Nicholas could feel the lump growing in his throat and his demeanor staggering.

Vuel was no stranger to his easy swaying under Arkady's words and spoke up. "Come on, Alloy, none of that matters. If the Spirits chose this heir, then they will be just. And what I told you earlier is true. We need to just leave."

"*Your companion is correct,*" *Arkady said sternly. "The Spirits have chosen. Though, as I am told, they predicted that this heir could lead to great destruction as well as peace. Follow the patterns of Dukhovia and lead to peace...*" *He put one of the tea cups closer to him on the table. "Follow the path of America and destruction will come.*" *He moved the next cup closer so that they were side by side again. "We all know that predications are ever-changing. Imagine the heir learning of their fate, the Spirits changing their mind, and the heir taking the country by force.*"

"*That has never happened,*" *Nicholas said, shaking his head uncertainly.*

"*No, it has not. As an heir has always been Dukhovian born and raised with Dukhovian values. Do you know the types of crimes that happen in America, Nicholas? How common it is for people to go missing, be taken captive, be murdered simply walking home from school...*"

The idea of children being murdered twisted Nicholas's stomach. He pictured Dukhovian school children walking down the street, being drug around a corner and beaten into oblivion—their corpses left to rot rather than be passed onto The Spirit Realm.

"*Nicholas...*"

"*Come on, Alloy...we need to leave. Now.*"

"*I...I need to do what is right by my family. I need to redeem them.*"

Vuel rolled his eyes and shuffled his feet.

"*And you will,*" *Arkady promised. "What will come of this predication is unprecedented. What we need is an heir willing to do whatever is needed to save this country. If something the Spirits could never see coming takes place, will you save this country? Will you honor your ancestors and be hero to all of Dukhovia?"*

"If someone is needed so bad why not do it yourself?" Vuel spat, fierceness in his eyes and in his tone.

He shifted in his seat, unwilling to respond. "It is likely my time will expire before this heir comes to our country or is found. Believe me, it was my hope I would not have to involve you children."

Vuel sneered harshly and rolled his eyes in response.

"And if the heir comes after—after they have lost their Spirit and tries to take over...why then must it be me?"

Arkady simply shrugged. "Because it has to be somebody. Do you not wish to be that hero?"

Nicholas's eyes had darted to the floor. He had now fallen completely out of his defensive stance. He was left, arms dropped to his side, thinking, waiting.

"Who is to say that, even if this heir lives in America, that the ideals would transfer on to them? Perhaps the Spirits have far more wisdom. Perhaps they have some type of protection against this happening."

Arkady sat up in his chair, a small smile seemed to spread across his aged lips. "I am glad you asked such an important question, Nicholas Tyler."

Nicholas recoiled in his spot.

Arkady was back to his tea cups, however, this time, he reached forward and brought a cup of sugar towards the two cups, sprinkling it only in one. "You see, people are like tea. They will absorb, to some degree, what is put into them or is centered around them. We see this as some of the sugar dissolves, yet we can still clearly identify which cup is without sugar. We can tell by sight, we can tell by taste. Somehow, some way—we can tell.

"Now, bring that tea into a new, clean cup of tea..." he poured some of the sugar tea into his untainted tea cup. "...and some of what was absorbed is brought in." He revealed soft speckles in the new cup and a small amount of sugar remains in the old cup. "Perhaps not all of it, but definitely some of it—and that is enough to understand we are risking losing everything we have ever loved. The unknown is terrifying, Nicholas Tyler, but the known can be an absolute nightmare."

Nicholas's tear-stained eyes stared at the tea, unwilling to blink, unwilling to move. A thousand possibilities, a thousand questions went through his head, and yet he knew...he knew what he had to do and he knew he could not face Vuel.

"You may leave, Nicholas. There is only so much I can do to stop you." Arkady was casual as he pushed his seat out and the tea was carried away by a servant.

"I am leaving," Vuel announced. "Are you coming or staying?"

Nicholas's eyes shifted, making the longest journey they ever dared towards looking his friend in the eye. "Vuel, please...stay with me."

"Stay? Stay with you? You must be completely and utterly insane! Did you not hear a word I spoke to you this morning?" He lowered his tone. *"Do you not trust me?"*

Nicholas only shook his head, fear and confusion keeping him locked in place. "I must save Dukhovia. I must stay."

"Fine. Then good luck."

And then he was gone. His only ally, his only confidant...gone.

Friends did not exist in Dukhovia—only allies and enemies. You were either on the right side of the war or the wrong. What would make that any different in Dukhovia? Friendship—particularly friendship with the heir—was undeniably impossible.

What was the purpose anyway? They did not support you; they did not attempt to understand you.

But Stacy did.

Ugh. He was glad he was not yet expected in any classes. After lunch had ended, he ran to the nearest exit and vomited out his insides. Yet, somehow, he still felt pain. He felt naked and exposed having revealed as much as he did to her. No chance to consider the pros and cons of the words, no chance to analyze their impact, no chance to slaughter her instead...

And also no will.

Friendship.

The word entered his mind as he raced back to his apartment near the end of the school day. The closeness and call he felt towards Stacy in discussing their families was almost...calming. Perhaps it was something he had been craving these many years without knowledge.

No, he had knowledge, had a wrench in his stomach every time he considered the word...It just...It was something he had not wanted, had not thought of so fully, in such a long time. It had become nothing more than a fantasy thought. Everyone ridiculed him and his family, no one understood what it was like to walk in his shoes...yet there was one person, one person in this world who might.

One person who loved their family selflessly.

One person who loved Dukhovia like their will to breathe.

One person whose family wore a title they did not earn, resulting in this person not getting a chance at fulfilling their future.

Stacy. She was the one person in this world who could make him desire friendship, and yet...he was aware of all the double-edged swords, of course. He found himself yearning to open up to the person meant to be his enemy. Yet, he wondered if she truly was his enemy. If she could serve Dukhovia justly...

Stacy asked questions about him. He watched her fumble over her thoughts and watched that anxious foot tap. She chose her words carefully—was that for her own advantage or his? Stacy seemed brave and intelligent beyond her academics—she was socially aware, a strong point for a Dukhovian ruler.

Ancestry, culture, and tradition are not minimal, they are non-existent. Once thought to be the "melting pot" of accepting and endorsing all cultures, America seems to instead wipe the slate clean, forcing their customs of non-practice amongst those who enter it. Names are stripped away, titles...

These aspects were also true. Although he did not know much on her views of ancestry, she did mention her grandfather teaching her the guitar, perhaps that stood for something. She also wished to preserve their feelings in not discussing matters of Dukhovia. Names stripped away...

Nick. Stacy had asked to call him Nick. In Dukhovia, nicknames were sometimes used by close family, however, it was thought disrespectful to use a nickname as the norm or with strangers.

But she had respected what she read to be clear on his face—that he did not like that.

And then there was the subject of their families and what he had divulged. Ugh. He swallowed sickness. Nicholas had not lied, not technically. He did hear of them from a young age and he did come here hoping that they would be traditional. He just did not necessarily believe it would make a difference nor did he believe the vast majority would have remained traditional. But he did not predict this knowledge either.

He also was not aware how much their families truly did have in common. He had considered the idea and was angry beyond belief that his family was shamed and ridiculed around the country while hers was not. However, he never quite heard their story described the way she described it and he almost wondered if they did deserve full pardon.

He also found himself begging for the chance for the conversation to continue.

He was desperate to know more about her. Not only at school—he needed to get her alone. He needed to see how she truly functioned and who she truly was. Not around others, not when they both needed to obey other rules—their genuine selves.

He supposed he should not have left school early. Not that he knew for certain he would be able to slip away into swimming class, but he perhaps could have walked her home or they both could have snuck back and attempted their bet at the cold-water race yet again.

Nicholas sighed, considering the pros and cons to everything that was happening with this heir. The fears that Arkady had put into Nicholas's head those many years ago were still true. No matter how much Dukhovian she was, mixing any part of those American traits that did exist with Dukhovia could be its downfall—especially with the war. Yet, he did not feel that way. When she spoke, he felt something so nonexistent in his life he could barely fathom he was naming the correct emotion. Shall he dare call himself hopeful?

Hopeful. It was a foreign word, yet an accurate word, a *full* word. Much of what he observed from Stacy was very traditional, and that was alarming, yet it was not fear that bounced off of him every time she spoke. There was always a lightness to the air. Then there were the moments she spoke the way any honorable Dukhovian would—again, he did not know what to do with that information, he did not know if it truly could make a difference in either of their fates, but it sealed him in—hope.

He felt hopeful of their futures. Hopeful of their choices. And simply hopeful because it was all he had to offer. He had nothing concrete.

Ha. Choices. He scoffed at the word the same way she had. *When I had a choice.* Little did she know just how minute his choices were: in being here, in fulfilling this mission, in anything at any point of his life. The idea of regaining his ability to make choices was laughable at best—and that was on a good day. An impossible day.

But hope.

But could the lies he spouted to Stacy somehow prove true? That if he could provide proof that the banished families, that Stacy, was traditional, would Arkady change his mind?

"The forms of transport utilized in Spain? Not only are they utilized as the norm, they are utilized for dangerous sport. Purpose is insignificant, they chase only monetary value. The dead are thought to be abandoned and forgotten the moment their corpses hit the cold, cold ground."

Those things, they were not true. They were not concrete. Arkady was wrong and he would continue to be wrong and that meant there was another choice for Nicholas. There was a way he could honor his family without disgracing his country, the Spirits, Stacy...

His brain began to hurt and his frustration began to rise. He knew the double standard—he always knew it. He had just always hoped that Arkady was right and there existed a danger that Dukhovia did not fully predict. After all, they did speak of both great destruction and great peace. They spoke of it without much explanation and that left room open for interpretation. Still, he could not shake the frustration of adding yet another person onto his ever-growing list of problems and tangibility.

There is, at the end of the day, only one choice...

He used to think Erlik was right when he first started telling him this sentence. He knew the ending of it by heart...

...The right one.

But the right one was never clear—at least aside from the mind of Erlik.

Nicholas shook his head, becoming aware of a pounding knock at his apartment door. He froze for a moment, neither expecting any visitors nor making anyone aware of where he was. But he had not contacted Arkady yet. He should have. He should have sent him a letter the moment he arrived. He expected him to also spend days in meditation, trying to connect with him, to share their thoughts and feelings. That was another mess Nicholas was caught in—it was not so much that he could not do it as much as he prevented himself from doing it. The last thing he wanted was Arkady to know he was second guessing his path.

The pounding came again. Nicholas took a moment to think. He did not recognize the pattern of the knocking, he did not feel a presence he recognized, yet it did not feel completely foreign either. He walked towards the door, putting his hand close to the middle. He closed his eyes and begged his Spirit to guide him. He felt no threat and swung open the door.

His eyes immediately took in a tall, decently built man, perhaps 20 years his elder. He was dressed in a uniform of some kind—with a badge of gold deeming him "Chief" on the chest of the black material. His face was neither welcoming nor did he feel warning fanning out from the deep green eyes, framed brilliantly beneath a pile of spiked, black hair…

"A police officer," Nicholas said with shock and affirmation. They were meant to enforce the laws in America. Arkady deemed them the only possible savior of American soil.

The man nodded. "My name is Richard Grayson." He lowered his voice to a softer tone. "I'm Cody's father and Stacy's uncle."

"Oh!" After pondering in his mind why he could be here and how he could be helpful, Nicholas was brought back to reality. Cody—the cousin who hated him— had a father with the power to not only hold him accountable for hurting Rachael, but enforce American laws restricting minors from living alone.

"Chief Grayson, it is an honor to meet you," Nicholas bowed, his left hand balled into a fist with the right holding it tight. It was a way to greet people of dignity in Dukhovia. A reserved right and honor. "I assure you, I did not mean any harm to your son or niece or any of the like…"

Chief Grayson held up his hand to stop Nicholas from going on. "That's not why I'm here, son. May I come in?"

Nicholas stared at him blankly for a moment, then moved to the side, holding out the door to welcome him inside.

The officer's eyes looked around the apartment once quickly, likely performing some type of assessment—was he really alone? Did he have food? Shelter? Among these questions the chief likely had, Nicholas had only one— how did he find him?

Paperwork.

He cursed the landlord and the blasted school once more.

"Stacy tells me you are planning on seeking help for your anger, is this true?"

"Yes," Nicholas agreed quickly. "I already have. I have been praying for guidance and diligence throughout the day." Okay, so he had not quite figured out how to root that back to his anger, yet—but it was true. He was trying.

"Well then, sounds like that much is taken care of," he agreed with a warm smile. He gestured over to the couch where the two of them sat side-by-side. The officer seemed unsure of himself, yet in total comfort with what he came to do and say. "I hear you came to the country alone—without any family or guardian."

Nicholas paused, now back to cursing Arkady, wishing he knew more about the American law system so that he knew how to move his way out of this. What would happen to him? Would they force him to stay with someone else—an orphaned child? He shuttered at the thought. He was already prisoner in Dukhovia, he did not want to be kept prisoner here too.

Then he pondered over the officer's word choice and wondered if it held any merit. He had stated that Stacy told him about his anger, yet that he heard he was in the country alone. Were both from the same source? If they were different, what did that mean? Did Stacy truly have the remorse Nicholas thought he had noticed when he spoke of his family—or was she only concerned with his anger?

Frustration rose in him for not knowing where he stood with her.

Nicholas nodded once. "It is customary in Dukhovia. To venture out on one's own and find their own path typically begins around the age of eleven or twelve."

Richard nodded. "Yes, I remember that quite well. Of course, in The States, we do things much differently. There are laws and such we must follow—remaining with our parents until we turn eighteen." Richard's eyes seemed to drift off, then he came back, his eyes fully focused on Nicholas. "Fortunately or unfortunately, I was much like you growing up. I did not seem to have a place and was on my own from a young age. A very young age." His eyes scanned the left side of the apartment. "I suppose there were times I was not that great at following the law and times I realized why it was in place—and why it shouldn't have been." He smiled.

"Times you have disagreed with American practices?" He questioned daringly.

Richard nearly laughed. "Oh, most definitely. Sometimes it takes submerging yourself in a broken world to learn all about how to fix that world, how it became broken in the first place.

"I think that's how I ended up in the spot I'm in now," Richard went on. "The desire to not only no longer be the broken, but to heal the broken. To have an endless array of resources at my hands when I find them—or they find me."

"Did you never feel…angry?" Nicholas pressed.

"Oh, of course," he laughed. "I was angry at my circumstances. I was angry at those who discouraged me from finding my way. But I knew that I was not alone and that I had the desire and ability to help those like me—those alone, those lost. So, I did."

Nicholas watched him, understanding flickering in and out of his mind. Arkady had explained that the Grayson family had their trials in America. Only, he never made it sound so—heroic? He described them as mass murderers, cunning, and deceitful. Arkady spoke of children whom—whether out of learning or hurt—lured innocent people into their clutches to harm and support the evil doings of their parents. One of those children was the man in front of him right now. So, who was lying?

Nicholas let his thoughts go quickly, searching for the best words to say. He doubted Richard could fully relate—that there was a man on the other side of the globe gifting him a lifetime of pain without the promise of an early death. But he saw a similar difficulty—if the world was hurting you, do you hurt it back? If choice did exist, then…

"How did you choose?" He felt the words fall out of his mouth without control. "What to do, I mean?"

Richard looked off into the distance, a memory or two flashing in his mind. "I think it came down to who I wanted to be. Then there weren't many choices left. What about you? What brings you here now?"

Nicholas looked down, shame rising up in him. "Not choice," he decided. "But I have nowhere else to go and nowhere else to be." It was true enough. He had tried and he could not go anywhere Arkady did not want him to be.

"And so, The United States of America made sense?"

Nicholas shrugged. "Maybe so. Maybe a complete and total opposite of what I was used to was exactly what I needed, perhaps it is what Dukhovia needs."

"I'm not sure a total opposite Dukhovian exists," Richard disagreed. He seemed to be shifting back into officer mode, his eyes starting to look around the apartment again. "But I like your train of thought. And now that you are here—how are you feeling? Is there anything you need?"

Nicholas rattled his brain. Good, he had decided. The officer was good and Arkady was a liar. What else was he lying about? "Just time," he answered. "To find myself."

The officer's half-smile pulled larger on his lips, a small hint of happiness escaping. "Fair enough."

The officer stood to his feet and walked around his apartment, examining the broken objects and holes in the walls with fleeting precision. Nicholas had his surroundings examined many times and the familiar lump in his stomach grew as he awaited to find out if he passed the test. Only, this time, he was observing quite different body language. Richard walked with his pleasant, half-smile traced on his lips. He walked slowly and gently—not checking off a list, but building one. He did not look disgruntled; he did not look ready to induce pain.

The lump grew and spread, sparking like a fire that roared through his chest and into his throat. He was itching to scream, to run, to assert his dominance.

No. No.

He closed his eyes. He pictured Oona. He pictured Onla.

Fear. Anger. Loss. Grief.

He grit his teeth.

These were the things that trapped him—not himself. He pictured the things which caused him discomfort and pushed them into a different space in his mind—a space not occupied by the Spirits. A space that he would soon push out of existence.

"Do you mind?" Nicholas's eyes flashed open and he saw the officer standing next to his refrigerator, his hand on the door handle.

Nicholas was not sure what he quite looked like, he made to nod, but was certain the confusion in his brain caused some other type of movement. Then he noticed that the lump grew smaller. Only just, but smaller.

Richard had opened the door to the nearly-empty fridge slowly and shut it once more. Slow. Precise. Gentle.

Gentle. That was the word that described the movements, the language, the persona of the officer. He was gentle. He was kind. It was decided. He was, in fact, good.

"Well, Nicholas, I can tell you have a lot to think about and you seem comfortable enough. If it is okay with you, I would like to send up a few welcome gifts from the town and my family and I."

Nicholas nodded, unsure now if it was in hesitation or moderate-eagerness.

Friendship.

"I would also like to extend an invitation to you. Our door is always open: for dinner, company—anything you need. Please do not hesitate to accept."

Nicholas stood to his feet to see the officer off properly. "Of course. I am indebted to you and your kindness, sir. Thank you for your time."

The words felt dry and undeserving for the man that had just walked in his presence, but they were all his mind new how to find.

CHAPTER 25

INDIGENOUS BEHAVIOR

Stacy was waiting outside the minute her uncle's car pulled in the driveway. They spoke very briefly and he was gone again, but she stayed—sitting and thinking and thinking and sitting.

He had gone over to interrogate Nicholas. At least, that was what Cody had told her. The palpitations that rose in her heart the moment he said the words sent her spinning. Would he find out more or actual straight answers? If so, what would they be? Then there was the small, miniscule side of anger that something Uncle Richey might say or do would upset Nicholas.

Protect them.

When he returned, he seemed almost in somewhat of a daze of thought. Fair enough, she figured. Uncle Richey spent the majority of his life helping runaway kids after living on his own since age ten. It was something he loved, but also something that caused a lot of pain. It was only natural that he would have some type of feelings going back into the game.

Stacy was concerned with Nicholas. She was concerned when Uncle Richey returned home and conveyed that his apartment was totally empty aside from a small bag of things. She was concerned that the only items in his fridge were whole carrots and three potatoes. She was more than concerned, her heart broke as she thought of the overwhelming number of things her very much alive parents bought for her.

But then she would shift, focusing all too much on the rest of the information. Nicholas admitted to looking for her family specifically. Nicholas lied about being a fan of the band. Nicholas was secretive about being from Dukhovia. And the biggest, the one-hundred and ten percent direct lie…

He had said that he came here by choice. That he decided to research the banished families on his own, but then what she overheard in the office was quite contradictory. Nicholas did not come to Dukhovia by choice and he was not at all gentle with the information.

He had told Stacy he decided to come here at his mother's recommendation.

He had told Uncle Richey that he had nowhere else to go and that complete opposite was potentially what he needed. That choice evaded him.

But Santifini? He had *barked* at Santifini that he needed to be here. It came off almost that he was *forced* to be here. Every evident piece of bitterness and distaste thick in his voice.

CHAPTER TWENTY-FIVE

What you already know... Help me do what I came here to do and maybe we could both return to Dukhovia.

Stacy felt for Nicholas, but the clench in her stomach told her that mission was anything but innocent.

And her principal? The principal they spent years pining against? But that Terra was best friends with? Stacy had not even known he was Dukhovian, but it explained enough about Terra and his relationship. They always acted like old friends. But...

What did the way Nicholas was speaking to him reveal about either of them? Who was friend and who was foe? Stacy did not know, but it was evidence enough to prove that it was at least one of them.

Then again...could he be just referring to his own plan? That they were both banished and if Nicholas was able to sway Dukhovia that the banished families were traditional, they could both return to a more peaceful Dukhovia than the one they left? Was Santifini also banished or did he leave by choice?

Stacy threw her body into the snow, letting the back of her hand glide against its wetness, the chill intensifying her. If she was wrong, then what did he come here, not by choice, to do? Why did he need to keep secrets to do it? Who sent him? What did it have to do with her family? With the dream? With Dukhovia?

Research was what he had told her. Research to end the war, though he had hardly elaborated on what that meant and the role he played. What type of solider was he? What side was he on? Why did she not ask?

She breathed. Trying to focus on facts she knew to be true...

She knew that he was right as far as that Dukhovians started their 'independent lives' sooner than Americans.

She knew that he was, to some degree, a traditionalist. But did traditionalist automatically mean good over evil? Perhaps that was the gray area he meant. There were bad and good intermingled on both sides—hence no need for banishments.

She had not yet told Rachael what she overheard in the office, mostly because she already knew what she would say. "You have grandparents and now a fallen angel literally sent from the Dukhovian skies above, the stars could not align in a better way. No more wondering". And she knew what she was doing to herself, all the back and forth, and she knew she only had one option. Whether she wanted to protect her family or learn more about Dukhovia, she had to get closer to Nicholas.

But that protective shield went up, confusing her every time. Protect her family. Protect the dream. Protect Dukhovia...Protect Nicholas.

Protect them.

She never knew her purpose in life or Dukhovia, but the stars truly were aligning, fake Rachael was right, and it was time to listen.

"You're keeping something from me," Rachael said in a sing-song voice, popping up behind her.

"Did your parents indirectly bestow mind reading upon you too?" Stacy chastised.

Rachael shrugged, her face poised as she waited impatiently. Stacy spilled the details and watched as Rachael sifted over the information, going through the same internal battle as Stacy. She went from hopeful to biting her lip and then back again for several minutes before deciding to stick with what they already had. After all, they already were suspicious and nothing had changed— and keep your friends close and enemies closer and all that.

But one thing had changed. Instead of complete dismissal or acceptance, Rachael now ended her thoughts with a warning, "Just play it safe". It became Stacy's new mantra as she sifted over every thought and decision and decided whether or not they were examples of her playing it safe.

Stacy and Rachael squinted as they made their way over to Cody's house. Wednesday morning had not only brought the sun, but an alarmingly warm forty-degree day. A day that made it warm enough for others to want to walk to school with Stacy. Still, Rachael dawned her infamous red earmuffs that seemed oh so fitting despite her teal-blue jacket and yellow knit scarf. She was wearing stylish boots that were not made for winter, but that was nothing Rachael did not plan on. She was not only good at making fashion improvements to clothing, but realistic ones too. She never wanted to be forced with the choice to look practical instead of fashionable.

Stacy, on the other hand, was in a thin, light blue and purple windbreaker with black gloves and open winds thrashing around her ears.

"But imagine it wasn't anger problems that had him screaming at the principal," Rachael reasoned, causing a small smile to find Stacy's lips. "Maybe he's hard of hearing? Orrrr maybe it *is* just his anger problems and they aren't closely related or planning to expunge your family."

Stacy shrugged, considering the possibilities. "We've known Santifini for a long time and he definitely has reason to hate us, but he's never done anything to put us in danger."

"Not yet," Rachael laughed.

No sooner did the mention of anger issues run through their ears did the screams of Cody's mom fill the household they were standing in front of.

The girl's go-lucky smiles quickly exchanged for tense, panicked ones. Fear flooding their bodies, they ran up the last few steps to Cody's house and barged in to a scene of chaos and utter shock.

"PICK THIS UP! I DON'T WANT TO HEAR THAT MUSIC!" Yasana was howling from the kitchen, gesturing to what no one could even guess amongst all of the torn and broken remains of the house. Shattered glass, knocked over and dismembered bookshelves, trampled on paperwork scattering the floor of Richard's office.

"Mom…"

Cody was standing feet apart from her, in the dining area of the kitchen—though no table was anywhere to be found and only a single, broken chair lay on its side to his left. His dragging eyes and poor posture reflected a desperate lack of sleep His blue and white striped pajama pants and tattered white t-shirt still clothing his body only confirmed the neglect on himself. But it was the look on his face that the girls could not ignore—it was full of complete and total emptiness. Emptier than they had ever seen it. No trace of sadness, no hint of remorse. Even fear eluded him.

Below Yasana's feet lay a shattered coffee pot, accented by spilled coffee grounds. Her body was arched low; in a position a bear might take before charging. Around her, every cupboard was flung open, some dishes daring to spill out while others stay in perfect austerity.

Anger seemed to flood her like a wave that ceased to fall, continuously crashing up and getting louder and more powerful. It was not until they made eye contact with Cody, who seemingly ignored them, that they fully took in the scene, noticing that Cody's favorite guitar, his most prized possession as a musician, was clasped between two fists, held high like a bat to be swung.

The small gulp they noticed in his throat seemed to tell them to back away, to be careful. Stacy looked from Yasana to Rachael, whom nodded. Taking slow, deliberate steps, Stacy made her way around her aunt and over to the side of the kitchen, immediately next to the open cupboards. She needed a distraction. Not something that would make her angry enough to break Cody's guitar or hurt him, but enough to cause confusion for her to let it go.

Assessing her options, Stacy began tossing plastic cups from the sink to the floor. Yasana turned, but maintained her stance, growling like the animal that she had become.

Stacy changed her course, registering her aunt's face. "I'm sorry, I was looking for a plate. You want some toast?" Then she sent the whole stack of plates flying. Yasana lowered her arms, immediately dropping the guitar which would have sent it flying across the floor, had it not been for Stacy's agility, quickly catching the guitar and tossing it to Cody.

"The police will be here soon, I know you don't think Uncle Richey is going to let you get away with this."

Yasana looked at Stacy angrily, then sent the same message with dagger-like eyes to Rachael and Cody—both of whom avoided eye contact. She seemed to be looking around—assessing her options. Then she bolted up the stairs.

Stacy immediately chased her to the edge of the kitchen, a look of indecision and frustration pent on her face as she decided to remain with Rachael and her cousin. Today was not the day and this was not the moment. Cody needed them in this moment and she felt her role was support rather than vengeance.

Huh.

Stacy turned to face her friends. Rachael had immediately raced to Cody's side and handed him his guitar, slowly and silently, her eyes searching his.

He took the guitar and leaned it against the wall. Not a second later, Rachael was reaching her arms around his shoulders and he was pulling her waist close to his. She closed her eyes and leaned against his neck; he buried his head into her shoulder.

And then he was calm. Just as every time before—no matter how regular a routine between the two.

The heat of the emotion he previously felt turned into passion for the girl he held, into a desire to have her never have to feel what he was feeling and to wash any fear that could have possibly transferred over to her. He let himself be comforted, consoled, and his emotions recognized.

She leaned down from his shoulder and pushed back his hair, peering into his eyes as if she were saying everything that he needed to hear. She was assuring him that she would always be there, that she cared, and she was confirming that he was alright.

And his gazed back, thanking her, answering her.

"My dad's working midnights this week," he sighed in a muffled voice, looking back at Stacy. "I'm not feeling good, so I was going to stay home…"

A crash and bang came from directly above their heads—Cody's room.

Stacy looked up with anger flaring in her eyes, she was already prepared to call her uncle the moment she stepped out the door. "You should stay at my place—at least for the day. I'll talk to my mom when we get there."

"Yeah, you're probably right." The words sounded almost as detached as Stacy's. Then he grabbed his guitar and looked back at them. "I'll be better by this weekend, I promise." The promise was to himself; both the girls knew it.

Rachael took his hand and set it on his heart, shying away from the instrument. "Just take care of yourself."

After hearing his mom disappear, Cody ran to grab shoes and a blanket before heading over to Stacy's. Once they parted ways, the girls headed straight to school an hour late, but with no punishment thanks to Rachael's convincing.

As planned, Stacy and Rachael had called and spoken with Uncle Richey on the way over. He was mostly silently urgent as he heard the words, struggling as he mulled over in his own mind what next steps to take. Knowing he needed to protect Cody, knowing he promised to always care for his wife, knowing that the two no longer worked in unison.

"I just wish we could do more," Rachael said solemnly.

"Hm? Oh yes." Stacy's words were stuck and incohesive.

Rachael smirked knowing she was distracted. "You're still thinking about Nicholas?"

"And Cody too!" She retorted, then fell victim. "But it is *so* weird, Rache. You have to admit."

"And I do," she said casually, nodding her head. "Okay, so we don't upset the balance of Sir Nicholas and risk matching casts, we don't expunge Terra and Tom for all they're worth—what's stopping us from a little conversation with our dear principal? Finding out what he knows?"

Stacy's eyes widened, both surprised by the good idea and dumbfounded she did not think of it. "Can we really trust him though? I mean, he was so dead-set on me getting detention when I didn't even do anything and keeping us together to serve it like he's you trying to play match-maker."

Rachael snickered at the comment.

"And then Nicholas said he knew his parents were dead. If that's true that makes him an absolutely horrifying person to ask about them." She considered the options she had thought of earlier—unsure which one would be victim, but she had to admit, if she was willing to talk to Nicholas about everything and find out more, she should very well be willing to ask the principal she had spent years around and never felt threatened.

Rachael nodded in agreement. "Well, I think you do the same thing you're doing with Nicholas. Listen to what he says, then take it with a grain of salt and fact check it as you get to know more about Nicholas."

Stacy agreed to the plan and it was decided they would pay a visit to Santifini at the end of the day. With the plan for Nicholas and Cody both filed away, the girls continued to the school, pushing open the doors at a completely acceptable 9:00a.m.

Instead of going to class with Rachael post their argument with the office staff (she was already late, what was the point?), Stacy wondered over to the middle school. The building was a smaller, but more put-together version of the high school. They had made modest updates since Rachael left the school. Modest— but not complete updates. Stacy smiled at that fact as she passed the wall just outside the auditorium where her, Rachael, Cody, Jade, and Miranda once carved their names. Not a single letter weathered.

It had been the last day of sixth grade; they were laughing together after successfully smuggling an industrial box of pop tarts away from the cafeteria staff while Rachael distracted them. Though Santifini—who was the middle school principal as well due to such a small school district—wanted to blame Cody immediately, they were never able to find any proof and the search went on for months before becoming forgotten.

"Knock, knock," Stacy sang in a high voice before entering her mother's classroom. Though just as passionate about the sciences and everything related as probably even her own science teacher, her room failed to be decorated with posters with witty jokes on the periodic table and instead grabbed even the furthest eye with fluorescent bright streamers, lava lamps, and posters.

Grace smiled and looked up at her homemade clock, giving her daughter a mischievous look. At the strike of the new period and late bell, the clock would spray confetti outward into the class. The confetti had long since covered the floor and she knew it without the need to look. "What might you be doing here halfway through second period, my lovely daughter?"

"Skipping class to get away from the torture of another history lesson on pirates versus Indians." Stacy plopped down into a chair next to Grace and started examining all of her pens with tedious attention.

"Enthralling, I don't blame you one bit," Grace decided. She dropped her pen and gave her daughter her attention, knowing that while Stacy was not student of the year, something more had to have brought her out of class and over to the school.

"Cody stayed home sick today," Stacy began, her eyes and hands still preoccupied with pens. She finished twisting the cap back onto one and looked her mother in the eye remorsefully. "Yasana was going crazy when we went there this morning, mom. It was the worst we've ever seen."

Grace's eyes filled with worried sadness. "In front of you children?"

"*At* Cody this time, mom. She had the whole house thrown around—you should have seen him."

"Is he okay?"

"He wasn't hurt," Stacy assured her, but cringed considering the hollow look in his eyes.

"Was Yasana still at home?" Grace asked, prying open the locked drawer in her desk to dig out her cell phone.

"Yeah, destroying his room. She threw his signed, acoustic guitar from Scott Danesville, Cody's favorite singer. The thing that he literally cherishes almost as much as his football trophies."

Grace shook her head, disgusted. She dialed her father's number and set it on speaker. Stacy could not determine if the feeling in her stomach was comfort or disgust. Tom was the savior of the family. The glue. The butter to the bread. Calling him meant safety, it meant peace. It meant a solution. But calling him also meant this was serious.

"Yes, my dear?" Tom's voice was polite and welcoming. He was at the hospital, that was clear before he even spoke his first word. The blaring of the sirens and voices of hurried staff in the background allured to that.

"Hi daddy, are you busy?"

"I can talk...what's up?"

Grace was still concerned but she smiled a little at the way her father avoided answering the question. She explained everything that Stacy told her and Tom revealed that he had just gotten off the phone with Richard, but was planning to go over to his house after he got off work. Grace volunteered to go along.

Stacy sat in silence as she listened. Her heart rate did begin to calm down as she realized Cody would be helped, but then circled the thoughts of the crazed woman they were protecting him from…the woman who was supposed to love him, whose feelings of love and safety were so quickly overcome with rage, with violence…

She shook her head as the bell for third period rang, bringing Grace's free period and her phone call to an end. The classroom quickly started to fill with eighth graders who sent paper airplanes flying and the noise of trampling feet rampant.

"Alright, hooligans, I'll be back in a second. Take out your books, turn to page forty-four, and get ready to learn." Grace gave the call before shuffling Stacy out into the hall to say their farewells.

"Oh, by the way, Cody is staying with us. Although I don't think he'll do much other than play Xbox and sleep, be prepared to come home to an empty fridge."

"Take out for dinner it is," Grace smiled.

"We have takeout every night," Stacy laughed, picturing her mother's horrid cooking.

"Not when Kevin preps for me," Grace argued, slightly defensive. She let it drop, perhaps remembering the last two or three roasts Kevin had prepped resulted in a visit from her on-duty Fire Chief brother.

Stacy walked back over to the high school with a faint smile, feeling a little more reassured both for Cody and herself. The more she thought about the similarities between Nicholas and Yasana, the more differences she saw. There were similarities in their anger, but anger existed between most people. When Nicholas's anger broke, there was remorse, there was a willingness to make amends and ensure the behavior did not repeat. The same could not be said for Yasana.

It was then that something hit her—a wave of relief, maybe. But suddenly, she felt more confident in her decision to get closer to Nicholas.

"How are you able to get out of detention and not attend a single class? Should I be taking lessons from you?"

Stacy looked up at Nicholas. There was something different about him. Not physically, but mentally…emotionally. A smile? She took time to assess him in the full lens of every thought she had in the last twenty-four hours. When he reacted, she found herself asking: victim or assassin?

"It's Rachael you want to take notes from," Stacy explained, eyeing him up and down. "I'll probably get extended detention while she's given Student of the Year."

"I shall remember that," he smiled. He had his hands behind his back casually— he was without a care. Clearly, he saw nothing amiss with their conversation. Of course, he did not know what Stacy overheard.

"And what has you out of class, Mr. Andrews?" Stacy used a sophisticated, chastising voice. "Or have you yet been allowed to reintegrate into the normal classroom life?"

"Yet to reintegrate," he confirmed, holding up a folded piece of paper. "And therefore, acting as messenger for our fearless leader." He raised an eyebrow at the description.

"Ooo, top secret," Stacy said, reading the words etched across the seal of the letter. "Have we already peeked and resealed or did you save the fun for me?"

"I cannot say that I was all that curious," Nicholas said flatly, now eyeing the envelope with curious eyes. "However, I was able to make a bargain for its safe delivery."

Stacy's interest now turned. "Oh?"

Nicholas nodded. "You see, if this crucial recycled piece of tree makes its way to its destination, then I have been guaranteed a spot in sixth period swim class— no matter the rest of my schedule."

"Is that so?" Stacy said with an interested voice. "Then you'll be able to lose to me in the cold-water race every single day."

"That was the plan," Nicholas agreed.

"And when might this start?" Stacy pressed.

"I have been told by the end of the week, so let us hope it is sooner rather than later."

Stacy nodded in agreement. "Then I suppose you better safely deliver whatever needs to be kept top secret in a high school."

Nicholas nodded, nervously tapping the paper against his other hand once. The two both moved to go onto their classes, then stopped, starting each other's names at the same time, then laughing in unison.

"Go ahead," Nicholas said with a bow of his head in her direction.

Stacy smiled. "I just wanted to see if you wanted to have lunch with us today. Cody is out for the day, so it might be a good day to test the rest of the waters, without the sharks…" She hated the comment as soon as she made it. Without the sharks? What the… Who says stuff like that?

"I would love to sit with you and meet the rest of your friends. I will meet you at our usual spot?"

Stacy nodded her head in agreement and bid him farewell, her cheeks blushing in response all the way to third period.

CHAPTER 26

THE FEARS OF OUR OWN

Lunch was only one period away—assuming Stacy actually went to class. She decided that she might as well— lessen the chance of her getting pulled out of lunch to get in trouble. Not that she had much luck of paying attention. The promise of seeing Nicholas at lunch was both exciting and nerve-wracking.

Exciting for the obvious reasons— she was finally moving forward on what had been pushed so far back already…getting to know Nicholas and therefore closer to getting to know Dukhovia. Then nerve-wracking for more obvious reasons—her friends. There was the fact they would think her utterly insane and grill her for continuing to bring him around, despite what had happened. She was not sure if it was her agreement with them or not wanting to hear it that made this one onto her list.

Then there was the risk he posed to hurting another friend. But again, her newfound analysis of him versus Yasana led her to believe he was not the maniac waiting to snap that she had grown up with. He was hurt. He was lost. He was confused. And that led her to her last concern that had nothing to do with her friends as victims at all—but of Nicholas.

Nicholas was someone to be protected. The idea was crazy, she knew that, of course she knew that. But he was sensitive. He was lost and alone. He needed someone to understand that. He needed to be around patient and kind people. Those were words that typically described her friends, but given the circumstances… She could see someone who was in his position…whatever the heck position that was…not wanting to be surrounded by people who mocked him and did not understand.

Which was why she likely needed to prep her friends for this.

Then there was the plan to meet with Santifini. If they did not all suffer a bloodthirsty wrath at lunch, there was promise that she would be able to find out more at the end of the day. Ugh. The wait made her want to claw at her desk and shrink into nothingness.

Focus on the now, she assumed. And now—was fourth period. Fourth period was math—Stacy's worst subject and another one of her mother's best. Apparently, she was some mathematics prodigy and everyone had to obsess over the fact, waiting for Stacy's math genes to kick in if the science ones would not. They would be disappointed.

CHAPTER TWENTY-SIX

Her mother did not even go to the same school, she did not understand why they were so concerned. And yet, ever since she began school, she could not remember taking a single test without teachers boring over her shoulder; expecting and anticipating her success.

"Welcome to class, Ms. Matthews, you're just in time for a pop quiz," Mrs. SohKahToa was just as cheery and fun as ever.

Stacy was not at all surprised when she watched the other students fly through the exam while she stared onto the distance and every so often attempted another question until the bell rang. It was not that she did not want to try, or even that she did not understand—she just had more to focus on. Or at least…she felt like she did.

This period specifically, however, she truly did. She tried with failure at her only attempt to tap on Miranda's shoulder during the exam, but Miranda was too focused on her test and Mrs. S was too focused on Stacy. So, she sat back between potential attempts at Miranda and attempts at math questions to anticipate her friend's reactions. She even practiced what to say over and over on repeat until she decided she knew herself better than that and it would just be word vomit the moment she met their faces.

So, it waited until the moment the bell rang and she rushed to their table, glancing up every so often at the place her and Nicholas agreed to meet. *Their usual.*

"I invited Nicholas to eat with us today," Stacy said coyly the moment she sat down.

Jade spit out her food, Rachael did some form of broken wrist clapping, and Cara gasped happily.

"Do I hear wedding bells?" Cara celebrated.

"No," Stacy said, crossed, her eyes dodging around the cafeteria. "You do not hear wedding bells. It's just lunch. I'm eating lunch with you without a proposal, aren't I?"

"Do you think this counts as an official first date?" Rachael chastised. Cara squealed.

"Stace, I think it's great you're giving him a chance," Miranda agreed, patting her on the back.

"And I love a little death wish," Jade laughed. "See, we're all supportive." She tossed her milk in the air as if she was toasting and chugged it down.

"Yeah, I don't know," Dylan jumped in. "Cody's gonna ask me his every little move and I'd rather report less than more."

Stacy felt hot anger rise. "He's going to *ask* you about him? What does he seriously think is going to happen?"

Dylan shrugged, backing off. He suddenly became as interested in his lunch as the rest of the cafeteria was at figuring out what it was. "He just thinks he's bad news, can you blame him? He wants to make sure he stays away from you and Rachael."

"Me and Rachael are perfectly capable of taking care of ourselves," Stacy shot.

"Speak for yourself," Rachael said wittingly, examining her arm. She winked in Stacy's direction.

"And why does one little incident make him think he's such a bad guy? He had a bad day. People have bad days for all types of reasons."

Stacy looked at Dylan's face and calmed herself. She did not want to get into it with him when it came to trying to convince that someone who physically and intentionally hurt others was innocent.

"My last bad day, I didn't send anyone to the hospital, but…"

Stacy ignored Jade. She knew she would not find acceptance with her. "Look, guys, I asked him to sit with us so can we please just give him a clean slate? I don't want to invite him here just to be attacked. If he throws the first punch, then by all means, have at it, but otherwise, can we just error on the side that it was a one-time thing and he's totally normal?"

"I don't want any problems and it's probably better to test it when Cody isn't here," Dylan jumped back in. "But say he's not totally normal? Say something does happen again?"

Stacy swallowed the lump in her throat. "Okay, fine. Look, Rachael has spent the most time with him. She knows that there are certain things he gets upset over…mention of his parents being one and involvement in arguments being another."

"So, let's have those two things off the table, give him a fair chance, and if he dropkicks Jade, we'll reassess," Rachael finished with a warm smile.

"I can take him either way," Jade said with a brutish grin.

"Oh my god," Stacy murmured the words as she got up to leave the table. Nicholas had not appeared in their agreed upon spot yet, but she needed to do something to stop the screaming in her mind and stomach and eating was typically a solution that worked in her favor.

She passed through the line in a daze, taking turns glancing back over at her table and then around the cafeteria for Nicholas. When she exited the line, she glanced over to see that the half laughter, half-grimace-eye rolls continued from her table, telling her it was not yet time to return. Her eyes subconsciously fell to the foot that Nicholas was so observant of—it was tapping a mile a minute in unison with her brains anxious thoughts.

What would she do if she was wrong or something just went out of her control? She could not stop what her friends said. What if someone mentioned Nicholas's parents and he lashed out and knocked that someone unconscious? *Not like Yasana.* He did not hit Rachael just because. He was in defense mode. The other guys started it—he just responded. If they did not go for him, he would not go for them.

But he *could* get upset. And that could impact either of them. Stacy's friends, yes, but also Nicholas. She wanted him to feel support...not the opposite.

Her jitters stopped when her eyes passed to the spot Nicholas always sat at. She found him opening and closing his brown bag multiple times, looking up and back down to it, before finally delving in. She smiled faintly, a warmness approaching her stomach that she tried to both reason with and push away as she made her way over to him with her tray poised high.

"So good to see you made it back from the secret mission, Mr. Andrews." He seemed to wince when she said his name, probably he preferred 'sir' over 'mister'. "And what delectable substances do we have before us today?" Stacy asked, eyeing his plate with suspicion as she downed her milk and attempted to scoop the remainder of her peas into the empty container.

Two years ago, a boy finished all of his vegetables and ever since, teachers monitor student's throwing away their trays and make them sit back down and eat 'at least half'. Stacy had never been successful in this mission and was not about to start on pea day.

"I could ask you the same," Nicholas said through gritted teeth.

Stacy looked at her plate and shrugged, then lifted a spoonful of mystery meat to her mouth. "It's certainly something. Not pork, but also definitely not chicken. Beef, maybe?"

Nicholas's eyebrow raised above a disgusted and perplexed face. "Do you often eat unidentifiable food?"

"At school or in general?" She asked.

Nicholas was quiet, not seeming to think there needed to be a differentiation. He was quite wrong.

"At school, I very rarely ever know what I'm putting into my mouth, but I'm about ninety-percent certain it isn't going to kill me, so I live a little. At home, if my mom cooks, I'm about ninety-percent certain I *am* going to die and so I generally stay away from that unless I'm feeling risky."

He continued to stare at her with the same disgusted face before sighing. "America truly is as wonderful as they say."

"So, you didn't come for the band and you didn't come for our rare cuisine," Stacy noted.

"Hardly," Nicholas half scoffed, half laughed.

Stacy wanted to press more, but felt like the admittance to the first half of that was already a giant leap, so she stayed on the subject of food, glancing at his tray again. "So, where did you manage to find whatever items you did deem healthy enough for your plate?"

Nicholas pushed his bag toward her. "These are beet roots and dahlia beans— at least they are supposed to be. I was not informed of how scarce the choices of

American food would be so I stopped at the Dukhovian based grocery store just outside of town." He stirred his beans around with his finger. "But it is heavily Americanized."

"Well, it is America, so…"

"Very unfortunate." Nicholas looked up and seemed to get distracted.

Stacy turned to meet his eye-line and found all of her friends staring over at them. "Ah. I suppose they are ready for us."

"Great," Nicholas said, but he did not move from his seat.

Stacy eyed him up and down. "Are you still okay with this?"

Nicholas looked at her for a moment then nodded his head. "I am great. It is great. Let us not keep them waiting."

Stacy walked to the end of the row of tables and waited for Nicholas to join her. Together the two walked over to the table and sat down. Stacy was in her usual seat and Nicholas was to her left—away from the others.

"Nicholas! Hi!"

"It's so nice to meet you."

"It's so nice to hi meet."

"Hi. Nicholas…meeting."

Stacy immediately shot warning eyes at her friends. They all welcomed Nicholas with feigned enthusiasm and stumbled over their own prepared words which they delivered in unison.

"Thank you for your warm greetings. It is great to meet you all as well."

Stacy wondered if Nicholas's own over usage of the word *great* was his rehearsed line. He did not look all too nervous and if she had not heard the word forty-seven times in the last five minutes, she would have no idea—he sat with the same eloquence and poise as always.

"Listen, Nicholas," Dylan began. "I have no doubt that you're a stellar guy, but Cody has pegged you as public enemy number one, so if I have to give you a bit of a hard time, just go with the punches."

"No problem," Nicholas assured him. "I have had to play my fair share of different roles over time and they do not always nicely align. I can also imagine Cody is quite upset with me." His eyes seemed to drift to Rachael.

She welcomed him with a smile and extended her good arm over to lay on top of his. "We are just grateful for your friendship." Then she transformed. "So, Nicholas, how are you liking America so far and, from a Dukhovian perspective, what is the meaning of life?"

Stacy gave her an odd look and kicked her from under the table, muttering a silent *what?*

Nicholas seemed to catch the exchange, but laughed and formed his own unsure reaction. "America has been…different." He seemed content on the word.

"What you expected?"

He seemed to juggle with that question for a moment. "I am not yet certain." He settled on, looking at Stacy who continued to look straight ahead at her food. She began shoveling it into her mouth, choking in response, then continuing onward.

"As for the meaning of life…" Nicholas chuckled. "It is different for everyone, but we are all meant to please the Spirits."

"Oh," Rachael emphasized the word with peaked interest. "The Spirits, you say?"

"Yes. All of our decisions, all of our beliefs, serve to please them. However, we all also have individual purposes we are meant to fulfill. So, in that way, I suppose the meaning of life is individualized."

"Huh." Rachael said stabbing her salad with a fork fiercely, her eyes looking directly at Stacy who rolled hers.

"Moving away from that subject," chimed in Cara, who sat up on her knees and leaned over the table with poise. She modestly extended her hand to be shaken. "Cara Mayue, Dylan's sister. Lovely to meet you!"

Nicholas looked from her to Dylan as if taken off guard. He accepted her hand, but seemed distracted as he shook it. Rightfully, so, Stacy thought. They were dragging him all over the place, but it was not negative, so she took it.

"Now, Nicholas, I must ask," Cara went on with a question that she most certainly did not have to ask. "Is there a special someone back home for you? A girlfriend or betrothed, perhaps? I heard that arranged marriages are common in Dukhovia."

"Who did you hear that from?" Jade asked condescendingly.

"Yeah, who are you talking to about Dukhovian marriages?" Dylan asked through squinted eyes.

"Papa," she answered simply. "Nicholas, you may continue."

Nicholas looked back and forth between the twins, over to Stacy, and even Rachael before answering. "Dukhovia is actually the opposite place to find an arranged marriage," he stated matter-of-factly. "We're known to be a country of romance and charm. Most find their significant others at a very young age, they grow up together, learn together."

"So that explains why you're here," Jade laughed, receiving an elbow in her ribs from Stacy.

"*Aw! It's so romantic, I can't stand it!*" Cara muttered the words in a dreamy, Spanish voice.

"Care, no one speaks Spanish, no one knows what you're saying," Stacy remarked.

No sooner did the words leave her mouth, Nicholas was shuffling in his seat to face her, his own words responding in the same tongue. "*It is quite magnificent. They are definitely the lucky ones.*"

The others stared at him, bewildered. It was Dylan who broke the silence. "Alright! Another Spanish speaker. Welcome to the group, bud." He stood up and clapped Nicholas on the back, to which he responded with a half-grin, half confusion.

"Wait, wait, wait," Stacy started, turning on him. "So, you speak Russian, English, Ancient Dukhovian, *and* Spanish?"

"I speak seven languages," Nicholas offered the information willingly. "Russian, Ancient Dukhovian, Spanish, French, Japanese, English, and Italian. Though, I am not perfectly fluent in Japanese."

They continued to stare at him. "*How?*" Stacy asked, anger starting to rise. She thought she was doing well with two languages, so it was easier to accept her struggling to learn ancient Dukhovian, but now learning how weak she was in comparison to Nicholas, in comparison to a true Dukhovian—how common was it that other Dukhovians spoke this many languages too? And what, she had to go sit in *Algebra* when she had five more languages to learn?

Her head ached as she thought of what other shortcomings she had as a result of being stuck in America. Perfect swimmer until the Dukhovian came along. Skilled at languages...until the Dukhovian came along. And...okay, fine, she was failing classes and he was advanced regardless, but there were more important things to focus on.

Nicholas shrugged. "I have a lot of spare time, I suppose. And a lot of interests."

It was Rachael who latched on to that one. "So, you had interest in other countries, you mean? America may not have been your only or first choice?"

Stacy eyed her with suspicion, her heart leaping into her throat then plummeting into her stomach. *What* was she asking? Was she calling him out?

Nicholas looked down for a moment and nodded. "Definitely not. There was a time in my life that I would have rather been anywhere other than Dukhovia and I suppose I prepared myself to live that life." Nicholas's voice was detached as he spoke, flat, and uninterested. But the more he spoke on the subject, the more the others wanted to know.

"Have you visited the other countries?" Miranda asked. Suddenly everyone's interest was piqued by Nicholas. Every person sat eagerly listening—even Jade. And Nicholas seemed to begin to grow from uncomfortable to comfortable with each tempted face.

"A few," Nicholas answered. "Not often and not for long enough to truly know about them. I have been to France and Spain. America has its charms, I suppose." He let his eyes look in the general direction of Stacy which Cara and Rachael quietly squealed in response to.

Stacy bit her lip and tapped her foot, her mind running a million miles a minute. So little she knew, so much confusion over Nicholas. He had interest in other countries? Further encasing her point of why he would choose America. Was it really because he wanted to know if her family was traditional? Was it really because he planned to do something positive with that knowledge? Or was it a mix of truths?

His words echoed in her head. *We can both have a chance of returning to Dukhovia.* So thrilled to get out and begin his independent life, to choose America over countries like Italy and Spain, and yet so intent on leaving. When would he know when to go?

Noticing that she had left the conversation and others were beginning to notice, Stacy snapped herself aggressively back to the subject. "Well, you've had the pleasure of being around the worst part of America so far—what do you think of our old friend, Santifini?"

Nicholas nodded his head slowly, his eyes searching. "He certainly is tantalizing, no? Strange as it seems, I have actually met Santifini before."

The others shot confused, alarmed faces once more.

Stacy felt her attention snap too quickly towards him, her facial features leaving nothing to the imagination.

"He is actually from Dukhovia. Our families did not get along well." His eyes started to drift as he spoke.

Stacy noticed the far-along look in his eyes begin to get deeper and she decided to let the subject drop. Did that explain everything she overheard? Did it explain why he was speaking so cruelly to him? Generations of fighting? But why then did Santifini act like he did not know Nicholas? About his parents? Now it was Nicholas's words that made sense, but the principal, the man they were trusted under for eight hours a day, whom needed the cross examination.

You already know... Santifini knows their family. Confirmed.

*Help me do what I came here to do and perhaps we can both have a chance at returning to Dukhovia...*hostility because of their past. Fine. But also definitely a threat.

What I came here to do...help me to find my independent life that my mother told me would be promising here? No. Help me prove that these families were wrongly banished and maybe we can end the war? Okay...fine, maybe. She accepted it for now, but again, it felt too...cut and dry. There was more. There had to be more.

Perhaps it was just his tone that had her thinking the way she was. He had said it so...absolute. It was not as if he made a choice based on the war, research, or her family to leave the country—it was absolute force.

"Really? Fini is from Dukhovia?" Dylan laughed. "Ha! They probably chased him out too."

Stacy shot him a glance, but was grateful for the comment. "I'm sure that's hardly how it happened, right Nicholas? Or is his story not as famous as ours?" *Crap. Why did she give him that way out?*

He seemed to mull over the question before shrugging. "It is not nearly as famous." Their eyes locked for a moment and, seeming to sense her suspicion, he added on. "Mostly because it is rather dull—family turmoil, a dispute amongst his cousins. That is half of Dukhovia these days. They remained behind."

"Well, I'd hate to take his side, but if we had to pick a winner of yours and old Feen's dispute based on surviving family members, it seems he is in the lead— haha."

Stacy's eyes began to widen but as soon as she heard Jade's cryptic words begin, she knew she would have to act. Snapping her head back before she fully even had time to engage her, she tore up from the table, her heart racing. How long did she have? Did Nicholas pick up on what she was saying?

"Oh, Nicholas," she said in casual, rushed words. "I forgot I wanted to show you something. We have to go."

With speed, she darted her hand across the table towards where Nicholas already stood. She flung her hand over his, readying to pull him away—then immediately retracted herself.

It was like a volt of electricity had been sent through her hand, except instead of sending a response of pain, it sent a response of—peaceful light? She could neither describe it nor make any sense of it. A wave of comfort and joy simultaneously washed over her at their touch. She felt calm, security, and trust.

When she was finally able to recover, she saw he had shoved his own hand into his pockets. Had he felt the same thing?

Stacy's friends had become aware of the strangeness and she remembered she had a goal—get Nicholas away. Without any question, he was up and following her to the opposite side of the trophy wall, away from the cafeteria.

Away from the table, Stacy stopped in front of Nicholas, unsure where to go next. So much had just happened. Did she say something about Jade? About him? Did she distract him? Did she bring up what she felt with his hand or would he think her utterly insane?

She thought about it only for a fleeting moment before deciding. Not that she spoke much of Dukhovia to her family, but when she did, it seemed the unique oddities she experienced were just that—unique to her.

He would have her committed.

Deflect it is.

"Nicholas…" Rachael appeared, her hands folded gently in front of her as she approached slowly and hesitantly. The bell had rung and people were surrounding them now. She glanced at Nicholas who seemed surprisingly calm, given Jade's comment. Stacy assumed they were safe enough.

"I wanted to apologize. I'm sorry I rushed you into meeting everyone that first night. I had wanted everyone to meet you to help you with the transition, but you respectfully told me about your boundary and I broke it."

CHAPTER TWENTY-SIX

To Stacy's surprise, an immediate, small smile formed on Nicholas's lips. "I could understand why you were so intent on my meeting them." He reached for her hand, which Rachael graciously gave, and clasped it between both his hands. Looking from her to his hand, he brought it up for a kiss.

"I'm glad we could do this," Rachael celebrated. "See you tomorrow?"

"Absolutely," Nicholas promised, returning his attention to Stacy.

"Well," she started. "I should probably get to social studies."

"You had social studies already," he corrected.

Stacy nodded slowly. "There's probably a class I need to be in."

Nicholas nodded and began to turn away. Before either of them had time to disappear, Nicholas paused and turned slowly on his heel. "Thank you, Stacy."

She looked in his understanding, knowing eyes and nodded once.

"I wondered, if it would not be too bold of me to ask, perhaps we could have lunch together again tomorrow, regardless of your cousin's attendance?"

Stacy shifted her eyes to look out at the gusts of snow beating viciously against each other in a battle of strength.

She nodded once. "I'd like that."

CHAPTER 27

AN INNOCENT ASSASSIN

Stacy tore across the hallway at the sound of the bell, leaving shouting students waving their fists and a sea of papers in her wake. She and Rachael had decided on meeting outside the office door and cornering Santifini in his office. It seemed like the best option in order to avoid his suspicion or the office staff telling them no.

She came to a squeaking halt outside the office door, darting to the side to sit in between the lockers and the janitors closet to avoid suspicion.

"What are you doing?" Rachael pressed, coming up behind Stacy minutes later.

Stacy responded by gripping Rachael's upper arm and pulling her toward her. "Avoiding suspicion. We can't be seen lurking right outside the door! He'll run before we can seize the day."

"Okay, well I heard at least three people talk about how Stacy Matthews is acting like she did one too many cold-water swims, so let us continue, shall we?"

Rachael guided a gawking Stacy off into the office. The girls tried to blend in with the array of vacating students and parents as they pushed their way to the back office and into Santifini's small, dimly lit cave of torture…um…office.

It was just as dark as Stacy remembered. Everything from the dark colored, leather chairs that her and Rachael now occupied to the blazing black walls. Even the walls of books boasted faded color, paling amongst the lack of appropriate lighting.

"Homey," Rachael chastised.

A moment later, Santifini entered the office, a complimenting dark suit accenting his tall figure. Surprise flickered on his face at the sight of them, but it was quickly replaced by his usual unmoved facial expression and accompanying tone.

"Girls," he said in a sultry tone. "What can I help you with?"

"Now is that anyway to speak to your star student who just wanted to come for a visit?" Stacy felt sarcasm heavy on her lips, half regretting them. She knew she should keep an even playing field—they were not on the defensive this time. But it also bought her time as during her incognito spy mission, she failed to consider how to even bring the subject up to Santifini. Again, what if he did not want to talk about it?

"What Stacy is *trying* to say, Mr. Santifini," Rachael interjected before Stacy got them expelled. "Is that we just wanted an update on what's going on with

Nicholas. We haven't seen him in either of our classes, but we've talked to him and we believe his actions were a mistake and he deserves a chance at reintegration."

Stacy nodded her head slowly. Well played.

Santifini looked from each of their faces as he rounded his desk and took a seat. He seemed to be reading the hidden message, but took what he heard at face value. "Well, Miss Leighton, your safety is my top priority and you have every right to know. As with any behavior student, I like to get to know them before they reintegrate with the rest of the classrooms. I want to ensure that I know what led to the issues and that putting them back in the classroom won't result in a secondary attack."

The girls waited, then Rachael spoke. "And do you think you've found what led to the issues?"

Another damning glance. "Nicholas is a new student. A lot of change at once can be rather…stressful." Dismissive.

"So, totally safe then? He'll be coming back to class soon?"

The principal's eyes locked on Stacy's for a long moment. Almost in the same way Nicholas's did. As if he was looking for something, as if he was waiting for something to happen, looking for it to happen. "It's unforeseen at this time."

Stacy and Rachael exchanged a glance.

"Do you think he could still be a danger?" Rachael asked, batting eyelashes over faux terrified eyes.

He shrugged, glancing towards the door. "Unfortunately, I need more time with him to determine that, ladies. I am certain that the unfortunate events of Nicholas's life are what led him to make the decision he did, however, that does not mean that my student body is safe. And after all, this is in fact a place of learning and not a place of great destruction."

Stacy was not sure what it was that made her heart leap when the words left his mouth, but it seemed to ring a bell that had long been silenced. The way that he said it… The way that he locked his eyes again upon hers, reading her, *waiting*…

Flashes of Dukhovia *beat* viciously behind closed eyes. Packing. Running. Fire. Tears. Sailing away. Death. Loss. Family.

She could not beat around the bush anymore.

"What unfortunate events? Do you mean in Dukhovia?"

He nodded his head slowly. She noticed the tapping of his fingers, not out of impatience, but almost as if it helped him decide what to share. As if he intended to share it in whatever portions he deemed fit.

Yes.

It was something Stacy wanted but was never used to. Santifini was far from the kindest person in the world or greatest conversationalist—but he was going to answer their questions. Anything she wanted to know about Dukhovia—he was an open, yet very forward book.

"Well, his parent's deaths for one thing. That you are aware of."

They both nodded.

"I haven't asked him about them," Stacy said with a taste of guilt. "He says that they were killed because of...because of the war. Because Dukhovia fears anything that's different and there was some...lie...I don't know the specific details, but that something happened where people think badly of his family. Sort of like mine."

He sneered at the comment. *Sneered.* Santifini is as callous as they come but he never did anything to show such outright *disgust.* "Ms. Matthews to know anything of the Andrew's family is to know that they are nothing like the Grayson's."

Thes girls exchanged silent glances, every bit of confusion and yearning etched on their faces. Was that a compliment? To the family of Cody Grayson? The kid who was suspended more than he was in school? Perhaps he had good talks with Uncle Richey. Then again, there was his close relationship with Terra—thwarted by the nothing more than formal head nods when Tom was around.

Former star-crossed lovers, perhaps.

"So, they were non-traditionalist?"

His face hardened in response; his line of vision went back to whatever was so memorizing about his door.

They waited.

"While this was long before young Nicholas's time, his family carries the burden of the start of the revolution, the attempted overthrow of the Dukhovian throne, and potential dismantling of our entire nation."

Stacy's heart faded into her chest. She knew by the coldness that rushed through her that every palpitation had to have stopped. A murderous, conniving family. The reason for her dreams, the reason for her banishment, for the fire and despair... The man who claimed to come here looking for her banished family was the reason for their banishment to begin with...

She struggled to align her thoughts and focus. Struggled to sort through the array of danger and fear that flecked her entirety.

Her voice shook, but she managed to get out her next words. "I...I didn't realize you were from Dukhovia."

His tight jaw shifted to face her, seriousness that never left solidifying. "I grew up with your grandparents. Terra and I were great friends. Has she never spoken of those days?"

Stacy shrunk into herself. "I don't ask."

His eyes were piercing now, as if he was desperate to know what she had said regarding their past. Star-crossed after all?

CHAPTER TWENTY-SEVEN

"Nicholas, he says that your families didn't get along in Dukhovia…"

"Ask what you intend to ask," he beckoned.

Stacy gulped, Rachael joining in to finish her sentence. "What led to the disagreement?"

He thought for a long moment, hands folded too gently and neatly on the desk for the conversation that was taking place, for the thickness and potency of ominous terror that hung in the air.

"Nicholas was a trained solider in the Dukhovian army. He fought under the Czar's command. Whatever he commanded. Nicholas had freedom to make his own choices too—if he wanted to use any means of force that he desired.

"Nicholas made his own choices in my family's village. We lived in the far northern part of West End, nearly to North Bridge. A raid took place on the village to seek out those who were traditional and those who intended to support the newly named heir…."

Stacy's heart stopped; she was uncertain if she was hearing anymore.

"It did not matter what Nicholas supported and what they did. If they spoke to him with so much as a tiny bit of what he considered disloyalty, they would be slaughtered on the spot.

"This village was known to defy The Czar. To do anything against his dictator-like commands. They would remain traditional as needed and they would support the newly named heir to their graves. As a result, nearly that entire village found themselves slaughtered. My family included."

Stacy's arms and legs were shaking. She did not know whether to run straight to her uncle or straight to Dukhovia. Fear stretched across her mind. Then she thought of Nicholas, the feel of their hands together, the gentleness in his words at lunch, the appreciation in his stare following…

Protect the heir…

They're coming…

Nicholas. Nicholas was coming. For that entire innocent village.

She looked over at Rachael, her lids heavy, tears welling into them.

Rachael inclined her head once. An agreement.

"Do you know why he's here now?"

The principal's eyes had become distant again. This time they did not return to Stacy and they did not seek anything in return. Instead, he stood up, walked over to his windows blocked by blinds and brown curtain panels and waited. "That I cannot say."

"But…" Stacy started, and looked to Rachael for confirmation before continuing on. "I heard him in here the other day…saying that he needed you to help him do what he came here to do. That he didn't make the choice to come here…"

He craned only his neck, eyeing Stacy for a split second. "Then I suppose you have your answer."

Confusion stopped Stacy in her tracks, giving Rachael time to take the conversation back over.

"What happens to him—if you decide he is a threat?"

Santifini sighed heavily, hands behind back, still staring out to nothingness. "It is rather a decision of state affairs than it is mine."

"What do you know of The Czar? Is he…I mean, he doesn't seem the right person to be ruling Dukhovia." It was an honest enough question. Nicholas seemed somehow tied to this Czar—doing his bidding to raid the village and if Nicholas was not sent here now by his own accord…

Santifini made no sudden movements, but said in a flat, dry tone. "He brings himself and Dukhovia closer to dictatorship every single day. He acts just as Nicholas has learned to act—with tantrum-like violence the moment he does not get his way. Ah!"

The girls both flinched, looking up at their fearless leader as he grabbed his arm as if in pain, then straightened back up as if nothing ever happened, a mutter of pinched nerves whispered under his breath. "But you can understand why I am doing my own homework on the subject and will only reintegrate him if I feel it best serves our nation. As I've stated, a nation cannot function when it's two strongest allies are at war."

Stacy was shaking her head. "But what does that mean? That because we're from Dukhovia we shouldn't be fighting?"

A shrug, and then a dismissive response of… "I'm sorry I could not be more help to you girls."

The girls looked at each other as if to prepare to leave. Rachael stood and waited patiently next to her chair, but Stacy sat, her eyes counting the pieces of shag in the carpet below. Then, she spoke in a broken, nearly whispering voice. "So, Nicholas…is dangerous. He's killed people, innocent people. He does as the Czar commands, the same Czar that commanded our banishment—and he said he was looking for us. For the band and my family…"

Rachael's eyes met Stacy's as if they wanted to add more, but in the same moment Stacy started to ask, the room shuddered and Rachael looked away.

"I will not allow harm to come to you or your family, Ms. Matthews. You may bet on that."

It was the most she ever trusted him and the safest she ever felt. The words were strong, damning. As if he could take down the Czar himself if he set foot in that room.

The two girls nodded and got to their feet. Stacy's hands were clammy and her knees wobbly as she attempted to find grounding in the spinning room and make her way to the door.

"Oh, and Ms. Matthews?"

Stacy paused.

"Listen to your instincts. Your Spirit will lead you justly, but at the end of the day, you should keep your distance from Nicholas Tyler Andrews."

Stacy and Rachael hurried away, feeling the rush of the cool wind on their faces, seeing the emptiness of the parking lot before them, but they were suffocating.

Evidence. Finally, they had solid evidence of whether Nicholas was friend or foe, safe or dangerous, whether his crime against Rachael was truly a one-time-incident of the boy struggling to cope with change after all. Evidence that said not only was he likely to reoffend, but that his history of offenses ran much deeper than a fractured wrist.

This evidence and first-hand account told Stacy so much that she so desperately needed to know. Was Nicholas here to harm her family? Was he someone she could truly gain valuable information from as an honorable Dukhovian?

The answer seemed clear. Stacy needed to help Dukhovia from the oppressive evil that clearly lived inside Nicholas. Clear from this first-hand account, but not clear from the instincts that screamed the opposite at her from day one...

"Well, that was...shocking." Rachael's words seemed to mimic Stacy's thoughts—clear of the danger, but aware, so aware of what they both felt, of those instincts that only confused Stacy all the more...

Stacy felt she barely heard Rachael or that she spoke from a dimension somewhere else entirely.

Rachael swallowed, her voice shaking. "You still think he's innocent?"

Her only response was one slow, hesitant, but unmistakenly obvious nod.

CHAPTER 28

EMOVINYA

icholas pulled his hand out of his pocket, darting his eyes towards it before it was shoved aggressively back into his jacket. He rolled his shoulders and snapped his neck. It only increased the tension that rose from the ground up around him, sending spirals in a fury of gray and black and red around him.

Stupid girl. Stupid and clueless girl. She must know something of the presence of the Spirit inside her body. She must feel the power leaking from her body. So quickly it could shift to another if she is not careful.

He felt his eyes roll subconsciously back down to his shaking hand—he still felt the power that she had left behind. Perhaps she did not know. She had mentioned her family being leery to speak of Dukhovia and her being leery to ask. He sincerely doubted then that she knew anything about the power she held. All the more dangerous. For her and Dukhovia.

Yet how easy for him. It would be all too easy to drain her of her Spirit power. It would be quite simple if she were leaking power to that degree. At least, he assumed. He had a much harder time connecting to Arkady's. Though, he assumed Arkady made it as difficult for him as possible. Power was centered in their hands due to the location of the Spirit energy. When he and Arkady would practice, they would lay their palms flat against each other and both would push outward— Nicholas to latch on and Arkady to release.

Stacy did not have to push out at all and the amount that hit him like a ton of bricks. Though, he could not quite make sense of it. Was it simply because she did not know how to control it? He had been around other, lesser heirs, children even, and never felt what he did when he touched her.

The complexity made his brain hurt. He gripped his temples and paced the school grounds. He was not certain what his plan was—but he needed to be doing something. He needed to find a way to earn her trust so he could complete his mission. He needed to find out more about her so that he could deny that entire mission. His hands covered his face. He needed *something*.

He had not even considered what the experience felt like for her. What would she be thinking and feeling in this very moment? Was she currently seeking answers or did she shove it off as normal and move on? UGH. It infuriated him even more. If only he could just speak with her, openly speak to her…without fears, without concern…without the mission.

CHAPTER TWENTY-EIGHT

He played back lunch in his head up until the incident. She had gripped her hand afterward as if it were on fire. Normal reaction, he supposed, if she never felt Spirit energy. But would her family truly have such little connection to Dukhovia? Did she never worship?

He knew everything there was to know of them, of course. However, he doubted much truth was among his knowledge, especially after speaking with Stacy his first night. If she did not know, there would be no harm in him draining her and returning to Dukhovia. She did not lose anything and Dukhovia was safe. She would be safe. He would not be a traitor.

He threw himself to his knees, drawing in a deep breath, then let it out as he rose back to his feet, closing his eyes the entire time. He centered his anger and frustration in his center and let it pass out as he rose himself. He took another breath. Prayer to the Spirits had been helping him guide his anger, but it was still there. It was always still there.

Arkady had told him to not attempt anything. To just bring her back to Dukhovia to be '*dealt with*'. He was not to harm her. He was not to drain her. She had to come to Dukhovia and she had to come willingly or disrupt the Spirit connection within all of them.

Assuming he could even convince her to come back with him. She may not have asked her family questions in the past, but what was stopping her now? What was stopping her from asking her principal? Ha. What a joke. She would be more curious than ever having met him, and him having harmed Rachael. She must want to find out who he was…especially with all the secrets. Especially with him having divulged what he did at lunch today.

IDIOT! He knew better than to make any mention of her family. They were banished and he was here seeking them, could he paint a more fearful picture for her? She was suspicious, she had to be suspicious and just waiting to gain as much information as possible before acting on her suspicions…cunning, decisive, smart…

Just like a leader.

What would be said of him? If she were to ask her family? If she were to ask *Santifini.* He grimaced. He knew that anything he would say of him or his family would be vile, cruel, and untrue.

And if he uttered even a single truthful event, he was certain Stacy would understand—would she not? If he could talk to her. If he could get her to understand the monster within…if he could understand himself…

He had only told her of him knowing Principal Santifini in order to save face. He felt her presence in the office the day he had argued with Ruslan Santifini over whether or not he should be allowed in regular classes. While the man who hid behind his suit and tie claimed Nicholas was a danger to the class, Nicholas reminded him that it was his lack of choice that allowed things in Dukhovia to play out the way they did, that if he wanted Nicholas to make better choices, he himself had a choice to make… the man in charge did not like that much.

He was unsure for certain whether or not Stacy was present, not having detected her until after he had calmed himself. *Miserable failure*, he thought to himself. He was in defense mode, the one time he should have had all senses activated at once—able to sense an attacker, able to hear and see everything that happened even remotely close to him.

He had only been able to detect a slight calming after he had said the words— several moments after. She had already gone, if she was really there. He figured allowing her to hear the most peaceful aspect of his relationship with the man would explain his reaction to some degree.

He hoped.

But he did not have the luxury of hope.

His brow began to sweat; his knuckles were so tightly held together he noticed the color nearly drained. He breathed in once and the force of his exhale could have put out a forest fire.

Then suddenly, the broken door to the school slammed shut and his nerves calmed—Rachael and Stacy stood before the school, whispering words to each other with faces that reeked of disappointment, rage, and utter complexity. The more he studied them—their body language, their unsteadiness—the more he found. Blind fury, bitter anxiousness, obvious discontent…

The sight of the heir washed him with a wave of relief he failed to ever before experience, but he knew that if he felt a feeling of comfort near her, it only meant one thing—he was on the right path.

The two girls did not seem to say much else to one another. Instead, they began walking towards the back of the school—to the sports fields, he knew.

You are becoming quite the stalker.

Nicholas shuttered, shaking off the voice he tried day after day to lose. He knew what he was doing. He had to follow Stacy around. He needed to learn more about her. He needed to know what she liked and disliked. He needed to know if she would be a fair ruler. UGH.

He typically only watched—watched from afar as she lifted her head towards the sky each time she laughed, joy radiating from her very being. Watched as she cheered her cousin on, made a joke with a friend, or managed to do a likely deadly maneuver had she landed any other way…

But today…today her face was deadly stone, her body the matching statue. The only movement that came of her today was the occasional tapping of her anxious foot. When it moved, it beat at a pace faster than his well-trained eyes could nearly comprehend. Her eyes were not full of life, but instead drained completely of their soul, replaced with a thick sheen of dust and dread.

CHAPTER TWENTY-EIGHT

Seeing her this way intrigued him to the point he felt strain he could not understand tug on his chest. He needed to know...needed to know...

And then his steps were taking him where they had not yet. These days he tried so hard to get to know her from afar, letting her in whenever possible at school, in the least overwhelming and most casual of ways—a run in here or there, a brief interaction in the packed school cafeteria—now he would approach her specifically, her intentionally...He did not have enough space or time to talk himself out of the decision.

"Stacy Grace, Rachael..."

He was surprised to see both girls jump at the sound of his voice. Rachael's face turned into a forceful smile, but Stacy remained that stone-cold, distant look. It was as if someone removed every ounce of her personality.

"Nicholas," Rachael managed. There was a shake to her voice.

What had been said? What had they heard? His heart was in this throat, thudding at maximum speed. Run. It was not too late to run. To say that he messed up and needed to start over. Would that look better or worse? What had he *done?*

No...no. He needed to fix, repair. Whatever it was what they were thinking, whether caused by himself or something someone else had said—he needed to repair.

He looked off at the game with them—football, he had learned. But he knew nothing about it and therefore not a single phrase he could utter that might make sense. Facts. Focus on facts. They had teams. It was a game. Her cousin was playing—but not today. He was out today. Why was he out?

"Is all well with your cousin?"

Stacy snapped her head up at him. *Danger. Threat.* Her eyes said that he was a threat and that snap was her way of guarding her family like a beastly animal—ferocious and terrifying. But—there was something there too. Deep in the gaze of the beast, if he could hold it for long enough without breaking, was something softer, some chance for him, some desire from her...

And a mask to maintain.

"No." She glanced down at her phone when she said the words. He recalled that she had it up to her ear on their way to walk behind the school. She had paused briefly and then exchanged what appeared to be difficult words with Rachael. He could not quite make them out, but there was some type of turmoil within the family.

"I am sorry to hear," he mused. "I am pleased to be of any assistance—shall you need me."

She seemed to scoff. "Can you stop a crazed lunatic from harassing, abusing, and emotionally damaging her child and husband? If so, sign right up."

So, was that the reason for her face? The reason for her to completely disappear? Did it have nothing to do with him? He sank into the seat next to her, causing her to push a few steps closer to Rachael. No. It was him too. There was more.

"I am sorry he is experiencing that. It can be rather...difficult." It was all he could muster as images of his own life fled through his brain. His father, once loving, kind, and compassionate, turning into a man known to terrorize, brutalize, destroy...

Stacy looked him up and down, her eyes lingering for a moment on his tense shoulders. Then she looked away. Not another word.

Confusion ran through him. He cleared his voice. "Rachael, may I have a word in private?" He gestured to the side of the bleachers in which they stood. Tall, metallic things that no one in their right mind would choose to sit for long periods of time. At least he assumed as much.

Stacy's face was immediately taken aback. That ferocious beast returning.

Rachael's face flecked with surprise and some reluctance, but she graciously nodded her head and stood to her feet.

Stacy snapped her head in Rachael's direction, a silent plea and perhaps even a shout echoing on her facial features.

Rachael simply squeezed her friend's shoulders, gave a small grin, and walked towards the end of the bleachers—out of earshot, but not eyeshot. Smart girl.

"What is going on with Stacy?" He asked the moment Rachael stopped and turned to him. "She seems very...frustrated."

Rachael looked over at her friend, biting her lip. "That's just how Stacy gets when she gets angry. She detaches; she becomes sort of...cold. Ruthless, even, if you don't watch out." She added with a half-hearted wink.

Nicholas took the words in understandably. Could he judge her reaction when she felt for her cousin experiencing something he knew to be horrible? Could he judge her angry response when his own was the reason her best friend now hung onto the handrail of the bleachers with pink-encased fingers.

"I understand." He looked back at Stacy. She was facing towards them. While she stayed in her spot, her stance was ready—feet apart, hands at her sides, fists clenched, eyes unapologetically on Nicholas—perhaps her family taught her a thing or two after all.

"She seems—leery of me. Of course, I do not expect the forgiveness of you two after my actions, but...it seemed as though I was earning them and now we have gone backwards. I do not know what I did."

His disappointment was not feigned, but he hoped she read its sincerity, the desire making him feel just as cunning as he was meant to be. But it was the most honest he had ever been. Honesty seemed to flow naturally and carefree when it came to conversation with Rachael. No one in Dukhovia was easy to talk to—he would be screamed at, beaten, or worse. From Stacy, he feared this reaction, but Rachael...she was peace, she was calm.

CHAPTER TWENTY-EIGHT

She gave a sincere warm smile, even reaching her good hand over to rest on the top of his, giving it a gentle squeeze. "I already told you she's difficult, it's too late for regrets now," she smiled. "Fiercely loyal and fiercely stubborn. *But* you want the real secret to her heart? *Honesty*, Nicholas. No matter the severity of that honesty, if Stacy has your full trust in her, she'll be an open book to you."

Surprise flecked across his face. He arched his back, his own hands gripping the handrail for support. Total honesty? He considered it. She had already forgiven something that, for someone so fiercely loyal and devoted to her friends and family, was as good as murder. What if he truly did fully open up to his own reluctance? Would she be understanding, sympathetic even?

He gulped. "No matter the severity?"

Rachael tensed her jaw, but nodded nonetheless. "She doesn't know—that you asked specifically about her. I only said that you were interested in the band. She knows that to not be true now." Her eyes narrowed. "Promise me you won't hurt her. Or I won't be nearly as forgiving."

He was shaking his head with fierceness. "I have no desire to harm anyone, Rachael. I swear my allegiance to you. I do not want anything to happen to Stacy or her family." It was true, if he could find a way to prevent it, he would. But if he could not find a way...

"I never meant for anyone to get hurt," he hoped that, whatever she may know, he knew that he extended that past her, past America. "I just want a chance to get to know her."

Rachael looked into his eyes and back to her friend, still in her defensive state. Then, there was a crack in the bleachers and one of them split behind them. Rachael turned and grimaced. She looked at Nicholas and the crack grew louder, split louder. All at once, he turned to see Stacy bolt—not away from the disaster as one might expect—but towards them. The groan in the bleachers grew louder as they started to give out.

Rachael's eyes grew wide with horror and she pushed Nicholas off the bleachers towards the field, where the players were now beginning to turn their heads, some coaches rushing over. Caught off guard, Nicholas began to fall, but reached a large arm upward to pull himself back up.

He looked over and saw Stacy still running, until the bleachers split down the middle and Stacy fell through the opening, screaming as she fell between. Nicholas's eyes widened, he craned his neck attempting to see the bottom, but if she fell all the way through, he could not see it.

Rachael was grabbing her head, backing up slowly, more of the bleachers cracked, then the ground itself began to shift and widen. If he did not know better, he would have guessed it was an earthquake, but he did know better.... He knew all about this gift Rachael had been somehow blessed with.

"Rachael! You have to relax!" He shouted over the creaking and sliding of metal on metal. "Center your emotions, imagine the energy you feel is a ball!"

Her trembling body turned with caution to face him, a slow and nervous motion, carefully removing shaking hands from her ears. Her face twisted into a puzzling look, but she seemed as though she attempted to obey.

Then failed miserably when the earth began to widen to her left—just outside of where the bleachers were.

Simultaneously, Stacy crept out of the bleachers, planting her palms against the walkway, and lifting herself with seeming ease. Nicholas looked towards her, ready to run to her side, but then the group of filth he fought on the first day of school started making their way towards Rachael, pointing and laughing. Her body started to convulse and she shrank to her knees.

The coaches from the football field had two of their team members pull Stacy off the bleachers as she tried to get to Rachael. Another coach bellowed at the group of boys to back away. Then they were coming for Nicholas…

He quickly looked around him, then at Rachael. Objects were flying around them now—bricks, shards of sharp, piercing metal. Nicholas dodged the bellowing coaches and chunk after chunk of hurling debris until he was with Rachael.

Stacy was shouting for him to back away—whether out of anger or his protection he did not know or have time to consider. He approached her as quickly as he could while maintaining gentleness. Her eyes widened at him, shaking her own head to back away. But before she could move herself, he was grabbing both her wrists. He extracted his engraved knife from his pocket, slashed into her cast, and threw it into the crack in the earth.

"I apologize for this," he mumbled quickly, before pressing both of his thumbs deeply into the inner part of her wrists.

She howled in pain, dropping to her knees as the rush of power and pain coursed through her body, centered back *into* her body. The wind stopped howling, the world stopped moving, and Rachael's silent body fell into his lap.

He caught her gently, cradling her head in his arms. "Doctors!" He shouted, holding two fragile wrists as he scanned for her pulse, the already injured one now a swollen bulge of black, blue, and purplish hues. "I need doctors NOW!"

The shocked mass of onlookers stood frozen in their spots until the urgency in his voice called them into action. Moments later, phones were being flipped open, whether to spread the word of what had happened or to call for help—he could not focus on. He only focused on maintaining the positioning of the girl in his arms.

Remember, head aligned with stomach, remainder of body down. Nicholas nodded, a one-time thank you to Erlik. *Center her power,* he recalled. *Power in the stomach, spiritual connection in the head…*

Yes, Nicholas, yes… Nicholas swallowed. The words were Erlik's he knew it, they were comforting and gentle, *encouraging*…but the voice he heard them in were that of his fathers.

CHAPTER TWENTY-EIGHT

With shaking hands, he relaxed Rachael's body, propping her up against the left side of his body so that her stomach and head were at equal lengths, then allowing the rest of her body to drop.

"What's going on? What did you do?" Stacy's words were rushed and anxious, but he could tell she was not certain whether she meant them to be blameful or thankful. He was helping, certainly she could tell he was helping.

Before he had time to answer, the ambulance arrived and Rachael was rushed into the back. Stacy quickly tore off after her, pausing only a minute in which she beckoned Nicholas to follow her—then kept running. A single command.

Shocked, but unwilling to miss out on the opportunity—he rushed to follow, jumping into the back of the quickly speeding, loud vehicle before him.

Nicholas had never traveled in a vehicle before; save for the two aircrafts he had the unfortunate pleasure of experiencing on the way in. He had been in carriages and obviously on fast-moving horseback—but none of those felt like this. None of them mimicked the fast pull around corner, the loud noises and bright lights echoing around both the inside and outside of the vehicle. He felt himself turning white and leaning over with nausea before they were nearly a mile out from the school.

Stacy eyed him curiously but said nothing, instead turning her head to a focused, direct woman who appeared out of the front of the vehicle.

"Lawl, do Tom and Terra know she's coming in?"

The short-brown haired woman's head bobbed once in the affirmative. "They will be waiting once we arrive. Don't worry, Ms. Matthews, we know the drill when it comes to Ms. Leighton."

Stacy nodded her gratitude.

Nicholas felt his blood run cold and freeze over. *Tom and Terra?* Her grandparents. Her Dukhovian grandparents, who knew all the secrets of his family, likely of him? He could not face them. They would find out he was involved whether he faced them or not, but to meet them now? Under these circumstances? To question why he knew so much on the subject of her powers?

No. *Have to run, have to run...*

Nicholas could barely hear anything over the roar of the vehicle, the thudding of his heart, and the racing thoughts of sheer panic that occasionally yielded to thoughts of his proximity to the nearest window. He nearly missed the woman's barking order of "you'll need to be able to repeat to them everything that happened", until he heard Stacy's response of "don't worry, we will".

Panic. Clear and yet complicated and inescapable panic. The enclosed vehicle and his inability to access fresh air made it all the worse. He felt his fingers begin to tap and his heart begin to race. He was already running.

They came to a halting pause at the front of a tall, beige colored building. It rose and rose with so many floors; he wondered how it stayed upright. No building was like it in Dukhovia—not even the palace. Rows and rows of windows aligned the outside of it, with a bright red sign deeming the Heart of America Hospital—just like the airport.

Her grandparent's must have owned both.

Nicholas was thrown forward when it came to its stop, then it backed up quickly and the back doors were thrown open. Nicholas looked at every angle for an exit, thanking the massive rush of people that surrounded the ambulance the moment the doors were pushed open.

He looked out at the sea, then down at Rachael. He was certain her grandparents would know exactly what was going on, but it had gotten to this point, she had seemed so uninformed and ill-trained, perhaps they did not…

He had one foot out of the ambulance, but paused, turning towards Stacy. "Her Spirit energy is centered in her head and the power in her abdomen—that is why they need to remain level. The rest of her body lying dormant helps it to flow appropriately. Emovinya is the name of the power."

"What?!" Stacy asked in wild shock. But, then she and the rest of the onlookers became perfectly distracted by Rachael's shuffling of breath and opening of her eyes.

By the time they looked up again, Nicholas was gone.

CHAPTER 29

THE ACT OF CONFIRMATION

Stacy flung her head around wildly, her heart racing as she ran up the corridor with Rachael on the stretcher. She was quiet, attempting to remain as calm as she could—but she looked like she would snap at any moment.

"Just…c-center it," Stacy stuttered, racking her brain for the words Nicholas had said amongst the confusion and jumbled mess that was once a functioning mind. Where the hell was he? The only person in the world who had ever been able to give her any type of help with this curse and he just disappears after likely her biggest fall out since her first...

The earth cracked. She had never done that before and, again, it was during a talk with Nicholas. But he had not touched her. He had not looked at all angry and she did not hear him raise his voice—she stood just a few feet away ready to pounce the moment she did.

Understanding clicked in her mind and she gave a grateful but annoyed look at her friend. *She was protecting me.* Nicholas was likely just asking her what Stacy's problem was. After all, he had no idea what they found out after the conversation with Santifini. They went from inviting him to lunch, laughing and getting to know him, making plans to hang out again to…this.

What. The. Hell.

So much had happened in the last two hours, Stacy could barely keep her head on straight. Nicholas being a murderer, Santifini being an open Dukhovian history book, Rachael having another incident around Nicholas, Nicholas *knowing* about this condition—all while still reeling off the spark of the two of their hands touching. She still felt the tingling sensation left behind.

Beeping sounded from the machine that connected Rachael—her blood pressure was either rising or falling, she did not know—but she heard people yelling and saw Rachael's facial features fading in and out. But then she felt a tug.

Stacy looked down and Rachael was shaking her head. "It wasn't his fault this time." Then she was gone again.

Stacy was pushed out to the waiting room without so much as a word. Hours of uncertainty passed. No one asked Stacy for her account, they just worked relentlessly to figure out—how. She felt isolated and in the dark, just the same as anything that ever had to do with Dukhovia—which was apparently where this strange power somehow originated. She had never heard of it and never got any information—not from anyone other than Nicholas.

She could only hear from the whispers of other passing nurses, doctors, aids, and specialists that whatever was happening in Rachael's body was strange, unexplainable, and totally senseless.

Senseless—was it not all? Stacy closed her eyes, trying to center herself. She had spirituality in her somewhere, right? What better time to find it.

Protect them. They're coming.

They're coming. More than one person. Nicholas was only one person. Did that mean that her dream was not speaking of Nicholas?

She smacked her head intentionally off the wall. Maybe it would start making this make sense. She did not want to keep going hot and cold on Nicholas. She knew it was not practical or mature and she knew it would fail to solve her problem—but it was simply her go-to. Shut down, fill with rage. It protected the people she loved from stuff she could not find a practical solution to—because she did not have enough information. She never had the information, the history, the knowledge.

He told Rachael he came because he wanted to meet the band—not that he had interest in their music. So, was that technically a lie? Stacy and Cody were Grayson's who were part of the band. Looking for the band was the easiest and most known way to find them. Nicholas's explanation of comparing family shunning's made more sense than him wanting to be in a rock band.

Fine. But he was still looking for her family specifically. That still made her leery. But she felt comfortable with him. He was not cunning and full of anger. He was kind and inquisitive. She supposed he could have been trained to use charm to deceive. Dukhovia did seem like a mess, after all.

Then there was Dukhovia. Flashes of the war had started coming to her during class, when she showered, when she breathed the wrong way. Now that she was wrapping her head around the outcome of what war actually looked like, she wanted more answers—why? What was being done to help? What were the odds? But most importantly, she needed to know how she could help, and the reality of that felt like the equivalent of finding a pot of gold at the end of a rainbow.

So, then she was left with Nicholas. Nicholas who, even if he was a bloodthirsty killer, gave her answers. Except...

She rubbed her hands together. What she felt was definitely more than a shock from static cling. It was like the time Cody and Rachael were messing around with the heart defibrillator machine at the hospital. It sent a vibration through her hand and up to her arm. But then it seemed to veer off, sending a similar, yet different sensation throughout her body. Then it faded, replaced by a sense of warmth that she felt she did not have all the words to explain. It was like the aftermath of waking from a dream where she had everything she ever hoped for—purpose, appreciation, recognition, answers, peace...

She was surprised to still feel some of that lingering behind. She was even more surprised when she felt the feeling resurge the moment Nicholas was near her, despite finding out...

Ugh. Santifini had never been their friend, but this seemed like something pretty off-the-wall to make up. He seemed so concerned and so ready to tell everything...

She could have asked more. That much was clear. She shut down under the weight of the information. Logical, she supposed, but now a hinderance. What exactly were Nicholas's orders that led to the murders? Was it even Nicholas's call or was he just part of the order?

She narrowed her eyes and drew in a breath. Santifini had said that the ruler of Dukhovia was at least nearing dictator-like behavior. He said that Nicholas was mimicking that behavior. If that was true, she could infer that Nicholas did in fact make that call. But all she had was his side, his information, and she had lived long enough with hearing untruthful statements about her own family to know that opinion was just that—opinion, formed one-sided from things that were witnessed. Witnessed.

At least some of it had to be true and if Nicholas was as close to this dictator as Santifini said, taking direct orders from him—*danger. Run.*

She craned her head back again and then threw her head into her lap, covering her face with her hands. The abnormal dryness of her usually sweaty palms reminded her that she had not had anything to eat or drink since lunch time. And she could not even remember if she ate then.

Their first interaction with Nicholas as a group seemed so long ago, weeks instead of mere hours. Everything had gone so well. She was getting answers, she was feeling confident—and then everything shifted. Just like it always had and she never knew why. Just like it would again and she would never know why if she kept running and shutting down instead of demanding answers.

Her eyes closed under the weight of the day and her lack of sleep. She was not anticipating that would change anytime soon, so she gave into their heaviness.

...

She was not sure how many hours had passed by the time someone finally acknowledged her, but the sky was darkening and she had said no to at least three people requesting she "go to the café and eat". She refused. She was certain she should eat and was hungry beyond belief, but the resistance that rose in her stomach the moment her thoughts resurfaced told her otherwise. Besides, if people were finally ready to listen, she needed to be ready and able to talk.

Stacy was not surprised when the first footsteps she heard rushing towards her were Cody's. He had a look of craze in his eyes, seemed to be struggling to stay straight—and he was badly beaten.

"What the hell happened?" Stacy proclaimed the moment he was before her. She could tell he was still sick—worse than this morning. Snot drenched the outer parts of his nose until he smeared it with his sleeve, his eyes were encased in a fogginess that forced struggle on him to fully open them, and he looked more physically exhausted than she had ever seen.

"That fucking asshole," he breathed.

Stacy's heart sank—but she was surprised it took him this long to figure it out.

"That fucking asshole hurt her again!"

"So, what did you do, find out where he lives and show up on his door step?"

"Dad's office is perfectly organized. It was easy to find his address."

Stacy was surprised at the anger she felt towards her cousin, but found it nearly coupled with understanding. "*Code,*" she said directly. "You're joking, you have to be joking." She assessed his face and body language. He was bent over his knees out of breath—he had to be sick. Did he run all the way here or just up the steps?

"Did he hit you?" She asked, registering again that his snot covered sleeve also wiped his face clean of blood, revealing a gash on his cheek to match the already clear swell above his eye. His knuckles were also both caked in dried blood, several of them leaking fresh.

He was quiet for a moment, then shook his head. "You'd think if he's going to keep acting like such a stupid fuck, the least he can do is fight back like a man. He just stood there, dodging me." He glanced down at his hands to answer Stacy's confusing glances. "I punched out his windows and then fell out of one onto the fire escape a few stories below."

Stacy could not help it—she stifled a laugh.

Cody shot her an angry look.

"He didn't even fight back and you look like that?" She laughed again. "So, what did he do?"

Cody shook his head. "Tried to help me, but I tried shoving him off. Guy is like a freaking ape. He caught himself with one arm and flung himself back up to his window. He might have superstrength too."

Stacy lifted her eyebrow with humor. *Any excuse to make this less humiliating.*

"He went back in and called for help—which is when my dad showed up."

Stacy squinted. "Ooo I know Chief Grayson was full of disappointment at the sight of that."

"Well, he's not happy with your boyfriend either," Cody retorted, earning an instant dark glare. "He's downstairs now talking about filing charges and sending him back to Dukhovia."

Stacy was instantly defensive, her heart in her throat. "He didn't do anything— I was there the whole time."

"What happened then?"

Stacy bit her lip, realizing what revealing everything they found out to Cody meant.

She had a long time to sift over the information—what Santifini said, what Nicholas said and how he had acted. She thought of everything he had said, everything he had done. All of the inconsistencies—but she focused on what Santifini told her too and she focused on today.

Her gut instinct. And her gut instinct told her on repeat that Nicholas was safe. But she still had yet to decide how far she was willing to take that. If she was back to taking it slow, or if this would be as far as they'd ever get—just talking in between the halls whenever they happened to run into each other or if they would ever both be afforded the conversation they deserved. Well, she deserved.

No matter what, as she sat there, being ignored and left without so much as an answer to whether or not Rachael was conscious, one thing stuck with her—she was sick and tired of being told *nothing*.

She shrugged. "We found some stuff out from Santifini about Nicholas. He found us afterwards and I wasn't sure I wanted to talk to him so he asked to talk to Rachael. I had my eyes on him the whole time. He didn't say anything wrong; he didn't raise his voice. He didn't lift a finger. I think Rachael just got overwhelmed. She didn't know whether to lead us closer together or further apart."

Cody sifted through the information. He relaxed hearing that he did not harm Rachael, after all, but she was still in the hospital and she was still confused...

"What did you find out about him?"

She knew she could not get away with it that easily. "Just—family issues. Their families didn't get along and Nicholas has a heavy past with the military."

"Heavy past with hurting people you mean? He's dangerous? That's why Feens isn't letting him back in class? Why hasn't this idiot just left the country?"

Why indeed, she wondered. If it just so happened that the family he sought lived in the same town as the man that hated him, why did Nicholas not abandon his mission and return to Dukhovia? A man with the power to make a phone call and send him back to Dukhovia... but he was more intent on learning about Stacy's family than he feared getting sent back home—or worse. Why?

Stacy said nothing, and the silence was filled the sudden appearance of Tom and Terra.

Both of them jumped to their feet.

"She's stable," Tom said in a gentle voice. Both he and Terra glanced at Cody disapprovingly, but said nothing, and she assumed they had already been in talks with Uncle Richey.

"The amount of power she used and fear caused her body to shut down and put her in shock. No major issues—she just needs rest." Terra added with a smile. Then her brow narrowed. "Something was different this time." She looked at Tom whose face let on to nothing, but Terra took it as confirmation. "So much of her power was centered in her abdomen—it seemed to help her. Usually all of the pressure builds up in her head and makes the pain much worse."

Stacy hesitated, biting her lip as she sifted through the information. She wished so desperately Nicholas stayed. It was the most information they ever learned and it was still nothing without him there to explain. But she could not blame him. Everything was so new, the mix of his lost look and pale skin made it look like he was going to vomit all over the back of the ambulance. He would have witnessed Cody blaming him now when genuinely, he was just trying to help.

But what kind of murderer also genuinely wants to help an innocent girl suffering? One that he could easily just walk away from and not give two craps about.

"It was Nicholas," she replied. "He told her to center the energy she felt from her power and then…" She gulped, looking at Cody, but decided he would likely find out anyway. "She couldn't do it, so he ran up to her, cut off her cast and gripped her by her wrists. Everything that was moving stopped and Rachael passed out."

Cody was forming a fist; she heard heavy breathing and then he tore towards the stairs.

"What are you gonna do, fall out another window?" Stacy called over.

Cody stopped at the door, paused for a long moment, then came back towards them. He did not release his tension. "I need to see her."

Terra nodded and began leading them down the hall. "So, he applied pressure at the pressure points in her wrists which triggered the rest of her to calm down. Fascinating. Some type of anatomical relaxation response?"

Tom began to speak, but Stacy interrupted. "I think it's spiritual," she blurted, then lowered her voice to a whisper, knowing these types of talks were forbidden amongst their family for this very reason. "Emovinya. Nicholas called it emovinya."

Terra and Tom both stopped walking and looked at each other. "Emovinya? What else did he say about it?"

"N-nothing," Stacy stuttered out the words. "That the spiritual connection is in her head and the power in her abdomen. Why, what does it mean?"

"We'll let you know if it's what we think," Terra answered, her and Tom began shuffling off down the hall to the left. "Rachael's room is the last one on the right. 203."

Stacy watched them go eerily. She was used to not getting answers, but this was a time she thought she would be included. Rooky mistake.

Her and Cody continued down the hall. She was ready to give the lovebirds time before she found a way to get Cody to leave and rehash the exact details of their day with Rachael. She had her own opinions and thoughts, but she needed her to weigh in—both in aid and out of respect.

Cody paused in the hallway and flung himself into the empty room next to Rachael.

"What are you...?"

Stacy watched as he glanced in the mirror, fixing the spiking of his hair and washing all the excess blood from his body. Then, he went to the floral vase against the window and removed the flowers, carrying them back out of the room with him.

Stacy smirked. "Very smooth."

Cody gave her a chastising smile in return.

"Ready?" Stacy asked, breathing in until her feet remembered how to move.

Cody started to nod, but then his brow creased and he stopped. "I want you to know that if she says even one thing that contradicts what you told me, that if her side of the experience was that he did even the slightest thing to harm her—he's dead."

Stacy tore her burning eyes away from her cousin. She balled up her own fists and swallowed hard. "Agreed."

CHAPTER 30

THE DEVIL'S GAME

*N*icholas ran his finger along the white trim window, fingering the edge delicately with Raspcyrt powder. Its concealment properties did its magic as he blew onto it. It would render any trace of him by anyone—heir or other—impossible. He smiled and thanked himself. He had gone over all of his mixtures before he left and struggled to decide which to bring—he decided right.

At the same time, he wondered how quickly he would die if he threw himself into the path of an oncoming vehicle. Would he be able to succumb to his injuries before he healed?

He had already scaled the outside of The Matthew's Residence. It was all clear. Not a soul was home. Perfect. Except for the fact that he had hoped he would not need to succumb to this type of…intrusion. It was invasive and horrific—not at all an act one should commit when they were attempting to gain trust. He should not need the cheat, should be able to rely on his own skill. Except he could not. Because the skills he needed in America, to earn American trust, were not nearly as congruent to a Dukhovian as he had hoped, nor were they as identical to an American as he had been trained. Stacy was her own monster. Her family was their own monster.

And that was the biggest reason this intrusion weighed on him so heavily—her family. They were all nearly as highly trained as he was—able to detect, able to hear and sense. If he was caught, he might as well just head back to Dukhovia himself. But it was worth it, now, it needed to be.

Stacy was acting so strangely around him today and he did not know why. Where they were to where they now existed simply did not make any sense and he had no other way of knowing the reason without doing some type of prying.

Perhaps it was simply what was going on with her family. Rachael had said that she shuts down when bad things happen. Or perhaps it was something about him. He had seen those daggers before and he knew them. He knew when they were meant for him.

He scaled the house one more time for measure—up and down to best his ability. He had never cleared such a large structure before. They did not have the luxury of two-story homes in Dukhovia, save for the palace. Any larger bases or camps he infiltrated were one ground level as well.

Nicholas sighed. It probably would have been more favorable for him to stay at the hospital. He would show that he knew he did no wrong, he would be supportive. Instead, here he was, crawling through her window in order to invade her privacy.

It was the wrong choice. He felt it in his gut and in his mind. But it was too late now. The darkness in the sky confirmed that. Hours had passed, surely things had been settled by now. Yet, the family was not home. Were they all at the hospital? He recalled from the day he followed her home that Rachael and Cody lived right next door. Their homes were also dark and appeared vacant.

He lifted the bottom of the window up easily. Did they really lack such security? He would have been shot by at least three different spotters by now trying to get into the castle. How easily it would be to simply sneak into the heir's room and slash her throat. He was ordered not to harm her, but a million people in Dukhovia wanted her dead and *could* make the trek to find her. Did her family perhaps not know?

He gritted his teeth as he crawled through and was greeted by absolute darkness. His eyes would adjust. He was confident he was alone, but remained as still and silent as possible, uncertain when he could expect his hosts to return home.

The house was nothing like he anticipated—though, he failed to truly anticipate anything. From what he could tell in the dark, it was large and spacious. He entered through a back window that led him into a small room littered with shoes. A purr in the dark corner told him that laundry was washing.

He moved slowly, staking out the rooms, hearing them, sensing them, smelling them, before he moved. Then onto the next. He was not sure where he would learn what he hoped to learn, but he was certain he was looking for her sleeping chambers—her bedroom.

American homes were, in fact, something that Arkady went over with Nicholas. Of course, the one technique he did not intend to utilize. He knew to expect them to be lavish, he knew to expect, at minimum, a living room, kitchen, multiple bedrooms and bathrooms. He knew to expect it—yet the realization of it was still unnerving.

Stacy's home had not one, but what appeared to be three living areas. After entering the backroom (a mudroom, perhaps? He did not quite understand the term), he was in the kitchen. The kitchen alone was the size of his cottage back in Dukhovia—perhaps larger. Most Dukhovian homes were one room, though having one or two bedrooms was becoming more common. They did have indoor plumbing for restrooms and showers, though, it was nothing quite as extravagant as what he utilized even in his simple apartment.

All Dukhovian homes had some type of open living space with a fireplace that was generally cooked over, and a separate space for prepping the meals and doing any washing. He did not feel he was missing out with that experience. It felt comfortable, perhaps that was why Dukhovian families were generally closer.

His stomach twisted at the thought alone. How dare he make such an accusation, knowing it was his own father whom delivered the large scar barring down his right arm that Stacy stared at for the duration of swim class. He wondered if she would have kept her eyes to herself if he were like the other men and removed his shirt. He would do no such thing—they would all have their judgmental, condescending looks glued to him.

He tensed his shoulders, releasing the memory, the thought, and smells of his own home. Barley, stock, and vegetables. It always smelled of barley, stock, and vegetables. It was always warm, even when there were icicles in his bedroom.

No matter what he did, whatever type of day he had—a warm bone-crushing hug was waiting for him. He had his mother, he had his clothing, he had a warm meal. He always had all he needed—until the home of ash no longer smelled of barley, stock, and vegetables. Until only the lasting smell of singed bodies and wood was all that remained.

Nicholas blinked a wetness out of his eyes, making his way over to the fridge. The fridge, Arkady had mentioned, sometimes held memos—appointments, accomplishments, notes. He could not risk turning on a light, but again coated his fingers in Raspcyrt and ran his hand down its side, attempting to angle anything he found against the moonlit window.

Congratulations on your demotion, Grace! Wishing you many more failures ahead – Your second failure

He recognized Stacy's handwriting, but was cautious of the note. Was it pure sarcasm? If so, to what did it reference? Why did she call her by her first name? In Dukhovia, to honor your elders and family meant to call them a chosen respectable title. His mother was his mama—someone who gave their all, who cared for his needs above their own. To call her Anecka was to dismiss all of that…but he supposed things were different here.

He continued to check the fridge. They did, in fact, have memos—a lot of them. The entire fridge was cased in some type of photo, joke, or encouraging or damning comment. Nothing useful, nothing practical.

She is loyal, kind, is close with family, a sense of humor is the way to her heart…That tells you more than you need to know to see she is a right fit for Dukhovia.

Nicholas hissed at the voice in his head. "She does not need to be a fit for Dukhovia," he whispered back. "She needs to be talked into coming home with me. I can use all these things to talk her into coming home with me."

Just like Arkady always planned. Use your charm and looks to trick her instead of your brains and brawn to fight for her.

Nicholas heaved deeply, catching his breath before his anger caught up to him. He sent a glass magnet shattering to the ground.

"Bleestay," he swore, quickly gathering the pieces and depositing near the trash can.

Good person, fine. Moving on.

He abandoned the kitchen, shifting into the room next to it—a living room. It was quite simple for American standards—a television set and a long couch. He sat in the living room for a moment. It gave away nothing, yet he wondered, only for a passing moment, the hype behind the television. What did it look like? What was its purpose?

He supposed he could ransack the area to find out which type of movies she liked, but she would—or at least *should*—know that he would never have seen a movie in Dukhovia. She had been there before, he knew, she had to have known that much.

He sensed an unreasonable anger rise in him at the thought of her trip to Dukhovia. He knew little of it, but she was there, she had met another solider and...

He rose from the couch, pounding down his fists as he went and continued on. There was a type of extension on the kitchen, though it was still a part of the same room, housing a long wooden table with more chairs than family members. *The family dinners*, he vaguely remembered. If they bought a large table specifically for their once-a-week dinners, family must be more important than he realized.

Noted.

To the right of that, the house shifted into a smaller sitting room. He quickly moved out of there and then across the hall. There was yet another sitting room, though this one housed a large desk and smaller, square screen—computer. He had one in the apartment as well, though he had not gone near it.

At the end of that room, was a hallway. He casually walked down it and seemed to strike gold.

Bedrooms.

He tore from one end of the hall to the next, working quickly, yet quietly. He blew Raspcyrt on every door knob and in every room. Yet they all seemed empty or nearly empty. At least of what he needed.

One appeared to be a simple guest room. He would not even know the word had he not been raised in the palace, no ordinary homes in Dukhovia had them—or could even fathom having them. It was complete with a dressed bed and dresser with a few miscellaneous items: a toothbrush and soap. A journal and a few books lay next to the bed. He wondered if Stacy read and if so, what she liked.

He sat on the bed for a moment, strumming his fingers along the edge of the pages, feeling the smoothness of the spine and delicate lettering. It had been so long since he read a book on his own accord. So long since he was able to lose himself in a different world, feel connection, feel hope, dream...

He had to keep moving. There was no time for dreams.

The next room was definitely lived in, though not by Stacy. It was neat and tidy to a fault, stocked with men's clothing, men's magazines and everything a growing man could ever want. Her brother.

He exited quickly. Another guestroom and then finally a room that appeared to be an office of sorts. Except, instead of paperwork, machines and maps littered every table top. He spent the most time here, wondering what they were building, what they were attempting to solve by making what they were...

As he sifted over page after page and tool after tool, he learned her father was a rather skilled inventor. Whatever he set his mind to, he usually accomplished— but he played by the rules. He frequently noted Dukhovian serums that could easily do what he needed to do, but broke down those serums to finding legal, American ways to mimic the behavior.

Honest.

Valued family, valued honesty.

She's shaping up to be quite the ruler.

Nicholas flung his arm backward, ready to strike, ready to send the papers before him everywhere.

He paused.

Breathe in.

He extended himself to his spirit.

Breathed.

He walked out of the office, shutting the door behind him. Curious that the bedrooms were so separated, he began to make his way back towards the front door. And directly across from that... lie a flight of stairs. He ascended them carefully, but, feeling anxious for his time, he tried to glance into these rooms rather quickly.

The first he immediately knew belonged to her parents. A large, open space opened up to a nearly-equally large bathroom and attached closet. The remainder of the upstairs rooms consisted of closets, another spare bedroom, another bathroom, and finally...

There was a long, dark hall that split from the main hall upstairs. He made his way down and breathed in. Connection. He had not even tried to rely on his connection. He supposed he wanted to look around the entirety of the home—to learn of the family as well as the heir herself. But now he felt it—the small tug at his heart and veins, the feeling of calm encapsulating him. The sweet smell of vanilla and pine swirling around him...

He immediately chose a door knob and walked into the bedroom of Dukhovia's strongest heir.

CHAPTER 31

A NEW PERSPECTIVE

Stacy had decided against going in with Cody entirely. At the last second, she determined that agreeing on separate visits would be the best way to get Cody out. Depending on the state of Rachael, he would never leave her side, otherwise. Besides, she had a visit with her uncle to contend with.

Cody agreed with some suspicion, but he was focused on his goal and his goal was Rachael, so there was little disagreement.

She immediately started heading for the hospital office, her feet flying down the stairs, two steps at a time. She ignored any attempts of onlookers telling her to watch where she was going. She had a clear path and she would make it there anyway she had to.

She shuffled past a field of nurses and radiologists, through large double glass doors, past large brass ones, and into Tom and Terra's office. The room was huge and it was easy to get lost within its borders. It was not nearly as dark and dismal as Santifini's office, but ran a close second.

Walls upon walls of shelving encompassed the perimeter: open, closed, lined with books, lined with papers or medical equipment. Large glass meeting tables littered the far left and the far right, leaving the middle open to a large, oak desk.

Then there was another sectioned off part of the office to the right—a more private area with lounging and an attached restroom. This is where Stacy flung herself over to, expecting to find her doomed uncle.

She heard muffled voices from beyond the door, but was met with a locked, steel knob. Shaking it constantly, she began shouting, repeating 'open up, open up' until it finally crept open and she filed in with Uncle Richey and her grandparents.

She assessed the situation for all of two seconds—taking in Richey's concerning, desolate eyes and Tom and Terra's worn, nearly drained faces. Richey was in uniform, but it was haphazard, as if he put it on in a rush. She looked at the clock briefly, realizing he was likely off hours ago and then responded to Cody's distress call and donned his uniform. Perhaps he was even home for a few hours to deal with Yasana.

She gulped, not wanting to regret her words, wanting to be gentle towards her uncle, but needing to back Nicholas. "Uncle Richey, you can't report Nicholas. None of this is his fault, he didn't do anything, I swear it. You can talk to Rachael, talk to the entire football team. Everyone was there and Nicholas was just trying to help. It's my fault if anything, it's my fault. Please don't call anyone. Please."

She started out strong and intimidating, demanding her desires. But, her last plea had it and her eyes welled with tears.

Richey's face was stone as he locked eyes with his parents, then back to Stacy. "A call was already placed this afternoon." He said the words as if they pained him as much as Stacy.

Stacy automatically began to change her stance, ready to scream, but Richey held up a hand. "He had all the proper papers for a shortened stay in the country. Because they do not recognize Dukhovia as a country, they cannot—or at least *will* not— say that he should be detained for any reason. What he did as a member of the Dukhovian military is of no concern to them as they cannot speak on the state of Dukhovia or its', quote, 'confusing military and civil war' and therefore are 'uninvolved' in whether or not he is war criminal. This will obviously change if anything happens on American soil."

Stacy breathed, watching the fallen faces of those around her. She did not know whether to jump for joy or howl with anger. The fact that America wanted nothing to do with Dukhovia and hardly recognized it as a country was not news to her. She could assume it was a majority of the reason that the restrictions placed on Dukhovian practices was so heavy following her grandfather's court case. Still, perhaps if there was a bit more concern, the country would not be in the state of war that it currently was. It shook her to her bones.

But, in that discrimination was solace for Nicholas. Thank the Spirits.

"So…he's staying? He's safe?"

Uncle Richey nodded his head slowly. "Stacy… we need you to understand that some of the things Nicholas may have done are very dangerous. He has had a difficult life, yes, but these things sometimes change people for the better and sometimes for the worse…"

"He's not Yasana," she interrupted. She hated herself immediately and was not even certain on what context she made the statement other than her gut feeling— and that was not something she could expect others to understand and agree on. "I'm aware of who he is and what he's done and I'm smart enough to make my own choices to stay safe."

Uncle Richey nodded once as Stacy continued on.

"I don't know why he's done it—that's just the thing. We don't know if it was force or choice. Do any of you even know anything about the war or are you too afraid to face your pasts to even think about it?"

She felt her insides crumble the moment the words left her mouth. Regret seeped through her, settling into a muck as she watched Terra's hurt, shocked face, Uncle Richey's uncertain one, and Tom's always stoic, always straight, always refusing to give away anything.

She wanted to backtrack, but the sting of tears filled her eyes and she knew she had to leave. Cody had plenty of time, it was her turn to solidify her thoughts with her friend—with the only one whose opinion on Nicholas she could trust.

Moments later, Stacy knocked gently on the door. She was pleasantly surprised to see Rachael up and alert—looking just as much like a supermodel as any other day. It was Cody who looked more like he should be in a hospital bed. She was certain Rachael had done her scolding, but she watched as their intertwined hands separated from each other the moment Stacy's knock sounded.

"Stacy!" Rachael sat up with enthusiasm the moment her friend bound forward. She threw her newly-casted arm around Stacy and squeezed with all her might.

Stacy instantly squeezed her friend in return, then stepped back to glance at her up and down. Not only was every hair in place and her make-up immaculate, she had changed out of her shredded clothes and hospital gown and into some brand new, showstopping ensemble. Stacy wondered without too much curiosity where it came from. If Rachael had a will, she had a million different ways.

"My time with the queen, yeah?" It was all she said by way of kicking out her cousin. He furrowed his brow at her, but responded by grabbing Rachael's empty cup of ice and shuffling away with minor grumbling. Her last-minute plan was a blessing after all.

"How are you feeling? How are your wrists?" Stacy asked the moment Cody was gone and she was certain the door snapped shut.

"Absolutely fine," Rachael said with enthusiasm. Then she frowned. "Cody..."

"Will never listen no matter how many times we tell him," Stacy finished. "But with that in mind...I need to know what he said to you."

Rachael knew she did not mean Cody and understanding and memory flickered on her face as the windows began to rumble and then...stop. Not just because the feeling disappeared, not because someone interrupted, but almost because Rachael...

She shrugged. "He said to center it so...I've been trying. I don't really know what that means or what I'm doing, but I'm just trying to imagine that I have the capability of controlling it and...it's working."

Understanding and further concern flicked across Stacy's face. He was telling the truth about wanting to help Rachael.

"I mean what I said earlier...he didn't mean any harm. He came over wanting to know what was going on with you. You have more in common than you do different, you know," Rachael chastised. "You shut down the same way he shuts down. Perhaps he's a bit more theatrical..." She rolled her eyes, then continued.

"He notices the difference in behavior you're giving him and he's confused by it. I told him to just be honest with you. We were just sort of talking about how to get on your good side and I...I honestly wasn't sure I was doing the right thing.

He seemed honest, so sincere and genuine. He swore he never meant any harm to you, like he truly did just want to get to know you. And I want so desperately to believe him, but… what if?" She bit her lip.

Stacy nodded her head. She mirrored her thoughts exactly. "Santifini told me to go with my gut. My gut is telling me to trust him. But is that some weird Dukhovian Spirit telling me that or is it just hope? Because the dream is telling me otherwise."

Rachael nodded, thinking it through. "We have intuition, we have the dream— imagine we go one way or the other. What else do we have to sway our opinion?"

Stacy frowned. "I should have asked Santifini more. I mean, maybe he's biased towards whatever happened in Dukhovia, maybe Nicholas was forced or it was just a misunderstanding…but he was forthcoming and—ugh, I can't believe I'm saying this—someone we can trust."

Choice. *When the choice was mine.* And that was the ticket that made her decision—Nicholas said he no longer made his own choices. So, who controlled him and when did they start?

"What more can be asked?" Rachael did not mean the question to shut Stacy down, but to egg her on. To prepare her.

She thought about it. "Details. Any exact details he knows—what brought Nicholas's family's dishonor exactly, what was his upbringing like, the reason he's here…he knows and he'll tell me. I knew he would tell me anything it was just like he wanted me to ask it first or ask a certain way. Maybe it was a way of backing himself up. We can't see it as slander if we asked?"

Rachael shrugged. "The whole situation is strange. We know nothing about him being Dukhovian now he's suddenly an open book. I know your grandparents don't mention it much, but why didn't he talk to you about it? You've asked questions about Dukhovia in school before. You've been sent to his office before for being a 'threat to the school'."

Stacy rolled her eyes in memory. In her early years, when she was more naïve, she would ask any teacher who would listen questions about Dukhovia…what was it like? Who was there? What were the Spirits like?

And what was an heir.

That was now the most crucial question she had for Santifini.

And so, her and Rachael took the night listing out every single question they would ask their fearless leader the following morning. All the way until the nurse entered to give Rachael her medicine and send her home.

Stacy smiled solemnly at her best friend. Gratitude overwhelmed her. She could not imagine a friend so incredible. A person who would back Stacy to the grave but not without making sure she did her research first. Rachael was a blessing, an angel worthy of all the protection the angry ball of Cody had to offer.

"How are your wrists?" Stacy asked her gently.

Rachael rolled her eyes. "The left only slightly worse than it was and the right totally fine. It was strange. The moment he pressed down on them it was like this wave of nothingness overcame me. I didn't just feel normal, I felt—like I had exited my body and was living in a different world. Then I crashed back to earth."

Stacy looked down at her hands. She knew a similar feeling and made note to add that to their list for Santifini the next morning.

CHAPTER 32

CONTROL SLIPPING

*N*icholas! Nicholas! It is time!"

Nicholas scrambled to his feet, fleeing from his chambers without so much as tying his boot all the way. He had little reason to hope ever since the death of his parents and his imprisonment in this castle, but if he was going to have any, today was the day to have it.

"Uniform?" The word fell lazily out of the demeaning man in front of him. His very presence was enough to put Nicholas's heart in his throat. Still, he had learned that there was no room for fear in these castle walls, no room for emotion. Only sacrifice—and he was happy to oblige.

"Scrubbed, sir!"

"Sword?"

"Shined and at the front of my hilt, sir!"

"Soldiers?"

Nicholas fell silent. What was he referring to? What was his response supposed to be? A wave of fear and angst washed over him. He knew the repercussions for failing to respond within seconds. He readied himself for whatever form of abuse The Czar would utilize. His already scarred, bleeding back tensed.

The Czar stopped; the cruel resonance of stone-cold silence echoed around the dark, stone corridor.

"S-soldiers, sir?"

He rounded, standing just feet away from Nicholas, and his full features became realized. The Czar had been looking more and more ragged these last few weeks. Not that he ever looked particularly grand in the years that Nicholas had come to know the man, but he was either faltering or strengthening, and that frightened Nicholas all the more.

"This is your first solo journey, Sir Nicholas III. Of course you will need an arsenal of men to command."

Nicholas's heart stopped. Men to command? His own men? Him in charge? A position of leadership, of gratitude? His heart leapt. He knew he made the right decision to stay. This was already enough to please his ancestors.

"You will have Beta platoon at your command today. All twenty of them. Your mission is simple enough. The people of North Bridge are struggling to find enough shelter after the battle destroyed most of their houses. The soldiers are to *rebuild. The quicker the better before they all freeze to death. Most remaining settlements are housing about four families, but a few have as many as eight.*

"They know their mission. You will simply direct them, keep them on task, ration out their meals and schedule break times. Are you up for the job?"

Nicholas blinked. The task seemed simple enough and yet such an honor. He knew he could do it. He knew he would do it with his best efforts.

He bowed to his mentor.

"Good."

Nicholas followed The Czar as far as the throne room, then he exited the front of the castle himself. He found around ten horse-drawn carts waiting for him. All of them filled with either men or supplies. Then there was a single horse awaiting its rider—his horse.

He passed the men one-by-one on his trek to the front. He found his palms began to sweat as he walked by, taking them in. Their looks ranged from blankness to disgruntlement he could not place. He started to question what their intentions might be—would they try to overthrow his command? Would they give him any type of trouble? Did they look down to him?

He alternated from nodding a hello to avoiding eye contact, until he was nearly certain he would lose the contents of his stomach and then he beelined his vision for Karaby, his mare.

Hitching himself to the animal, he looked back in ensuring all was ready. Then, he yelled out the warning and they were off.

It was a long, but relatively simple journey to their destination. They covered most of their ground the first day. Nicholas judged the incoming storm as a better time to be sheltered than it would be to travel, thus they continued to push as far as they could until the sky began to rumble and snow began to fall.

Nicholas attuned his well-trained ears to the sounds around him and noticed that some of the carriages began to veer the moment the snow fell.

"Aye!" He called back. "Is everything alright back there?"

"Aye," the solider called back. "The storm is beginning; we are veering off for the night."

Nicholas's stomach began to knot. He did not yet say to stop, he was leading this journey, whom did these soldiers think they were disobeying orders?

Nicholas envisioned the faces of the ones who mocked him on his walk up and attempted to swallow his disgruntlement.

"There is a tunnel of caves only a few miles north. We will fare better there for the night. The horses should not be left exposed with the type of weather conditions that are coming."

He swore he heard snickering and a bit of commentary, but he buried it. He never heard that type of pushback towards Arkady, why would he hear it now? Then again, he thought of what Arkady would do if he heard it...no. Nicholas would not copy the behavior. He would do nothing until necessary.

"The horses need rest; this is a long haul for them. Many of them have not travelled this distance in a long while. We should rest here."

Nicholas looked around. Other soldiers began to poke their heads out, wondering what was going on, others because they simply wanted a front row seat to the show. He gritted his teeth. To listen to his fellow men or to make the call? How did one decide what was being walked on and what was entering into compromise?

"We will travel further. If the storm worsens, we will stop sooner than the caves."

There was another murmur, but Nicholas did not entertain it. He continued onward, even as the snow began to fall thicker, he knew they would reach the caves in time.

Just as the wind began to howl and the horses began to whinny, Nicholas guided the men with pride into a thick cave. He gave directions to set up: to smoke the meat they brought and divvy up the bread and dahlia beans. Other soldiers would prepare camp while others tended to the horses. Nicholas's eyes watched the men who disobeyed him, but he made no comment.

The following morning, the horses were rested enough and the sky calm enough for the remainder of their journey to continue. They hitched up and arrived in North Bridge hours later without much concern.

Nicholas gave the orders for who would do what, separating the men based on skill level and strength. There were thirty-two total displaced families, thirty-two homes destroyed and six remaining. Two of the homes had eight families as they had barns to accommodate, the others had four. Four families, with numbers ranging from twenty people per house up to thirty.

Thirty. Thirty people in one to two-bedroom homes.

Nicholas swallowed.

After giving his orders, he found a group of children. He sat near them, getting to know their names, their story's, their dreams. He watched while he chatted, watched as the men worked and others stared—stared with a look one should never give a superior, right in his direction. He did all he could to ignore them.

A while had passed before his stomach growled, reminding himself that he needed to pass out the rations.

He made his way to the wagon carrying the goods and glanced in. He grimaced. He did not realize how much the meat would cook down, did not realize how little they would have for the duration of their stay. Why had they been given so little? He quickly realized that they would be able to eat no more than half a portion each if he did not solve this predicament. He decided that would be a problem for him to solve once they at least had something in their stomachs. The priority was to not halt production. The priority was with the citizens.

CHAPTER THIRTY-TWO

As Nicholas began to pass out the food, he became aware of the now familiar feeling of tightness in his chest, of the sweat glistening on his palms. He looked around, trying to close off his ability to hear as he glanced around at the disheartened soldiers, livid at their portion size.

"Aye, Andrews."

Nicholas felt anger rise inside of him at the name. Not only at the name itself, but the disrespect in how he was addressed, the disrespect in the tone.

He turned to face the solider who had disobeyed him on where to take their rest. "That would be Sir Nicholas or Captain, soldier. What can I do for you?"

"Are you trying to starve us? What, so used to your cushy lifestyle in the castle you can't bear to split rations, so you keep them for yourself?"

Nicholas bared his teeth. The last thing his life in the palace could be referred to as was glamorous. Anger and aggression began to boil in his center, but he pushed it down, forming it into a well-controlled ball. As long as it was in his ball, he could hold it, he could control it.

"Unfortunately, this is what we will have to work with for now. There was a miscommunication with the kitchen staff and not enough food was packed. This is what we will work with until we have a solution. In the meantime, anyone who feels comfortable can share their ration can and I will skip my meals as often as possible."

The soldier's thick eyebrows creased, threatening to meet his untidy, curly brown hair. "Oh, what a selfless leader we have found ourselves with. If there is not enough food, that is a problem that you need to solve and you need to solve now. We did not sign up for death sentences."

"I will update you as soon as possible."

Nicholas began to walk away, but the soldier was not backing down. He began following Nicholas up to the wagon, holding the rations. He tore off the cover, eyeing what they had.

"There is enough for us to at least have our full portion this first meal after the journey."

"I have already calculated..."

Nichlas was interrupted by the whispers and shouts of other approaching soldiers who had overheard and began to crowd the wagon. Some began to take the food, others simply backed the first solider.

Nicholas tried to block it with his body, but his eyes widened in horror as he realized what the amount they were taking meant for the remainder of the trip.

"Maybe Czar Arkady should not have sent you out if you were so incapable of making life-saving calls."

Nicholas clenched his fists. "Solider, you are already on thin ice for insubordination. Would you care to backdown or have that punishment be announced to your brethren?"

CONTROL SLIPPING

The solider, whose name Nicholas did not even know, smiled a chastising smile, cocking his head to one side, spreading that widening grin. "We are already being led by a solider whose entire family is treasonous scum, do you not think that punishment enough?"

That was it. Nicholas snapped and others began to riot. He withdrew his sword, pointing it at the soldier's neck, shouting at him to obey his commands. They were met with laughter, with cunning, disgusting words. Shouting back at Nicholas, the soldier reached up, touching Nicholas's shoulder, then...

Nicholas sliced down, cleanly and neatly, dismembering the solider. The solider began to scream, but the names he called Nicholas were only more vulgar. Some of the soldiers began to back away, others tried to stop Nicholas. He simply slaughtered them too. Slaughtered them all. Until ten men had fallen at his hand.

He caught his breath and looked down, realizing what he had done. With disgusting shock, he shoved his sword into his hilt and looked around, breathing in and out deeply, looking around—anxious. Angry. Confused. Alone.

"If no one else would like to meet their fate, I suggest you return to your posts."

And they had. And the children whom he befriended hid for the remainder of the trip.

Nicholas remembered the first time he caused others to fear him. The look matched that of Rachael's hollow, shaken face and mirrored Stacy's glaring ridicule. He had never wanted to cause it again, to lose control in such way again. But, over time, it became...not necessarily habit, but...a defense. Yes, it became a defense. If people would not listen to reason, they would always listen to fear. And he was triggered, so easily triggered.

He did not want to be triggered anymore and he did not want to be fearful anymore either. He wanted to make mistakes and learn from his mistakes, taking the strongest with him and letting the weakest learn.

After he and his remaining soldiers had returned from rebuilding the homes in North Bridge, word had already spread around Dukhovia that the great grandson of the most disloyal family in all of Dukhovia murdered his own soldiers. Arkady did not react nearly as bad as Nicholas had anticipated. Instead, he had poured Nicholas a cup of tea and explained the importance of maintaining control.

"You are going to fail, Nicholas. You are going to fail on your first mission; you might even fail on your last mission. What matters is that you learn from those missions. You learn what to do, what not to do, and how to maintain that element of control so that your people listen to you. A ruler cannot have insubordinate subjects."

It seemed like great advice at first, until Nicholas learned that it was Arkady's plan to cause the food shortage to begin with. He had set him up to see if he could problem solve. He failed. He failed miserably and now Dukhovia hated him even more.

He had to admit, it was almost nice to get away from that, to have a fresh start. In America, he could walk the streets as anyone he wanted to be. His name meant nothing here, his face did not tell the people to fear. He could just be Nicholas Demitona. And Nicholas Demitona could be whoever he found himself to be.

But, for now, he needed to find out who Stacy Grace Matthews was. He needed to find out what caused her to have that look of stagnant rejection that he knew meant that one thing—fear.

He had now searched her room for an entire hour. He found nothing useful as far as what she had discovered of him or why she was not speaking to him, but he did find her interesting.

In here, he dared not turn on a light, but was thankful that a small, oval shaped, purple lamp with thick bubbles of lighter purple swirled around atop her dresser, lighting his way enough to make out enough of the area.

He was initially greeted by the Dukhovian flag, hanging proudly next to her dresser. He ran his fingers over it. He wondered if she felt the same stab of the double-edged sword that he did when his hand hovered over the symbol for peace, for unity…

In her top drawer, he had discovered more Dukhovian relics. There were a few miscellaneous notes she had jotted down. He analyzed them with curiosity and humor. A part of him wanted to roar at the simplicity of her thoughts and questions, but it was a small part, the part raised in the castle, the part that his true senses did not yet phase out.

She would clearly be curious of the differences and unknown—she was not allowed to ask questions. Just as he faced a similar ban. She knew nothing of her country and no way to find out. All too similar.

Then there was a necklace. He lifted it up just high enough to dangle at eye level. His eyes could have burned a hole in the necklace. A small, golden heart-shaped locket. He glanced down at the note he recognized as signed by the Dukhovian solider she had met during her trip. He wondered why she kept it.

He felt anger and anxiety wrestling in his chest as he bore into it. He thought of one hundred ways to rid her of the piece of jewelry until he finally decided to leave it where he found it. His emotions were balls of energy and he needed to control them. It had been so long since he put that practice into use. So long since he felt he could create a big enough ball to contain himself.

He had searched longer, finding she listened to mostly heavy music, she was rather unorganized, and she ate quite a bit of chocolate covered granola bars if her trash can was any indication.

He wondered what her days looked like. How long did he listen to music? How often did she reach for a granola bar? When did she know she was satisfied by her music?

Just as he was about to leave, he stopped near a desk that was piled with papers. He had picked through them, but one must have clung onto the other as he saw writing not previously noted.

From Dukhovia

War sent? Why?

Parents dead. Murdered?

Santifini knows him

Help me and we can both get back to Dukhovia?

He sunk into her desk chair. It was a list. A list of everything that she had learned of him thus far. Everything she found curious, everything she was cautious of. Stupid girl. Stupid and ridiculously brilliant girl.

This was exactly what he was looking for and it told him everything he needed to know. She had not believed a single word from his lips. She had been questioning him and stringing him along until she found out who he truly was—just the same as he was doing to her.

What a joke. What a mysterious and laughable joke.

Nicholas spent more time reading through the list, playing back their conversations in his head. He needed time with the paper. Time to work out what he could say and whether or not any type of truth could or should be within those walls.

Nicholas perked up. He saw the front porch light come on and the door slam shut. He readied himself to scale the side of the house, but he could not leave. He was not ready to leave.

Instead, he glanced around quickly, choosing instead to hide himself in the back of Stacy's closet. It was disaster enough, he doubted she could find her favorite shirt let alone him.

Mere seconds passed and he heard Stacy's door open and then slam shut. He leaned his head against the wall, listening. The instant she walked in his heart warmed, his body calmed, save for his racing heart. He wondered if she felt their Spirits connect as well.

Stacy seemed to be frustrated. She came in, kicked her desk, yelped, and then seemed to fall to the floor. The wall he hugged mirrored her Dukhovian flag on the other side. He felt her approach closer, possibly reading it, running her hand over it. He closed his eyes, breathing in her scent, imagining the touch of her soft, skinny fingers. Watching the trembling of her full, pink lips.

Why here? Band? A line had been drawn through here. War? Banished? A break? Find out about if banished families could be forgiven. Hope? Help?

His heart stopped. If what he had told her was truthful, she wanted to help him. How much simpler could his task be? To woo her into returning to Dukhovia under the impression that together the two of them could prove their mutual innocence and end the war. To think that they could show themselves as individuals, redeem their family histories, and be known for who they truly were...it was laughable.

Yet, what a strong heir she was. So little did she know of the war, so little did she know of Dukhovia as a whole. Still, here she was, ready to risk her life to throw herself into the fire to end it. For the sake of whom? Her country? Her family? Her people.

Nicholas was quiet, stashed in the back righthand corner of her closet. He listened as she exited the room, heard the rush of water pour from the shower across the hall, and then returned moments later.

He let his head rest back against the closet as he listened to her, experienced her. Strange and stupid as his action may have been, it was this...intimacy with which he needed, craved. To not only have fleeting conversations with her, but to know who she was beyond both opened and closed doors. To know what captivated her. To know if she was worthy after all.

Nicholas lost track of time between the moments when Stacy was in the shower and he stayed behind. He did not know why he did not move. He heard others rustling around downstairs, but was still certain that he could have escaped out her window without cause for concern. Even though it was a side window rather than the back, which certainly was not helpful.

Nicholas was so lost in his thoughts, he barely noticed when Stacy tore open the door to her closet. He sat alert, prepared for this moment. She made an immediate right, throwing, tossing, and rifling through everything on that shelf. She was a menace with no cause, but seemed to suddenly stop. She had found what she was looking for and sunk to the floor with it.

It returned—the feeling he felt when their hands connected. The softness, the gentleness of the world around him. No matter how many times he connected to Arkady's spirit, it was never so...reassuring.

Then, as if she felt it too, her back stiffened, she whipped her head left to right, sighed, then returned to fondling whatever it was she had in her hand.

He tried to crane his neck to see what was before her, trying so hard to see, yet so gently to not make a sound. It did not help that the house was dead quiet. No other noises from other inhabitants, no music playing in the background. She could hear him if he breathed too loud. He was simply grateful the closet was the size of his boyhood home's bathroom.

When he caught sight of Stacy again, he realized that she held a Dukhovian relic—a small, stone wolf statue. They were given away around Dukhovia to people with special purposes by soothsayers. When they would pass a person they felt called to in the street, they would tell the receiver that The Spirits spoke to them about their purpose. It was a great honor to receive one.

Stacy held it and stroked it intently, as if hoping it might speak to her. He wondered with awe just how much she knew of its intent and if she intended to extract her purpose from it. She had clearly given thought to it, she had said she was uncertain if her band was in her future, but how much did she truly wonder? He had to get to know more of her…he needed a moment with her…

So often did Nicholas wish he could pass a soothsayer in the street. Then he would know more about what he was supposed to do. He would question them, he would ask what they heard. That he was supposed to follow the Spirits to the T or that he was supposed to listen to Arkady? He simply needed guidance.

Eventually, Stacy returned the wolf to its previous place and left the closet, leaving it slightly open. Nicholas tiptoed over nearer the door and watched her climb into bed. Once the lights were out, he extended a hand into the box she left the wolf and caressed it gently. Nothing happened, but the feeling he felt when Stacy touched him jolted him in his place. It took all his effort to not move another inch and risk knocking over Stacy's things.

He held onto the wolf longer, feeling like he was supposed to hold it, like he was supposed to stroke it, like he was supposed to never let go. He needed to protect the wolf, that was it. It needed his protection, his guidance.

Time passed. Nicholas knew darkness had consumed the household even greater than it had upon his entry. He felt the stillness and silence of the air telling him the occupants of the home had drifted off to sleep. He felt his own eyes begin to drift, but this was a risk he could not afford. It was time to go…

"No! No stop! Help me! Help!"

Nicholas was on his feet like lightning. He did not care what the consequences would be, nor did he even have time to consider them. He heard the piercing shouting of Stacy's screams and ran to her side. Visions of Arkady coming to her window bombarded his mind. Had he connected the three of them and called him by caressing the wolf?

Alas, when he flung himself out of the closet, he only found Stacy's sleeping body. She thrashed and kicked against the bed, but she was, in fact, asleep.

His eyebrows creased and his eyes searched her body for a way to help. It was like no nightmare he had ever seen—and he was quite familiar with nightmares. No, her body jerked around as if it were responding directly to everything happening in the dream. As if she was running and hit a dead end—her body halted. As if she was hit and her face ripped to the side. As if she were full of fear and her breath left her body—then hit her like a train as it filtered back into her lungs. And then he looked at the blackening mark on her arm and fierce panic flashed across his face.

Nicholas looked around wildly for a way to help, a way to stop the pain. Then he froze. Footsteps he scarcely processed deciding on making carried him back over to the closet where he took the wolf from its wrapping, carried it back to the bed, and placed it in Stacy's hand.

He could tell the dream continued, but her body did cease thrashing and maintained some sense of stillness.

CHAPTER THIRTY-TWO

At a loss of what to do next and too invested to do anything else, he held onto her arm and spent the remainder of the dark hours of the night holding onto it.

CHAPTER 33

NO MORE HOT AND...

$\mathcal{Y}$ ou look God awful—when was the last time you slept?"

Stacy slammed the door shut tight behind her, barely acknowledging Rachael's words. Her face appeared just as disheveled as her hair—which appeared much more like a bird's nest than usual.

"I haven't been," she sighed, heading directly over to Cody's house. His mom was supposedly gone for a few days.

"Wait, wait, wait, wait, stop..." Rachael swung forward and latched onto Stacy's arm. "I'm not letting you walk in the door looking *that* horrible. Are you still wearing your pajama pants?"

Stacy glanced down. "I guess so."

Rachael gave her friend a remorseful look and a pitiful sigh. "Come on."

Grabbing her hand, Rachael walked Stacy up the stairs of her house into her bedroom. The Christmas wonderland was ten times more than what anyone expected to see walking into your average home. But the Leighton's were not your average holiday decorators.

Kenny loved the holiday ever since any of their parents could remember—or at least cared to talk about. Each year found him and Kevin inventing some new decoration. Ellen was not always so gung-ho towards celebrating, but everything changed that approximately sixteen-years-ago, when she received her Christmas miracle.

A sea of multi-colored lights lit their path from the front door to the stairway. The rail was draped with thick, green garland and red bows placed in exactly the right places. Stacy knew Ellen enjoyed helping set up the decorations as part of their tradition, but Rachael always plotted out the journey.

"Sit." Rachael demanded of Stacy, pointing to the chair in front of her vanity table.

Stacy obliged, squinting as Rachael lit the clear lights that hung around her mirror. "And what, you slept fine and dandy after last night?"

Rachael shrugged, happily. "I know more than ever before. I for one am excited at the prospect of speaking to Sir Nicholas today to find out more."

Stacy cringed. The two had spent a majority of her last few hours in the hospital debating whether Stacy just bite the bullet and ask Nicholas all the questions she had herself or sticking with her plan to ask Santifini. On the flip side, Rachael was certain she was going to ask Nicholas and implored Stacy to as well. She was on the fence.

CHAPTER THIRTY-THREE

She continued to think about it after she went home that night, debating what the Spirits would want from her and praying so desperately they would give her an answer. The only thing they really gave her was the worst dream of her life.

"Hmpf." It was all she offered.

Rachael took a brush and tore through Stacy's hair, her tone lightening. "I know you're worried about Dukhovia, Stace, but country's go to war all the time, I'm sure they have groups set up to help."

"*Other* countries go to war all the time, Rache, *other* countries, not Dukhovia. They don't have programs ready to go give them aid; they're not on any alliance for help. I told you what Uncle Richey said last night—we don't even acknowledge them as a country worthy of recognition let alone aid. They're dying and I can't even help them. I'm stuck here learning about…cells and mitosis."

"Well, first of all, we aren't even covering that anymore, so at least you're not entirely wasting your time." Rachael laughed and rolled her eyes. She bent her head down to level with Stacy's and looked into the mirror. "Isn't your entire culture based around trust? Trust the Spirits. If they need you or anyone else…they'll let it happen at the right time. Before then, everything will be okay. Nothing that can't be reversed will happen."

Stacy sighed and nodded her head once. Though Rachael's words made sense and resonated deeply within her, her own reflection in the mirror only made things worse when she did not like the background surrounding her.

Rachael went to her own wardrobe and took out an outfit. Stacy gave a reluctant sigh when she saw the ensemble, but began stripping all the same.

A horrified gasp left Rachael's lips. Stacy dropped her arms after pulling off her shirt to see her friend standing with cupped hands over her mouth in the corner. She followed her eyes down to her torso which was covered in heavy, purple bruising along her ribcage.

"Oh," Stacy sighed. "That."

Rachael's eyes bulged demanding an explanation.

"The dream was rather…intense last night. I just woke up this way."

"Stacy!" Rachael's voice was condescending and horrified all the same. "*The dream?* If this is really from the dream you need to speak to Nicholas asap!"

"You've seen how I get when I dream," Stacy shrugged, keeping her eyes away as she pulled on the pink, glittering top Rachael chose for her. She frowned at it as it hugged her curves.

"I've seen how you get when you have *the* dream. Just that dream. Otherwise, you sleep like a log. This is not normal, Stacy. Either you're becoming so chaotic you're hurting yourself and we'll need to hire a bodyguard while you sleep or…" She drifted off.

Stacy knew what she was going to say. They have had the talks before, of course. This was not the first time Stacy woke up with bruises or unexplained wet hair—but it was certainly the worst.

It was strange. It was different. It was otherworldly. But so was Rachael's…condition. Thus, they found little to puzzle over regarding the matter. Neither had an explanation for either so it was just something they accepted at face value.

"It was different this time," Stacy started to say, her voice drifting. "It was almost as if they're…rushing me. The words were the same *they're coming, protect them, protect the heir*… but there was urgency in the words, harsh urgency. I still couldn't see who was after me, but it *felt* like they were after me. I kept running, crashing into trees, I felt like something had me but in the end, it was just…" Stacy paused, understanding flickering on her face. "It was just me."

"No hot and cold," Rachael said gently, ready to head out the door.

Stacy nodded. "No hot and cold." But she had already decided that she was not going to go back to giving Nicholas the cold shoulder. She simply was uncertain what she *would* do. To ask too much could mean to reveal too much. And if he was someone who murdered whoever The Czar saw fit…she would play it by ear. Because she also knew what her family experienced, and she knew that murderer did not equate danger…

What a sentence.

Stacy finished changing into what Rachael chose to dress her up in and the two headed out the door. She supposed she owed it to Rachael, after all, she had been through a lot at her hands.

They ended up proceeding without Cody, who said he woke up late and was still getting ready. Stacy realized there was more than one person she had a lot in common with at the moment. They tried to keep the conversation light on the walk, but eventually, Stacy looking back and forth at her wrists caught Rachael's attention.

"What on earth are you doing?" She finally asked.

Stacy had raised both hands to her face, nearly an inch away, and examined them from every angle. "When I woke up this morning, I felt this like…tingling…on my wrists. Then like an insane amount of energy but it was in my stomach?" She felt the strangeness of the words as they left her lips, but again, strange was her middle name.

Rachael's face did not seem confused by the information or like she was trying to solve the mystery. Instead, she looked concerned. "That's exactly how I felt after Nichlas touched my wrists." She rubbed them gently. "It was like he took everything I was feeling and bottled it up…"

Stacy arched her eyebrows, her eyes not leaving her hands. "That's sort of what happened in the dream. Everything went from the worst it's ever been to…mild."

Rachael mirrored her puzzled face. "But no one was with you to do that so…did you do it yourself? Did the Spirits do it?"

CHAPTER THIRTY-THREE

Shock dawned on Stacy's face. "When I woke up this morning, I was holding the wolf statue. I don't remember getting it, but hey, I don't remember dodging coconuts either and here I am." She lifted her arms and examined her ribs.

Rachael rolled her eyes, a gentle laugh breathing through her lips. "The one that's supposed to like communicate with the Spirits for your purpose or something?"

Stacy grimaced, wishing she knew the right words to correct her, but her guess was as good as Rachael's. "She said that the Spirits tell her when someone with a powerful spirit passes by. Then the statue guides them to making sure they fulfill it…"

"So, it protected you from getting internal bleeding in order to fulfill your purpose once you got it?" Rachael guessed.

Stacy shrugged, holding the door open to the school as Rachael pushed through. "Seems like it."

When they entered the school, the entire student body seemed to be buzzing about something. People were rushing by them in a sea of excitement and chaos, talking quickly in hushed tones. No one openly told them what it was, but the exciting chattering ceased when they walked by, eyes dropping to Rachael's new cast. They were no strangers to being talked about, but the extremeness of it had not been done in quite a time.

"What do you think is going on?" Rachael asked Stacy.

Stacy shrugged, but a smile crossed her lips moments later. "But I know who will give us the ugly truth."

Planning to head straight to Santifini's office anyway, Stacy slid into the office, standing a distance back as she waited her turn to speak with Ms. Frito Lay.

"It seems to be the only way and they've been getting along…"

"…talking and getting along are different things. Do we have any alternative ideas?"

Stacy rolled her eyes, ignoring the conversation between the two secretary's the same way they ignored her presence. She started bouncing a golden apple back and forth in her hands as she waited for their oh-so important conversation to cease.

"Well, it wasn't just a one-time thing. They've been seen around the school loads of times; believe me they're the talk of every class."

Stacy cocked her head to the side. Although there were several students she knew had problems with one another, she could imagine there would only be two who would be "the talk of every class".

"Well, Principal Santifini said to keep them separate at all costs. But if he wants him in advanced science, they're going to have to be in the same class eventually, anyway."

Stacy's heart dropped into her stomach. She dropped the apple, only snapping back to reality when the sound of it bouncing off the counter, escaping her hands, and shattering to the floor awakened her.

Both secretaries turned to see Stacy's face, then the floor, then back up.

The larger secretary, Ms. Behaz, walked over to assist. "May I help you, Ms. Matthews?"

Stacy was still trying to collect herself. Her and Nicholas in the same class? They were really going to allow them to be in the same room as each other? And prior to their detention sentencing? Without guards, guns, or backup? Well, she supposed that much had not been disclosed.

"Um...y-you're going to put Nicholas and I in the same class together?" She asked in a voice she did not recognize to be hers.

"It appears that way, yes," Ms. Behaz sighed heavily, her dark blue suit rising with every breath. "Unless you want bumped down to remedial biology."

Stacy shrugged. "I mean I wouldn't really mi—...actually, that sounds like a fine idea. We appreciate your trust." Stacy bowed.

The secretaries both gave her a strange look. "Did you need something, sweetie?" Ms. Frieda requested. She folded her prim and proper hands over the paperwork neatly.

"Oh," Stacy lifted her head to peer around the back of the office, towards Santifini's room. "I just needed a word with His Highness."

Ms. Behaz gave her a death glare with her dark as night eyes, refusing to accept the bait, but Miss Frito Lay chimed in, slowly. "Unfortunately, Principal Santifini is not in."

Dread and defeat wavered over Stacy, but she swallowed her disappointment. "Will he be in later?"

The two women exchanged worried and apprehensive glances. Then Frito Lay shook her head, sadness penetrating her young features. "Unfortunately, he is out until further notice. Family matters."

Stacy's heart dropped into her stomach. If she had breakfast, she was certain it would be all over the office. "Family matters? Are you sure or is that just what you're telling me?"

"That's enough, Ms. Matthews," Ms. Behaz said forcefully, her large body bounding forward as if she could cast Stacy's questioning down with her invisible shield. "His reasons for being out are no concern of yours."

"Sure, but you can just tell me that, but you didn't, you said family matters. So, is it ambiguous family matters or is he dead? If he's dead, you can tell me he's dead. You can tell me he has cancer, car accident...." Her heart was racing, but she had a game to play. She needed the truth. *Family?* He said his family was dead. So, if it was a family matter, did that mean he was in Dukhovia? And if so— was it by *choice*?

"Family matters are family matters, Ms. Matthews. Now, happy as Mr. Santifini will be happy to see you so involved and not just eavesdropping since the moment you walked in the door, please find your way to class."

"In my defense, the door literally rings when anyone opens it. It was sheer negligence on your part."

Stacy smiled at her satisfying comment, but walked out of the office in a daze, running straight into Rachael.

"Graceful," her friend commented, handing Stacy her science book.

"Like a duck on ice skates," Stacy commented, wondering with too much curiosity how that combination would unfold...and then trying to remember the last time she was on her skates.

"Soooo class with the superstar?"

Stacy made a face. "Of course you found out."

"You took too long," Rachael chastised. "But it's unclear the reasoning. What did you find out from Santifini?"

Rachael and Stacy linked arms, beginning the walk towards their lockers. "That he's away on 'family matters'." She raised her eyebrows.

Rachael mimicked the look of puzzlement and intrigue. "Family? Like actually?"

Stacy threw up her hands. "It's uncertain when he'll be back, so no one to supervise Mr. Andrews. He's a Grade A genius so—guess who will be in our classes today?"

"Well, he'll be in mine," Rachael joked. Then her tone got serious. "That's a lot of info. He's out of town and now we're face to face with how we're going to interact with him. Not just at lunch time. What are you going to do?"

Stacy gulped. "No more hot and cold."

Rachael smiled approvingly, her lightness returning. "I actually just had the pleasure of speaking to Mr. Andrews," Rachael grinned, in an attempt to hold nothing back.

Stacy perked up, cursing herself immediately when Rachael's reaction resulted in a fit of laughter.

"And?" Stacy pressed.

"Well, first of all, he was 'concerned for your wellbeing'," Rachael quoted in her best imitation voice which was not even slightly close to accurate.

"In what way?" She grimaced.

"He saw that I was well and asked how you were then talked in circles about how he needed to know if you were safe and how you were and what your favorite color is."

Stacy rolled her eyes, but she squinted all the same. The last interaction they had was Rachael in the back of the ambulance and Stacy fighting to protect her best friend. Once he saw Rachael was okay, that should have led to a segway to assume Stacy was okay, or at least not seem so panicked about it. Unless...

Hot and cold. He was so interested in getting closer to Stacy...only Stacy...he wanted to know which Stacy he was going to get today. Hot...or cold...

"What about the indifferent mitosis?"

"He said that stories of my type of power are common in Dukhovia, but they're more like a fable. Not many people are known to actually have the...power. We obviously didn't have time to go into detail, but I asked if he could possibly get together after school to let me know all he knows."

"Rachael!" Stacy squealed with excitement. This was the closest they had ever been to answers. Even when her grandparents began working on the case and there was a flash of hope, it still did not compare to someone who actually knew what this was supposed to be, as opposed to someone who had no idea, but was good at working with mysterious and unexplained. And if Rachael was willing to sit down with him alone after school, should she do the same?

"I know! Now let's get to class so I can snag a seat next to him."

Stacy did not want to burst her bubble by telling her Cody would allow no such thing, but they had not seen Cody since they arrived at school, causing her to worry that perhaps he was aware of what Stacy was now certain the student body was whispering about...

As they travelled to class, Stacy learned that Nicholas had not just made an impression on her, but with many others and not all for the same reasons. Sure, some were prepared to label him as a monster and call for him to be deported right along with Uncle Richey, but then there were those who felt the complete opposite about Nicholas. And suddenly their opinions were coming out of the woodwork...

Stacy felt her cheeks burn and her nostrils flair as she heard words tossed around like "dreamy" and "genuine". He was "genuinely a good person" and "the most genuine man" they ever met. Stacy could not necessarily disagree, he was rather good looking and very open on his opinions, clearly, but she could not understand the feeling of anger at hearing the other girls speak of him this way. That was what she *wanted*. She *wanted* everyone else to see his goodness.

"Do you think him and Stacy Matthews are dating, or just talk a lot?"

"No way, she's nowhere near pretty enough for him."

"Wha..." Stacy tried to interrupt the conversation a group of freshmen were having right in front of her, but they flitted away too quickly, clearly not aware of their surroundings.

Whatever. Stacy did not fret over the words of others. Her focus was getting through first period without flames and demons popping up in her brain—or falling asleep. She sighed. Too late. The flashes of Dukhovia on fire were the first thing she saw every morning and the last thing she saw every night. The screams and shouts of mothers and fathers became her lullaby. And they followed her anytime she dared shut her eyes.

"Ready?" Rachael asked, appearing with a bag of items Stacy was clearly meant to have but could not even recall a memory of it being mentioned in class.

Was she ready for class? Did class even matter? Was she ready for anything? Basketball practice? Band practice? Could Dukhovia wait for all that? Could they even wait for second period history? Here she was fretting over what was in Rachael's godforsaken bag while Dukhovians were afraid to sleep in their own homes.

She shook her head, attempting to focus. Though it did not help for more than mere moments, she was beginning to realize if she told herself worrying did not help, she moved on quicker to get closer to whatever would.

"It's not that hard to reach me, really," Stacy whispered to Rachael as they took their seats. Nicholas took the only open seat which was directly across from Rachael.

"Forget you, my bones will be pieces by the end of the period," Rachael retorted.

Stacy looked stealthily over shoulder. Nicholas was making no secret that his entire focus was on her. She fully met his gaze, looked to Rachael...then decided to push her chair out and towards him. No more hot and cold. Uncertainty in how much to reveal, sure, but she would never find her answer by remaining distant. The path forward was guarded, full speed ahead.

"Hey," she said quietly, lifting her hand into a gentle wave.

Nicholas nodded towards her, giving a similar sheltered smile. "Hello."

Then the two spoke in jumbled words at the same time. "Listen...I..." Strained laughter.

"I apologize for yesterday," Nicholas said in that soft, caring voice. It melted through her like butter and she hated herself for it. The god-like face and body, the impeccably heavenly eyes—he had to have known the effect he had on women, perhaps used it to his advantage, and she refused to be dumb bimbo number whatever. But yet...the gentleness in his tone was like a warm hug at the end of a trek through a deserted arctic snowstorm.

Stacy shook her head. "You have nothing to apologize for. Listen..." She looked at Rachael who was trying hard to look distracted. "Thank you. Whatever you said that would help with Rachael—it did. I can't explain how much that means to us."

He fluttered his lashes in an appreciative notion, a small smile gripping on those beautiful lips that Stacy would never admit made her heart throb.

Cody filed in. He started to pull out his chair then looked over to Rachael, behind her, and back to the front of the room.

"Mr. Galley, you aren't really going to let him sit that close to Rachael, are you?" He asked, gripping the back of the chair angrily.

"Mr. Grayson, I assure you everyone in this room will be completely safe. There will be two teachers and a security guard in the back at all times." Mr. Galley waved his hand to reveal that there was, in fact, a security guard blending in with the back corner.

"Wow, they're pretty serious," Stacy indicated, looking closer at the uptight security guard. Out of the corner of her eye, she saw Nicholas glance over at him and grin the widest, most devilish grin she had seen yet and she knew the security guard would not serve his purpose if the need arose.

"Well, I feel safe," Rachael declared happily for the benefit of all involved parties.

Cody grimaced, eyeing her wrist. "I'd feel better if he were on the opposite end of the room. Wasn't that the reason for putting him in other classes to begin with? Why make it so simple for him to get to her next time he has a maniacs reaction to absolutely nothing?"

Stacy looked back at Nicholas. Their eyes locked for the first time since she practically pushed him out of the ambulance. It was like the ball of energy was back and her body ignited into flame with it. His eyes were piercing, but in a less menacing and more meaningful way.

She started to turn back around, but she stopped herself *no more hot and cold.* She shielded half her face from Cody and whispered a quick, 'sorry' towards Nicholas. Perhaps he was a murderer, but perhaps he was a murderer with a voice in his head telling him he had to be—or a voice from a throne in Dukhovia.

He shook his head and kept his eyes straight. His left hand was in his mouth, pretending to nonchalantly chew on his finger nails while the other allowed its digits to strum the table beneath them.

She turned back, impressed that he was able to control his temper so well. Perhaps he too recognized that there were more important things at stake in the world.

"Mr. Grayson, Santifini was very clear that this open spot worked well in favor of this transition. I assure you it is tried, it is true—it is fool proof!"

"Santifini said that?" The words flew out of Stacy's mouth quicker than she could stop them. Her eyes caught Nicholas's staring at her from the corner of her eye.

"That's right," Mr. Galley cleared. "And Nicholas has been on his best behavior in every class as well as far exceeding the marks of most of our students. He shall not be treated as a criminal for one outburst. Now, please take your seat and back down or *you* will be the one removed."

The teacher's words were only fuel to Cody's fire and his next actions flew out faster than Stacy could comprehend, especially as she mulled over Santifini's choice in seating arrangements. "Oh, so that's all it takes at this school to be able to get away with anything is to get good grades! Didn't know that!" Cody threw his book on the ground and pushed over his chair. The officer began to walk over, but Mr. Galley held up a protesting hand. "Is it okay if I do this as long as I ace the next test?"

"Cody..." Rachael reached her hand for him, but he was already too far gone, and she could not be confrontational enough to stop him.

"Better sit down, Grayson," Stacy butted in.

"Mr. Grayson!"

"Can I do this if I get good marks on all my proficiencies?" Cody put his hand on the papers of his classmates and threw them on the ground. Some of them were quiet as they understood his frustration and were in agreement that they did not want Nicholas around. Others shouted for order.

"Oh, no, Kent, can't stick up for your friends—that's frowned upon in this school! He didn't even get ANY PUNISHMENT! Is this okay?" Cody asked, now throwing the teachers belongings across the room. "IS THIS OKAY?" Cody stood on top the new tables and kicked everything off.

"CODY ROBERT GRAYSON! OFFICER MILES!"

The officer came forward, waiting for his que. He got out his hand cuffs and readied his position to begin forcing him to the ground.

Suddenly, Stacy saw Nicholas push out his chair and shoot up. In a grace almost like a dance, he was at the side of the officer, resting his hand upon his shoulder.

The officer jumped in response, shock following Nicholas's gaze from his shoulder up to Nicholas's piercing, blue eyes.

"Sir, Cody has every right to feel angered by the injustice in my punishment and I believe he has several problems in his home life at the present time..."

"DON'T TALK ABOUT WHAT GOES ON IN MY HOUSE."

Nicholas flashed him an annoyed warning look, but continued. "If you could please give us a few moments to sort out our differences, I can assure he will be better behaved."

Officer Miles looked at him for a long time not saying a word, the two could have been having an unspoken conversation. Then, the officer nodded his head and stepped back into the corner.

"Stay in view," the officer warned.

Nicholas nodded his head and guided Cody by the shoulder roughly over to the front corner of the classroom.

"What is your problem?" He demanded. "What happened with Rachael was an accident. A horrible one, I will admit, but an accident that I am doing all I can to make amends for. Everyone else has forgiven me, so why are you so intent on refusing?"

"Oh, you want to know what my problem is?" Cody asked, madness in his blazing, green eyes. "You're my problem, Andrews. You know so much about my home life, then I guess you know how I need to be on the tip of my toes every second of the night just to make sure my dad's safe. Then I come to school and have to worry about my best friends because of you.

"They think you're just some lost soul, but I see past that. I know who you are. I know what you are." Cody was speaking hostilely through gritted teeth, ready to burst at a moment's notice. "You're worse than any of them can see and I'm not giving up without a fight."

With that, Cody sprang forward, latching onto Nicholas's head and searching for his neck. Nicholas's arms seemed to instinctively go up, but he spun around and his gaze met Stacy and Rachael's wide, panicked eyes. He seemed to take a deep breath before wrapping his arms around Cody's waist, lowering him to the ground, and tossing him with likely much more ease than he wanted to against the back wall.

"GRAYSON! OFFICE IMMEDIATELY! THREE DAYS OF OUT OF SCHOOL!"

"Oh, come on!" Cody shouted, messing with his disheveled hair to get it back to its natural disheveled look.

"March!"

Cody shot Nicholas a look of deep hatred and a bitter promise of vengeance before shaking his head and trailing out the door, pulling his shirt smooth.

"Sir Nicholas, please take your seat. I may need your help teaching these students our lesson for today."

"Of course, sir," Nicholas's voice was a soft, caressing promise. Just as gentle and kind as the words pouring from it always were…but his eyes were on Cody and they did not return the feeling of hate—they shook with regret.

"I am truly sorry," Nicholas whispered in Rachael's ear as he took his seat.

Rachael nodded once, swallowing hard.

Stacy put her arm around her and stroked her hair. She turned slowly, her eyes taking a slow journey towards meeting his eyes with a sorrowful, but meaningful glance—a grateful one.

He now helped two of her friends—she supposed she was up next.

"Now, before we begin, we have a small presentation from Marysville School of Science in Washington. If I can open the email…"

He put on his spectacles and began fumbling around, trying to pretend like he had ever gotten anything related to electronics working on his own. Eventually, one of the other students rose up and helped him open his email and project it onto the screen for them all to see.

It started with a dark green background and light green scientific symbols dancing around it.

"P-p-p-passion," the video sang. "P-p-p-purpose. Future. Vision. A better tomorrow. Find it all here at Marysville School of Science! Whether you find your skills serving you in engineering or pharmaceuticals, Marysville is here to assist you along the way!"

The video went on to talk about all the different programs, how much money you can make doing them, how in demand they are, how you can climb the educational ladder with them…The only thing it did not mention was going down these paths for personal fulfillment.

At the end, a video of Jessica, the Marysville representative gave an overview of how her school had possibilities for absolutely any person. She was phenomenal.

"Okay! What a great video for those of us planning on going into the science field which I believe we all have the potential to do!"

Stacy rolled her eyes and sunk into her seat, waiting for the usual next ten minutes to play out where they all talked about their futures and she hid her face wishing she could disappear, run out of the room, or blow up.

"But college isn't the only way to become successful, Mr. Galley, right?" One boy raised his hand high in the sky. It was common knowledge amongst the class that he planned on joining the military. The Air Force in particular. If his locker, truck, and notebooks did not make people aware of that, his clothing certainly did. He was one of the only ones Stacy could attempt to admire.

"Oh, no, and if something doesn't work out you can always try something else."

Stacy was ready to let it go, but out of the corner of her eye, she watched a student scratch something off his list in frustration. Suddenly, her passion flared inside her.

"Wait, Jared, why did you just cross that off?" Stacy asked him.

The class looked around shocked, including Jared who was not aware Stacy knew his name.

"Well, I don't know, I just have this list of things I might want to do and I've been thinking this one certain thing is impossible and he was talking about not always being able to do things so I figured it was a sign."

"And that's okay, if something is too difficult or too expensive, you can change," Mr. Galley…encouraged?

"Wait…why are you telling him that? If you want to do it, if you're meant to do it—you do it, nothing can stop you," Stacy stood up, aggressively shoving her chair out from the table. "It doesn't matter how much it costs or if it's hard. It just means that isn't what you're meant to do, it doesn't make you any less capable of a person.

"Just because we can't or choose not to do it doesn't make us any less intelligent, it means we weren't meant to do that. People are good at what they're meant to do, not everything."

"A very good point, Ms. Matthews! The sky is the limit! Now…for our project today…"

Mr. Galley began to ramble on about how they would pick partners and go outside or something to complete some type of activity and so forth. She glanced out the windows, watching the chaotic snow waver, wondering if Mr. Galley had finally lost his marbles. But she hardly listened or thought much more than that. Instead, she found herself lost inside her head, watching flame after flame lick the sides of hutches and farms, chasing after screaming mothers and children from shoreside to shoreside.

Stacy gripped her head, trying to control the thoughts that bounced around in her mind. There were too many. Anger at the teacher, anger at her situation, desperation for Dukhovia, frustration at how to move forward with Nicholas. Too much. Too much. The walls were closing in. She could not breathe.

Run.

Just as Stacy rose to her feet, the entire rest of the class did too and the distraction was enough to slip her somewhat out of her head.

Rachael had not seemed to notice. She was likely still recovering from her own emotions from watching Cody. The two really were two peas in a destined pod, the matchmaking gods could not have done a better job. But neither would admit it anytime soon.

But, directly behind her, and somewhat to the right, another person did notice and she could feel their heavy gaze encapsulating her.

CHAPTER 34

TRUST

The class was shuffling outside in a sea of panting and commotion. They anxiously pulled on jackets and hats, some chatting with enthusiasm while others were downright aggressive about having to bear the winter weather. Nicholas wondered how long they would last in Dukhovia. He wondered how they would survive. But he did not wander too long. No. He was preoccupied watching the steady gait of Stacy Grace Matthews as she whipped her head around every few seconds to look at him. He was not sure if she was attempting to be inconspicuous, but he did not care.

He found that he liked the feeling that surrounded him when she turned to look at him. Whether it was just confirmation that her look said little about never wanting to speak to him again or another option, he was unclear and uncaring. She was speaking to him today and though he had spent most of the early morning anxious over which Stacy he would get today, he found immediate solace in that fact.

The last time he had seen her conscious, she definitely wanted nothing to do with him. He wondered whether talking to Rachael worked—in some roundabout way, given all that transpired. Then again, the way Rachael greeted him this morning told him that they anything but feared him. In fact, he was able to provide some type of assistance to them, to introduce them to answers and ideas they never knew before. If that worked for Rachael, would it work to solidify Stacy's trust to him?

He considered it. They were definitely at odds with each other, yet in the same predicament all the same—no matter how much she realized that to be true. He needed her to return to Dukhovia and end the war. She had mentioned several times that she could not ask her own family about Dukhovia, no matter how desperate she was. As strong of an heir as she was, some part of her had to yearn towards him. Both for answers and their connection.

That was it.

He needed her, she needed him for answers. If only he could solidify one final way to trust him, or simply show her that he was able to answer anything she sought to question, he could then at least attempt to earn her trust. Right now, they were conversational, but they were at an absolute, boredom-transfused standstill.

He felt confident he could approach her in their normal way. He just needed the teacher to stop talking about whatever they were doing.

"How are you feeling after your outburst, trouble maker?" He whispered into her ear from behind. The response caused her body to tense in a way he found he enjoyed more than he would have thought.

She turned, eyed him from head to toe, then turned back around, waiting on instructions comfortably as the rest of the classmates shivered in the cold. She sneered. "I didn't cause any problems; I'm just trying to stick up for what's right." She paused. "Do you disagree?"

"No," he answered quickly, huffing as he shoved his hands casually in his pockets. "Your line of thinking is the belief system of an entire nation in Dukhovia, only here is it more obsolete. I imagine that would be very isolating."

Stacy nodded her head slowly. "Perhaps as isolating as being alone in an unfamiliar country?"

He shifted, feeling the intensity of her words, of her realization. "Perhaps so," he agreed.

"Then it seems we're both not quite living our purposeful journeys either, are we?" She gave him those side-eye glances again before she moved with the rest of the class toward their partners.

He watched as she went towards Dylan. He and Rachael had already decided to be partners. He was desperate for more time with Stacy, but he knew that solidifying his friendship with Rachael got him just as far.

She bounced towards him, her book open and ready to go. As it would turn out, they would not have that difficult of a time completing the assignment. It was a rather basic assignment involving the measuring of different plant growth at various seasons and points of time. Being a farmer from a cold country, it was second nature to know this type of information.

He and Rachael watched with little remorse as Stacy and Dylan seemed to be stuck on the first question and worked with much difficulty to come up with an answer that even feigned accuracy.

"Do you mind if I ask you more about the...about..."

Rachael's small, fragile voice interrupted his thoughts. He looked down at her with a grin.

"Emovinya," he finished with a smile. "It means that your mind is able to control movement of objects through your emotions."

She planted herself on the ground, considering the words. Clearly it was something she had been doing, but the realization it was known or intentional must have resonated with her. He could not blame her. It was not common in Dukhovia and when someone with the power was known to exist, it often resulted in ridicule or disbelief. Home sweet home. But perhaps it was simply because the power existed within his family. Specifically, with his mother, whose entire family abandoned her for marrying his father.

Stacy and Dylan had turned in some rendition of what they considered to be completed work and sat on the ground next to them. Stacy was warm as she approached him, but seemed distant all the same. She came up to sit next to him, but then backed away, moving closer to Rachael and Dylan.

He assessed their interactions. Dylan seemed like a good enough person, though he was curious of his background. They spoke Spanish and noted that they came from Spain, they even had Spanish features, but they seemed mixed with other features as well.

There did not seem to be any type of relationship between Dylan and Stacy. No type of flirtation took place between them. They were merely friends just as well as she and Rachael were. He was not certain why he focused on this detail, but he supposed it was important to know whether or not she was romantically involved with anyone currently.

"So—like telekinesis?" Rachael finally asked delicately. The other two turned to him for response.

"Sort of," Nicholas began. "Telekinesis means to move objects with your mind. It's unknown whether or not that is a true power, so it is difficult to say where the energy stems from, but Emovinya stems from your emotions. It is a matter of putting all of the energy stemming from your emotions into one clear path and using that to control the elements around you." As he spoke, Nicholas was drawing swirls in the snow. Basic drawings of swirls of energy coming from a person's stomach and head.

"But still move objects?" Stacy asked.

He nodded slowly. "Move them, control them, change them. Because we know so little, the possibilities are endless, however, we do know that this energy stems from your chakras."

Dylan, Rachael, and Stacy simultaneously exchanged a glance telling him that he had uttered a foreign word.

"Which aarree?" Dylan emphasized.

"Your chakras," Nicholas began, back to drawing in the snow, "are where every aspect of energy in your body is stored. Energy relating to spirituality, to emotions, and so on." He drew a body and etched out two x's—one in the head, the other near the stomach. "Emovinya is a gift from the Spirits. It is believed that they have given part of their gifts to you and therefore you utilize your skill by communicating to them through that chakra which is located in your head."

Rachael gripped her head, knowingly. No fear encapsulated her, not even confusion, she only absorbed the information as if her life depended on it. Perhaps it did. Emovinya unchecked was dangerous.

"The second aspect of your power lies in your stomach. It has to do with power and control over that power. Since your gift deals with controlling your emotions in order to control it, it would make sense that this chakra be crucial. That is why

I recommend imagining that your feelings are a ball of energy, centering them, and then doing with them whatever you wish."

Rachael looked hesitantly out towards the woods that encapsulated the back of the school. He guessed, based on what he knew thus far, that she had spent so much time running from the power that she believed to be a curse, she never imagined wanting to summon that power. Yet, now, it was evident—she wanted to take back this part of her life. Good for her.

"Alright class! We have frozen long enough! Let us head back to collect our findings! Onward towards exploration!"

Nicholas watched as the feeling of defeat washed over Rachael's face. It was just barely noticeable, but noticeable all the less. She bit her lip, looked down, and then smiled towards the others, getting to her feet. He wondered how long she had to play it cool, how long she had to pretend like everything was okay when it was far from it.

He knew that feeling.

"I am more than happy to teach you about connecting to your spirit, anytime, Rachael." The words felt rushed and out of proportion to what she needed to hear. Still, the way her eyes lit up towards him told him they were exactly what she needed to hear.

She started walking forward with Dylan, the both of them speaking excitedly about how thrilled Cody would be to hear she solved so much of her mystery. He wondered how thrilled he would be to learn from whom she had help.

He attempted to stay back, watching Stacy's soft footsteps, she appeared to be doing the same thing. So that was where they were? Willing to speak to one another, but not willing to admit it.

Surprisingly, it was Stacy whom stopped her footsteps first and spoke. "So, how do you know so much about this? Is it just common in Dukhovia or...?"

He smiled. What a simple and expected question, yet a good one to introduce the topic. "Most people in Dukhovia know the legends of Emovinya. They have been passed down through generations, so, the more one person knows today depends on how much their ancestors believed in the past. Many families know no more than Rachael."

Her face seemed to relax and crinkle in confusion all at the same time. "That must be my grandparents. If they had known...They've been trying for years to figure Rachael out."

Nicholas kept his eyes plastered on her face. It revealed so much about her, it told so much, yet never enough, never everything he needed to know... "Yes, I'm certain that is it."

She shook her head, concentrated hard on digging her feet into the same snow-dug footprints ahead of her, and crinkled her nose. "But your family believed?"

Nicholas tensed up, anger flaring through his nostrils—an automatic response to anyone talking about his family. It had never been genuine curiosity, no— no one was curious, they had already cast their opinion and spoke only to voice it to the masses.

But Stacy was not people. No, she was not saying what they were or what they believed, not like the others always did, no, she was asking. Genuine. And he needed to earn her trust. He needed to get her to see him as good.

So, he went vulnerable.

"Yes, my mother was Emovinya."

Her head shot up towards him, as if he had just confirmed all he had been telling them. "Really?"

He nodded once, swallowing the same, familiar, lump that formed whenever he spoke of her. He thought he would be better by now, he should be better by now. "That is how I knew how to calm Rachael. Pressing on the wrists is not a chakra, but a Dukhovian spirit pathway. It calls for immediate control in the body—but only between two people touched heavily by the Spirits."

She eyed him more cautiously, but intrigued all the same, her green eyes bobbing up and down. "Then you're Spirit touched too?"

Now was his chance. His chance to pull her in, to prove to her that he could be everything she needed him to be. He could be a wealth of knowledge. He could be honorable and worthy of giving her answers.

"Not in the same way," he replied. His eyes darted to the side of the school where a few dead bushes grew. He reached for one as they passed and pulled off a branch. "But I am rather attuned with my nature spirit."

He held out the dead stick he had pulled, twirling it before her intrigued eyes. Not losing her eyeline, he closed the branch in hand, squeezed, and opened it back to her, revealing a perfectly green, lush vine.

Her mouth gaped and he knew—he had her interest and she had her proof. Now onto trust.

CHAPTER 35

FOR MY PEOPLE

Stacy's feet crunched in the uneven snow beneath her. Wind whipped and lashed stronger than it ever had, but she needed a minute to feel the cool air, to feel the openness and relief of the harsh windchill. It reminded her of serenity. It reminded her of simplicity. It reminded her of…

Dukhovia.

She had made it a whole five minutes after science concluded before giving in to the chaotic, anti-rhythmic thudding in her chest. Taking deep breaths only intensified the tightening sensation.

No more hot and cold—she had decided. But aside from that, she was stuck. What did she reveal to him? What did she keep secret? Secrets. She was sick of them. She had enough of them her entire life and now…Nicholas was an honorable Dukhovian. He had to be. He had been blessed with a Spirit gift, just as Rachael somehow was. That confusion tore her a bit. Rachael was not even Dukhovian, but she had a Spirit gift? Blah.

She replayed the moment when she watched the greenery spring from his hand. She had never seen anything like it, had never confirmed that the beauty of The Spirit Realm existed outside of her chaotic dreams—until this moment. That determined for her that he was her key. That and his wealth of knowledge and his ability and desire to help Rachael.

That was where she found herself currently. Sitting outside the school gymnasium, desperate for escape. They were given a free period during what was supposed to be math class—something she could care less about not having a sub or something. Ironically, the same thing happened to Nicholas and Rachael's advanced math class. Thus, they met up in the gym where Nicholas had promised to teach Rachael more about her powers.

Two for two. They were really allowing him around the common folk now that Santifini was gone. She half wondered whether that was his order or something that naturally happened due to him being gone. She also constantly wondered where he really was.

Nicholas and Rachael had planned to meet in the coming moments once the bell sounded, but Stacy had run. She needed to. She closed her eyes to keep herself from glancing towards the omniscient, snow-covered woods—a vague reminder of her home. She could not face the darkening skies, beckoning drifts of uniquely orchestrated flakes, knowing the moment she did, there would be nothing to stop her thoughts…

CHAPTER THIRTY-FIVE

The war, the turmoil...the fear of the people. Her torn heart felt weary and desolate. She felt as though she was stuck in an area completely blank of anything in existence: No air, no people, no life...and she was thousands of miles away from anything that could possibly bring her back. Worse, it was impossible to bring anything back.

The bell sounded and students started pouring out of class. The sounds were menacing. The bell. The laughter. The discussions.

The longer she stood by and watched the simplicity of everyday life, the more she felt a paining stab of guilt that while Dukhovia's war raged on, she did nothing. It was not in her heart to stand by. She wanted nothing more than to run directly into the line of fire, stop the forces which threatened the peace of her land, and expand restoration...But that well thought out plan was easier thought than done.

She slowly looked around at the passing students, trying to figure out how she could escape off the campus without anyone noticing. Certainly, on a typical day, they would not so much as bat an eye at a student walking out the door—they were all too absorbed in their own lives to care. Even if it was a member of the band, the school did not find themselves deeply concerned in their whereabouts.

Usually.

With the band getting signed and them recording new songs, the buzz about going to school with *The Rockers* was much more enthusiastic. Stacy could barely pass through the halls without someone congratulating her or asking her what her new songs were about, if Rachael had any new ones, if Rachael and Cody were dating yet. Not to mention the continued staring and pining since the explosion in first period. People practically had her under a microscope anticipating the next move. Even now as they gawked at her through closed windows.

She shook her head, pulling her hood up over her head and deciding to chance any notice from her classmates. They could tell the paparazzi she was a delinquent school skipper who was on the verge of expulsion, they could tell them anything—and she would tell them things ten times worse to rebound. And anything they said, the turmoil would nowhere near measure up to her true concerns.

Dukhovia—The population of Dukhovia was 2,874,976. That was 2,874,976 people whose lives were at risk. Over two million people who could not live in the peaceful ideals that they were fighting to protect.

For the first time in her life, the wind slashing against her face was not freeing, it was suffocating. The chill that ran through her veins, that ran through Dukhovia—it no longer stood for freedom and individuality. It meant chains. It was a sign of enslavement.

Stacy walked back and forth down the school sidewalk for a long time trying to decide if what she needed in that moment was to stay or go. In the end, she realized that what she needed to do was get on plane to Dukhovia and never look back. Simple except that she would be dead without the knowledge one person could give her...

Nicholas…

No more hot and cold. No more…

The wind blew harshly against her face, throwing piles of snow at her. Suddenly, the temperature seemed to drop twenty degrees and ice appeared around her, causing her fingers to stick to the sidewalk. She stood to her feet then fell again, her entire body becoming covered in a snow drift that blew out of seemingly nowhere.

And it was that event with the thought of Nicholas in her mind that made her turn around that allowed her to choose to put her guard…not down, but at half an angle with a panic button. It was as she had been saying—she would never know if she did not give herself the time to find out. But she struggled so much with letting someone potentially dangerous come close that she was losing out on what someone who was not at all dangerous had to offer—like the answers to her best friend's lifelong dilemma. If she had not been killed yet, Stacy could stand a chance to let her guard down long enough to find out.

And so, she returned to school, threw open the doors to the gym, and in the final seconds before the bell rang, Stacy approached Nicholas and Rachael, the two both looking almost as ragged as she.

Then she froze, paralyzed as panic started in her chest and spread.

"Stacy? Stace? Are you okay?" Rachael's words sounded like a hollow echo in the back of her mind until she latched in on them.

"Yeah," she breathed, exhaling deeply. "I think I just need more air. Being inside after this morning is killing me."

"Okay, well, I am most definitely not walking home with you today, there is freezing rain and I can't risk another injury. But, I will porch sit with you in my blanket when we get home." Rachael winked.

Stacy rolled her eyes. "It's fine, I could use the time to think."

Lights seemed to dance in Nicholas's eyes as he pulled himself into the conversation. "If you would allow me, I would love to walk home with you, Stacy Grace."

Stacy paused, reeling in her panic. She breathed in, taking the moment to look towards Rachael's over-approving head nod.

"Yeah," she breathed. "That would be great. Meet you up front after school?"

He smiled. "I will be there."

CHAPTER 36

THE WAR OF DESTINY

S tacy Matthews had skipped the rest of the school day and Nicholas was not sure where that left them for their walk home. This was it. Finally, he would have uninterrupted time to talk with her, to see who she truly was when she was off guard—well, to some degree, hopefully.

Yet, could her absence be telling? He noticed by lunch time for certain that he was not just missing her between classes and that she was, for certain, gone. They did not have any other classes together, but he was in all of Rachael's. Even asking her did not seem to yield any answers. She shrugged as if this type of thing were normal, citing that sometimes Dukhovia called to her and she answered in whatever way she could muster.

Huh.

"Hey!"

Nicholas spun around, there she finally was, bounding towards him with a crushed, brown bag in her hand and a completely empty parking lot in her wake.

She bounced towards him without fear, seeming to pause and hesitate as she raised and then lowered a hand the closer she got to him. "Sorry, I'm late," she started. She looked down and began rummaging through the bag in her hand. "I already skipped most of school and I knew there was no chance of beating you in swim class today, so I decided to skip the last two periods to bring you these."

He eyed her questionably before taking the bag. What could the gesture mean? What could be inside? What was her angle? He peered into the bag which seemed to be filled with an array of vegetables. His eyes widened and his heart fell into his stomach as he realized the specifics of the contents. Carrots, dahlia beans, eer root, even navar.

"From my grandparents garden," she explained as his puzzled and bewildered eyes met her gaze. "I figured you can't starve and we certainly can't expect you to live off our horrid Americanized groceries."

"Stacy…" He stared back down at her and the food. Her foot did not tap. Her eyes ensured she believed the message. She delivered the words lazily and carelessly—she was telling the *truth*. She truly brought him the food simply to nourish him. To *help* him. Just as her uncle did.

"Well, surely you must help me eat them," he offered.

Her lip seemed to tense, but he continued to hold it out to her.

"I didn't get enough for two," she revealed. "I want you to have them." She seemed to cross her eyebrows, infuriation at herself written across her face.

"I insist," he said, forcing the carrots into her palm.

She looked from him to the carrots, her lip and foot now in their assumed positions. "Okay," she agreed with a reluctant smile. "Would you like to sit down or is it acceptable to eat and walk?"

"It is whatever you desire," he told her.

Stacy grinned, seeming to find humor in something he said, then planted herself on the curb. She slowly began munching on a carrot, passing the rest of the bag to him. "In Dukhovia, we eat sitting down like civilized human beings."

He raised an eyebrow as he sat down to join her. He took out a dahlia bean, examining its perfection with care before taking a long bite. It was the best thing he had eaten in a week. Perhaps longer. "Is that truly what you learned on your trip to Dukhovia?"

She bit the carrot, seeming to mull over her words as she stared out into the empty lot. "Meals are a symbol of culture. Recipes are passed down by generations and time together as a family or with friends is an honor."

She recited the words poetically, but he could almost laugh at the redundancy. The thought left a metallic taste in his mouth as he processed. How ironic he wished she knew the words were. "At a point long ago, certainly," he began. "However, now most Dukhovians can scarcely eat let alone together. They are lucky to be able to obtain three meals a day, never mind follow any recipes. Many become so…enthralled when they find berries in a forest that they swallow the bush before getting them home for supper. That is not Dukhovian like—not at all."

His thoughts drifted to another time, a simpler time that he knew so much about in theory, but so little in execution. He lost focus himself and felt his focus shift to the empty parking lot as he tapped each individual finger against each other.

"What happened?" Stacy asked aloud.

"The war," he answered slowly. "But I suppose it has been a variety of things since then and over time—building."

Stacy waited. He knew she wanted answers and he so desperately wanted to be the one to give them to her.

"At the rise of WWI, our people began to fear that our simplistic ways would be our downfall. Rightfully so, some thought, there had been times in the past where fighting came close to our borders and we questioned whether we would need more protection, more security. In those days, rebel groups started to form, but nothing as severe as now came of it. Other times we had war over farm land, fear came essentially anytime Russia went to war, and so on... but we always relied on the weaponry of our ancestors and our fighting techniques—never anything stronger. We would also rely on direction from the Spirits whose voice became quieter and quieter the more we rebelled and the further we broke away from what was meant to be.

"This time was different. A boat of Russian refugees was coming for us and we only had so long to decide what to do. Not wanting to leave them stranded, but also not wanting the rest of the world to target us for breaking our neutrality, we did what we thought the Spirits would want from us and accepted them.

"Bombs fell down on us that night like rain. Those who were alive to see it, documented it as if the sky were falling, bringing every fiery ball of gas down to the planet with it. We assembled as one, with every weapon we had in an attempt to fight back, to ward them off. But so many of us died so quickly and we became each other's enemies.

"Immediately the fights began—we needed to update and use modernized firearms, we needed to listen to the Spirits, the Spirits got us into this mess, and on, and on."

Nicholas paused for a moment before continuing. Stacy was facing him full on now, her arms wrapped around one of her knees.

"Our death toll..." his words disappeared and he swallowed the lump in his throat. "It was unprecedented. No one knew what to do after that. Russia offered us aid and it was with their support that we were able to fight off the enemy. We signed a petition stating we had no stake in the war and we were left alone after that—but the fighting amongst ourselves only continued. Meeting after meeting, protest after protest, war after war. People were frightened and wanted to train our military to use the weapons Russia wanted to give us. The majority refused. Thus, the greatest tear our country has ever seen was born.

"Ice sculptures began to melt, the Spirit's presence withdrew even more, people were deceiving, murdering—Dukhovia became a country of fear. Families torn apart, father's and son's not returning home..."

Nicholas paused, a single tear falling down his cheek as he spoke.

Stacy paused, starting her words slowly. Nicholas could barely see from his line of vision, but he watched as her lips mouthed words, decided against them, and then tried on new ones until audible words finally escaped. "Is that...is that what happened to your parents?" Even still, she seemed hesitant in the response and out of the corner of his eye he saw her back away an inch.

Reveal something to her, earn her trust.

And he would. He would not lie.

"No. Not exactly. My parents were murdered because of me. Because I was weak and stupid and foolish."

"Nicholas, that can't be true..." She was protesting strongly, immediately— but he sensed her fear all the same.

"It is. I needed to be trained and I could not focus with worldly attachments."

But that was all he would reveal. If he was going to tell their story it would not be to further his stupid and foolish gain, it would be to honor them, it would be, dare he say, to heal...

Stacy seemed on the brink of vomiting, perhaps she even had with the level of disgust written on her face. So, American's did not have corporal punishment. At least, not in her life.

"That's what they wanted to do to punish my family," Stacy revealed.

Nicholas shot his head in her direction. He had never heard any such stories of The Grayson family receiving any punishment for their crimes—be it in Dukhovia or America. Simply some restrictions.

"To your grandfather?" He asked slowly.

She nodded once. "And my grandmother and my mother and Uncle Richey. When they finally healed my grandfather and everything was ending, they had the trial. Dan, my older brother, he was a baby, I think, and I hadn't been born yet. The court wanted them all to experience what they put the world through. They bounced different ideas around like electric shock, torture, stoning…" Stacy shook her head and closed her eyes, the very thought conjuring up tears. "My mom was only sixteen. My age."

The significance pained him. "I was six," he offered. He would not use their story to disrespect the Spirits, but he would use his story to…provide comfort? To connect? To understand… "Six years old when my mentor took me to our home, chained them to our chairs, and…"

Stacy put a gentle, but affirming hand on Nicholas's shoulder, begging him to stop. But then immediately withdrew it, leaping backward and glancing at her hand as if she forgot the spark that would ignite between them. In the process, she seemed to forget what she meant to delay originally.

Nicholas swallowed the lump in his throat and pushed through.

"…engulfed the house into flames, and made me watch everything." He shook as he spoke, tears now pouring freely down his face. His own chains seemed to be melting. His own thoughts, thoughts he long ago hid, flowed freely. "I can still hear my mother's screams, her piercing screams. I tried so hard to get free and save them…I tried so hard."

He felt his body shake and crash the way it always did when he thought of their deaths, remembered their pleas and he stood, a stone statue that could not bend or break. Yet, the words fell differently from him. They did not leave him scarred and beaten, they felt almost freeing. And the more he revealed, the more he wanted to. Perhaps he was making a mistake, perhaps it was too much to reveal simply to earn her trust. But he was letting his gut lead and she was listening.

Nicholas's glistening, bright blue eyes found Stacy's round, huge, brilliant green pair and the feelings of anger, of loss, of devastation seemed to be nearly replaced with that of words he did not know the name for. They had not disappeared, surely not, however, he felt—less isolated.

Stacy's eyes were searching his, looking past his words and seeming to look into the world he described to find some new version of the person she thought she knew, the person she thought she had pegged. He knew, of course, that she was still wrong. That as long as his duty called him, he could never be entirely honest with her. She could never know him completely and therefore, he would not know all of her. All of who Dukhovia was meant to be led by.

"Oh, Nicholas. You were just a baby." She fell silent, finding that the right words did not exist. "I can't imagine the guilt you're carrying. You must have lost so much that day."

That day. Ha. Yes, he had lost a lot. In that she was correct. However, his loss dated back well before that day. He was destined for failure the day she was born. The day they were both born and the Spirits decided they had pegged her for greatness and him for doom.

That was what the prophecy meant. That was where the differentiation between great destruction and great peace came in. That was why he *was* curious to meet her and her family and see *why*. Why they were chosen to lead Dukhovia to greatness while he was chosen to play a pawn in a game and rot.

Anger rose inside of him, despair and vengeance fighting for rights. He had always thought it. Always thought that the prophecy meant not that the world had two fates, but that she had one and he had the other—great peace or great destruction. He balled his fists, began to shift his feet.

No.

It was not the Spirits whom had decided this fate. It was not them who decided that he would be the sacrifice, the great destruction. It was mankind. It was Arkady who had formulated this plan and put him in the middle.

He breathed. Did that mean that he had a choice? Did that mean that if he did do his best to obey the Spirits, that he could still lead the country to great peace? Even if that meant allowing Stacy to take that lead?

"That day, before, after..."

Stacy was quiet, kicking her feet for several moments, watching the slosh of snow and slush fall from her boots lazily. "It's horrible the way they want to treat people. You're right about what you said at lunch the other day, about things not being black and white. None of it is. My grandpa did do horrific things, but he did so many more beautiful things that never would have happened if they decided his fate by only looking at the crimes—not the explanations or the person."

He forced his chin up to look more closely at her. Tears still sat in his eyes the way they always did when he thought of that day, but he needed a chance to bury them. "It is disgusting, what they do—wanting to punish our families for crimes they did not commit based on fear and lies."

"Fear," Stacy agreed, her voice sounding far away. "My grandfather used to tell me that fear was a weapon—the strongest one we have."

"He is wise," Nicholas agreed.

She seemed to smile at that, just a small perk of the sides of her lips, but enough to tense his stomach. "He is the most wonderful, kind, intelligent, resilient person I know. I think if they did try to destroy him, they would find him indestructible."

Nicholas smiled back and dabbed at his eyes, gathering himself. "He seems fit to rule Dukhovia, let alone live there." The two laughed.

And then he considered his next words.

He considered these words carefully, turning them over once, then twice, examining them carefully for holes—for anything that felt like pressure.

They were his choice. They were what he wanted to share. His story. Not a story forcibly told. Not a story told to sway. A story his own, told for his own purpose.

"My mother. She was as perfect a mother as you could ever dream. A saint amongst demons. She was as pure a Dukhovian is meant to come. Honorable, kind, loyal. She taught me everything I know about joy and love and patience. She *was* joy."

Nicholas felt his hand began to shake just as he tried to move his fingers up and then down up and then down. He could not manage. He was breaking.

"She sounds beautiful."

"She was," he breathed, a gasping sound escaping him. Where did he stop? What benefit did divulging this information have? Could he stop? He had to tell, *wanted* to tell. Perhaps it was not out of his own selfish gain, but to tell her story, to share her legacy so that more people knew of the brave, selfless woman that he owed his life. "I remember her mostly tending to her garden. She was always so nurturing to each and every plant, to every creature. Especially her strawberries. She taught me that each form of life yields its own purpose and thus we have a duty to ensure every life is preserved in order to reach its fullest potential. It was then I decided to become a vegetarian."

He watched Stacy suck in a breath that seemed to get stuck on its way out, the sounds of her exhaling were rigid. "Tell me more about her."

He smiled. "Nurturing. Kind. Compassionate. Purposeful. A woman worthy of Dukhovian soil."

"And worthy of raising a son that shares those qualities, I'm sure," Stacy responded.

Nicholas was unsure whether he liked that—the comparison of himself to his mother. He sat in uncomfortable, stumped silence for a long time, seemingly null of emotion.

"What would you have done?" Nicholas asked, his words pulsating in the back of his mind, begging for release. "If anything like that did happen to your family?"

She thought about it for a long moment, her facial expressions bouncing between contemplation and rage. Finally, she breathed deep and relaxed. "I'd avenge them—anyway I could. I would make sure the world knew the injustice, knew their stories, and I would burn every bridge in my way to get there."

Nicholas was struck with the power and passion behind the words. "And if your efforts failed?"

She thought only for a moment before turning to him fully, a fierceness he had seen so many times—always regarding her family—flared from her. "The only way you can fail at what you were born to do is if you don't try—or so it wasn't meant to be."

And then the words knocked him from existence. The words did not seem they could ever apply to him, yet he sat with them. The only way you can fail at what you are born to do is if you do not try…or if you intentionally do the opposite, he theorized. He was not certain, in full, what the prediction given from the Spirits regarding the two of them meant, but he knew that it was not damning. Not unless…

But his eyes flashed with the fire of his family home, of where he remembered his mother making his favorite dinners, of where he sat on her lap and sang songs, of the moments that seemed they would last lifetimes… If he abandoned his mission, they die in vain. If he fulfilled his mission, they died in vain. But if he strayed from it…he had seen it enough times to know…that fire would spread.

"Would you break the rules then?" He asked calmly. "If you knew it would protect your family?"

She seemed to read something on him that was, dare he say, damning, but she nodded her head with diffused confidence. "Every time."

Stacy looked at him for a moment, her eyes going up and down as if reading him, taking him in. She chose to not say anything else related to the subject after that. Instead, they both chose to sit in silence for a long time. "What about your father?"

Nicholas's face turned from nothingness to automatic stone—death etched on every inch of him. "If my mother taught me all there was to know of joy and love, then he taught me everything there was to know about hate and evil. I suppose you saw that side of me."

Stacy was shaking her head. Shaking it—confidently. How strange the difference from only a day ago.

Without a second thought and before he knew what he was doing himself, Nicholas was stripping himself of his jacket and shirt. The cool breeze directly against his skin felt freeing…and trapping. *For me. Choices.* He was doing what he wanted for the first time in his life. Sharing his story, making choices.

"During WWI, my family was dishonored. We took the blame for a crime we did not commit. My father wore the repercussions of that decision like a badge of shame, willing to do anything to regain it. When I was given my birth reading, he thought I may have a chance to redeem our family, he wanted to make sure I was as *focused* as I possibly could be."

Nicholas ran his hand down his arm. He watched as Stacy's gaze flitted to his horrendously scarred back and water began to well up in her eyes. He sensed her pounding heart, her remorse, her pity. He had no use for it.

"If I showed the slightest hint that I had my priorities crossed: any mention of a break, failure to know what he expected next, a mistake…the punishment…well, the punishment never quite fit the crime."

"Oh Nicholas…" Stacy's words evaded her. She lifted a hesitant hand and ran it over his mutilated arm. Her touch was soothing, soft, nothing like he had experienced in the last ten years. Her hand hovered over his back—his worst spots. The burns and once-infected, poorly stitched gashes were a display of red and purple hues.

"Losing him changed me for the better. I no longer had to pretend that I could ever love a monster."

Stacy's eyes met his, silent, solemn, but most importantly… understanding. "You're not dangerous at all. You're hurt. You're lost."

Nicholas looked up at her. It was not a question, but he felt the need to be able to give an answer, confirmation—something.

"I only ever wanted to make him happy," Nicholas choked out. "But now that I look back, I realize what a failed mission it was. How there was no happiness within him to ever conjure up." He paused, swallowing sadness.

"If you being you and being as true a Dukhovian as you could be didn't bring him happiness and pride in you, then he was broken," Stacy asserted. Her body was close to his, her fingers so very close to grasping onto his, inching closer and closer… "You didn't deserve any of that, Nicholas. No one ever does. We all deserve to be treated like people."

Nicholas sized her up. Her words, the truth they held, the comfort, and the wisdom. "Perhaps that was something he should have known. Were he the best Dukhovian himself."

"People operate out of fear," Stacy repeated the words simply. "My grandpa told me that once too—about my own father."

Nicholas looked at her, perplexed.

"Kevin, my dad, well—he isn't *technically* my father. My biological dad's name was Rodney. He and my mom dated on and off when she was young, but her and Kevin always loved each other. My grandpa says he knew that and he knew that our family was a lot and children were a lot…so, when my mom told him she was pregnant, he ran and never looked back."

She smiled a not pleasing smile. "Tom says he was afraid of what he didn't know me to be and that he is missing out. I've wondered a lot about him. About why he couldn't even give me a chance. Maybe I wasn't so hard, maybe our family wasn't so much to handle…but for him it was, and that's okay because it could never mean anything about me—he didn't even know me."

She paused for a moment. "I suppose that's similar to your father. He was afraid you wouldn't be able to erase your family's past, afraid of what would come of it if so…so he just tried to control as much as he could and lost himself and you in the mess. And he would have had someone worthy of Dukhovia and the Andrews family if he gave you the chance."

Nicholas's palms went rigid, the heavy feeling in his chest seemed to lower into his stomach before slowly dissipating. The girl next to him had gone from public enemy number one, to someone passionate of Dukhovia, to someone potentially *worthy* of Dukhovia. She held the passion, the love, for their country. She held wisdom. She held kindness for her citizens.

Granted, she was still American in aspects as well. Those would be the things Nicholas needed to focus on. How worthy she was and how likely the other side of her was to cast out that worth. But how much would they matter?

"Demitona," Nicholas corrected after a while. "My family's true last name is Demitona. After we were dishonored, we were stripped of our Dukhovian identity and given a new name. My true name is Nicholas Aloyshenka Aleksis Demitona."

Stacy seemed to be studying the information before responding. "Sir Nicholas Aloyshenka Aleksis Demitona—priyatno poznakomit'sya."

Nicholas smiled and laughed. "It is a pleasure to meet you, Stacy Grace Matthews."

CHAPTER 37

PROTECT THE HEIR

S tacy and Nicholas walked in what seemed to be years of silence after talking nonstop for so long. She wanted to learn any and everything while still keeping her reservations. Still being aware of his ambiguity. Still being aware of the red flag statements. Yet, the more she watched Nicholas come undone, the more absolutely certain she was that he was sent to her for a reason—the exact reason she needed him.

Accident. She had deemed well enough by now that Nicholas's blowup at Rachael was a total and complete accident—even twice. It was not who he was, but rather a reflection of so many more frustrations—to what?

She felt she had him figured out. Nicholas was like Dylan. Nicholas was like Cody on the bad days. It was not the monster within that made him unsteady… it was the monsters around him. And him being hell bent to earn Stacy and Rachael's trust and forgiveness was a silent plea to not see him as the monster his father was.

He was afraid, he was lost. Deciding to come to a country (one he had always been told to fear or disregard) in order to learn if his family was alone in being wrongly dishonored, was a daring task. She wondered if he had felt his task was successful—that her family was in fact unjustly banished.

Her family. His was gone. Murdered so that he could focus on his *mission.* How serious of a mission was it if they wanted him to pay such close attention that they were willing to murder his family over it? Especially in such a gruesome manner. Also, who is they? Maybe she failed to ask the right questions, but right now, watching him grieve their loss for what seemed to be the first time, did not seem like the time to ask. Even if she was comforting a trained assassin.

Ugh. She could only imagine what Rachael would say. *You finally find a guy you're into and he's an axe murderer.* Not that Stacy was *into* Nicholas, persae. At least, not in the way Rachael intended.

But at this point, she was locked in. Nicholas was a wealth of knowledge when it came to Dukhovia—even if she had to swallow the innate sense of fear that bubbled up inside of her when she pressed. Don't ask questions about Dukhovia, she had always learned. Don't ask questions about his parents.

But she had asked the questions and so far, she was still standing. With a lot more information than she knew what to do with. What even was Dukhovia? She knew they had to stay hidden due to their banishment, but it still seemed like the peaceful Dukhovia she knew and loved. Yes, they saw some soldiers, but murdering families? The type of fear and anxiety Nicholas spoke of? That could not have been her Dukhovia. There was no way.

The information nearly scared her out of asking anymore, but she knew she had to, especially with the information divulged as they stood to finally leave the school...

Stacy had reached for his shirt and jacket to hand to him. "Here. You must be freezing."

Nicholas took the items, but instead of immediately putting them on, he leaned back in the snow and closed his eyes. "The cold doesn't bother me. It's comforting..."

"Like a hug..." Stacy finished, her breath nearly gone.

Nicholas opened his eyes. "Perhaps. Other times it's an emotion—like fear."

Her heart turned into a brick that hardened, cut loose, and landed in her stomach. So many years of searching for another person who was not bothered by the cold...wondering why it was only her when her entire family was from Dukhovia...Yet the pain he described...

That was when the silence began. Her head had not stopped spinning: running through word after word, how to phrase things, how to just not. What did she ask now? What did she save for Rachael? She could not. She could not. There was no way.

Deep breath.

"So...what exactly is your plan now? Or, I guess, once you figure out what you came here to figure out?" She felt the unsteadiness in her words as she spoke them and Nicholas, with his keen observation skills, did not miss the trembling of her lip. She saw the slight upward curve of his lips before he responded with a confident "Your family is safe, Stacy Grace."

Okay. Now what? He's avoiding. He's not avoiding, you are. Gr. "But?"

"There is no rebuttal as far as that statement goes," he declared and the sureness of his voice seemed to settle the majority of her nerves around the subject. "There is no intent to harm your family."

Stacy's eyes darted to the ground as she thought. She hopped up on a curb, watching Nicholas's eyes bulge and watch her like a hawk would its dinner. He followed down to her steps and then up to her watchful eyes. Her words seemed to flow with less ease now that they were out in more of the public eye. Not that there were not custodians and other staff eyeing them with pretensions at the school, but now they were front and center for any fellow passerby. Throw in the distraction of the speeding cars, the risk of slipping on ice, and the wafting smells reminding her to never skip breakfast again...it was a type of purgatory.

Nicholas looked up now as well, his own gaze as far away as his memories. Finally, he shrugged and in a raspy voice said, "I told you I came here because I was interested in the comparison of our family trees. That much is true. However, I wonder what important information I might learn. Will I convey to Dukhovia that even those families thought the most untraditional are worthy? If so, will that show them that things are not so simplistic? Will it be a cause for change?"

"Change in what way?" She pressed, her blazing green eyes as urgent as her words.

He shrugged, and she wondered if it was because he truly did not know what came next. "A call for peace. A call to see patriotism and brethren before death and destruction. As we are meant to be."

Stacy tried to breathe, but felt as though all the air was sucked from her lungs and there was no oxygen left in the world to replenish them. "And you'll return to your role in the military to accomplish that?"

Nicholas tensed. "If they will have me."

Stacy stored the information. "What if they won't?"

He breathed. "Then I assume I will have to pray the Spirits guide me wherever I am meant to be and that I still have a place in Dukhovia."

"You mentioned something earlier that I...I don't know what it is," she stuttered over the embarrassing words she had been too embarrassed to ask Tom. "Your birth reading?"

His body tensed. She saw his eyes rapidly fire back and forth once and then settle as if he was currently trying to read some type of spiritual, unseen words. "A birth reading is the Spirit's prediction of your life's purpose. The moment you are born, families and Shaman pray over some type of spiritual or ancestral relic— sometimes a locket, sometimes an orb. The relic will hold the purpose inside of it for purposes of prayer in order to ensure the purpose comes to fruition.

"Once prayer begins, Shaman utilize objects and boards to determine what the Spirits have relayed to them regarding the purpose of the individual."

Stacy waited. When he did not go on, she prompted him further. "So, what was your birth reading?"

He had never fully returned from drifting away, but his eyes seemed to further disappear inside his head, inside his thoughts, perhaps inside his memories. "Mine was different. I was born on the floor of my family's barn. My reading was meant to be stored in my great grandfather's military medal." He reached into his pocket and fingered the antique, weathered golden medallion. It clung to a dark blue cord that looked nearly in mint condition.

"But, instead, when Shaman arrived, they already knew my prediction. It was given to them directly from the Spirits in a vision ritual..." He paused and laughed lightly in response to her confused, asking face. "...A vision ritual is when Shaman gather together to attempt to enter The Spirit Realm and hear direct warnings or predictions from the Spirits. Usually, they relate to the country as a whole rather than a specific person. In fact, they have never related to a specific person."

Stacy waited, hooked and begging for answers. It was like a door was opened and she snuck away from reality and into the world she always belonged in. The usual thick, stifling feeling that existed around her in some capacity no longer existed.

"My reading was not direct. I was predicted to bring Dukhovia either great destruction or great peace. That was all, nothing more."

There was more and Stacy knew it. She knew it from the solemn way he hung his head. She knew it from the emptiness of his words. That, or he felt he knew which one it would be...

"It's great peace," Stacy said matter-of-factly.

Nicholas looked up from her clumsy feet only a moment before darting back to trace their every step as she hopped over ice patches and around snow banks. "What makes you so certain?"

"It's obvious," she mused. "Great destruction isn't fitting for you. Anytime you lose your cool, you catch yourself. It isn't intent to cause harm. So, I know you don't *plan* for that. And I know you're able to catch yourself before any accident would lead to something a Spirit might determine to be 'great destruction'."

His face tightened, registering her words. "You do not understand the choices I have made in the past."

Her stomach knotted, but she shrugged. "Past being the key word there. You are who you choose to be and who you are now, not who you were five minutes ago or a year ago. Who you were doesn't determine who you are."

And then that tightened face seemed to fall freely. "A choice?" He scoffed. "I have not had a choice in my life since this war began. Everything was determined for me from the moment I was born, as you see. So, I am not so certain. Not so certain I get a say."

Stacy wanted to remain optimistic, not because she knew any more than he to be able to reassure him, but because she fully felt as though he deserved that reassurance.

"Who were they?" She whispered, finally. "The people who hurt your family? What did they want with you?"

Tears filled his eyes as bitter rage and intense sadness flared his nostrils. She noticed his body begin to shake and his fists begin to clench.

Too much. It was too much to think about. He had already said enough.

"The leader of the military," he choked out. "If I had the promise for either great peace or great destruction, he needed me on his side. He needed to make sure my upbringing was swayed the best way he could manage it."

Stacy bit her lip. "And what about on the flip side? What happens if all us banished families are just as horrific as Dukhovia deemed us?"

He inhaled deeply, whether to cope with the realization that may be fact or to buy time, she did not care. "Then I suppose we continue in the patterns of judgment and empty-mindedness that we have been circling around for years and years."

Continue in the world she could not think existed. Continue with the fire and smoke of her dreams in her beloved country. Her stomach turned. To her, they were just in her dreams, but miles and miles away—those dreams *were* real.

She swallowed a lump in her throat. "How bad is the war—now?"

Nicholas inhaled deeply, his nostrils flaring as his brilliant eyes flickered with feeling. "I do not like to think about it."

"I'm sorry," Stacy said quickly, looking up from carefully watching her feet only a moment, then she waited expectantly.

"It is a heartbreaking subject, however, it is the only thought that has entered my mind in my nearly sixteen years."

Also almost 16. Noted.

"The war is in a stalemate of sorts, currently. Both sides are tenser than ever, however, they are holding out for…something."

"For you?" She asked with a raised eyebrow.

Nicholas shrugged his shoulders, trying to ignore how her feet were starting to slip on and off the curb thoughtlessly. "Yes, in a manner."

Her stomach twisted into knots.

"I have told you about the divide our country faces as far as whether or not to modernize," he went on. "There is another dilemma that divides us—the heir. Watch!"

What felt like a million things happened at once. Stacy stopped dead in her tracks, causing her to slip into ice and go crashing backward towards the street. Her breath already taken away from the weight of the word on her chest, let alone the spinning in her head as her thoughts played out the dream, played out thoughts of Nicholas, of his words, of her knowledge, of her fears, of her family—over and over and over.

It was only Nicholas's shouting of her name that brought her attention to the bright headlights flashing up beside her. She looked only for a moment, the moment before she knew her head would smack the pavement and send her on her first hospital trip. She felt a weight fiercer than she could ever imagine crash into her body and roll her to the other side of the street, then there was blood splattering around her, in front of her eyes, on her face…but it was not her own.

"Stacy? Stacy, are you alright?"

It took a moment for her thoughts to register. The car swerved and drove on, honking fiercely at her. She watched it go, seeming to zone in and out before her face met Nicholas's—latching onto his ice blue eyes. They never looked so concerned and pleading, wild with panic as they bore into hers, darting back and forth across her face, down her body, and back again.

His right-hand rest underneath her head, his body on top of hers entirely. He was so close she could smell the sweetness of his cologne and the fear on his breath. She wasn't quite sure where his windbreaker ended and hers began and each of his heaving breaths pressed into her chest with force.

"Nic..." It was the only sound she could get out, capsulated by a fear she never felt. What had happened? She had fallen off the curb and laughed about it a million times over. What had distracted her thought so much that she was nearly crushed by a car instead of Nicholas's body?

The heir.

They're coming. Protect them. Protect the heir.

"Stacy..." He lifted his left hand to brush hair from her face; it was then she caught notice of where the blood was coming from.

The heir would have to wait.

"Your arm," she muttered, then she bolted up. "You're bleeding."

He looked at it as if it were the first time he noticed. "It hit something on my way down to you. Are you okay? You should be seen at the hospital immediately."

"No," she was shaking her head and standing. There was a gash down nearly the entire length of his forearm that was gushing blood. It looked deep and she was certain it would need stitches. She looked around for any sign of help, but the usual bustling street seemed to die down and no one in the businesses seemed to take note of the incident. How could that be?

Choosing to ignore the strangeness, she rushed to pick up a pile of snow and throw it onto his arm, wiping away as much blood as she could. Nicholas tried to protest and make her sit down, but she continued on, wiping at the blood. "You need stitches," she told him in quick, panicked words as she worked.

He shook his head. "I heal quickly. I will be fine. Stacy..."

She failed to hear the rest of his words, focusing on tuning out what he just revealed. *Not bothered by cold, like me. Heals quickly, like me.* Her hands were drenched in blood and shaking, the scent of metal and snow filling her nostrils. Something seemed to silence him now and he gave up trying to get her to sit down and let her work.

She bit her lip, working quickly to whip off her long sleeve shirt and tie it around his arm as thick as she could, leaving herself stranded in a camisole.

She grimaced as she moved her shirt over the waxy grafts of the brittle burn scars that wrapped around his left elbow and partially down the side and back of his forearm. When she finished, she paused, holding pressure onto his arm. They were both quiet as they met the other's gaze.

Stacy swallowed. "You saved my life."

Nicholas was still out of breath as he watched her, now lost in his own thoughts. "I suppose I did. You need to be more careful, Stacy Grace. You could have been killed. Promise me?"

She could only nod, unable to make audible words. So, what if she did die? What concern was it to him? Other than another hit on his record as far as violence, she was no sweat off his back. Unless Rachael was right and they were destined for love. She thought about her own feelings as she rushed to stop him from bleeding out. Perhaps it was less so that he loved her and more so that he needed her for whatever this *mission* was—just as much as she needed him for her own.

She felt his heartfelt conviction that her family was safe to be true. Then again, was she falling right into a ploy? And was the ploy his or her own? No, she felt the sincerity in her soul and his. She felt the genuinity (right?) pour from his heart as he talked about his family, his struggles. Nicholas was a safe person. Her family was safe. And if he wanted her dead, his one-way ticket to do it completely guilt-free just took flight.

Nicholas was safe. She was certain of it.

***

"Tell me what I can do for you." She had asked the question at least three times on the walk home after pledging to him that she would be more careful. She decided she likely should anyway. If this dream truly had meaning and Nicholas was here, talking about the heir, on a mission to find her family and end the war, then she likely had purpose beyond just being able to maintain stellar balance on the icy curb.

He had nodded his appreciation, but rejected the notion. "You have done enough. I should be getting you home. Your family will worry."

Stacy hesitated, but shrugged the comment off. "I think by now they consider me indestructible enough that I can go off with even the most dangerous of students and survive."

Nicholas attempted a smirk, but was certain the various emotions resulted in more of a grimace. "They must not know how frequent your near-death experiences are." He joked.

"Hey, that was only one," Stacy chastised.

"I'd argue it was two with the way your cousin thinks of me."

They both now walked side by side. Stacy's house was finally near enough to ensure she would make it home without another threat to her life. The closing in of the tall pine trees in the back brought dismay to both of them as the walk dawned to a close.

Stacy grimaced. The last few hours had been filled with so much between her and Nicholas, she had forgotten about Cody being over and the issues that led him there. A sense of guilt immediately washed over her. Her thoughts continuing to wander to Dukhovia while there was someone who needed her fifty feet away on American soil.

"Well, I'll be coming home practically unscathed so that'll earn you major points in the trust department."

"*Practically*," he emphasized. "Would you truly not allow me to lend you my jacket? At least make a show of me being a gentleman and not sending you home in your undergarments?"

Stacy flashed him a condescending look. "Sir, this is considered a full ensemble in the warmer months."

"Hm."

Stacy looked as the pines were now half showing and stopped Nicholas. "Cody did have a rough morning though and showing up covered in blood with you is probably not the best way to continue it. Or us being…together," she swallowed a lump of fire at the word. "That's his house, Rachael's, and then mine—I can see myself the rest of the way. If that's okay with you."

Nicholas could not hide the hope that fell when she uttered the words, but he reluctantly agreed. "You would know best. I wish him well."

Stacy nodded her appreciation. The two stood facing each other in stillness four houses from their intended destination. The sun had started to disappear now and cool winds whipped at them from all angles. Neither shuddered. Neither moved.

Not cold like me. Heals fast like me.

"Have you ever been sick before?" She asked the question with confidence.

"Excuse me?" He asked.

"You know like a cough, a runny nose, stomachache."

His face seemed to understand what she was asking. He averted his eyes only for a moment, Stacy assumed in an attempt to dodge suspicion, but she was locked. "Not really, no. Perhaps once and as you can see, I am susceptible to injury." He gestured to his back and she flinched. "The wounds simply close sooner than anticipated. Outwardly, anyway."

Stacy attempted to convey an empathetic, remorseful look. She was not sure how well she succeeded, but she knew that she felt with her entire being that she needed to be there for him now. She needed to understand, to protect, to heal.

"I know this will sound strange given the adventure we had, but I had a really nice walk with you."

Nicholas took a step towards her, his good hand hovering around the side of her face. With the back of his hand, he grazed her face lightly. "Are you certain you are alright?"

Stacy's knees felt weak and her stomach fluttered at his touch. Perhaps she was not feeling okay after all. "I promise. Once I wash the blood off it'll be like it never happened. And you?" She stopped herself short as he unwrapped his arm— the bleeding seemed to already clot.

"Fast healer," he reminded her.

"Fast healer," she confirmed. "See you tomorrow?" She asked walking backward toward the house.

"For a full school day?" He chastised.

"Swimming class?" She asked, eyebrow raised as if it were a promise.

Nicholas nodded his head once. "Swimming class."

Stacy bounded forward, towards the house. Half of her wanted to continue to watch Nicholas as he walked away, wanted to stop him and return to their previous conversation, while the other half knew she had responsibility elsewhere– and a slight fear of falling in the street again if she kept walking backwards to watch him.

The heir. What was he going to say? Something about how Dukhovia was torn over the heir. Was that why they needed protecting? Maybe this new heir believed strongly in modernizing or not and the opposing team made them public enemy number one. That would make sense why the country was further split. But if that even was the case, what on earth could she do to help? What did the Spirits expect of her?

Tiptoeing as slowly as her clumsy feet would allow her, Stacy tried to make it to the bathroom to wash the blood off her face before Cody found her. The only two rooms she really had to pass were the sitting room and the kitchen. If he was in the computer room to her immediate right, he would be back further and out of her line of sight. There was about a .1% chance he was hanging out in the sitting room and an at least 90% chance he was in the kitchen.

With slow, deliberate movements, she made it just outside the bathroom door before she heard Rachael's sing-song voice behind her.

"You maaaade it!" She sang with joy, throwing her arms off. "See Cody, one last thing to worry about for today. How was your walk?"

"Too long," Stacy said quickly. "I've had to pee since Main Street. Give me two mins!"

"Two quick minutes before you give us all the details! Ah!" Stacy felt Rachael's voice getting closer but couldn't think quick enough on her feet to decide what to do. Rushing into the bathroom would yield suspicion just the same as approaching them covered in blood– but at least this way she could prove it was not her blood.

"Stacy, oh my gosh, what happened?"

Cody came leaping forward, quickly and gently taking her face into his hands. "I'll kill him, Stace. Where is it coming from?"

"*His* arm," she quickly emphasized.

Rachael looked down at her own arm then back to Stacy confused.

"It's not what you think– at all. This is his blood. I got covered in it after he dove in front of a car to protect me."

Cody was quiet, a death glare in his eyes as he examined Stacy's face. He rushed her into the bathroom and began wiping at her forehead. She quickly tore the wash cloth from his hand. "Look," she declared, wiping it quickly and aggressively. "I wouldn't lie to you guys. I don't have a death wish."

Rachael and Cody were both quiet as they looked from each other to Stacy. "Why were you standing in front of moving vehicles?" Rachael's voice was light and full of humor so Stacy just rolled her eyes and thankfully let that part of the conversation roll off. "Enough about me and my problems. What's going on with you?"

Cody shrugged. "Nothing new. I'm not suspended. Something about understanding 'the turmoil I'm going through'."

Stacy rolled her eyes. "Any update on that turmoil?"

Cody shifted. He looked like someone who wore the weight of the world, but would take on another world to help someone else. "Dad came by to talk to me. He apologized for everything, talked to me about school, but still says it isn't safe for me to come home." Cody rounded the corner and did, in fact, take a seat in the sitting room. "So, what am I supposed to do? Live like a recluse forever? I feel like I'm the one who did something wrong."

"You're not, Code," Stacy told him gently. She reached forward to lend a comforting hand on his shoulder, but backed off, realizing it was still coated in blood. She quickly ran to the bathroom and returned. "It's just more complicated to get her to go, so he's doing the best he can to keep you safe right now."

He looked to the ground, Cody had been known to struggle with anger on and off, but the person she saw now she hardly recognized. He had dark circles carved around hollow, sunken eyes. The look of desolation and despair robbed him of the happiness and joy he typically felt. Gone was the class clown who could cheer anyone up. In his place, was a stranger.

"Well, that's another thing, isn't it?" Cody went on. "I shouldn't have to be kept safe from my own mother. Isn't that her job? Isn't that what your parents do? Keep you safe? Why not mine?"

The girls both felt a blow to their insides. Rachael began to cry as she embraced him. But it was enough, enough for him to close his eyes, drop the look of danger and death in his eyes, and release. He shut his eyes, seemed to release a breath as he held Rachael close, breathed her in, rubbed her back.

The two denying feelings for each other dated back to when they first became friends. After their parents had a falling out, the three were forbidden to speak to each other. But it was Cody and Rachael who broke that barrier first. Cody approached Rachael after one of her episodes in preschool. She was alone and crying. By the time Stacy wondered over, the two were laughing and comfortable. Safe. That was what they provided each other with—safety from the darkness within and the darkness at home.

Yet, they never made it past playful flirting, blushing cheeks, and any excuse to get close to each other. Always taking the seat next to each other at the movies and restaurants, always standing next to each other for practices, Rachael always being the first to fling herself onto him after the winning football game, Cody always planting a more passionate than thankful kiss on her cheek.

Happiness. Safety. Two words brought on by these two being together—and something they each deserved so wholeheartedly.

"Anyway, I'll be here or bouncing around for a while," he delivered the words with a touch of lightness. "Sometimes it's hard to be so close to home and not home. Jade and Miranda both offered their places." His eyes averted away from Stacy's as he looked at the ground. "Dad says they're starting the process for divorce."

Stacy was silent for a moment, then she threw her arms around her cousin's neck. "So maybe there will be a calm to the storm."

Cody looked at her for a moment then back down, nodding. "Yeah, maybe."

Rachael watched him with sad eyes, gently caressing his upper arm with both hers, warmly. "Change will be hard, but calm will be a good change."

"A good change," he agreed, nodding his head.

Stacy and Rachael met each other's eyes signaling that it was time to end that conversation. They spent the rest of the night running a few of their original songs before Miranda and Jade stopped over to practice the others. The night went on in rigid, tense joy and paralyzing wonder.

Cody was silent most of the night, responding when needed, but mostly quiet. The music helped, as did leaving closer to nightfall when Dylan stopped over, football in hand. He was out until late that night and it was close to ten when Stacy heard him crash in through the front door and sink into one of the guest rooms below her.

Rachael did not seem to miss the lack of concentration displayed by Stacy. She would look over to her with questioning eyes prompting an explanation that Stacy did not feel ready to give. Not that she did not want to, but because she could not even make sense of what took place on the walk home. Because there was so much to process, so much to feel.

She had learned so much and yet so little. She had learned of Nicholas's tragic backstory—the deaths of his parents were no peaceful accident (if such a travesty could occur), but brutal attacks that he had to witness and carry the burden of responsibility for. A responsibility he felt only half guilty for and then maybe a quarter guilty for not feeling guilty over his father's death. Blah.

It was tragic and Stacy could not help but let her thoughts wander to her aunt and uncle. How different would Nicholas's life have been if his mother had left his father? How different would Cody's life become if Uncle Richey decided not to leave Aunt Yasana and the abuse became worse?

She did not want to let the outcome of those thoughts continue. She could not bear the thought of imagining Cody covered in the welts and bruises that scarred Nicholas's back…and then her focus stuck to Nicholas's back. Not the rippling muscled patterns, that was a second thought, thank you very much, but of the fact that the scarring was *fresh*. Meaning that not all of those scars were from his father whom died several years ago. No, meaning Nicholas was still around someone who was hurting him and she could not smother the annoying thought continuously telling her to protect him...protect him...

Protect them.

The heir.

The heir. What was he going to say? What on *Earth* was he going to say?! And when would she be able to start the conversation up again? Certainly not in swim class when they're running drills every five minutes. No, she needed time away with him—*alone* with him, as much as she knew that would not go over well with her friends.

But she had to! She needed to know what he knew...what did he know? They had been talking about the war, about the separation due to modernization or some other words...then the heir...the...dilemma that divides them? Yes! Those were the words he used. Whatever this situation was with the heir, it was something that had the country torn. But how? Why?

She supposed if she could even stifle a guess, she needed to know what an heir even was. Of course, she knew what it meant in lamest terms—something passed down to you. But what did that mean to Dukhovia? Was Dukhovia being passed onto someone? What type of political system did they even have? Is that even the right word? Or was it the passing of some spiritual gift or duty? Maybe part of some type of ceremony?

All that Stacy knew was that she was being told to protect them and she felt with absolute certainly that Nicholas was the person meant to fill in the rest of the blanks. It was the way he spoke of Dukhovia, the way he carried his uncertainty in his journey. It was just the real feeling she experienced being around him. The closeness, the near-trust...

Born in Dukhovia. History of abuse. Torn country. Degraded family. Not wanting to be here. Having issues with Santifini. Murderer. Spirit touched. Looking for hope in banished families.

Nothing was adding up into any equation that made sense. Was America some safe haven for Dukhovian's? From what she had managed to pick up from her grandparents, this was not where they chose to go—but where they *had* to go. They tried to go to another country, but they would not let them in. From what she picked up from Nicholas, America was the last place on Earth a Dukhovian would want to go—so why did he? Why did Santifini? Were these murders true? And most importantly, Nicholas had made the comment of them getting out of here. So, if he did not plan to stay, how would he know when it was time to go? How long did she have to ask her questions? Would he tell her? The thought caused her stomach to drop.

And then there was the most confusing part of all. The part she understood so little about she would not even know how to put it into words for Rachael, she barely knew how to form an audible thought besides pure shock and pure desire.

PROTECT THE HEIR

All her life she wondered why she was different. Why did she not get cold? Why did she not get sick? Why was no one else like her...except Sir Nicholas Tyler Andrews the Third? And why did that make her feel more connected to someone and seen by someone than anything she had ever felt in her life?

CHAPTER 38

THE PRICE OF HONESTY

*T*he wind whipped and tore around his ears violently, he did not shudder, but he was aware of the lack of comfort. It was a strange experience, though he did not really understand it. He had ridden horseback several times. Then again, mama always made sure his ears were wrapped. Mama always made sure she kept him close to her chest. Mama never rode with such harsh violence.

Where were they going in such a hurry? Nicholas had only been training with The Czar for a little more than a year, but he knew by now to not ask questions. Although, he noticed that since mama yelled at The Czar in the kitchen a few weeks ago, the beatings had become fewer.

Eventually, the speeding horses came to a pressing halt. Nicholas blinked hard. They were at the family farm? They were not due back until late in the evening. Was it a surprise? Was he being given the day off for his birthday? He smiled with glee.

Last year on his birthday, he and mama went to the Moon Tunnels together. The most spiritual place in South Gate. At night time through the early hours, the moon reflects in the pools of hollowed out stone, allowing lit passage for the water. She had taught him about his spirit there. He had never felt calmer.

Each year, their birthdays were to be spent doing something to connect to the Spirits to get closer to their Spirit gift. Mama always said that the day should also be spent celebrating the person you are as well. After the Moon Tunnels, they went for a ride on Nicholas's favorite trail, they made blueberry and lemon muffins— the Dukhovian famous treat—and she later made him his favorite dinner.

He thrilled with excitement of what they would be doing this year. He had been forced away early this morning. He was deeply sad, but it all made sense now. His mama just needed time to make the surprise. She was the best mama ever!

"Come on, boy."

The Czar yanked him down by his arm off his horse and threw him down onto the grass below. It was not out of character for the man, but Nicholas felt braver knowing he was getting to celebrate his birthday.

"You cannot touch me like that! It is my birthday!"

The man had already started heading towards the house, but he stopped and paused, "Oh, your birthday, is it?" He asked in a condescending tone. "Then by all means, have a more comfortable seat to the show." He again, yanked him up and this time had him sit on a bale of hay facing the house. They were still so far from it.

CHAPTER THIRTY-EIGHT

Arkady walked into the house. Nicholas could hardly hear what was happening, yelling of some type, he assumed arguing about the day's events. Then.

His heart stopped, his soul on fire.

He tried to jump to his feet, but Alexander and Albert were now holding his arms. Albert wrapped his arm around the bottom of Nicholas's and then lay his other hand lightly on Nicholas's bicep. Alexander had a more vicious, painful hold.

Arkady slammed the door to the house shut, threw something behind him—and the house burst into flame.

He could hear his mother and father's frantic screams, their ear-piercing pleas. Until his own wails covered them up.

"We are men with a mission, Sir Nicholas. And men with a mission cannot be distracted with thoughts so idol as birthdays."

Nicholas's face was covered in heavy red blotches, a look of fear he had never known plastered to his face. His stomach hurt, his heart screamed in pain, he tried so hard to break free.

And then he did. He ran up to the house. At first, Alexander and Albert chased after him, but a barking order stopped them at first.

Nicholas touched the doorknob but a moment later, flame erupted, sending it to oblivion. He screamed and rounded to the front window. He had a clear view of the kitchen, albeit, riddled with smoke and blackening windows. But he could see them. He could see his mother and father, both tied to chairs, brown cloth bags over their heads.

His father's chair had fallen, he was on the floor, attempting to kick with all his might. He was attempting to do what Nicholas would do—thrash against the weak chairs, hoping they would give out.

But his mother. His mother was so frail, so weak. She had scarcely eaten in the last few months, scarcely slept. Her thin body was already leaning over the side of the chair, limp, but not quite motionless...

"Mama!" He yelled the word as he thrashed at the window, then, taking his left elbow, he angled his body to utilize all his strength and smashed into the glass.

The pain shot through his body like an electric shock. Wave after wave crashed through. He could not breathe, he could not see straight. He grabbed onto his elbow, but the touch only escalated the pain. He heard his mother shouting his name through his own howls.

Then Alexander was there, forcing him up off the ground. Pain seethed through his arm as Nicholas continued to thrash against the man's body, but he held him firm, squeezing onto the burnt elbow, layers of burnt flesh peeling away. The more he tried to move, the worse the pain, the more energy he lost. Eventually he tried to close his eyes and look away, but his eyes were forced open and he was made to look.

He remembered vomiting on the ground before him. He remembered watching with eyes and a body void of emotion as the house turned to rubble and ash.

And then he remembered the worst feeling he ever felt as the mix of utter fear and hatred that penetrated his bones leaked out and the sound of slow, purposeful, proud footsteps approached him.

"Stand and look me in the eye."

He refused.

"Sir Nicholas."

He could not think. Should he fight? Run? Obey...

So, he did nothing. Nothing for anyone. And then Arkady lifted him by his burnt elbow and threw him against the burnt house. He howled in pain as the heat tore at his shirt and melted the skin off his back.

"Men cannot be distracted by hopes of tomorrow. We must be strong enough to focus on creating what we want tomorrow to bring. I want you to remember this pain. I want you to remember what it feels like when you fail to listen to me and when you fail to do everything I ask. From this moment forward, there will be no games, only work for this country and perhaps you can avoid the same fate for your future ancestors— do you understand me?"

Silence. He forgot how to speak. He forgot every word in the Russian and Dukhovian vocabulary.

A sneer and then hot glass sliced down Nicholas's arm, through his burn. "YOUR ANSWER SOLDIER OR SHOULD YOU JOIN YOUR PITIFUL, DISGRACEFUL FAMILY NOW?"

He looked over at the debris one last time, stifled a tear, and stood to his feet. "I will redeem my family, sir."

They were his last words before walking away, remounting his horse, and returning to the palace where Albert would clean his wounds.

Steal. Lie. Cheat. Kill. It was the code of dishonor that Nicholas was taught to live by. If you wanted something, needed something badly enough, there were no rules. No emotion mattered enough. No voice was loud enough to silence pure desire.

That was why Nicholas knew he was making the right choice now.

Nicholas lifted his head over the large set of doors that led to the natatorium. They were heavy brass that one could tell had been here since the school had been built and taken a beating or two from hurried students or a busy janitor. An offensive grayish-beige encapsulated the entirety of the door except for the one small window that Nicholas now peered through, taking in the emptiness of the chilled room.

He was early for class, obviously. Not a single student or teacher had yet entered the area and that was where he would put his plan into motion. After last night's events, he spent much time thinking about his next move—both what it should be and what he wanted it to be. Although the two would never end in unison, he decided that he would make his decisions based on getting the two as close to unison as possible—hence his plan for today: getting Stacy to agree to spend alone time with him.

He needed purposeful, meaningful time with no expiration. The walk was a step, but fear blazed through him at her hesitancy towards the end. She had said they should not be seen together, that they needed to end before even fully making it to her home due to the opinions of her family members. And he sent her home *covered in blood.*

What on earth was he thinking? He should have insisted they go back to his apartment and clean up. At a minimum, a public shop where he could have purchased her a new shirt. UGH. He had been up all night playing out the scenario and everything he did wrong. And if he was, he knew the girl who already had hesitancy would be doing the same.

And he could not afford hesitancy.

He should get her alone. He should be earning her trust. He should be winning her over to convince her to come to Dukhovia. At least—he was supposed to be.

And then he had considered the *feeling* he experienced. He understood, in part, that the feeling of closeness he experienced around her gravitated from the pulls of their Spirit connections on one another, but there was something more that he did not experience around Arkady. Perhaps it was simply because this heir was stronger. Regardless, it drew him to her like flame to the fire. He needed more of the feeling, he needed answers.

Therefore, he needed to come to class early, he needed to convince her to race him again, and he needed to sway his win. This was his only choice, after all. She seemed open and accepting towards talking with him in classes only a day ago, and then today, a day after declaring they should 'not be seen together'—nothing. She had turned around and given him a shielded smile and wave a handful of times first period. But every time he so much as shifted in his seat, her cousin gave him daggers that sent a crystal-clear message—move and die.

Lie. Steal. Cheat. Kill.

He had not gone to lunch out of nervousness. His own choice, certainly, but he spent the short period of time franticly wondering if it were the right one. He had somewhat of a better time emotionally when in classes with Rachael. She spoke softly, purring reassurance into his ear whenever possible. And asking him question after question about her gift. She had been wanting to practice getting it under control, but she wanted him to help with guidance. He was back in her good graces. Win.

He dipped his hand in the second pool, the one the cold-water race took place in. The ice melting was so fresh that there were still heavy chunks floating around the midsection—giving them space to safely swim, but dropping the temperature as close to the freezing point as physically possible. That was his angle.

Stacy and Nicholas both had a large piece of the Winter Spirit living inside them. The Winter Spirit activated in the cold. They also had a piece of the Water Spirit inside of them. This enabled their swimming desire and abilities. The combination of the two created the Spirit that made them both heirs.

Therefore, lowering the temperature of the pool as much as he could would give him an advantage. The cold temperature would "shock" Stacy's system, releasing power she never felt and, likely and hopefully, paralyzing her long enough to plunge himself forward. If that failed, he would have a better chance of connecting to his Spirit powers and lunging himself forward. Of course, the Spirits would only grant him this power if it was their will for him to spend alone time with her, but it was, he knew it. It had to be.

He stood over by the temperature gauge now, the twist in his stomach that started the moment he thought of his plan becoming a tighter and tighter knot...

Lie. Steal. Cheat. Kill.

Really? Is this how low we've stooped? Trickery?

Nicholas dropped his hand from the gauge with a start, slicing his finger open in the process. "Ah! Devil's Spirit!" He swore in a whisper, sucking the blood away.

How proud you will feel when you have beaten the girl through games and deceit.

"It is not about a fair game," Nicholas retorted, returning his attention to the gauge. He had spent the morning memorizing the manual to find out if the machine was even capable of having its temperatures reduced. He had recalled a time not long before he departed Dukhovia where Albert approached him at the King's Baths—the Dukhovian equivalent of the swimming pool—and noted it as one of the differences he would find in America. He did not take much note in what Albert had said, as no one ever took much note in what Albert would say, but he did have an annoying way of usually being correct, and so he stored the information away just to be safe.

"It's about getting her alone by any means necessary."

And the girl is already heavily suspicious of you; it is practically plastered on her face. What about winning her over like a gentleman?

"What about it?" He shot back, feigning naivety.

Imagine the girl of your dreams agreeing to dinner with you because she is interested in you, likes you, even wants to be around you—not because you tricked her.

Nicholas's hand slipped again at the comment. He caught himself this time, but stood to his feet and aggressively punched the large metal cylinder next to him, puncturing a hole in the side which immediately began to let out a disapproving hiss.

"She is not the girl of my dreams!"

Tell that to the beating of your heart when she is near.

"She is an heir. Even you should know how we react in each other's presence. This is purely business." He added the last comment before Erlik could offer any other criticism on the subject—and before he became too accusatory. But he felt his anger rising.

Business that you are not even bought into. How very cavalier, an owner not supporting his own market, a mentor not certain of his own agenda, his own gains.

Anger hissed from his entire being. "I just need to get her alone. That is all. I do not care how I do it. I do not care if it is fair or cheating. None of this is fair. None of this is how it should be and yet it is happening. And yet that man continues to sit on the throne and have the control and power over me that he does! So no, I will not play by the rules when not even Dukhovia is playing by the rules! I do not care about any of that! I do not care about this stupid mission!"

Silence.

Well, that is certainly the most honest you have been during this conversation, perhaps ever.

Nicholas steamed as the words flew out of his mouth and off his shoulders. What had triggered the release? He could not place it, but he knew that as soon as the words had been uttered, he needed to consider them, to feel them. He felt his body go rigid, it was as if he had run twenty miles and then had a boulder dropped on top of him. His breath evaded him, his knees felt weak. He stood, bent over, hand on what he was nearly certain was the lever to reveal the buttons he needed to change the temperature in the pool.

Yes, he was aware of the double standard and the trap this entire time, but for some reason the more he got to know Stacy, the more twisted the ploy became. All the more confusing. All the more unnerving. He did not care about any of it, and that resulted in careless mistake after careless mistake. He did not understand the unfairness, he never did.

Lie. Steal. Cheat. Kill. *Is that your agenda or his?*

How could Arkady still rule? Truly. He was known to have ended so many lives and plan so many invasions that resulted in the loss of lives. Yet he did not make the final call. Yet he did not lead them. Yet the Spirits were so, so forgiving for Arkady. But never for him. Never for his family. How? Why? HOW.

How could his parents have been taken from him? The Spirits were meant to preserve life, to protect the plan that they had for each individual. Surely the plan he had for his mother and father was not to be burned alive in their family home with him pinned down with his eyes forced open made to watch. Surely, they had never planned for his father to ruthlessly hold him still, stripping him until he was bare while the Czar branded him, lashed him…

How could the Spirits abandon him in the way that they did? Leaving him utterly and coldly *alone*?

If this is what you need to do to win, you are not following the call of the Spirits.

Nicholas swallowed the lump in his throat. He sat with the words, with the realization that the Spirits abandoned him long ago and so what did that mean with his faux decision? If he no longer cared about pleasing them, could he then leave?

A short-lived thought. No. Arkady would murder him either way. Would he rather die attached to the Spirits and pray for some hope that the afterlife they promise is better than the physical life?

With that thought, a faint sound of the school bell sounded off in the distance, followed by the closer banging of the heavy iron door. Nicholas quickly hurried himself from his present location and into the bathroom stall to change, abandoning his plan to chill the water.

He took an extra moment before he heard the footsteps of the other male students entering to close himself in the stall and breathe, relinquishing his thoughts, lifting himself to the Spirits for calm, but feeling anger, for strength, but feeling deceit, but searching for peace, begging for it...

Avoiding eye contact with any of the other students despite their whispers, Nicholas made his way out, anxiously looking for Stacy. Finally, as he saw her whipping her head back and forth as if looking for someone, the Spirits answered his prayers and filled him with a sense of ease.

Stacy smiled, looking him up and down as he approached in his swim gear. She had on her form fitting black suit. He had not noticed the last time they were together the way it hugged her thin hips perfectly and clung to every shape and curve. He quickly pushed the thought away.

He watched her eyes drop immediately to his injured arm. "How's your arm?"

He lifted it to her line of vision without hesitation. "Good as new." The sight revealed that there had been damage, just as with all his other marks, however, the opened gash from the day prior had become a closed scar with moderate scabbing. Staring at her dropped jaw, he noticed her disheveled hair, thrown into a pile on her head. Her eyes were etched with dark circles surrounding them.

"It appears so." Her eyes immediately took in the fact that he was already dripping wet.

"You look awful," he blurted, the first distractor coming to his mind.

She looked up, surprised. "I guess pushing me out of the way of that car was just your conscious and not chivalry, huh?"

"I apologize," he quickly began to speak, seeing his error. American's took offense to simple observations. Noted. "I simply mean you look...like you had a difficult night. I hope that is through no fault of mine." He leaned into her, his fingers brushing the top of her arm delicately, his eyes pouring into hers.

She was shaking her head, seeming dazzled. Then, with a blink of her lashes, she was herself. "No. Nothing. I mean—it was just a bad dream. I seem to get them a lot."

"I see." He tried to discreetly look at the parts of her body that he had witnessed her violently thrashing against. She had severely beaten her ribcage and tried to hit her face twice as hard until he stopped her and handed her the wolf. Still, he had not known what had made her so...difficult. "Is there something you are fearing?" He waited hesitantly, unsure what to do with the information she had given him. Had these dreams just started since he came into the picture? He supposed he did not know the specifics of what he had witnessed the night prior. And she has had a lot of stressful days as of late on top of the chaos he brought to her life. It would make sense that she would have nightmares, yet...

She shrugged, seeming hesitant to answer further.

"Stacy, you can trust me," he whispered. He was now close to her face, his hand grazing across her cheek as he tucked a stray hair behind her ear.

"It's Dukhovia," she choked out, seeming to have a lump in her throat. "I worry about them. That's all."

"That's all?" He pressed.

She nodded. "Now you owe me one. Yesterday, you mentioned something right before...the incident."

"Ah, yes, your fall of shame."

"It was with grace and class."

Nicholas nodded. "We had been talking about the war and I mentioned the divide over the heir." He watched her reaction carefully, curious of what she knew and what she yearned to know.

Stacy nodded, her trance seeming to disappear at his final word. He watched how her eyes and body responded, how her Spirit responded. Did she seem worthy of even the term? Could she even understand the gravity of what being an heir meant?

"What...what exactly is the heir? Why is there a divide?"

Nicholas considered her question, then chose to smile. "You said I only owed you one answer."

He laughed again as her face turned into a stubborn pout and her foot began to tap anxiously as she tried to form both questions into one without success.

"What about a deal?" Nicholas said, eyeing the cold-water pool now with raised eyebrows.

Stacy seemed to catch onto the plotting in his mind and she seemed to take the bait with eager anticipation. "What did you have in mind, my cunning companion?"

"I challenge you to a rematch on your original challenge," he spoke slowly, deliberately choosing each word with care. "The cold-water race."

Stacy grinned and held out her right hand. "Stakes?" She asked.

"If you win, I will answer any question you have regarding Dukhovia." Her eyes were automatic lights. She was shining as brilliantly as a child on All Spirit's Day. "If I win, you will grace me with your presence at dinner tonight."

She lowered her hand, closer to his. "Deal." They shook and sealed the deal in stone.

A whistle blew and both of their attention was drawn over to the swim coach. A group of students was already huddled around the pool and the heater area where Nicholas had previously been. His nerves began to kick in as he thought about what he had done.

"Alright troops, listen up. Seems something happened to the pool heater and caused both to slow down, so we may just be running stretches today."

There was a groan amongst the class.

"Ugh. There's no way we can if the pools are down," Stacy sighed, but continued eyeing the cold-water pool with precision.

"Sorry, gang. I can't have you in water this cold."

Stacy and Nicholas automatically walked in a disappointed daze to sit with the rest of the class. The coach had begun muttering about lessons and swim techniques, but he would glance and check the temperature of the pool every so often.

Nicholas found himself glancing over at Stacy, whom sat behind him, every so often. They did not have permission the other day and they jumped right in, what was stopping her now? Her eyes too seemed to be looking over at the pool, perhaps questioning it herself.

"What are we to do?" Nicholas finally whispered to her.

She seemed unmoved, answering quietly, but as if she were simply waiting for him to ask. "We just need the right moment so he doesn't stop us. He keeps looking in our direction so he's expecting us to test him." Then she broke into a devilish grin. "Well, he's expecting *me,* anyway."

"Are you truly such a horrid student?" He asked, humor and curiosity battling for tone.

Stacy shrugged. "I like to test the limits."

Nicholas laughed, thinking of his own behavior as a student. Fearful of his mentor one moment, but pushing any button he could the next. It was the only way to make it through the monotony. Through the pain.

"He does not seem to be changing his mind. He is quite focused on the swimming positions."

Stacy put her hand up to her chin and rubbed it. "Hmm. Quite." She continued to look at the coach for a while before speaking again. "But look…" She pointed down towards the coach's wrist. "Every time he glances at his watch, he also glances at the water. I suspect that means he's waiting on it to warm up or at least that something is happening with it."

Nicholas nodded, impressed with her level of observation. "Very well noticed. You would make a great spy back home."

Stacy seemed to take just a fraction of a second longer than expected before responding. "Would you rather be a solider or a spy?"

He breathed in deeply. "A choice, ah." He sat with it for a moment. "Sometimes the two jobs intertwine. I suppose that is what I enjoy most—possibilities."

She nodded her head in understanding, accepting and (what appeared to be) appreciating his answer.

"And you? If you were to return to our motherland, would you find yourself a spy or soldier?"

Suddenly Stacy's face went blank, she dazed off for so long Nicholas was certain that she was back to spy mode and noticed something about the teacher. Then she finally spoke. "I don't think I would be either. I think I would be more like you—whatever I needed to be. But I have a feeling what I need to do isn't covered by either of those job titles."

Nicholas eyed her with suspicion, so deeply wanting to know what she knew, what she failed to realize, and so deeply wanting to just have their damned race and find out.

"What about in America? What would your purpose be here? You had mentioned the other day that you were not certain music was in your future."

"Ah, that." Stacy rocked backward, either not having revisited the topic or having spent far too much time in its presence. "Well," she started, shaking her head, her whisper voice beginning to crawl higher by the octave. "Definitely not music, but only because I don't think my purpose is in America. If it were, then I suppose music. What about you?"

Nicholas took in her words, the words rendering him paralyzed. She did not think her purpose was in America and she seemed to *want* to chase something outside of music. That made this easy, all far too easy. All he would have to do would be to offer to take her to Dukhovia. No coercion, no manipulation. He would still have to ensure she trusted him to go with him, but if her concern is he is a danger to her family would it only be all the better, all the easier if they leave alone?

But then she had asked him—*what about you?* What if he had a choice? Would he be the person to take someone else's choices from them? Who would he be if he had never crossed paths with Czar Arkady.

"I might be a police officer," he answered certainly.

Stacy's eyes narrowed, a small smile on her lips. "Really?"

He nodded. "Why not? I could do a lot to help those in difficult circumstances." Nicholas's heart welled up at the thought, a rush of peace seemed to overtake him. It was like the world silenced itself of not only sound, but sight, touch, smell, taste. He was only in the moment of sacrifice. He was only in the moment of goodness. The only feeling comparable was when he was submerged fully and intentionally in the ocean.

"You would make a great police officer, I think," Stacy smiled. She moved her hand as if to pat him on the back, then retreated, going for a thumbs up instead. "You should talk with my uncle. He'd help you. I think you have a lot in common."

Nicholas looked at her and nodded, smiling at the thought that he could have anything in common with the selfless officer that entered his apartment.

Both of their eyes shifted back to the coach who was now making his way over to the pool. The entire class was on their feet, lifting necks and shoving shoulders in order to see over the next person, waiting for the verdict.

"What's the temp, coach?" Someone called out.

Nicholas watched, a lump growing in his chest as the coach walked at a pace slower than a sea dove. *Just 40 degrees, give me 40 degrees,* he whispered to himself. He felt sweat dripped from his brow as he watched anxiously, tapping his fingers.

Coach was next to the warmer pool. He deemed that it was an appropriate swimming temperature and the class immediately sprang forward, jumping and pushing to get a spot in.

Stacy reached back for Nicholas's hand, seeming to forget the impact it had until she held it. She recoiled some, latching only onto his fingers as she pulled him forward, running to join the others.

A helpless grin that Nicholas could with absolute certainty say he never felt before broke over him and he willingly chased after her into the pool.

Immediately, Stacy was on the other side, pushing the water around her with grace. Her arms grazed backward and the water seemed to curve around her with ease, helping to push her along. The work looked effortless.

She flipped onto her back and her lips could be seen pulled upward until the tips reached her cheeks. Grace. Ease. Home.

Her motion came to a stop at the far end of the pool. Nicholas stood, watching her in awe but aware of the uncomfortableness around him. The coach had not yet returned order and the other students were foolhardy as they splashed in the water around him. He had never seen the water to be such sport.

Uncomfortableness saturated him as he sat in the middle, his eyes darting around, contemplating how he should be acting. Stacy was swimming on her own, should he join her in the lap lanes?

As soon as he thought it and glanced that way, he was met by her warm smile. She parted the water in front of her with her hands as she made her way back towards him. The water looked stunning around her. Once she grew powerful enough, he imagined she could simply close her eyes and imagination alone would call the waters to bend to her beck and call.

The closer she came, the more he found the uncomfortable feeling slip away, the pounding in his chest subsiding. She stopped just a few inches from him, the smile never leaving her.

"Well folks..." The class drew their attention to Coach in the cold-water pool. He seemed to be checking multiple times, even sticking his own foot in to test the accuracy of the thermometer below him.

"Yikes." He shook his head and read the temperature allowed. "A crisp 36. I can't allow any of you in this one today. That means you, Matthews."

Stacy and Nicholas were both stuck in their spots for a moment, both seeming to consider next options. Then, Stacy looked at Nicholas and beamed the broadest smirk he had ever seen. In perfect unison, Nicholas responded with the same chastising mask.

Then the two were off, ignoring the shouts of the coach behind them. They climbed out over the side of one pool and, pausing only for a moment to nod their start to the other, dove straight into the ice, cold water.

Nicholas prayed as he dove in that his plan would work, but he had no time to turn and look for Stacy. He needed to focus. He needed to win.

Ignoring the shock to his own system as he realized he had not felt water this cold since his fight in the Kara Sea, he swam on. Images of Stacy in her perfect form, the water holding her with comfort battled memories of vicious regret. Memories of surfacing from the brutal waves of the Kara Sea and being beaten by Arkady with his ore. Faster, stronger. Never enough. Never enough.

The piercing, tearing feeling of Arkady's rusting chains digging into his back washed over him. Fear. Anger. Isolation. Alone. Alone. Always alone...

He rose on the other end of the pool and immediately pulled himself out. He timed it to less than a minute. His quickest time ever. He breathed heavy, tapping his fingers against the pool, the residual of his memories refusing to leave him.

That was when he heard a cough and turned to see Stacy, tapping her feet next to him.

"Finally," she chastised, smiling next to him.

He started blankly at her. But, before he even knew what he was doing, before defeat could even set in, he was on his feet. "Best two out of three?"

Stacy grinned broadly and nodded. The two dove in, resurfacing in unison on the other side.

"NO! NO! THAT IS ENOUGH! YOU ARE BOTH GOING TO GET SICK!" The coach was howling like he did at meets and everyone failed to listen. He stuck his arm in to fish them out, but Nicholas's death glare was enough to keep him at bay.

"Last run, coach!" Stacy called. And then they were gone.

Nicholas closed to his eyes, feeling the water, feeling his Spirit, opening it up, connecting to it. *If I am meant to succeed, I will succeed. If I am meant to succeed, I will use their power. No pain. No pain. No pain, only purpose.*

And then, as if his body just realized it was in a race, he was shooting across the pool, feeling lighter, quicker, than he ever had. He did not break. He did not breathe. He just swam.

Comfort. Unity. Peace. The water was cold, but he felt warm arms around him, carrying him to where he needed to be. Not alone. Not alone.

Without any acknowledgment of time, he climbed out of the pool and stood front and center. A second later, a gaping Stacy's head popped out of the water below him.

"Well, well, well, looks like you're not the slowest man to ever enter water after all."

There were a crowd of cheers and people ran over to surround Nicholas. They grabbed a medal from a ribbon with Stacy's name and plastered his name to it, then hung it around his neck. Confused and overwhelmed, he wanted to run away, but he could also not help but sink in to the feeling of wanting to celebrate as well.

"Pick me up at my place this evening?" Stacy asked. "But I get to pick the place."

Nicholas nodded in agreement. "That is only fair as I do not know the area."

"It'll be only the best," she promised. "Oh, but come prepared. We will not be partaking in any healthy foods."

CHAPTER 39

ONE REVEALED TRUTH

Stacy looked at her reflection in the mirror, criticized herself, then made for her closet to change. She had no idea why she was so bothered by her appearance now, but it seemed like the night to have everything go perfect.

"I'm not sure where you think you're going because you certainly won't be ruining those designer shoes by putting on a baggy t-shirt and ripped jeans." Rachael scrunched up her nose in disgust when she said the words.

Stacy rolled her eyes. "Rache, I just want to feel like myself."

"You said you wanted to 'look good'. I love you, Stacy, but if you want to be yourself then fashionable you will not be."

Stacy blushed at the reminder. How stupid she felt being stupid excited for this dinner tonight. For the uninterrupted time with Nicholas. For the opportunity to ask as much as she wanted.

Yet she felt much more ridiculous when she got home and realized not only did she want to spill the details to Rachael, she was anxiously excited, practically sprinting home to reveal the news. Then came the horrendous realization that she not only wanted to hear Nicholas's words and be prepared with her own adequate wording to protect her family, she also wanted to look pleasing to him. Or, at least as pleasing as he is to look at. Not that she finds him pleasing. Who uses the word pleasing?

"I'm sure you just want to have the upper hand and that's why you're going for fabulous," Rachael taunted.

Stacy grimaced, second guessing her choice. Was she being stupid? Did she have the famed crush that Rachael always said she would have when she met the right boy? If so, what type of person was she if the 'right boy' was some mysterious assassin sent here to end her family and break the arm of her best friend?

Ugh.

"I'll tag along and give you the upper hand." Cody sat hanging upside down on the bed, his lips a thin line of protest. It had taken a solid hour for him to stop yelling about the decision to go out with Nicholas…alone. But, once she reminded him that she had zero intentions of going back to his dungeon/lair afterward, he lightened up.

She shot him a remorseful glance, too upset by his own circumstances to give him much flack. He had every right to be concerned and she knew that. *She* was concerned. And she desperately wanted to open up to him about the very real risk to their family, but she knew Cody would not give Nicholas the same benefit of the doubt that she was. That potentially, *maybe* he was not here to kill them all in cold blood.

Hesitation tugged at her insides, but beaten senseless by the excitement within, by the realization that after years of begging and pleading for answers, tonight was finally her night. Nothing was off-limits.

Finally, just as six neared, Stacy and Rachael finally compromised on an outfit. She looked herself over, admiring the shimmering silver shirt, calmed by a black sweater. Her dark red, skin tight jeans blended nicely with her black, low-cut boots. Although a difficult task for Rachael, Stacy was allowed to leave her hair down and by the end of it, she retained the ability to please Rachael, look nice, and still feel like herself. The evening was off to a good start.

"Remember, you make him come to *you* for the first kiss," Rachael instructed, followed quickly by a loud groan of protest from Cody.

Stacy darted a dangerous look in Rachael's direction before dancing down the stairs, swinging the door open to meet Nicholas's eyes. Immediately she felt some type of feeling in her stomach looking at him. Nervous, maybe? Was she nervous? Self-conscious? Of what? They were going to a fast-food restaurant and he was standing before her looking like a God. Not that he was attractive like a God might be. He was attractive, she was not putting him down, she just…

Ugh!

Either way, she sank looking at the perfection of his outfit against hers. The white button-up decorated with blue stripes only emphasized the blinding brilliance of his eyes even more. The sleek and shine of his black pants and matching dress shoes she could practically hear laughing at her.

It's what's on the inside that counts, she reminded herself. Decorated and wonderful as he looked, he might be a coldblooded killer—and that mattered— right? *Of course it matters, Matthews, you idiot.*

"Why don't we look dashing," Stacy said with a smile.

"And you look absolutely ravishing," Nicholas said, peering at her with large eyes.

It was the deer in headlights look that got her. She hated every minute of it. But she took a gracious bow as she gave him a cocky smile.

"Thank you, sir," Stacy said in her best British accent. She held out her elbow for him to take and leapt down her front steps onto the sidewalk, unlinking arms at the bottom. She eyed the curb with precision, knowing she would eventually turn to her usual ways of dangerous-backward curb walking, but she tried to restrain herself in the name of respect for Nicholas's arm.

"Thank you for accompanying me tonight," Nicholas started his words slowly, almost reluctant to allow them to escape. "It becomes rather dull to be alone each night."

Stacy nodded her head confidently, her thoughts wandering somewhere between hesitant fear and empathetic despair. Alone in the country. Alone in a country that he did not want to *really* be in, wishing for a way to get back peacefully.

"So, you know nearly all there is to know of my family. May I ask to know more about yours?"

Stacy felt herself bite her lip too hard. The pain reminded her he was just as observant as she. Dukhovian spy material.

Before she could give a verbal answer, he let out a very real chortle of laughter. "They are safe, Stacy Grace, I promise you. Do you really not trust me so much?"

The musicalness to his voice had her hooked. Her name on his lips put her into almost a dream-like state, but she shook it off. He probably knew the impact he had on women—look at him. It was probably part of his game.

"I don't know you so much," she reasoned with a shrug.

He chuckled lightly. "You know me better than most anyone else, believe it or not." He paused. "Ask me anything." He looked deep into her eyes as he spoke the promising words.

She swallowed the lump in her throat. It was time now, she had fully turned and was walking backward, patterning between meeting his gaze and staring at her feet. She found herself looking down more often than not, for a variety of reasons.

"Favorite color?" She decided on.

He barked out a laugh so fierce it made Stacy jump. "A color?" He spoke as if it were the most ridiculous thing he had ever heard.

"Yeah, you know: purple, orange, green, blue…"

"Yes, yes," he hushed her. "I know what the colors are. I simply never fathomed a moment to consider having a favorite. Hmm." One point for Arkady. He finally got something right.

He paused for quite a while, putting much thought into his answer.

"Mine is light blue," Stacy said to aid in his decision, hopping on the curb.

"Light blue?" He asked lightly, his eyes watching her feet, anxiously. "Why light blue?"

Stacy looked up at him, then to the sky. "Because light blue is the color of hope. It's the color of Dukhovia and the color of all things that bring peace: water, clear skies, the posters at school that decide it's the color that best represents calm."

Nicholas smiled, nodding his head. He seemed more relaxed than usual, yet still the master of being keyed up. "Very reasonable choice. I suppose then that my color would be light gray."

"Light gray?" Stacy asked with humor.

Nicholas nodded. "Because it is the color of all things I consider to be home. The color of the clouds before the largest snow fall, the color of the sky just before dusk in the winter time." He stopped, his brows coming together as his face grew glum. "It is also the color of ash. Ash falls in Dukhovia just as often as snow anymore, and while that does not bring me a pleased feeling, it does remind me that this is my home and I must continue to fight for it, anyway I can."

Stacy dropped her arms from balancing and walked glumly, a pit growing in her stomach that had nothing to do with hunger.

"What else do you need to know to trust me?" Nicholas pressed.

Stacy brought her gaze back up to his. "Trust is pretty major, Sir Demitona. Trust is more of a feeling than it is a check off my list." She looked back down. He was quiet, letting her thoughts go, his eyes so closely on her it was as if he were trying to read her thoughts and force them out, or just waiting for her to tumble in front of another car. She wondered if he would save her again or leave this one up to survival of the fittest.

"When is your birthday?"

"December 25th," he answered quickly.

Stacy whipped her head up, then spoke excitedly. "Mine too! You'll have to come over so we can celebrate together. My mom always throws a big party— both for that and Christmas." She felt herself rambling but let it continue, thinking it would lead her somewhere. "We'll have turkey and casseroles and pies—oh! Favorite food? And don't say a vegetable."

Nicholas laughed at her train of thought. "I am a vegetarian," he revealed, to which Stacy made a face but then seemed to register he had already revealed the information previously. He responded by holding out his hand to her. "May I?"

Confused and hesitant, she obliged, sticking just the tip of her fingers into his hand. The response was electrifying, not nearly as much as it was the first time they connected hand and hand, less so than when she grabbed his hand at the pool, but a wave of shock was sent through her none the less.

She watched his response, reading him to see if he felt anything. He gave no indication, only rubbing her fingers gently as he led her off the curb and knelt down until they were sitting on the curb she once walked.

"Hold out your palm," he instructed and was enthused when she immediately obliged. He dipped his hands downward, cupping snow off the ground. Gently, seeming to avoid making contact with her palm, he laid the snow into the center of her palm and pressed down.

Stacy felt herself lose grip on reality for a moment. If laying in the snow and swimming in the water brought her any form of closeness to Dukhovia, this sent her spiraling. It was more than any natural expression of emotion she had ever felt. It was not happiness, it was not comfort, it was everything all at once. It was as if she had been elevated, every naïve or slightly nervous thought lifted. Everything she saw had not disappeared, it was as if she was seeing it for the first time, every aspect of every object heightened, brightened.

Finally, Nicholas folded her fingers over the snow and lifted her hand to his lips. Her mind was not even able to react, or she was certain her insides would be screaming. Cupping the bottom of her hand lightly in his, he brought her hand as close to his lips as he could without them touching and blew the snow away.

Stacy blinked hard, trying to find the question to ask.

Nicholas seemed to smile, both pleased with himself and—something else? As if he were wrestling with a thought. "You have a special connection to the Winter, Water, and Moon Spirits. They allow you the ability to fight off sickness, withstand the cold, swim beautifully and effortlessly, and more than you could ever imagine.

"Because of this, you have a sense of duty to those elements, no? A sense of loyalty, a sense of respect?"

All Stacy could do was nod slightly. Her entire life she wondered what made her different, why it was just her, and Nicholas was reading her mind.

"I have those Spirits in me as well," he revealed. Stacy snapped her head up to meet his eyes. "Though, not quite as strong as they are in you, still stronger than most. I have one more Spirit present in me, that sort of turns the tides—the Nature Spirit. Therefore, I feel a sense of lineage to the earth and all her creatures. As long as they will not eat me, I will not eat them." He chuckled softly.

Stacy felt like she was drowning, but that she wanted to drown. These were the only words she could deem worthy enough to explain what was happening inside of her. So much information, so many different directions to run with the information—but she welcomed it. She never felt more at home in her life.

"What makes us different?" She asked.

Nicholas smiled a soft smile—he was waiting for the question. "We all have different purposes, yes? Our purposes depend on which Spirit lies in us. So, while your family may not be at their height with The Winter Spirit, they have other strengths?"

Stacy thought. "They're scientists and doctors—most of them, anyway. My grandfather and grandmother, my mom and dad and brother." She rolled her eyes. Everyone except her—but also *only* her and not them.

"Then they may have the Intelligence Spirit. It can vary, depending on their branch of science. There is a Spirit responsible for air and space study, for humanity...There are also Healing Spirits, responsible for study in medicine and the understanding of natural remedies."

"Suppose we're supposed to have that one," Stacy joked.

Nicholas smiled in response, helping Stacy to her feet. "Varkan, by the way. Varkan is my favorite food."

Stacy blinked. "Sounds a little bit like a disease."

He recoiled a bit. "Varkan is a casserole layered with a variety of vegetables and mixed with a hearty soup base and cheese."

"Varkan," Stacy noted. "I'll have Terra and Tom add it to the list for Christmas dinner."

The two began walking again. "What is your favorite meal?"

Stacy smiled. "Well, now that I know I'm connected to Spirit's I can finally get my mom to let me give up water, snow cones will be a sacrifice though."

Nicholas's smile faded.

"But you'll just have to see when we get to Wally's."

"Fair enough," he smiled. "I suppose I found out a tad of your family, after all. They are all quite brilliant."

Stacy nodded. "My grandparents came over from Dukhovia as healers. When they weren't allowed to practice anymore, they decided to take on modern medicine. My grandfather said they had already started adapting some modernizations into their technique anyway, but it was hard to give it up completely." Stacy's demeanor changed, feeling herself get lost in the words. "It's something I wish I could ask them more about."

"In what way?" Nicholas pressed.

"How hard it was for them," she responded, openly. "Was it difficult to do something they were told was a huge no-no while giving up everything they knew to be right? Or did they see the benefits of modern medicine and run with it?"

Nicholas was silent, perhaps seeing the dilemma. "What do you think?"

She thought about it. "Difficult, for sure. I wonder if it was something they learned about at their birth reading." Her thoughts drifted for a bit, considering it.

"What about your mother and father?"

"My parents are incredible. They allow me so much freedom to practice and learn more about Dukhovia, but also keep me safe. Mom did everything she could to try and keep me safe and secret on our one trip to Dukhovia. We made it."

"What did you think of it?" The questions seemed to be coming easier from both of them now, spilling out like cups that had long been at the brink and were now overflowing.

"It was everything. I remember feeling like I was abandoning everyone in the country when we left, even if we didn't meet many people, even if I wasn't specifically doing anything to help. It felt like if I stayed longer, I could have."

Nicholas was quiet, his series of question after question seeming to end. She thought back on her words, worried she revealed something deadly. She could find no hidden meanings.

"We tried to have secret identities," Stacy laughed. "It failed pretty quickly. We only ran into one person who we revealed our true selves to, but I wonder how many knew anyway. I also worry all the time that he told someone we were there. I worry that consequences are coming."

"You worry I am that consequence?" Nicholas read on her.

Stacy shrugged sheepishly. "Sort of. If not because of that for something else related to our banishment."

Nicholas stopped abruptly. Stunned, Stacy stopped too and stared at him. That was it. She had done it. She had made him irrevocably angered. They were right across the street from the restaurant, but it was fairly dead and not a single other thing was on this side of town. How very convenient, Matthews, how very, very, hideously convenient.

Her next question was more difficult: accept death or fight back? Easy. Fight back. But how did one fight against a trained Dukhovian solider?

But, when he finally stood face to face, inches away from her, his demeaner was calm and nonthreatening. A scare tactic, no doubt.

No.

He lifted his hands onto her shoulders, making an effort to avoid laying his palms onto her. Then he brushed her cheek with his hand and lightly caressed her face. "Stacy Grace," his voice was a delicate whisper that sent chills down her spine. "I cannot promise you much. I am a very broken person sent from a very broken land. But I can give you my word, on my family's honor, that I have no ill intent to your family. From the day my plane landed until the day it leaves again, I shall do nothing but protect your family, princess. You have my word."

And then, to seal the deal with fate, he bowed into the most binding way to seal a Dukhovian promise. He bowed to her, palms together close to his face. Then, he lifted his hands to the Spirits and fell to his knees.

It was in that moment Stacy decided that she could potentially trust the Dukhovian solider.

Potentially. Because in his swear, he had accidentally revealed too much: sent from a broken land. *Sent.* Sir Nicholas Aloyshenka Aleksis Demitona the Third had been sent from Dukhovia to America for something. It was something that Santifini knew about. It was something he had to do in order for both of them to return. And if it had nothing to do with her family—what was it? And why could she not know?

CHAPTER 40

THE DAMNING AMERICAN

Nicholas was not sure what to make of "Wally's Burgers", nor Stacy's etiquette. She could go from totally normal one moment to practically savage the next. He had to remind himself, as much as she did appear Dukhovian, she was also American. That shined through often, including now.

Stacy had burst through the door of the establishment on her own and stuck one arm out behind her to save the door for him. He tried his best to maneuver around her in order to be holding the door for her, but she left no leverage. He could not read her response to the promise he made just before she sprinted across the street into this place. Did she believe him? She did not let on. She went from looking at him grimly to grinning so broadly he thought her cheeks would tear, then she took off across the street.

Nicholas seemed to move his thoughts away from Stacy's reaction for a time— either intentionally or force as he tried to understand what he was looking at. The inside of the…erm…restaurant sent Nicholas's heart tightening in his chest. He was reminded of the feeling he had when first exiting off the plane and realized how little of America he still knew—their day-to-day activities, their shops and eateries. This one was as American as America could get.

The blinding fluorescent lights did not surprise him, but they certainly annoyed him. The left of the restaurant was riddled with white booth-type seating, red cushioning providing comfort, were it not for the tears in many of the pieces. The place looked clean enough, were one to not think of the amount of people who likely sneezed on the device one poured beverages from. Then there was the blinding smell of dirty grease and spoiled food. He knew that smell all too well, but none of the American's patronizing it seemed to. Or they did not mind if they did.

Stacy had immediately grazed off to the right where a long counter with two workers stood—black boxes in front of each of them. He glanced up at the choices in meals and immediately felt his stomach kicking him. What had he gotten himself into in allowing her to decide where they would venture?

"Now," Stacy turned, gesturing for him to take a seat. "I know that this food isn't anything like what they have in our great motherland, so I'm going to order for you and blow your taste buds out of the water, and you are going to cherish every decision I make."

CHAPTER FORTY

"Understood," he remarked, gulping as he looked up at the menu and around the restaurant once more. Stacy went up and ordered something he only understood when she mentioned vegetables—or the lack of—and the name of their country. His country. Theirs?

"Okay." Stacy walked over with a huge smile, carrying two wrapped objects and two small fries. She gestured to a table and the two sat down.

"Yours is this one…the Veggie Lovers Supreme!"

Stacy slid over a bun with lettuce and tomato spilling out the sides. Indeed, there was no meat inside, and he could not help but feel a small piece of affirmation that she ordered within his dietary restrictions, but the cacophony of unknown was disabling.

"What is this?" Nicholas asked, finding something that looked like a meat patty.

"Veggie burger," she answered simply, unwrapping her own death sentence.

He eyed it with indecision. "What is a veggie burger?"

Stacy thought about it and shrugged. "Got me. Veggies held together by something? It looks terrible."

He grimaced, picking apart the rest of the sandwich piece by piece. Nothing looked even remotely close to anything he had eaten back in Dukhovia and none of it looked to resemble what it was meant to. He sighed, lifting a shriveled up, browning slice of tomato. "This is a vegetable?" He asked.

"As is this," she said, lifting a fry into her mouth. She opened her burger up and allowed grease to pour out the bun, bacon and three different kinds of cheese were falling out the sides.

"And this is a sensible meal?" Nicholas asked, staring at it.

"No," Stacy answered. "Not for people with an agenda to live past thirty."

"You do not wish to live past thirty?" He asked, eyebrow raised as he calculated how many years he had to go and how Arkady felt about relying on natural selection. He battled relief and sickness over the thought.

"Eh." She shrugged and shoved a few fries into her burger then took a bite.

"This would hardly be considered suitable in Dukhovia…" Nicholas began. He pushed it away, refusing even a single bite.

"Oh, I know," Stacy said, but clearly having no regard for his culture, as she finished off the burger in another two bites. Ugh. He looked back down at his own meal. She had ordered him as vegetarian a meal as she could, perhaps it was unfair to assume she did not care for a culture she understood so little about.

"When we were there, we couldn't find anything edible to eat. Unfamiliar equals unappetizing to this palate," she sang, now picking at the remainder of her fries.

"Just because it is not familiar does not mean it is not edible," Nicholas told her. "And it was probably not familiar because it was not heavily processed," he added, moving the straw around in his cup filled with a strange, dark and bubbly liquid.

"I could say the same to you," Stacy noted as grease dripped down her chin. "You're afraid of a pickle."

He looked at his food with understanding. Perhaps she was right, he was not giving the food a chance. But he also did not want to dishonor himself. "In Dukhovia, we believe that we honor the Spirits with our bodies. While we are perfectly aware that we will not live forever, we know that they have a plan for us and we want to be in perfect health in order to fulfill that plan. We may need to live past thirty in order to accomplish it as such."

Stacy paused after he said the words, letting her last fry dangle in her mouth with regret. She let it fall back to the tray.

"We do not eat like barbarians simply because the rest of the population deems it appropriate," he looked at her disapprovingly.

"I don't know that anyone deems it appropriate," she was saying, but she still did not pick back up her last fry. "Some people just don't know the bad effects. Others know but are too disappointed by their lives to care…" She looked around, guessing at the choices of the people in the building.

Nicholas looked at her, intrigued. Dukhovian spy, he remembered. "Which are you?"

Stacy's eyes found the ground, lost anytime someone asked her to identify with a specific group. "The one intent on my Spirit keeping away heart disease?" She mused, but her tone and face told him she already knew the ridiculousness in the statement.

"And what if heart disease does someday find you?" Nicholas pried. "What if someday you get sick and you never get to fulfill what you were meant to do? What if the lives you were meant to change go uninfluenced? What if the people you were meant to love go lonely?"

She grimaced again and pushed her food to the side. "Then I suppose I'll eat more apples," Stacy decided, the lump in her throat not willing her to say anymore.

He breathed and looked back down. "Is this truly your favorite meal?"

She looked at him as if deciding whether or not to answer with the truth. "Favorite and I could usually go for seconds."

"Fine." He pulled his tray back over towards him and, with much difficulty, found the least mutilated vegetable and forced it down his throat.

Stacy's eyes lit up, her smile the widest and brightest he had ever seen. "Well?" She pressed.

He choked as it went down, immediately went for a drink of his pop, and spit that out as well. Stacy roared with laughter.

Nicholas smiled and stood up, holding his hand out for her to grab onto and rise. She obliged.

"Let us attempt to find something real to eat in this horrid country?" He mused.

CHAPTER FORTY

She laughed and accepted. "Lead the way, master."

This time, Nicholas held both doors open for her and she exited with a smile and a twirl, then ran across the parking lot and street just the same as before, willing him to join her, though he would refuse.

CHAPTER 41

THE FIRST WORLD

S o, what did you find out?" Stacy asked as Nicholas came out of a convenient store. He had decided that he was going to 'get to know the American people' by asking everyone he passed for restaurant recommendations. However, he continued to question them on the recommendation and also was keeping a tally—none had been good enough for his highness quite yet.

"We will have to take a bus to get there," Nicholas explained, hurrying out of the store.

"Ooo we have a winner!" She celebrated, clapping her hands. The growling in her stomach had her immediately chasing after him towards the bus station, realizing that she would absolutely go to her death if it meant the possibility of food.

"You're taking me to a remote area on a bus all alone? Cody was right, you're killing me for sure," Stacy teased.

"Is that what he thinks?" Nicholas asked, unsure by the tone of his voice if he wanted to come off as sarcastic or playing dumb.

"Most definitely," Stacy agreed. "And now here we are, walking together in the deep hours of the night, without anyone around. I played right into your game."

"It is 8 o'clock and the bus station is well lit," Nicholas argued.

"On a school night?" She protested. "Just promise you'll let them use a nice picture on my missing persons poster."

The two arrived at the bus stop on the west side of town—the less developed side. There were several broken down buses littering the lot. The fence which was meant to encompass it had rusted and caved in in so many places it may as well have been taken down. Every edge of the bus station's building was spray painted in some form of pornographic or otherwise derogatory profanity.

And there were homeless as far as the eye could see. Several people held up signs, clanked cups, wheezed, and shivered in the cool breeze of the chilling night. Stacy and Nicholas could see where they had mock tents made of ripped tarp around the station. This was the only section exempt from the profanity. Instead, creativity raged even deeper, spraying: "Get a Job" and "Waste of Space" or "Menace to Society".

Nicholas held his hand out to Stacy's as he helped her onto the nearly empty bus. She grasped the ends of his fingers and climbed aboard. She would never get used to the electrifying jolt that coursed through her, but she was finding ways to avoid how intense it felt. The feeling was far from negative, but confusing and she already had enough on her list.

Stacy followed Nicholas closely, unsure who was protecting who, but as she watched the way he defensively moved around her, she partially got a feeling she should allow herself to be protected and partially felt like she should run him down and take a bullet.

She could not say she was surprised by the appearance of the interior. The filth of the bus compared to the sounds they were hearing: in fear and extremities. Food was scattered on the floor, crushed into undefinable crumbs. Bags of fast-food leftovers were abandoned on certain unoccupied seats.

As they walked to the back of the bus and the driver threw it in motion, Stacy felt any anxious thoughts wash away. The few people who were on the bus stared at them, but not in a way that seemed of concern, it was more of a back and forth between the two with curiosity, as if they were expecting and *wanting* something to happen.

"Very sturdy," Stacy commented as the two were thrown backward by the ricketiness of the bus as it drove down completely paved streets. The sounds of creeks and the shuttering of the frame blared well over the music and any other sounds, but every so often they were quiet enough to hear the whispers of the onlookers.

Stacy looked over at Nicholas's grim and focused face. He looked as though he might be sick.

"Not the preferred transportation method in Dukhovia?" She asked.

Nicholas shook his head immediately. "I have never been in a vehicle before, aside from the ambulance. And my first trip on a plane was getting here. It is all much different than a horse and I do not like any of it."

Stacy could not help but laugh as she watched him bend over with sickness. "So, you can ride boats across the seven seas but the city bus has you down for the count?" She laughed loudly, the sound of her laughter echoing around the bus.

"I regret trying your horrid vegetables," he said through clenched teeth.

Uncomfortable as he was, Stacy was bothered as she watched him hide that discomfort as much as possible.

Finally, the bus came to a halt and as quickly as if it never happened, Nicholas sat up from his sickness and followed Stacy off the bus. The doors opened revealing a very clean and exceptional looking restaurant. Bright, gold lights hung over every ivy-covered arch leading up to the entryway. Bushes of exotic flowers that Stacy had never seen in person lined the pathway. Everyone whom entered in their wake were in their best dress and on their best behavior.

Now she hated herself for not dressing fancier. But they were only supposed to go to Wally's.

A prim and proper valet greeted them with a wide armed wave, pleasantly waiting to be of assistance. He showed them the way up the elegant pathway where the doors were held open for them by a bubbling, larger man.

"Right this way!"

Nicholas was smiling a chastising smile as the two were escorted to a table covered in a beautiful velvety, red tablecloth. It was completely set with a fork and spoon for every item and a crafty, folded napkin. Two candles lit either side of the table while a vase of flowers formally decorated the center.

"Alright, Sir, so far so good, I'll give you that, but we'll have to see how the food fairs." Suddenly her eyes fell and she found the flowers. "Wow, we got lucky," she said, feeling the soft petals of the ice thistles between her fingers. "We're the only table that got flowers."

"Those are for you," Nicholas told her, pulling out her chair carefully.

She sat down in a mesmerized trance, unable to distract herself from the beauty of the flowers. "Ice thistles?" She asked, surprised. "They're my favorite." He truly did think of everything.

"Did you know that they are the national flower of Dukhovia? Because they are known to grow where great destruction took place."

Stacy drew a flower out of the vase and took in the scent. She loved them from the first moment she saw them because they were unalike any flower she had ever seen before. They did not seem to simply sit idly by, but instead waved themselves with a certain allurement that dared to be noticed. Their color was enough to draw attention: pale, but deeming themselves to hold story, to hold truth. They got their name as the tiny, pale lilac-blue bulb would hold ice and glisten in the moonlight, reflecting the light and making them appear to be lit like powerful Christmas lights.

Then there was the scent. The scent was mesmerizing in and of itself. The strongest she had ever smelled and the least floral. It reminded her less of a flower and more of something powerful, stronger.

Nicholas watched her with envious and discerning eyes as she took the scent in, continuing with his tale. "In the past, they were thought to be a symbol associated with death and darkness, because the way they reflected the light was confusing and unfamiliar…but now we see them as rebirth, as a possibility that it is possible to regrow what once was and find beauty from the ashes. To…make sense of what we do not comprehend until we can be certain we do not bear the burden of careless mistakes."

Stacy closed her eyes and took in the words. Visions of Dukhovia flashed behind her eyelids. The feeling of home, of peace coursed through her. She envisioned the people, envisioned Nicholas, and felt devotion. Then she saw fire coursing through the country, unexplained. Unstoppable.

"Nicholas," she whispered softly. "You promised to tell me anything about Dukhovia…"

"Anything," his voice sounded sincere as he made the empty promise, taking her hand gently into his only for a moment.

Stacy hesitated, thinking of just the right way to word it, to not cause him upset feelings of his home or memories at the loss of his parents. To keep him calm. To keep the conversation on track. Yet she knew. This was her chance and it was time. She waited long enough in isolation.

"You said that the war wasn't just over modernization anymore, there's something else our people want. Something to do with...with an heir?" She felt the lump growing as she spoke the words, only confirming she was crossing into dangerous territory when she watched his neck stiffen ever so slightly and then back again to hide the indication—too late.

He drew in his breath, a deep sigh he wanted to prolong. "What do you know of The First World?"

When Stacy blinked at him blankly, he laughed and continued.

"The First World is what we call the original world, the world in its prime. Currently Dukhovia is the only traditional country that remains in our land. Long ago, it was our entire planet, split into different sections, guided by different Spirits.

"There was the Nature Spirit, the Sun and Fire Spirit, the Winter, Water, and Moon Spirit, the Spirit of Ancestry, and the Spirit of Loyalty. They each had their role that they would teach the people of their lands and those people would travel across other lands to then exchange and share gifts. It is how we obtain our value of cultural acceptance and growth.

"The Nature Spirit represents the value of nature. We are to have respect with every living thing under the impression that they each serve a purpose and to alter that purpose could change the way of our world forever. Even something you may deem small, such as smashing that spider..." he pointed to the right with his head, "...could prove a disruption.

"Then there are the Spirits of the Sun and Fire. They share gifts and teachings, but are also their own. They bring warmth, light, protection, growth. They are responsible for our meals, our value of agriculture.

"The Spirit of Ancestry." He paused for a moment and looked down. "This is one of great value to me. You can guess that it is where we obtain our value of ancestry, of respect for our family names. We are taught to preserve our families and carry on their names, their legacies. We are taught family always comes first."

"We can take a break," Stacy interrupted, watching his face fall and a dark color begin to fill his cheeks. He seemed to heave out the last of the words between breaths of exhaustion or holding back the empty contents of his stomach.

He was already shaking his head. "No. I would like to tell you the story of our people." He shook his head again. "It is an honor to tell this story to you, Stacy Grace."

She paused, waiting and watching for more words, for more of a reaction. "It's an honor to hear it."

Slowly, Nicholas went on. "The Spirit of Ancestry works to maintain our lineage with…accuracy. They will ensure our tales and legends get passed along so that our story and culture continue. It is of upmost importance that this continues. Some considered this Spirit to be the most important at the time. Without accuracy, there is nothing worthy of believing. Without accuracy, we only have stories, not history."

Nicholas was quiet for a long time after discussing The Spirit of Ancestry. Stacy knew exactly why and did not press him, but she also did not move away from it. Rachael had said he probably needed somebody he could open up to, someone he could lean on for support. So, she waited and she listened and prayed they would push past and talk about the heir.

It was funny. The only moment she was willing to lose the conversation of the heir completely was when she saw Nicholas come undone and she knew he needed her more than she needed to fulfill her own selfish need. At least, until that annoying buzz in the back of her head reminded her that it was not entirely selfish.

"And then there are The Warrior Spirits, or The Spirit of Loyalty. From here is where we derive our value of patriotism. They were known as The Warrior Spirits at one point, since they are always interacting as a team. They are where we originally obtained our value of the martial arts. We learn it out of honor to them and the Spirit that would further it.

"Our Spirits are not all-powerful beings, they do not exist to rule over us, but rather to balance us. The stronger we believe, the stronger they and their gifts are present. When the world started to lose its way and act in opposition to what the Spirits deemed appropriate, the Spirit Connection was lost, those Spirits drifted from that land, and it would eventually become part of the modern world.

"Dukhovia's strongest Spirits are those of the Winter, Water, and Moon because our land is currently all that remains of The First World. The only remaining sector is that which they oversee. To lose them means to lose our entire world, our entire culture. It is for this reason that maintaining traditionalism is more important than it has ever been."

"And the…heir…" Stacy could hardly form her words as she took everything in. It all felt like information she knew for years—or should have known and yet how little she did know ate her alive.

Nicholas nodded. "The heir is the most important person to Dukhovia. The heir is the person with the strongest connection to The Winter, Water, and Moon Spirit. They may be able to speak with them, harness their power, there is much known and not known. The heir will be the ruler of our people."

Protect them.

They're coming.

The heir.

CHAPTER FORTY-ONE

Protect the heir.

"So, they're safe then? The heir? They have the strongest connection that makes them safe?" Her voice was like a shaking plea.

His laugh was a sneer that melted her bones and left everything that remained numb. "No. It makes them the most vulnerable person in all of Dukhovia."

Stacy's eyes widened in a horror-stricken response.

"They will rule our people, Stacy. Imagine your own political system. You do not want to choose someone who does not align with your views. Dukhovia is torn more than ever before—imagine the Spirits choosing a person with modern ideals?"

Stacy squinted, shaking her head at the nonsense. Perhaps it was his hunger. "But they have the closest connection to the Spirits. Of course they would remain traditional, right?"

Nicholas's eyes were looking into hers, but past her at the same time, searching, yet understanding. His fingers twitched, her foot tapped. It was the longest nonverbal conversation she felt she ever had that gave her the most.

"Maybe. This heir is said to be different. The strongest we have ever seen and that sets fear in all of Dukhovia. The people are saying that because they are so strong with the Spirits that their stance will be the one that ends the war, the one that decides the future for all of Dukhovia."

Great destruction or great peace.

Stacy's eyes widened. But she had other questions, she needed to be sure, she needed to know...

"Nicholas...a few days ago, I came to the office to talk to you and I overheard you talking with Santifini."

Nicholas's face went cold and he became white as a ghost. A lumped formed in Stacy's throat telling her to stop, but she persisted.

"You mentioned returning to Dukhovia...as if you're not allowed. As if something you need to do here will determine if you both can return."

He looked down at the table as he thought, his fists twitching in his lap and his jaw clenching and unclenching unevenly. "You heard that, did you? I apologize, I lose my temper quite easily, as you know."

She waited.

"Santifini means you no harm, I can assure you. Nor your family. He is amongst the banishments in Dukhovia, there are so many that have started after the war on modernization and now the tension surrounding the heir. I only meant that if I can figure things out here, that it will be safe for those wrongfully banished to return. Your family included."

Stacy drummed her fingers against the table. She looked around the restaurant as if the courage to say what she needed to say would fly out at her. "It sounded like you coming here wasn't exactly your choice. Like someone sent you here. The military maybe forced you?"

She watched sweat form around his brow as he distracted himself by taking a long drink of water which he then choked on.

They both recoiled in their seats as the waitress finally approached them, distracted and distant.

"Can I get your order?" She asked, glancing at her notepad and speaking to no one in particular.

"Yes, thank you." Nicholas was the first to snap out of their conversation, though the distant look in his eyes seemed to persist. "Stacy?"

Stacy continued to stare at him, searching him. There was more, she knew there was more and she needed to know whatever it was that he continued to keep under lock and key.

Shaking her head, she took out her menu for the first time and chose a few of the first couple of items she saw. "I'll take a family order of mushroom soup— actually make that three—four or five whole chickens, whatever you have in stock, aaaannndd for me—hmmm…maybe the sushi?"

The waitress and Nicholas both stared at Stacy in disbelief. She stared back from one reaction to the next. "Oh, I'm sorry," she finally said after a moment. "Nicholas—go ahead." She granted permission with a wave of her hand.

Nicholas continued to stare but blinked hard once and turned his attention to the menu. "What is your least refined meal?"

Stacy laughed quietly as the waitress stood dumbfounded.

"I don't know," she spat as if it was the most absurd thing she ever heard—it probably was.

"Ah. Well, in that case, I will try your homegrown vegetable platter with the Basmati rice."

The waitress said nothing, but walked away in a haste.

Nicholas stared after her for a long time.

"You want me to get her number for you?" Stacy asked, smiling as she rested her chin on folded hands. "I don't know that she'll be much of a conversationalist, but by all means, I won't judge your taste in women."

"Then you thought her rude too?" He asked slowly, astonished. "I apologize greatly. This place was so highly recommended and now…"

"It's okay," Stacy smiled. "Maybe she's just having a bad day."

"A bad day? She did not even try to acknowledge us appropriately. If one has a bad day, one still has a duty to perform."

Stacy raised her eyebrow, humor on her face. "One is also allowed to be human and have a bad day."

Nicholas averted his gaze to his water glass. "Perhaps it is my own upbringing swaying my thought." He drank for a long time.

Stacy nodded her head with more empathy. "Perhaps so." She waited, hesitant before she went on. Then she was all in. She folded her hands over top the table, leaned forward, and dove in. He had promised answers and she had questions. "Alright, I'll play naïve for a moment. Let's pretend like you did come here because you thought learning about us might help end the war—what's the next step? When will you have enough information? What will you do with the information?"

Nicholas's eyes penetrated her deeply before he spoke cold, affirming words. "That *is* the reason I am here," he protested. "And it is rather complex."

"I'm a bright girl," she smiled, tucking her hands under chin. "Do we simply storm the castle and tell The Czar how it is?"

He barked out dark laughter. "No one ever tells The Czar he's wrong and survives. No."

"Well then?"

Nicholas looked her fully in the eyes. "You were permitted to ask anything regarding Dukhovia, not anything regarding me."

Ouch. She felt the shift in the mood between them and the whole restaurant seemed cooler. "Fine." She said with poise. Whether he answered her questions regarding her puzzlement over him right this second did not matter. She had other questions unrelated to if she could really trust him. And if he could not answer those questions, whether she could trust him or not did not really matter. To a degree. "Then, regarding *Dukhovia*, what do you have to do to help *Dukhovia* and how can I help?"

"Help?" The word sounded foreign on his lips.

"Yes, help." She nodded her head to seal the deal. Then her voice broke, becoming more authentic. "All I think about lately is Dukhovia on fire, Dukhovia no longer existing. I don't know what that means, but I know it means I'm not supposed to just sit by in American and watch."

Nicholas seemed to relax, his neck muscles untensing. His eyes closing and opening again. "You mentioned if your future was in America, it would be music because you do not believe your future to be in America."

Stacy nodded slowly to confirm the detail. "And—if this mission of yours is really to provide a safe way for the banished families to return—then I need you to succeed in your mission so that I can return safely to Dukhovia."

Nicholas's eyes penetrated her for a long time. They spoke nothing, they revealed nothing. They only sent a message of intensity, a message of mystery. "My purpose in Dukhovia is not exactly—traditional. Though it is meant to protect tradition, strange as that sounds." His voice trailed off, sounding more cryptic, more isolated, lost. "It is something I was told at a young age that I would have to do or many lives would be forever altered—lost, destroyed, whatever the means. I agreed in the beginning, only because I did not know better. But, as I have grown,

I have recognized this purpose to be more flawed than it is coherent. And I am not so certain it will truly aid in ending the war. However, if I do not complete my mission, I run the risk of hurting millions of people and disgracing my family—and that is a risk I cannot take.

"I know that does not fully answer your questions. I know it is vague and perhaps seemingly misleading, but it is the best way I am able to explain."

She sat, relishing and soaking in the words that he said, the words that he thought were not enough that to her ended up being just enough—just enough to confirm her original thought....

It made sense. It all fit. He was predicted to cause great destruction or great peace—end the war or intensity it. His broken family would tear the world to shreds and cause for total focus to ensure his upbringing was traditional. *Sent* to America to find out if the banished families could help end the war or cause it to worsen. A mission that would indeed be perceived as very black and white in Dukhovia—the banished families were either just like everyone else or pure evil. That would absolutely explain the contention he seemed to feel. Not to mention her intense urge to protect him.

And so that confirmed one thing for her if nothing else—Nicholas was the heir. He was the heir. He was the one she needed to protect. And she knew exactly who she needed to protect him from. She need only the confirmation from him, but she knew better, she knew by now when to ask questions and when to silence her thoughts.

Her mind was a rush of thoughts, ideas, and outcomes, spiraling and piling up on each other, fighting for resolution. Slowly she back pedaled through every interaction, every conversation, every hesitant moment. If Dukhovia's future ruler was on American soil and he was talking to someone from one of the most famous banished families, it would make sense why he would have his reservations about her—as well as the other way around. She could also assume the amount of stress he was under would cause him to do some rather uncharacteristic like things—perhaps even kill. And if she was right, if Nicholas was the heir, if his purpose was to take over Dukhovia and end the war—what was hers? How was she meant to protect him?

CHAPTER 42

NO WAY OUT

icholas looked around the restaurant ready to throw up.

What a mess! What an absolute and total mess! He never planned for her to be traditional. He never planned for her to want to go to Dukhovia. Never planned for her to be so damned observant! But she was and she did. Did she trust him? Perhaps not. He had alluded any direct question she had—there was no way she did. But she would travel with anyone if it meant going to Dukhovia safely and he set himself up to be that very person. How simple his mission would be, were he to want to accomplish it.

But he did not want to accomplish it and taking her home, even if for her own wishes, meant fulfilling a path he tried for his entire life to avoid. He knew it his entire life, but he knew more than ever after this conversation that he *needed* out of this.

She seemed to drop her pressing interrogation of him, but he knew that only made him all the more suspicious. He knew he would eventually have to give an answer—which is why he gave her as much as he did. But now he realized…he was only digging himself deeper and if eventually her Spirit told her he was to be feared rather than drawn to each other….

What on *Earth* was he going to say? What could he possibly say to entirely ensure her that her family was safe when she had figured out where he had come from? What else did she overhear or simply already know about his relationship with the principal?

There was silence at the table for a while after they spoke their last words. After she declared her suicide mission to help end the war and he gave his half-answer… She had more turning in her mind, he did not want to touch whatever it was, he did not want to respond, but the reality of the unknown was clawing at his mind viciously.

"I apologize for my outburst. You have other questions, please tell me." His voice was gentle yet pressing all the same.

She eyed him with suspicion then swallowed. "You told Santifini that you needed his help. How would he help you?"

He bit his lip tediously. "It was sort of more of a…threat," he spoke the word hesitantly and was not surprised when she straightened herself up, but kept her poker face. "He…" He felt his throat close and sweat drip down his back. "I… He knows my purpose here," he blurted it out, not fully considering the consequences. But it was as honest as he could be without giving away everything.

"And he has a vendetta to ensure I fail. I do not truly believe he will help me, but it was my polite way of asking him to back down or else." He did not dare make eye contact with her after that, but instead chose to swirl around the lemon in his water, watching the seeds and juices spin to the bottom of the cup.

"Why would he want you to fail?" She whispered the urgent words.

He looked up at her and then back down, shame dripping from every inch of him and he knew it. He expected she knew, he had seen her go into his office the day she came out hating him again. But, if he was wrong, now was not the time for her to find out, not before he had a chance to let her know what she suspected—that she needed him and he needed her.

"I already told you—family disputes."

She seemed unsatisfied with the answer, but took it for the time being. "So...is there a way to help you? To get the banished families home quicker?"

He shook his head. "No. I hardly believe in the goal myself. As I said, to tell The Czar he is wrong is to commit treason. Even if I found the families to be promising, I would need to return to relay the information before anything could be done. We would all need to plan."

She was quiet, but maintained hard eye contact. "Have you found them to be promising?"

He looked at her. He knew perfectly well he was lying and he was almost positive she did too. But another thing he was almost certain of hindered his answer—she was the only person he had been around and she had to have known that.

"Much more promising than I had imagined, but I am still learning." She seemed to catch his drift.

"So," her voice was casual as she chugged back her water like it was a tall glass of brandy after a battle. "Who is this heir then?"

Nicholas spat with a sound close to ridicule, but it was pure humor. "Irrelevant. You would not know them."

She raised her eyebrow. "Fine. Tell me more about the risk they're in."

Nicholas looked at her now, tried reading her. What did she know? He desperately wanted to ask, but to tear down her walls meant to tear down his own—and he would not, he could not. "It is unprecedented."

"Is the divide just over whether or not they'll modernize then? Who is their biggest threat? Is it The Czar?"

He reclined in his seat. He had promised answers, did he not? What in the world was he thinking? Yet the more she asked, the more he realized—they were on the same side. "Possibly, but it is complicated. The Czar is concerned that this heir will modernize our nation due to their upbringing and family status. The Czar has power on his side, however, there are more intelligent and cunning men who are in support of the heir. Then again, the numbers seem to fair against the heir." He sighed, the uncertainty of his country making him sick.

"But if the heir is traditional, then at least we're just back to whether or not to modernize. What if the heir isn't traditional? What if they do want to modernize?"

Nicholas swallowed. "Then I fear the dissolution of our world and I fear that traditionalists will respond tenfold to bring the heir to their demise."

Stacy's mood seemed to shift the same way his did, her poised attitude sinking into a sea of thoughts. "Are they safe now?"

He swallowed. "I hope so."

Her eyes held deep suspicion. "Can The Czar or anyone do anything to hurt them now?"

Hesitation. "He always can."

The widening of her eyes and the way her body froze in place sent fear down his own spine. For the first time, she had the most knowledge about the actual risk to her life and she was frightened. To go any further would be for him to be the reason for her fright, for him to be the monster who hung his mother upside down in a cave, for him to be the monster that lit his home to flames.

He imagined her banging on the door of her beautiful home, shouting her parent's names. Her, fighting tooth and nail, screaming and shouting more than he had, *demanding* everything to stop. But no one would listen. No one would listen to what she wanted. No one would protect her. Even if she was the heir that would cause great peace.

He wanted to throw up.

Stacy had thrown herself back in her seat defeated, her eyes searching for more and more answers across the dark, unknowing vortex of her mind.

"There has to be a way to protect them."

Nicholas raised his eyebrows. "Protect who? Dukhovia?"

Stacy lifted her head to meet his eyes, but her own gaze was far away. "No, the heir. If they have the ability to bring great peace, they could very well be traditional. But we know The Czar has persecuted innocents before, and they could be easily hurt by him at any time. We need to find a way to keep them safe."

His blood went cold and the sound of his already thudding heart had to have reached back home by now. She wanted to *help* the heir? For God's sake, she *was* the heir! The best way to protect the heir was him leaving and her remaining right here. The way her thoughts were totally distracted told him she had some inkling that the heir existed, whether she knew it was her or just an important person in Dukhovia. Was that what she was so intent to ask? Did he have no way of diverting her now?

Him leaving. It was the only answer. Arkady needed him to secure Stacy. He needed him. If he left, he would track him down, but he would be far from Stacy.

And then he finds another way to get the girl, Mr. Hero.

Nicholas did not know how to please Erlick or the situation. If he stayed, the demon was unsatisfied. If he ran, he was unsatisfied.

Honest as he could. He needed to be as honest as he could. There was no way to get her off this topic without lying to her. Ugh! He ground his feet into the floor trying to hold back his angst. He'd be pushing through the floorboards soon.

"I suppose the heir's greatest chance at safety would be their own strengths."

Her head cocked to the side. "What do you mean by that?"

Nicholas breathed. She seemed to be taking the bait. "They were chosen for a reason, surely they must have some type of strengths, some type of internal instincts, be it intelligence or spiritual power, that would keep them safe."

Stacy thought on that for a long time before she spoke, the sound of tapping underneath the table ceased and she sipped her water with care. "What exactly makes an heir an heir? Does it mean they have a certain strength like super intelligence? Super strength? Super spirit connected?"

"Well, as I stated, they have the greatest connection to the Spirits, however, different heirs have different gifts, depending on what Dukhovia needs of them at the time. For example, King Yuriy thrived in his time as the war was just starting and the people were frightened, he had strength in gifts such as empathy and resilience, courage. I imagine the world needs another person like Yuriy with the ability to make armies fall by fear alone."

Stacy seemed to shudder in her seat, he was uncertain if it was his words responsible or the lack of assurance they provided.

"What else do we know about this heir? Do we know what strengths they have?"

Nicholas looked her up and down. *Brilliant. Patriotism beyond her realization. The Ancestor Spirit probably runs through her veins more than blood.* "No more than what their birth reading revealed. She might have any number of Spirit gifts."

"She?" She flung herself forward at the hint.

Nicholas tried to not reveal the horror at his mistake. *Keep something vague,* he told himself. Now she had more and more information to narrow it down… until she realized it was herself she was so desperate to protect.

"Or he," he added casually. "Assuming the birth reading even remains accurate—they tend to change. But it can be assumed that the Spirits did not leave this heir completely defenseless. He or she likely has a gift that will cast enemies to the sea and beyond. We also believe that one cannot die until their purpose has been reached, so if this heir's birth reading was correct—they will be safe."

That seemed to allow her to breathe for a moment, even if it was full of gaps and lies.

"Well, at least tell me what their life is like now. Do they have soldier's protecting them? Family?"

Nicholas considered the benefits of answering honestly versus the opposite. He could see difficulty in either path.

Honesty.

"Yes. Yes, they have protection."

Stacy seemed to be sifting the information. Nicholas sat uncomfortably as he waited for the next question that would cause her to throw back her chair and storm out of the building. It was in her head and he knew it. It was not enough, telling her she could do nothing. It would never be enough for an heir and it certainly would not be enough for the stubbornly protective Stacy Grace Matthews. And that tore his heart in two.

Ask me again, he pleaded. *Ask me who the heir is. I will tell you so can run from me. I will tell you everything. Just run.* Run.

Follow his mission or follow his heart. *Run.*

Follow Dukhovia or follow Arkady. *Run.*

Follow the Spirits and his family or follow a fearful man…. *Stay.*

He had looped his family and the Spirits together. To do what was right by his family was to do what was right by the Spirits…right?

Stacy opened her mouth to press further, but the waitress returned with their food, taking her mind in a completely different direction like a child that had just seen something shining and new.

The waitress set their food down on the table (the majority of Stacy's on the table next to them) and walked away without a word.

"Hungry tonight?" Nicholas asked.

"I'm always hungry," Stacy retorted. "Jot that down, you'll want to remember that for future reference."

"Consider it stored in my memory for all of eternity." It was. No matter how miniscule a detail.

The two ate rather quickly, Nicholas was surprised at how much he ate, despite the fact that the food was bland and his stomach felt on fire. He was in quite the hurry to leave the friendly restaurant, even after they graciously provided him with extra sea salt.

"Do you not eat carrots?" Stacy had asked, eyeing the orange pile pushed off to the side. "They provide an essential set of nutrients."

Nicholas looked from her to his carrots and back more times than was likely necessary, but he tried to find a way to deflect the keen observation. "I do not like the flavor. Plus, they do not offer any essential nutrients not found in anything else on my plate."

"I see," Stacy accepted. "And how are the rest of your healthy vegetables?" She asked him, tearing through two sushi rolls at once.

"Rather bland. Where is our waitress? Excuse me, could you please get us some salt, our waitress finds herself unable to perform at the current moment." But it was the waitress who returned, tossing the seasoning towards him with the final word of "enjoy" before disappearing until her final appearance of the night.

Stacy seemed unable to stifle her laughter at his reaction.

"Any dessert?" She asked, a bit more lifelike.

"Yeah, does the chocolate cake slice come as a whole cake?" Stacy asked, peering at the menu with great interest.

"Yes, it does," the waitress confirmed anticipating the amount Stacy would request.

"I'll take two."

The evening finished in mostly silence as they chewed and processed details of the other's information. At the end of the evening, Nicholas pulled Stacy's chair out for her and she rose to her feet, taking the check book in hand.

"What are you doing?" Nicholas asked her, extending his hand for the book.

"What did you want to do, dine and dash?" She pondered. "Dinner and a show—I'm in."

He shook his head. "No, but I will pay...we will keep it legal for tonight."

Although she wanted to make a joke that there was hope for tomorrow, she watched with a heavy heart as Nicholas pulled out his wallet.

"Nicholas, you don't really think I would make you pay, do you? I mean..." she paused, trying not to stammer over her words. Trying not to offend. "I know you're perfectly able to take care of yourself, but, you're on your own. It doesn't really seem fair."

"On the contrary," he stated, comfortably pulling out the exact amount in cash from his pocket. Stacy saw several hundred-dollar bills filter passed her eyes, shocking her. Worrying her. "They made certain I would have all I needed to stay as long as I needed." He said the words with opposition thick in his voice.

"As long as you need..." She repeated in a distant voice. She fell silent as the two walked back outside and started towards the bus stop.

"So," Stacy's words began shortly after they left the area of the restaurant. Their surroundings were nearly desolate in the late night. Wind whipped at their faces as the nighttime chill set in, threatening to freeze any puddles that had dare melted. "Who exactly is *they*? Is it just The Czar who asked you to come? Made you come? Whichever." She leapt onto the curb, slipping and laughing in response.

Nicholas's lips turned into a half smile; he pulled one hand out of his pocket and reached for Stacy's arm to steady her. His hand softly stroked her upper arm, then retracted, allowing only his fingers to dance across her sweater.

"I had a wonderful night with you, Stacy Grace. To bring up the confusion of my family life and my upbringing would only upset you," he said.

Stacy was silent for a moment. Whether she was thinking of her next tactic or focusing on not having the evening end in another near-death experience, he was not certain. He supposed it was likely both.

"Are you sure you would describe the evening as wonderful? You looked sick half the time and we haven't even gotten back on the bus yet." She smirked.

Ah. Deflection was what she settled on, then. "Ha!" He surprised himself at the barking out of laughter. "Fair enough, then." He stopped walking, surprising

Stacy. She stopped too and watched as he let the hand which held onto her arm fall lightly down her arm, just onto her wrist. He held out his opposite hand as an invitation. One he owed her after failing to keep his promise to answer any and all questions.

She looked from his hands to eyes with puzzlement, with hesitation…but with intrigue. Slowly, she lifted just the tips of her fingers into his hands. Immediately he let her hand fall to his. Cusped, yes, but fully settled into his own. Instantly, the hand holding her wrist slid down as well.

He watched and listened as he felt the quickness of her breathing intensify, her heart pounding in her chest. Her mouth seemed to go completely dry, as though for once in her life, she had forgotten how to speak.

His body responded in unison, not quite the same. Of course, he had felt the pull of another's spirit before, plenty of times as Arkady taught him how to sense and track, how to transfer Nicholas's power into Arkady's. The aftermath of the transfer always left him so weak afterward, so defeated and helpless and lost. It was as if he was draining himself of who he was. It felt so wrong.

Yet when they were simply touching for transfer, he felt electrified. He felt so full of power, so unstoppable.

This feeling with Stacy was nothing like that. On the contrary, Nicholas felt a closeness he never experienced, a fullness. His nerves seemed to relax and the glow of electrifying power became one of joy and connection and peace and…

"What I enjoyed about the evening was being near you, Stacy Grace. Even if your decisions repulsed me and made me question my sanity, I enjoyed our discussions, I enjoyed watching the passion in your eyes and your heart."

She was blinking at him absently, shock and bewilderment on her face. He squeezed her hands once and then released them.

He smiled, then transferred their hands around so that he was cupping her hands together over top one of his. Then, he took the fingers of his free hand and danced them in her palm. "That feeling…" he pushed into her palm. He quickly steadied her back before she fell and brought her down safely to the sidewalk, returning their hands to the previous position. "Those are our Spirit's getting to know one another. It's so strong."

"What does it mean?" She finally choked out.

He shrugged gently, he considered the most basic explanation he could give her ever since he saw her reaction in the cafeteria, knowing that she would have felt something, but never imaging how *amazing* it would feel to hold the girl's hand, to be so close to her. "Perhaps that our destinies are intertwined."

Stacy looked down at his hand now. She lifted her own and felt her way along his arms. She lingered at the white, healing patch where he had cut open his arm saving her. He had spent the entire night with his own fingers over it. The only one he could ever say he obtained out of loyalty. A scar he could be proud to wear.

Her hands moved further, up his biceps, tracing the muscles beneath his shirt, then up to his neck. She paused. He saw the flush red fill her cheeks as she brought both hands gently to his neck, his cheeks. She took a step forward, placing her body so very close to his. He could no longer breathe.

"Stacy Grace..." His hands had fallen limp to his sides.

She picked them up and placed them on her waist, then waited. "You're the only other person I have ever met like me," she whispered. He closed his eyes, breathing her closeness in. "How can that be?"

He opened his eyes. "I told you," he croaked in a whisper. "Our Spirits make us one."

In the distance, a wolf howled and the wind beat fiercely at their faces, blowing their hair around each other.

"We should go," Stacy laughed, lifting the bag of her to-go order that Nicholas had set on the ground next to them. "My food will get cold."

Nicholas came out of his daze more slowly, continuing to look at her for answers. Answers on who she was, on if she would be a good fit for Dukhovia, on where that left him, on anything.

Finally, he smiled and began walking. "And your cousin will think I have murdered you for certain."

"Oh absolutely."

They walked back to the bus station in pitch black, the only light came from the Christmas lights surrounding the area that made it almost beautiful—that and the fire the homeless had going around their tents.

The remainder of their walk had been light conversation. Stacy told Nicholas of her family's holiday plans, Nicholas listened, not daring to say anything that might upset the peace of the evening. She was suspicious and pressed him, of course, but she would then all too inconspicuously avert the subject to something else when she sensed he did not want to answer. She was the only person to ever sense that and the only person to ever grant him the respect to mourn the life he would never know again.

Arriving at the station, Stacy bounced towards the tents and the men and women standing around the fires. They welcomed her as if she were a long-awaited guest. She quickly emptied her purse of rolls, delivered the soup, and handed the cakes to a man who gratefully bowed to her and wiped his tears on her shirt.

Stacy laughed with them, cried with them, sang for them. And Nicholas watched as the heir with the power to change his world responded to a situation with grace, with restraint. She ushered him over and he helped ladle out the soup and pass it around.

Most notably, the man who first greeted Stacy observed her lack of jacket and handed her his raggedy, old jacket. Stacy accepted, feeling too ungrateful to explain the man's error.

NO WAY OUT

And Nicholas's insides crashed down around him. *Run.*

CHAPTER 43

A FOOL'S GAME

*F*ire. Ice. Swords. Animals racing by.
A forest, lively and free. And then destruction.
A world brilliant with color and birds...but no people.
Then a face, always the same face. Laughing. No. Howling with joy.
Nicholas.

It was the third time that night she had the dream and she was not willing to tempt fate a fourth. Each time the dream repeated, Stacy would wake up, walk herself through the evening, walk herself through what she knew about Nicholas, and fall back to sleep. Each time, more sweat soaked her pillow and more bruises littered her body.

Why would the dream be showing her something like this? That Nicholas was the one who caused all this destruction? Was it her own thoughts coming in, like a normal dream? Heck, she did not even know for sure if the dream she was having normally *meant* anything. But her gut instincts told her that it did and if so that meant...*what* about Nicholas?

Ugh.

She threw back her covers and sat at her desk, quickly throwing out a notebook paper and a pen. She already had been keeping careful record of everything she knew about Nicholas. It helped to analyze his character. It helped to make sure she was not crazy. But last night...last night added...a lot.

Of course, there was still some things she did not know. She knew that it made him sad to open up completely and she did not want to put that pressure on him. Still, she felt deep within her soul that the reason for this *was* that there was something worth hiding rather than fear.

Don't ask about Dukhovia.

The innate response that had been burned in her since she was a child. So much that only Dukhovia could explain. So close to answers and yet so far away. Finally, she had been given a pass to ask everything she ever needed to know—but did that fear hold her back? Did she not ask enough? Is that now what her dream meant? That she was the monster and she limited herself with Nicholas?

Ugh.

Okay.

Born in Dukhovia.

Plays the Lyra.

CHAPTER FORTY-THREE

Parents murdered in front of him, he had to watch—by who? Who was he with now? The same people who hurt him?

Answered—somewhat. The leader of the military. But who was the leader of the military? And how was Nicholas able to get away now? Was he really able and seeking this out on his own? Perhaps not his first choice, but new it would bring him promise? Or was it force after all? If so, what were the stakes? And how safe was she really?

Safe. Nicholas had told her, had been adamant. Why would he be so adamant if it were not true?

Abused—some marks recent. Not all from dad.

Another piece of evidence that it was force that brought him here.

Vegetarian.

Sent to end the war—why him? Why does he seem so much like he doesn't want to? He likes the war? He supports the other side?

Huh. She supposed she never asked if he was a traditionalist or not, but she seemed she could make a fair enough guess. Sent. Sent. He had used the word sent. He was told to come here. He was told to find out if the banished families were traditional or not. Unless he was not told that at all and part was his choice— or his cover.

Why him? His family. He had to earn back respect for their name. Plus solidify his birth reading.

She thought over everything he told her again and again. She had been so certain that he was the heir—everything pointed right to it. But then the more he spoke, the more…loose his words became, she questioned it. The way he seemed so certain and yet so fearful told her otherwise. Then he mentioned that it was a female and that totally threw her—which could be exactly what he wanted. But then he said it could be a man too. UGH.

Ask. You're allowed to ask.

Or so she had been told. She was given full access and then he shut her down. But she supposed he was right. She was swaying. She was asking questions about him and why he was really here, she was feeling out if he was trustworthy of answering her questions rather than simply asking.

And so, she began to run down the pros and cons of asking—which were safe and which might pose a risk to her family. The fact was, she did not know enough about Dukhovia to determine it. What if something she thought nothing of was actually a secret spirit mission that he deemed worthy of whisking her away into the night to slaughter in a field?

He did not seem slaughter-in-the-field material.

But he was.

Murdered Santifini's family.

But Tom had murdered too. And Nicholas was only a child. What could that mean?

Ask.

She probably should. But asking why he murdered people seemed to be where the line should be.

Ending the war because his family was shamed—potentially banished. Needs to be the one to do it for them?

That was reasonable enough.

There was no family back home waiting for him. No one to care for him.

She leaned back in her chair, dropping her pen. Dazing off into the rising sun, she sat in that thought. No one to care for him. She thought of her family. Her uncle, running over to meet the new terror at school, albeit, because it also fell in his job description, but not really. Cops did not typically make house calls because a fight happened at school. Not unless charges were pressed.

Were charges pressed? She had not talked with Ellen and Kenny on it, but Rachael's grace came from somewhere.

She shook the thought from her head.

Even the idea that she could talk to Ellen and Kenny, to her uncle, to her other aunts and uncles and grandparents, to the parent of her friends, to all of her friends and cousins…. Nicholas had none of that. Not even a best friend. Not even a mom. In fact, in place of those things he had to endure the repeated thoughts of watching his parents burned alive.

And then she realized what she had done. She realized that she had spent so much time pressing him, so much time being adamant to let him know that she did not see past his story, that she forgot he was human too. Whatever this was, whatever he was telling the truth on and what he withheld—it was out of force and fear, something they discussed being oh so powerful.

Her heart sank; tears flooded her eyes and disgust with herself took over. She needed to talk to him, needed to make amends. She needed to focus less on what he was today and more on the path that got him there. After all, her family was the picture-perfect vision of that. *Not who I am, but why I am. Who I was.*

She needed a moment to not be his ally or the one who would crack his code, but his friend. Because at the end of the day whether his purpose here was good or evil, he would need one of those.

The sun had risen. People were beginning to clunk around downstairs and Stacy's lids were getting heavier and heavier. Thank God it was the weekend. But that meant no Nicholas. Nicholas…

The leaves on the trees waved over the dirt floor, thick and lush. Their coverage provided shelter from the sweltering sun, though the opaque surroundings of the forest seemed to deem them unnecessary enough.

Stacy's eyes drifted, granting her the pleasure of viewing a streaming waterfall—beautiful, gentle, cascading waves. She felt the water—it was the warmest, most comfortable water she had ever felt. It was soft, more like silk than any liquid she had ever felt.

A rustling behind her caught her attention. Again, her sight moved to the dry, moss-covered thicket. Nothing but silence. Silence and peace. Peace and purity.

Then another rustling overhead and vibrant, colorful wings flew overhead as bird after bird flew carelessly....no...were they fleeing? Her head spun wearily around. Another rustling, another spotting of something out of the corner of her eye. Something moving, something moving fast.

"They're coming, Stacy Grace."

"Who is?" She spoke boldly. She could not remember ever speaking in the dream before. "Tell me." So much more she wanted to say, but she felt limited, as if the oxygen was being stripped from around her and at any moment gravity would give out and she and this beautiful place would be turned into oblivion.

"Protect them. Protect the heir."

"Who?"

She seemed barely able to make out the words that came out, but she felt her legs pulling her closer, positive the word 'see' was coming out of this person's mouth.

"Who?" She repeated.

Then she froze, eyes wide with fear, paralyzed in her spot. The face looking back at her was dark, nearly threatening, certainly not there to help and support.

The face was her own.

She shot up in a pool of sweat, gasping and panicking. Pens flew off her table as frantic hands moved in every wrong direction to catch them. She gripped the pulsating veins of her forehead.

Her eyes flashed and the last thing she saw before waking flashed back in her mind. Then the dream began to fade…

No…no…no…She was frantic again, reaching for her fallen pen as she tried to retort every disappearing detail…

Herself. What did that mean? Was she the reason for the destruction? The banished families? Nicholas had come here asking about her, about her family… Was she a bigger piece of the puzzle than she thought? This role that she had to protect the heir was clear, but why was nothing else?

Tears flooded her eyes. She fought them away with a rage that expanded inside her.

Heir is the ruler. Closest to Spirits. Those closest to Spirits have special abilities.

Can be multiple heirs.

She froze. Multiple heirs. They are close to their spirit, just like her and Nicholas…

But he had also said that her other family members had Spirit Gifts, that they were connected...

But that Spirit didn't prevent them from getting sick...

Maybe because Dukhovia was The Water Spirit's land and the other lands had faded, resulting in her being stronger, more protected...

The heir will be the ruler of our people... and so they would need protection, they would need to be traditional, and they would be the savior of all of Dukhovia...

CHAPTER 44

THE LOST DUKHOVIAN

Cody had eventually joined Stacy in her room. They killed some time before class, exchanging stories and jokes about their situations. The two laid back in her bed, considering their choices, their circumstances. Soon, Cody had to leave for football, but Stacy stayed back rather than attending her own volleyball practice. Her lids were too heavy and her thoughts too foggy.

She closed her eyes and reopened them frequently, trying to fight sleep as best she could. She knew it was not practical and knew there was no solution even if she did manage to for the moment. What was she going to do, never sleep for the rest of her life or figure this stupid dream out?

The day went on in a daze. Stacy went back and forth between fighting sleep and returning to her desk. Finally, she lost the fight and found herself slipping into a four-hour nap, only to be awoken hours later by a quiet rapping at the front door.

She stretched, waiting for either whoever wanted to sell her whatever to leave, or someone else to have to deal with it. But the tapping persisted.

With a roll of her eyes, she rolled herself out of bed and dragged herself down the steps, grumbling with each step, ruffling already messy hair beyond saving.

She tore the door open with a harsh pull—and slammed it immediately in return. Frantically, she looked to the mirror and began flattening her hair, checking for drool stains on her shirt.

What was Nicholas doing here *now?*

Taking a deep breath, she opened the door and met him with a brilliant smile that she was not all that confident did not contain at least some remains of the chocolate bar she choked down for her 1pm breakfast.

"Hey…what are you doing here?" She asked, leaning against the door in a poised position, certain she looked laid back and sophisticated.

She took him in as she tried to look decently normal. He stood, dressed nicer than anything she had ever seen someone wear on a casual Saturday morning walk, holding several brown paper bags as if they were as delicate as a newborn child. The black and white stripes of his button-up top clung to his chest in distracting ways. His face was flecked with surprise and genuine curiosity.

"I thought you might be at the school this morning, but you were not. Rachael said you were not feeling well. I feared that perhaps there was something I said yesterday that frightened you or confused you…" He went on when Stacy said nothing, but looked shocked. "So, I brought you medicine and nourishing foods. Then I recalled you do not get ill in that manner and so Rachael recommended some of your favorite foods. I thought we might go to my apartment and I could cook them for you. If you would be willing?"

Stacy tried to push down the scream in her throat as her mind ran a million miles a minute, fighting with her heart for speed. She peaked into the bags as he lifted them towards her, revealing flowers, chocolates, medication, and fresh fruits and vegetables. Ha.

Unsure how to respond and certain the heaving in her chest made her look like a potential heart attack victim, she slowly nodded her head.

"Is it okay if I make myself look decent?" She asked, gesturing to her appearance.

Nicholas smiled a small smile and walked through the door after she held it for him. "You always look ravishing, but whatever would make you feel most comfortable."

Okay, Stacy thought as she heaved herself up the stairs. *So this is what Rachael means about all this gushy stuff.* She had to admit, it did send butterflies to her stomach—or whatever Rachael would say—when she heard Nicholas compliment her.

But who needed butterflies. Who had the time.

Deciding against calling Rachael for her advice, Stacy decided on a purple sweater dress with black leggings and boots. After running a comb through her hair a few times, she deemed herself presentable and flew herself down the staircase.

"Ready." She presented herself, meeting him in the sitting room with a grin.

Nicholas turned to meet her gaze, his eyes seemed brighter than normal, his tension well—less intense. He was almost relaxed, almost not so...alert. He walked toward her slowly, bowing his top half down until he was bent at an angle. Then, he slowly brought the back of her hand to his lips. "As I said, always ravishing, but extraordinarily beautiful."

Stacy imagined these butterflies in her stomach as a person and decided to throat punch that person from existence. Focus. Focus. *You're going to his place.* She had not thought of it exactly the moment he asked her, but now that her brain had slowed down and continued to as they began their walk, the idea crept closer and closer to the forefront of her mind.

She was not sure what to expect or what she was walking into—but she was positive that if she told anyone they would have already sent her parents in after her. Which was exactly why she left a note saying she was going ice skating. That was typically a good couple of hours for her—they had time.

Nicholas's place. What type of place would or *could* a fifteen-year-old have on their own? Stacy did not even really have any chores. Nicholas had to cook, clean, shop, go to school, do homework, and he was making *her* dinner? She felt the knots in her stomach surface.

Be a friend, she reminded herself. *He needs a friend.*

Alright, she supposed her parents grew up raising themselves. They had their own place at a young age and it was hardly a cardboard box, the way the story was told. Also, she doubted Nicholas would invite her for dinner if he did not have a means to cook. Unless they were eating fireside.

Yikes.

Still, she worried about what she would see and what she would do if she did in fact see that he was—in need. Would it be absolutely ludicrous of her to invite him to stay with them? Especially with Cody also staying with them? Would Kenny and Ellen take him in? Probably, but Cody would sooner burn the house down. He did not really interact with Jade and Miranda much. Cara and Dylan seemed to hit it off with him but yikes. She would just be sending him from one hell to another.

Okay, so she was not at all sure what to expect from a fifteen-year-old who lived alone. But she was also not sure what to expect from a Dukhovian soldier's home. Would he have weapons lying around? Would that make it all the more dangerous for her to watch what she said? Maybe she should have told someone, after all.

No. *We're figuring him out. We're figuring ourselves out and we're just being his* friend.

"So, you are not ill, you do not wish to avoid me, what had you missing practice today?"

Stacy felt her body tense. "It was more so the wanting to avoid everything else. And I didn't sleep well."

"The nightmares again?" He asked gently.

She nodded fervently. "The nightmare."

"And this nightmare, it deals with your worries of Dukhovia, yes?"

She considered the words. She was not quite ready to divulge the details of the dream, but she could entertain baby steps. She nodded slowly. "That's correct."

"Anything I can do to help?" He asked.

The change in direction took her by surprise, but she was also struck with the question. Realistically—was there anything he could do? She raised her eyebrows curiously. "Not unless you can promise me our people will all live to see happy and fulfilling lives."

Nicholas looked at the ground, a small, forced smile on his lips. "You care an awful lot about a people whom have left you out to rot."

Stacy shrugged her shoulders. "I'm used to our family getting hate. I'm also used to it usually stemming from a place of not understanding—for whatever the reason may be. It doesn't make anyone any less valuable."

She felt his eyes watch her for a while. Her feet felt light as the snow crunched beneath her, hollowing around her ears. The air was just as light, filled with scents of smoke and wafting smells of freshly cooked foods.

"That is a perspective that Dukhovia could benefit from—not condemning people for a mistake or even a misunderstanding."

She considered his words. "Which was it for your family?"

"My family," he breathed in deep. "I…I have never really spoken about it with anyone."

Stacy shrugged. She hopped from the curb down to his side. "You don't have to," she promised. "I was just curious."

He hesitated for a moment, silence and unknowing thoughts trapped in an icy whirlwind. "It happened back in WWI," he began, his voice uneven, but confident all the same. "My grandfather, Nicholas the First, was one of the first members of the Dukhovian army. He was a traditionalist who wanted to protect Dukhovia from modernizing after we were unintentionally pulled into the war. Part of his mission was to infiltrate the non-traditionalists, find out their plan. He was excellent at his job, having stopped multiple village raids and saving countless lives, all while remaining secret."

Stacy shook her head. "Why would they want to end lives either way?" Her stomach was in knots, hoping he would answer honestly for more than one reason.

"It is as we said—fear. And lack of critical thinking. If they suspected that eliminating a certain people would help their side—for example, sacrifice the teacher of martial arts and end one life in order to have gun makers be the only ones left and save thousands…"

Stacy was disgusted, but could see how the line of thinking could lead to justification in the mind of a maniac. So, what was Nicholas's justification?

"Those of us traditionalists believe all life to be sacred. We hope to inspire and change minds, not destroy everyone until all we have left are traditional thinkers."

"So, it sounds like your grandfather should be hailed as a hero. What happened?"

He nodded, his lips drew together and his fists clenched. They were beginning to enter a darker side of town now, with less lighting, less people. "Nicholas was informed by the non-traditionalists of a plan to overthrow Czar Mikhailov, the current Dukhovian ruler." Nicholas paused. "He was disgusted. If the Spirits had chosen Czar Mikhailov—then he was the right choice and we are all called to defend heir's and rulers with our lives."

Stacy's eyes widened. "We are?"

Nicholas was silent for a moment, but seemed grateful for her question. He seemed to freeze after his last words ended, not that he did not want to go on, but as if he could not. "Yes," he choked on the word. "We are called to honor and defend the Spirits and that means honoring and defending their choices as well. Otherwise, our world would become chaos rather than peaceful by thinking we know better than the Spirits…" His voice drifted again and he was white as a ghost.

"Which is what is happening now," she finished.

He nodded.

Stacy could see difficulty in him going on, the strain in his eyes could not be hidden beneath the glowing moonlight despite the shadow of the clouds above. So, she continued to move away from the subject of his family.

"What is happening in the war right now? I mean…" she rubbed her neck, embarrassed at not knowing the right way to ask her question. "What are we trying to do to stop the non-traditionalists?"

Nicholas drew in a deep breath, but, as he promised—dispelled everything. "The goal is to find out their plans and prevent them from happening. Prevention rather than attack and then reason." He spat. "It has failed for the last 80 years. I am not certain when they think a miracle will pull through."

Stacy's heart leapt in her chest. "You think they should do something different?" She held her breath in response for his answer.

Yes, they should slaughter the banished families one by one.

No, he had plenty of chances if that was his angle.

"Weaken them from the inside out. It is a classic technique but also an outdated one due to its difficulty."

"Infiltrate them like your great grandfather did?" Stacy asked.

He nodded. "Everything falls down when the inside is broken."

Stacy looked around as they moved closer in to that rough part of town. She was not certain what to say to answer her leery questions, but for some reason, despite everything, even though she could possibly be the victim of a stabbing in the next second, she felt safe with Nicholas.

She just felt safe.

And she did not know if he did and she was supposed to be a friend first and see where that led them.

"Are you scared?" She asked him, not even sure why she did.

He cocked his head towards her. "Of what?"

"Being here," she reasoned. "Or returning home. Whichever."

He considered it. "I am not permitted to have an opinion on anything I do. I simply must do it."

She paused, putting her arm on his. She did not care about the feeling; she cared about his words. "No. Everyone deserves a chance to be themselves, no matter their circumstances."

He looked away. "Even if that person has committed crimes you could never envision? Even if that person put their own selfish needs before the needs of others?"

Stacy gulped. Fear was certainly on her face. But she nodded. "Even then."

He nodded slightly; his eyes locked onto hers. The brilliance of them was blinding and dazzling all the same. She felt as though she would pass out.

"I do not think fear is the word for what I feel."

CHAPTER FORTY-FOUR

"What is?" She pressed.

He breathed in. "Trapped. Suffocated."

She reached up again, putting her arm on his and gently rubbing it. "Then let's figure out how to breathe."

The way his eyes penetrated her soul felt like something she had never experienced. She was on fire, ignited, feeling...fulfilled. But if what Nicholas had said was the truth, if she was meant to protect the heir and that was not him—what was she supposed to do?

The remainder of the walk to his place was nice. They spoke more of their families, of school, of...each other. Befriending Nicholas seemed not only like a good idea, but easier than she imagined. He became lighter as they moved away from the subject of Dukhovia. He was open, easy going, *funny*. Her only complaint was that each moment Stacy felt closer to him, was a moment she felt the butterflies that she tried with much difficulty to ignore, resurface.

"We are nearly there," Nicholas told her after recovering from laughter.

Stacy looked around at the tall, should-be-abandoned buildings. She thought they looked more like the backdrop for a haunted house than a place someone should consider their home—even temporarily. But she had anticipated...okay, she did not know what she anticipated, but her expectations started to drift off the more she saw. Soon they were surrounded by homes without roofs, broken windows, and loud sounds. A chill went up Stacy's spine as she took in the decaying fences and what would be over-grown earth and tree beneath the safe-haven of the snow.

Nicholas stopped when there were a few scattered houses to their left and run-down, buildings with piles of glass to their right. Her stomach was in knots. She kept her thoughts to herself, but it looked like the perfect place to hide a body. What was she doing?

"If I were in Dukhovia," Nicholas began slowly, "I would never dream of taking you here. I would like to take you somewhere—inspiring. Somewhere comfortable and worthy."

Stacy smiled softly, leaning her head towards the buildings. "You don't need to impress me. And I'm hardly impressed or unimpressed by your living quarters. You could take me to a tent." It was true.

Nicholas grinned only slightly back and she questioned whether or not he likely knew what a tent was. Did he? Should he? Oh well. She took in his words and compared the area they were now in to Dukhovia—she would likely be on edge too. Dukhovia was a land of vision and pure beauty. It was awe-inspiring and encapsulated every heart, every eye. This was...well...none of those things.

"What was your home like?" She asked, unable to shut up her stupid mouth, really trying to sell the whole dead body thing. "Back in Dukhovia?"

Nicholas scoffed at the term as they began walking again. "Dukhovia is definitely my home. It is where I belong, but it has not felt like that in a long time."

He stopped at probably the most secure-looking building on the block—thank God. The faded yellow brick and dark, small windows were not all too alarming and she felt better once he opened the door to the stairwell and it just looked like a normal—albeit, in desperately outdated—building.

Nicholas held the door open for her and waited for her to walk through, then he continued to lead them up the stairs as he started talking again. "I grew up on my family's farm. The home was in my family for generations—until..." He drifted off.

"So, what about after that?" Stacy prompted, climbing the stairs with caution as she was confident that she just stepped on either a broken pen or needle and she did not want to weigh the odds. "Where did you go?"

Nicholas shifted casually as he came to a stop at an apartment door deemed "3B". "I grew up in the palace."

Stacy halted in her spot. Stuck like a wave that crashed down around her and glued her to her spot, yet told her to flee all the same. Her heart pounded in her chest so loud she was certain he could hear it or at least sense the sweat that drenched her hands.

The palace? The palace?! It was just as Santifini had said. Nicholas was raised by the rulers of Dukhovia—the traditional non-traditionalists? If that were true, and based on what she knew about Nicholas, what he said about himself, did that make the other parts of his story true? That Nicholas truly was a murderer?

It did not matter. She already decided. Life was not black and white. But it certainly...solidified how real things were.

Raised by the leader of the military. Was there a reason before he failed to mention that the leader of the military was also The Czar? Perhaps he was not. Perhaps Santifini was wrong. He was raised in the palace by a kind, military leader who had an inside job to train Nicholas and overthrow The Czar.

Oh, except he tortured a child for his entire life and murdered his family.

Nicholas continued walking casually in the apartment and over to the kitchen. He paused and looked back at her.

Unsure whether her next move was prompted by sheer stupidity or empowerment, Stacy stepped forward. Her feet slowly guided her in the home as her brain was plummeted with a million new thoughts, drawing conclusions to unanswered questions, creating more, uncrossing problems she thought she had solved.

Stacy was frozen by the new information and while she knew her reaction was not subtle, Nicholas offered no further explanation without prompting.

"You grew up in the palace? Like royalty, like the rulers of Dukhovia?" He did go by Sir Nicholas.

Nicholas's mouth turned into a slight smile but it vanished almost as quickly as it formed, turning into a thin line on a face of stone. "I would not consider myself royalty, however, I was to be treated with respect due to my close status in the castle."

"But—you're banished too?" Respect for a murderer, at that. *What the...?*

Nicholas shrugged, seeming to not know how to explain himself. He shifted about the kitchen, grabbing different things from the fridge and the cupboards as he worked to begin cutting vegetables. Stacy decided to try to be of use, even though she knew she would fail at helping even if she asked for guidance. She needed to act natural. She was in the midst of a skilled, observant, mass murderer—it was no time for obvious curiosities. Though hiding her intentions was also never her strong suite.

"The Czar needed a job done and I volunteered. It was a chance to redeem my family's name; the choice was hardly a difficult one to make."

Stacy considered his words. He *volunteered,* yet his family was also murdered because he had to do this job, the job he was sent to do. *Choice.*

Sent by who? Answered. *The Czar.*

Reason why? Still ambiguous.

"So, sort of like a plea deal?" Stacy asked. "You find out some way to end the war and your family name is cleared?"

Nicholas was quiet for a long time as he either considered his answer or focused on cutting—noodles? Rice? Beans, maybe?

He finally decided "yes" was enough of an answer.

Stacy allowed the conversation to drift for a moment, taking in the surroundings of the apartment. Again, it was not nearly as awful as she had expected, but she also did not anticipate the number of holes in the wall either and that sent a good number of nerves throughout her, although she was pretty confident she could either scale out his window or knock him out with a little karate. Either one.

"I thought you said it was the leader of the military who took you in?" She tried to sound casual and not forceful. When did she get so bad at friendship?

"They are one in the same, unfortunately."

"Hm."

Nicholas looked up at her from his fervent chopping of vegetables. What happened to making a favorite food?

"What?" He asked with a slight grin.

Stacy shrugged. "I just don't know that being both the leader of the country and the military is a good idea. It seems there might be some...favoritism."

"Favoritism?" He both recoiled and laughed. "For one's own nation?"

Another shrug. She walked up and bit the edge of a thinly sliced cucumber. Gross. "Well, if your role is to protect your country and the people expect you to do that, I can see it causing stress and wrong decisions. It seems it should fall to someone who can be more neutral to make clearer decisions for the wellbeing of the country."

Nicholas eyed her for a time before speaking. "You do know that the president of the United States is also the leader of your military, correct?"

Stacy felt the room turn to silence. "That I did not. I know very little of anything."

He shook his head, slight annoyance and slight humor battling for victory. "What would you do then? To end the war in Dukhovia?"

And then it seemed he was at full attention, waiting and anticipating her answer, even as his eyes looked at his work, his mind was fully on her.

She thought about it for a long time, considering the right words to say when she struggled with any type of political or economic knowledge. "The path of least resistance," she finally said. "Whatever cost the least amount of lives for the most amount of change. I'd compromise lightly."

"Even if they wanted to update?" He pressed.

She considered that, how far would she be willing to go? What Americanized answer would he expect of her? "Rachael despised our visit to Dukhovia. Well, I shouldn't say that. She was able to appreciate the aspects of beauty and culture. However, she knew she could never adapt to such a life—spas and make-up or go. I appreciate that. I appreciate that that is her normal and her culture, something she finds appreciation in. So, I would listen. I would listen to what aspects they think are important and why. We have updated some things within reason and I assume we did that by weighing the pros and cons, maybe holding a vote, anything but force and ending lives.

"I wouldn't do anything that would jeopardize Dukhovian culture, that would silence a Spirit. In fact, I think I'd make sure whatever change honored a Spirit in some way, sort of a way to 'check' ourselves, you know?"

Nicholas started to agree, but suddenly, he let out a powerful "AH!" and blood splattered the walls.

Stacy jumped as Nicholas swore loudly and the sound of his knife came clattering to the ground. Shock overtook her. She looked over to see the sharp part had detached from the handle and blood was spurting everywhere.

Immediately she rushed to his side.

"No." His voice was a direct, hostile order.

"Nicholas, please…" She said the words without much plea to them as she took off towards his bathroom. She found it to be completely empty save for the roll of toilet paper, a tooth brush, and a single, clear glass tube she assumed was tooth paste. Frustrated, she ran down the hall and tore open his closet door.

"Seriously?" There was nothing but a single bath towel. Ignoring his calls after her, she tore back into the bathroom and threw open the shower curtain. She was met with a wall stained with yellow-reddish coloring that deterred her only for a moment before she grabbed the single, black wash cloth and ran back out to the kitchen.

"Stay away," Nicholas ordered. He stood backed up against the kitchen sink, holding his wound. "Please," he got out through grunts. "It will heal soon."

Choosing any decision but to listen to his words, Stacy approached slowly. Thinking through what to do, she concentrated on her thoughts, on her feelings, and taking her hands gently, she moved closer to Nicholas.

As she approached, he backed away, but the moment her hands gently cupped his, he seemed to succumb to her. No, not only did he succumb, he looked surprisingly up at her...relaxed.

Stacy did not know if what she intended had actually worked. She considered the times that their hands had touched. Each time it was like a manifestation of what she was already feeling. It turned her hope to joy, her ease to comfort. She had hoped she was able to convey something to Nicholas now—trust.

"I'll help you," she whispered while she worked. "You're safe." She switched on and off between different phrases: *I'm here for you. You didn't deserve this.* He said nothing, but the emotion in his face conveyed everything.

She worked quickly, just as she had when he was injured by the car. But this time, she took extra care to stroke his hands, his arms—anywhere but his back. And Nicholas seemed acutely aware of this.

"Just rest for a moment," she ordered, leading him over to sit him down on the couch. She pushed the hair out of his eyes and wiped sweat from his brow. She briefly went to the kitchen to rifle through his cupboards of nothingness in search of a cup, a bowl, a literal *anything*. Finding an empty mason jar, she filled it halfway with water and returned to his side.

His eyes never left Stacy's face for a moment. The moment she returned to the couch, he reached his free hand up and cupped her face. Stacy's eyes met his.

"Thank you." His voice was calm now, gentle. He continued to cup her face and explore her from her cheeks to her hair, down to her neck. His fingers lightly danced across her collar bone, sending a chill throughout her. He dropped his hand.

Stacy's lips turned into a smile. "You messed up. You save me, I save you has been our routine. I need another near-death experience."

Nicholas released a sound that sounded like a mixture of a disgusted laugh and choking. Unsure how to respond to the noise, or even what to make of it, she chose to avoid, hopping up to walk back over to the kitchen where something was burning.

"I'm no cook so I'm hardly one to judge," she began, turning off a burner and walking the smoking pot to the trash can. "But I thought we were supposed to be making my favorite foods? What the heck is this?"

Nicholas leaned his head back against the couch in disappointment. "Pasta Skadash," he groaned.

Stacy raised an eyebrow.

Nicholas stood to his feet, coming towards her and the remaining food. "Rachael said that you enjoy pasta and fried foods. Dukhovia does not fry any foods, however, we do make a pasta dish with crisped meat. I was attempting to incorporate Dukhovian food into your favorite American meals—to give you both your worlds."

Stacy's heart stopped in her chest, her breath immediately becoming uneven. *Cunning murderer or great guy? Cunning murderer or great guy? Black and white...gray.*

Friendship. Just go with your gut.

And so she did. She reacted as she would any other friend and flung her arms around his neck, squeezing him close, closer to herself than most anyone had ever been. Feeling the exposure of his tight muscles rippling across her in a startled response, she felt tears well in her eyes.

His strong arms tightened around her waist and back, drawing her nearer. Her face had been buried in his neck, but he drew back just far enough to feel the softness of her hair tickling his nose.

Finally, she pulled back, her eyes meeting his with longing. "Thank you, Nicholas."

His eyes met hers, slowly reaching up a hand, he stroked her cheek gently, the electricity igniting her like never before. "Anything for you, Stacy Grace," he said through a raspy voice. Then, his eyes seemed to get distracted and wander to his injured hand.

"How did you know what to do for me?" He asked, mirroring the same desperately grateful tone she had.

"They hurt you," Stacy reasoned in a slow, steady voice. She felt like a child whispering as they admitted wrongdoing. But she knew she was right, the more she learned, the more she saw his actions and reactions, she knew he was the victim in his story. She went on when his face seemed cross, but not objecting. "Your scars on your back. They weren't all old. Some of your wounds are fresh. That tells me force had to be used to get you here—where you don't want to be. And it tells me you don't have a safe home to go back to."

His eyes searched her face for a long time, glances continuing between his hand and her face. "You are partially correct."

Stacy waited, expectantly. "This is exactly where I want to be."

CHAPTER 45

A PLAN WORTHY OF DEATH

Nicholas was flabbergasted by the keen observation of the American heir. Stacy. Stacy Grace Matthews. The most brilliant and fiercely loyal of perhaps those even in Dukhovia. And caring, so very caring. And here he sat, stumbling over the fulfillment of a doomed mission for a doomed country. Their country. A country he knew he did not stand a chance saving alone or by fulfilling this mission. A country he could perhaps only save with her.

He looked at her as she spoke the words of his scars. Of course, she was right and of course she would notice. The last of his lashes were so new they still stung in the shower. They still bled if he scrubbed too quickly. He had taken to utilizing the blood as paint, tallying up his days here, his accomplishments and failures. He hoped she had not taken notice. She had to have had bad enough thoughts as it was. Yet here she was.

Why? Why on Earth was she near him? Was he truly as cunning as he tried to be? The thought repulsed him. Certainly, he wanted to be as great as he could be in his purpose—were this his purpose. And the longer he stayed in America, the more certain he was it was the last thing he wanted. Still, even if he was forced to wear the skin of a monster, he never wanted it to truly reflect the inside.

Stacy. Stacy Grace. The American heir he sought to destroy before she destroyed the country first, yet everything that he learned of her so far revealed a strong, confident heir. It revealed someone whom he might team up with in the war. It revealed someone whose right to rule he might defend—so, then where did that leave his mission?

More than a wonderful heir, he began to see her as something else too. Something he could not quite put his finger on, but his heart did not need him to.

He watched her moving about the kitchen. Now that she was comfortable, she moved with persistence, intentional in all her decisions, even if they were strange or out of order to the norm. Such as when she began to spoon things out of one pan before prepping another.

She had returned to their meal preparation. He pulled out the card where he had written down all he could recall and gave it to her.

"I'll do the meat part so you're not committing a crime against vegetarianism." She made the joke lightly, but immediately looked for direction on what to do next—clueless as she appeared. She was selfless. Humble.

Nicholas wondered if she saw him—how she saw him. Did she see beneath his facade? The shameless flirt as he tried to play the role and win her over with

~ 350 ~

his poisonous looks… Did she buy into it all? Or did she see him for the miserable, lost human being he truly was.

He was not sure whom he wanted her to see.

But Stacy was clear to see. Beneath her wildly unique nature, she was pure, she was kind, she was genuine. What would she think of him if she knew the truth? What would she do? She turned her back the second she thought he intentionally harmed Rachael. If she knew the worst of him—the pieces she had been trying to figure out—she would be done altogether.

Maybe that was in her best interest.

And maybe that was something he cared about.

He held onto that piece. Perhaps he was wrong, perhaps he had leverage there. She had no reason now to trust him and be around him—yet she was. Because she needed answers and he had them—he had all of them.

Always cunning. Always, always.

He closed his eyes, breathing in deeply as he tried to gather his thoughts, to keep himself calm for the duration of their day together.

Dukhovia

America

Stacy

His mother.

He threw back his shoulders, breathing out frustration. No thoughts, no thoughts were better than any thought.

"Who taught you to be such an expert chef, was it your mother?" Stacy's nonchalant question broke his thinking patterns, snapping him back to the reality that she was here—she was the now. She was most important.

He walked back over to join her and began cutting the dough he formed earlier to make noodles. "No. Mother was as wonderful a cook as she could be, she learned from my grandmother. However, we were always poor and seasonings are a luxury for most of Dukhovia." He lifted up the canisters he had purchased for hardly anything at the supermarket in town. "Yet these were a breeze to come by here." His tone was soft and muffled.

He felt Stacy's reluctant gaze over her shoulder for only a moment before she returned to breading the chicken. Trying to improve the tone of his voice, he added, "I learned from a friend."

He felt the excitement as she turned to him, smiling fully. "Really?"

He nodded, meeting her eyes for only a moment before returning to his cutting. "Is it so hard to believe I have friendships?"

"Sort of," Stacy laughed. "No. I've just never heard you mention them before is all and you seem very—suspicious of others. Which I'll permit, given your circumstances."

If only you knew half those circumstances. "Knowing how to act around people has been a challenge for me. Act one way and I am harmed, act another way and I am the one doing the harming. I only want to be myself and have my world align from there."

"And were you yourself?" Stacy asked. "With this friend?"

Nicholas nodded. "Vuel was the only person I have been myself with since moving to the palace. On nights we went without dinner, we would sneak into the kitchen and he would cook us meals."

The scent of boiled carrots and potatoes still hung in the air even though the freshly baked blueberry and huckleberry pies were wafting over them, fighting for rights. The lanterns flames were dim and nearly extinguished, but for the moment, everything was illuminated just enough.

"Okay, let's see what we have here..." Vuel had shuffled over to the cooling box and began rifling through—tossing aside vegetables, fruits, and juices.

"Vuel!" Nicholas whispered, whipping his head around. "We'll be caught."

"Live a little, your highness. We need to eat and we sealed the treaties that brought in half this stuff, we're entitled."

Nicholas agreed, but kept his senses alert. "Just be quick."

"Quality food is never quick, Aloy, remember that. Grab the zucchini, eggplant, and chatar. We're making a casserole."

Nicholas and Vuel worked steadfast for hours. Keen listening turned into laughter and joking around. Finally, Vuel removed the casserole from baking, listening to the clang of the pan hitting the countertop the same time the sound of thick, steel-toe boots sounded from the corridor.

"Someone is coming!" Nicholas howled, eyes lit with panic.

"Come on!" Vuel grabbed the casserole and two plates and headed for the door, but paused, grabbing a pie.

"What are you doing?" Nicholas asked shocked. "A pie? We will be massacred."

Vuel shrugged. "No, we won't, he needs us. But we will get beaten so we might as well make it worthwhile."

"Is he still in Dukhovia?" Stacy asked. "At the palace?"

Nicholas set his knife down, his mind drifting away. "No," he answered slowly. "He was smart, he left."

Stacy had finished her chicken and started a pan to boil for the pasta. "So, why didn't you leave with him?"

"We both had the same mission, but only I was doing it for my family," the words flowed from him as natural as the thousand times he recited them to himself, confirming their truth. "It seemed to be abandoning them if I did not comply."

"And would your family want you to complete this mission?"

Nicholas was silent for a long time. "I do not know. But I know there is not a single part of me that wants to unless I force it and that tells me they would agree."

As soon as he said the words he realized he did not fully think them through. But he was doing something he never did before, something he felt comfortable doing—living in the moment.

Stacy shot her head up at him. "You don't want to end the war?"

He realized the gravity of his error and paused, mulling his words. He bought himself time by walking her through the making of the sauce and then plating their meals.

"Of course I want to end the war," he continued on as he pulled her chair out at his make-shift dining room table. It was complete with more Ice Thistles and candles. The candlelight illuminated the crystallization of the flowers, creating a dancing light show across the darkening room. "But this is hardly the way to do it. If you ask me, it is a waste of time and innocent lives are lost day after day as I sit here doing nothing."

Stacy's hands were secured on her knife and fork, but she dropped them and met his gaze. "I feel the same way," she finally confessed. "All my life I've felt like I'm supposed to be in Dukhovia or that there was something about Dukhovia that called me in. The more I hear about the war, the more convinced I am..." Her words drifted away. "On our one trip there, I could hardly bear to leave." Her words were becoming harder to form, her voice cracking, shaking. "I couldn't stand it. I was leaving because it was 'too unsafe' yet to leave set my bones on fire and felt like I was walking to my death."

"It was unnatural for you," Nicholas finished, gulping. Her wide eyes met his, shocked but confirming. "You do not seem to be someone who holds the same ideals as the other Americans."

Stacy laughed without humor, stabbing a piece of chicken. "Hardly." Then she frowned, a look of disdain on her face that she recognized all too well. "It's so unsafe for me, yet it seems unsafe for everyone. Who gets to decide that? Who gets to say that I sit here safe and sound while others die? Screw banishment. There's a war to end." Her eyes seemed to soften when she finished her words, then she looked up at him again.

"But you don't think anything you find out about the banished families will help? I'll do anything, Nicholas."

"Anything to return to Dukhovia?" He asked, his soul on fire. So simple. So *stupidly, irritatingly* simple. The girl he needed to bring back to end was handing herself over. His mission could be over right now. He could pack her up, drop her on the steps of the castle, and begin rebuilding his family home as he awaited the announcement that his family would once again go down as loyal, honorable Dukhovians.

He had considered the moment a hundred times over. How he would walk out of the castle a free man. Free to explore, free to fight the way he wanted to fight.

Free to visit his mother's and father's graves and perform the ritual that should have been performed long ago to help them crossover. Free.

He would wear his great grandfather's formal military uniform. It was kept in the chest in the barn and so survived the destruction of their home. He loved the chest. It was the one reminder that they were an honorable family. He knew the truth about The Demitona's and as soon as the next few days, all of Dukhovia could too.

But what was he thinking? What was he doing? He undoes one curse only to hold a secret one over his next generation… He was able to envy his great grandfather, even if the rest of Dukhovia could not. His children and grandchildren would never be able to if they knew how he restored their honor.

Certainly, perhaps it would be honorable if he were truly protecting Dukhovia from the wrath of Stacy Grace Matthews. But Stacy loved Dukhovia with a stubbornly selfless heart. She was deserving and keeping her from Dukhovia would be just as treasonous as he was always told by the opposing parties.

But what was the alternative? What would happen if he never decided to bring Stacy back home? His insides twisted making him want nothing to do with the dinner they had stalled on eating. Were either of them even hungry anymore?

Arkady could hunt them both. He could and would find him and that would lead him to Stacy.

Run. The only thing you can do is run far away from her.

Perhaps Erlik was finally right.

"There are no secrets to being Dukhovian," Nicholas said after a while. "The banished families have no special traits, no evil to them. All Dukhovians are imperfect. They were all wrongly banished."

Stacy stood to her feet, motivation taking over. "Then we should be allowed to come back and have a fair trial! They can't just say whatever they want about any family. What made them a target anyway? My family would maintain traditions. I mean, sure we've adapted to America, but we still celebrate Dukhovian holidays. When I was a child, I would sit my family down every single night for three years and teach them about Dukhovia—things I don't even really know myself because I can't go!" She turned and kicked the couch.

Nicholas had not yet seen this frustrated part of Stacy. It was even more ruler like than he had thought.

"Let's just go!" She yelled. "Let's just go and tell them we're going to fight and we'll kill anyone who gets in our way!" She seemed to pause as soon as the words left her mouth. She stood before him, breathing in and out with each heavy puff of her chest.

Nicholas outstretched his hand and reached for her. She latched onto the tips of his fingers and together the two rose from the dining area and found a seat on the couch. She half-glanced at his hand as they did so.

"I didn't mean that," she said softly. She felt like that same school girl, peeking over her shoulder to him as she spoke, trying to gauge his reaction.

"You are frustrated, I understand. I have definitely stood in your shoes several times over the years." His voice was strong and honest, but the detached look on his face held a story his lips did not dare tell.

And Stacy knew it.

"And have you ever…" she stopped, stammering over what to say and whether or not to even say it. "…you know, hurt anyone?"

His face tried to find humor in her reaction, but it contorted, unable to complete the action before turning into an unappealing grimace. "Actions are not black and white in times of war. Sometimes you do to survive, sometimes you do because you have no time to think. Right and wrong no longer exist. Not on opposing sides, anyway.

"Still, my failure to navigate my own emotions and reality resulted in an unforgiveable burden I will carry for the rest of my life."

Stacy was quiet, he sensed her heart thudding full speed in her chest.

"My grandpa hurt a lot of people when he was…not himself. That's the thing, he wasn't himself and we all know it and him with all his extensive scientific brain should know it—but he still has a lot of guilt." Stacy shook her head. "My grandpa is the kindest and softest person I know. Sometimes we're not ourselves when something else takes over—fear or extreme chemicals."

The two laughed softly.

"Still…My mom always says that good people and bad people don't exist, only good and bad actions…because we have forgiveness."

Nicholas was silent, the thought filling his mind. Forgiveness. Forgiveness for slaughtering a town? Forgiveness for caving under pressure and watching a life end? Forgiveness for not knowing how to respond to a situation resulting in the death of a child?

As if reading his mind, Stacy reached out and squeezed his hand. The jolts of electricity brought him back to her. "Forgiveness for anything," she confirmed.

"Stacy Grace you are worthy of Dukhovia beyond words. And those are the people we need to keep safe. There is nothing that would benefit Dukhovia more than you marching to the castle and demanding every wrong be righted. But it is merely unpractical and those willing are the ones we need to keep safe."

"I don't want to be safe, I want to be useful," she spat at him through gritted teeth.

"Understood—but unless you learn the proper way to fight and all the history of this war, we will lose a strong, passionate warrior that we cannot afford to lose."

Stacy was quiet as she calmed herself back down slowly, her color returning to normal. "Then you'll teach me? As long as you're here, you'll teach me and if you feel I'm ready, you'll bring me with you?"

Nicholas's throat swelled and he found himself unable to think, unable to breathe. If he could return with Stacy not as his prisoner, but as his companion, would that help Dukhovia? Truly help Dukhovia?

Or even if it were with pure intentions, would he be confirming his destiny as a murderer? He could not do *nothing*, he knew he could not do nothing—but he could stall. "I will teach you anything I can on Dukhovia, but I will not bring you there."

She shot up, stubbornly. He did not know whether the vicious attitude was growing on him or if he was learning to handle annoyance better.

"You are more valuable alive, Stacy Grace," he added before she could say anything in her spit-fire mode. "We both need to do as the Spirits command us. If, after you have learned, the Spirits command you, we can talk about your proposition. Otherwise, you will remain our secret weapon in America."

Nicholas watched the light leave her eyes the more he spoke. The life had drained from her, flushing her face of color and poise. But, something in her peaked when he mentioned the Spirits. Normal, he supposed. She reacted positively towards anything even remotely close to Dukhovia. But her searching eyes seemed to hold more, except for this time, she kept her lips sealed. The realization that she still did not trust him fully ate at him more than it should have.

He rose to his feet, extending both his hands out to pull her from her forearms, to her feet. He folded her against his chest, feeling her warmth slowly spread through him, as if he could absorb her goodness, her bravery, anything but her Spirit.

"Please trust me, darling," he whispered and felt her body go weak. "I promise to not keep you safe only for my stubborn selfishness, but I will keep you safe long enough for you to fulfill your own purpose."

She was silent, but her arms fell like he pushed a simple button and they wrapped around his waist. "Thank you for everything," she whispered. "I'm sorry we wasted the popikosh."

Nicholas laughed at the ridiculous name. "It will make for a fine lunch tomorrow and you will need your energy, anyway."

Stacy lifted her head towards him, as if snapping back to reality. She was not in Dukhovia, she was not going out to war. She was in America and she was going to be playing in her band. Pitiful as that may have been to them both, that was how she was safest. That was what was best.

And he wanted to protect her.

"Tomorrow," her words fell unintelligibly out of her mouth, as if trying to piece together ramblings. "We have to practice for the recording then Rachael and Cody and I had plans to sled ride. I'm not sure when I'll be able to see you again."

Nicholas pulled her in closer and then apart, pulling the hair out from behind her ear—the way she liked it. "I would wait a lifetime if I needed to. I wish you the best of luck and I cannot wait to hear about it. And I cannot wait to begin teaching you more about our home."

Stacy stayed back for a moment, and he wondered if she was drawn not to the icy blue chill in his eye or the promises of her future he potentially held, but to something else. It was something both their minds started working in overdrive to figure out, only to be interrupted by a fierce pounding on the door.

The crease in Nicholas's eyebrow arch should have said enough, but Nicholas partially heard Stacy's voice asking if he was expecting anyone. She was more curious than she was cautious, which he could not pinpoint whether it was good or bad.

"Stay back," he warned and, to his surprise, she half complied and half looked like she would be ready to take whoever stood on the other side down herself.

He tried to see whom it was through the door peek, but to no avail. No one planning an ambush would make themselves known.

Nicholas took another moment, assessing his surroundings. His sword was in the back bedroom so as to not frighten Stacy. The best he could grab was a kitchen knife. Then stood the issue of protecting both of them. It had been a long time since he fought as a team and protected anyone other than himself. Did he even remember how?

It was a quick decision. If he could not protect them both or if they were outnumbered, he would save Stacy.

Preparing as much as he could, he threw open the door to immediately meet a hand that pressed against his chest, gently but firmly pressing him back.

It was the Chief of Police—Stacy's uncle.

"Thought you might be thrown off if you were in," he said, greeting Nicholas as he pushed past him and forced his way into the door. He did not seem full of worry or anger, but he was on a mission.

Stacy stepped forward, looking relieved but confused and moderately...irritated? "Uncle Richey? What are you doing here?"

"I should ask you the same, missy. Your parents are worried and have the whole family searching around town for you. Do you have any idea what time it is?"

A lump in her stomach began to form because for the first time she realized—no. She had absolutely no idea and it was the last thing on her mind to keep track of. Her eyes desperately began searching the room for a clock.

"It's 2a.m.," His narrow tone answered the question in her head.

Her eyes automatically bulged from her head, but her mouth went dry.

"2 o' clock in the morning and you left hours ago not telling anyone where you would be, when you would be back. You're not with Rachael, you didn't tell Rachael. You're not with Cody, you didn't tell Cody..."

"It is my fault," Nicholas interjected. "I did not ask her for her curfew and I was lost in our conversation. I did not consider the time to walk her home may have passed."

Richey was quiet for a moment, looking back and forth between the two of them. "Conversation?" He asked, waiting for more to come.

Before Nicholas had time to prompt what the officer meant by questioning his words, Stacy was huffing, rolling eyes, and heading towards the door.

"Really, Uncle Richey? Yes, all we did was talk. No harm, no foul, no crime. Can we go?"

Nicholas's heart sank into his stomach, but he tried to understand why the night was ending what seemed to be prematurely. He bid Stacy farewell, wishing they had longer to discuss—when would they see each other again? Surely it would be sooner than the next day of school. He meant what he said, he could wait. But he did not want to.

***

Stacy and Richey drove home with the windows on his police cruiser down. She knew he was off duty, so she tried racking her brain for reasons that he needed to come look for his delinquent niece in full uniform with all the bells and whistles on. She did not rack it for long.

"You know the police didn't need to come find me," she said quietly, trying to keep an even tone on the topic. "Regular ole Uncle Richey would have done just fine."

His face stayed focused for a long time, then it slowly began to soften, and landed on middle ground. "The world is a dangerous place, Stacy. Sometimes we spend so much time fearing the enemy across the world, we forget to fear the one right next door."

Stacy swallowed hard. "Don't worry," she said bitterly. "I'm aware of the one right next door."

CHAPTER 46

THE GREATEST REVIVAL

ere it is, folks. December 10, 2006. A small, miniscule day for some, a huge, monotonous day for others!" Jade put her foot on a stool and lifted her microphone into the air as a salute.

"I don't know that you're using that word correctly," Miranda snickered from beside her.

"Mutinous might be a better term," Rachael chimed in. "Revolution!" She banged her drumsticks hard on her drums in random places.

Jade reached over and high-fived Rachael.

Stacy could not blame her friend's excitement and she would be lying if she said she was not excited too. After all, they all wanted this from day one—to get signed from a great company and have their music reach thousands, millions even. Stan was great as they came for that.

But Stacy had a hard time finding her passion in it today when the night prior her thoughts and desires were on boarding a plane and fighting Dukhovian soldiers. The three hours of sleep probably also had something to do with it. She struggled to find sleep after surviving the berating by her friends for not letting them know where she would be only hours after confirmation that Nicholas was a ruthless murderer. Fair enough.

At least the dream evaded her. Perhaps the Spirits remembered she was, in fact, still human and needed to close her eyes without being startled awake at least once a week—give or take.

Still, she had another theory as to why she did not have the dream last night. Certainly, if the Spirits wanted to get something across to her, they could do it in a milder form. But for the months and years since having the dream, she stood idly by and did nothing. Now, finally, she has the conversation with Nicholas to do *something* and the dream stops. Problem solved? Solution started? It meant something… she could feel it.

It made the itch to return to him even more stubborn. What if she did not see him again until school? Would the dream return by then, reminding her that people were dying and things were more important than songs being played on the radio? Or, if she did see Nicholas and the dreams failed to return, did that mean she was on track to return to Dukhovia? How much more would she need to learn before she was ready?

Blah. Ready for what? Nicholas had said he would not take Stacy to Dukhovia. He would not put her at risk. And what if she was just as incapable of learning about Dukhovia as she was learning about America? If the Dukhovian from America came pledging her allegiance to the United States of America but not knowing the year the revolutionary war started in Dukhovia, she suspected her chance of death increased. Likewise, if she knew every Spirit by name and not every state's capital, her chance of survival would double.

Columbus was probably somewhere. Kilimanjaro? Was Puerto Rico a state?

It was a shot in the dark, regardless.

"Okay, three songs that we're sending to Stan. Are we all in agreement?" Dan asked, his palms sweating as he ignored the relaxed band and opted for a stress infused atmosphere.

"*Freedom Rider*, *Keep Me*, and *Tainted Memory*," Cody read off in agreement. The songs were all by the original three. Surprisingly, Dan was not willing to try anything new when it came to performing for Stan.

"Yeah," Stacy chimed in. "Can we use a recording for my guitar solo, though? I'm not really feeling it today?" She asked, with a crack of her fingers.

"Stacy, we're doing this live," Dan replied.

"What?!" She shot up, outraged. "No one told me this."

"He can hear our edited crap anytime, Stace, he wants to see if we suck raw," Rachael, whom Stacy had not yet shared the excitement with, described.

"Okay, rule number one: never refer to your music as crap, it reflects every one of us in a negative light. Stace, do you need time to practice?"

"Ugh, no," she said, rolling her eyes. *Whatever gets me out of here faster.* "I guess I'll just show him how raw I am today. Sucky by the end of the week…take me on my bad days, as well as my good."

"Do you have bad days?" Miranda asked, curiously.

Stacy smirked. She had not been completely honest with all the bad days she had been having recently. Not that today was necessarily a bad day, but her head was full of thoughts and theories and there was not a piece of her that was focused on music.

Why was Nicholas still being so secretive? Okay, okay…Dukhovian ideals. Maybe he had *some*. But she noticed when he tensed up and when he seemed to be an open book and the pattern was…off. His willingness to say the things that would leave him as an enemy were open, the things that could possibly make him a friend were where his lips were sealed.

Lie. The word entered Stacy's thoughts most of the time when she conversed with Nicholas. She was certain that his complicated stories meant he was telling her half-truths at best. But then she could not ignore how in sync they were at the same time.

Both never getting sick. Both withstanding the cold. Both quick to heal. Both feeling drawn to their purpose. Both having their guard up. He was a liar, but he was a liar for a reason.

"Then you're going last," Dan was saying as he typed some highly important information into his keyboard, bringing Stacy back to the present. He adjusted the lights on the band, blinding Cody and Jade in the process.

The lights were new. In order to impress Stan even more, Dan bought new equipment to really make them pop, even going as far as hanging a curtain along the entire length of the back wall instead of just the center. On screen, it was almost as if they were not in a basement at all, although that caused them to lose some of their nostalgia.

"Everything set, captain?" Miranda called over.

Ugh. Stacy exhaled. Perhaps she did need that "time to practice"—the state she was currently in was not fair to her friends. She glanced at all of them and dissected those words. Family and friends. How they became friends. They were not just people there because they liked to play music, it was more. They would love her if she sucked raw or if she belted out a tune like she never had in her life. That was what made them amazing.

And those were the people the world deserved to know.

It was not just about letting their sound fill the world, it was about showing the country who they were. More than their family's past mistakes, more than their last names. It was about restoring family honor by showing the world through their lyrics who they and their families truly were.

She was ready.

Dan was silent as he entered in a few more codes, allowing two more smoke machines to come down from the ceiling. Bright lights then shot on, encircling the smoke machines instead of anyone's eyes. Then, the moment he flicked on a powerful overhead light causing everyone to shield their eyes and scream, the thumbs up was given.

"Okay, guys, huddle up..."

The band gathered in a circle, arms around arms, like before every major performance.

"I'm really proud of how far you guys have come. I know I've been hard on you these last couple months, but you've more than surpassed my expectations. You carry your sound, you have a voice, and there isn't a doubt in my mind that once we start with Stan, you guys will be able to achieve everything you want to. Ready?"

"Set!" They all chimed back. In the same instant, their hands flew into a pile before them then shot up into the sky with their final word. "Rock!"

The band took their place at their designated spots.

Dan turned on his computer and faced a camera towards them and dialed Stan.

"Good evening, Daniel."

"A pleasure to almost see you in person," Dan laughed through a frenzy of sweat. "I'd like to introduce my band to you. On the far left, my sister: Stacy."

Stacy waved.

"Jade in the back on the microphone."

She shot a peace sign.

"Cody, our lead singer."

"A pleasure to meet you, Mr. Simmons." Cody was always very professional when it mattered, it was definitely one of his strengths.

"Miranda, on backup."

She waved quietly.

"And Rachael on drums."

She gave a flirty wave and bright smile.

"Very good. Let's see what you can do."

"We've prepared three songs for you today. Our first song is called *Freedom Riders*. This is a song sung by Cody that he and Stacy wrote together a few months back."

Rachael started out on a mellow tune on her drums.

After a few beats, Stacy strummed on her guitar, a single note.

Rachael picked up, then Stacy.

Cody came in with lyrics, Jade and Miranda hummed in the background.

"Mmm.
They say we're all meant to be someone.
The opportunities are never ending.
Line up at the gates, they say.
We'll help you find your beginning.

Watch the line shrivel down.
Memories recounting.
Watch the line shrivel down.
Opportunities are slimming.

I can't fi-i-i-ind, what I came for.
I can't se-e-e-e, what's before me.
The force of us on unholy ground,
We were never meant to be tamed...

So ri-i-i-i-ide Freedom Riders.
No longer will they tell us what to do,
Imminent loss of control.
Ri-i-i-de Freedom Riders.
A chance to take the world by storm,
Live happily, ever after.
Ri-i-i-de Freedom Riders.

THE GREATEST REVIVAL

So you find yourself stuck in this trap.
A world you can't break from.
So you find yourself in this life,
But you're free to break away from."
Jade and Miranda joined in on the chorus this time.
"So ri-i-i-i-ide Freedom Riders.
No longer will they tell us what to do,
Imminent loss of control.
Ri-i-i-de Freedom Riders.
A chance to take the world by storm,
Live happily, ever after.
Ri-i-i-de Freedom Riders."

Cody was alone again.

"Here we're at the golden stand,
A land I call my own.
Here we'll start a land our own,
A place to rise and call home.
"So ri-i-i-i-ide Freedom Riders.
No longer will they tell us what to do,
Imminent loss of control.
Ri-i-i-de Freedom Riders.
A chance to take the world by storm,
Live happily, ever after.
Ri-i-i-de Freedom Riders."
The music cut and Cody's voice was alone:
"Ride freedom riders."
Stacy ended the song on one final chord.

Dan pumped his fists in excitement, then rolled his hands giving them the sign to announce the next song.

"Our next song is called *Keep Me*. This is a song sung by Rachael, so I'll be switching to drums. I think you'll find her voice is very eloquent."

Rachael smiled a quick thank you to Cody as she pushed passed him to get in front of the microphone.

"1,2,3."
"Time's at a standstill now.
Wind keeps blowing by
And the ocean still sings its rhyme, but I'm, Oh...
Jade and Miranda joined for a single line.
"Time's at a standstill now."

CHAPTER FORTY-SIX

"I'm looking back on the past.
Taking memories for forever,
Just trying to make it all last.

If I sing here
Darling, oh darling won't you keep me here?
Grounded now rooted to our same game
Loving and reminiscing in the same way
Promise you won't forget to hold
Every promise down the road.

Will you remember?
If when these times pass, we're no longer together
Every moment, every picture we took near
Every laugh, every splitting fear
Even my wildest dreams
Will you remember them, my dear?

If I sing here
Darling, oh darling, won't you keep me here?
Grounded now rooted to our same game
Loving and reminiscing in the same way
Promise you won't forget to hold
Every promise down the road."

Several moments passed where the music wisped around them and Rachael danced, eyes closed with the microphone close to her heart.

"No need to fear, now
The distance between us only lessens from here, somehow.
And I will always hold the moment when you promised that
Even if we never spoke a word
The truth would be heard in our world."

The three girls finished the song:

"If I sing here
Darling, oh darling won't you keep me here?
Grounded now rooted to our same game
Loving and reminiscing in the same way
Promise you won't forget to hold
Every promise down the road."

"Wow." Stan had his hand clasped over his mouth, wide-eyed. "Wow. Wow. Wow. You have an absolutely stunning voice, Rachael. Raw talent like that doesn't come along every day."

Stacy laughed, Rachael turned back to wink.

"Stacy is singing one of her new ones up next...*Tainted Memory*," Rachael announced and then danced away.

"Good luck to me having to top that," Stacy said loudly, handing her guitar off to Rachael. "Get ready for the greatest rock song to hit the speakers in a long time."

Dan shook his head. The others started to play a song that was almost heavy metal, transforming into hard rock.

"Stop singing to me about your broken dreams,
The twists and turns down this rigid scene.
I've been there before, I've heard your cry.
I don't care anymore....

Every broken promise
Every twisted lie
A hit in the face would be a better lullaby

I've thrown out all the broken pieces now
I'm gathered
I'm healed.

And you're nothing but a tainted memory
I'll remember the first times but omit your name from my vocabulary
The fair
The fun
The park
Where we run..."

Stacy hit her guitar hard and loud. The other members backed out. Stacy let her solo play through, keeping herself on task to not get carried away—like she always did.

"You think you have a hold on me
But you're
Nothing but a tainted memory."

"Perfect. That's different than anything you've done in a while, Stacy."

She bowed with a fake smile, then grimaced as she walked out of camera-shot.

"Listen, Dan, your band is exactly what I'm looking for. You hold yourselves to a certain way you want to be regarded as and I admire that. As soon as you're able to come down, let me know. Aim for a couple weeks in advance so I can book your hotel rooms and flights."

"Thank you, sir, for this wonderful opportunity. We're aiming to come down there the weekend of February 16th. We would be able to leave the evening of the 15th and return by the following Monday night."

Simon was silent for a moment as he turned to his assistant. "It's all booked. I'll send you your tickets. See you then, Daniel."

The computer clicked off. The band immediately got together and screamed loudly.

Dan gave them side eyes for a moment, but joined in on the celebration.

"Wooo, celebration!" Stacy cheered, crashing down on her guitar in the most obnoxious of ways. She was doing it. Whether she was going to Dukhovia tomorrow or months from now, she still had purpose here—and she was doing it. "I'm thinking four pizzas, two tubs of ice cream, and every topping imaginable."

"Are we celebrating or drowning our tears in soap operas?" Cody recoiled. "Let's at least throw some chips in there."

"Done!" Stacy replied, clicking her phone shut. "My dad will be home within the hour."

"Pool?" Cody asked Stacy expectantly.

"Oh, yeah!" She pumped her fists with enthusiasm, awaiting the return of their pool match that they put on hold several months ago. Time had gotten away from them.

"Alright, don't stay up too late!" Dan countered. "We'll practice in the morning. And remember, just because I'll be leaving doesn't mean I don't expect you all to be practicing!" Dan called after his band who were all already scrambling up the steps and out to the garage.

***

"Are you ready, young grasshopper?" Cody asked Stacy as he lined up the ball, ready for the showdown of a lifetime.

"Ready as the rising sun in the east," Stacy replied, masking her game with the awful pun.

Cody took his shot, sending the ball into another one, then two, causing both to fall in the hole.

"Nice shot!" Stacy cheered. She lined up her eye, squinted for added enthusiasm, and knocked a ball close to the hole, but not close enough.

"Good eye, cuz," Cody congratulated. "It's all about assess and response." Cody squinted again, taking his time before slowly sending his next ball flying across the table and into its home.

A total of eight balls later, Stacy was raising Cody's arm into the air and pumping her fist. "The champion!"

"He doesn't have room for anymore trophies," Rachael said, squeezing his arm. "I declare a rematch."

"He has to go against me this time!" Jade said, grabbing the stick off Stacy and running around the table.

"Come on, guys, there's plenty of skill to go around," Cody argued, as the girls laughed, deciding who would be the biggest challenge. "I can whoop all your butts and teach you how to pass on my legacy by the end of the night."

"Pizza's here!" Stacy declared, running out of the garage to meet her father.

"Finally!" Cody abandoned his pool stick and all plans of demolition.

The friends gathered around the pizza and each took a slice.

"To success and a positive future with Stan!" Miranda toasted.

"To our band!" Rachael added.

"To friendship!" Stacy rejoiced.

"To rock n' roll!" Jade celebrated, already biting her slice.

"To Victory!" Cody chanted.

CHAPTER 47

THE EVERLASTING PACT

O kay, guys, now remember. I'm going to leave everything you need for the show the day after Christmas and if anyone needs anything…"

"Just wing it and hope for the best," Stacy cheered, clapping her brother on the back. She, Cody, Rachael, and Dan were out on the front porch; sitting on the frozen stoop, laying in the snow-covered yard, whatever seemed appealing to them in the present moment.

Dan gave her a threatening look. "No. You ask dad. If dad is unavailable, there's a direct list of who to ask, in order, and what their specialties are. Now, just to recap, what exactly is your plan if something malfunctions?"

"You do realize we've rehearsed all our songs acapella in the event that science fails us, right?" Stacy chastised with crossed arms. "You'd think we never managed ourselves before," Stacy added thoughtfully with a scornful smile and a roll of her eyes.

Dan rolled his eyes then broke into a smile, swinging his arm around Stacy and Cody. "You guys are gonna do great."

"Thank you, Danny!" Rachael called, shooting up from her position on the ground with a smile. She pulled her knees up towards her face, resting her chin on the comfort of her snow pants. "We'll miss you, though. Are you sure you can't wait until after the show to leave?"

"My externship begins the 22nd and runs until the day we return to school. I was thankful they would even let me join with such little experience. This will truly be beneficial for me."

"Guarantee you he already knows double what those guys do," Cody snickered.

The harsh tear of a door being slammed to the point of falling off the hinges jolted the kids heads in the direction of the house next door. Yasana came out the door, stomping towards her car, fumes of bitter fury bound into every aspect of her body language.

She pushed her long sleeves up, over her forearms, making extra sure that every strain of hair was back behind her ears. Her arms revealed hollow wounds, mostly circular in shape. Her face was brimming with a purple gleam from around her eye over to her ear.

"Cody, why's your mom covered in bruises?" Stacy asked. There was little care in her voice, mostly shock.

Cody tore his face away and looked down. "Her newest game. Hurting herself so people will think my dad did it." His expression was pained with sorrow but there was too much irritation resonating with it.

Rachael climbed up on the stoop next to him. Reaching forward, she grabbed onto Cody's hand. Without a glance, he latched on with a grip tighter than he meant, loosening his grip immediately.

"I haven't been home since the other day," he assured her in a whisper.

She knew it. Whether he was at one of their houses or Jade or Miranda's, he was in good hands. He was protected. But Richey was a different story and what Cody did not know about his dad was eating him alive.

"When did she start that?" Stacy questioned. She had been replaying her terrible but true words to her uncle on their drive home the other night. Guilt plagued her, but also a feeling of bitter annoyance.

"A few days ago. Then dad told me he tried to talk to her yesterday about ending their marriage and her moving out and she took a knife to her arm doing that." Cody gestured to her bandaged-up arm.

Stacy shriveled up, feeling responsible.

"Strange choice," Dan noted. "If someone wants to hurt someone, they go for a more painful spot. If someone wants to hurt themselves for show, they go for a less painful spot." He shrugged, closing his computer and walking in the house. "Just a thought."

The three were left with the images running through minds, fighting for attention with everything else the other was considering. It made Stacy feel weak and selfish. She knew she did not want to focus on the band entirely because of Nicholas and Dukhovia, but what about Cody and his mom? Or Rachael and her arm for that matter? Her abilities?

"Let's hit the slopes!" Stacy suddenly shouted as thick snow fell from the roof and onto her face. She passed it between her fingers delicately. They all had their things ready to go, they were just waiting for the snow to pick up enough and get thick enough to blind their vision. And her thoughts worthy enough to leave.

Rachael looked at Cody. He nodded and grabbed his snowboard. "You still sure about this?" He asked Rachael, looking at her wrist.

"Absolutely," she said with a smile and nod of her head. "Just innocent sledding for me."

The three took off towards the edge of town, where (through no purpose other than nature), a large hill stood. It was rather steep and dangerous, and several signs warned them not to go anywhere near it, but they had consistently for so long, it seemed like obligation now. To not go would be betrayal.

Cody ran towards the hill, readying his snowboard at the top. He secured himself, observed his path, and set off straight down, yelling with enthusiasm.

"Sure you'll be okay?" Stacy asked, looking at Rachael.

Rachael grinned brilliantly and nodded.

Stacy readied her skis, planting them firmly on either side. Rachael had been known to delve into skiing a few times, but not with one arm.

Rachael smiled at her friends. Down below, Stacy had slid past Cody, falling to the ground laughing. Cody helped her to her feet and then the two fell on one another due to the ice below their feet.

With her sled straight and path away from her friends, Rachael set off down the hill, speeding with eyes shut toward the rush of the chilled air. She felt her sled start to tip, but she did not want to throw it off course—Cody was usually in charge of steering.

Her eyes remained shut, a small scream escaping from her airways as the sled threw her overboard, into a large bank of snow.

"Rachael!" Cody and Stacy yelled in unison, starting after Rachael.

Rachael shot up from the snow drift, laughing as she wiped snow from her face. She took off her hat to get the snow out, revealing that hat hair was apparently not a thing for Rachael Cassidy Leighton.

The other two glanced at each other then back at Rachael. Cody clasped his hand on Rachael's left shoulder; Stacy attached her hand firmly onto the right. Together, they pushed her into the snow, all three falling into the snow bank in fits of laughter.

"You two are absolutely incorrigible!" Rachael laughed.

"We don't know what that means, but we're absolutely certain it's bad and so for that we thank you," Stacy said back, barely able to breathe through her laughter.

"Ugh." Rachael rolled her eyes, sitting up with the other two. Assessing her surroundings, she shoved the two by the chest with either arm and dashed back up the hill, shouting "Time for round two!" after them.

"Get back here!" Cody called after her.

In less graceful attempts to climb the hill, Stacy and Cody reunited with Rachael, staring down the hill.

"Race ya!" Rachael challenged.

It was on for the two most competitive people in all of Toristh Hill High. With unfair advantages clearly on the side of some, the three flew down the hill, ending up all on top of each other in the end.

"This is fun," Rachael breathed.

"Yeah," Stacy agreed. "Dan would say we should be growing up and practicing."

"And wouldn't we all want to be as uptight as Sir Daniel," Cody mocked.

The three laughed.

"That's why he's not part of the Unfathomable three," Cody added.

"Hey, that's catchy, let's change the band name," Stacy said, the wheels turning.

CHAPTER FORTY-SEVEN

"There's five of us," Rachael reminded her.

"Oh, right," Stacy sighed, back to the drawing board. "The Fabulous Five, The Frightening Five…eh? Make people too terrified to mess with us?"

"Or too frightened to see us and lose half our audience," Rachael reasoned.

"Guess we're sticking with the old name," Stacy decided. "Face it, world, we're not creative people."

"As long as we stay the three absolute best friends ever that's all I care about," Rachael revealed to them, her voice rich with desire.

"And we always will be," Stacy promised.

As always, almost on que, almost as an unspoken promise, the three reached up an arm up in the air and linked hands.

"Beat you to the top of the hill!" Cody taunted, dashing up the hill quicker than anyone had been yet.

"You wish!" Stacy dared.

The three were back at it, racing after each other and causing the perfectly pleated snow to be a memory of the past.

CHAPTER 48

THE AMERICAN WAY

$\mathcal{I}$f he did not know any better, Nicholas would think that the looks he was receiving as he walked through town were meant for a monster. Perhaps they were properly aimed, but they could not have known that. Still, that passerby did not run, nor did the next. Perhaps monster was not the correct term…dangerous? Fearful?

Either way, they might not have been wrong. Whether it be here or in Dukhovia, people generally saw Nicholas, assumed the worse, and ran. He supposed it was a bed he made for himself. Today though, he ventured people were looking at him for an entirely different reason—and that reason might even be concern.

Nicholas had not slept since the night before Stacy came to his apartment. Though, he slept like a baby the night prior, feeling as though so much was left unfinished and that so much had changed between them, Nicholas found himself incapable of sleeping Friday night and then again Saturday. He had certainly dealt with worse, but adding in the mixture of the torment of his thoughts…

Stacy's entire demeanor had seemed to change. Though she still seemed on the fence of trusting him, she was becoming undone. She was exposing herself as well as beginning to treat him more like a human being and less like a terrorist under investigation—and he did not realize how much he needed that treatment. He did not realize what having Vuel did for him and found every calming word that Stacy spoke to him to melt him like butter, to be soothing, to be…addictive.

School was tomorrow, but after shifting in his apartment for hours and hours, trying to distract himself with thoughts of anything other than Stacy, he fled. He had decided that he would not interrupt her at home, this was a big weekend for her and he doubted she was as distracted thinking of him as he was of her. No, he would not invade directly. However, if he were to run into her in town, well then…

He had been walking around all morning, another reason for his haggardly appearance, he was certain. Though he did not react to it, the air still flushed his cheeks red, the wind still whipped his air around unevenly. He sighed, breathing in frustration as he dove into the nearest café. It was useless.

He placed his first order since the night he and Stacy went out. He at least needed to eat something if he was not going to be sleeping. Something needed to help him think straight. He decided on a cup of hot chocolate and a Danish. It was the most appetizing thing he had seen in America thus far.

He sipped at his hot chocolate with ease and care, savoring the time it took to enter his mouth and empty down his throat. He closed his eyes, breathing uneasily.

This was not how this was supposed to go. And yet, he was not sure what he was expecting. He knew he wanted out of his predicament and he knew that would not come easily. He supposed unless Arkady rode in to tell him the deal was off, it would be messy.

And he certainly wasn't holding his breath for that.

The bell to the café dinged several times during his hours long stay. The worker of the café, much to Nicholas's surprise, was welcoming, refreshing his hot chocolate as he waited and even offering him a second and third Danish—all of which he gladly accepted.

He appreciated being seen. He appreciated taking the moment to soak up what he needed. He realized what rest there was in supporting oneself.

As the evening went on, Nicholas finally decided that he had not given up. He had decided that he should continue to walk not just wherever his feet would take him, but where Stacy's feet would take her. What types of places would she frequent?

His stomach twisted at the thought.

But then, as if the health gods heard an unspoken prayer, the café door swung open and three familiar classmates bounded forward—laughing, eager, and covered in snow.

Nicholas took a moment to observe Stacy before making himself known. Her hair was obviously windblown from whatever nonsense she had been partaking in. She laughed with Rachael and Cody with ease and comfort, seeming relaxed and aware. And yet…there were still the same dark shadows under her eyes. The ones he pointed out in swim class. The same ones he himself had.

She still was not sleeping. She still was not worrying. What thoughts had kept her up since their last interaction?

Or was it simply the band?

Finally, angst got the better of him. Not thinking at all what he would do or say, Nicholas rose to his feet, the stool beneath him causing a deafening screech that called the entire café to attention.

Stacy, Cody, and Rachael turned towards him with gawking eyes. Then three different responses took place as they registered who they looked at.

Rachael waved with brilliant enthusiasm and joy.

Cody rolled his eyes and turned back to the counter.

And Stacy stared back at him the same way he now stared at her—blank longing with no direction.

At least he hoped he placed the first adjective correctly.

"Hello," he finally said in a weak, broken voice.

It was then Stacy broke into a smile. She whispered something into Rachael's ear and strode over.

She stopped abruptly in front of him, almost as if she was not sure what she was supposed to do next. Then she smiled. "Hey! Guess we didn't have to wait until Monday to meet again after all."

He grinned back. "A blessing." Then he paused. "How was your recording?"

She breathed in, sighing heavily before she continued. "Great, actually. Stan loved us, well, he loved Rachael especially, but everyone does. Unfortunately, we can't go down to record anything new until at least February."

"Why is that?"

Stacy rolled her eyes. "My brother and charming manager feels that we simply cannot miss a single day of school and he has prior business to attend to over winter break."

"Well, he may be correct," Nicholas stated. "After all, with all your difficulties, you may be getting close to truant."

A devilish smile spread wide over Stacy's entire face. She playfully punched his arm. "Thankfully I'll have you to blame."

Nicholas laughed back, surprised at how easy it was to let the feeling exist. "And how do you feel you did playing your music? After the prior nights events?"

Stacy pondered that for a moment. "I thought about it a little differently than normal. Normally when I feel overwhelmed by thoughts of Dukhovia or confusion, it feels like a headache that will be the death of me and that headache is turning into a cage I can't escape from." She shook her head. "I remembered my muse, our muse, had more to do with regaining a positive name for the Grayson family more so than it did comparing the best beat. We became known for that— for having a positive impact, for not stepping down, for showing the world who we were fearlessly instead of just becoming the next in the family to screw up and make headlines for bringing the country to its knees."

Nicholas was silent. Stacy seemed to expect this, but when the silence grew uncomfortable, she looked over at him, watching his chest heave up and down, up and down. His face was a ghostly white that was void of all emotion.

Stacy skidded to a halt. "Hey…" She reached up to gently touch his arm, but he withdrew it in a haste, making Stacy feel like she had fire for fingertips.

"I am sorry." His words were quick. "Just a bad memory," he muttered the words slowly. He glanced up, noticing that Cody had his eyes on Nicholas like a hawk, even as Rachael tried with vibrant effort to get him to focus on her, even swatting a red mitten-covered hand in his direction.

Stacy shook her head. "You don't need to apologize for that. I never really experienced any of the repercussions of my family's decisions, but I have more than enough memories of people screaming insults at us—even with the start of the band."

Nicholas cocked his head to the side, interest peaked. "How do you mean?"

She rolled her eyes. "People didn't take us seriously at first—with all the background. When we first started getting offers for shows and battling other bands, they would make digs at our family to try and gain leverage—but we were too good. We always knew how to one-up them."

The memories Nicholas spoke of ran through his head. "What did you say? How did it not bother you?"

"It did in the beginning," she answered plainly, tapping her fingers delicately as she looked back at her friends who were now being given their drinks. "But then we realized the only people who still thought those things were people who didn't know us and didn't listen to anything about us. We weren't the things they were saying, but they were judgmental and cruel. You can't fix those things and no matter your strengths and weaknesses, they'll always find fault. So, in the end, it says more about them and their character than it does about ours." She turned, accepting a tall cup of hot chocolate from Rachael. "That's what my mom says, anyway."

Nicholas looked at her with admiration, the simple way she was able to live so…simply. So relaxed, letting go of everything…

She sipped her hot chocolate slowly then beamed with satisfaction.

"I was surprised to see you here," Nicholas offered as a change of subject. "Nothing looks like it will cause your heart attack nearly as quick as you'd like."

She barked out laughter. "Then you haven't seen the right stuff." She took another deep swig. "We love Coller's, especially after a long day like today."

"More music?" He asked.

She shook her head. "No, today was all about bonding. We went skiing, snowboarding, and sledding. Rachael fell twice. It was great."

He tried to imagine the scene. "Seems very…entertaining."

It was then she eyed him with strange curiosity. "Fun," she said in a corrective tone. "It was fun."

"Stace, let's go!" Cody called over from a booth near the door. "Seriously?" He muttered not so quietly. "Why does this guy keep showing up?"

Stacy looked at Cody, rolled her eyes, and returned to Nicholas. "What were you doing today?" She asked after eyeing him up and down, taking in his dreadful appearance.

"Lacking, as you called it, fun," he quoted.

She raised her eyebrow in response. "Do Dukhovian mastermind soldiers truly not have time for the simpler things?" She asked, her curiosity seeming peaked.

He grimaced. "I cannot say that I have ever been snowboarding nor had much time for such casualness."

"Not even with the mystery best friend?" She asked.

He shook his head, forcing back a small smile. "Not even with Vuel."

Stacy's eyes brightened. "Well, Vuel would want you to have fun now. Maybe a little American break was just what you needed." She perked up, her head whipping around. "Rache! We need to show Nicholas what it means to have fun!"

Rachael's eyes mimicked Stacy's, growing as she forced down her mouthful of hot chocolate and jumped up, leaving Cody panic-stricken.

"Absolutely!" She declared and his hand was pulled, leading him out the front door before he could be offered another Danish, though he planned to return for a scone.

Cody slithered out behind them, attempting to whisper advice against the plan to both girls, then making no show of how he 'should not be around them' because he was 'a menace', sure to 'kill us all'. Nicholas could feel anger and hatred rising inside of himself. But he relaxed. He was being shown around by two girls who genuinely cared about him having a good time. That was something he had not experienced since...

He dared not think.

As the evening went on, he found himself relaxing. He found that once he was around Stacy and seeing that she did not lose faith in him, that they were still exactly where they left off, he could breathe. He engaged with her and Rachael both, neither seemed to fear him, neither seemed to dislike him.

It was as though he had friends.

Though, his stomach did churn at their idea of fun. It was not that he could not remember a time when such a life existed. There were times that he and Vuel snuck out of the palace to play pranks around town, skate on the lakes of North Bridge, practice putting their spirit power together...this was different, at least it seemed to be...

Perhaps the only differences were the.... untraditional activities they partook in. They laughed the same, they joked the same. But Nicholas felt his breath quicken and his pulse shake when they showed him the arcade games in the center of town. His comfort further evaded him when they tried to show him Cody's favorite pastime, erm, video games? He tossed the handheld device and walked away within ten minutes of attempting to follow the way the light reflected off Rachael's television as sound shot out of hidden speakers—despite them telling him he was doing excellent.

Still, time passed by easier than it had when he was on his own. He was at least learning something, he was at least proving himself, he was at least not alone...

Yet, at one point he felt Stacy's hand gently rest upon the side of his shoulder, the one not nearly as scarred as the charred left. Her smile was gentle, understanding, questioning. The type of smile that automatically put thoughts of unease to rest. The type of smile he never knew he longed for.

"Not super traditional ways to have fun, huh?"

Nicholas sighed, unsure what to say, unsure what hidden meaning lie in her question. He only shook his head, unable to decide quickly enough what one answer might mean.

Stacy only smiled larger in return, the same assurance coursing through him. "I have another idea. Come on."

She linked her fingers into his, tightening them when sheer power coursed between them. She pulled him along, towards the back of the house where they entered a room enclosed entirely in windows, beauty in the disguise of snow and icicles tracing the outdoors behind them.

He only noticed the contents of the room when Stacy released his hands and began to look around. "This is one of my guitars," she smiled cheerfully, pulling it up. Around her there was a drum set and a single microphone lay on the ground. "We usually play in my basement," she went on. "There's a whole stage down there, but I requested a change of scenery."

He smiled, breathing it in. Rachael's backyard was immaculate. Rolling hills of pristine white faded into a clearing of coniferous trees. The tops were decorated with gleaming flakes of white, all overseeing a large, white carved wooden bridge. Nicholas cocked his head, questioning Stacy on it.

She nodded. "Kenny, Rachael's dad, he carved it for her one year for her birthday. Her birthday is Christmas Eve."

"Christmas Eve is a very spiritual day, and the bridge..."

"Mimics one in Dukhovia," she finished with certainty.

"Not just any bridge, though, it mimics Umai's Right."

Stacy now looked towards him, a questioning and embarrassing look on her face.

He smiled a cocky, but reassuring grin. "It is not your fault that you are not well versed in Dukhovian history, Stacy Grace, you were never taught to be."

She grimaced. "Who is she?" Her voice was a mere whisper.

He kept the same smile. "And you can ask me anything."

She kept patient, waiting for the answer, but the gratitude that reflected in her eyes was overwhelming. It was something he never experienced. To not only be appreciated, but to be of a positive use to someone—it was a purpose he never knew he could serve.

His voice changed, becoming more powerful as he told the story. "Umai is our fertility goddess, often regarded with the Moon Spirit since the First World crumbled. Some regard her as the most important determiner of purposes as she makes the first crucial decision for us—which family we will be born into."

He paused. He could not talk about Umai without wondering why she chose to put him in the family that she did, and then guilt overpowered him. Not that he did not appreciate his family. He could not have begged for a better mother if he tried, he loved his grandfather and his grandfather had loved him more than anyone else. He was his protector, his hero. He looked up to his great grandfather. And yet....

And yet he could not help but compare himself to the other soldiers. To those who chose to come and go and serve as they pleased. Lightness in the military did not necessarily exist—there was a job to be done and the end goal had to be reached no matter the strategy that was used to reach it. Yet he wondered what it would be like to not carry the weight of his family's honor on his shoulders. To be able to walk away from a place, a situation, a stance, without risking everything...

But Umai had to have a reason.

"Your family must be able to raise you up appropriately in your purpose: guide you, support you."

Stacy's face had fallen into a look he recognized. A look of thoughtfulness, of confusion, of remorse and sorrow.

"In Dukhovia, couples who intend to become pregnant or expecting couples, will go to Umai's Right to pray for the purpose of their child, for an honorable purpose, a peaceful purpose."

Stacy seemed to remember why he was telling the story and looked back out at the replica. "Rachael's parents went. When they were trying to conceive. They went to Dukhovia after their fifth miscarriage and brought Umai a gift—I don't know what it would have been. They prayed to her and Rachael's mom, Ellen, returned every night, even soaking in the freezing waters."

Nicholas's eyes widened. "That would be rather extreme for a non-Dukhovian."

Stacy nodded. "They seemed to truly earn Rachael." Her face fell. "Nicholas, I just have one more question..."

"Of course." His voice was light.

"What happens if you were never given your birth reading? How do you find out?"

Nicholas's eyes bored into hers. It was the first question that he did not necessarily feel wary answering. In contrast, he was intrigued and implored that she wanted to know. And he could not quite put his finger on what it meant that he would be the one to answer her. "Well, it depends whether or not you were truly never given it or if you simply are unaware what it is."

She looked as though she would protest his statement at first, but then something took over her mind and her thoughts drifted away.

"If your family truly fled before it was given, you would need to find a shaman or attempt to connect to The Spirits yourself. That is no easy feat—you have to be selected as a Shaman and it typically takes years."

"And if my parents know..." she began her sentence never intending to finish.

"Then there would be a reason they have not yet let you know," Nicholas murmured, lifting her chin into his hand until their eyes met each other's.

Whatever thoughts plagued her mind seemed to slowly drift away as she looked back and forth from one end of his conniving, wicked face to the other.

Stacy shook her head, seeming to focus. "Anyway, I know that you have played music before, music exists in Dukhovia, and I did promise to teach you the guitar, so…" She took a seat on the couch, lifting the instrument into her lap. She flashed her eyes to the left of him, motioning for him to sit down.

He obliged.

From the time she strummed the first chord, he felt his heart fall into his stomach. His mind slipped into a place that time could not keep him from and memories could only scarcely recount. She strummed again and again and his mind pictured the ice and snow. He forced the image away until he pictured the school, his apartment, anything else. He wanted to hear Stacy's music. Not just the music, focus on her chords, anything but the music…

Stacy's voice was beautiful, melodic and passionate. Her face and eyes carried the same tone as she carried out the words. Soft, gentle, caring. She reminded him of his mother. The way she would close her eyes and let the music carry her, take her to a new place. A place of love, a place of hope…

He had not noticed how deep he had gone until he was past the point of return, until Stacy's sounds had faded and all that remained was her touching, gentle voice asking him if he was okay.

Until the welled-up emotion of nearly sixteen years poured from his eyes like The Una Falls in North Bridge.

And then he was running out the door, Stacy chasing behind him.

He threw open the door into the cold night. Rachael and Cody had turned with confused looks on their faces, but Cody easily enough kept Rachael back.

Air whipped harshly at his stinging eyes, he looked around, trying to reorient himself, remember where he was, where he was going, why. Sickness filled his stomach as a lump grew and grew.

All because of the music. All because of the stupid, stupid music. He knew better than to listen to the music…

"Nicholas…"

"Stacy, no, please, just get away from me. Please." His voice was shaking; his entire body unsteady.

His mother twirled and danced around his room, playing the lyra with energy and flare.

His mother picked him up as his father came in and took over, the two taking turns dancing with him and playing the instrument.

His mother spinning him in his room, picking him up and tossing him, before dinner, before bed, any moment he needed the music to calm him down, to save him…

"Nicholas please!" She shouted loudly over the roar of his protests and the wind.

"Stacy, please hear me. I am not trying to be cruel. I am not trying to dismiss you. I cannot control myself when these feelings come up and I cannot risk harming you. Please understand me."

"And you understand this," she said the words with forceful certainty. "You don't have to do this alone anymore." The words looked uncertain on her lips, but she did not take them back.

He was quiet. "Neither one of us know what the future holds."

Stacy merely shrugged her shoulders. "But we can find out together."

CHAPTER 49

WE ARE ONE

*N*icholas flung himself forward, wrapping his arms around Stacy's shoulders and squeezing her into his chest. He breathed her in, seeming to absorb any part of her. Stacy could not say it was alarming, it felt too natural, it felt right, it felt good. Then she had burst into laughter.

"I'm sorry that our day of fun was torment for you."

He laughed in return.

Then she took him in, brushing loose hair back out of his eyes, her hands searching his face for the right position, the right spot to land. She took a cheek in either hand and leaned her forehead against his. "Nicholas there's so much I don't know. I don't know what to do about Dukhovia, I don't know what's going on with me. But I'll be here for you. No matter where, no matter what." She was not even sure what she was saying, but she knew the words were right.

If looks could kill was a phrase that did not hold a candle to the emotion Nicholas conveyed when he looked back at Stacy. The eyes of gratitude, the face of wonder, all previously masked by the persona of pure torment, the prison of expectation.

"I owe you the world, Stacy Grace."

She brushed his cheeks in response, the feeling to her conveying the same message, the feeling to him like a flood of heart-stopping ease.

"But perhaps I can start by showing you how us Dukhovians truly have fun."

Stacy grinned broadly. "It's a date."

CHAPTER 50

DETENTION SENTENCED

Stacy put her hand over mouth, yawning as she came down the steps the following morning. She had tossed and turned all night, her dreams battling with her mind when she woke up in a sweat after having narrowly escaped death for the fifth time in a row.

The dream returned last night with a vengeance, occurring so frequently in one night, that she expected to see her pale white face the moment she closed her eyes, Nicholas's fierce grin and villainous stance in suite as he chased her with a large knife.

She always awoke before he caught her. She always told herself that he was a great guy who would never do anything to hurt anyone—but her subconscious clearly *always* disagreed.

She partially wondered what these spirits expected out of her. That she would never have a day off? That her and Nicholas would spend endless time together until the end of time? Ugh. Maybe they just expected her to get her butt moving and make *something* happen before Dukhovia fell to ruin. She had all the time in the world, they did not.

They were dying. It was a fact that she tried to lose sleep over, but it was as if the Spirits sucked her in, practically forcing the dream upon her. Maybe it was not so nightmarish after all. She spent all of her awake time picturing Dukhovia slaughtering their people—it distracted her in biology, lunch, basketball practice, you name it—so maybe having someone screaming at her to do something about it was the wake up call she was ignoring.

"Why does six am always come earlier on the week days?" She asked no one in particular as she entered the kitchen.

"It's a lifelong curse from sleeping in too late on the first day of school every year since you started," Grace joked.

"I'd like to say I'll try to do better next year, but I'm making zero promises."

"You don't have to promise, just attempt it," Dan advised.

"Eh." Stacy shrugged. She grabbed an apple and a plate of wheat toast and eggs, choosing to skip the bacon, before taking a seat at the table. "What's for dinner tonight?"

"Uncle Fred and Aunt Jenny are teaching us how to make their famous lasagna," Grace said with much anticipation. She danced on her feet as the words flowed out.

"How does anyone in our family make a famous anything?" Stacy wondered.

"Excuse me," Kevin protested. "Tom and I have saved Thanksgiving every year for how many years now?"

"I don't know," Stacy replied, lazily. "Probably all of them?"

There was a half-attempted knock at the door that was already opening before Rachael and Cody appeared in the kitchen several seconds later.

"Morning fellow family members!" Cody welcomed. "Can I stay here tonight? If I have to sleep on Mr. Leighton's twenty-year-old futon one more night, I'm going to have to sit out the rest of the season."

"You're more than welcome," Kevin chuckled.

"We should get to school," Stacy encouraged, setting down her orange juice and kissing her parents. "I'm one tardy away from another detention sentence."

"Blah! I forgot about that!" Dan recoiled. "You'll have to…"

"Work extra hard while you're away…got it," Stacy finished, winking at her brother. Though she actually wondered if she was even serving detention with Santifini gone.

"Get another detention," Cody instructed. "You'll know what it's like to live like the other half." He broke into a broad grin, swinging his arm around Stacy's shoulder.

The three heaved themselves over the blowing swirls of white as they walked to school that morning…some with slightly more ease than others. The sun was shining, threatening to tear the wonderland away and replace it with puddles and muck, but the weather man was casting a different prediction.

Stacy found herself looking behind her shoulder every once in a while as they walked. She was not sure whether she was hoping or anticipating, maybe even expecting? But she knew that she *wanted* to see Nicholas.

She tensed at the realization. How had things gotten to this point? Where she still felt so leery she had not divulged anything about the dream, but found any thoughts that were not preoccupied with Dukhovia in flame were bursting at the seams with thoughts of Nicholas, of her concern for him, of his unwavering dedication to his country and his family, of how they would bounce witty comments off each other, of his heart-stopping blue eyes and that smirk that pulls up only parts of the corner of his mouth.

No. She refused. If she was going to have a crush, it was not going to be surface level, perfect-smile crush. That was exactly what people were expecting, what they wanted. No, it was going to be hardcore, life purpose's intertwined, awestruck…mesmerized…non-surface level crush. AGH. Who was she?

Regardless, she knew she needed to start trusting Nicholas. The more intense the dream became, the more aware she was of one thing—if Nicolas was not the enemy, someone was, and intentionally running from someone who could help her save her country was not only foolish, but selfish. Even if he meant harm to her family, she needed to find out how to level out the risk so that she could protect both them and Dukhovia.

She bit her lip, acutely aware of Rachael staring and giving her questioning looks. How on *earth* was she supposed to figure out how to do *that?* She trusted Nicholas, her gut told her to trust Nicholas. Anything that happened she now had explanation for. He had a horrible upbringing. He struggled to control himself when reminders were brought up. But that did not mean he came to America to slaughter her family.... But he was leery as to why he was here.

She was simply certain—and last night confirmed it. Certain that Nicholas was innocent. Certain that Nicholas was a good person. But also, certain he was lying to her.

Perhaps this unexplainable feeling to protect Nicholas was the strongest reason she immediately chose to jump to his side and protect him. Perhaps it was her innate sense to do that for anyone. What other response would there be? Tell him 'eh I haven't figured out if I trust you yet, suffer on your own'. She could never. And so, she had not.

Instead, she spent time with him, she comforted him, she talked until the stars gleamed high and laughter erupted from each of them. It was calming, it was freeing. It was right.

No more cold shoulder. Be his friend. She did not mean for it to be an angle, but her showing her true self was revealing his, or so it seemed to be. She supposed she could not be certain. But the lightness between them, the way he looked at her, the ease of being around him...

Ask. Her gut was telling her to ask. She was desperate to know what this dream meant and the dream was clearly desperate to have her find out.

"Stacy!"

"Oh, come on!"

Cody's grumbling caught her attention before the sound of her own name. She glanced over her shoulder to see her cousin's face scrunched up in the deepest level of hatred she could recall at the present moment. She followed his gaze, down his line of vision, until her eyes met Nicholas tracing after them.

Her heart was immediate butterflies, a whirl wind of emotion fighting against logic. Her instinct was to run into his arms, but she played it a bit cooler than that.

"What does he want?" Cody had a vein bulging at the top of his head. He rolled his sleeves up to his elbow, giving perfect access to the fist that was forming.

Rachael quickly pushed his sleeves back down and latched onto his arm. "We'll give you two some space," she sang, giving Stacy a wink before leading Cody away.

Stacy heard him begin to bicker, but tuned it out the moment she turned back and raced towards Nicholas, leaping next to him and meeting him with a bubbly smile.

He returned the expression, a statue of pure perfection in a light gray jacket which hung open in the cool breeze. She glanced down at his injury from the other night and noticed it had mostly healed. Again, she fought the urge to nurse his every injury back to health, but she reeled it in.

She tried to assess him, to assess *herself* and see why her mind was telling her that he was so dangerous once she was asleep and out of her own control. But she failed to see it. Perhaps it was just the words of others, perhaps it was the lying. On the flip side, perhaps it was just his good looks and Stacy was human after all. Perhaps it was just the fact that he used sweet words and knew about Dukhovia. Either way, only one was right and the other was a façade with potentially fatal consequences.

"Walking today?" Stacy asked with a raise of her eyebrow. "How civil."

"Walking and intending on skipping at least half of my classes," Nicholas replied with a chastising grin, glancing at Stacy from the corner of his eye as the two began to match one another's pace. "Something new to me, I would have never dreamt the idea back in Dukhovia."

Stacy gave him a flabbergasted look. "I'm appalled that you would become so reckless simply by setting foot on our land. Perhaps it should be condemned after all."

Nicholas gave a snort. "Though I do not want you to get all of the credit, you are my muse."

She turned up her nose and faked disappointment. "And here I was thinking I was inspiring life-long change."

The four entered the school early for a change. The hallways were a lot busier during this time, which acclimated Stacy with the newfound realization that she had to squeeze against multiple people just to get to her locker. How on Earth was she the only one ever late?

"What are you skipping the afternoon for?"

Nicholas seemed to grimace in response. "Just catching up on some things related to Dukhovia. It seems the last few days I have been rather…distracted."

Stacy blushed. "I wonder who could be to blame for that."

Nicholas hesitated a moment, then grinned. "See, a truly poor influence after all."

The two continued down the halls, finding themselves walking into clouds of smoke and steam from a poorly executed science project. Nicholas grimaced.

"This…catch-up work," Stacy began, her words hesitant as they walked around the spilled volcanic contents. "Is it something I could potentially do with you? We need to begin my training."

Nicholas nodded his head once. Annoyance trickled throughout him as the subject he was dying to have happened to come up as they were battling gaggles of giggling girls and loud conversations.

DETENTION SENTENCED

Students were lining the halls with posters for the upcoming school elections. Stacy usually ran for office, but this year she did not seem as interested. Holding a leadership position seemed to speak to her, but once she was actually doing it, she felt meh at best. It always got a good laugh out of Santifini, though.

Hm. She glanced into the office on her way to her locker. Still no sign of the grand principal.

"I agree," he accepted immediately, filling Stacy with confidence. "And actually..." he cleared his throat, nerves kicking in from him stomach and up where he felt the sensation of something being stuck in his throat.

Stacy was automatically at attention, concerned eyes watching his closely...drawn to them.

"I wondered if tonight would be an appropriate time to have our date? I have planned an evening fit for any Dukhovian princess."

The words struck a chord, but she buried it. "Oh really? A night of royalty from Sir Nicholas himself. Were you this gentleman-like with all the ladies back home?"

He smirked. "Hardly."

She arched her eyebrow. "So, there aren't, like, any lovely ladies in waiting sitting at the castle doors awaiting your homecoming?" She felt her face turn red as the paint on the mismatched lockers as she said the words, but she felt like they needed to be said. Was she reading his flirtatious signs appropriately or did he have a love interest back home?

A loud snort escaped him. "No arranged marriages, no ladies in waiting. Stacy Grace, I can assure you that you are the only lady I have ever had interest in."

That silenced them both until Nicholas cleared his throat. "So, tonight?"

Stacy shook her head as if clearing a fog. "Tonight. I would love to," she began, biting her lip. "But Monday night is family dinner night. My whole family comes over and we play games, tell jokes, cook dinner. No one has missed one since the beginning of time unless they were dead or dying." She bit her lip at the horrendous joke once she realized who she was talking to.

He did not seem to react. He only shook his head. "No, of course. I would never ask you to miss something so momentous."

She smiled, ducking her head down. Showing care for her family. Someone sent to hurt them would not do that, unless it was a head game. Blah. "But they usually leave around 8. I can sneak out and come to your place?" If she could turn a shade any deeper, it just happened. What on *Earth* was she saying? Sneak out? Go out that late on a school night? Was this kindness, desire, or desperation? She was just glad options existed.

"I would not wish for you to travel over to that part of town past dusk on your own," he said reasonably.

Stacy hated herself immediately. "Okay thennn—tomorrow? I have basketball until 4 and then band practice, but I can sneak out around 6?"

Nicholas smirked, looking impressed. "It is a date," he promised. Then he bowed to her in the strange way he always did and bid her farewell until they met again first period.

After that, the passing of the day seemed much slower than ever before and much more irritating. She had passed through first period *advanced* science class with much more ease than usual. It was test-day and she didn't stand a chance. So, she guessed in the normal pattern and moved on with her day. Upon turning in her test, she was informed that her grades were beginning to excel so high that she could attend the school of her choosing in the future.

Fantastic.

She had never wanted to get through a Monday more. But it was not so much the angst of wanting the day to hurry, of how she desperately wished they would get to work in groups in science and not have an entire day of lecture, no—it was the rest of the day that was the problem.

It was excruciatingly slow. It was the pressure. It was everything. The career fair staff returned with extra information for those who requested it. They gave a speech in third period math and threw in an extra spiel in fifth period social studies for added measure…and frustration. If she was not already prepared to slam her head into a wall by second period, she certainly was now.

Was anyone else painfully aware that you can get a bachelor's degree in one thing and then a master's degree in a completely unrelated topic? In case there was not enough to become overwhelmed with. She thought of her family again—of how Terra was a teacher by day and doctor by night and airport owner by midafternoon. But then she considered her own newfound realization and figured Tom and Terra were doing the same thing. They were not overwhelmed with choices and could not decide—they were trying to give back and restore the Grayson name.

The Grayson name. Nicholas discussed how his family was banished and his name changed because of it. She wondered, for the first time, what The Grayson name meant in Dukhovia. It was not stripped, but they were removed. Was it one or the other? What type of treatment would she get if she uttered it over there? She assumed the same mix of awe and blood curdling fear she received here.

And then she realized no one outside her family could ever understand that frustration—besides Nicholas.

And then she wondered how many other Dukhovians felt the same way.

And then she remembered that someone existed who was open to her about both of their families. And that that person had mysteriously vanished.

Swimming class being cancelled for a presentation in the auditorium was just the icing on the cake to Stacy's crappy day. On the plus side, she sat with her friends, laughing and joking around. Nicholas sat a row behind her with Rachael due to being in another class, but his sheer presence made her feel—comforted? On the downside, well, everything else.

"We all have things we want to become and we all have reasons for these desires to manifest: interest, finances, employability. For example, I hear we have a pretty famous band in the audience today."

A majority of the school broke into a sea of applause, screaming and cheering on the band as they pointed them out fiercely until the speaker found them. The remaining ten percent rolled their eyes and tried to fall back asleep.

"*Pretty* famous?" Stacy ridiculed.

"I bet you all plan to be in your band for the rest of your lives."

There was some half-hearted denial from the band and other reluctant head nods just to shut the man up, but Stacy rolled her eyes and sunk disgruntled into her seat. She knew the speaker's eyes left her, but she felt another pair boring into the back of her head.

Almost like an intuition kicking in, Stacy turned to meet Nicholas's shining, blue eyes.

Her body wanting to gasp, but, not wanting to draw attention, she tried to swallow it. The resounding sound mimicked something between a hiccup and a donkey—and drew in much more attention. Nicholas's face hinted humor, but he continued to have the glassy eyed look from this morning.

"Well, I'm here to teach you how to exert yourselves in order to climb the business ladder, make the most money, and become the very best!"

"I bet," Stacy mumbled. The eyes had not left her direction.

***

Stacy was ready to slam her head off her locker by the end of the day, even more so when she arrived at said destination and found a flyer for class president taped right on it...over a flyer for an advanced arts degree. *What*?

Nicholas had quickly left the auditorium after the speech was over. In fact, so fast, she was convinced he either had super powers and could snap his fingers and vanish or he hopped over the back of the seat. While the second was more likely, she held onto promise that the former was an option, making travel to Dukhovia much more convenient and safe.

Stacy slammed her locker shut once and then again, frustratingly shaking the lift to go over the taped papers that had gotten stuck.

After several failed attempts, someone walked up behind her, removed the papers, and closed her locker with ease.

Frustration only moderately subsiding in lieu of curiosity, she turned to meet the eyes of a tall, dark-haired man in a blue polo and a pant color so hideous Rachael would have surely gouged her eyes out. What even were they? Khaki? Green? Blackish gray? She shuttered at the very thought of her best friend's reaction.

"Ms. Matthews, I presume?" He asked in a charismatic, but to-the-point tone.

She nodded slowly.

"I am Mr. Antezi. I'm the substitute until Principal Santifini returns. It is an honor." Except his body language failed to make it seem like it was an honor.

Stacy stared back in response, a lump forming in her throat. So Santifini was going to be gone long enough that he needed a long-term replacement? She eyed him with suspicion.

"It is my understanding that you and Mr. Andrews were to serve detention together. That seems to have gotten pushed back quite a bit."

Stacy felt her blood pressure rising as he spoke. Where was he going with this? She slammed her locker shut in frustration, catching her thumb in it as she did so. "So what?" She forced out.

He looked taken aback. "*So*, it seems that this issue should be rectified immediately with your detention occurring after school tonight."

Stacy was certain steam could be seen shooting out of her ears. "No," she automatically argued. "I can't tonight. I have plans."

He laughed. "Then I suppose the consequence is working, isn't it?"

She was not sure why, but even more anger flared, bursting through her like a wildfire the moment he uttered her name. Who was this guy to come in and tell her to miss family dinner?

"It's a family thing, Principal Santifini never makes my mom stay late and has never had my cousin serve detention on a Monday."

"Well, I'm glad to hear how family oriented he is. Unfortunately, I am not Principal Santifini and I will not be making any adjustments. Good day, Ms. Matthews." And then he strode on his not nearly formal enough heel and strode away.

Stacy could not help herself. The ringing of the bell meant nothing, the whispering of the students was null. She exploded. "My mom will be in your office to complain. My whole family will."

He was quiet for a moment, as if slowly contemplating, and then, without turning around or missing another beat... "Grace is up for a performance evaluation anyway—I look forward to it."

She saw red, swinging her arms forward before she even knew what she was doing—until strong, muscular arms came in from behind her and brought them gently behind her back, replacing the feeling of anger and violence with that of safety, of security, of hope.

"I see you have met the new principal," he whispered into her ear gently.

The sensation nearly made her forget her name. Then she readjusted to Earth. "I never thought I'd want Santifini back! He basically just threatened my mom. No doubt someone who just hates our family."

He was quiet. "Does that happen often?"

"All the time and I'm sick of it," Stacy knew her anger was displaced, but she did not care. It was warranted. "Be mad and frustrated the past happened, we are too, but blaming our family? It's a joke. It makes everything complicated. Fair jury? No. Fair job interview? College application? Band gig? Nope, no, no."

He waited, patient as a saint, quiet as a mouse.

Then realization struck her. "Is that how it felt for you? People hearing your name and automatically making assumptions about you?"

He nodded slowly. "It seems we have more in common than perhaps we realized." Then his eyebrows twitched. "Including our detention time."

Stacy rolled her eyes. "UGH! I can't miss family dinner. This is something we've done every year since Tom was freed and our parents started talking again. Everyone makes it top priority. If I miss it all because of…ugh…well it's not like *I* did anything wrong." She stopped herself, realizing her anger was just going to return to Nicholas whose fault it was not and then to Santifini who was now her favorite person alive and also not around to blame. She settled for the new guy.

"And then you have your thing…" she rattled on. "Connecting with the mysterious Dukhovian channels of war and heirship."

Nicholas gave her a sideways glance. "More of a paperwork trail." He wiped sweaty palms against his pants. "However, I think there is a way we might be able to continue on with our evenings."

The halls were starting to quiet down now. The hustle and bustle began to creep behind classroom doors and nerves were splitting.

"How so?" Stacy asked.

The final bell rang out and Nicholas began trailing away. "Just follow my lead—see you in detention."

CHAPTER 51

AN HEIR IS BORN

American school in general was agonizing but the last few hours when he had plans as grand as tonight was absolutely excruciating. He found himself staring at the clock more than his paper—which he supposed was not much change from the norm.

Everything about this country was a waste of time and a waste of his abilities. Especially with the war raging on. He realized that more and more as Stacy spoke. He had been worried about his family, his future, and of course he cared about doing what was best for his country, but he felt he was finally seeing his issue clearly for the very first time—family values versus love for one's country. How did one decide how they were weighted?

His family loved his country and thus they would want him to do right by it, just as Nicholas the First had done. Despite what would or could be said about him, he was ready to move forward with the pride he did the right thing. Could Nicholas III make that same choice?

Then again, his country also boasted doing what was best for your family. So, did that mean that in order to honor his country he needed to do what was best for his individual family, as part of his own purpose?

And there was the catch-22 in which he always seemed to find himself—one end always chasing the other.

Five more minutes. He only had five more minutes to endure and then he would be on his way.

Of course, tonight's plan certainly did change—but for the better. It was true, what he told Stacy, he was not focusing where he should be. And Arkady had ordered him to use their spiritual bridge to connect and update him. Nicholas had told him he did not know how, to which Arkady simply told him to figure it out. Thus, Nicholas thought it was time. At least as a test if not to actually update him. He would be doing no such thing.

He had not yet fully decided his opinion on the female, American heir—and that was enough for him to postpone his return to Dukhovia as long as possible. He was not quite certain when The Czar expected him back—specifics were deemed a waste of time. Then again, perhaps that was something they were supposed to discuss over their channel connection. Hm.

He supposed even thinking he had a choice in what to divulge was an idea Stacy instilled in him—and that he did have a choice in the matter of his future. That he could decide what he would be known for. And so, he needed to decide:

natural Dukhovian heir that he should break every rule he ever made to save or traditional nightmare that would end the war by destroying the last piece of the First World?

Stacy was brilliantly wise. Her keen observation skills would win many a diplomacy meeting in their favor, it would protect them from war, it would be a strength Dukhovia could feel safe under. Then her ability to find reasons why imperfections were maybe not so—imperfect. How they were useful, how they were unique—it spoke Dukhovia through and through. Did that make her strong enough? Did that convince him?

His stomach tore into knots at the simple thought of breaking from his mission—yet no more than the mission itself. He found the anxiety that trapped him enough to make him question whether he was better off ending any purpose altogether. When he considered the question of breaking from it—it was less ill provoking and more stress of the confusion, of the how.

Thirty more seconds left…Twenty…Ten…

Ding! Ding! Ding!

Nicholas flew out of his seat. He was to meet Stacy in the detention hall—just past the gym and after the choir room. He discreetly and quickly moved through the halls, maneuvering through a flood of overly perfumed and underdressed classmates.

His destination was bleak. He was not certain what to expect of detention, unsure how sitting in a room for an hour was even a punishment, but he would certainly take it in comparison to what he had experienced in Dukhovia. However, the blank, cream walls and ear-piercing sound of metal on metal as the pencil sharpener was cranked seemed an expected nuisance.

Stacy had not yet arrived, nor whomever would be residing over them. He chose a desk nearest the windows and sat his bag down, then he began his mission.

It had been a while since he staged a distraction as grand as this one. He and Vuel did it only a few times, before the beatings became too significant. However, he knew the basics. He would stage a trap to be triggered at a random moment so as to not cause suspicion. The distraction would allow him to help Stacy and himself navigate to safety.

A few moments later, Stacy entered the room. Her body moved slowly, almost in hesitation as she assessed her surroundings. She settled into a chair next to him.

"So, what's the plan?" Her voice was a whisper, despite no one being anywhere near them to hear it.

"The plan is patience, Stacy Grace." He smiled gently.

Her eyebrow perched up. "When did you become such a cunning mastermind?"

"A lifelong skill," he said with confidence. Their eyes were locked on each other. Her brilliantly bright, green pair searching his for meaning.

She smiled a coy grin. "And cocky too. Full permission to judge you for the rest of your life if this fails entirely?"

He feigned upset. "Fails?"

"Fails," she solidified. Her head turned only for a moment to look towards the silent hallway. "Plans so epic that instead of glory and freedom they crash and result in our detention extended until the precipice of midnight."

"We might as well settle with the mere hour," he condoned.

"And go down as failures not even willing to fight?" She feigned disgust, holding her chest. "While I could never."

Moments later, dead silence fled the hall, filled with the noise of clacking, heavy shoes. Nicholas's heart leapt into his chest at the sound, but quickly relaxed once the door was opened by a scrawny, feeble looking man. He doubted he needed half his theatrics.

"Mr. Sanders!" Stacy shouted with enthusiasm. The social studies teacher walked in, sweat dripping from the fake hair encapsulating his forehead. "How did you get trapped in this?"

"Poor timing," the small man told her, undoing his tie and relaxing into the chair. "I am rather disappointed to see you here."

Stacy rolled her eyes, as if tired of the explanation. "I didn't do anything—and mom is not happy with this replacement principal."

"He certainly is different—however, we must persist." He folded his hands promptly and looked up. "Okay you two, the easier this goes the better. You're in here for a fight so separate to the opposite sides of the room, allow me to watch my show for the next hour, and it'll be smooth sailing."

"Really, Mr. Sanders?" Stacy begged. "The opposite side of the room? We didn't fight, Nicholas just has anger issues and they reintegrated our classes so we're practically as well behaved as a gaggle of nuns on a Friday night."

Nicholas glanced down at her. Was that truly how she portrayed him? Even now? Still? *Has* anger issues. Not past tense. He decided to interject. "I have been working on my anger and feel completely healed."

Mr. Sanders responded by looking from his watch and back up lazily. "And we're already down to 50 minutes. Time is going to fly by with you two far apart."

It was no matter to Nicholas: he knew his plan would have them out momentarily. He could care less of the teacher's request—but he understood they had to play like they cared. He did care, however, quite a bit, of the look Stacy gave him when the teacher made the request. Those large, gentle eyes looking to him for guidance, for reassurance. The look they held had something with which he was unfamiliar.

Trust.

The two sat in idle silence for time. Then a snapping noise came from around the back of Mr. Sander's desk. Nicholas glanced at Stacy who was looking to him inquisitively. Mr. Sanders had whipped his head around and was furiously looking for the source.

Then the noise stopped.

"At attention you two," he ordered, adjusting himself in his chair until he settled back.

And then a spring on the chair flew out.

And then the chair dropped him to the ground.

Stacy looked over to Nicholas, those doe-eyes brilliantly surprised. She laughed softly, hiding it quickly behind her hand.

"What on Earth…" The teacher began to examine the chair, resulting in him knocking his head on the desk. This trialed more noises which then led to a light smoke filling the room.

Nicholas jumped up from the desk, nodding to Stacy. Stacy quickly jumped up, trailing after him.

"Wait! Wait! You two get back here!"

Stacy and Nicholas laughed loudly as they entered the hall together. Stacy danced down the hallway with grace and a lightness he could only beg to know. She pulled abruptly on the fire alarm as they passed, laughing as she did so.

Nicholas could not remember a time when it was so easy to laugh, when he felt as…normal…as he did in this moment. He looked at Stacy with newfound eyes, with opened eyes.

They continued laughing until they ran out the back of the school, running together until they were in the clearing of thick forest. Then they fell to the ground, catching their breath.

"Pulling the fire alarm was a nice touch," he breathed. He lay just inches from her, their heads aligned but bodies shifted in opposite directions.

"I thank you," she grinned. "Now we can just say we were scared. How did you do all that?"

"Observation and science," he replied confidently. The chair breaking was likely to cause some type of shock which led to him triggering the traps in the desk. If I had been wrong, we would have needed a plan B."

Stacy breathed out another laugh. "I had a few tricks up my sleeve."

He turned his head to meet her eyes, intrigued. "Oh?" He pressed.

Stacy began to list things off her fingers, her tongue sliding along her perfect teeth as she spoke. "Yell fire, say I hear screaming, fake a heart attack."

"Oh, the fake heart attack would have been golden. So simple."

"Next time," Stacy laughed. Then her eyes fluttered and she too turned her head to meet his eyes. Her voice was soft, like honey. "Thank you for buying me time."

He responded with the same quiet tone. "Of course. I hope to prove to you that I am more caring than I am demonic. At least, I try to be."

She seemed torn as she responded, but she laughed and nodded her head. "You succeed."

His eyes searched hers for a time. *Charismatic. Intelligently wise. Compassionate.* The list grew and grew of ways that proved the Spirits to be indeed right. She not only was an heir, encompassing care for her country and moderate strengths, she encompassed the passion and devotion and strength to take on all of them. Perhaps even each Spirit from the First World.

Nature. Sun/Fire. Winter/Water/Moon. Ancestry. Loyalty.

"You would risk a second detention for a night with your family?" He asked softly.

Stacy nodded her head slowly, their eyes still locked on one another. "I would risk anything for my family." Her voice nearly broke. Everything about her was gentle. Was whole.

The Spirit of Ancestry was definitely in her.

"What about returning to Dukhovia? What if it was what you were called to do, but it would mean you having to leave your family behind?"

Stacy thought about it for a while. Her eyes searching his for the answers, but they gave up nothing. "That's a question I ask myself all the time. But I refuse to accept it as an issue. Will my friends come? Will it be made safe for my family to come? I don't know. But I know my purpose is there and I know my family needs me and I don't think the Spirits would ask me to choose between the two. So, until they do—I won't."

Nicholas was blinded by the amount of loyalty in which she possessed. Even he struggled with the question of family versus nation for his entire life, not understanding how to not alienate the two. "I have asked myself the same question all my life as well—I never land on an answer."

Stacy gave him a questioning look and it took every ounce of his being to not unleash his entire situation onto her. Never before had he come so close to someone understanding. Sure, Vuel was also being held against his will, his parents murdered to keep him there—but he did not have his ancestry on the line. The ability to bring the entire family name honor again by saving all of Dukhovia.

But he would not be saving Dukhovia if Stacy was meant for great peace. He would be damning them. And his name would deserve to rot in shame. And his ancestors would fully deserve to block him from a spot on their afterlife gathering, and block him any entry into The Spirit Realm.

"I have been given...a way to redeem my family, to restore our honor," he struggled for the right words, the most honest words he could divulge. It made his throat swell.

"That's wonderful."

He was shaking his head from the moment he heard her upbeat tone. "The Czar says he will make the announcement official, but I need to do something for him first. And that would bring great harm to the country."

Stacy was at full attention, her fists beginning to clench. *Loyalty.* "Why would he ever want that?"

Nicholas swallowed the lump in his throat, his mind racing. "Because he does not know." Does not know what a wonderful person she is. Does not know how strong her Spirit is. Does not know how much love she has for her country, how much *true* sacrifice.

She stared up into the tree line, the blowing wind wisping fallen pieces of pine onto them. It was freeing. It was imprisoning. He closed his eyes, feeling the chill, feeling the snow crunch beneath him, fill him through his palms and surrounding. He used the power, used it to mend his thoughts, to silence them. Nature.

"Do you have any animals?" He asked, the question seeming as sudden and out of place as it was.

"Like a pet?"

Nicholas nodded. He once had a pet. It was a cow. His father had gotten it for him as a gift and his mother was livid. He loved her with all his heart—caring for her, brushing her, cleaning her. He would be out at the barn everyday if he could.

Until he no longer could.

A tear rolled down his cheek in memory. He believed she was a trick of his father's, to win him over and then dangle over his head.

"We have a dog—Buddy. He's a Siberian Husky so he's like my own partner in crime. When no one else can withstand the cold, there he is." She smiled.

Nature.

He looked at her, just as comfortable in the freezing cold snow as he. She did not shudder nor did she curl up. No. Instead, she was basking in the fluff of the soft, chilled snow. He considered her swimming speed. He considered her inability to fall ill. It was evident just from the prediction that she had The Winter, Water, and Moon Spirits. But this solidified everything.

Stacy propped herself up on her elbow, looking at Nicholas. "What about you?"

"A cow," he answered, looking away. "My father brought her home from a trip when I was four-years-old. I called her Sila."

"Strength," Stacy stated the Russian translation of the word automatically.

He nodded. "I remember my mother scolding him. I was so afraid she would take her away. It was the one time I felt bonded to my father. But as always, she was simply trying to protect me. I sided with my father, did whatever he said as long as in my free time, I was able to care for her."

He could no longer form words, fire burning in his throat. Darkness encompassed his memory. He felt like he was falling, falling down a deep, dark nowhere. He wanted to be there. "Until he burned down the barn my uncle and I built for her with her inside."

Nicholas felt the hole in his chest grow until it felt like he no longer existed. The heaviness of it broke him in two. He could not breathe. He could not fathom another moment living the life he came to know. And so, he wept.

And then Stacy reached forward, the tips of her fingers entwining around his. "Everything is okay now," she whispered. "I'll keep you safe."

Sun.

It was true. Stacy was the strongest heir there had ever been. She encompassed not only every Spirt from the First World, but embodied them to the fullest extent. And that meant that if he was going to take her away from the world, he was going to be the sole reason Dukhovia would fall.

CHAPTER 52

THE REASON WHY

Well, they decided against lasagna."

"Oh my gosh, Stace, no one is asking about what you had for dinner. I'm referring to detention. Tell me about detention!"

"Very dingy and lacking color."

Stacy had never kept any type of secrets from Rachael before. She was not even exactly certain that was what she was doing now. She thought that she perhaps simply did not know how to put into words what took place, what she was feeling, what she wanted to do next.

But she felt like she saw him. Yesterday in the woods. That was the first time she saw him without any lens—without wondering who he was, without fearing her family, without wondering how he became the way he was, his past, or his current reason for being here. She was not with the mysterious Dukhovian. She was just with Nicholas.

And now she was ready to move forward.

She took the phone from her ear, thinking for a moment. "I don't know, Rache, I just…I can *feel* him, ya know?"

"No, but please continue."

She smacked herself, frustrated with the lack of ability to come up with the phrase. The pull she felt towards him, the net of safety, of security that existed when he was around.

The net of purpose.

"I don't know how to explain it, but he's pure. I know it."

She struggled for a while longer to explain to Rachael just how certain she was. But Rachael understood and eventually filled her with the supportive-Rachael-y words that Stacy was looking for.

She was still so uncertain. She was still so unclear on her next move…But she was ready. She was ready to tell Nicholas everything and see where it led. She felt his heart last night, his pain, his dreams. He was a victim of circumstances, yes, but he was not willing to play the victim. He wanted to take his life and Dukhovia back—and she was going to be the one to guide him.

CHAPTER 53

FREEDOMS CALL

Nicholas closed his eyes and pressed his fingers to his temples. It did not help.

He could not organize the thoughts that battled inside his head, waging a war against right and wrong. Reality and dreams.

Every thought of the unknown fueled this war. Unknowing how best to protect Stacy. Unknowing, if that was the choice he made, how he could still avenge his family, and unknowing how to even go about making this choice—because the choice did not even exist. Just the same as always.

He ran. He stated a desire to change his mind…and he was useless and therefore dead. He could not die. He could not die and be the only one in all of Dukhovia who knew of the heir that they had.

Which was why he was working day and night to work on everything he should have perfected before ever leaving Dukhovia. The thought irritated him beyond reason. They had always said that they would wait until he knew how to wield his gifts better, yet here he was, stranded in America, not knowing how to connect their Spirit's without great effort, not knowing how to deliver a message to another heir, simply nothing.

The unknown had become the mantra of this entire mission and it made him ill.

He sighed, lifting a heavy pack of nails and a hammer as he went door to door in his neighborhood, making negligent repairs. He had been spending too much time alone with his thoughts, frustration growing every time he glanced around the decaying region.

It was not as if he needed to pass the time, no, he had more than enough to do with attempting to make sense of what he was to do with his situation, figuring out the next best way to train his heir, and most importantly, practicing controlling his Spirit channels—primarily for tracking and connecting purposes.

Tracking. He winced again. The closer he and Stacy became, the heavier the lump in his stomach became.

Arkady was the most advanced tracker he ever knew. Rumors circulated that he could track even those with the smallest piece of their shared Spirit. He believed it. He had no reason not to. He had seen Arkady hunt down and find every person he ever sought after—and he was ruthless when he found them.

CHAPTER FIFTY-THREE

Nicholas gulped. If he was not back soon enough or did not figure out how to send word to Arkady where he was in the mission, he could find Nicholas in a heartbeat, or worse, he could find Stacy...

Stacy.

He closed his eyes, allowing the wind to whip at and theoretically burn his cheeks. The burn intensified when he pictured her long, soft hair flowing around her shoulders, whipping across her face, doing whatever it wanted so carelessly, so free. That was what he admired most of her. The way she threw her head back into laughter, the way she said anything that came to her mind without fear, with passion, with grace. She was careless, she was free.

Free and safe. For now.

Nicholas knocked on a door of a residence and waited for the door to be slammed in his face, only for them to reopen it when he flashed several hundred bills in their faces—typical Americans. But people in need, nonetheless.

He had not needed nearly half the money he had been given thus far, and he was getting sick and tired of looking at the rundown area and nothing being done to help. *He* was sick and tired of not being any help. Of doing nothing. Of feeling useless.

Even if he still was not helping Dukhovia, Dukhovia was always just a stepping stone to changing the world. Perhaps he did not lie to Stacy in their initial encounters, perhaps his purpose did lie in America.

At least for now.

"What the hell do you want, boy? Get off my property."

Nicholas swallowed his pride, imagining the Spirits, imagining the differences of others, letting his anger wash away. "Hello, sir. I have recently started volunteering in the area to make necessary repairs to homes using donated funds. I noticed the tarp on your roof. Might you allow me to attempt to fix it?"

"Fix it?" He spat, then laughed as though it was the most ridiculous thing he had ever heard.

"That is right, sir."

"Boy, what sort of scam are you trying to pull?" The man's tooth snagged his lip and the edge of his cigarette when he spoke, causing for a slight slur in his speech. "Get a good angle on the house to look for the best way to break in?"

Nicholas only shook his head. It was not the first time he had heard that. "No sir."

"Where's your crew? Your father?"

Nicholas shook his head, tapping his fingers against his leg. "I am here as part of a volunteer program to prove my skills and assist those in need. I am alone. I received several years of training in building and am qualified to fix a minor hole." Though Nicholas doubted that the hole he was looking at was considered minor. It was nearly the size of his end tables at the apartment and appeared to go clear through to the attic.

The man's demeanor began to shift as he listened to Nicholas's words. "That there hole's been there for years. Ain't no fixing it. There's rot in the floor boards from all the leaking."

"Then I shall fix that as well."

The man stared at him blankly for a moment, then, glanced around him, shaking on frail, bony legs as he did so. The shape and stature of the man reminded him much of Nicholas's father towards the end and it gave him all the more reason to want to rush past the unpleasantries and simply repair the roof. Most of the people gave him difficulty, but this one was certainly the worst.

As if on que, Chief Grayson pulled up in a blank truck with material. He had offered to help him further, but Nicholas refused.

"Alright then, ladder's round back. I'll see you up there."

Nicholas went in the direction of the man. The only one who saw him safely on the roof. The only man who then later brought him a warm drink and spoke with him about his life, about his imprisonment, about his change of self, about how different life was now that he was free. Free, not only of prison, but of his poor choices, of his past life, and now of the one thing he could not fix that was a daily reminder that he was still a failure. Free of the negative self-outlook. Free.

Free.

Freedom was a feeling Nicholas had never known. Not at home, not in the palace. His every move watched, judged, scrutinized. His life planned out from the moment he was born, his purpose, exactly how he would fulfill that purpose. Never time to even consider what he wanted, why he wanted it, and how he wanted to get it.

Not until he met Stacy.

Being with her was a sense of freedom and safety he never knew. It was being able to say what was on his mind without thinking of a potential consequence, a punishment, pain. It was doing and planning with ease and precision—not rushing and fearing his response, not taking his time and fearing his mentor's response. Just…free.

Gone were the chains of his life in Dukhovia—where he was prisoner to Arkady, to his family ideals, to everything around him.

He winced, feeling guilty for the thought. He had never felt that way before, at least, he had never made the connection that he was, perhaps, chained to this destiny due to his value of ancestry. The thought set his nerves on fire as he wrestled with the thought.

It was not *his* value. It was a *Dukhovian* value which made it *his* value—right? Yes. A proper Dukhovian cared for his family, cared for their character. It had been done in Dukhovia for generations. Each family was known for something and bestowed that characteristic with honor.

CHAPTER FIFTY-THREE

The Vestiv's were known for their skilled martial arts. They were called upon to train others for generations.

The Makhilov's were known for their healing, their ability to concoct any remedy for even an unheard-of ailment.

And the Demitona's...the Demitona's were known for treason. They were known for being treacherous traitors. They were ridiculed, they had lost their minds, their integrity, their goodness, their lives...all to prove their innocence.

And now that fate rest in Nicholas's hands.

How? How after his family members went through all of that, years of shame, years of torture, can he be standing in the perfect position to redeem them and change his mind? Say no? Run away? For WHAT?

For what...

For the chance to do the right thing—clearly. For the chance to create a new name for the family: the loyal ones, the strong ones, the impenetrable ones.

For the chance to see Stacy Grace, an heir more worthy of the Dukhovian throne than himself, than Arkady, than anyone he knew, rule to her fullest potential.

For a chance to save Dukhovia.

"Perhaps this heir will be a fair ruler. Assuming they will be terrible simply because they live in America is judgment, the thing we fear, is it not?"

A hot, metal bar struck him across his back, followed by several lashes. He howled out in pain, scrambling to run away.

"Guards!"

He was grabbed by both arms and his head, his chin was yanked upward, forced to look into the eyes of the Czar who was mere centimeters from his face.

"Do NOT undermine me, Sir Nicholas."

Nicholas was too afraid to speak.

"SPEAK TO ME!"

The metal rod came down on his back again, this time being held on until he could swear his insides were on fire.

Nicholas only howled out in pain.

"Until you learn how to speak to me properly, this will be your punishment! Again!"

Nicholas stood up, lifting the guards with him as he went. He turned his body and, in a grunt of anger, flung each man into the ocean below.

Arkady's smile broadened. "Very well, my student."

Nicholas received no lashes for that. He slowly began to realize that when he tried to reason with the Czar on why his plan would upset the Spirits, he was only punished until he learned his lesson.

He soon stopped having those opinions at all, until recently...because he was right.

Stacy Grace, their brilliant heir, was not doomed simply because she was from America…she was not even doomed for being female. This heir was a product of her culture, no doubt, but her wisdom surprised and surpassed him. Not to mention the fact that the Spirits were so strong in her, she had a desire to leave the country with a man she barely knew in order to protect a country she knew very little about.

Her love for her country, and for people for that matter, was awe-inspiring. Her bravery covetous worthy.

But then there was him…

If Nicholas's destiny was not to stop this heir from ruling and was not to rule himself—what was it? And where did that leave him according to the Spirits? Where did it leave his family?

Icicles began to form on his lashes the longer he worked. He did not mind. This job needed done now most of all and everyone he helped so far either told him that no one would do the work in the winter or they could not afford the repairs in the summer.

How utterly ridiculous.

For as long as he could remember, his only desire was to regain the family honor—even if that was not what the Spirits predicted of him. Afterall, in the past, his father, and his father's father for that matter, had never been given the option to fulfill their spiritual purposes due to their shame. Whatever they were called to do was swept under the table and a minor job handed to them.

As long as they lived under the shame of their falsified treason, they would never be free to serve the Spirits anyway. At the very least, he would be able to rest easy knowing he brought back the family name, right?

The day was bright. The morning air tickled the edge of a young boy's nose as he gently clasped onto the tips of his mother's fingers: for security, for strength, for warmth…

Nicholas's mother had led him down to the water. It was night and he had not seen his father all day, unusual as he typically made sure to punch a hole in at least three walls and break a few of his mother's ancestral relics before dinner time.

It was just as he remembered it, the last time they came, which seemed like so long ago now…

The bridges, white and brown, floating almost in mid-sea. They did not seem to connect to anything. The water, perfectly still for the reflection of the bright and brilliant moon. And the lanterns, dim, but present all around. He could swear he felt another, stronger presence…

"I love it here, momma," Nicholas III said, leaning his head into his mother's hip.

She tried to muster up a smile, but all that she revealed were sad and panicked eyes as she squeezed him closer to her. "I do too, my son. And you must never forget this place as long as you live. You must never forget that when you lose sight of direction, to come here. This place will always help you, to push you where you are meant to be."

"But momma, you will be here to take me, yes? This will always be our special place, just like it is now."

Annecka reached down to the boy, her eyes wildly searching his face. She held onto his shoulders. "Tell me what you feel right now, Nicholas. Tell me your desires, where does your heart call you to be?"

Nicholas was confused. He knew all about the Spirits and their call, he knew what his mother was asking, only he did not know why...

"Peace, momma. I feel peace."

Her body seemed to ease. She stood back up and the two looked over at the water, in loving conversation as they had a million times before.

"You will always make your momma proud, Nicholas, remember that."

"And I will make you and daddy proud too," he announced, a sense of humility showing through. "I will bring honor to our family."

The pair pierced the sea with adoration in their eyes. Comfort was bliss and they could remain there for an eternity or longer.

"The waters are so calm tonight, Nicholas. Funny for such an extraordinary element. It can be soft and frail, or protective, weathering even the strongest rock to make way for its purpose. Coursing through the river, determined to stay on its proper path.

"The waters always know their direction and they will do anything to travel on that way. But sometimes...sometimes the earth softens and steers it down a different path. It adjusts and follows the new path, but continues to fight.

"I admire the water for fighting for its true path, but fighting for even the most honorable cause is futile if that is not where it is meant to be."

And so, his mother had been right. The years he spent recklessly and tirelessly wearing away at a purpose not his own left him weary and deterred. The cause which his mentors spoke of appeared fruitful and just, but it would be just as dishonorable as any if it were not his to fulfill.

He glanced down at the ground, still not entirely convinced he believed that argument, still unable to come up with a reason why it would not be so.

Nicholas closed his eyes one last time, allowing a fairly recent memory to enter his mind. One in which an heir asked him a very important question and gave him a very straight response.

"And is that what you want to do? Spread peace in America?" Stacy asked him, her chin turned up toward him.

Nicholas laughed, coldly. "I do not get a say in what I want to do with my life."

"Of course you do," the heir was quick in her reply. "Everyone deserves happiness. No matter their circumstances."

FREEDOM CALLS

Nicholas reflected on every smaller call the Spirits sent his way. He had answered. He always answered their call. This was not their call.

CHAPTER 54

THE PURPOSE OF PEACE

Stacy stood looking out her front door, waiting and watching for Nicholas. She was on her tip toes, trying to not be super obvious she was looking. Unless you were on the inside looking at her—then she was as desperate as one could get.

She did not care. Her and Rachael had briefed today. They had discussed what to talk about and what not to talk about. They discussed not trying to analyze anything out of him, but enjoying him and seeing where it went. Getting to know him, letting him know her. They were treating it as what it was, a...a...a date.

The lump that had been staying at the base of her throat dropped down into her stomach where it began to bubble and erupt. Her very first date. A month ago, she had no interest in ever being on one. But now, with Nicholas...

She asked herself over and over whether she truly felt she *liked* him or just the idea of the promises he held. She tried to separate him from what he brought her regarding Dukhovia. And she supposed that brought them to today.

BUT.

Now, as she looked out the door for him, knowing perfectly well she was not hanging out with him to probe him of deep, dark secrets—she was still brimming with excitement. She was looking forward to the feeling she experienced around him, to hearing his deep laugh, to laughing at his jokes. To *him.*

A few more moments passed until Stacy saw him out the fogged-up window pane. Her heart leapt in her chest as she took him in. He dawned the same light wind breaker he wore most days, complete with black pants and a plain, blue button-up top. He took slow, deliberate strides, but seemed to be mumbling something to himself. Perhaps his own jitters.

She gave him no time to get to the door, flinging herself out on the sidewalk, just inches from his body. "Hi!" She grinned by way of greeting.

He paused, surprised, but seemingly impressed. "Good afternoon. How was band practice and sports?"

"Fine and fine," she declared happily.

"May I?" He extended his elbow out for her to grab onto.

She accepted graciously. "So, Dukhovian fun. I can't wait to find out what we're going to do. Learn how to lengthen our sentences? Go to the park and choose random, happy families to kick out?"

"Ah," he said slowly, his arm securing around hers. "So, you *do* hate Dukhvoia?"

"Fair enough," she replied. "Ice skating? Prayer? The cooking of mystical food that never quite gets finished?"

"Do they have patience in America?" He smirked.

Stacy laughed loudly, she felt her arm automatically tighten around Nicholas's, her head leaning into his shoulder playfully. Against all her previous concerns, she pointed out a field of pine trees covered in snow where her family was planning to get their tree this weekend. She showed him all the spots marked significant by her childhood: the first place she fell off her bike, the first place she beat Cody in a race. She told him about the old woman at the local bakery who always used to give her and Dan their own mini loaf of bread, because they would fight over who would carry their groceries.

She grabbed the tips of his fingers and danced down the sidewalk with him. Every moment, her heart growing closer to something other than fulfillment from Dukhovia.

"Oooo and that's where Dan got his leg stuck in the bicycle rack and my dad had to call EMT's to yank him out. They had to use pliers to get it apart. Hasn't gone near a bike since, poor soul."

Stacy pushed her hair back as the cold wind beat at it, but it flew out again despite her attempt.

"Your family," Nicholas began whatever he was prepared to ask slowly, licking his lips as he tossed different words around in his brain. "Other than Cody, what do they think of you spending time with me?"

Stacy smiled, acknowledging his insecurity. "You're Dukhovian, you're in. They're very understanding, my whole family. Not Cody. Mom's the most loving person I've ever met, she believes in the good in people and that any bad is just because of something that went wrong in their lives. Dad's the same way, but he's more insecure—guarded, I guess I would say."

"Guarded is understandable," Nicholas replied, unsteadily.

"My grandparents are the same way, of course. No mistake goes unforgiven."

He seemed to soften at that comment, while still maintaining the stiffness that descended down his body and to her arm every so often.

She paused, both her arms brushing down his as he became rigid, aware—guarded. "They would see everything I do in you and like you just the same," Stacy told him, she felt her cheeks flush with an unfamiliar feeling, but did not regret what she said.

Nicholas's own redness reflected that of her glowing face. This time, he pushed her hair back and brushed her cheek gently. Her big, green eyes gazed into his calmly, igniting a heat of passion within him. His hand held her face for a moment, his forehead pressing down on hers as he whispered to her.

"If they are anywhere near as exceptional as you, then I would be honored to meet them."

"Then you shall," Stacy said cheerfully, but a solemnness suddenly appeared across her face.

Snow began to fall faster around them, sweeping down over the houses as yards began to vanish and clear roads were a thing of the past. Traffic slowed and salt trucks became most of the remainder.

"Are you still having your dream?" He asked as they began to walk again.

Stacy bit her lip and nodded slowly.

"And worry of Dukhovia?"

She nodded again, unsure how to answer. She wanted to keep the focus on them, but she supposed they were Dukhovian. Her mouth went dry. "Always."

"I worry of them too. I worry about what could happen in the amount of time I am away."

She looked up from keenly watching her feet and met his eyes. "Is that what you were trying to figure out last night? Did you?"

He nodded. "I failed."

The word rang in the back of Stacy's mind. "What happens next in Dukhovia, if you don't succeed in helping the banished families reintegrate?"

That one was easy to answer. "Then Dukhovia falls and I earn the shame my family has worn for decades."

The thought made Stacy sick. "Is there no other plan?"

He shrugged lightly. "The war has raged on for centuries, I suppose ideas are bound to run out. Right now, the strongest security we have in terms of protection is our alliance with the United Nations."

"But I thought that meant you sided with a country—that you would help out in times of war?"

Nicholas shook his head. "Not necessarily. The United Nations is centered around maintaining global peace—the very thing Dukhovia strives for. The help is there, if necessary, but it is never an automatic obligation to join war. Different countries send peacekeepers to aid the people in times of great turmoil."

"And are they there now?" Stacy asked. "The peacekeepers?"

"No," Nicholas answered, his voice sounded uncertain. "At least not when I left. They are sort of a worst-case scenario that we do not want to utilize if not necessary."

"And then the heir, right?" She prompted. "If the heir is meant to bring great peace, the heir could end the war?"

She felt his muscles tense and then relax. He shifted his arm to stretch his muscles out before gripping back onto her arm. "Yes, that is the idea."

"Then we have to make sure the heir gets to Dukhovia. We have to make sure they're safe and that they can rule. There's only three we need to choose from, right?"

Nicholas exhaled deeply. He knew it only made sense for her to be curious about the country. It was also in her as an heir to be curious. And he supposed he owed her all the explanation he could comfortably give, all things considered.

"Technically," Nicholas said in an uncertain voice. "There can be a vast number. One may be meant to rule from this year to next, another might be destined to begin five years from now. So, it complicates things a bit. However, three were named to be stronger than any other and two of those were said to help end the war in Dukhovia."

"Fascinating," Stacy said. For the first time she used the word commonly used as a joke in her classes in a serious manner. "And you still won't tell me who the heir is?"

Nicholas held back at a smile at her attempts. He knew he would have to tell her eventually, that he was being selfish for not. But he could not lose her. He needed time.

It was only a matter of time. Her family knew and if she asked them, there was nothing stopping them from telling her. He should at least be the one who did that.

"The Czar's brother is one, is that not enough for you?" He asked with humor.

"No." She smiled. "I need to know who I'm here to protect."

Nicholas hesitated. "I am one. Second strongest. Still stronger than any heir that has ever existed, but second to the heir mentioned in the prediction."

Stacy sat with that information for a moment. She was not shocked, yet the fact that there was still another heir out there threw her through a loop. So, she was right. Nicholas was an heir. He did need protection. But he was not the heir that was at risk, not the heir that Dukhovia needed. What on earth did that mean then? That her and Nicholas were supposed to work together? Did her dream then mean him or this other heir?

"You would be an excellent ruler," she finally decided on. "Fair, kind, knowledgeable, honorable—and not at all patient."

Nicholas's cheeks filled with color and he smiled. Then the two veered off toward a thickening of trees—the same wooded area that eventually led to the spot they were in behind the school.

They kept walking as the snow continued to dance beautifully around them. Their trail of white and slush started to head into a far-off field, away from the town. The tall trees stood in the background. Dark and although so close, they seemed far enough away to not be of much concern to them. They now seemed to be too far for anyone to hear them and too far to be seen.

"Dark and dreary screams fun to me," Stacy joked. She felt no fear.

Nicholas looked at her crossly but mustered up a chuckle. "Do you have any other guesses, my dear American?"

Stacy clicked her mouth as she leaned her head back and thought. "Amusement park, concert...simply a casual walk in the park?" She added, noting his tensed expression.

He turned his expression quickly back to a smile. "We do things a little differently in Dukhovia."

Nicholas suddenly placed both of his hands on either side of Stacy's waist. He lifted her into the and spun her in a graceful loop. It felt like the most freeing moment in the world. Then he made for her hands, hesitating as he held onto the backs of them—a jolt still rushed through her. It felt faster than ever. Peace. Comfort. Assurance. Exhilaration.

He dipped her down, his crystal blue eyes meeting her large, green pair innocently. She grinned broadly at him and he could not help but smile a shy smirk in response.

"So, *this* is what Dukhovian assassins do for fun?" Stacy pondered curiously. "I could get used to this."

Nicholas was taken by surprise again. Although her actions and expressions clearly told him that she was not afraid, her words added onto the reality. He dropped his hands and looked at her.

"You do not seem like most Americans." It was a merely curious observation, but she knew he was digging and wanted to learn more about these strange Americans.

She chuckled. "Oh yeah, in what ways?"

"Well, for example, you came off into a dark and dreary forest...alone...with a...Dukhovian assassin, as you put it. Happily, instead of cowering in fear of the evil that is right beside you."

"I don't see you as evil," Stacy said with a smile. "I see you as lost."

Their eyes met for a moment of silent voices and chattering minds.

Nicholas's heart stopped. Stacy certainly was unlike the American that was described to him and certainly different than anyone he had ever met. Even in Dukhovia. He was expecting someone who just went along with the crowd, unable to think for herself, and only thinking about how things would fair in her favor.

To be entirely truthful, he had a moment of thinking she was that type of person when she reacted to her detention, but then she went on to show care for a—as she put it— Dukhovian assassin. She went from watching him mercilessly attack her classmates, no, her *friends*, to making him feel like he had a choice in this situation. Before their conversation, sure he debated it with himself, but never actually saw himself as having the option to back out. She made it seem like such a simple option. To simply say *no*.

And now here they were, swaying to the sound of unheard music, close as he ever hoped to be. Close enough to kill her before she even had time to take her next breath.

Her eyes beamed into his with happiness. She was growing close to her purpose, a purpose of true honor and dignity. But he...he was nothing but a criminal with not even his fellow cronies to return back to.

"How can you be certain I will not bring you harm?" He asked her calmly, her face hidden in his shoulder as they danced.

Stacy shook her head. "I can't. But I can trust who you seem to be and if I turn out wrong, then I'll deal with it then. But I just know."

He was silent. His lips grazed across the top of her head until his chin rest lightly there. "Come with me, there is more."

The two walked carefully through the thick of the trees, darkness pouring in around them, yet somehow their path seemed clearer than ever before. Suddenly, when the winding path came to an end, Nicholas paused, holding back a tree branch for Stacy to hesitantly pass through, heart thudding the entire time.

Her gasp when she looked around echoed throughout the trees, causing a flutter of wings and crows throughout the tree tops.

The sight waiting for Stacy looked straight from—Dukhovia. She was not sure how he had done it, but he had sculpted to absolute perfection, intricate buildings, temples, and statues mimicking their land, all purely from ice and snow. She had known him to be talented, to be thoughtful, but to go to such a measure.

She walked around each and every sculpture, her eyes brimmed with tears, but giving each one the care and observation it so deserved. They did not seem fit to only be looked at for a mere hour or less, they were fit to be longed after for all of eternity.

"Were we in Dukhovia," he began through a raspy voice, "I would take my time to properly court you. I would never display the temper you have seen, I would never beg your forgiveness and trust as I do now. I would not feel the rush and pressure that I now feel.

"I would find out your interests, your loves and displeasures." He partnered this statement by revealing to her the contents of a nearby picnic basket. Inside there were a variety of foods: from Dukhovian traditional to the greasiest Wally's burger she had ever seen. He then lay his hand just to the side of the picnic basket, where a small, ancient radio sat. He pressed a few buttons until light, gentle music poured.

If Stacy's face could hold anymore shock, could elicit anymore tears—they were now present. She looked almost in a daze, the world spinning around her as she realized just what she had in front of her.

Protect him. Care for him. Trust him. She had to.

"I so desperately want to bring you to Dukhovia when it is safe for you, Stacy Grace. To take you to our finest plays, to walk our more sacred streets. But until then, I will bring every piece of Dukhovia to you—and every piece of you to Dukhovia. It is what we all need."

CHAPTER FIFTY-FOUR

"Oh, Nicholas." She could not stop herself any longer. She lunged at him, nearly knocking him to the ground with the force of her embrace.

He clutched onto her, tightly, breathing her in, squeezing as if she might disappear as if this all might just be a dream.

Stacy was not sure what she imaged out of the date—but this was everything she could never fathom.

"There's one more thing…" And then he bent down, clicking his tongue and rubbing his fingers together until animals began to creep toward him. A silent fox, a gentle raccoon, a fearless chipmunk.

She laughed a sound of pure delight to all who could hear it.

"All heirs have one particularly strong gift. Mine is nature. Even if I had no one to talk to back home, no one to be there, the very trees I felt bend to my comfort."

She remained absolutely speechless. Joy and awe similar to when she watched the plant wither and grow in his palm that day in class. She had learned more and experienced more in this moment than in her entire life. This was truly the moment for which she had been waiting.

Nicholas made to the picnic basket, opening it up with care to deliver her a few options.

"I wish I could have met you in Dukhovia," she began her words slowly, licking her fingers as she sucked down a burger as if it were the first meal she had all day—she was pretty certain it was. "To have all the time in the world, to learn all the things, to save each other from loss and disappointment and confusion. And I'd give you my forgiveness and my trust every single day—because you deserve it."

Tears brimmed Nicholas's eyes with a deeper message seeming to scream out from their shine. But he did not say it, instead, he began to speak in words that could have been a lesson. He returned to her earlier question, not refusing to answer like so many times before, but simply returning to it at the proper moment.

"To protect *any* of the heirs is not an easy task," his voice was gentle as he delivered the words. "It's as if you are going up against a nation's entire army and only you stand on the defensive."

She took her time replying, staying just as silent as he for as long of a moment as he. "I don't know who this other heir is and if I can protect them." Her voice was the same gentle, soothing tone. "But I know I'm meant to protect you. And I know you're worth the battle."

He froze, backing away to face her now very close face. She was tracing his jawline with her hand, studying every inch of his face with detail. Her hand made its way down his neck and lingered just for a moment over his chest before grazing the scar along his arm.

And then she made her way to his hand. She held it up until his palm was facing her. Slowly, cautiously, she traced the outline of his hand. The wave of intensity hit her, but it was manageable. She slowly moved in, working her way further and further into the center of his palm.

As she did so, the intensity of the feeling only grew. She found it difficult to stand, overcome with heaviness from the feeling, rather than lightheadedness. Her vision began to blur, but her heart, her entire self, felt—stable. Confident. At ease.

Nicholas caught her hand before it dropped and took the other one, bringing them both close to his mouth. He hesitated for a moment, then stopped himself from what he was about to do, instead deciding to go back to spinning and dancing with her quickly.

She laughed, trying to catch up with him until she fell dizzily in the snow beside him.

"Hello." He whispered to her. He was now on top of her, breathing hard. His hands held her head and they looked adoringly into each other's eyes.

She laughed. "Say hi, you dork." She pushed him off and they both chuckled softly.

He smiled at her dreamily as they rose to their feet, swaying once more.

"You are an incredibly brave and selfless person, Stacy Grace Matthews, do you know that?"

Stacy looked at him with a challenging smile. "And why's that?"

He looked her up and down, unable to keep the smile from growing with every thought. Unable to stop his brain from telling his heart that it did not deserve such pleasure.

"You have a heart of gold," he stated plainly. "You care so much about saving a person you don't even know from a person you just met." He wanted to say more but froze.

Stacy remained quiet, waiting for him to continue. What on *Earth* did that mean?

"And…I have never had anyone to speak with about my parent's deaths or my family. I have never felt comfortable with allowing anyone to listen to my thoughts and feelings—about anything regarding my life." He paused a moment. "It's helpful to have someone who also—understands the battle."

Stacy's heart was racing. She was not certain why she felt so safe around him, why her heart was telling her to stay while her brain told her to run or at least think twice. But here she was. And here she'd remain. At least until the oxygen returned to her brain.

Out in the distance, music began to play. They did not know exactly where it was coming from, but the soft, slow tune melted their hearts and drew them to one another even more. Their hands synched up as best they comfortably could and they rocked, or stood, or moved, or remained still, anything to just be close to the other in that moment where they both knew the other was what they needed.

CHAPTER FIFTY-FOUR

Neither Stacy nor Nicholas could describe the bond they felt in that moment. It was more than their destiny's intertwining. It was more than the glory of figuring themselves out. Their hearts and boundaries were beginning to come undone as their heart strings tightened around one another. They felt close to one another, they understood each other in ways no one ever had.

Nicholas put his arm around Stacy's waist and her arms went instinctively around his neck. Next thing she knew, he was spinning her and dancing with her in the most magnificent of ways. She felt like a princess.

She loved this moment. She yearned for this moment all her life. Someone to understand, someone to open up to. But again, Nicholas had said too much and yet not enough. She wanted to protect someone she did not know…the heir…from someone she just met…that had to be Nicholas. So, if Nicholas was sent here to protect the heir and reunite the banished families, why was he talking as if he was the threat?

CHAPTER 55

THE GIRL PROPHESIED

$\mathcal{N}$icholas closed his eyes. The swelling around his temples seeming to rise as he did so. How simple it was to block out his surroundings in Dukhovia—when people gave two thoughts about another's privacy and sanity in general. Here, in his apartment…Here, in this country…There was too much noise. Too much shouting and unnecessary scolding. It made zoning in on his senses difficult and meditation near impossible.

Even now as he stood in the shower, his hand resting against the blood-coated shower wall. He had made a promise to himself, well, to Stacy really, although it was a secret promise. He was going to stop hurting himself. Ever since the night she came over and ransacked his apartment looking for something to clean his wound, he feared her worst thoughts. Did she see the shower? What did she think if so?

Well, she was still coming around him, so either she knew it was self-inflicted or she assumed he was murdering people in his apartment and was okay with that. He doubted the latter.

He scoffed at the idea, thinking of the difficulty he had been having in meditating on his feelings, attempting to ring in his anger. It felt like no use much of the time. He had too much to be angry about. Even as he got closer to Stacy, he found the anger became worse rather than better—he had no way out. Here he was in this picture-perfect life, a girl of immense bravery whom loved Dukhovia and was born for greatness. But sentenced to death.

He smashed his fist into the shower wall, blood poured from his knuckles as the sound of crunching plastic brought him to attention.

So much to be angry about—including his apartment. Doable and livable for his short stay, certainly, but the poor construction irritated him beyond belief on a daily basis. The walls crumbling, the windows allowing howling winds to enter in, the continuous banging of his neighbors in the odd hours of the night. That one certainly tested his ability to restrain himself. In Dukhovia, he would have gone up to their room and killed them both then slept peacefully. He could not leave such messes here.

Although he could cover up his crimes before the police even knew about them and would be able to free himself from prison without much difficulty, Nicholas could not risk losing what he finally had gained—Stacy's trust.

Huh.

Their very first encounter he proved to be a menace. He would have never expected anyone to trust him under the circumstances. To trust a man whom brought harm to her best friend and was keeping too many secrets. To willingly befriend a man who was unsafe and insane was merely a wish.

But she did.

He supposed he thought it rather expectant. Of anyone, he would expect a dimwitted, American to be the one to go after the man surely for his looks. That was his plan, after all. How shallow.

But that was not Stacy.

Nicholas rinsed the blood off his body and turned off the shower. Stacy. He closed his eyes and breathed in her name, her presence. Her everything. She trusted him. And while his goal was to travel these many miles and earn that trust to wear as a badge of honor in completing his mission, having it now fulfilled him in a different way, in a different place.

He squinted against the sound of a large, metal object hitting the same wall for the fourteenth time. It happened every night—usually at six, when the couples below him got home, but it could also happen at one am, they did not discriminate.

Everyone in this country was everything he expected them to be. The arrogance, the ignorance, the complete disregard for the planet and common sense...

Except for Stacy.

Stacy was not like that at all. His heart welled up at the thought, a feeling of safety, of desire that he had not felt in such a long time he did not think he could ever fathom to again. Stacy. Stacy Grace.

He was wrapped in a towel, sitting on the bathroom floor. His eyes were closed, picturing her face. Muttering her name on his lips felt good. He considered her lips, the ones he so desired to feel yet had not. Out of fear. Out of respect. Out of waiting anxiously for the proper moment.

No, she was not the expected American to any degree. Even when she should have been angered beyond words with him—she only showed him kindness. So unfamiliar. So unique.

He struggled with the impulse to put his clothes on and travel to see her right now. To wrap her in his arms and run. No, he had to do things right. He had to do things carefully. But what was right? What was careful? How on Earth was he to get out of this mess?

Stacy had proved to not be entirely selfish and proved to love Dukhovia—but did that mean she was not a threat? No. He hardly wanted to have the thought. Stacy was exactly what Dukhovia needed. Her assertiveness, her passion, her devotion. And her American customs...would those, if brought to Dukhovia, even be a downfall?

There was her band. The instruments, the sound, they did not synthesize the way music did in Dukhovia. She could not bring that type of sound to Dukhovia.

Still. Stacy did not have blind ill-intent when she played. She showed passion towards it, but was not blind to her individual potential either. In fact, she felt called to the exact purpose she was meant to fulfill. Rarely did that happen, even for an heir. She played to save her family. She played *for* family.

Ancestry. Passion. Purpose.

All Dukhovian qualities.

It was not black and white. It was never black and white.

There was the way she spoke. Completely barbaric, not at all as though she came from a civilized, respected place. But that was how she was able to maintain that assertiveness. Perhaps Dukhovia was confused on what was traditionalizing and what was simply…different. Adaptive rather than blunt change.

He shook the thought from his head. He was beginning to lose himself. Befriending Stacy, falling in… No. Understanding American ideals, learning about the culture… what was he *doing*?

And then, complimentary to everything else, there was his complete and total loss of control. He had never come so undone in front of anybody. This country was truly getting to him.

No, Stacy was getting to him. And he wanted her to. He wanted her to be the calm to his fire. He wanted her to cover his wounds, to be the peace that he so desperately needed.

Thinking of Stacy, it was suddenly much easier to tune everything else out. He got up from the floor, throwing on a pair of shorts, and sat crisscrossed on the floor. He breathed, reaching the state he desired.

He was at peace. His mind was blank. His heart beat slow. Wisdom entered his mind and his heart.

He breathed.

He felt direction, guidance. A tug on his heart to follow the train of his previous thoughts. Then stop.

He breathed.

"Czar, I am certain that it is a complete mistake, but some of the country has heard that you plan to rebel against the next heir when he comes to power?"

The entire capital city of Vodva as well as several others surrounded the palace in a formal manner. Green shrubbery lined the castle as flowers that were not in the greenhouses bloomed fresh from the grass around them.

It was the Czar's weekly address to his people. Every week he stood outside the palace and delivered his plans for Dukhovia, his worries, his victories…

"Though unfortunate to admit, for several reasons, your rumors speak to the truth."

No one spoke. They waited for a completely sound and logic explanation, they waited for a punchline…they trusted their ruler.

THE GIRL PROPHESIED

"On December 25, 1990, our noble Shaman told of an heir stronger than any we had ever seen before. They told of an heir strong enough to influence our entire country if not the entire world. This is the type of heir we have long awaited to bring the ideals of Dukhovia to the universe!"

The people waited.

"However," he hung his head. "Such will not be the case. This heir is living in America! While many of you know of the ideals and customs brought up from this country, there are several who do not. This country is shameless, solving all of their problems with violence and rage." He closed a fist and formed a very convincing look of anger. He did not have to falsify much.

"Americans are quick to follow the path of others, never finding their own. Americans will judge a person they just met based on visible criteria on a mental checklist that deems this person invaluable, never attempting to know the person's story, their individual strengths..."

Half of the people looked frightened, another half enraged, and a handful skeptical.

The Czar overlooked his subjects and said with a final boom of his voice, fearlessly and patriotically: "In the era of our nations birth, listening to the call of the Spirits without questions took precedence. But we live in a different world today. A world where our fellow man has decided to turn its back on tradition. A world where banishment has taken place and Dukhovian's have become outsiders whom cannot be trusted.

"The world has updated and no longer does having Dukhovian blood mean those born of it are virtuous. We must never let these types of ideals infiltrate Dukhovia. We must never let these ideas destroy all that we have worked to build! Dukhovia is the only country still following the ideals we were always meant to. Let us not prove to the Spirits that we are anything less than deserving of all they gave us! On-la!"

"On-la!"

Soon thereafter, several of the people known to openly protest The Czar the night of his admission began to disappear. The ones who eyed the growing greenery around The Czar with suspicion and fear.

Even later, the country began to split. Fighting in marketplaces and such public arenas became frequent. Still, there were those who were not at the meeting that night, those who denied that any such rebellion was even happening...

The Czar told the country of an American leader that they all had to fear. Nicholas himself was disgusted with the thought of what was described to him coming in to rule. And meeting any of the people he had met confirmed that he did not want any Americans leading his land.

But Stacy was not the girl he foretold of. She was much more.

CHAPTER 56

FAMILY HONOR

"Nope, you're done. Never speaking to you again."

"I would like to make up for it, Stacy Grace. Please."

Stacy sashayed through the halls, a broad smile on her face as Nicholas tailed her. He had been late to school today and thus missed their lunch date. Forgiveness could not be extended around mealtimes.

"May I walk you home?" His voice became that tender, magical sound that she melted under.

UGH.

Stacy nodded her head once, her own hesitations growing at what she had planned to ask him over lunch. "Actually, I wondered if you would want to stay over for dinner tonight. It's totally up to you, my entire family will be there so it might be a bit awkward, but I'd love for you to meet them and they're all really nice and…"

"I would love to."

Stacy grinned, joy at his answer and the fact that he stopped her rambling before it could get too far.

It was perfect. Not only would she see how he interacted around them, but she would be able to expose him to something he had not had in a long time.

"It is not even Monday night," he seemed to question as the two began their walk.

Stacy smiled at the recognition. "You would be correct. We're actually celebrating. Dan is leaving for some big fancy trip at the end of the week and it's sort of a good luck send off. Wednesday seemed to be the most flexible day."

Nicholas's eyes flickered. "Are you certain it is okay for me to attend?"

Stacy nodded once, so certain she saw the assurance wash over his face, despite the fact she failed to actually tell anyone in her family. "Absolutely."

Nicholas moved the papers he was holding to one side, aiming for a trash can at the end of the hall. He seemed to pause, the contents of the paper catching his eye.

"Class president?" He questioned.

Stacy nodded, beginning to lead them out the door. She took the paper off him and chucked it at least semi-close to the trash can. "Yep. It's, um, sort of like the leader of the class. They plan fundraisers, school trips, things like that." She noticed a change in her mood as she talked about it, wanting to kick over the trash can and stomp it to pieces.

"You do not like this presidency?" He asked her, reading her face.

She shrugged. "I was class president for the last few years, it's just…it's stupid."

"Nothing you have to say or have an opinion on is stupid, Stacy Grace. Whatever your feelings are, I am certain they are justified and I am interested to know them."

Stacy felt the burn of her cheeks again. How could she argue with such confident flattery? "Well, I guess it just feels too—insignificant." Who was she using these big words? "It's not like if I ever get to Dukhovia I expect to overthrow The Czar and sit on the throne while the people worship at my feet, but it is meant to mimic holding a position of change and power. I just don't feel strongly about changing anything at school. But Dukhovia…"

Nicholas seemed to be letting her words sink in. For a second, she was half afraid he was going to overreact again, but then instead of the intensifying look of disdain growing, he became almost softer. "Tell me more of your plan…to help Dukhovia?"

She sat with that for a moment before responding, coming to terms with the reality of her answer. With the fact that she could add little onto what she already told him last Friday. "Okay, full transparency—I failed government. Not that they would necessarily teach the Dukhovian political system, *but* I'm not exactly sure how I would maneuver everything. *But* my mom mentioned how Tom was part of the military. I forget the name they had for themselves. I think I would start there. Hear each side.

"Embarrassing as it is, I feel like I don't know enough about Dukhovia to help nearly as much as my heart is telling me to. But I know that as the options presented themselves to me, there's nothing I wouldn't do to revive Dukhovia to what it was in the First World."

Nicholas responded by removing one hand from his jacket and dipping it down between them. As if asking for permission, he put his hand out towards Stacy.

She responded by glancing anxiously in its direction, her stomach twisting from Dukhovian confusion knots to first love, erm, first crush thoughts. She forced a nervous smile and their fingers intertwined. The power that shot through her felt different now. Not something that knocked her off her feet, not something to run from, but something she craved.

"The beauty of your views on Dukhovia are liberating. Dukhovian history has been rather unfair to many of us and I am not certain there is a good enough reason for that, but there is reason. I do believe that the Spirits watch over us as much as they can, even given our circumstances, and sometimes our trials are meant as the training that prepares us for the final battle. Perhaps that is why you are in America."

Stacy thought about it. She asked herself the question time and time again—why would the Spirits lead her family to America but leave her heart in Dukhovia.

A trial, a test. Nicholas was right, it did seem unfair and unjustified, but there was so little they did not control, perhaps they had to work with what they did.

"I think that's what I like to believe," she agreed. "That these things happened to improve my family, to build them into who we are. I mean, we were always close and resilient, but who knows, maybe Tom and Terra never would have opened the hospital or the airport if they didn't feel like they had to make amends for all the people they hurt or safely get Dukhovian's into America."

She paused, watching Nicholas stiffen back up.

"How do you feel about them? About the circumstances and how American's and Dukhovian's view Tom and Terra?" Nicholas asked the question gingerly, worry seemed to be increasing within his eyes.

"Well, I don't know how Dukhovian's feel about them. Maybe that's why it's so hard for them to talk about Dukhovia: they were already banished wrongly and now Dukhovia hates them?" She looked to him for guidance on the subject and his response reflected regret on pushing the subject.

"Tom and Terra are well known for several reasons in Dukhovia and I would assume the split of those who support them and those who despise them is about as even as it is here in Dukhovia."

"Half and half? Seventy-thirty?"

"Half is fair," Nicholas responded, carefully. "If anything, the pool is more in their favor than not."

That thought improved Stacy's mood. Perhaps it would be something she would share with them, if they did not already know. "I feel ashamed," Stacy finally answered. "I feel ashamed when I think about the circumstances, but when I just think about my family, I feel angry. Angry because I know the truth and I want everyone else to know too. Not only do I want them to know, I want them to fully experience what I do. I feel like that's the main part. That's the part that matters most. I know they're happy and they love us, but are they fully happy if they can't share these things with the country that means the most to them? The people that do."

Stacy paused for a while, then asked. "Do you feel that way about your family?"

And then the face was back—the ghost, the white, the pain. Everything that the last ten minutes worked to undo had been restored and he was stone. "Yes," his answer was slow, as if the words themselves hurt coming out, as if he had to force each syllable... until they flowed like an unlatched river gate. "I feel disgusted and humiliated to know that people believe such horrendous lies about my ancestors. I feel trapped, screaming to let everyone know the truth and even though they stand right before me, they do not hear me. It is the most infuriating feeling I have ever felt.

"I feel like I must hide, as though I cannot show my face, say my name, wear our family crest. I feel disappointed, rejected, and hopeless."

Stacy waited for him to finish, the desire to touch him again resurfaced, but she decided against it this time, waiting patient. "What can fix it? What do we need to do?"

Stacy watched as a simultaneous huff in Nicholas's chest fought with an exasperated breath—a breath of relief that seemed trapped for a long time. "Honor Dukhovia. Honor it in such a way that the heroism I exhibit outshines the plague of doubt that has already been cast."

She watched the flash in Nicholas's eyes as the words seemed to flicker from grief, to regret, to frustration, and back. He swallowed and with the lump in his throat, all emotion seemed to follow.

"It seems you might already have an idea in mind to do that?" She waited patiently, determined to get an answer.

He nodded his head slowly, reluctantly. "Anything and everything The Czar demands of me. Whether I agree with it or not, whether it is truly honorable or not. That has been the tale of my life for the last fifteen years. Eventually I will do something grand enough to earn back the respect of my nation."

Sadness filled Stacy with each word. It was not necessarily his story, she already knew it. It was more. It was the feeling of resorting to this lifestyle. It was the passion and devotion for a country that he loved that did not show him the love in return. It was that he was willing to risk everything for that country, those people, and his ancestors.

It was the pull to do something about it.

Almost immediately, she was shaking her head. "No."

He stopped in his tracks, raising an eyebrow in her direction. They were coming up closer on the houses now and both wondered how the conversation would fizzle once they reached the destination. Stacy was not blind to the slowness Nicholas's steps began to take.

"No?" He questioned lightly, with almost a tone of humor.

She stopped too and eyed him directly, firmly asserting herself. "No. No one else gets to determine what matters to your family and what makes them unique and honored. They might never know. Dukhovian or not. *You* know what makes a Demitona a Demitona and so *you* are the one who gets to decide what would bring them honor."

Nicholas was smiling, that brilliant, shining, worn smile. A smile that perhaps used to reach the tops of his cheeks and stretch all the way to his ears, but now stopped short just at his jawline. The sparkle, the familiar, dazzling and comforting sparkle of his eyes shining even greater with pools of tears welling in them.

"Stacy Grace…" he was reaching for her again, but his hand seemed to stop at the midpoint of its destination, then he just looked at it and dropped it. "You are right and yet—yet the Demitona's want and need Dukhovia to have a respectable name for them. Not just ourselves."

Stacy shrugged her shoulders. "Maybe the two go hand in hand. Maybe they honor you because you stood your ground as a proud Dukhovian, unwilling to take anyone's crap."

The two stood eye and eye for a while. Neither willing to break the trance, neither willing to lose the moment of connection.

Then, Nicholas looked towards the houses on his right and back to Stacy. His lip quivered before he spoke. "I am dishonored and disliked by much of my home in Dukhovia. I am disliked by your friends. What if I am also displeasing to your family?"

Stacy considered his words and took the shot through her heart that it rattled inside of her. Then she looked towards the three homes making up her little family and smiled. "They aren't often displeased, your highness. Come on!"

Wrapping her hand around his wrist, she pulled him along. Hopping over snowbanks and twirling beneath his arm over patches of ice, the two finished their journey on Stacy's front porch.

"Ready?" She asked, encouragement reflected in her eyes.

Slowly, he nodded his head in agreement and watched as Stacy pushed open the door to her home.

CHAPTER 57

INNOCENCE BROKEN

$\mathcal{T}$he home was extravagant. Far more impressive than any Dukhovian home he had ever seen, including the palace. The walls and furniture were neatly kept. Each piece of furniture made of some type of soft, luxury material of which he was unfamiliar. Dukhovia did not have soft arm chairs and…she had called them…couches? In their place would have been wooden carved rockers and chairs.

Accenting each piece of furniture were more, seemingly unnecessary objects. Faux plants and other decorations sat atop tables holding light fixtures.

As if the furnishings were not enough, the house itself boasted glossy and elegantly placed tile. Countertops which perfectly complimented tiled…um…backsplash…also begged for attention.

Nicholas swallowed the lump in his throat, though he had to admit, standing next to Stacy, he felt much more confident that he could handle the new changes around him. Though struck with fear and nerves, he followed closely behind her as she made her way through a sitting room and into the large kitchen, in search of the woman whom raised such a passionate, caring, devoted…

Marry her already, will you?

Shove off.

The brilliant smile, the one that he was beginning to notice warmed his heart and brought him back to reality, flashed up at him. All thoughts emptied, all worries. She had said something that was important, he assumed. She seemed to be waiting for a response. Unwilling to explain his internal battle, he opted for a soft head nod and hoped that answered whatever she asked appropriately. She responded with a wide grin that seemed to seal the deal.

"Mom!"

The moment the word left her mouth, he was at attention. Sweat formed at his brow and neckline, dripping down his back. His heart raced so loud he was certain the woman entering would be able to hear it.

But the gentle woman who entered gave no indication towards his reaction. Nor did she seem to carry any suspicions from that of which Stacy's friends or cousin may have told her. Instead, a tall woman with dark hair and brilliant green eyes identical to Stacy's approached him. Her smile and body language were as relaxed and welcoming as he might expect her to approach an old friend. She was gentle and kind and eager.

"Mother," Stacy had moved forward in front of Nicholas, presenting her hands in his direction. "May I introduce to you, the talented, the exquisite, the fantabulous... Sir Nicholas Aloyshenka Aleksis Demitona the Third."

Nicholas bowed the Dukhovian respect bow, closing one hand around a closed fist and leaning forward ever so slightly. He watched Stacy's expression change out of the corner of his eye, but could not make sense of the reaction—confusion? Likely.

"Ma'am it is an honor to be in your presence and I am grateful to be in your home."

Grace smiled and nodded in return. "Please, call me Grace. And the honor is all mine. I have heard many things."

Nicholas tensed up.

"All good," Stacy assured him.

"Eh, mixed," her mother offered, honestly. "But I will make that decision on my own." She started moving about the kitchen, thrashing through pots and pans as she continued speaking. "I was always told that there are three sides to every story: his side, her side, and the truth. I've learned the opposite from my life growing up. There's only one side and everyone else is just too stubborn to admit it."

Nicholas watched with awe as the woman moved about the room, laughing and joking in moments where a typical person might be stressed. It was easy to see where Stacy's humor was passed down from—as well as her poise and her mannerisms. The mother-daughter duo were complete copies of each other.

And he could see where she got her warmth.

Grace took any chance she could get to include Nicholas, to ask him questions, to check on his comfort—and provide it. From a simple placement of her hand as she moved around him, to a one-armed hug as they spoke and laughed. Grace made the thick tension that rose up in Nicholas when he was around new people subside and in its place was a home-like familiarity that he had never known.

And it made him sick.

They are good people.

He knew it. He knew it was a chance before ever getting on the plane. Yet, he expected...perhaps he was not fully certain what he expected. Decent, perhaps. Instead, he found a goodness he never knew existed.

Slowly, other members of Stacy's family started to trickle in. Her father—Kevin. Nicholas was surprised, acknowledging what Stacy had told him about him not being biologically related. They too shared similar physical characteristics—the infamous black hair and green eyes all Grayson's possessed. The way they shadowed each other, interacted, their words bounced off of each other as if mirroring each other in perfect unison.

CHAPTER FIFTY-SEVEN

Then her brother walked in. Daniel, whom they referred to as Dan. The star of the evening. If Stacy and Kevin were similar, and Grace and Stacy were clones, Kevin and Daniel were also each other's doppelganger. Not only did the green eyes and black hair match, but a slight elongated face and a continuously pained, albeit, stressed, expression.

Kevin and Daniel seemed to watch Nicholas a bit more wearily. Though both just as accepting and warm in their words, their body language and eye movements told a different story. Nicholas could hardly blame them.

"Nicholas, what part of Dukhovia are you from?" Grace asked as she improperly kneaded bread. He watched as she glanced back at her recipe, squinted, and threw it off the counter with a shrug.

He felt his stomach drop. Questions. Anytime there were questions, he did not know how to answer. He could not respond with the snideness he would in Dukhovia. He was not meant to tell the truth, but a lie could ruin everything. Opening up could ruin everything.

He weighed the pros and cons fervently and found himself with the truth.

"South Gate," he replied, swallowing the thick lump forming in his throat. "Near Plodor."

Nicholas watched for her reaction. Plodor was farming land—known to be the poorer region of Dukhovia, at least by those whom inhabited it. The Grayson's, he doubted, had any stake in Plodor. But surprisingly, Grace reacted with pleasure at the news.

"Ah Plodor, near where daddy grew up."

Nicholas jerked his head up. The Grayson's were thought to be from North Bridge, Lunovny, specifically. Rich military background in the beginning. Then his wife, Terra, she was a bit more difficult to track, not knowing her own history, but was thought to come from the industrial part of East Valley.

"I did not realize..." Nicholas began.

"No, likely not," her facial expression seemed to change now...almost fade. "Dukhovia seems to be a mess of half-truths these days. The one place we didn't expect it." Her face fell then brightened again as she made direct eye contact with him. "Is that where you grew up?"

Nicholas blinked away. His thoughts seemed to be jumbling together in a rush, like books flying off a bookshelf into a pile at the floor. "Sort of."

Grace seemed to absorb the emotion he put off. She looked from her bread to him slowly. "Stacy filled us in on your family history. Who took care of you after your parents?"

Nicholas looked around for a lie, but he considered the upbringing of the woman he spoke to. The woman whom, as it was told, practically raised herself for years after her own parent's lives were turned into an unspeakable nightmare. The woman whom risked her life to search for them and restore the family she now celebrated and made tough bread for.

Nicholas cleared his throat. He decided to walk up to her and start to offer assistance. "Do you mind if I help?" He asked.

"By all means," she laughed, backing away without a second thought.

"The bread is going to be dense," he mentioned. "You want to work it just enough then set it on the stove to raise as you wish."

Grace shot an impressive glance at her daughter whom was sitting perched at the kitchen island watching with wonder and awe.

"He was taught to cook by his long, lost best friend," Stacy informed her.

"Aw. Long and lost?" Grace sighed sarcastically.

"And best," Stacy agreed.

Grace put her hand over her heart with remorse.

Nicholas formed a small grin and continued to speak as he formed the bread and set it on the stove. "I trained in the military in my early years and quickly became a leader of sorts. The Czar had handpicked me for a mission that I apparently proved in the military that I was able to fulfill. So, here I am."

"Here he is," Stacy finished.

"The military?" Dan interjected. "How old are you?"

"Life is a lot different in Dukhovia than it is here, Daniel," Kevin jumped in. He had walked upstairs to change after work. He apparently worked in some type of shop which did not fit the expectation of what he was known for—advanced scientific work that was near sorcery.

"Twelve used to be the age to join, but now it is closer to nine or ten-years-old."

Stacy seemed to tense up at the counter.

"Why the change?" Dan prompted. His gaze was analyzing of Nicholas, giving him the chance to speak his story, but preparing to critique any answer he might receive.

"The war breaking out led to a number of different reasons for the spike." Nicholas had finished with the bread and was now walking back over to Stacy's side. "Patriotism to work for the cause if a man was able-bodied enough. Dukhovia fights purely with martial arts and swordsmanship, so yielding a weapon is relatively simple from a young age. Many were left without parents and so they did not have many other options. But I would say a majority of explanation rests in our mortality rate. Too many of the twelve and up had already been killed and our numbers were too low. We had to start searching younger or forfeit the war."

Silence spread throughout the kitchen. Nicholas stood with Stacy, his hand close to hers on the countertop. The more he spoke, the more her fingers began to curve and that anxious foot began to tap. She was in a total desolate state now and seemed to not even be in the room anymore.

"Wow," Dan finally replied. "It's a good thing you got out of there. Happy you're here now, bud."

Nicholas nodded his acceptance, but the perspective turned his stomach. What did it matter if he was safe in America? That only made him a runaway, a coward. His country still suffered and other men still risked their lives, died, so that he could bake bread.

"What is your mission now, Nicholas? Will you be returning to Dukhovia?"

Nicholas played close attention to how Kevin phrased the question. His voice was soft, curious. He was not analyzing. He was not tricking. He sought an answer only out of small-talk and to get to know him, not for any other perverse reason.

"God willing. I must find some idea of how to end the war, then I can return."

Dan's face squinted curiously. "Here?"

"How can we help?" Grace asked, seemingly as a way to hush Dan.

"He's here for two reasons..."

It was Stacy who spoke next and the words that flowed from her mouth next set his blood on fire. His heart began to pound like a caged lion breaking for freedom. His head pounded like a violent storm raging against a dauber home. *Why did he tell her so much? Why did he say so much? How could he stop her now?*

There was no way. There was no way. There was absolutely and without austerity *no* way.

What did he do? Stacy would tell them everything. She would tell them of the heir, which her family knew was her. They did not tell her for whatever reasons they had, but as soon as she spoke of information surrounding the heir, they would have him figured out. They would know he was sent there, by The Czar, The Czar who banished her in the first place, and they would know he was sent there for reasons surrounding him finding her. They would know it was not innocent.

Why did he not shut his mouth? Why did he not shut his stupid, *fucking* mouth?

You will not divulge you are Dukhovian. Ruined.

You will earn her trust. Ruined.

You will bring her back. Ruined. Ruined. Ruined. EVERYTHING.

His thoughts were in such hysterics he nearly missed Stacy's words. "One is to save Dukhovia and the other is to sit there and look pretty. So far, he's only fulfilling one of his duties."

He looked at her, but did not see her. His breathing labored as he began to notice movements around the room. Grace rolled her eyes and returned to her prepping. Kevin and Daniel continued to eye him, but glanced away.

And Stacy. Stacy had her eyes locked on him, perhaps locked onto his very soul. Then, in a flash, her hand was on his and the electric shock flowed through him, restoring his focus, his comfort, almost his ease. But not quite. His heart continued to race, his vision continued to remain cross, but warmth flowed through his body.

"Mom, I'm going to show Nicholas my room, we'll be right back."

"Okay!"

Nicholas glanced back and noticed Kevin shoot Grace a look. "I mean, you're nearly the age I was when we were blessed with the conception of your brother—use protection."

Stacy groaned and rolled her eyes. "I'm giving him the grand tour, not stealing his innocence. We haven't even kissed yet."

Nicholas looked at her surprised. Either she did not notice what she had said—or she meant it.

He followed her up the grand staircase, etched in colors of cream and white. The home was nearly as grand as the castle, if not more.

At the top of the staircase, they were met with a long hallway. To the left at the end, a door and another door on the wall opposing them. Stacy made way down the right where there were several other doors. She took another right down another hallway and made for the only door in the middle of the left of the hall.

Nicholas continued to struggle to control his breathing, the pull of her hand the only thing keeping him grounded in the moment. She shut them in the room and immediately faced him, pulling his face into her hands.

"Breathe," she commanded in a gentle tone. "Shh. It's okay. I'm here. We're here."

Then he choked and the tears began to well in his eyes and fall without a hope of stalling. "Stacy...Stacy I...I do not know what I am doing. I do not know and I need help and I..."

She threw her arms around his neck and cradled him close to her, stroking the back of his head with just enough force to comfort him.

And he cried. He cried and cried, expressing a level of emotionality that he may have held in for years. For his entire life.

"Then I'll help you," she whispered to him, pulling her body away. She took his hand and sat him on the edge of her bed. Then sat and patiently waited for him to catch his breath. "Tell me what we need to do."

Continuing to gasp between words, Nicholas tried to collect himself. "I am not...here...to help end the war for the army...I am not here...I do not know why I am here.... I need to help my family but they are asking me to do so much. They are asking me to lose myself and everything that is right in order to do it and I cannot...I cannot."

Stacy seemed to let her eyes fall to the ground, perhaps admitting that she would not be able to help him or even fully divulge and understand what it was he needed help with.

"Then you won't," she said simply. "You'll do what you think is right and you'll do it the best way you know how. You'll stand by your values and what you know to be fair and true and if that earns your family their honor back then great, but if it doesn't then you have a whole new thing to be considered honorable for—your dedication."

His breathing evened. His heart began to control itself. The words did not fully submit themselves to be analyzed by his brain, he could not. He was breaking. No, he had been broken and he no longer had the capacity to keep all his secrets.

"We will stop anything, fight for anything, and I'll be with you, every step of the way. Always."

"Oh, Stacy." He flung himself toward her, burying his face in her neck as she stroked his arms and back—gently, swiftly, as if remembering the patterns of his wounds and scars.

Eventually, he lifted his head to meet her eyes and pushed her hair gently back behind her ear. She shook it free and he laughed, caressing her cheek softly.

If touching her hand ignited a flame, then this type of intimacy created a blazing inferno of wildfire. It started in his stomach, warming him, calming him, then flowed to his chest and steamed up into his head, silencing his thoughts, filing them away for careful analyzation later. Then it settled in his heart, burying in and nestling. It was peace. It was home.

"You said something earlier, on our way up the stairs…"

Her cheeks immediately flushed bright red—so she was aware of what she said. She meant it.

"You said we had not kissed…*yet*. Does that mean that you want to?" He waited, his heart not pounding like it always had before, but fluttering, lightly, softly.

She bit her lip and her foot began to tap. She averted her eyes and stumbled over her words in a way that made her charm and true beauty radiate. He had never noticed the amount of beauty she beheld until this moment. This perfect moment. "Um…well…do you want to?"

Nicholas cupped her face again, his eyes softened and his mouth curled into a gentle smile. Slowly, he bent his lips towards hers. "I do…" His voice was a whisper. He could feel her breathing quicken, practically hear the thudding of her tender heart.

Suddenly, a loud crack came from down the hall. Fast footsteps flailed, bounding closer and closer towards them. Nicholas's trained ears should have heard them much sooner, but he failed to maintain dual focus.

He darted back, a cloud of thick disappointment looming over the wildfire that had just existed.

Stacy's door burst open and three or four children came running in. The youngest jumped into Stacy's lap, flattening her against the bed.

"Woah there!" She burst into laughter picking up the child and placing him on the ground. "Nicholas," she said, her breathing uneven. "Meet Nicholas, Garrett, Katie, and Fred. My Aunt Sara's kids and my nieces and nephews. Garrett is the baby, Nicholas is two, and Katie and Fred are four."

Nicholas had never been around small children before. He had seen them, certainly, but had never been expected to interact with them. He felt strange as the more he watched them, the more a warmth different than the one Stacy filled him with seemed to set in. They were free, innocent. They were the age he was when his life was taken from him.

He watched the youngest waddle over to Stacy's desk, picking up pens. Stacy gently kissed his hand in a successful effort to pry it away.

He would have been beaten beyond recognition for the same action. Ridiculed and left a statue robbed of the ability to learn and make mistakes. His eyes watched as the older children danced in a circle around the room. He could not imagine it. The very thought put pain and torment into his soul. To beat those children. To burn them. To tie them up and torture their parents. But he had endured all those moments at their very same age. He and other Dukhovians.

The sickness in his stomach was beginning to return.

"Nicholas…" Stacy noticed and reached for his hand, clinging to the ends of his fingers.

"Is this your boyfriend?" The oldest chastised.

"Um…" Stacy started.

"Do you love him?" Katie asked. "Do you want to marry him?"

"Do you like kissing him?" Fred retorted.

"Ah…I don't know," she blushed, looking over at Nicholas. He smiled, laughing at their shared disappointment.

He glanced back at the children, tightening his hold on Stacy's fingers.

CHAPTER 58

DIVIDED LOYALTIES FINAL RECKONING

*N*icholas was able to meet the other members of Stacy's family who had arrived. Her Aunt Sara and her husband Jeff. A kind, yet very nervous girl whom did not seem to act the same as the other Grayson's, despite her identical appearance, albeit, being the shortest of the family.

Jeff was also a rather serious man. Straight-faced, long, pale face with glasses he frequently pushed up on his freckled nose or scratched at the light fuzz on his bald head. He wore business attire, rather formal.

Fred was Stacy's younger uncle. Another kind and charismatic man. Fred was a firefighter married to his wife, Jennifer, a nurse. The two of them had older, twelve-year-old children, Jimmy and Jamie. They appeared close to Stacy and were eager to meet Nicholas.

Cody arrived late with his father, the officer. While Richard welcomed Nicholas with a mighty handshake and pleasure to see him, Cody reacted with evident distaste that he made no effort to hide as he chastised his aunt for allowing his attendance, commenting on the "obvious danger" the family was in.

"And none of us have seen danger before, so we'd never be able to suspect it." Grace had told this to her nephew, but seemed to also wink in Nicholas's direction.

Nicholas attempted to keep his distance, but he and Stacy were closest and they found themselves together in the basement with Jimmy and Jamie just as the family had put the lasagna in the oven.

"What made you want to play to begin with? Before you realized you could use it to restore your family name?" Nicholas was asking. She had shown him the setup of where they would practice—an elaborate arena of cords and chaos. It was much more intense than anything that he had ever seen or could even comprehend.

Stacy smiled. "It connected me to my family." She turned and gave Cody a smile and his hand a squeeze. He managed a small smile back at her, but it seemed wrought with frustration not aimed at her or her comment. "Our parents say that they don't remember much from before Tom's accident, but what they do remember is that they were singing and dancing all the time. Playing instruments. When Tom taught us to play guitar, it was like a rite of passage, and then starting the band was like our way of maintaining the family tradition and our way of showing the world the true Grayson's."

Cody's smile brightened and he nodded.

"Do you think it worked?" Nicholas asked. "Does the world know your family for who they really are?"

Stacy dropped her smile. She eyed him lightly and put her hand comfortingly on his shoulder before answering. "It's seventy-thirty," she winked. "But it seems now that most people...appreciate us. I feel we are more accepted than we are ridiculed even though there are still certain states we aren't allowed to travel to and the occasional person who calls us names and brings up Tom's past."

"They're idiots," Cody commented. "They don't understand or know anything so why give them a thought."

Stacy shrugged but agreed. "It's like there's a descending order of people who know you best. Yourself, your family, your friends, then society. And who you are to those people, even to yourself, depends on your own beliefs and values."

Nicholas nodded his head. It was as if his mind had formed a gate, refusing to let in more. But whether he let it in or not, it caused the ache at the base of his skull to grow and spread.

"This is my guitar," Stacy smiled bringing it over for him to see with joy on her heart. "My grandpa gave it to me after teaching me and Cody when we were little."

Cody made a disgruntled sound.

Stacy stuck her tongue out at him. "Some of us are just upset because the skill didn't span across the entire family."

"You cannot play?" Nicholas asked him calmly.

Cody shot him a look, refusing to answer for a moment. Then he sat next to Stacy and grabbed the guitar, stringing at cords. "I *can* play. I prefer to sing."

Stacy pulled back at her guitar. "He's also not allowed to use my guitar ever since the last time he played it on stage. He broke half my strings."

"It was an accident," Cody said with a heavy roll of his eyes and deep bitterness to his tone. He sat like stone as they spoke, seeming unsure whether he wanted to even be there, or whether he was there as a friend or a guard.

"Mhm," Stacy groaned.

"Tom taught me how to control my vocals the first day my mom left me." Cody's words hit like a ton of bricks and silence spread over the room. "See? We all have a sob story. Doesn't mean we can do whatever we want."

Stacy shook her head, ignoring the comment, and turned to Nicholas. "Think you're ready to learn?"

He eyed it suspiciously. "It is rather similar to the lyra," he said. He reached his hand toward it and then pulled it back. "We never had a guitar, but I suppose..." He accepted the instrument as she placed it into his hand. His palms went rigid the moment he touched it. He had not held an instrument since his mother passed away.

He could not think of that now. Not now. Everyone was around him, watching expectantly. Everyone was being so kind and accepting. Save for Cody. This was what his mother would have wanted. This moment.

Suppressing a tear, Nicholas strummed a few times at the guitar. It made an unpleasant sound. He attempted to think back to his mother playing, how she held it, how he should hold it, how he should strum it just so.

His thoughts became a whirl of buzzing and flashes of flame and screaming infiltrated the wake of peace. He shook his head and pushed the guitar back towards Stacy.

"Apparently no," he said with a heavy breath.

Behind them, Jimmy and Jamie were banging on the set of drums. Rachael's drums. Nicholas took a few moments to breathe, grateful for the destruction and desperate for the topic to not return.

"Rachael plays the drums?" Nicholas clarified. "She seems as though she would rather something a bit softer."

"You don't know Rachael!" Cody snapped, his teeth were grinding together heavily, his fists had become balls of violence and threats.

Stacy stood to her feet, fuming. He half expected steam to roll from her ears. "Cody!" She spat his name through gritted teeth. "Nicholas is here as our guest. He has been nothing but kind and courteous. The only person doing anything close to what you expect from him is you. So, shut your mouth or stay away from him."

Cody responded with a glare so deep Nicholas could have sworn they were having a whole other conversation between those eyes. He shot the look to Nicholas then stomped off up the stairs.

Stacy sighed heavily and flipped her attention to Nicholas. "I'm sorry," she commented. "Cody can be protective and nurturing and then he can be...Cody."

Nicholas nodded in understanding.

"We should probably get upstairs too; it'll be time to eat soon."

Nicholas nodded but stayed in his position, a million thoughts speeding through his head at maximum speed, crashing into each other, knocking some over while others disappeared completely or grew beyond capacity. The pain grew worse.

Do something.

Do something. Do *something.* His heart ached for Stacy, that was something he was beginning to no longer ignore. Yet he was meant to see her as a detriment. He was meant to bring her downfall. He could not—so what did he do?

He was meant to trick her. To trick her and her family. Her caring, bubbly, understanding family. The family whom, even knowing him and his family history, treated him with kindness not because he or The Czar had manipulated them into doing so, but because they were worthy people—and worthy people saw the truth.

That was what Stacy and Cody had been trying to drill into them—what the entire Grayson family had been trying to drill into him. Not caring about what parts of Dukhovia had to say about his family because those whose opinions mattered, those whom, if Nicholas the First was still alive, would matter to him.

Nicholas the First did not care when he was murdered. He did not care the rumor that spread, he cared that he did a good thing. And he knew that the people that mattered—his friend, his son, his grandson, his grandson's wife, is great grandson—they would all see his worthiness, they would feel and carry on the pride he created.

And the movement he created held so much to be honored of. He saved Dukhovia. He held his ground on his beliefs and because of it, Dukhovia prospered.

And everyone Nicholas cared about knew it.

But his name...but the bond that tied him to Arkady, to Stacy, to every heir that ever lived... What power did he truly have to change his mind without putting them all at risk? His mother's screams rippled through his ears. Arkady had made it abundantly clear over the years: you can run, but you will never hide.

"Nicholas?" She had repeated his name at least twice; he was certain of it.

"I just need a few moments of space," he whispered in a voice he did not know would be so hoarse.

She nodded, rubbing his shoulder as she slid away. "Stay as long as you need. I'll save you a plate."

He sat back down on the chair he previously occupied. His mind ached, plagued with thoughts, choices, and bitter memories he no longer wanted to remember.

He thought of Stacy. The brilliance in her bright, beautiful face, full of life and desire. She had not only the heart to save Dukhovia, but a bravery that willed her to a country she should fear. A country no one should have ever feared.

He needed to make the change. He knew he did. He needed to forever alter his goal from destroying her to pitying himself to saving her life. No matter the consequence, no matter the difficulty. There was a solution, there had to be.

The Spirits willed it so.

Great destruction or great peace.

Or.

Stacy was that or.

The power to end the war.

Stacy was that power.

Nicholas's ears were suddenly alerted to the sound of shoes clanking down the stairs. He would have suspected Stacy bringing him food, he failed to pay attention to the amount of time that passed; however, the steps were heavier.

His head lifted as the figure revealed himself and he was staring face to face with a tall, older gentlemen. He was the spitting image of the officer, but with a face that reflected more years—more and very difficult years. Still, there was a shine to his green eyes that even took focus away from the light blue tube connected to the side of his temple and around the left of his skull.

Nicholas jumped immediately to his feet, a feeling of nausea and conflict overtaking him. He had always been taught to look at this man with disdain and disappointment. However, he had been taught many wrong things. Perhaps the first step to analyzing if he and his family could be given grace would be to extend it himself.

"Hello, Nicholas, I assume?" The man asked with a pleasantry to his voice. He had a small smile when he spoke, maintaining a light, upbeat attitude.

Nicholas was before the man in a heartbeat, bowing. He folded her hands, kneeling as he bowed the way one would do to a mentor or someone of high praise. "Yes sir."

"Tom Grayson. It's nice to meet you."

The pair made vague and yet penetrating eye contact for a moment, perhaps telling unheard stories, then Tom spoke again. "I knew your father."

Nicholas perked up. "You did?" He had not heard any stories of the two interacting. Ever.

Tom nodded. He strolled over to a refrigerator behind a bar and grabbed a bottle of water before proceeding to speak. "We were stationed in the same camp for our initial military training. We were rather good friends."

"My father..." Nicholas could feel the look of confusion that must have been heavy on his face, perplexion setting in. "I was unaware he served in the military. I thought him only a farmer and he attended university."

Tom nodded again, then his face fell. "He struggled in the military—which led to him attending university where he met Anecka."

Nicholas's heart leapt at the sound of his mother's name. His voice fell to a whisper. "Did you know my mother?" He asked pleadingly.

Tom cocked his head to the side. "Unfortunately, no. I never had the pleasure. Though, I hear wonderful things. My wife, Terra, she did have the privilege of knowing her."

Nicholas's head was back to that overwhelming feeling, that loss of control feeling. The swimming that felt more like drowning and fighting for his life. "What does she say of her? The type of person she was?"

Tom smiled. "Likely the same person you knew. Brave, caring, and stubborn when she believed in a cause."

Nicholas laughed with Tom. He could feel hot tears burning in his eyes. "And...and what of my father?"

Tom took a seat next to Nicholas, inviting him to sit with him as well. "Nicholas II... he was fearful. He always was. But he always volunteered to assist recruits. He was loyal beyond measure. That is the trait I remember of the Demitona family the most."

Nicholas sat for a moment as he let the name seep in. Tom viewed them as Demitona's. He did not agree with their dishonor. Did that mean others felt the same way?

"He was as honorable as they came." Tom looked specifically at Nicholas, choosing words intentionally. "I wish that was the man you knew."

"So do I," Nicholas whispered. "I cannot understand why he changed so drastically."

"Fear," Tom answered quickly, sounding sure of himself. "Fear during times of war will change a person into everything they never wanted to become. Adding in isolation doubles those odds. Your father was once a good person, Nicholas, however, the more degraded he was, the more lost he became. He was tormented for the choices your great grandfather was said to have made and he lost himself in an attempt to prove his innocence."

Fear. Isolation. Innocence.

Tom's eyes were penetrating Nicholas's now, wanting his message to sink completely in. "I tried every single day to get him to let go. To accept what he did not have the power to change and celebrate what he did. There was no changing his mind. Nothing that made resiliency stick. It destroyed him and ruined that reputation of loyalty for most of those who knew him."

Suddenly Tom's face fell. "But it is truly a challenge. I suppose I understand now more about his internal battle than I did back then."

Nicholas looked at Tom, curiously. He wondered how easily he typically shared this information, information about the darkest time in his life.

In Dukhovia, Tom was known as Beit—the Dukhovian word for death. He was portrayed to be a true monstrous villain, like that straight out of hell. Some called him a demon, others described him as a being completely out of the realm of understanding. Something not of this world or any world. A creature all his own being.

It was hard to believe that was the man sitting next to Nicholas now. A man who was gentle, whom was giving him advice, who was a listening ear when he never had one. This whole family was the support system he never knew, the warm embrace at the end of a long, adventurous day.

"How do you cope? With people treating you as if you are a monster..." Nicholas's words were slow and even, genuine curiosity rather than accusatory. He needed to know with desperation that he attempted to conceal.

"When I first returned to the world as my true self—it was horrible. A time perhaps even darker than when I was away from my family, because the promise hung so close for the first time, yet was so distant as well. I was lost as I so desperately wanted to be forgiven for my crimes, yet wondered if I truly did deserve to be forgiven."

"Yes," Nicholas's voice broke.

"We know now that it was a combination of Dukhovian botanical pharmaceuticals that caused the alteration in my brain. It would shift on and off from minor to disastrous. I physically could not control myself. And yet...I could have controlled locking up the herbs. I could have restricted myself in those minor moments—I didn't. I researched for years and years with my wife until one day she found a way to cure me.

"In the meantime, countless lives were lost. I will wear the shame of their lives forever. Mothers who no longer have their children, children who no longer have anyone to care for them. We do what we can to make amends, but that is something one can never, ever heal. And I do not expect forgiveness.

"When Terra came up with the solution," he pointed to the blue wire on his head, "it seemed like it was time to move on. Yet, people were livid. A monster such as me walking free amongst the innocent. They rallied in the streets, there were death attempts weekly, if not daily. I could not even hide—covering the wire is prohibited."

Tom sighed heavily. "I started to question whether I wanted to live at all and whether it benefited my family. That was when I was able to get through, when I was reminded that I was here because of and for my family. Life was not over; I had received it back.

"I attribute two things to saving me: confidence and my family. The confidence to acknowledge that I knew who I was, even if the others didn't. And I dedicated my life to doing things to assert who I was. Not to satisfy the others, but so that I could see my strengths at the forefront, rather than my failures.

"And then my family. I turned to those things because the alternative was to have what the public was saying eat me alive and I did not want to lose my life, I had already lost so much. I wanted it to start over. And so, it did. I focused on rebuilding my family, being by their sides no matter how difficult it was. That was the ticket. How much I cared for them and how much I wanted to return to the family we had thirteen years prior."

Nicholas's heart was flooded with emotion. He was not sure whether he was containing it or not anymore, whether he wanted to or not anymore.

"It helped to recognize my failures as mistakes—not intentions. I realized that many of us in the world are not so innocent after all. We all have our burdens to carry, no matter how publicized. In the end, I learned a lot about innocence and a lot about grace. The burden is still very heavy on several days, but we have become stronger over time."

His eyes turned to Nicholas, again, with that plea for understanding. "My wife carries a lot of grief for the state of Dukhovia—you will have to forgive her if she has difficulty around seeing you."

Nicholas nodded his head and cleared his throat, tears now flooding his cheeks. "Of course," he choked out.

Tom stood to his feet, ready to head back up the stairs. "I am sorry that your father did not realize the importance of family, Nicholas III. I am sorry that you carry the burden of that failure. But know this—as long as you are part of this family, you are safe, you are cared for, and nothing and no one, *no one* can touch you."

Nicholas stood to his feet, gratitude overflowing his ability to remember how to stand, how to breathe. Emotion welled up in every part of his body, rendering him unsteady.

"Yes, sir."

"We'll see you upstairs," he said before disappearing up the stairwell.

There was silence for a few moments before it was filled with the sound of thudding feet returning. "Oh, one more thing, Nicholas."

Nicholas's blood ran cold and his heart stopped.

"I do know why you are here. I know exactly why you're here, your entire mission, everything that The Czar has ironed out for you. I believe you are a better man...I *know* you are a better man than to fulfill that mission and a stronger man than your father to remain honorable for your grandfather and great grandfather. But let me be clear, if I am wrong and you bring any harm to my family, I will not hesitate to turn that promise into a threat. Do we have an understanding?"

Nicholas's heart was outside of his chest. He tried to speak, but nothing but dryness came out. He could feel his every part of his body shaking, on fire, any and everything. Finally, he was able to muster the slightest head nod.

And then Tom disappeared up the steps, Nicholas eventually trailing in his wake.

CHAPTER 59

THE WAR BETWEEN US

Stacy adjusted herself in her chair, shifting just so that she was positioned well enough to see the basement door—should it open. They had eaten and cleaned up and still Nicholas had not come back upstairs. She thought she should check on him, but when Tom returned saying he 'really enjoyed meeting him' she thought that meant he was better off coping the best way he could—or the opposite.

She second guessed herself. Second guessed whether or not she should be helping him more because she was not sure exactly what he was feeling. He did not want her family to know about the mission—he feared judgment, simple enough to figure out. But he had been on the verge of what looked like a breakdown either in the form of running away or slaughtering the town all night— his usual, sure, but the intensity tonight was…. different, eerie.

Finally, as the final game of cards came to an end, the basement door pushed open and Nicholas crept out. He looked side to side as if assessing where he should go next and if he was still welcome. The look of disaster had not fled his face, but was dripping to his outward appearance as well. His hair was disheveled, his usually neatly-tucked shirt pulled out from his belt with stark unevenness.

Stacy started to approach, but stopped herself, remembering he had yet to eat. She turned and made to grab his lasagna off the stove, giving Terra the opportunity to swoop in on her target.

"Nicholas." Tom approached him, his hand on the small of Terra's back as he drew her close. "My wife, Terra."

Terra reached a rigid hand towards him. She shook it with hesitation, then bowed to return his gesture.

"It's so nice to meet you, Nicholas. I'm… I…"

Stacy's own nerves went stiff watching her. She was shaking, uneven, uncertain—she was going to snap. Nicholas had been the talk of the table and the entire night she looked nearly as miserable and uncomfortable as Nicholas— would meeting him be her final act of resistance?

Finally, Nicholas interrupted her and lifted the back of her hand to his lips. "Terra Grayson, of course. I have heard many stories. Many great and wonderful stories. You are considered as blessed to Dukhovia as our Great Tereni. Perhaps your names are not the only commonality."

Tom gave a grateful and approving nod and made to say goodbye to Sara and her children as she wrestled them into coats.

"Your dinner," Stacy hopped over to him with a smile, presenting the freshly heated plate. "Meat-free lasagna. You'll give me your fully honest review?"

Nicholas looked down, his own gratitude radiating from the plate to shine through tearful eyes over to Stacy. He nodded once and took a bite. "Even better than spakosh."

They both laughed, then Stacy straightened, following Nicholas's eyes as they landed back on Terra. She was cheerfully helping the children into their jackets, but she was still…off.

"You can see why I never mention Dukhovia around them," Stacy noted, her eyes drifting away.

"Perhaps it was a bad idea for me to come tonight?" Nicholas began.

Stacy was shaking her head. "No, of course not. They…they'll get used to it." She found herself using the words that she herself negated for so long from so many others. But this was different. There were other Dukhovians nearby and they survived. Santifini was Dukhovian and they were the best of friends—unless, of course, Terra did not know he was Dukhovian.

The thought was fleeting. Important, but not enough to take over the moment right now. She filed it away for future inquiry. Focusing on the fact that if Terra did know about the others and did know about Santifini—what made Nicholas so different that she could barely zip Garrett's coat with her trembling hands?

"She feels guilty, I think," Stacy continued. "She wonders what her beloved country really thinks of her when she's been so…done so much."

"She has nothing to feel guilty of," Nicholas replied in a steady tone. "We have all failed the Spirits, we all should be on our knees in forgiveness."

Stacy inclined her head towards him. The thoughts battling with questions known and unknown as she sifted through different information she knew and knew from him. "What about you?" She asked gently. "Are you feeling okay? Being here?"

The look of dread returned to Nicholas, if it had even left for that moment. His knees seemed to buckle, his eyes immediately welled with tears that were blinked away a moment later. His lower lip trembled in unison with his Adam's apple.

"Hey," Stacy reached a hand out to stabilize him. The support seemed to cause further deterioration in his eyes. "Let's go out on the porch."

"Who's Tereni, by the way?" She asked by way of small talk on the way to make their exit.

Nicholas looked up as if confused, then recollection flooded his face. "Oh. Tereni is a mother Goddess. She is known to be caring, devout, gentle but would go to war to protect her children."

Stacy smiled as she opened and shut the door gently. That was certainly Terra.

The two walked out into a dark and starry-skied night. The brisk hair lashed snowflakes and whisps of wind at their faces, but neither shuddered. Beams of light from the street and surrounding Christmas lights bounced around the yard, but both remained focused. Both unmoved.

They sat next to each other on the stumps. Nicholas rubbed his hands together nervously, puzzlement etched on his perfectly structured face. His passionate, ice blue eyes darted around the area nervously.

"Imagine a world where Tereni didn't need to go to war for her children," Stacy said flatly. Bitterness coated her tongue heavily, but it was a taste she could not spit out no matter how hard she tried.

Nicholas laughed cynically. "That is a world I have been imagining my whole life. Ways to escape and start over, ways to stay and change all I ever knew…"

Stacy's stomach turned into knots. "How did you do it for so long?" She whispered. "Witness all the pain and misery?" Stacy was tactful in choosing her words, still not exactly sure what all Dukhovia truly was and what he witnessed. Aside from seeing a few soldiers on their trip a few years back, Stacy found Dukhovia to be as beautiful and peaceful as she had ever imagined. But Nicholas had told her it was not the place she remembered. Had so much really changed in such a short period of time? Or was she truly shielded?

Pools filled Nicholas's eyes but he did not blink them away. Instead, he let them fall and stain his red cheeks. "I became a monster," Nicholas replied. "You cannot think clearly…you cannot think *passionately and purposefully* when you are fighting for your life every single day. I did not make a decision to become the evil that I became, it was a timed switch that manipulated all of my decisions to become destined by one question: live one more day or die tomorrow? And I could not do it. Whatever mess I was making I could not die and leave both Dukhovia and my family disgraced. And if I can only save one, it has to be Dukhovia…"

Stacy realized she had been holding in her breath, her lungs tight with air. She released it slowly, in an effort to say his name. "Nicholas…"

"I told you upstairs that I do not know what I am doing here…"

"You don't need to know…we can figure it out…" Stacy interrupted.

Nicholas held up his hand in silence. "Please," his voice was a broken whisper. "Let me get this thought out before my cowardliness returns to stop me."

Curious, Stacy stopped talking and listened. As time went on, she felt her mouth dry out and eventually wondered if she even remembered how to speak.

"My entire life, my goal has been to save my family honor. I do not even know if the goal was truly mine or my father's. Of course, I care what mark my ancestor's leave. I just wonder if when I told my father that I did not want to rule Dukhovia and he held my head over our hearth and blocked the exit with his sword…did that shape my decision? Was my decision lit with passion or was it truly only lit by fear this entire time? Fear of him, fear of disappointing him, fear of the ruler I would be raised by…"

Stacy gulped, finding a hoarse voice. "But…Nicholas…"

Nicholas's icy blue eyes seemed darker than normal. They seemed not so isolated, but instead filled with memories that were never intended to be conjured up. "Stacy, I must tell you everything. I want to tell you the entire truth of my past. And I cannot force you to promise to stay. I must understand that you will never want to speak with me again. But if you can, if you can find it in your heart, please allow me to tell you my story. Please try to understand my perspective. And please try to not leave me because I truly do not know what I would do with myself if I lost you."

Stacy nodded her head slowly, her voice gone, her heart racing. A pit had formed in her stomach where every movement or word she ever knew how to make leaked out into the abyss of nowhere. She truly did not know what to expect from the words that would flow from him. She felt she already knew and understood so much and yet…she knew there was so much she did not. And there was so much she still held back from him, unsure whether or not she could trust him. Now, now she would have all the answers and she would be able to determine what to do with them.

"My entire family is Dukhovian bred. Even in the First World, we were always of the Winter lands. I was born in a small village near the end of South Gate called Vier. My mother came from a poor family from North Bridge. At the time of her birth reading, it was determined that she would be a 'prosperous and daring person'. A person full of 'flare and unwavering dedication'. Very ambiguous and vague. Typically, birth readings are very direct: healer, teacher, farmer… I suppose we realize now it was because she was to be my mother and being my mother required her to be all those things predicted…and to be my father's wife.

"My father's family is of South Gate—from Plodor to Vier. Generations of highly trained militiamen whom have dedicated their lives to protecting Dukhovia and whom have gone down in our history as saviors. Until my great grandfather, Nicholas the First. Nicholas the First was every bit as dedicated as the rest, however, he found himself set on a suicide mission. He was only meant to infiltrate the enemy army to find out their plan and carry it back to his platoon. However, what he found out was alarming. They planned to overthrow the Czar that night.

"So, instead, he went straight to the ruler to warn him. He was grateful and planned to honor my great grandfather and my family. We were to have a plaque made and he would be celebrated in the Gathering Festival."

Nicholas's face fell and he was silent for a time. Stacy bet he was imagining what that life would have been like, how different his life would have been if his ancestor had never been sent on that mission, had never been murdered…

"It never happened and our contribution was never known. The enemy army told a faux story blaming my great grandfather and still attacked. That faux story was heard around the castle grounds and spread like wildfire. They went to my great grandfather's cabin, the cabin that would become my childhood home, and shot him and his wife beyond recognition. The next morning, my family was publicly disgraced."

Nicholas swallowed hard. Stacy wished there was a way to turn back the clock as he recounted the details of the story he only before mentioned. With all her might she was ready to charge the streets and not only demand people to know the truth, but to alter it.

"The only saving grace was that one of the men who stormed the house that night had a conscious. He was mortified by the killings and so he saved my infant grandfather, David Christopher, and raised him and ensured he knew the truth of our family. But, no one else ever believed him. He was seen as a traitor and outcasted the same way my family was. Already known to be an enemy to one side of Dukhovia and then betraying the side he was meant to defend.

"My father was humiliated his entire life for our supposed crimes. People would call him names, attempt to hurt him, to kill him…several times false accusations were brought against him in order to get him banished. Thankfully, we had a fair justice system at the time."

"What about the new ruler?" Stacy asked, finding her voice.

Nicholas nodded, as though acknowledging the key element to his story.

"King Yuriy. Yuriy was a fair ruler and loved by all. He was said to be the greatest ruler of all time." He paused. "I do not blame King Yuriy. He was given false information and so came up with a fitting punishment. Dukhovia was not yet all bad and the line was not yet blurred. It was definitive, at least mostly. He was attempting to keep a chaotic situation contained. We all make mistakes."

Nicholas breathed. "King Yuriy would eventually be murdered and in his place, his son would rule. It is not typical that heirship follows families. In fact, it was a big story at the time. Both of Yuriy's sons were named heirs at birth. They both trained, however, one found another call and felt comfortable in that decision. Arkady not so much. Arkady wanted to rule and he wanted vengeance for the murder of his father.

"Many say that he was a calm and genuine person before the murder. But they were so young and it was so ill timed. Some say he feared ruling and that made him the person he became. That the fear became pride—he needed to continue to rule once he failed to avenge his father. To rule forever…

"Arkady intercepted my birth reading the day I was born because it was the biggest news in our nation's history since the start of the war."

"What was it?" Stacy asked, eyes wide. She felt her nails digging into the concrete stairs with angst.

"A prophecy. Two new heirs had been born. The Spirits predicted them to be the strongest heirs ever born. They were predicted to be both the fall of Dukhovia and the saviors. The Spirits predicted that the war would intensify ten-fold…"

As Nicholas spoke, flashes of Stacy's dream plagued her thoughts. Unprovoked and unable to be stopped, flashes of the utopian rainforest she fell asleep to lit up in flames, each hot, burning tail licking the forest with greed and without mercy. Her knees became weak, but her body felt…almost at ease. It was as if it was information she needed to know, was perhaps born to know…

Nicholas was still speaking. "There was never any explanation as far as what that meant. Would the ten-fold be because of the heir's and their choices or because of how the people reacted to these two heirs?"

Stacy's head whipped towards him. "Why? Who are they?"

Nicholas swallowed hard. "As I said, I am one. From the most highly disgraced family in all of Dukhovia, said to rule. You could imagine the uproar."

She could. "Similar to the uproar of murderers being set loose on America, I imagine," she empathized, thinking of her grandparents faces at just meeting another Dukhovian.

He nodded.

"The other?" Stacy asked expectantly.

Nicholas's Adam's apple shivered in unison with his weakening arms. "That is what I am here to find out. One heir of a disgraced family, the other of a banished family. Certainly, that would cause war and certainly that would cause great destruction."

Stacy considered the words. "Then we cannot be the ones to take that perspective. They would feel that way because they do not trust the Spirits. We trust them. We act justly to honor them and their call and the world will right itself."

Nicholas managed a faint smile and nodded.

Then, Stacy's eyes did that thing when they wondered, wondered things he wished she would not wonder and asked questions he prayed she would not ask…

"You've no idea who the heir is then? Just of a banished family?" Stacy racked her brain. She obviously knew her family, but there were others whom her grandparents helped pass into the country safely through the airport. The only issue was she did not think they stayed in the area and she wondered how she might help protect those heirs…and she wondered if she was meant to.

Protect the heir. One heir. Single. Protect the heir. Nicholas was the one she felt drawn to protecting. Nicholas was the one that was being controlled and manipulated to be here. Unless…

"So, what happens after you find out who this heir is?"

Nicholas's eyes fell. He folded his hands into his lap and twiddled his thumbs, raising each finger up then down, up then down.

"As I said, Arkady was said to be a just man in the past. That is not a man I knew. When I was named heir, Shaman arrived at my home to deliver the news shortly after my birth. That is also uncommon. Usually, it is within the coming days. A celebration is held; family is present. We call it Reading Day. Rarely do they ride in with horses, storm into the barn, and deliver the message in the form of a warning.

"My mother was worried. She worried about what this meant for me and what it meant for my father. She was right to worry. I remember my father being a good man. I remember loving him and wanting to protect the image that he was a good man that I loved, so much so that I would bury the truth. If no one else knew, I could pretend it was not real. Until I no longer could.

"My father was always hard on me, wanting me to train and do well, but when I was not training fast enough, when Arkady began threatening him, he began threatening me."

The tear-stained cheeks had dried, but new pools filled and replenished them. Nicholas's fingers twitched as he spoke, his own anxious foot tapping at maximum speed.

"The country was already so divided over whether or not to modernize. The idea of having an American-raised, banished ruler set the world on fire. And if my family carried more shame, if I could not learn quickly enough and be the one named ruler over this heir, I would further humiliate my family and be responsible for destroying everything we know of Dukhovia to be true.

"I had to do this. I had to. There was no choice." Tears spilled from his eyes to the ground beneath him as he told his story. Stacy cupped his face, catching them as they fell. She slid closer to him, their thighs meeting. She reached for his hand gently, then decided holding his forearm would be the safer bet.

"I understand," she whispered, leaning her head against his shoulder as she held onto his arm. "I understand," she cooed again.

"Everything hurt so bad every single day," he sobbed. The words held such emphasis she knew he was sick of holding them in, sick of putting on the brave face he always knew. "Every hit, every stab, every burn..." He inhaled heavily. "It did not matter how well I did it or how bad I did it, he would hit me over and over and then sent me to that *monster*." He said the word as if he had always wanted to say it and never could. He breathed in again deeply, hyperventilating before catching his breath.

"He would train me by teaching me in the beginning. He wanted to help me grow and I wanted to make him proud, to make Dukhovia proud. And I loved my country with everything I had. Then Arkady told my father that he did not understand the stakes, he told him that I needed to do more or else...

"The farm started to suffer and I knew he was to blame. Every time an animal disappeared or a meal was skipped, he would take me out and work harder on it— and apparently, I only worked hard enough if I was beat hard enough.

"He was apologetic the first time. He broke down and held me, promised he would never do it again. Then he snapped again and the light in his eyes showed remorse, but he must have thought it was helpful, or he just did not think at all. Soon the remorse left his eyes completely.

"I started to work one-on-one with The Czar more. Sometimes father was there, sometimes only us and his brothers. They were never kind, but they were helpful, instructive. My father taught them how I functioned best. The Czar would not hurt me at first. It seemed…seemed as if he thought it wrong.

"Then, one day, we were practicing Connections. I would connect with Arkady's Spirit in order to increase our power—stabilize and protect each other. There are other things we can do when we are connected, such as track, but… I was… never very good at it."

Stacy squeezed his arm. She had begun gently stroking it as he spoke, patting his leg—anything she could do when everything was so helpless.

"I could not keep my connection from breaking when under stress, so, my father struck me from behind. The Czar was upset that I could not even block or dodge, so he decided I needed to be given more incentive. He wrapped a rope around my neck and pulled. The longer it took me, the longer he pulled. I nearly passed out before perfecting my dodges. I am very skilled at blocking now. The best."

His eyes looked solemn, he was not proud he acquired these skills. "The only moment that I ever felt in control, was when I was calling the shots. When I got older and led the military, I got to lead the people. It never felt right, but it healed a small part of me—until someone argued with me. Until someone made a comment of not having to listen to a child, not having to listen to a traitor—the moment someone gave me a hard time, the moment I felt out of control, I released all my aggression on them. I screamed, I beat, I killed—I was becoming the monster."

He sobbed, wiping away the streaks on his cheeks. Stacy noticed her increased slowness at the comforting patterns she was tracing on his thigh, she noticed him noticing and the sobs got harder. She faltered, her hand shaking as she wanted to soothe him, but felt the very real threat beside her.

"I would hurt myself after," he said the words as if they would reassure her. "I did not want to become them, but I wanted to feel better. I did not know how else to feel better or who I could tell. I had no one to tell. Please forgive me, please."

"Oh, Nicholas…" Stacy threw her arms around him and held him close, the stroking of her fingers returned, feeling right, feeling justified. She drew back, cupping his face in her hands. "You were scared. You were scared and hurt and confused and…" Everything. He was everything and nothing. What would she do differently? She could not say. She did not wear those shoes. She never would. "Promise me you don't hurt yourself anymore."

He sobbed harder, shaking his head ever so slightly.

"Promise me," she commanded, keeping their eyes on one another. "And promise me you'll forgive yourself because that is the only person's forgiveness that matters now."

He looked at her, seeming years away, and began to nod his head slowly but nonstop. "I promise," he whispered.

She held him for a long time, stroking his hair and whispering hushes into his ear. Eventually, the two separated and Nicholas peered off to the ground. Stacy knew his story was not over, it was far from over. The thought made her sick.

He licked his lips, contemplating the next part of the story. "Training to be the best ruler was not enough and it was always a double-edged sword, a double plan. I did not know of that plan until after my parent's deaths. A few years ago, I believe I was ten or eleven, I overheard the Czar mentioning the other heir to enemy troops. He planned to use me not to rule fairly, but to force me to find the other heir and bring them back to Dukhovia so that he could find a way to prevent them from ruling. Death, eternal imprisonment, I do not know—but stop them. Permanently."

"No." Stacy shot up. Her heart was racing in her chest, flame ignited inside her. That energy to always want to run, to *go*.

Nicholas turned to Stacy. He grabbed her forearms in a gentle plea and poured into her eyes. "That is why I am here now, Stacy. Why I am truly here. After all my years of training, I came to fulfill that mission. To disgrace Dukhovia, my family, and myself by not listening. I would give up my throne one hundred times over if it meant the right heir sat on the throne, if it meant all of this stopped…but it never well. Not until the other heir is silenced." He gulped. "I am here to find the heir, to lie, to deceive. I have murdered before. I have taken countless lives in this war. I am not a safe person. I am not the man you think I am."

Stacy could feel the shock in her eyes as she stared back at him, unsure what to say or how to change things. But she wrestled with his last words the most— that he was not the man she thought. On the contrary, she had stopped herself from forming an opinion until she held all the facts. Now she had them, now was the time to focus on what she knew, what she did not know, what he controlled, what he did not control…

She was uncertain of so much—but certain she cared for him. Certain she knew the true him and his true motive.

"This is the part where you decide to run away," he explained.

Stacy shrugged. "Well, technically, this is my house. So, if anything, I go in and get my uncle, he arrests you for terrorism or something of the sort."

Nicholas nodded, uncertainly. "It is what I deserve."

Stacy shook her head. "That is how you were raised and that is what you were sent here to do. But that is not the question we are stuck with now. The question that matters is are you going to do it?"

Nicholas looked into her eyes, her generous and kind and considerate eyes. For the first time, he spoke the truth. "I do not know what to do. I do not know what to do or how I am going to do it, but I will not hurt the heir. I will not fulfill this mission. And I will take any punishment that comes from it as an honorable man."

Stacy continued to stare at him expectantly, whether she was waiting for the perfect words to enter her own mind or sensed that there were more coming from his own.

Then, Nicholas caved. He threw himself into his lap and the magic act of blinking his tears away was nowhere to be found. The calm and collected man of no emotion was gone without a trace, with no chance in the world to rekindle him.

"I know that if I do not complete this mission, he will have no use for me and there is a good chance that I will be killed. I cannot run forever. I cannot delay my return forever. I do not know how to get out of this and still preserve the life of everyone." He spat the words between heavy, exhausted sobs.

Stacy said nothing at first. She fixed herself back into her previous position— head tucked into his shoulder, arms wrapped around his. But this time, she wrapped her arms fully around him and he responded by accepting her fully into his space, tears pooling into her sweater, her neck. She did not care. It was what she wanted.

"It's not your burden to figure out on your own anymore, Nicholas," she told him in a gentle, but firm promise. "We'll figure it out together and I won't let anyone hurt you anymore. You're safe now, you're safe."

The words were like honey to his soul and seemed to make the sobs that could not worsen intensify, everything that had been stored for so long spilling into her lap for her to decide what to do with, how to treat it, how to give care to not just his entire being, but each individual wound. They would all need their own treatment, their own time.

The two remained in that position for the rest of the evening and into the wee hours of the morn, moving only to grant Stacy's relatives access to depart. Not much was said, yet everything was conveyed. And Stacy could not stop the overplaying of thoughts in her head as she maniacally decided what to do, where to go from here, and how they could find this new heir.

CHAPTER 60

WALLS DOWN, TRUST UP

*T*hirty-five families.

Thirty-five.

Stacy stared at the list, distant and detached from every name on it. She dropped the list to her side, angst and agitation setting in.

Protect the heir. Colors that burst into wild fire. Wildfire that burst into rays of sun and then falling snow and Nicholas on the throne...

The dream had never changed before. But now it did. Now that he had finally been nearly fully honest and transparent. Now that she had so many answers to so very many questions. And it all fit—except one thing.

Of these thirty-five Dukhovian families that lived in America, none of them felt heir-like to her. None of them seemed to match what Nicholas described. They left Dukhovia in Dukhovia and they nearly trembled at her very presence on their doorstep—they were not about to bridge the gap between oceans and fight for the broken land.

Two heirs. One he was sent to find—yet he was not looking. He was only spending time with her, trying to earn her trust, to get in her good grace's.

She shook her head. Another heir. There had to be another heir. There had to be.

Stacy and Nicholas had decided that the next day after band practice would be their first training session together. Stacy got through the day with anxious anticipation, even more so as Rachael was absent that day getting her cast looked at and Jade hardly offered the same type of encouraging advice.

"You think he'll train you well enough to turn it on him and kill him?" She laughed manically.

Stacy had rolled her eyes. "I don't want to kill him. I train beside him and fight beside him."

"One wrist at a time."

She had gotten up and stormed away after that. She could understand to a degree. Just like those thirty-five families were afraid, so too were her friends. They left Dukhovia for a reason and now she was laughing in that reasons face, ready to negate everything they did by escaping and return.

A flash of her father's mangled leg flashed in her mind. A memory that she was not sure was truly her own or one she crafted from hearing the story so many times.

After her birth, her mother was in a coma for two long years. It was Tom and Terra's job to successfully get her home and Kevin would protect Stacy. The story was told that he outran a group of cloaked men chasing after her—one shot his leg and badly injured it. The injury was made worse by the fact that he could only make his escape by hiding on a row boat where he and Stacy floated for several days until they were found by a large, thankfully American, ship. Kevin had lost a lot of blood and Stacy was nearly starved. But he never let her out of his sight.

The knots in her stomach returned. Could she really just run back to Dukhovia after all of that he endured for her? The fear and panic he must have felt as she cried and cried for food but he had used the last bottle a day before their rescue. The amount of sadness and agony when his painful screams matched those of the infant he held. When he had to undo his homemade tourniquet in order to keep Stacy warm—unbeknownst it was an unnecessary notion.

But she was not just throwing that away—she was fixing the reason it existed in the first place. She was picking him up off that boat and not settling him in America to have to search hospitals to find his wife. She was sending him back to his home, a peaceful home with no fighting, no running, no fear...

And it was not just him—it was an entire nation.

Stacy closed her eyes, trying to figure out what this new information meant, putting it into the puzzle pieces that her and Rachael crafted over the last few weeks.

Rachael.

They spoke on the phone last night. She wanted to know how dinner went, of course, and obviously saw them on the front porch at one point—though she hardly knew how long she watched. She gave her nearly all of the information she needed to know—nearly.

She told her what she wanted to hear—about the almost kiss, about how nervous he was, that he stayed in the basement for a long time dealing with what was likely either culture shock or awkwardness at meeting her entire family.

But...she felt herself grazing over the major details. She did not tell her about the connection between their two families and how much guilt Nicholas held in attempting to regain his family honor. She did not tell her about his confession on the porch nor anything about the new heir.

She figured she had two reasons behind not yet opening up about the conversation. One, she wanted time to process it on her own first. That way she would have already thought out and analyzed whatever Rachael came up with. Two, because if Rachael thought out and analyzed the answer she was not yet ready to hear...

Stacy managed a smile as she saw Nicholas approaching her. They were meeting in a secluded field surrounded by a wood of intimidating pines that rose nearly as tall as the sky. No one would be able to see them, save for the two houses that cut off the neighborhood next to the field. But they were far enough away and close enough to the tree line that they would just be two, small specks that might even be deer.

"Perfect spot," Nicholas commented, glancing around.

She observed him for any telling signs—but he acted just the same as always and how would she expect him to act in the presence of an heir? What differences were there in how he treated her compared to anyone else?

He was training her. If he did not want an American ruler and did not want to kill her, this would be the next best bet.

He put his hands together and bowed entirely at the waist. A vision of him flashed in her mind—him bowing to her relatives—when he only bowed his head the way she was taught.

"Why do you do that?" She asked him flatly, void of all mannerisms.

He looked taken aback. "Greet you?" He asked, tone of shock and surprise.

Stacy cocked her head to the side then straightened and presented her case. "Fully," she said, copying the behavior. "But for others you only incline your head."

She could have sworn she heard him curse under his breath, but she watched him avert eye contact and wonder further into the tree line as he set down the large, brown case he carried.

"It is how you greet someone of higher rank, perhaps someone you admire…" he added.

Stacy's insides burned.

He walked up to her and cupped her face with both hands, rubbing her cheeks. Stacy could not help but almost want to burst away. He was still only telling her half-truths. She was not interested in him only telling half-truths.

She wondered why, with everything else he divulged, why it would be a big secret to reveal this to her. It changed nothing between them or their plan.

But he feared losing her.

So, she had to show him she could not be lost.

"I am glad you came today," he whispered, their faces only inches apart.

"Of course I came," Stacy choked back. "It's going to take more than being a war criminal to get rid of me."

Nicholas laughed, seeming to swallow the bitterness in the comment. "Even if I bring danger to you and those around you?"

Stacy grabbed his hands and shut her eyes preparing for the impact of the power that would radiate through her. It was stronger than ever before. Instead of a direct shot, one thousand separate shocks were jolted through every part of her body, vibrating, floating, comforting.

"Even then," she promised through closed eyes. She gave his hands a squeeze and backed away, recoiling as she recovered from their power.

"Why does that happen?" She pressed.

"I already told you," he began, but she cut him off with a shake of her head. Demanding more.

He breathed in deeply, thinking. "We share the same Spirit. We are connected."

"Why?"

Nicholas stared back at her, his lips a tight, thin line. Stacy turned on her heel, then stopped. *Trust.*

She bent down, and chucked a snowball at him.

"So, I can tell when you're able to do that," he laughed.

She was angry, but returned to his side, grabbed his brown bag, and sat down. "So, what are we learning today?"

"To me, ones understanding of the nation in our position begins with two basic traits: history and fighting skills. You must understand what it is you are fighting for and you must be prepared to defend that physically if it comes to it."

"In other words," Stacy summarized back, watching in a trance as he opened his bag and drew out a long, thin piece of paper that looked like it had withstood the test of time. "People will try to kill me for what I believe, so I must have the ability to fight back."

Nicholas nodded. "Unfortunately, that is what Dukhovia has become."

He flattened out his paper which turned out to be a map. He used his knees to keep it flat and pointed to different sections with his fingers. "This is North Bridge, South Gate, East Valley, and West End. They do not serve to separate Dukhovia into sanctions of any type. Though, some areas are known for producing different types of goods and some are wealthier simply due to proximity to the capital city of Vodva and the largest and most sacred city, St. Karsburg.

"North Bridge has the lowest population. It has the most turbulent snow storms which few have been able to withstand since the decline in interaction with the Spirits. When we were closer to them, there were bridges and temples we could travel to and find communication or worship with the Spirits, resulting in guidance and calm weather. When it stopped, the storms picked up. Now, only the most spiritual live in this area, as others think it cursed. Many Shaman live here."

"What goods do they produce?" Stacy asked, intrigued.

Nicholas's mouth formed a small smile. "The North is known for producing literature and musical instruments—the arts, mostly. This is where one would travel to visit the orchestra."

Stacy nodded understanding, then immediately felt like a horrendous student for not bringing anything to take notes.

"East Valley," he frowned. "I said that there are not specific sanctions, however, East Valley is rather well known for having a lot of rebels."

"Which of the quadrants is Das Denivya in?"

Nicholas was silent a moment. "East Valley."

Stacy's mouth went dry. She guessed Nicholas already knew why. "My grandparents lived there for a while."

"Much has changed in the many years since they left the area," he offered either by way of explanation or sympathy. "Many travelers avoid the area, but it also supports the ships that dock in and out of the country. All the other ports are too frozen over. That is why your escape from the country was so difficult. You were truly in the most dangerous waters."

Stacy squinted, confused by the statement. "But if they are rebels, don't they defy what Dukhovia has determined to be fact, which is our banishment? Wouldn't they support us?"

Nicholas made that face he made when he regretted something. The realization of what it meant this time made Stacy want to throw up.

"Remember, there are no lines. There are no colored jackets or black versus white faces. I could be a rebel one day and traditionalist the next. I could support execution of the heir while still wanting to maintain traditionalism and vice versa. There has even been talk of calling those of us who support the heir rebels. The lines are very blurred."

"So," Stacy began slowly, trying to egg him on without being overly direct. "The rebels are non-traditionalists. They want to update the country. If they heard of a banished, American heir ruling, they might want to secure that heir to their cause, at least initially?"

"Something to understand about Dukhovia, no matter how much we hate each other's views, we hate Americans more."

Stacy swallowed. What was she getting herself into?

"The non-traditionalists, or those who want to update, want the American heir to rule because the heir will bring them into the new world. The non-traditionalists who do *not* want this heir to rule, might want change, but not corrupt change. They still want Dukhovian ideals, just tweaked to their liking.

"Likewise, the traditionalists want everything to be as traditional as possible and that means either excluding the heir or trusting the Spirits and seeing where that lands them."

Stacy nodded in understanding but she felt dizzy considering all the different ways Dukhovian was torn and what would happen if someone spoke their mind.

"And what's that split?" Stacy asked with hesitation at the response. "70/30? 50/50?"

Nicholas eyed her cautiously. "90/10."

She shrugged her shoulders back as if she could shake away the meaning, as if there was still a chance she could change that response. "And I'm assuming that's not in the heir's favor."

Nicholas did not respond. She did not need him to.

"East Valley imports many things—fruits and vegetables from neighboring countries. They also are our builders. They manufacture what is needed for our homes—inside and out."

"West End?" Stacy asked, reluctantly.

"West End is sort of a catch all. Not really known for one specific thing. Part of The Palace is located in West End, so I suppose it is more high-end. Vodva is not said to be in West End, though the lines are not definite and East End and North Bridge argue. St. Karsburg, however, is definitely in North Bridge. It is considered not only our largest city, but the holiest."

"Have you ever been there?" Stacy asked, looking at its proximity to the very top of the country and knowing it was likely in the do-not-enter area.

Nicholas was quiet. "A long time ago. My mother and I tried to flee and she took me through St. Karsburg. I did not know until after we were leaving that was where we were."

"What was it like?"

Nicholas shrugged off his fears. "Exhilarating, for an heir. I had never been surrounded by such power. If I were there now, I bet I could take Arkady down. I was so young and naïve at the time. I…"

"You couldn't have known," Stacy offered, interrupting what she was certain was a painful memory. "You were just a baby, Nicholas. You are the victim here. You should have been loved and given patience and grace. You did not deserve the abuse you endured." Stacy gulped, wanting to mend him as much as she could but feeling the words fail before they even left her mouth. They felt so powerless over the emotions he had, so narrow-minded.

Nicholas hung his head. He blinked hard and tapped his fingers. "I have visions of it, sometimes. Of snow swirling around in a fashion quicker than any human could comprehend. It is far North it is dark nearly all the time, but stars shine brighter than anywhere else on Earth, especially America. You can nearly see the fire.

"The air feels—free, light. Open spaces and trees exist without fear of anything. There is no traditional and non-traditional, no war—only peace."

Stacy smiled, her own visions popping her mind, fighting and rejecting the idea. Bright, colorful. "Is there anywhere colorful in Dukhovia? Tropical?" She tensed, remembering how things played out with her grandparents the last time she asked the question.

Nicholas immediately shook his head. "Not exactly, anyway. The Spirit Realm, it is full of different seasons, for the different Spirits. For example, the Summer Spirit might like a more tropical setting whereas Winter would obviously be more chilled."

CHAPTER SIXTY

He offered the information up simply, but his face became inquisitory when Stacy said nothing else, but instead stared into the distance, lost in her memory. If she was connected to the Winter Spirit, why was she envisioning the Summer?

"Do they ever feud? The Spirits? Especially since the other First World Spirits were destroyed."

Nicholas shook his head. "Of course not, they act in harmony. What is it you have seen?" He asked the question with careful precision.

Stacy chewed her lip and tapped her foot. Should she really divulge her most trusted and well-kept secret if he was not being totally honest with her?

Trust.

"I've been having this…dream," she chose the word carefully, tossing it over in her head for minutes upon months. "It's almost always the same. I'm in a tropical setting, almost like a rainforest, but the colors are out of this world: bright yet calming. The air is thick, not enough to be suffocating, but enough to cause anxiety. I know that I'm trapped in that spot."

Stacy watched Nicholas's face both eagerly and apprehensively as it flecked with understanding and inquisition—the look her insides had been burning and screaming to find.

"Then there's a voice. Sometimes the peace stops when I hear the voice. Lightning bolts shoot off or thunder sounds somewhere… the feeling gets more…eerie and I get more fearful, like I need to make a decision soon."

"What is the voice saying? How does it sound?"

A feeling of calm fell over Stacy at the sound of his questions. There was something in his tone that told her he was not just wanting to know, he was having thoughts and running down a list to help her find a solution. A solution. After years of wondering and months of angst, whether the solution he came to was a suspicion or fact, she would have *something.*

"It's terrifying," she breathed, as if the confession would make everything go away or come right to her. "But maybe just because the tone of the scenery and the quickness, not really the voice. But it's bold, it's important. It's a command, not something said out of fear. It's a warning."

She gulped before going on. "It's coming, they're coming, the heir…it's time…protect them. They want me to protect someone." She stopped, meeting his gentle, concerning eyes. "I thought it was you. Ever since I met you, I've been pulled towards you. Even when I pretended to hate you, I still didn't want to, I wanted to be near you, to help you."

The two exchanged longing looks for a time. Looks that spoke a secret, silent language conveying understanding, conveying hope. Finding in each other not just another Dukhovian, but guidance and healing.

Then, Nicholas took a step closer to her, his head bending so that their foreheads met, hands interweaved in her hair. He closed the space between them and breathed, "Your soul is beautiful, Stacy Grace."

The comment filled her, set her on a fire that did not destroy, but lifted and made itself known. A fire that gave her strength and courage. "I'm so confused anymore," she admitted. "Now I don't know if I feel like I want to protect you or if I just want you." The bravery quickly snapped away the minute she admitted the statement. She felt her face go white as a ghost as the blood rushed from her body.

But Nicholas did not respond with ridicule. On the contrary, he lowered his arms and embraced her, with hesitation at first, but then realizing that perhaps Stacy was the only home he ever truly had or would have again, he took her completely in his arms and brought her to his chest.

Everything about the notion was intoxicating. There was the obvious—his strong, muscled body up against hers made her blood boil. The relaxing sigh of his breath that had been held for too long in anxious anticipation. The way he held her with such profoundness, yet still had the underlying fear that she would disappear.

Then everything built into the hug. His fear, his safety, the meaning in his life. He was home.

Stacy swung her arms around him, not just in return, but squeezing him with all her might to get that message across to him.

"Your dream," Nicholas said, taking a step back from her. "I think the Spirits may be trying to communicate with you. In fact, I am nearly certain of the fact."

Stacy felt like she was standing on the edge of a cliff leaning over to see what else would fall out.

"Only... I am a little uncertain what it truly is that they are trying to communicate to you." His face was puzzled. He was looking into the distance as if the platform of his mind had become entirely overrun by uncertainty and options.

"Not to protect you?" Stacy asked gently.

Nicholas gave her a small smile. "Perhaps," he agreed. "However, there are other things that do not add up. Why is the voice and the atmosphere frightening? Is it just your banishment and how you feel when you think of Dukhovia?"

Stacy was already shaking her head. "Dukhovia is my home. I have no fear of it or anyone there."

Another small smile and a squeeze of her shoulder. "Assume they mean the other heir," he began softly, aware of his every word. "Why ask you to protect them? Why would the Winter Spirit speak from somewhere tropical?"

Stacy shrugged. Her thoughts loomed over what he refused to say. *You.* The word *you.* Why would the Spirits ask *you* to protect *yourself.*

They both exchanged a look in understanding what was coming—war. If the new and feared, modern, American heir ruled or did not rule—it would be the turn the war in Dukhovia needs for its grand finish. But why would the Spirits warn

Stacy to protect herself from this coming threat? Why in such a threatening way? Was it a mere suggestion or a command? A purpose?

Regardless, until they figured it out, she was set on sticking with her original thought. She knew so little. She sought so much to gain. But that one thing was clear—she was going to help Nicholas.

CHAPTER 61

WRECKLESS DENIAL

Let's do one more take and call it a day," Dan ordered, pressing a few buttons on his laptop and then pointing to the band. They had him set up via virtually as he had arrived at his hotel for his internship mere hours ago.

It was Friday afternoon and the band was practicing some of the newer songs they had written. Sports were done from now until after break, so they were able to get done at the perfectly reasonable hour of five, instead of just beginning. Today, Rachael and Cody were practicing a duet which involved them dancing together and getting closer than the two were ready for. It was a beautiful song and something fans would go crazy over, and who was to say they were not secretly in love with the idea?

"Perfect, great job, guys," Dan smiled. He fixed a few things before taking his earphones off and acknowledging them.

"Where would we be without our flawless manager?" Rachael grinned and teasingly playing with his cheek.

"Out of here twenty minutes ago," Stacy complained. She was throwing things together in her purse and hurrying to strip off her uniform which she wore over another outfit.

"Oh, don't tell me you're going to see that guy again?" Cody complained walking over to her grumpily.

"What business is it of yours what I'm doing, Grayson? Shouldn't you be more concerned with the drool that's been on your chin since you started dancing?"

Cody went to wipe his chin causing Stacy to grin and chuckle lightly. He caught her prank and blew it off angrily.

"Stacy, I don't like you hanging around him. No one does. He's going to hurt you."

"Don't get your panties in a bunch, cuz, I'm not hanging out with him. Me and Rache are going shopping."

He stood down. "Why wasn't I invited?" He asked in a hurt voice.

"You can be," Stacy said, reorganizing her makeshift-purse. "But then your present wouldn't be a surprise, would it?"

Stacy and Rachael laughed and waved to everyone as they exited the house and headed for town.

As usual, the town was bursting with people doing their last-minute Christmas shopping as well as just starting out. Decorations hung from every street lamp and every shop while carolers were bullied from block to block.

CHAPTER SIXTY-ONE

Stacy and Rachael knew exactly what to get Cody, but (as happened every year) they always felt like he deserved more. Aside from watching over them like a hawk, Cody was an all-around great friend. He was always there when someone needed help with anything, he was reliable to anyone. If one of the girls needed help with homework, he was there...for moral support more so than educational, but still...

If the neighbor needed their grass cut, he was there. Nothing kept him from helping. He was also a very good listener. You could tell Cody anything and know he would be there for support, comfort, and any words of wisdom he could come up with.

"It needs to be the mixture of perfect, awesome, and unique. Basically, nothing that exists already," Stacy said, feeling defeated.

"Something that says: 'you're as amazing as you are overbearing," Rachael offered. The girls laughed. "So, you've been holding out on me," Rachael went on with a smile, her eyes criticizing her friend as they looked through clothes.

"With what?" Stacy laughed, avoiding eye contact as she pretended to be interested in overalls for Cody. It had only been two days since Nicholas's confession, but Stacy was still mulling over how she would tell Rachael. Not that she was too put off by anything she had confessed to her thus far.

"Oh, just the most exciting thing to happen to us since ever!" She proclaimed. "Sir Nicholas! One minute he hates everyone and everything, now he's beaming every minute of every day and the girl hell bent on dying alone has googly eyes for him!" She narrowed her tone into a mixture of condescending mother and the 'give me the details' friend she was rightfully portraying. "Everyone is talking about seeing you two around town together, skipping detention, eating lunch together, walking to school..."

At the end of it all—Rachael was right. Stacy had hardly explained anything to Rachael since things had gotten so...heated. It was not intentional. It was simply becoming difficult to balance everything inside her head let alone explain it to someone else.

She was getting answers on Dukhovia. She was fearing the fate of her beloved country—that they would meet their demise before she had a chance to try to save them, meanwhile she was banging on her guitar to lyrics about nothing. Stacy tried to juggle her thoughts enough to explain to Rachael, but she was also blatantly aware that as she spoke, she tried with failure to hide the radiance she beamed with as she spoke Nicholas's name. And then she thought of them in the woods, them walking home, how the tips of their fingers just barely touched...

She felt herself drifting as she thought of what a brave and honorable man he was, so caring, so...

"It's nothing, I think..." she forced herself to say, to regain her thoughts. "He's had an unimaginably hard life. I think he just needed someone to vent to. Anyone." Her cheeks turned crimson.

Rachael saw right through it. "Aww. Evil Dukhovian gets turned around by the nice little American girl," Rachael put her hand out like she was reading a headline in a newspaper. "The perfect love story."

Stacy shook her head.

"Aaaand," Rachael started walking backwards so she could see her friend's expressions. "What about after we hung out last week? What about your date? Ugh! I know you're going through it and I'm trying so hard to give you Dukhovia space, but I neeeed Nicholas deets! Leave out not a single detail."

"He's sweet," Stacy began but as soon as she used one term, she realized simple adjectives would not do Sir Nicholas justice. Images of the extravagant date he planned flashed in her mind. The detail, the thought, the time… "He's the sweetest and most dedicated man I've ever met…He listens to me, really listens and wants to give me answers. And when he shares his feelings, I never want to stop listening. He can understand anything and if he doesn't quite, he'll do everything in his power to be able to. He understands everything that I'm going through in my struggle to find my purpose and his knowledge for Dukhovia is extensive…"

Rachael lifted an eyebrow. "Extensive, is it, Mrs. Andrews?"

Stacy ignored her. Now that she started, she could not stop. She did not want to. "He's so dedicated to trying to please his family and the Spirits at the same time…it's admirable."

Rachael's smile spread wider. "Well, I'm glad I forced him to meet you." She laughed, wheeling Stacy into the next store.

"And in regards to our more practical use for him… What new have we found out about the heir?"

A lump formed in Stacy's throat. Suddenly she felt like she was wasting her time on something as miniscule as shopping, when she had a life that needed protecting. A life that she still needed to find…

Stacy grabbed Rachael's good wrist and pulled her in a section of elder women's clothing. She looked around her shoulder, Rachael smirked at the lack of necessity.

"He is *an* heir."

"*An* heir?" Rachael repeated, mimicking Stacy's whisper. "What does that mean?"

"There can be several," Stacy told her. "Sometimes ones who are predicted to rule end up going down a different path and their purpose changes. Or, they are called to rule at different times. He's *an* heir, but he's not the strongest. He's the second strongest."

"How demeaning," Rachael laughed.

Stacy urged her to be serious, it was a difficult and confusing task. "Promise that you trust him?"

Rachael looked down at her arm and shrugged with a radiant grin.

Stacy smacked her shoulder.

"If you trust him, I do too."

"The war in Dukhovia... Apparently, feuding over whether or not to modernize isn't the only concern...now the Czar wants to dictate who rules, instead of listening to the Spirits."

Rachael's face had now turned into ridicule and disgust, she learned enough while in Dukhovia to know the severity. "What? But that's hypocritical..."

Stacy made a face of agreement. "And people are dying and are more torn than ever—the people who think he should be allowed to stop an indecent ruler from ruling and those who think it isn't his place to interfere."

"Why would an heir be indecent?" Rachael wondered, Stacy knew she was just as confused as she started out.

"Nicholas says it started out over the fact that the heir was stronger than his brother and so he would never get to rule. He wanted the line to remain in his family as long as possible. Then the Czar learned that this heir was living in America and he told the country that they would modernize for certain, worsening the war."

Rachael looked up, trying to piece it all together. "So, we have people who want to modernize that would probably be okay with this ruler, but also those who are okay with him changing the method of ruling. Then we have the ones who want to stay the way they are and not change what the Spirits predict...what a mess."

"And Dukhovia is at war because of it."

"How does Nicholas fit into all of this?" Rachael asked, remembering how they got on the subject.

"Trust him?" Stacy offered her pink to Rachael.

Rachael shook Stacy's pinky with hers.

"Nicholas was sent here by The Czar to find the heir and bring them back to prevent them from ever ruling."

"What!" Rachael shouted. Several of the employees looked over, then, recognizing them, waddled over to be of assistance.

"Ugh, come on!" Rachael grabbed Stacy by the arm and they marched out of the store. Rachael looked around the mall cautiously, a woman intent on fulfilling a mission as they sauntered over to the largest store in the middle of the mall.

"Is this private?" Stacy asked with heavy sarcasm.

"This, madam, is the largest, busiest store in the mall. They don't have nearly enough employees to pay attention to everyone, so they pay attention to no one and all the customers are too focused to on the sales to care about anyone else." Rachael was momentarily distracted by a pair of black boots with a buckle. "Now spill!" She urged.

"I don't know much more. He says he doesn't want to do it, that he never believed in the cause."

"Do you believe him?" She pressed, wide-eyed.

Stacy nodded. "With my whole heart." She looked off, momentarily blinded by fluorescent lighting. "I have no idea who it is, but he seemed to know. Seemed to think they would make a good ruler, but I haven't noticed him around many people besides us and I just..." *Protect them.* "If this heir is at risk, I feel like they're the one my dream is telling me to protect, but I just feel so *drawn* to Nicholas."

Rachael's face was now inquisitive, nearly forgetting completely of the shoes. "And Nicholas is an heir?"

"Correct."

"And he says this nonsense happens with your hands because you two are connected? Your Spirits?"

A lump landed in Stacy's throat as Rachael connected what Stacy had feared. "Yes."

Rachael stared at her friend for a moment, marveling over an unspoken thought. She seemed to answer a question that brewed in her head and smiled. "Let's keep shopping."

The girls continued on, they searched store after store in search of Cody's perfect gift all the while, Stacy thought of Nicholas and Rachael's odd response to the conversation.

She thought of how grateful she was for Rachael and having so many people to talk to about what was going on. And then she thought about how utterly alone he had always been.

She thought about how confident she was she had finally found her purpose. Then she thought about how afraid Nicholas must be to fail his mission and never find his purpose. To bring his family more shame instead of honor, or honor and a loss of identity for himself.

Overwhelmingly, she thought of the urge to comfort and support him, to be there for him in any way, despite the danger. The thought thrilled her to happiness. But with thoughts of Nicholas, came the overpowering and unshakeable thought of what came along with him: the heir.

Who was the heir? The longer she waited to find out, the more danger for both this heir and Nicholas... Her heart felt so strongly about saving this girl's life, while her body stressed itself out for having no leads and no way of getting Nicholas to cave and tell her. He was too smart to be tricked.

Then again...she swallowed...would he confirm to her something she already knew?

"Crazy thought," Rachael said, putting down a football jersey. "But why is the Czar having Nicholas do his dirty work for him in the first place?" She stopped herself. "Okay, maybe that's the wrong question. He's lazy, clearly. But why bring the heir back to Dukhovia at all? The man obsesses over the fact that he can snap a neck quicker than I can French braid, so why doesn't he just kill the heir here?"

Stacy was stunned for a moment, unable to process how she did not think of that. Her heart raced with a million different explanations, but none held merit. For Nicholas, it was obvious—he did not really want to. But for The Czar to expect him to bring the heir back in the first place? There had to be a reason. "Maybe they want to put it on display for the whole country to see," Stacy mused. "Lynchings of the future."

Rachael shook her head. "They really do refuse to update."

The girls laughed, leaving the subject behind them.

Rachael was able to find the last four jerseys of Cody's favorite NFL team that he did not own. She also went to a personalization store and had them make a plaque deeming Cody "the best running back in NFL History".

Stacy bought him a new gym bag since his mom "accidently" ripped his along with vitamins and protein powder. Those things, of course, would only be given after the joke gift of her plaque of an award deeming him "the most overbearing human alive". He. Would. Love it.

When the girls returned to their street, Rachael ran home to scribble a lengthy note in her homemade card about how grateful she is for Cody's overprotective side. Stacy made note that she would do the same, but the second she opened her door, it was like she was hit with a brick of reality.

Her flag of Dukhovia was staring her in the face, but it seemed brighter and more necessary than it ever had been before. She threw the bag of his gifts on her bed and sat on the edge, the obvious crashing down around her.

She desperately wanted to trust Nicholas, especially as her heart started to feel so strongly for him, but he was not being truthful with her. There were small pieces that he casually let slip since the day they met—but she knew now why he was here. She could understand the uncertain feeling. She could understand why he would need to get to know Stacy first before spilling something as drastic as that he was, in fact, a trained assassin.

A normal person would be done from the start if not now. But Stacy...Stacy felt the draw she refused to ignore. Yet at some point, she needed to think realistically. Be practical. Was the draw spiritual intuition or did she fall right into the trap of Sir Nicholas's master plan? Did he even have this traumatic backstory? Was it all show? Where was Santifini? He was in on it all these years and did his part and disappeared?

She was spiraling and she knew it. But it was time to be forced with the obvious.

And Rachael had a point. Why did he have to bring the heir back to Dukhovia? As proof that the crime was done? Or was that just what he was telling Stacy so that she did not know one way or the other whether he was good or evil.

Then there was that look that Rachael gave Stacy when she asserted the fact that she knew she found her purpose. She recognized that look. It was the one she used when Stacy mentioned how strange it was that her parents did not make any vacation plans for the first two weeks of summer as if it was "some trick to get her to go to summer school". She was going to summer school and Rachael knew it.

Stacy knew what Rachael knew this time, but she did not want to admit it…she could not admit it. Because admitting it meant that the one redeeming fact that Nicholas had spent no time attempting to ensnare an heir into his trap had gone out the window.

No. He had spent *all* his time doing just that.

But she pushed the thought away. She had to push the thought away…She wanted to trust Nicholas.

CHAPTER 62

RUNNING WITH WOLVES

Stacy inhaled deeply, filling her screaming lungs with air. Her face had been barricaded in snow long enough to have ice crystals form on her lashes.

"Not quite what I meant, but a fair skill," Nicholas told her in a concerning, yet lazy tone. Stacy had come to him for her training session today, curious about Spirit gifts. Curious if only heirs could have them or if she might possess one. Ugh. He was uneasy the entire night and morning and this did not help.

He knew he had to tell her and he knew he had to tell her soon. It had to be before someone—such as the principal—told her and twisted it in such a way that he would lose her. He could not bear the thought.

Yet, he had been up the past two evenings wording the breaking news differently, changing the emotion to his tone, finding ways to comfort and explain after—yet for every option there was a heart-shattering response he anticipated.

And so, he continued to hide her truth for his own selfish gain. Until today, when the guilt ate at him so heavily, he knew he needed to find the right way and find it today. Because there were two things he cared for more than his own short-lived happiness—even if this was the first time in his life he considered putting it before his mission— his country and the girl who would save it.

"I bet I just broke a world record for holding my breath, though," she grinned. "Okay, fine. So how did you know that the gift the Spirits gave to you was your connection to animals?"

He considered that for a while. "I suppose it was more of a hope. Even on the darkest days, surrounding myself in the trees with the wolves could make me feel carefree. The more I did it, the stronger I became. It was not until I began to train more that a former shaman told me I was spirit-blessed. Most people don't believe I should be."

Stacy gently lifted her hand to his face. "The Spirits do," she said comfortingly. Then her face changed to a more serious, inquisitive type. "I guess I have hopes. But my hopes have always been more—concentrated. Maybe that's just because I'm not in Dukhovia? My hope has always been to be there until I found out about the war. Now it's to end it."

Nicholas considered this. "And then there is your dream."

Stacy nodded. "Yep, there's that."

CHAPTER SIXTY-TWO

"I have an idea for how to figure out more about your dream—if you would allow me."

She looked concerned, but nodded.

"I believe that the Spirits are trying to connect with you. They have a message for you beyond just what your dream is revealing. They want you to attempt to connect and speak with them."

He could tell her interest was beyond peaked, but confusion ran through her. "What do you mean? How?"

Nicholas grunted. "It is my weakest point, but perhaps because I was always doing the opposite of what they expected of me. I believe that I might be able to help us both enter if I use what I know to connect while you dream."

"So," Stacy began slowly, the words sinking in. The sun had peaked in the sky and flashed across her face, highlighted the brightness of her eyes in the most brilliant way. "You'll watch me sleep?" She was doing her usual climbing over icy rocks in the most dangerous of manners.

"To some degree," he laughed. "I believe if we can enter at least some capacity of The Spirit Realm that we may be able to contact The Ancestry Spirit."

Stacy's eyes squinted. "Not the Winter?"

Nicholas shook his head. He began pacing, his mind racing to make sense of his ideas, his abilities, and hers. He could barely keep track of what he was saying and what he was thinking. "The Spirits do not get caught up in human hardships, but because such a large element of your heirship is likely rooted in your family's banishment, it would likely be most beneficial to at least start there."

He continued to pace, but paused when he saw Stacy's face. Her eyes were wide, but she continued to sit comfortably, transfixed and frozen on his face. What on Earth did he say to yield such a reaction? He tried to trace back his words, but he could hardly keep track of what he was going to say next let alone what he already said.

"Stacy?" He asked with concern.

"Continue," she choked out in a throaty voice.

He continued to ramble on about Spirit's and gifts and the ways in which they would interact in the Spirit Realm versus the Physical Realm, all the while her eyes darted back and forth with a look of something that crossed fright, sadness, and understanding.

"So," Stacy asked when he paused. "This type of thing might be normal? Since I'm an heir, dreams leaking into The Spirit Realm are somewhat common?"

"Yes and no. They will often speak to…"

And then he paused.

And then he realized what he said.

And then his world crashed down around him.

He paused where he stood, slowly turning around. His hands dropped to his side and his eyes slowly floated towards Stacy.

She sat, the perfect image of calm, eyebrow raised in question.

And then he flew to her, dropping to his knees. "Stacy…I…" His heart was pounding, his ears screeching. The world seemed to be moving faster than it ever had before, and the longer he looked at Stacy's quiet face, the faster it spun.

Until he flung himself over the rocks and vomited over and over.

"Nicholas!" Stacy was on her feet, part of her touching his back, part of her wanting to maintain her distance. The truth was out for the first time; it was time to press for all the answers.

"I am sorry. I am sorry. Please. Please." He heaved the words between deep breaths, some interrupted by more vomit, some by simple dry heaving.

"Nicholas, Nicholas. I'm here. I'm not going anywhere. I'm here. Breathe. Breathe."

He turned slowly, latching onto her words. *I'm here. I'm here.* She was here. She had not run. She now knew everything and she had not run. He started to move, started to breathe in and out, to catch himself, to relax himself.

Stacy reached around his front, despite him trying to hide his sick from her. She latched onto his wrists and pushed down with all her might.

The rush that jolted through them was like a strike of lightning. Nicholas could have sworn he saw a flash of bright light, his body being thrown backward.

And then a rush of silence. Of peace.

Stacy was first to get up and rush to him. "Nicholas? Nicholas, are you okay?"

He felt the hot tears pour down his face, not realizing the sting in his eyes until they were already flowing. "Please do not think of me differently, Stacy Grace. Please do not run. Please do not leave me. Please do not leave me." He repeated the words, sobbing into her shoulder.

And she pat him, his mind blank with where to go. And then she stepped back. "Tell me everything. From the beginning. No more half-truths, no more secrets. Everything."

And so he did. Unsure at this point what he told the truth on and what he had not, he chose to begin as far back as he himself knew. With their birth readings…

"Shaman tend to have a better spiritual connection on highly spiritual days— All Spirit's Day, Festival of Lights, and so on. Therefore, they typically tend to attempt connection with The Spirits on these days as well as every few weeks in order to hear any messages they wish to pass on.

"Typically, when a message is received from the Spirits, it is through vague interpretation. The Shaman might have some type of relics that react in a certain way, telling them their message. Similarly, the Spirits may enter our world to attempt to convey a message to us. They might send small 'invitations'—such as your dream."

He saw something flicker in her mind.

"December 25th is considered a holy day in Dukhovia as it celebrates the birth of a Spiritual Messenger and the further spreading of spiritual values. On this day in 1990, Shaman entered the Spirit Realm closer than they ever have. There had been previous times they received direct warnings from the Spirits, but nothing quite like this.

"They spoke of two new heirs born that morning." He swallowed hard. "Born to parents of banishment and those of disgrace." He stroked her face and then pointed to himself. "These two heirs would be stronger than any other and were predicted to cause either great peace or great destruction. They were said to potentially be a refuge for Dukhovia, but that the chaos of Dukhovia would tenfold before a solution came out."

At that, Stacy's pupils flared. Her fists clenched and she was ready to go to war. Dukhovia's strongest heir.

"Shaman told our families immediately. They helped your father escape safely with you and they came to the barn moments after I was born."

"How do you know that?" Stacy asked, her words sounding more accusatory than he was certain she meant them to.

Nicholas's eyes bore into hers, utter stillness and sheer pain etched on his face. "Because I have been training since birth to learn all there is to know of you, Stacy Grace."

He could nearly hear her heart leap out of her chest, but she waited patient.

"When The Czar found out the prediction that was made, he was full of anger. His wrath caused many of The Shaman to flee as he was intent that they should re-enter The Spirit Realm to attempt to alter the call that the Spirits made.

"Arkady, at some point, was a good ruler. He always sought to maintain traditionalism in Dukhovia and was someone the country could be proud to have as a leader. However, he went into an immediate downhill spiral when our names were announced. A female born to a family who was banished, living in the most modernized country in the world—surely she would update. Surely she would turn the tides of everything he fought for."

"But I wouldn't!" Stacy protested loudly. She seemed to get knocked backward by realization. "I mean—I have no idea what this means, what *ruling* means." She grimaced with anxiety. "But I love Dukhovia for what it is. I would not change it."

The words were like magic to his ears, soothing him, comforting him...reassuring him of what he was now doing. "I know you never would, darling. I knew that from the moment I met you."

She seemed uncertain. "So, what happened? How did you get involved this way?"

"As we've already seen, clearly a disgraced family held a bit more merit than a banished one. The Czar took a few years to come up with his plan, or perhaps fine-tune it. During that time, I lived a decent life. My father was stressed, I know now because he wanted me to fulfill the pressures of my role—a disgraced family given the chance to bring glory. I had to succeed—or else. Sometimes I felt the pressure of that or else—but not always. Not nearly as bad as once The Czar decided.

"I remember the day vividly. My mother forced me into the back of my bedroom so that I could not see or hear. She did not trust our leader. I wish I had her intuition."

Nicholas looked away solemnly for a time, then he stretched his fingers across the cold, pleated snow and continued. "I do not know what all was discussed, but after that my training began. I met with The Czar and my father showed him my technique so far. He was impressed and disgruntled at the same time. Much like my father—he was under pressure.

"I never knew what I was being trained for until much later in my life. I thought I was being trained to rule. Eventually, my best friend, Vuel, joined and underwent the same rigorous training except it did not seem that the same pressures were on him. It made sense—he was an heir, but not as strong as us. Not nearly as strong as us. We would bring great destruction or great peace. We would. Not anyone else."

Stacy's eyes were glistening as he told his tale, her arms tucked in at her sides as though she might be cold. He might think her frozen solid if he did not know better. If he did not know so much more...

"I was learning of our history. I was learning to strengthen my Spirit's gifts and track and kill. I was put in the military when I was 12." He gulped, choosing to move past the subject for the moment. "That was when Vuel and I discovered what we were really meant for—finding you. We were really being trained to track so that we could find you. We were being trained to hone in on how to pursue and convince you to come back to Dukhovia with us."

Anger was rising inside of her; he watched her chest rise and fall despite her making no movements.

"This was my particular skillset back home. Flattery. The country jested that I would have no problem convincing you. They claimed every woman wanted me—whatever that meant.

"Once we found out—Vuel left. He wanted me to go. He begged me and I know he resents me for not. But I simply could not bring myself to give up on my family. I never believed in the mission, Stacy Grace. You must understand that. I beg of you. I prayed and thought about a way out of this mess while still bringing my family honor each and every day. But meanwhile, I trained. I learned everything I could of your family, their past. Everything Arkady deemed important enough.

"Then it was time to come. I never felt sicker than the moment I boarded that plane—and not just from motion sickness."

CHAPTER SIXTY-TWO

A small smile.

"I felt like I was screaming inside. Time was up to find a way out of this. Now I needed to do it or be killed and that would be the end of my family. We all die for shame."

He looked at her now. His eyes pleading, full of more truth than they ever had been, of more yearning but of less pain than ever before. "And then I met you. And I knew immediately that what Arkady spoke of, what he had forced me to believe for so long was inaccurate. I would not be dismissing Dukhovia of their destroyer, I would be destroying their savior."

"I did not know what to do. I still do not know what to do," Nicholas said the words slowly, through a flood of hot, heavy tears and exasperated breaths. "But I know I will not bring harm to you. I know I will not bring harm to Dukhovia, no matter who hears of it. With that said, Stacy Grace Matthews…" He rose to his feet, bowing the unique way he always did to her, then bowed his head, shut his eyes, and dropped to his knees.

"I humbly ask your forgiveness. I can never earn it; I will never deserve it. But I beg for you to not only forgive me, but bless me with the new purpose in ensuring your safety and ensuring you will someday sit on the throne of our great Dukhovia."

CHAPTER 63

THE PEACE OF PURPOSE

Stacy felt like she was looking at life through a lens—unsure of what she was really supposed to be thinking or feeling. Her feelings were everywhere. Her thoughts. Her fears. But one thing took precedence over all of it…

It was right.

She was meant to be in Dukhovia. She was meant to protect an heir—right? She was still fuzzy on the dream.

Nicholas was good and pure and whole.

She moved closer to him, shaking her head. "You don't need my forgiveness, Sir Nicholas. You are the son, grandson, and great grandson of the Demitona family—a family of honor, a family that all of Dukhovia will see as just."

That was when he grabbed her, perhaps with more force than he meant to, but the bone-crushing hug was everything he needed for so very long. To be totally out. To be totally undone.

To be accepted.

"You must understand who I am," he cried, looking back at her. "I am evil. I have done so many bad things…I-I-I led raids on villages of people whom Arkady suspected to be modernizing—making weapons, building technology. I thought I was saving the country but I…" He fought through tears to attempt to find his way to express her thoughts. "I'll always remember the first life I took. How disappointed my mother would have been. When I think of them, I think of their face and I think of my mother holding them, protecting them now. And I think what a monster she must think her son."

Nicholas was quiet again. He looked towards Stacy for a reaction, but she either had none or was still deciding. The silence continued until she finally shook her head. "You're not a monster."

"I understand if you fear me. I understand if you want to run and never speak to me again. You have that right. I have killed before; I will kill again. I cannot be trusted."

She was shaking her head. "No, no I don't believe that. You were doing exactly what you were told to do. Your judgment didn't exist. Your rights didn't exist." Her voice was intense and demanding as she hammered down the facts. "You were *stolen*. *Stolen* from a family of love and honor and tradition and brainwashed into believing a narrative that helped someone with horrid motives. There is a monster in this game, Nicholas—but it is not you. Even if for a minute you believed in that cause—who you were doesn't define who you are."

Then she stood to her feet, power and rage overtaking her. If she knew half of her power, she could bring the world to its knees here and now. "You were not the first this happened to and you won't be the last. So tell me what to do. Enough sitting around, enough waiting—tell me what to do and where I need to be. We're bringing this Czar down."

***

They had talked for another hour. In which time, Nicholas begged her to tell him at least six times that she did not think him a monster. She did not. So, it was easy.

The difficult part was wrapping her mind around ruling a country when she could barely pass a single class. The difficult part was figuring out how she was supposed to rule a country that was at war over keeping her alive or slaughtering her in the town square. The easy part was trusting Nicholas.

Which led her to the next difficult part—understanding why her family kept this from her for so long. Nicholas and her were not able to come up with a set plan for what they would do next. Nicholas became too overwhelmed sorting through all the possibilities and Stacy became too agitated being so close and yet so far. So, they decided that they would sleep on it and revisit the subject tomorrow after school during their regular training time. After that she could only focus on one thing—why had her mom not told her?

It did not make sense. Her mother's whole life was kept from her and she vowed to never keep a secret from Stacy. Yet she watched her struggle every day in darkness and said nothing. Why? Surely she could have told her something. If not everything, *something* would have been better than the absolute abyss of nothingness she had lived in for the last sixteen years.

Yet she knew her mother. And she knew her father. And she knew any choice they made was never done in selfishness.

So she went home, walked up to her room, and sat on her bed until she heard her mother's car pull in the driveway. She was silent when her mother first walked in, her eyes distant, but telling everything. Her mother knew. She had to.

"Why don't you go up to your room for a moment and I'll meet you there when I get these things put away?"

A moment. Since when did Rachael Marie Lin Grayson use phrases like 'a moment'. She knew.

But Stacy obliged.

"Knock, knock." Grace's voice came from behind Stacy's door *a moment* later. She had hardly noticed her coming up the steps.

"Come in," Stacy responded without emotion.

Grace kicked open the door and came in the room smiling. She had a basket of clothes which she set at the foot of Stacy's bed and leaned against.

"There's something I want to show you," Grace said with a huge smile on her face.

Oh something you want to clue me in on.

Stacy sat up and scooched near the end of the bed to sit next to her mother. She noticed her own hands shaking, but tried to keep it well hidden as Grace pulled out a picture and handed it to her.

"This is my favorite aunt."

Stacy looked at the picture of the young woman—forever frozen at age thirty-two. She looked like all the other Grayson's with black hair and hazel green eyes. The one thing she had that no one else did, was curly hair. Aunt Grace.

Aunt Grace's story was one that Stacy had heard many times. Her mother told the story of a woman braver than all others, kinder than all others, gentler than all others. She stayed in Dukhovia, despite the banishment, to stay close to the man she loved. Stacy was not certain of the details that led to the complications, but knew that it ended in Grace taking a bullet to protect the love of her life. Grace did not make it.

For the first time, Stacy felt more anger than ever rise inside of her. She thought of Nicholas's mom—also a strong and kind woman lost to stupidity in a country that was supposed to be the majority of peace and love, not the minority. And to think the weapon of choice could even be something so modern.

She had to hand the picture back before she tore it in two.

"She was beautiful," commented Stacy, laying her hand over the photo. She knew how much Aunt Grace meant to her mother. It was after her death that her mother decided she wanted to be called Grace. It was her way of ensuring her aunt got to live on, that her name, that her persona, was never forgotten.

"Very. She always had a way of making things that seemed messy and complicated not so bad— no matter how…unique the situation was," she searched for the right word with a smile. "I always tried to think about what she would have said to me when I found out the truth about my past. I was so angry that no one told me, that they kept me guessing, that they kept me in the dark. I realize that your Great Aunt Terra was trying to keep me from getting into the trouble I willingly went into, but it never seemed like a good enough reason to keep me from knowing who I really was. Until I realized that I never would have found who I was meant to be without the adventure to find the truth."

Stacy nodded understanding. Her heart was a caged lion, tamed but beating wild and free and turbulent all at the same time. So that was the angle. The 'you have to find your own path' angle. Bull crap.

"Come here, take a walk with me," Grace invited, seeing the indecision plastered to her daughter's face. She held onto her daughter's hand and guided her downstairs, out the backdoor, and into their fenced in yard. Neither of them wore a coat.

Without much reason other than was Grace's way, she lifted a loose board from the fence and the two started down the sidewalk together. Nothing was before them but the moonlit path in the night sky, and the beauty of it was mesmerizing.

Grace found her way to a spot that looked like most people tended to avoid: it was in the middle of nowhere; desolate from people and contact of any kind. The stars shown down brightly, and a bridge free from any lit wreaths or Christmas décor stood before them, over a completely still stream. Now that Stacy thought about it, she did not believe she had ever seen the stream before. She felt like they were not even in Kansas anymore.

Stacy breathed in the sight and smell of fresh snow—and it heaved at her gut. Confusion and fear coursed through her as the understanding of it all began to sink in closer and lock into place.

"We had to leave Dukhovia when you were a baby and again when we went to visit due to safety reasons, I trust you know that, Stacy," Grace began. She put her arms up over the bridge and looked out at the wide, open field. There were no houses to be seen, no lights from buildings, though Stacy did not believe they walked too far from town. Still, only a blanket of white lay before them.

Stacy nodded. "We were—*are* banished." Her voice rang with annoyance.

Grace nodded in return. "Yes. Yes, we are. And it was the beginning of a very difficult time for Dukhovia. I don't know how much you know about the war, I know your grandparents don't talk about it much, but right at the time of your birth, tension formed around the announcement of the greatest heir Dukhovia had ever seen.

"This heir was predicted to change the world, reunite Dukhovia, and do things bigger than any heir ever had. It was a purpose that was much needed."

Stacy felt a lump forming in her throat, her stomach twisted.

Grace bent down and picked up the snow from the ground. She held some out to Stacy and, confused, Stacy held out her hand to receive it. Grace let her fingertips become red and raw before dropping the snow to the ground, watching it flutter in the most graceful of ways.

Stacy copied the behavior, although her hands remained the same.

"There *is* a reason that you have always been able to withstand the cold more so than any other *normal* human being." She laughed at the word. "A reason that you feel called to Dukhovia. You search for a unique calling because you were meant to do something that only you could do. Which I suppose isn't much difference than everyone else...except that you were chosen.

"A series of people and gifts must be used in order to restore Dukhovia and the world to its original glory, but only one person can help lead them. Only one person can convince an angry and unforgiving army that the people they fight against are just as human and good in their cause as they are, they are merely seeing unclearly.

"Almost sixteen years ago, in Vodva, Dukhovia, that powerful purpose was chosen for a brave and talented young girl with a heart of gold. This girl will soon find out that the most astonishing of things are set to happen in her life and whether she choose to accept and embrace that part of her life or turn away, I know that she will choose based on her own abilities. Her own ability to be strong and her own ability to think of the needs of others.

"A day will soon come when this girl will take over and rule the country of Dukhovia and on that day, she will need to do things she never thought imaginable, but her family will be there for her through anything."

Grace put her hand on Stacy's face and smiled. "And we always will be."

Stacy smiled. She closed her eyes and seemed to feel the falling snow as well as all the mounds that lay around them as an extension of herself. She felt drawn to them and drawn away from them...

"I'm the heir of Dukhovia." She said the statement with fear and certainty and, for the first time, noted the unbearable truth that finding out the truth she pawned after for years may have been the easiest part of her journey.

The two watched as the water in the motionless stream began to flow as though it had never been stopped. There was not a single ripple, but it flowed over rocks and stones toward a destination that was virtually unknown and perhaps nonexistent.

"I wanted to tell you when we were in Dukhovia, but I didn't believe it was the right time. I wished so many times during my life that someone just sat me down and told me the whole truth about who *I* was and *my* life, but I don't think it would have had the effect I wanted it to have. I think I would have lost more than I gained by not knowing.

"I was worried that if I told you before you were ready, it would have put an immense amount of pressure and tension on you and made you resent the idea of anything even remotely connected to Dukhovia. And I didn't want to put the pressure of your future going the way the Shaman predicted if that wasn't how it was meant to be. So, I waited until you showed signs that you were meant for that path.

"And you show such strong signs." Grace's eyes watered. She turned from the snow-covered field and held onto both Stacy's shoulders. "You truly are the strongest heir there ever was."

"I don't blame you for not telling me," Stacy managed to choke out, surprised by her own words. But it was true. Her mother wanted to wait until the right time, to not stop her from her destiny, but to make sure she got there. It could not have been an easy call to make. Regardless, she needed her mother now. "But I'm scared mom." She knew Grace would not understand the reason she was scared, she was not even sure if she knew, or if scared was the right word to use. Perhaps it was, but not in the traditional sense. Not in the way she should feel right now.

She simply feared the unknown. She feared how little she knew. She feared the number of enemies that faced her. How many of them were like Nicholas— kind and gentle? And how many…were not…

Grace grabbed onto Stacy's hand again and gave it a squeeze. "You have a number of enemies in Dukhovia, my darling, but not all of them are against you by choice. Even if they have intentions to harm you, that does not mean that person is who they really are. I have faith in you to notice that and faith that you will achieve everything the Spirits see in you. And you'll always have guidance. No matter what or where."

Stacy could barely nod her head. She felt like she was choking and by the time she returned to the comfort of her bed she could hardly even remember the walk back.

CHAPTER 64

BETRAYAL

Stacy did not recover by the time she made it to school the next morning. Just lifting her body out of bed seemed like an Olympic sport and pulling on her shoes felt like lifting hundred-pound weights. But it was the last day before break—she could survive.

But it was also a Monday. Who had Monday as the last day before break? What is this, prison?

It took that much more energy to drag herself down the sidewalks. How could she even begin to find school practical now? Not only was Dukhovia at war while she stood idly by, Dukhovia was at war while she stood idly by AND she was the one predicted to end it. And she was going to go learn Algebra?

Every part of her body was on edge. Every movement felt wasted. She wanted to run; she wanted to plan.

She waited outside the school doors for Rachael to arrive. When she did, she cheerfully approached, registered Stacy's face, and waited.

Stacy nodded her head. "It's me. I'm the heir."

Rachael was not surprised, but taking in her friend's reaction, she was hesitant. "And that means what now exactly?" She sat her backpack on the ground and leaned up against the school next to Stacy.

She shrugged, tears brimming her eyes. "I don't know. I trust Nicholas. That part is null. But everything else…I don't know how to get to Dukhovia. I don't know how to end a war. I don't know how to rule a country. But the hardest part is the *waiting*. I can handle not knowing those things, I have no reason to know those things but to sit by and attend freaking *gym class* while my people are being murdered for speaking their minds? No."

Rachael nodded in understanding. "What does Nicholas say?"

"He's a mess," Stacy answered. "He has no idea what to do either. We're supposed to meet after school today to figure it out."

"Then why don't we focus on that?" Rachael offered, shoving her hands into her jacket for warmth. "Why not skip school today, come up with our solutions, and then meet up with him?"

Stacy was alert at the suggestion, but realized who she was talking to. She smiled as much as she could manage. "This is your Dukhovia. It's important to you. I'll figure it out."

"You're a country's entire sacrifice; I can miss one day."

Stacy shook her head. "But I am going to break all the rules on our new, dear principal and attend all your classes. Nicholas and I figuring this out can put Advanced History on hold." She rolled her eyes.

"You should probably brush up on your advanced history—or any history." She smirked.

"I hate you."

But the plan was useless because Nicholas never came to school. Stacy waited and waited. She never went to class, never even set foot in the school, afraid to miss him. A few times she thought about starting her journey to his apartment. All she was doing was standing around for six hours, she might as well have. But then she realized she could easily miss him if he took a different route. So, she waited. And waited.

Until the school bell rang and the parking lot emptied once more.

Quicker than she would have ever previously planned, Stacy started her way to Nicholas's apartment. Unsure what to expect or what she would say when she got there, she took the time traveling on the sketchy bus to consider her feelings.

Was she mad? He did not show up today, on the day they planned to spend at least all of advanced science and swim class making plans to save Dukhovia. Had she pegged him wrong? Did he not want to save Dukhovia?

Was she wrong? Did they not actually plan to begin this today? Or, perhaps they had and he had some other Dukhovian problem to attend to. Or he was sick? Did he owe her an explanation for not being in school? How did she even expect him to communicate this to her if so?

Ugh. Communication. She should have gone to the office to see if he called himself out sick. Dead. Anything.

Was he dead?

Suddenly Stacy's heart flew into overdrive. The bus barely slowed before she was jumping out of the doors, flying up the sidewalk, and banging on his apartment doors. Her heart was unsteady, her pulse racing.

What if he was already due back? What if The Czar had come and decided to kill Nicholas and make his way off with her?

Come on Nicholas! Come on!

Sweat dripped down her brow, she ignored shouts from other neighbors who poked their heads out to silence her bangs and shouts at his door.

Not waiting another moment, she flew down the stairs, bursting open the managers door.

"I need a key," she breathed heavily.

The man only looked at her, his lack of urgency boiling her already racing blood.

"That's not how this works..." he began.

Stacy lost her patience. Every moment they waited another Dukhovian was dead. She had no idea if that next Dukhovian was Nicholas and she needed to care about the policies of an apartment? She could just as easily have her uncle come barge the door in.

She kicked his desk, sending papers flying to the ground. "If you don't give me a key to 32B, you'll have a sea of police officers giving you an excuse to buy a brand-new door." She gritted each word out unsteadily through clenched teeth. "Now, key for 32B, please."

He looked either petrified or concerned, Stacy did not have time to care enough to figure out which. But a shaking hand reached behind him and pulled out a row of keys, finding just the one she needed. "Oh, you never mentioned it was 32B. Of course, ma'am."

She rolled her eyes, half-wondering and half-knowing what Nicholas did to earn himself the fear.

She bounded up the stairs, tripping and dropping the keys in the process. She swore loudly, searching frantically for the right one.

"Yes!" Her shaking hands flew forward, quickly unlocking the two key-holes on Nicholas's door, then using every piece of strength and sheer luck that she had to break down the chain lock.

Quickly assessing the apartment, nothing seemed amiss. Would Arkady murder him in his apartment where it would be easy to spot, or would he catch him on his walk to school?

Her eyes grazed over the kitchen and living room. Nothing out of place—literally nothing. No pillow touched, no fork in the sink. She tiptoed with caution down the hall, quickly looking towards the nothingness to the left, and then hesitantly peeking in the bedroom.

The sheets were pulled back just at the corner, yet in a way that had her feel they were more haphazard than Nicholas would deem appropriate. She lingered here a moment longer then turned her head to face the bathroom—then she bolted.

Nicholas's unconscious body lay on his bathroom floor.

Her heart jumped up to her throat then landed in her stomach, erratic beating in her chest.

"Nicholas! Nicholas!" She shook him with shaking hands, tears streaming down her face. "Nicholas—please!"

Her panic overtook her, but she had to push through. Push past the fear and onto figuring out—what happened? What could she do?

Without a second thought, she was dialing her grandparents, urging them to come to his apartment.

"I don't know...I don't know what's wrong. He's not moving, he's not breathing. Please just get here. Please!" She did not know where they were or if getting here meant leaving the hospital, but she knew that whatever happened next, Nicholas would be okay. They would make him okay. He had to be okay.

She sucked in a breath, attempting to breathe. There were zero signs that anyone else had been in his home. There was not a single new mark on Nicholas.

She shook him harder, then her body calmed just ever so slightly, and she felt like she was pushed into a different world. Bright colors danced around her, stars sparkled brilliantly not just in the sky, but next to her, under her—everywhere. Her body was so light, so free, so untouched everywhere...except one spot. Something was gripping her hand.

"Nicholas!"

Rejoining reality, she noticed he had moved his hand into hers. Her eyes immediately shot to his face where she could just barely make out two, crystal blue eyes opening from behind heavy lids.

"Oh, Nicholas!" Her hands flew to his face, she touched him and felt him, trying again to look for ways to help. "You're okay, you're okay." She was not sure who she was assuring. "What happened? What is it?"

"I do not...I do..." His voice was weak, his words falling just as they started.

Stacy cursed the crappy apartment for the dim lighting and cramped space. "I need to get you out of here," she told him softly. She attempted to lift his body before crashing back down to the bathroom floor.

Moments later, Stacy heard her grandparent's voices through the front door and for the first time—she felt hope.

"Back here! Please help!" She called desperately.

She heard their footsteps turn into a jog as the two came rushing back.

Terra gasped, Tom automatically got to work, lifting Nicholas as close to 'on his feet' as could be managed. Stacy and Terra balanced his other side and carried him to his bed.

The Nicholas she knew was nowhere to be seen. He was delirious, lost...but he knew to grab her hand.

As Stacy stepped back, Terra and Tom moved his body back and forth, examining it, listening to it, talking in quick words that she did not understand. But then she realized why she did not understand them. It was not because they were medical terms—they were Dukhovian terms. The terms of Dukhovian remedies they were not allowed to have.

"It can't, Tom. He wouldn't.... surely..."

Whatever it was Terra was arguing against, Tom was not convinced. He turned to Nicholas. "Nicholas, son, before you left did you take Zhin? Nicholas, did you take Zhin?" Tom repeated it as Nicholas continued to look lost, his eyes opening more, but drifting to a different place.

"What's Zhin? Grandpa what's Zhin?"

He ignored her, continuing on with Nicholas until he seemed coherent enough to shake his head and mutter a sound that seemed to say 'what?'.

Then everything happened at once.

Terra stepped back and Tom grabbed Stacy. She tried to step back, to ask questions, but Terra simply side stepped around the bed.

"Your palms," Tom ordered Stacy. "Give me your palms."

"I can't...I..."

But Tom did not seem to care, or perhaps he already knew. He lifted her palms out and attempted to press them into Nicholas's, but he folded his hands in consciously, fighting and refusing whatever Tom hoped to accomplish.

But he was too weak, and in that moment, Terra was too strong.

Stacy returned to the land of stars and brightness. Except this time, Nicholas was there with her. The birds and colors from her dream floated around her, she felt light, she had no worries, no fears.

And then it slowly started to dissipate. She did not feel her fears immediately, but it was as if she knew they would soon return...

"What did you do?" Stacy asked, falling backward, her entire body feeling faint. "What happened?" Then her eye caught a small, blue tube that Tom grabbed out of his pocket.

"It won't be enough," he was saying.

"What is that?" Stacy protested. How could he? How long had he had that? How many others were there?

Tom paused, seeming to know he needed to provide answers. His eyes drifted from where his hands supported Nicholas's body and met Stacy's. "Zhin is a Dukhovian herb."

Her eyes bulged at the confirmation.

"I know the rule, but there are some things we Dukhovian's absolutely need and they were too stubborn to understand that at the ruling."

"You would put our family at risk?" Stacy choked out, her family's entire history running through her mind. If her mother knew it would be one thing, but if her uncle knew... Her uncle who disowned Tom for years until he proved his innocence, proved nothing was worth the risk of losing his family...

Terra and Tom exchanged a look with each other, Terra's eyes welling up in response.

"I will explain," Tom said in a hasty tone. "But Nicholas needs to get to the hospital. I need to monitor him."

Stacy nodded, but distrust quickly began to fall over towards Tom. She felt herself bounce back and forth as she watched him, knowing he was doing everything he could to save Nicholas's life, but knowing that he just risked his own innocence and that of their entire family.

And if he did it for Nicholas this time, she wondered how many other times he had done it before.

CHAPTER 65

ASHES OF THE HEIR

*N*icholas was rushed to The Heart of America Hospital where Terra and Tom pumped him full of an array of other unknown Dukhovian herbal remedies. Stacy said nothing. She glared at them as she watched them from his bedside, wondering what else they were willing to risk, what else they hid, but drew the line at helping their granddaughter.

She felt guilty for the thought—at first. But then it resonated with her. She thought they were so embarrassed, so scarred, so ashamed. She wanted to do nothing to remind them of their past and yet…hiding all of these things were a daily reminder. Or a way of life.

Her eyes remained straight, her voice silent when they let him know that they were done and he would just need to rest. She shuffled her shoulders and leaned forward, gripping his forearm. She did not let go. She did not leave. She simply sat.

She never noticed until now how innocent Nicholas appeared. Walking through the school, he was a warrior amongst peasants. But here, when he was so vulnerable, shielded from the need to wear those sparkling blue eyes and blinding white smile as a weapon, he was nothing more than a boy who had been so badly hurt.

She looked him over, his arms so badly scarred not just in one place, not just in a simple accident, but over and over, repeatedly punished for not disobeying his country. Brainwashed into believing he should harm his land. Broken and destroyed all out of spite. He was a person. A human being. A son. Destroyed.

Her eyes traveled along his chest and up to his face. Handsome. She was finally able to admit it. Maybe it made her feel better to be able to admit that the beauty she saw inside him first was confirmed to be true, but she knew she was lying to Rachael all this time—Nicholas was terribly, astoundingly handsome. He was soft. He was gentle. He was only human.

He groaned, moaning as he shifted his leg for the third time in ten minutes. Puzzled by what would be causing him pain, Stacy paused, looked to make sure he would not suddenly stir, and placed her hand on the top of his leg.

Nothing.

She moved down, slowly.

Nothing.

Then she hit his midthigh—the groans intensified, then he kicked and rolled over, remaining unconscious.

CHAPTER SIXTY-FIVE

Slowly, carefully, Stacy pulled back the sheet to find a gauze wrapped bandage around his leg. Strange. She had not noticed any injuries at his house or anything that could have caused him to get such an injury. Was it old? Or was she wrong and she missed something completely?

Maybe another Dukhovian secret her grandparents kept.

She threw the blanket back over him. More groans, then his lids began to flicker.

Hope spread throughout her body as he opened his eyes and glanced around the room.

He bolted up, attempting to get out of bed before losing his balance and plummeting back onto the bed.

"Nicholas, Nicholas…"

Stacy would be lying if she said her heart did not warm as Nicholas immediately settled back into bed once he registered Stacy's face.

"Stacy? Where am I? How did I get here?"

"You're at my grandparent's hospital," she explained slowly. He was comforted by her presence, by her grip on his forearm, but she saw the vein pulse in his neck when she said the words. "You didn't come to school today so I came to your apartment and found you passed out in your bathroom. What do you remember last?"

Nicholas seemed to be thinking hard, as if he had a very vague memory that he could not quite latch onto. Then he shook his head. "I felt nauseous last night. I had gotten up to shower and then…"

"And then this," Stacy finished for him. "Have you been eating?" It had been her first thought until Tom and Terra began pumping him full of unknown substances. Hunger seemed American enough to not require forbidden fruits.

He nodded his head slowly. "I had the leftovers from our picnic just before bed. It was the most I have eaten since I arrived."

"Have you been feeling sick?" She pressed.

He made the blank face again, as if focusing on how his body felt seemed so miniscule that he forgot to pay attention to such a thing, like he forgot it mattered.

"You had a severe Zhin deficit." Tom and Terra had entered the room, failing to hide the worry on their faces.

"Zhin?" Nicholas questioned. He seemed to remember the conversation at the house as he processed the word.

"Zhin is in all Dukhovians at birth. It is what connects our physical bodies to our spirit gift and the Spirit who gave it to us. The further we get from our spirit gift or from the source, in this case Dukhovia, our bodies begin to rapidly decline."

"That's why we have it," Terra said to Stacy quietly, apologetically. "We feared hiding it at first, but Tom is right, the American's simply don't understand that our bodies are different. We can't survive without it, so Tom has a friend send it."

"I've never had any Zhin," Stacy chastised angrily.

"You've never required it," Terra replied patiently. "Your Spirit is so strong you'd virtually have to leave the universe itself to feel the impact."

"Nicholas is just as strong as I am," Stacy protested in an offensive tone.

Terra tensed up and inclined her head, but Nicholas took over before she could speak.

"No, my princess," he told her in a steady tone. His words became soft, like a stroke to her hair, they melted her heart. "We are stronger than any other, but you fly above me."

"Nicholas's...alteration in path could also impact his connection," Tom said nonchalantly.

Stacy winced.

Terra noticed the tension and turned her attention back to Nicholas. "Nicholas did...did Ar...did he never mention this to you?"

Their eyes penetrated each other and the look told Stacy Nicholas knew exactly who *he* was.

Nicholas's face became vacant of emotion. "Must have slipped his mind," he uttered grimly.

Terra's eyes began to well, her face tightened as though she was holding back something—or everything—then she nodded her head ever so slightly and left the room.

Tom approached Nicholas with a light flashing into both of his eyes. Nicholas seemed perplexed, but remained cooperative.

"You need plenty of rest." He smiled warmly. "Terra and I would like you to come stay with us. We aren't exactly sure what to expect of your recovery and think you should have someone around you in case you lose consciousness again."

Nicholas's mouth dropped open. He began to protest, but could not form the words as he looked from Stacy to Tom and back again. "Oh, no, sir I thank you so much but I could never intrude..."

Tom was already shaking his head. "It would be an honor, Nicholas. Actually, you would be doing us a favor. We have two spare bedrooms that haven't seen use in years and we've lived quite lonely, unfulfilled lives when it comes to caring for others."

"I find that hard to believe," Nicholas smiled.

Stacy rolled her eyes.

"Consider it," Tom told him and disappeared after receiving an affirming head nod from Nicholas.

Stacy did not immediately make eye contact with Nicholas after Tom left, instead, she turned to him and looked down at his arm, tracing patterns along his forearm.

"Stacy Grace," he said in that voice that made her stomach do flips.

She met his eyes.

"What is it that is bothering you? Why are you being so closed off towards your grandparents?"

Stacy huffed, glancing out at the darkening sky and wondering if they were high enough to kill her if she jumped. "Tom and Terra aren't supposed to have anything from Dukhovia."

"As part of their agreeance to be released from prison," Nicholas finished from memory. "But they have said that they needed it to keep everyone alive. Otherwise, your family members would sit where I now sit."

She was silent. Partially furious at him for taking their side, partially furious at how accurate he was. "I know, but they just carry it around all willy nilly?"

A look of confusion.

"What if they were stopped in the streets? What if it fell out during one of their house searches? I mean, they could be more careful…"

"Perhaps," Nicholas agreed with a shrug of his shoulders. "But it is a risk no matter what and that will make things difficult to accept no matter what." He saw the persistence in her eyes and went on. "Deciding whether you are going to follow the rules or protect your family is never an easy decision."

Oh.

Then he did that heart-stopping stroke of her hair. "Sometimes you fail to find a reason to decide until you are looking right at it."

Her words and breath left her as she stared into the blinding beauty of Nicholas's brilliant blue eyes. Their bodies inched closer, their foreheads now touching, lips just inches apart.

"Thank you for finding me," he whispered.

She shrugged and whispered back. "You save me, I save you, remember?"

He swallowed. "You save me every single day, Stacy Grace."

She swore she threw up. She was biting her lip so fiercely it could have popped.

"Every. Single. Day." His lips moved in toward hers, she pulled towards him, ready for him, ready for everything that she never even once imagined a first kiss would be.

Until he howled out in pain, swore, and swung the cover from overtop his legs, revealing a deep, reddening mark around the bandage Stacy observed earlier.

Impulsively, he tore at the bandage, revealing a slashed cut that seemed to take the shape of an X. It was oozing with blood and pus, with purplish hues failing to compliment his tan skin tone.

He held his breath as he squeezed the X and watched as pus and blood seeped out from around him.

"I'll get my grandparents!" Stacy shouted, jumping up from her chair.

"No!" Nicholas shouted. "I can do it—please just find me something…no."

Stacy lifted more bandaging from a cart, but he refused it. Struggling to hold his leg and stop the bleeding, Stacy began tossing objects his way until he settled on simply putting a towel under his leg and allowing it to drip.

"Nicholas, you need my grandparents. It's horribly infected and might need stitches."

"No, not this. No one should have ever touched it."

Stacy gulped, fear and anxiousness over the drastic change in his tone spread throughout her body. "What is it? What's it from?" As if the origin of the rest of his scars were not horrific enough, she was terrified to find out why he was so protective of this one.

He glanced at her, then returned to holding his leg. "I do not wish to worry you."

She rolled her eyes and sat next to him. Swatting away his hand, she began to apply pressure on the wound. "Not telling me doesn't make me worry any less, your highness."

If looks could kill, Nicholas certainly had the highest body count. "It is something that people began to do in Dukhovia long ago—when the First World began to crumble. It was considered barbaric and out of practice until the start of the war when a few people began to do it again. Now it is far and few between, if someone sees the mark on you, you are regarded as someone who must have committed an unforgiveable crime."

"They branded you?" Stacy asked, horrified. "For your family? Nicholas, I..."

He was shaking his head, silencing her and bringing her to a halt. "No, no, Stacy. I did this to myself."

That was it. She had thought she heard everything. She thought there was nothing else that he could tell her that would surprise her or worry her any further. But this—this was the one thing that destroyed her. To not only hear about it and imagine it in the past or not real at all, but to *see* its realness, its severity...

She felt her knees buckle, her heart twist in her chest.

Then she turned to the side of his bed and vomited into the trash can.

"Stacy!"

Perhaps it was how innocent he appeared to her the moment before. Perhaps it was how clearly she saw the purity of his heart and soul. Perhaps it was the realization that if her role was to protect him, she was failing miserably. But the idea that not only would someone else fail to see that goodness, but that he would...she could not take it.

"Why," she managed to croak out.

He refused to say anything, understandably. But she took a seat next to him, playing the role of the innocent listener, hoping he would divulge everything she needed to know to actually start keeping him safe.

"Those of us who have committed the worst sins against the Spirits believe that we could possibly be cleansed of our sins if we make this mark on our body. Not just that, but we need to offer up our blood to be taken and cleansed or an opening for our body to be accessed through. If we sin again, we cut the mark deeper."

Stacy's chest began to heave as she looked at the depth and size of Nicholas's wound. It was just smaller than his hand and likely as deep as he could get it without cutting an artery. Did legs have arteries? Probably.

The more he dabbed at it, the more she was able to recognize the shape—and she realized it looked familiar.

She could not catch her breath. "Terra has that mark on her arm."

CHAPTER 66

DUKHOVIA'S VICTIMS

*N*icholas got out of the car with uneasiness. Most of it was motion sickness, but he had nerves as well. It was his first day out of the hospital after three days. Three days which seemed like a lifetime. He ran his hand down the forearm that Stacy held for the majority of those three days—it was the only thing that got him through.

He stood before a small, cream-colored house with dark green shutters. It was much more modest than Stacy's in most respects—both on the inside and out.

"Ready?"

Terra smiled at him as she lifted one of his bags, Tom the other. He nodded his head in agreement.

After much discussion with Stacy, he had decided to accept their invitation to stay. Though he felt he already knew Arkady lied to him and that they seemed to be good people, he was nervous that the rumors of Dukhovia were true and they were anything but the people they appeared to be.

Nicholas did not lie to Stacy—many people failed to consider the family meant to be banished, but rumors about the nature of Terra and Tom's mistakes were world-renowned. His gut worried that the source of rumors had at least some validity.

Still, he had never been welcomed into anyone's home, save for Arkady into the palace—and it was hardly a warm invite. He had never been given a tour of the home, walked over to a fridge and told to 'help himself'. He had never been invited to casually sit in the common area and mingle. He had never been walked back to the bedroom where new items sat folded on the bed as a welcoming gift.

After professing his gratitude to the point of near tears, Terra and Tom exited to allow him time to sort through his things and 'prepare for dinner'. Prepare. No rush. No demands. 'It will be ready when you are'.

Not monsters. Not deserving of their banishment.

Nicholas was certain he did not want to fulfill what he was sent here to do. He was certain Arkady was a liar and had no positive plans for his life. But he often found himself needing to verify the facts, to remind himself what was reality and what was a lie—it was the only way for him to determine who was telling the truth.

That and the issue with the Zhin was a wake-up call. It was clear to Nicholas—Arkady did not care what happened to him.

CHAPTER SIXTY-SIX

He returned to his bed—though smaller than the one in his narrowly missed apartment, it was much softer and offered bedding that felt like a hug. Strange how he now knew what that felt like.

Colors of red and blue streaked the top of the bed, standing out amongst cream walls and a speckled cream and brown carpet. The room was small—smaller than the smallest room in the palace, but it was comfortable. It was his. He was safe.

Shirts and pants. Shower gel and anti-perspirant. A journal. A relic of The Water Spirit. Nicholas slowly sorted through the items that had been placed on his bed. He unfolded all the shirts. They were button ups, but had only a few buttons at the very top and then flowed downward just the same as his tunic. The pants were also more like what he was used to.

He found himself quickly stripping down to change.

An hour later, Nicholas had showered, freeing himself of the scent of blood and hospital. He felt better and more comfortable as he seemed to moderately recognize the person looking back at him in the mirror. Except, he realized, he would never see the person whom looked back at him in Dukhovia ever again. That person was dead.

"There he is. And so handsome!" Terra welcomed him into the kitchen by embracing him and looking at his outfit. "Does everything fit okay? Tom took his best guess."

The terrifyingly gentle man shrugged. "I'm a brilliant guesser."

"Nicholas, Stacy told me you were a vegetarian so I made you a couple things, um…spakada, roast vegetables, rice medley, there's cata, mounite…" Terra's hands were shaking as she drifted over the plates.

"One of everything known to man—she's been working since sunrise cooking and she has done a beautiful job so, darling, please let the boy eat. He hasn't had a decent meal in days."

"Thank you." The word was beginning to feel dry and useless for the amount that was being given to him.

"Oh, Nicholas, we also wanted to make sure we gave you your choice of when you want to go down to the temple room. We usually go in the morning, but whenever you like to go, we can make adjustments."

Nicholas put his fork down and stared at each of their faces, waiting for the other shoe to drop.

It never did.

"I…I am permitted to partake in temple time?"

Heartbreak and confusion lined Terra's face. "Of course, sweetheart, why wouldn't you be?"

Nicholas did not answer, he only looked down at his food and suddenly did not quite feel like eating anymore.

Terra put her hand over her mouth and stepped away, she tried to return after three paces around the kitchen, but quickly disappeared again.

He could understand Stacy's hesitation in asking them anything related to Dukhovia.

Nicholas and Tom made small talk the rest of the meal, then Tom offered to bring Nicholas down to the temple to show him the proper way to perform the ritual.

Nicholas fought against his mind the entire time.

You think you deserve this?

I am honored and humbled to finally partake in this experience.

This is for honorable Dukhovians, not murderers.

Then Tom made to open the door and he stopped walking.

Tom noticed his hesitation and shut the door, waiting. Then he spoke in that even, calm tone he always used. The one that told Nicholas there was no way that voice belonged to the man responsible for the lives of hundreds of people.

"Do you know the biggest difference between man and the Spirits?"

Nicholas arched his eyebrow, unable to find his voice.

"Forgiveness and acceptance. Man can often times try for many years to earn the forgiveness and acceptance of others and still fail. But the Spirits? They can see your soul. They can see your true self better than even you and so they have forgiven you and already rewritten your story before you even asked."

He nodded, a small, confirming smile on his lips. He inched closer to the door until he was in the brilliantly white, pristine room. Before him were several lit candles floating in a circular tub of water, continuously circling a glass sheath depicting the symbols of Winter, Water, and Moon.

Nicholas dropped to his knees before the magnificent sight. Around him, the walls were decorated with the Dukhovian flag, symbols of the Spirits, several relics, and maps of the land.

"You'll begin by giving them an offering—a piece of knowledge, a confession showing vulnerability and trust…"

Nicholas thought on the subject for a while. Then he tilted his head forward and closed his eyes. "I am not worthy of this spot. My sins far surpass those of any Dukhovian. Yet I seek your forgiveness. I seek a purpose different than that which has ever been offered to me. I seek to protect Stacy Matthews…to bring great peace to my nation."

"Now you'll light the candle that aligns with your Spirit Gift."

Slowly, Nicholas lifted one of the other candles and made to the center where each Spirit was represented by a single wick across a long, cement board. He lit those of nature, winter, water, and the moon.

"Finally, you'll say Ailu's blessing over the water and wash it on yourself."

Nicholas nodded, both in understanding and gratitude.

Bless my spirit, bless my path and my ancestry. For good and bad, for near and far, for every knight of forever.

He sighed one more time before dipping his hands into the water. The cool felt inspiring on his skin. He reached up, splashing one forearm, then another and rubbing them together.

Immediately he felt the ground shake beneath his body. The cold, hard ground transformed into something soft, something smooth and comforting. He opened his eyes and looked around, but there was nothing to see. Nothing to hear. Tom was gone; everything was utterly silent.

Including the sound of his thudding heart.

Wherever he was now, his nerves did not follow him. He could breathe; he could feel without a weight trapping him in his place. That was it. He had no weight. He was free. He was free.

Then he heard a murmur of voices. Quiet and few at first, but growing into a sea of mixed whispers.

Follow. Follow. Lead. Lead towards great peace or there will be great destruction.

And then a wolf came out of the corner of his eye. He stood, proud, but nervous, waiting patiently for Nicholas. Then he seemed to nudge himself towards the left and went down the winding path, towards a tall, dark mountainside. He did not recognize the mountain range, but a memorable, path of naturally glowing light stretched down the middle.

The scene did not change after that. It only repeated. The words continuing and the wolf walking until it was over and Nicholas was once more staring at the gray concrete of The Grayson basement.

Nicholas blinked, looking up at Tom for his reaction—what had happened for him? Was Nicholas's experience normal?

Tom's face was expectant, holding some worry, but he seemed calm.

"Are you alright?" He asked, helping Nicholas up by the arm.

He nodded slowly. "I had a vision. Is that normal?"

Tom nodded slowly. "It's rare, but can happen. Being you are an heir and have never participated in temple time before, I would expect the Spirits have a lot to convey to you."

Nicholas bit his lower lip. "Lead towards great peace or there will be great destruction," Nicholas quoted. "A command. At least, that is how they conveyed it this time. Perhaps it changes? The way Arkady spoke it to me, it was as if the destruction was more imminent. As if it were one or the other—Stacy would cause peace, I would cause destruction."

"Hm," Tom shifted in his shoes as if he were stumped. "I do not know if I know exactly how the Spirits conveyed your purpose to the shaman, however, I can be nearly certain that two great heirs whom love Dukhovia more than their will to breathe would do more to save Dukhovia than could ever be done."

Nicholas's chest hurt at the words. He imaged what Arkady would have said. The pain he would have endured. Was it truly possible to live in a world where he could simply ask questions? Say his thoughts? Or would there be a time he went too far?

He pushed the thought away. Then focused on Tom—his calming presence, his kind words. He embodied trust.

"He—he never let me have temple time before. He said that my family did not deserve it, that it would be disrespectful to speak to the Spirits after what we did." Nicholas shook his head.

Tom was silent for a long time. "I tend to not apologize for actions that are not mine—perhaps a way of healing from my past." He laughed slightly, then grew as serious as Nicholas had seen the man. "But I am truly and humbly apologetic for the life you endured as a result of my family's choices."

Nicholas swallowed the lump growing in his throat, fighting a stinging in his eyes. "It is not your family's burden to carry," his voice quivered. "You have chosen to act honorably in the best interests of your paths and Dukhovia. As a result, you have created a family I can only dream of. I would have made all your same choices."

"You are part of this family now, Nicholas."

"I have not earned the right."

Tom shook his head. He approached Nicholas, firmly yet comfortingly setting his hand on his shoulder. "The right to be cared for does not need to be earned."

Nicholas could not control the emotion that rolled from him now. The questions he always wanted to ask, the opportunity never there. "How do you get over it?" He asked, tears streaming down his face. "How do you live day to day knowing that you've hurt so many people?"

"You don't get over it," Tom answered slowly. "No, you never forget, you never feel better about what you did—but you learn. You learn how to turn the devastation into empowerment, how to make their lives count. You think about them every single day and how to make their lives meaningful. I hurt so many people—whether I was coherent or not. But I've saved so many more. Saving ten does not outweigh killing one, but if I do it in their memory then maybe, just maybe, I can be forgiven."

Nicholas sat with the words for a time, mulling over their meaning. What they meant to Tom and what they meant to Nicholas were not really so different, after all. Not really. "You do deserve to be forgiven." He finally said.

"I hope you're right, son," Tom declared, clapping him on the back.

The two closed out the temple room and began to head back up the stairs. Terra could be heard moving around in their bedroom just beyond the kitchen.

Nicholas stopped before they got any closer, lowering his voice. "Terra deserves to be forgiven too."

Tom stopped where he stood, his head turned just enough to where the shadow of the light brightened his eyes. "Yes, yes she does."

CHAPTER 67

THE PLOT

"Well, well, well, in the flesh!"

"I even do summersaults and backhand springs."

Stacy laughed as she swung the door open for Nicholas. It was the first day Tom and Terra allowed him to get up and walk around, thus he insisted on making the trek to Stacy's for her first post-op lesson. She tried to talk him out of the idea, but they all knew it was a failed mission.

In the days following Stacy finding Nicholas in his apartment, they were together daily. Some days just for dinner, some entire days. Their lessons also continued. Nicholas seemed a better teacher surrounded by the growth of Dukhovian vegetables. Stacy was anxious, wondering what else they grew that was not so obvious.

Rachael often came over too, working on and perfecting control over her...gifts. She began to use them better than she could ever imagine, allowing herself to feel anger and sadness and fear and wielding them as a weapon to aid her rather than destroy her. The light from the confidence that shone from her on those days was enough to burn down a city.

But, speaking of burning down cities, Stacy had still not had a conversation with her grandparents. Despite Nicholas explaining it to her in a way that did make sense and he and Rachael ganging up on her daily over it, she simply could not find the words or the motivation.

Not even today, as her and Rachael spent the last hour talking about all the pieces of the puzzle.

"This sounds like the same amount of Dukhovian overthinking that you've been doing the last sixteen years," Rachael said with a chastising grin and flip of her hair. "And you did say they never denied you Dukhovian knowledge, you just didn't like to ask, right?"

The thought caused a tiny flicker in Stacy's mind that sparked an entire wildfire across her memory. "It was more like I ask and they walk away or avoid the subject."

Rachael took a last bite on her apple and chucked the core into the trash can behind her. "Okay, so exactly how we would expect them to feel given both their banishment AND feelings of perpetual guilt that they're continuing to harbor the substances that lost them their family." Rachael paused. "Have you told your mom?"

Stacy shook her head. "I don't want to worry her."

Rachael smiled. "So, it has a lot less to do with who is and isn't doing what and a lot more to do with shielding their feelings. Oh, my little heir, the Ancestry Spirit is strong in you after all!"

Stacy was not sure if she was looking for more answers, even had any more questions, or just needed the confirmation that she received staring back into Rachael's lifechanging eyes.

"Anywho," Rachael sang, with a smile. "Mom's taking me shopping for your birthday soon," Rachael squealed, holding her books up to her face as though her gift would be a secret and not the same red, dazzling heels Stacy refused to wear for the last six years. Albeit, and something totally amazing and unpredictable. "Gotta run." She saluted her and ran off.

"Later!" Stacy called.

Nicholas waved.

Through everything—Stacy overthinking and Nicholas teaching them—Nicholas remained independent. He would not rest, he never asked for help getting up, he fell often, and had to have stitches twice due to falls.

But today, today was different. Today was going to be different, it had to be—today they were making a plan.

She lightened up, gently touching the back of his neck and scratching at his hair. "You look much better than the last time I saw you."

He cocked his head to the side. "Are you saying I was not the ravishing, handsome man before you when I was barely conscious in a bed these last few days?"

"I'd never allure to such a thing." She laughed.

He extended his arms around her. "And how are you feeling?" He asked, rubbing her cheek instead of pushing the hair that blinded her vision behind her ear—she always shook it free.

She sighed. "I haven't slept. I constantly have visions of my family members frolicking in a glorious meadow that then turns into ash moments later. Oh, and in my dream last night, I finally got to Dukhovia, stepped out of the plane, and found my entire nation destroyed."

Nicholas's mouth tensed. "Well, we have accomplished one thing—determining that this *is* your nation. Now that we have half that battle out of the way, we can focus on what matters."

Stacy rolled her eyes as she shut the door behind him, trailing him over to the computer room. "Yeah, but what is that worth if I'm not doing anything about it?"

Nicholas sat down on the couch next to Stacy, he had not arrived empty handed and immediately spread out his map of Dukhovia, already marked where they had discussed thus far.

"Which is exactly what we will not be doing. I do not know exactly how we can get out of Arkady's game. My mother tried fleeing with me as an infant and he made it perfectly clear he was a skilled tracker—he could find me through our spirit connection in a heartbeat."

The words entered Stacy's head almost like a call. "But so could we. We can find him first and be one step ahead."

Nicholas nodded firmly. "Precisely. That in combination with our own spirit gifts and the fact we are much stronger will give us a significant upper hand."

"Not to mention the people who will rally behind us, right? We have supporters?"

He became silent, biting his lip so fiercely it nearly bled. "You have supporters," he said softly.

"Nicholas," Stacy said in an aggressive tone. "Our people are forgiving. Our people are kind and just. I know things have been difficult, but we are in a better position than ever—you are on the right path."

He hung his head, uneasiness in his stomach. "I am not even certain I know my path anymore."

"Well know this," Stacy spoke her words fearlessly. "Fulfilling your destiny, doesn't mean losing who you are, it means finding out who you're meant to be."

Suddenly, Nicholas's body was only an inch from Stacy's. Her breath began to grow uneven, her heart skipping every beat in absolute erratic rhythm.

"You care so much about the purpose of a monster."

She shook her head, sternly. "Wrong." She wrapped her arms around his neck, drawing him nearer. "I care about you."

He was silent, those brilliantly persuasive eyes not so cunning after all, but rather…comforting, safe…

Safe. From the man who was the spitting image of not a monster, but fear itself.

"What do your friends think now, your family?" His hands inched nearer, a lone finger loosely tracing along her collar bone and down her arm in abstract patterns. "Surely it isn't your life's dream to be with someone as broken as myself."

Stacy shook her spinning head. "I already told you—they see a man of brilliance and grace; they don't see your mistakes as who you are." Her eyes fell; she felt her face blush. "And I never quite pictured a 'man of my dreams', never even really considered it, had a fleeting thought about it…" She stopped herself before her rambling took off. "But feeling like…this…with you…it's easy."

She felt her heartrate accelerating, her breathing hardly existing as she held it in, afraid to move, afraid for the moment to end.

"I often thought of my future wife. Someone who makes the nightmares go away. I never imagined it could be so simple as merely looking into your eyes that sends even my strongest demons running."

With that, Nicholas leaned forward, his arms wrapped gently around her— holding her, feeling her, experiencing her. His lips lightly danced across her forehead, a sensual kiss pressing softly inward. Then he moved down, his eyelashes fluttering against hers, his own breathing uneven.

"I want to try something," he whispered, leaning into her ear.

Shivers went down her spine at his words, she thought it had to be evident now how embarrassingly wooed she was.

His hands slid down her arms, his fingers dancing along, sending more chills as they went. Until finally he reached her hand. He started slowly, his fingers lightly tracing the back, working his way ever so gently towards her palm. Then he danced his fingers on the bottom of her hand, sliding slowly into her palm.

Both of them drew in a breath, the usual whirlwind that only ever intensified sending them spiraling. Stacy hardly knew what was happening, but she felt his fingers continue to graze, to trace and claim undiscovered territory. He paused at certain spots, then added in a second hand.

Then he backed away.

Stacy blinked, freeing herself of the spell. "What was it?" She asked, curiously.

"I want to perfect my connection," Nicholas said it as a promise. "If I practice with you, then I can slowly start adding in Arkady."

"And he'll never see us coming," Stacy smiled.

"Never," Nicholas confirmed with a wide-toothed smile.

CHAPTER 68

THE POWER OF FEAR

Nicholas and Stacy had continued trying to connect to each other's spirit for hours after that. A few times they felt like they had it, but the amount of power that naturally shifted between them was difficult to differentiate between.

Eventually, Stacy deemed it time to head over to her uncle's and get ready for Cody's party. Nicholas quickly declined the invitation, stating that he was confident Cody's birthday wish was for him to not be there.

He was not wrong.

"Okay, so funny story, true story…" Rachael set down a large array of gift bags on Cody's kitchen counter, clueing Stacy into the obvious fact that Rachael continued shopping for Cody when she went for Stacy. It was to be expected. She swung herself on a stool next to the two, trying to suppress laughter.

With Yasana out of sight, Rachael and Stacy had fully taken over in helping Richard prepare for the party. Tom and Terra would be over to help momentarily, but decorating for a party was the type of thing Rachael lived for—especially when it was for the love of her life.

They were now working fervently on putting together a banner and blowing up balloons. Cody thought they looked juvenile, but Rachael insisted that there was a reason behind her master piece and they need not question it because their 'unfashionable minds' could not comprehend it.

Rachael continued her story. "There I am, in line at the store, minding my own business…"

Cody and Stacy exchanged a look.

"…When this guy behind me starts telling his friends about all the cool songs on our new CD. Well, clearly, homeboy didn't realize I was right in front of him because he starts going on about how we're trash and all this nonsense. Which, whatever, entitled to your opinion, voice it right in front of me, more power to ya…. BUT THEN HE STARTED SINGING ONE OF OUR SONGS. LOVER TRAILS WAS LITERALLY THE RINGTONE ON HIS PHONE."

"You don't sing often, he probably didn't recognize that we were the same band," Stacy offered with a menacing grin.

"How'd he download our song if he didn't know our name?" Rachael pushed, staring at their faces with intense pressure.

"Maybe he did know you were right in front of him and was trying to not come off obsessive," Cody offered plainly, tying a balloon around a string through the banner. "He was trying to impress you."

"Oh yeah, and bad mouthing my friends is a wonderful way to impress me." She rolled her eyes, smiled playfully. She hopped off the counter, beginning to dance around the house to decorate.

It did come together really well once they were finished. The decorations did not look nearly as *juvenile* as predicted. Apparently through previous help from Dan, Rachael managed to feed glow sticks and fluorescent lights through most of the decorations, making the house look like the stage at one of their concerts.

She meticulously set up their instruments around the house and borrowed a few of his football trophies for the football themed sitting room. It doubled as a tribute to Cody, displaying every award he ever earned in sports and music alike. The room was quite full.

Rachael sent Cody on a walk around the house to approve (and compliment) all of her perfections.

"You did an amazing job, Rachael, thank you so much for all your help." Richard beamed as he looked around the room, admiring all her hard work.

"I also do weddings and bar or bat mitzvahs," she said, admiring her perfectly manicured nails.

"You too, Stace. I really appreciate it."

"Happy to help, Uncle Richey," Stacy said, clapping him on the back.

"Don't forget I put the cake in the fridge downstairs," Rachael said matter-of-factly, smiling as she pointed to herself.

"The cake!" Richard slapped himself on the head. "I almost forgot. I never could have done this alone."

Stacy and Rachael smiled but met each other's sad eyes. Both for the situation and the lack of self-appreciation. Richard had been doing most of the parenting things on his own Cody's entire life.

"Where is my wonderful aunt?" Stacy wondered in a bitter voice.

"She stormed out this morning after telling him it was a reminder of the worst day of her life. She said she wished she never became a mother."

Rachael's eyes filled with tears, Stacy gasped, horrified.

"He never even mentioned it. He was quiet when we first got here, but he's been that way a while..." Stacy started as she thought of the empty look in her cousin's eyes that she was beginning to grow weary of seeing. She missed the bright flare that he always was and the happiness he emitted to an entire roomful of people. "How did he handle it?"

Richard shook his head, letting his head fall. "He was angry. He stopped himself from breaking everything in sight and ran outside..."

Stacy was quiet, approaching the topic sensitively. "He's not happy, Uncle Richey. I know you don't want him to lose his mother, but is keeping around someone so destructive better than nothing at all?" Stacy bit her tongue. She knew her uncle and Nicholas had begun to share a special relationship, but she wondered what he would say—if a murderer could be forgiven, could bad parenting?

She swallowed sticking to her guns. There was a sharp difference and that difference lie in accountability.

"I think he'd be happier with all love and no mother rather than a mother that brings around such terrible feelings," Rachael added in an almost whisper. Her balloon banner began to shake. She lifted two hands up in front of her, using the force of emotion to straighten the decoration. Then, satisfied, she smiled at herself.

Stacy gave her an encouraging hug.

Richard sighed, leaning against the kitchen counter with a thoughtful mind. "I know how these things work. I know that if she makes him feel inferior enough, he'll runaway... or worse. I don't want him to have a childhood to heal from. But I don't want to give up on Yasana either. She's my wife and I gave a vow: for better or worse."

"But the force always says: do the best for them, until it makes the worst out of you," Stacy quoted the phrase that was tossed around the police station daily as a pick-me-up. They taught them to always do what was best for society and for the offenders of the law. But if it got to the point where they were hurting more people or losing themselves, they had to make changes.

"You're right," Richard accepted. "Maybe we can talk him into staying put at your place for a few more days, after the holidays." He seemed less than thrilled about the idea. Cody had been wanting to come back home, trialing a night here and there. He was sick of the back and forth.

"My parents would love that," Stacy said encouragingly.

The clock struck 7p.m. and guests started arriving. Cody and Dylan spent much of the night discussing their plans for football in the coming year with family members. Other times, the friends all gathered in the basement to shoot pool and play air hockey. Tension only increased when they got into a heated game of darts. Aim was Dylan's worst skill but strongest focus.

For the most part, for the first time, Stacy felt herself able to relax, to be herself with her friends. Well, to a degree and situation dependent...

"Are you planning to run for office next year?" Tom's voice asked.

Stacy overheard the conversation with Tom, Fred, and Richard. She turned her head ever so slightly to listen in. The three were positioned near the bar, poised over drinks as they discussed the politics involved in some poor decisions the President was making and the backlash he received.

"Stace, you're up," Cody said, handing her a dart.

She got up and, without much effort, threw the dart almost perfectly in the center.

"Nice, Stace! She's on my team next time," Dylan applauded.

"I don't know that any of it makes sense, realistically," Richard went on. "I don't know what he'll do to fix it."

Stacy gulped. Since realizing she was the heir, most of her focus had been on ending the war and protecting her people. Rightfully, so, she supposed. But she had not stressed over the specifics yet. Like the fact that she knew little to nothing about politics in the country that she was raised in let alone another. She barely knew what form of politics they had. King Yuriy? Czar Arkady? Czars were socialist, right? No, communist? Were those even in the same realm?

And she could not fight the overwhelming thought that she had been trying to put out of her head all afternoon. If. Nicholas and Stacy doing this together was only an if... *If* he could get away from Arkady and out of this mission... What *if* he was unable? Then what? Then who trained Stacy?

She held her pulsing temples, her head groaning at her after trying to figure it all out. Deciding on a break, she grabbed her empty glass and headed back up to the punch bowl, taking an extra moment to linger in the breeze of the cracked window.

"I hear you're in love."

Cara had danced next to Stacy, singing the words cheerfully.

"Boy, word travels fast," Stacy commented, eyeing Rachael, who had been talking with Andy and Joey Leighton—her cousins by marriage and Stacy's by blood. Terra Leighton was Grace's cousin who had the twins with a man named Manny. When Manny decided to test the waters of infidelity, Dallas Leighton—Rachael's uncle—served as her divorce lawyer and the two wound up married.

Rachael waved and winked at the two, knowing Cara's drilling was soon to follow.

"Tell me all about him. Is he poetic? Charming? I already know he is. So, can I start planning the wedding? What will you wear to prom? Oooo shopping spree!"

The heaviness of reality set in the more Cara talked. It was not as if she did not want to be excited about those things too, she never dreamed herself thinking about this type of stuff. She never dreamed herself falling in—was she falling in...? Anyway, it was less so a matter of not wanting to talk about those things and more so having to be practical. "I really don't think he'll be here that long, Care," Stacy said, not even attempting to block her disappointment.

Cara's face fell. "Oh, why not? He's not here to stay?"

Stacy wished she had not said anything, she was not prepared for the welling of emotion that formed inside of her, the punch to the gut, the loss of breath in her lungs. What was she doing? What was she going to do? No trainer meant no saved country, no trainer meant Nicholas was gone, Nicholas being gone meant he was back to the pain and misery.

She froze.

No. No. He did not deserve that. He could not endure that. No. No.

"Stace?" Cara put her arm around Stacy.

She felt her eyes bulging, her body becoming weak.

"Stacy, let's sit down."

Cara walked her over towards the front door. They took a seat on the bottom step leading upstairs. It was quiet. Everyone was gone.

"Breathe, Stace," Cara said gently. "Breathe. Everything will be okay."

Stacy nodded her head, catching her breath. She did not know if it would be okay—but she had to try long enough to find out.

"I'm sorry," Stacy finally muttered, feeling herself still in a daze.

Cara shook her head. "Is everything okay? With Nicholas?"

She let out an exasperated sigh. "He's wonderful, Cara."

She squealed with delight.

"There's just so much to it," Stacy went on. "And I'm scared. I'm scared about what waits for him back in Dukhovia. I'm scared to think about what would happen to him."

She was not sure how much Cara knew about why Nicholas was here, but she neither led on to being fully in the know or confused. That was the beauty of Cara. She met you where you were at, no matter what. There was no judgment, there were no closed doors.

"Well, what do we know about him?"

"What do you mean?" Stacy asked softly, rubbing at her nose.

"Do we know him to be someone who gives up? Someone easily defeated? Or do we know him to be a fighter? Will he stand down if he is put into a dangerous situation? Will he think of every possible way to not get in that situation?"

Cara's voice nearly broke as she spoke, Stacy knew how raw the emotion was for her. The abuse her and Dylan endured was like that of nightmares or the most horrid film. And, continuing to live with said parents, it was not even something she could begin to heal from.

"Is he resourceful? Will he ever give up?"

"I love you, Care," Stacy exclaimed, swinging her arms around her friend.

"And he loves you," she whispered in her ear, earning a laugh from Stacy. "It's true," Cara went on. "It's the way he looks at you, and the way you see him, and the fact that you're the same person.

"And he's a wonderful man, Stace. His apartment is in my neighborhood. He's been working hard day and night to fix up houses, help elderly cross the street, building playhouses for little girls, oh it's so heartwarming to see."

What a great place for an heir, Stacy thought. A place to not only be of use, but fulfill a likely innate need when he had no other current use. At least, that was how she felt…

CHAPTER SIXTY-EIGHT

"Hello, ladies, what are we talking about?" Jade asked, coming over with a fresh glass of punch. One look told Stacy she had grabbed one of the fifteen glasses Stacy aimlessly poured.

"Just Stacy's new boyfriend, Nicholas. We were talking about what a sweetheart he is," Cara said with immense pleasure.

Jade raised her eyebrows, sipping her punch through a straw as an attempt to mask the smell of the other beverage she added to it. "Yeah, if sweetheart is defined by a lunatic impulse and a murder reflex. He's a real charmer."

She chugged the rest of her drink and walked off to meet the boys who were coming upstairs as the night wound down.

"Don't listen to her, Stace," Cara said, rolling her eyes. "We all have our weaknesses." She started twirling as she danced over to her brother. "Well, I'm off to find Dylan. We'll see you tomorrow night." She skipped off with a wink.

***

Surprisingly enough, it was another sleepless night for Stacy. She pulled the pillow over her head to silence all the voices inside, but to no avail... she was stuck with them. Every voice. Every vision. Every thought. Spiraling, spiraling away...

And every moment before she shut her eyes and made failed attempts to drift away again, a face of innocence flashed in her mind. Then she saw bright, blue eyes once full of hope and gratitude, fill with tears and desperation.

CHAPTER 69

THE MOST HONORABLE PURPOSE

December 24th

"Good morning!" Screeched Grace throughout the halls.

It was five-fifteen in the morning; everyone was rising to spend time with Kevin on Christmas Eve.

"Morning mom," yawned Stacy, coming around the staircase.

Everyone was already sitting at the counter eating their breakfast. Dan arrived on video call, looking like a zombie as he could barely get his eggs in his mouth. He picked up and sat down his toast so many times, soon it was just a crumbly mess that did not even make it onto the plate anymore. She guessed he was up all night putting the finishing touches on the concert.

Kevin was in automatic mode. He poured his coffee, as usual. He took his seat at the end of the counter, as usual, and he read his morning paper. He was neither wide awake nor tired, but his wife was bouncing with excitement.

"So, here's the plan," Grace began picking up everyone's plates and moving them to the table so they had to look at each other. Everyone else moved over slowly. "Your father's gonna get off early today for Christmas Eve and do his overtime on the twenty-sixth since they're off for Christmas. When he gets home, we will head over to Rachael's party together. I already picked out her present from all of us."

"Glad we did that together," Dan said slouching on his table.

"Oh, you'll love it," she teased him. "I just had to get it for her."

Stacy drained her orange juice glass and finished her last bit of toast. "Sounds like a plan…Wait, if dad's getting off early, why did I have to wake up?"

"There's no such thing as too early for family, Stacy Grace," Grace scolded, flipping a burnt pancake onto the floor as she spoke. Stacy saw a smirk escape Kevin's lips before he rose to help her.

"Yes, there is," Stacy claimed. "It's before six am on regular days and before nine am on vacation."

"When have you ever been awake by nine am when given a choice?" Dan joked.

"I was setting my limits," Stacy noted, defensively. "I haven't been sleeping at all, recently."

"Why's that, sweetheart?" Kevin asked gently, glancing up from the pancake debacle.

"Just too much on my mind," she let her elbow fall onto the table and her head collapse into her hand. Her eyes shut upon reflex only for a moment, before fluttering open to stare at the brown swirls on the dark, marble table.

"Is it that kid at school? The detention one? Is he giving you problems?" Dan asked each question slowly and with care, suddenly wide awake.

"Yeah, something like that," she admitted, feeling a punch to her gut as she did so. She only half-subconsciously rolled her eyes at the way Dan referred to the man he met and shook hands with.

"I'll go down to Santifini as soon as he's back and have him talk some sense into him," Dan offered in a threatening tone, as if the principal's mental abuse could touch someone as skilled as Nicholas.

Stacy was half-interested in if Santifini returning was a prospect on the table, but she could barely lift her head enough to care.

"I think you should invite him over again," Grace theorized, winking at Stacy. Kevin eyed Grace with a mix of confusion and adoration.

"What?" Dan asked blankly, a touch of shock peeking through. Dan had been kind enough after meeting Nicholas, but Cody had swayed him to join his cause as well. He was on the fence.

"Kindness is always the right thing to do, Daniel Joseph," Grace said the phrase in her best teacher's voice.

Dan argued against his mother, but the words resonated with Stacy. She was right and that was the mentality she wanted to bring to Dukhovia, after all. It was what they needed.

The vision of a world she imagined as a child blew into her mind. A bright world, full of color and peace had become the bitterness, hatred, and fraught of her desolation. And for the first time, she let the desires of that world fill her in a realistic sense—she could create that world. She could be the change she desperately searched to find. It was not only fulfilling to her people of Dukhovia, it was not only purposeful, and inarguably unique…it was life changing.

"Anyway, Stacy Grace," her mother began, poised and confident. "As much as I know mom and dad will love on him, I'm sure waking up Christmas morning surrounded by all of us would be a treat too."

Stacy nodded her head, a silent reminder to invite him stored in her head.

***

Nicholas pulled at his too-tight shirt for perhaps the seventh time that evening. At this point, he was uncertain whether it was out of nerves or discomfort. Or both.

He rang the doorbell and entered a home that was more Christmas décor than it was home. Room to breathe was a figment of the past. Though it was awe-worthy.

Rachael's father introduced himself at the door. A kind and gentle man, it was clear to see where Rachael got her kindness from. But he was also very strong and

Nicholas swore at least one bone in his hand cracked under the weight of his handshake—perhaps he deserved it, if so.

A moment later, Rachael came flying down the stairs, a vision of brilliance in her dress of gold, speckled with sparkles.

"Nicholas! You came!"

He greeted her with a warm smile. Lifting her as she jumped into his arms, he spun her around in a circle, watching her dress kick and trail behind them.

"Of course, I was honored to receive the invitation."

"Stacy should be here soon; her thing is to waiting outside a few minutes early so she can bang on the door precisely at 6pm."

Nicholas squinted. "Really?"

Rachael laughed. "You have no idea what you got yourself into."

"I thank you every day for getting me into it," Nicholas smiled at her.

Rachael seemed to wipe a tear from her eye before swallowing and saying, "You saved her."

Nicholas looked at her, perplexed.

"Truly. Maybe it was the timing of you coming and the Spirits knew exactly what they were doing sending her this dream, but she was breaking. I could see it more and more every single day. She was so confused and so worried. She desperately needed answers, but that girl will protect her family's peace with her dying breath. I know things were rocky for both of you, but there was a light in her the moment she met you and I didn't see that burn out, even after this." She gestured to her broken wrist. "I think you needed each other and I thank the Spirits I decided to work the airport that day."

Nicholas's heart swelled in his chest. He found Stacy incredibly difficult to read. She was not the average American he expected. No, it was as though she had spent so much time realizing the bigger picture to her existence, that she no longer made time for formalities, for stressing the little stuff others were preoccupied with.

And that was his leader. The leader of his country. No—the savior of his country. The strongest heir that was ever meant to rule and he played a role not in ending her life, but in saving it...in saving Dukhovia.

His heart welled in his chest. He could not speak.

Gracefully, Rachael looked over at the old grandfather clock dinging in the hallway. "Five till. That'll be her que. Grab a drink before you run out of time."

And then she strolled away.

Nicholas took her advice, hoping that swallowing the cool liquid would ease the unsteadiness he felt. It was no use. He had never felt so uncertain. The heir. The savior of Dukhovia. He helped the savior of Dukhovia. He helped Stacy. The girl who made him feel cared for and seen. The girl who put his stomach in knots and set his heart on fire. Was it possible she felt the same way for him?

He turned, looking for Rachael to confirm, but his heart froze.

CHAPTER SIXTY-NINE

There, standing in the doorway, laughing and swaying in a dress just as long, flowing, and sparkly as Rachael's, but donning the color red, was the girl he dreamt of. The girl he grew up hating only to meet and feel the same way Rachael described—healed from the moment he lay eyes on her.

He shifted, moving toward her, taking in the way the dress hugged every unfathomable curve of her perfectly sculpted body. Despite the beverage he had just partaken in, his mouth went dry the moment he was near her.

"Stacy Grace."

She looked up at him and he would have thought nothing of it had Rachael never spoken to him, had he not been so keen in his observation prior, but her eyes lit up. An actual flicker of brightness expelled from them, a glimmer of, dare he say, hope?

"Hey!" Then she folded her body into his, her arms securely wrapping themselves around his waist, in a way that he had never been held. Her body, squeezing his, in a way that he had never felt so needed, so cared for.

And a smile. A smile that could turn the tides of a country at war. But it was for him, all for him.

He reciprocated—his arms taking her in, taking in her feel, her scent, her everything. "I missed you," he whispered, his heart stopping the moment he said the words. He had not thought them, they simply escaped his lips and now they were out there, never to come back.

She looked up, that smile still on her lips, only now he noticed the dark circles under her eyes, the heaviness to her lids. He frowned. "You have not slept."

She shook her head. "I was thinking—all night."

"About what?" He nearly shouted the words. "Darling, the compassion you feel toward our country is beyond admirable, but you will not be of use unless we find a way to help this."

Her eyes avoided his for a moment, the motion made his heart sink.

"I was thinking about losing you."

And then it was back in his chest. "I am going nowhere, Stacy Grace."

"Maybe." She spat the word and he could see the hostility of everything she thought in a night pouring outward. "*Maybe*," she emphasized the word again. "*If.* We can convince The Czar. *If* our gifts are enough. What if they aren't? I don't want you to go back there, Nicholas. You don't deserve to be there; you deserve to be here."

The reality of the words trickled around them like a heavy fog, moving in closer and closer until it encompassed them. Encompassed them in the strange, alternate reality where America was safe and Dukhovia was feared. Where he did not want to go home. Where he was not certain where home was, or who it was with.

His head began to pulsate. He did not know what to tell her. She was right, of course. There were no guarantees. But he could not tell her that. He could not let her continue to go on losing sleep over him, no matter how much her feelings for him warmed his heart and saved his soul.

And he refused to lie to her anymore.

He held her closely and began swaying her to the softly playing music. He twirled her around the room and then, bringing her back up, whispered into her ear in a throaty voice. "Then I suppose we best make our time count." He raised his eyebrow at her—a challenge.

Stacy hesitated a moment, but then her own eyebrow perked and she pursed her lips in response. Keeping eye contact with him, she slipped out of her high-heeled shoes, losing a few inches of height as she did so.

Nicholas matched her, slipping out of his shoes, sliding out of his suit jacket. He undid his tie, tossing both items onto the armchair behind him.

Then they were off. Nicholas raced her at top speed, a speed only each other could ever match.

Stacy flung herself in the snow, laying full out, bare arms, bare feet, in total, comfortable bliss. She ran from the furthest end of the backyard, to the closest, throwing snow at him, rolling balls to build and fall over.

Nicholas matched her energy. He truly matched her energy. For the first time in his life, he was free, and she was equal, and they were laying barely clothed in the frosty snow, challenging destiny to stop them.

CHAPTER 70

SPIRIT BOUND

$\mathcal{N}$icholas and Stacy lay in the snow, tackling each other and feeling each other until the gawking crowd told them it was time for cake. Stacy had hesitated at first, but the excitement of introducing Nicholas to cake enticed her. It would not contain a single vegetable.

She was disappointed, however, at his announcement that he has been getting a Danish at the local bakery every morning and his perfect figure was now tainted by a mere pastry. Bitter disappointment.

The two spent more time around the music, swaying slowly in each other's arms. In those moments, Stacy felt close to Nicholas, she felt unstoppable, she felt like she could tear down a mountain, or save a country…

At least, there was a fighting chance. There was a chance to save Dukhovia. There was a chance to be unstoppable, to be what Dukhovia needed. And that was something she never had before. A chance. An ability to know—just like everyone else. An ability to feel at least like one other person in the room. She was not crazy, and she was not a lost piece of the puzzle. She had a purpose, and she had a destination.

Her head rested on Nicholas's thudding heart, beating rhythmically and erratically all at once, all the time. He would take a moment to either stroke her hair or move her body closer to his and the movement set her heart on fire while calming her storm.

"Stace! Come here!" Then it was the birthday girl herself who interrupted the moment.

Rachael came rushing over, pulling on both their hands. "Come over here, Cody was just about to give me his gift."

The two obliged, following Rachael through a forest of brightly lit and flashing evergreen. It was Kenny's magical touch. Each year he, Dan, and Kevin worked diligently to create a new decoration to add to the mix. This year, Santa and his eight reindeer were added to the sea of red and green, waving and whinnying at whoever drove by.

Stacy and Nicholas walked, as hand and hand as they could get (finger and finger?), towards the enclosed back porch where Cody sat tuning a guitar.

"Oh boy," Stacy said with mock tension.

He smirked at first, then his face became mundane and then repulsed as Nicholas sat next to Stacy, throwing his arm around the back of the couch behind her.

"Sit by me, Rache." He scooted over on the padded bench, making room for her as he began to sing and play.

The song was beautiful. His amazing, melodious voice was famous for hitting any pitch, low or high, which only added to his skills, making the fact that no one wrote lyrics quite like him an almost unfair advantage. His ability to move everyone's heart, make everyone laugh, and connect with people of any age or situation on a level no one had ever seen in music floored most of *The Rocker's* success.

"...So let your beauty radiate beside me, hold your head and laugh a little louder, hold my hand and walk with me, and show me, what it means to live with beau-ooty, you radiate beauty."

He wanted to make her feel as loved and appreciated as she made he and Stacy feel daily and judging by her tears, he seemed to do just that.

"Thank you, Cody, that was beautiful," Rachael hugged him.

He blushed.

"That's it?" Stacy questioned, meaning the insult to throw stones at the look Nicholas so effortlessly ignored.

Cody shot her a dirty look. "I gave her a necklace this morning."

Rachael moved her hair and the tip of the reindeer shirt she was now wearing over her dress (likely a gift from her father) to reveal the necklace. It was silver with several diamonds on it. Several real, decently sized diamonds.

"What about you, cuz?" Cody asked condescendingly.

"She's blessed with my friendship on a daily basis," Stacy said with fake hurt in her voice. Rachael nodded. "And we're going to the spa next weekend."

Cody gave her his now all-too-common judgmental look, shutting the conversation down.

Stacy and Nicholas spent half the evening returning to dancing, while the other half was spent laughing and joking around with friends. Nicholas seemed free, Stacy could almost breathe—it almost felt right.

But then she remembered it would end—and could end forever.

She lifted her head from Nicholas's chest, she did not know the time, her eyes could scarcely stay open any longer.

"We need to get you to bed, my darling," he whispered.

The soothing lullaby of his words alone could knock her out.

"I want you to stay," she muttered in a sleepy voice. She shook her head. "My parents. My parents invited you to stay over tonight. Terra and Tom too."

She felt Nicholas inhale deeply, moving her inward against his chest. "Well, I do believe your grandparents were very eager to have someone to care for Christmas morning, so, so long as they are invited…"

Stacy buried her head into his chest and groaned, but gratitude lined her heart.

Nicholas brought his voice down to a whisper, inclining his head until his mouth was nearly touching her ear. "This also gives us the opportunity to attempt to connect to the Ancestry Spirit."

Breathe, Matthews.

The Ancestry Spirit. She had not forgotten. Nicholas thought that observing her and connecting with her might help him figure out her dream, that it was likely the Ancestry Spirit that wanted her to figure out where to go from here. She was excited to move forward, but nervous to accept disappointment if they did not learn anything.

She nodded slowly. "I'm ready."

***

An hour later, the two were in her bedroom. Stacy had still not fallen asleep, so Nicholas had spent time after time attempting to connect to her spirit to no avail. Desperate and defeated, he fell next to her bed, head in his knees.

Stacy tiptoed next to him, placing her hand gently on his knee. "You're not a failure just because you can't do something, Nicholas. The Nature Spirit didn't need you for this. The Water Spirit didn't need you for this—Arkady did."

Nicholas peeked his head up, slowly. "But it is a gift given to all heirs as well…"

Stacy was already shaking her head. "To be used in time of need. We're in that time now and we're learning together. At our *own* pace."

Nicholas did not respond, he only wrapped himself around Stacy, who embraced him in return.

"I'm so very grateful for you," he told her slowly, his hands were shaking as he spoke, his eyes watering. "I…I never knew what it meant to feel free. I always answered to someone and always waited on someone else to tell me what course of action my life was meant to have. And then I met you, and you held that freedom to an extent I never dreamt possible. Your determination drove you towards a path you desired to take and were meant to take because you were always true to yourself. That is the only way to fulfill something truly meant for you, Stacy. You cannot fulfill a purpose if you are burdened with the pressures of doing so."

Stacy thought of her mother's words, her explanation for not telling her, and nodded her head.

"And now—now I feel like I have a choice. I may be horrendously lost in how to execute those choices, but I am here. I am with you. I can have a future and honor my family." He swallowed. "At least I hope."

Stacy reached a hand up, cupping his face gently. "Of course you can, Nicholas Aloyshenka. Fulfilling your destiny doesn't mean losing who you are," Stacy told him calmly. "Dukhovia knows. No matter what people hear, Dukhovia will see who you are inside and out. Whether that leads to you ruling or another path, it'll be the one meant for you to best care for our country."

Nicholas smiled at her concern for her country and how she was truly beginning to understand. That made it fall into place for both of them. Maybe they did not know what to do, who should rule, or what would be done to deal with Arkady...but Dukhovia did. There was a plan for both of them and as long as they did the right thing...how could they ever be swayed from that?

Their togetherness was enough now, part of the plan. They were in this together; strengthening one another and preparing for anything on the way.

"Then I suppose I have a new destiny," Nicholas said with the happiest look Stacy would ever see appear on his face. "Stacy Grace Matthews," he said proudly, holding her hand. "I vow to protect you for all my days. Whatever it takes, whatever may be lost, an incredible ruler will be gained." He lifted her hand up to his mouth, holding it delicately as he took in the feel of the softness of her skin as well as the feeling that swelled in his heart.

Stacy laughed, throwing back her head in the most freeing way she ever felt. "Are you even human?" She asked.

He looked perplexed. "Why would you ask that?"

"Because," Stacy said with a raised eyebrow. "People are predictable and you're not predictable. Are you a people?"

Nicholas laughed, the true beauty of his smile never shined through to Stacy until this very moment. The pearly whites and blue eyes never had the effect they were meant to—until now.

"The definition of humanity lies in individualism, Stacy. There is strength in unity and there is strength in separation. For in separation lies the purpose of our individuality, and that is who we are."

Beaming eyes penetrated each other as if they were connected, the lock pulling each other in. Then, Nicholas looked down and laughed once.

"I suppose Americans are the only ones as predictable as you make the rest of the world out to be," he said.

Stacy gave him a disproving look with a sly smile. "I would expect everyone in Dukhovia to be a huge know-it-all with an arrogance towards their beliefs."

He laughed loudly. "You would not be entirely wrong. Americans are the strangest species I have ever seen. Most humans are driven by a sense of fulfillment, but your people..." He shook his head. "Your people are driven by the ability to fit in and then the ability to make you think there is something wrong with you if you are not exactly like them."

Now it was Stacy's turn to agree. She smiled the same maniacal grin as he and let out one, soft spurt of laughter. "I suppose you're right; they are rather simple-minded and arrogant...but is that any reason to hate them? Or is it a reason to help? Perhaps their path is taking them somewhere else...Perhaps their purpose to right this world is based around caving in to the others so that people can see what happens when individuality is lost."

Nicholas smiled at her, that happy smile that she loved. "You'll make a fine ruler someday, princess," he said softly.

She beamed back at him, joy and fulfillment beckoning them together. Nicholas raised his hand, hesitating before caressing Stacy's perfectly soft, perfectly rounded face. He felt the warmth beneath her cheeks, felt the flesh and blood flow beneath his grasp. This was how he wanted her, this was how he was meant to preserve her. This was how he wanted to remember her now.

He touched her many times, but this time, he felt her. The softness of her skin reflected that of her heart. The flowing of her hair was a part of her that she touched and maintained, something she worked on daily. The shine in her eyes spoke directly to his heart, holding concern, holding hope, holding answers. The beauty of every aspect reflecting that of her very soul.

His hand slid down and landed on her shoulder. He slowly made his way down her arm, pausing at her hand. His reason. His reason for life. For freedom. And she cared for him back. He fulfilled her. She was whole—because of him.

The two now faced each other directly. Stacy watched his hand with precision as it slid further and further down, meeting her fingers on one hand, then another.

She could feel the electrical jolts piercing her before she recognized he had moved closer to her. Then she was gone, her vision blackened, her surroundings non-existent.

CHAPTER 71

A WORLD OF DARKNESS

$\mathcal{N}$icholas's world was color and music; birds and beauty circulated around him. Until fire and gloom took its place, circulating around him like a plague he could not fight off, he could not recover from. He tried pushing through, away and around the darkness, but he failed. He was slipping, slipping....

Then he was back in Stacy's room. The two were flung backward, breathing heavily as they each exchanged shocked faces.

"What happened?" Stacy asked. She seemed fearful, shaken up at the very least.

Nicholas's mood was...difficult. He had connected; he was certain of it. He latched onto her Spirit and felt the world as she felt it, her thoughts, her memories. He was ecstatic.

But to find out that she was in such.... distress? No, to confirm it, experience it through her eyes. It made him feel ill.

"I connected to your spirit," Nicholas confirmed.

"You did?" Stacy's voice was nearing congratulatory but plagued by something else.

"What was it like for you?" He asked her slowly. He recalled when Arkady had connected to him. He always just felt frozen. As if Arkady was blocking him...

"It was just black," she continued to seem unsteady. "I didn't know what happened. You kept squeezing my hands and I couldn't see or feel, and my head was spinning..."

Nicholas's stomach clenched. "I—that is often how I feel when I think of my parents. I have been thinking of my mother often this season." He looked down, ashamed.

Stacy did not seem to take on his shame, instead, she seemed to relax, and she seemed to think... "So, you're connecting to me and I'm connecting to you." The words were hardly a question. "Is that not what you experienced with Arkady?"

Nicholas shook his head. "I am confused. When he connected, I never knew about it. Perhaps there would be some sort of feeling I would get before or after, but it was definitely nothing like what we experienced. I cannot make sense of it."

"I have no idea," Stacy said shaking her head. Then she raised her eyebrow. "But I do know someone we could ask."

...

Stacy and Nicholas stood outside Tom and Terra's door moments later. Stacy's palms were slick against her sides as she sweat with nerves.

"You are nervous?" Nicholas asked gently. "We do not have to do this."

Stacy shook her head, stubbornly. Part of her reason for moving forward was likely selfish: if they could bring in substances for whatever reason, that told her they could at least hear what she had to say and then tell her if she was way out of line after that. But there was selflessness in her decision as well. "No. The foundation of Dukhovia is to update as needed. My tradition has been to keep myself in the dark to shelter them, that is a tradition worthy of change."

Nicholas smiled, his fingers dancing on her chin as his lips stopped just centimeters from her face. "As I said," he breathed, "A fine ruler, my princess."

Huh. Maybe this is what Rachael was trying to get her to see for.... years.

"Stacy, Nicholas!" Terra shut the door partially, simultaneously there was a rustling of what sounded like gift paper and boxes.

Stacy looked over at Nicholas and laughed.

Terra glanced over a few times before widening the door for them both. "Is everything okay?"

Stacy nodded, looking to Nicholas. "There was something we wanted to ask you about."

Nicholas nodded his agreement. "Do you know anything about Spirit connections?"

Tom's face was steady and unrevealing as he looked from each of their faces and then back to Terra's, who did not answer, but also looked towards him. He nodded slowly. "A bit."

Nicholas automatically bowed towards Tom. "We would be honored if you would be able to answer a few questions for us."

Tom agreed and Stacy and Nicholas both sat crisscross on the floor while Terra and Tom each sat in one of the blue armchairs in the corner of the room. Tom seemed to daze off before he said anything else, looking at Stacy uncomfortably. Clearly, they needed to have the discussion of closure.

Finally, Nicholas began. "Arkady always taught me that I needed to be able to connect to Stacy's spirit to be able to find her. He said that all heirs are connected by the same spirit, divided into us and thus we should be able to guide ourselves to one another. It was how he was always able to find me, but I was never able to connect to him and other than perhaps a feeling that was mere hope, I have not been able to connect to Stacy." His words trailed off and he looked at Stacy who nodded her head. "Except for now."

Terra and Tom exchanged a look. "Right now?" Tom asked.

Nicholas nodded. "But it was not like anything I experienced with Arkady. When he connected to me—I had no idea. Occasionally, as I learned, I would notice perhaps a slight headache, but otherwise—I could not predict he was tracking me. It would have changed my life if I could. But when I connected to Stacy, she also connected to me. Is it because of her strength, perhaps?"

Tom hummed casually, strumming his chin as he considered it. "Possibly," he decided. "It's possible it was easier for her to connect back because of the strength of her Spirit. However, in theory, you should always be aware when you are being tracked by another heir. After all, it is meant to be a way to connect heirs for the betterment of Dukhovia, not deception. He's blocking you."

"Blocking?" Nicholas said the term with confusion. "I have never heard of that."

Terra's face held a look of pain as Tom spoke, Stacy felt half guilty, but the information they needed was valuable.

"It is a very skilled talent. An heir would have to spend time getting to know their own spirit, getting to know the spirits themselves, how to twist them, how to manipulate them." Tom's lips were pressed into a firm line as he said the words. His eyes seeming to pour into Nicholas's for truth and meaning.

"Arkady manipulated the Spirits into blocking my connection?"

Tom nodded. "And tactfully at that if you never even knew. Are there any blockades in your memory? Anyone who was around you that would have made a comment about your consciousness altering?"

Nicholas seemed to think about it for a long time, his head down in his lap as he watched his fingers lift against each other. "I felt weaker," he finally mumbled. "Colder."

Anger arose in Stacy. He had already been victimized in every other way and now they could even manipulate his Spirit? "How can he be allowed to do something like that?" She spit out her words like venom.

It was Terra's soft voice that responded. "Oh, my love, the Spirit's reasonings can sometimes be so very complicated."

Stacy's voice remained hostile. "I don't care. I care that we find a solution."

"I have a theory," Tom said, paying no mind to the side-conversation. He grabbed a notebook and pen and began to draw a circle. In the center of his circle, he drew a person. "Think of your connection like an extension of the self. You are still fully connected, but willing your Spirit to go beyond your physical body."

"Like how Shaman travel into the Spirit Realm?" Nicholas asked.

Tom nodded. "Precisely. When you give your Spirit a physical shape rather than an idea of the shape, you can shape it and bend it at will. Have it follow your every command." He etched a person outside of the circle and drew extensions where the circle latched onto that person. First the top of the person, then the bottom. "Will it to enter their mind, their body, or their Spirit. Doing this can make transmitting direct, complex messages almost simple."

Nicholas's eyes stared at the picture. "Typically, we are simply taught to be attuned to our Spirit and listen to it, almost as if it will guide for us. But for us to will it, for us to envision it and control it…" His eyes were locked on Stacy. He lifted his hand up and paused—an offer.

Stacy nodded, her heart heavy in her chest as she continued to process the information they had just learned.

The two pressed their palms together and the world spun. Stacy saw this time not just darkness, but swirls of color, then swirls of more complex pictures. She tried to latch onto them, willing herself to not simply be mindful of the image, but to dig past the blackness and into the image.

And then she was on a farm. Panic and fear crippled her body. Tears poured from her cheeks as she flailed her head around. She was looking for help, she needed help.

But she was too late. The cabin was in flames.

Nicholas felt the force of pressure the moment his and Stacy's hands touched. Her world of color exploded around his mind in streaks and impossible-to-reach shots. He looked around, willing himself toward *something*. He chose a rainbow-streaked bow—nothing tangible, nothing too abstract or even concrete. Just *something*.

He immediately felt himself being pulled, pulled towards the streaks, past his darkness, into her color. But there was work to do. He willed himself toward it, but knew he had damage to repair. He needed to clean up the missing pieces. So, he did. Slowly, carefully, he pieced together her world of color, stitching and attaching it to his world of dark, one at a time, one at a time, piece by piece by piece.

And then they shot back.

Terra and Tom were both surrounding their bodies. Terra was holding Stacy in her arms while Tom was on all fours, his body positioned close to Nicholas, his hands hovering over top of him.

When their lids opened, both observers pulled back slightly.

"Stacy!" Nicholas shot up over to her.

She was immediately at his side, gripping his hand. The electric shock bolted through each of them, then fizzled only slightly. They both reached their hands back.

"I am sorry," he apologized before she uttered a word.

"You. Don't. Have. A. Reason," she said each word firmly.

And then he burst into tears, his head falling gently into her lap as the tears fell and fell. She stroked his head over and over. Then she bent forward, leaning her forehead against his, feeling the panting of his breath on her body. She pressed a kiss to his temple.

Terra leaned forward, mimicking the behavior with a squeeze of her own to Nicholas, gently patting his hand until his sobs ceased.

"It's late," Tom began, watching Terra walk out the door. "You two should get to bed and we can practice more tomorrow before the party."

The two looked at each other apprehensively, but nodded nonetheless. They knew there was no tricking Tom and Terra let alone anyone else in the house, so they made no show of Nicholas going to his room. He went straight up to Stacy's in her wake.

Once in her room, Nicholas drew back the blanket for Stacy. She crawled in and allowed herself to be tucked in.

"What did you see?" Stacy asked him.

Nicholas swallowed. "The same thing—your colors, torn by shreds of blackness. Me," he realized. His chest burned. "But I believe your grandfather was correct. It is not just a matter of waiting for something to happen, but you must reach and manipulate. *However,* part of it is waiting too. Part of it is listening to hear how the Spirits want us to move—and that is how Arkady is able to do what he is doing. He is simply connecting as he should, but bypassing that."

"Listening to himself rather than the Spirits," Stacy's voice was numb, vague. It had now been over forty-eight hours since she last slept and she was feeling delirious.

Nicholas nodded. He reached forward and rubbed her arm gently, then withdrew. She reached out and placed it back where he had it.

"What's the plan for tonight?" She asked.

Nicholas looked at her, bewildered. "You still want to attempt to connect to the Ancestry Spirit?"

"Of course. That was the point of all that, right? To give ourselves a fighting chance of actually accomplishing it?"

Nicholas nodded. "Yes, but, darling, though I admire your strength, you must rest. It is already so late into the night."

"We have to," she said, feeling her own voice slipping away. "People need us."

"And we shall be there," he said. He bowed close to her, his lips hesitating inches from her forehead before they landed there, hovering for a moment.

"Please don't talk me out of this," Stacy managed to beg. "I need to at least try."

He could understand that. "The plan, then. I believe the Spirits may be attempting to speak to you by inviting you in The Spirit Realm. If that is true, the Ancestry Spirit is likely to give us information, being the one most likely to share valuable information with humans. However, I believe the level of anxiety you experience around this dream may prevent us." He looked around then shuffled over to her closet. Quickly, he withdrew a lone wolf statue and placed it in her hands. "This. This is an ancestral relic that will relax you and may help us channel our power to connect."

Stacy was silent. She had lifted her eyebrow and had a smirk on her face.

CHAPTER SEVENTY-ONE

Nicholas looked at her with confusion—then he froze.

Stacy laughed as realization dawned on him. "Interesting how you know more about the items in my room than I, Sir Nicholas."

He tensed at first, then shifted, matching her energy. "I suppose the more curious thing would be a person sent here to find you *not* breaking into your home."

Stacy laughed as powerfully as she could in her condition. "Fair enough!"

Stacy sat for a long time after that, dropping in and out of consciousness, awakening herself in a panic so severe she thought she was underwater, but past her limit. She could not breathe, then she could not move. Her chest heavy, her limbs numb.

"I can't, I'm sorry," she finally expressed at half past three in the morning. "I can't sleep."

Nicholas looked her up and down, considering their options, his own chest tight. "I do not know what to do," he finally admitted sheepishly.

She looked at him, looking as if she had been through the flames and torture of his memory in real life. Out of energy, out of everything. Then she moved to the side, motioning for Nicholas to join her.

Hesitantly, he climbed into the bed with her, wrapping her in his arms, her head resting on his chest.

"Better already," she muttered, shutting her eyes.

Nicholas did not mean the noise that came out to sound so much like a sneer, he could not help it.

"Hmm?" She questioned.

"I am afraid," he answered after a pause. "I do not want you to have to witness the repercussions of my darkness. Any of them. Here, when we connect, my anger…"

Stacy lifted her head slightly, then her hand rested on the back of his hand. She moved it up and down slowly, warming up to the idea of moving closer to his hand. She connected their fingers, then closer, then further. "The good parts are easy," she yawned. "I want the messy. I want everything."

"You deserve more," he whispered.

Stacy shrugged. "You don't think the greatest heir in the world is up for a little challenge?"

Nicholas chortled. "Ah, and there is her American arrogance."

"There it is," Stacy whispered, then faded into sleep.

CHAPTER 72

ANSWERS

There was nothing but a mere twinkling of lights amongst total darkness. The world was soundless, worriless perfection. Peace amongst goodness. Goodness amongst grace.

Nicholas lifted his head towards the sound of running water. He pushed through the darkness, but did not move. Were he and Stacy connected? Did he have to will himself like before? He tried it, but did not budge.

Then came the screams. Horrific, terrified sounds, emanating from somewhere behind him. No—in front. No. No.

He was in such a panic as he realized they were Stacy's screams, he did not realize…he was moving. He was running full pace towards any direction.

Then the loudest one erupted, and the serenity of his surroundings were gone, shaking and throwing him forward.

He bent down, shielding the back of his head and neck with his arms until the shaking ceased. Then he glanced around—gone was his world of peace and bleak and in its place was Stacy's world of color and glory—except that it was on fire and someone was chasing her.

"Stacy! Get away from them!"

"From who?" She shouted, looking around wildly.

Nicholas realized she could not see the person and he paused in his tracks, analyzing them. Until he realized—it was him. And everywhere he walked black followed.

Nicholas ran forward, dodging flames, falling into vicious thorn bushes. He ran and dodged, panting aggressively, attempting to avoid the curiosity to lurk at himself. A crack in the earth erupted, threatening to further challenge his trek to Stacy. He looked in her path—beauty, lightness. He could not help it—he looked beyond himself—darkness, destruction, smoke, plague.

Then the scene flipped, and Stacy's side was flame encased. Then again and the entire world was in smoke.

Nicholas jumped, alerted by Stacy's screams that she was still in fear and panic. He ran alongside the cracks, readying his jump: one, fires roared up from the trees behind him causing him to shift directions. Two, a pack of wolves came in front of him, guiding him, until they fell into the canyon below. Three—the ground beneath his feet began to swallow him whole.

He had no choice. He lunched forward, somehow grabbing both Stacy's hands until they were both spit out, dry heaving on her bed.

"It's a warning," he breathed, dripping with sweat and vines. "Great destruction or great peace."

"What?" Stacy breathed. "Why? How?" Her sleeplessness was still impacting her thinking.

Nicholas glanced at the clock—they had only slept for twenty minutes. "The Spirits predicted that we would either have Great Peace or Great Destruction if one of us came to rule. I assume that meant that one of us would be responsible—I always assumed it would be me. Even before." He tried to slow his brain before he side-tracked. "But I think it's a warning...To protect the heir, find them, or there will be great destruction."

"It's coming, they're coming. Protect the heir." Stacy quoted the words slowly.

"I am coming. Arkady is coming and whether the heir is protected will determine the path—great destruction or great peace."

Stacy was shaking her head as it all fell into place. "Who is protecting who?" She finally breathed.

Nicholas looked at her, gripping his bleeding stomach. "We are protecting each other."

CHAPTER 73

BLACK AND WHITE

*T*hud!

Snow fell from the roof awakening Stacy and Nicholas simultaneously. They looked at each other through barely opened eyes.

"You're even more handsome when you're half asleep," Stacy joked.

"And you look much prettier when I can see you," he said, pulling back the curtains. "There. Beautiful."

She smiled in return, playfully batting at his arm.

Nicholas smiled, buried his head in his pillow and grunted. He looked back at her and rolled onto his back. "Merry Christmas," he said glancing at her.

"Merry Birthday," she replied with a grin. Then she frowned. "Last night."

He shrugged. "Indeed. Are you feeling any better?"

She stretched up, looking at the alarm clock next to her. "Welp, we got a full five hours compared to my zero, so that counts for something, right?"

Nicholas raised an eyebrow. "It is late. Will your mother come looking for you?"

Stacy looked from him to the clock and laughed. "No. She would be more surprised to see me before this time—or even at this time."

"So, a late sleeper?" Nicholas laughed. "Noted."

Stacy bowed in gratitude, then jumped out of bed, rumbling around for a robe, throwing everything out of her closet in the process.

"What about the state of your room?" Nicholas asked, standing to his feet in mounds of socks and pants. "Does your mother not discipline you for this?" He wondered.

"No," Stacy said simply, looking around with a puzzled look. "My mother doesn't believe in double standards." She exhaled deeply, unable to find what she was seeking and tore across her room. "I will be back in a minute—make yourself at home."

Nicholas raised his eyebrow and looked up. "We are missing at least four prison cells."

Stacy rolled her eyes, exiting the room. She ran down the steps, forgetting stealth, and quickly began rummaging through drawers, tables, and beneath couches.

Never leave things in your pocket when you're half asleep, she told herself.

"Ahem."

Stacy jumped up from under the couch to see Tom standing near the kitchen entryway. She supposed she could expect it would be him she would run into first.

"I know you're still angry with me," Tom began, hands casually dipped in his pockets, a gentle smile plastered on his always calm face. The fact that anyone could think that man a monster…

Realization dawned on Stacy and the flood of memories came back—both that night in Nicholas's apartment and last night. "I'm not. I was. I get it now."

Tom arched his eyebrow. "Oh?"

"Yeah. It's hard to choose between keeping your family safe and following the rules," she recited Nicholas's words perfectly.

Tom laughed softly. "Indeed. You need to know that Terra and I would never intentionally jeopardize our family. However, when the ruling came that we were to rid ourselves of everything Dukhovian related, Aunt Terra began to fight. She retained anything cultural: our relics, our holidays. However, due to the severity of my crimes and the lack of understanding for Dukhovian remedies, she could not get them to agree to any plants that had alternative uses.

"I explained to them that our bodies were different and needed Zhar, however, they refused to listen. They stated that if we needed something different to function, then clearly we were much more complex than the typical human and then Terra's entire argument with this went out the window." He pointed to the blue wire shooting out of his head. "Then there was the disregard for our spiritual beliefs.

"So, we discussed what this would look like. We discussed that it was necessary to keep our family alive and healthy so keeping it on hand was a moot point. However, we discussed risks, we discussed where it would be kept, how we would explain it. Everything. We were not willing to let our family suffer, but we were willing to let them live."

Stacy took in the words, understanding their suffering, their pain. She pictured Terra's face, the amount of guilt she carried. The harm she brought to herself—just like Nicholas. None of this was black and white. Just like Nicholas had said—none of it made sense and all of it was complicated. She had already decided to forgive him, but then he went on, his words no longer making much sense to her.

"We never wanted you to be in the dark, Stacy. I think we thought that if we left the past in the past that the future we all anticipated would not happen. Now that it is here, we are stuck with the complication of finding out what should remain in the past and what would shed light on our future.

"We owe you a world of apologies and a universe of explanation. And I would be honored to give that to you."

"I just don't want to lose you," Stacy said finally, tears brimming in her eyes as she let everything sink in. Dukhovia. Her family. Her friends. Nicholas. Keeping everyone safe. Making sense of everything. The weight of everyone's world was on her shoulders. An entire country on her shoulders. She broke down into her grandfather's arms. "I don't want to lose any of my people."

Her people. That was exactly what they were. Her people to protect, and she was theirs to find trust in—nowhere to be found. This could not go on. It would not. She closed her hand around the small box she was looking for and made a silent promise to herself.

Anything for her people.

CHAPTER 74

WHAT LOVE LOOKS LIKE

*E*yes closed," Stacy commanded upon re-entering the room.

Nicholas closed one eye and then the other, slowly.

Stacy's smile only widened. "Okay open!" He did so and she automatically thrust a small, golden gift box into his hand. "I got something for you." She revealed the small gift box.

He sat up, surprised, and excitedly opened the gift.

"I wasn't exactly sure what to get a Dukhovian assassin," she joked. "But..."

"It's perfect," he finished. He could not take his eyes off the solid gold medallion. It was large, about the size of his Stacy's palm, with something inscribed on it:

> *Heroes are heroes*
> *Because they are heroic in behavior,*
> *not because they won or lost.*
> *~Nassim Nicholas Taleb*

"I never want you to forget that you are a good person inside and out, no matter what you may be forced into doing, it is what you feel that makes you who you are. Choosing the right path makes you a winner, no matter the end result. Remember, fulfilling your purpose should never mean losing who you are."

Nicholas's eyes began to water, overflowing the more he considered the gesture and everything it stood for. From whom it came. He picked up the medallion and attached it to the chain lying in the box. Putting the two together, he lifted it to his neck and clipped it around.

"Perfect," Stacy announced.

Nicholas smiled at her. Although his mouth could not find the words to say, his face showed everything that was on his mind.

The two proceeded downstairs shortly after. Nicholas was hesitant, uncertain how to act or what to expect. But he was warmly greeted in the smaller living area near Terra and Tom's room. Terra and Tom, along with Stacy's parents, had gathered beneath the tree next to a tower of gifts.

At first, Nicholas prepared to take a seat on the couch, however, Stacy pulled on his arm, leading him to sit in front of a ginormous pile of gifts and a stocking with his name on it. He touched the dried glue mimicking an N slowly, a lump forming in his throat as he did so. He blinked quickly, wiping hot liquid from his eyes.

"I know it looks like we're terrible parents, but it is also your birthdays, so that is why there is more compared to our son whom we love equally." Grace seemed to have rehearsed the line as she explained, gesturing to the pile for Daniel.

"Also..." Kevin approached, carrying a large chocolate muffin covered in chocolate frosting in one hand and in the other—a Danish. Each held a candle.

"Traditional birthday morning dessert," Stacy said with a grin. She bound forward, blowing out her candle and annihilating her muffin in mere moments. "Sweet Kim always does the best for birthday muffins."

Nicholas blew out his own candle, a tradition he had nearly forgotten existed. Looking around the room, he felt such acceptance, he felt so seen, he felt...healed. Yet he struggled to also combat the urge to vomit up his Danish and run away.

Nicholas survived through present wrapping. He was rather impressed with what he received: clothing that was not as American as he thought he needed to wear. Tools for sharpening and polishing his sword. Shoes. An ancient scroll that Tom stated he discovered while exploring a cave in North Bridge. He felt an heir as strong as Nicholas would have more use for it than the shelf it was sitting on. Nicholas would be lying if he did not say he was bursting at the seam to have alone time to read through it.

He was certain his mind slipped a few times in and out of reality. He could not help but think of the last birthday he celebrated and then the last one he thought he was going to celebrate...

He shuddered, unable to think of it. Unwilling. The physical pain to his gut and chest, the emotional wounds were too much to bear in a moment that should have brought him joy. A moment that should not have him wondering what if... What if the house suddenly burnt down? What if Arkady tracked him here with no warning and attacked?

What if.

Stacy seemed to grasp onto the memory of him telling her what this day was and bit her lip. At one point she walked him into her room and let him breathe in and out until he caught his breath, until he remembered how to breathe. It was the best day. It was the hardest day.

They did spend some of it practicing. They practiced connecting their Spirits. They practiced tracking and they practiced simply trying to hold one another's hands. Later, Rachael arrived, and they practiced with her too.

Nicholas found himself separating to be on his own again a few moments before their party began. It was the banner declaring "Happy Birthday Stacy and Nicholas" that triggered him. It was the varkan. It was everything else too.

Good morning my little birthday boy. Four already?

Nooo! Five mama!

Oh my goodness! My apologies, I could hardly count that high.

A giggle as he was tickled and shot up into the air and sailed around the room like he was riding a wave on the sea.

"Well, at five we surely need to do something to celebrate greater than we ever have before!"

"Yes mama! Yes!"

"What do you say to making a stop at Ellie's and then a trip to the Falls?"

He recalled screaming with delight.

Nicholas swallowed his fear. He had to leave it in the past. He had to. There was only one way forward and that was by leaving his pain behind.

He stepped out of the room and found the house scattered with different friends and family members. He knew most, but those he did not, he was quickly introduced to and given a warm welcome.

Cake and food were served. He did not feel like eating but accepted a piece out of politeness.

Stacy remained by his side after that, sliding her hand into his every so often, ever so gently, and ever so briefly.

"And there will be a waterfall, and an ice sculpture..." Nicholas and Stacy eventually joined Stacy's friends near the tree. Cara was happily chatting away about...something.

"And a dancer throwing fire-lit batons?" Jade joked.

"Ooo," Cara jotted down a thought in her pink, diamond speckled notepad.

"What are we talking about?" Stacy asked. She motioned for Nicholas to take the last seat on the couch and then plopped into his lap. His entire body clenched in response.

"Just the best thing to happen since ever!" Cara exclaimed.

"Cara has decided that she wants to exploit your love for all it's worth," Rachael began to explain, humor glued to her face. She sat next to Cody who now glared in Nicholas's direction. He ignored him. It was an extra piece he did not need today.

"Meaning?" Stacy prompted with hesitation.

"We're having a school dance!"

Stacy raised her eyebrow.

Nicholas felt his own stomach curdle. What on earth could that entail?

"It'll be great! We're going to dress up and it'll be held on New Years Eve, so it'll be so romantic! Fireworks, nighttime. Now, Santifini said we couldn't have it as late as midnight, but we could still do it at night, SO..."

Nicholas looked up at Stacy, her face was just as shocked and confused as he expected it to be.

"Santifini?" She prompted. "When did you talk to him? Is he back?"

"He never left," she shrugged. "He was just taking some personal time."

"What are you, his secretary?" Jade asked.

Cara rolled her eyes. "He's been paying me to come over and water his plants and help with his garden since we moved here."

Nicholas's mouth went dry. He needed to leave.

He focused on Stacy. Feeling her arm, lightly patting the back of her smooth, soft hand.

"Well, I'll need a date to this shindig," Stacy said, eyeing him.

"It would be my honor, princess," he retorted. "Though I have not a clue what a school dance is."

"Please let me be the one that gets to tell him," Rachael intruded.

Everyone laughed.

And so, the night went on. No harm came to anyone. No firebombs sent through the windows. It was perfect, sincere, expiring bliss.

CHAPTER 75

ACCIDENTALLY IN LOVE

J'm just not sure what theme to go with yet," Cara continued. "Because if anyone shows up ugly, I'm kicking them out."

"Such flattery," Dylan commented.

The group of them had been sitting in the front living area, discussing plans for the Christmas concert that night. Talk of the dance crept in frequently, but Stacy found herself getting angrier by the moment as talks of the dance and the band filtered around—other things were more important.

"It'll be formal, for sure," Rachael offered. "It'll be so much fun and who doesn't want to get dressed up?" She looked off thinking about it. Ignoring Jade's answer of 'me' against Rachael's claim, Cara nodded and looked hopefully at Stacy for a response.

"Excuse me, but can we please get back on track?" Dan asked via web chat.

"Yes, what's track?" Stacy asked sitting Indian-style next to Cara and Rachael on the floor. Her stomach was in knots already, she wondered if everyone else saw the room spinning around in an uncontrollable circle.

"I can't get the light show for the opening song to work so we have to choose another," Dan answered, his eyes glued to something in front of him.

"Seriously? That was supposed to set the whole mood of the show." Stacy groaned and flipped through a list of possible song choices they had narrowed it down to. The original idea of doing it all acapella was beginning to sound more appealing.

"When are we going?" Dylan asked.

"Today," Cara answered matter-of-factly.

"Thanks, Sherlock," Dylan said sarcastically. "I meant what time."

"The limo will be here at four," Jade responded.

"Of today," Miranda added.

"Yeah, we established that," Rachael said with a bitter face.

"Two times already," Cody agreed, wrapping his arm around Rachael to agree with her. She laughed and shook him away.

"Why doesn't the band get some rest, Joey and Dylan, can you guys finish getting the stuff ready to be loaded?" Dan suggested.

"Amen to that brother!" Stacy said, already half asleep. "Oh, Jade—Happy Birthday." Stacy tossed her a small package. She hated the celebration but appeared grateful for the concert tickets to her favorite metal band.

Stacy was grateful for the few hours to attempt to catch up on sleep. She found it impossible at first, but then she replayed the last few moments. Time with her friends, time remembering that while her problems were so big, she still had so much positive surrounding her. And that positivity, that support would be what would help them save Dukhovia.

The hours passed by with Dylan and Joey working on loading up the van. Dan called several times to make sure they ran checks on the oil and tire pressure before departing. Dylan humored him for the most part, but eventually he just started ignoring Dan's calls.

"No, no your highness, and if anything did happen to it, I would be able to fix it better than any mechanic on this side of the country. Any other questions?" Dylan gave no time for other questions before clicking the phone shut.

The call was quick, but it was enough to make the band rise. No matter, they would not be taking the bus tonight anyway. Though the instruments would be carted in it, Rachael deemed a Christmas concert 'far too elegant' to be showing up in a 'rusty, old bus' and convinced Dan to book them a limousine.

"Alright guys, it is five o'clock, the bus is loaded, and the limo will be here soon."

Ring! Ring!

Dylan reached into his pocket, opened his phone, hit the end button, and continued on with his speech without missing a beat. "You guys are going to do amazing tonight. Watch each other's backs and have fun. Does anyone need anything?"

"He takes it over like a natural," Stacy said, holding back fake tears.

"Master never asks us if we need anything," Rachael admitted. "Master makes us crawl to the bus on our hands and knees. Master makes us scrub the instruments until they shine."

"He would never let them stop shining," Cody added for their benefit.

The limo pulled up to the front of Stacy's house in as *elegant* a fashion as could be achieved. Rachael clapped her hands together, lifted her entrance dress of the night, and made her way out, the rest of the members in tow.

Dylan and Joey piled into the bus and began backing out to lead the procession down to the *building* Dan had apparently booked long before requesting Stacy's approval. Last minute…not really his thing.

Behind the procession came their parents in their vehicles, driving closely by to help unpack once they arrived at the city building.

"Alright…instruments to the Fuhrer's liking," Dylan instructed, measuring the exact distance between instruments.

"Wow, he's really letting this go to his head," Jade snickered. "Isn't he normally the one pushing the instruments off an inch every time Dan turns his back?"

After a few hours of preparation, the lines were starting at the door. Grace came in declaring, "People are here!" and the band went into position.

"Thanks! Uncle Fred, Aunt Sara," Joey gestured the two to the door where they would be stamping tickets as the fans fled into their sold-out concert.

"Okay, behind the curtain!" Dylan urged his scattered band. "Seats!" He bellowed to the parents and other kids. Dylan watched as they went to their places, standing against the dessert table. He glanced down at it the moment they were in place. "Alright, great job. My work here is done. From here on out, I don't care what any of you do—just don't die."

"Not on the agenda, captain!" Stacy called back.

Those not in the band went in the front row seats Stacy had reserved them. They sat in their usual alignment: parents, grandparents, friends…then there was one extra chair there that night. One that Stacy kept her eyes locked on nearly the entire time.

As an observer, Nicholas seemed to be growing more comfortable. There was one occasion where he got up and left, Tom trailing behind him. But then he returned. He always returned. He always would.

He had to.

***

"Wonderful concert," Nicholas praised her.

"You came!" she smiled, stretching up to hug him. "And you wore a cut-off, how modern." She mused, ruffling the end of his shirt.

"What's winter without a little frostbite?" Rachael laughed, bouncing over. She extended her casted hand to shake.

Nicholas accepted. "A bore, I am certain," he replied. "How is your arm?"

Stacy cocked her head to the side, certain she heard a bit of an accent in those last few words.

"Wonderful. Tom and Terra said drumming was good for it—or maybe I made that part up," Rachael stated, looking up and down the cast. There was little pink left, her friends had coated it too heavily in permanent marker. What started out as simple names and get well soon suggestions turned into a way to pass notes in class, encouragement, and sarcastic messages. "Although I do believe it is lacking your name, Sir Nicholas."

Nicholas laughed as she rummaged through her purse for a marker. Finding one, she presented it with a bow.

Nicholas grinned and wrote in small, perfectly scripted letters, in the only blank spot he could find:

Thank you for everything ~ Nicholas

Rachael read it quickly and winked at him. "See you at the after party!" She laughed, running over to jump on Cody's shoulders. He lifted her up into his arms, beaming into her eyes, cherishing her smile.

Stacy and Nicholas watched, smiling as an awkwardness between them passed through.

"I really do appreciate you coming, Nicholas," she said nervously. "Thank you."

He grabbed both of her hands and held them onto his chest. "I will be here for every moment that is important to you, Stacy Grace. I promise."

A mere month ago she never found herself uttering the word, she never even thought the word, but now in this moment, surrounded by everything and everyone and every feeling—she was certain. She swallowed her pride, swallowed her fear and thought...

Nicholas. A man of more resilience than she could ever know. A man who knew what it meant to be in the dark, to be shielded from your future, your potential, could still be thoughtful and kind. And then there was what he was to her—he saw her, appreciated her, respected her dreams and ideas. And even if there were not all the things she was able to list and see...there was how she felt. Her heart pounding, her fears fading, every comfort she had ever longed for, every reassurance...

It was true. Stacy Grace Matthews was in love with Nicholas Aloyshenka Aleksis Demitona III—and that match could potentially bring all of Dukhovia devastation and ruin.

CHAPTER 76

IT'S COMING...

Stacy's body fell forward; she attempted to plant her feet firmly in the snow but tripped herself and landed face first in the cold precipitation.

"Again." She chanted, rising and wiping her face off.

Nicholas smacked his forehead. "We should take a break—reassess what is working and what is not."

"What *is* working is our ability to connect, what isn't working is our ability to maintain it for longer than thirty seconds—good enough break, captain?" The stress of taking time off to have the parties was weighing on her. She knew she needed to be gentle with him, Christmas was such a difficult day, but there were moments she let things slip out before she was even aware of them.

He raised his eyebrow toward her.

"Fine—you win. One last try?"

He threw his hands to his side. "Fine," he said lightly. "You win."

They prepared themselves. Hands raised, knees apart.

The feeling was exhilarating— it always was. No matter how many times they had done it.

Things seemed to be getting simpler. They had a clear look now into each other's minds and they were beginning to practice communicating to each other. One sound. One word. Repeating it back to check.

This time was different. This time they were not only able to see full pictures and sounds, but entire thoughts. They were getting stronger.

"We can't stop now!" Stacy cheered as they returned.

"Baby steps," Nicholas told her. "I need to test myself anyway. If the goal is to be able to connect to you when we are far apart, or track Arkady, I need to start practicing being further away. That way I can warn you of danger, send you messages, find you..."

"Okay," she shrugged. "Try me."

Stacy watched as he took a step back, breathing in deeply before closing his eyes. She focused on him, the feeling, then she figured maybe she should avoid that? If he was trying to communicate something, she may not necessarily be checking in. She needed to learn to rely on the sense of her Spirit.

So, she closed her own eyes, feeling the snow, removing her jacket, lifting a pant leg as she dipped her body into the cold. Then she felt it. The shudder, like a knock on a door that did not seem to exist. The pull of a body part that she could not see. The urgency.

Nicholas's eyes flashed open—he felt something too.

"Again," he said with flare in his eyes.

"Again!" She celebrated.

And again, she felt the same pull. Then she heard his voice.

She tried to send a signal back.

When she opened her eyes, Nicholas was jumping for joy. "Last time!" He declared.

Stacy nodded. But this time, she felt nothing. She searched and searched for him, tried to do what Tom had said and reach out towards his Spirit, but there was nothing for her to latch onto. Yet, Nicholas seemed focused. His eyes were closed, but his face was tense.

She waited calmly until the moment his eyes flashed open, and a panic look transcended his face.

"What happ…" She began to ask, but Nicholas gave her no time. Instead, he flew forward, faster than she had ever seen, eyes wild with fear. "Nicholas?" She tried to ask more, but he was pulling her with one arm, frantically packing up their things with the other.

In his hurry, he dropped everything, and responded by shoving his head into the snow, screaming loudly.

"Nicholas! What is going on?" Stacy shouted, this time frustration heavy in her tone.

Nicholas sat up, heaving in and out. His reddening face whipped wildly around, his arms moving chaotically from holding his stomach, to moving to his sides as if he would soon lunge.

"He is coming," Nicholas finally got the words out through a strained voice.

Stacy's blood ran cold. "W-who's coming?" She held her breath, anticipating the answer, racking her brain for any other person he could possibly mean.

"Arkady," he swallowed.

They're coming.

Immediately, Stacy's heart began to race, her body mirroring his panic. "What does that mean? How do you know?"

"I connected with him, or perhaps he with me…perhaps he was sending me a message. He was sitting in his private chamber, looking over maps and discussing strategy with his top men." For the first time, Nicholas's eyes locked on Stacy's. "I must go."

Protect the heir.

Now it was her turn to respond with bewildered shock. "Go?!" She shouted. "Why on Earth would you go?"

They're coming. Protect the heir.

"He needs me to bring you. If I do not bring you, he goes back to the drawing board. I…"

"And you go back to getting hurt," Stacy shook her head. "We already discussed this and promised each other—we stay together."

"But now he is coming. He is coming here and that puts you and your family in danger."

Stacy did not fully understand his line of thought, but she certainly saw the danger. She swallowed. "My grandparents," she managed. "They'll know what to do."

Nicholas cocked his head to the side, but nodded, reluctantly.

Together, the two of them raced back to her grandparent's house, dripping in sweat from urgency as well as the physical trip itself. Stacy was one of the best runners the school had, but the way she saw Nicholas move looked so effortless compared to her. He did not lose his breath. He did not need to exert himself—how in the world would she compete with an army of that? An army of *top men*?

"Tom! Terra!" Stacy called throughout the house the moment they entered.

Nicholas looked weary and helpless as he also went room to room in search.

"The garden," Stacy finally muttered in a wispy voice, turning out the back door.

"Stacy, Nicholas!" Terra's voice rang out in joy until she took in the panic-struck look on their faces. "What's going on?"

"The Czar," Stacy breathed. "He's coming. Nicholas connected with him and saw."

Tom looked at Nicholas and they seemed to exchange a silent conversation. "Come on." Tom's words were directed towards Nicholas. To *only* Nicholas.

As the two began to head out, Stacy quickly trailed behind.

"Stacy," Terra told her quickly. "You stay with me. We need to strategize based on your strengths."

It seemed like a backwards thing to say in the moment, but she agreed, watching Nicholas go with hesitation as the two tore off towards the house.

"What do you know?" Terra asked her quickly.

Stacy shook her head. "Hardly anything. Nicholas said he was in a...chamber...making plans with his top men."

Terra's face looked weary and then sick, but she quickly recovered. "Have you discovered your Spirit gift yet?"

She shook her head again. "I-I don't know. If Nicholas can do all the same things as me as an heir, I assume Arkady can too so healing quickly isn't it, not getting sick isn't it."

Terra agreed. "How are you doing with connecting?"

Stacy hesitated for a moment, eeriness beginning to set in as Terra jumped around. Perhaps she was not the best person for this. "Good. I'm going to go find grandpa and Nicholas..."

"No!" She interrupted her quickly. "They'll be out soon," she said slowly. "What about your fighting?"

Stacy lifted her fist, quickly moving her leg up in an offensive motion. Terra immediately moved to block it, successfully doing so, but not without a challenge.

"Good."

"Why can't I be with Nicholas? You're keeping something from me."

Terra bit her lip. "We're not keeping anything from you; we just don't want to worry you with what they're discussing."

"Ridiculous," she commented, tearing off into the house.

Terra quickly came off behind her. "Stacy! Stace!"

She made through the house, following the call she felt that told her Nicholas and Tom were in the basement—near their temple. She banged open the door, finding the two of them huddled together over maps and different, unknown artifacts.

"Whatever you two are talking about, I should know. I don't need guarded."

They looked at each other. Silence.

She did not want to play that card, but it was hard not to. "This is my country, my people, I should be the first person to know what's going on and what we're doing!"

Nicholas gave her a weary look. "I agree with you, my darling, however, there is just still so much that you are unaware of, so much that would confuse and overwhelm you and we need to act quickly."

"If I learn while the world is on fire, then that's when I learn. You really think so low of me?" She intended to wait for an answer, to at least see his response, but the frustration of the realization rocked her, and she was tearing out the door before Nicholas even had a chance to call her name or ramble off the danger she was putting herself in.

CHAPTER 77

FIGHT OR FLIGHT

icholas's feet plodded towards the tall, white house, too familiar to cause any gut-wrenching feelings now. His heart raced in unsteady patterns, his brain a fog. He had tuned every other sense out and focused on his hearing, to recognize the sound of aircrafts. Every time he heard one, he prepared to dodge and prepared to be the last man standing. Every time a chopper's blade completed a circle, he felt a slash of pain against his back. With every start of the cycle again, he found himself more empowered to run than ever before.

Danger. Nicholas had one job, if not to let Stacy know the full extent of Dukhovia's bloody history, it *was* to let her know that she was in danger and it was to protect her. Yet, surely, she knew? Surely, she knew to come straight home and not go anywhere unprotected? On her own? Not letting anyone know where she was...

He imagined the independent, self-righteous girl he knew.

She was in the middle of nowhere alone and he knew it.

Reaching Stacy's yard, Nicholas felt his wild eyes searching frantically for the girl he was meant to protect but only finding Rachael and Cara casually talking as if their bodies were not about to be blown to smithereens. It made him feel the insanity within himself spread.

"Why, hello, there," Rachael greeted, standing to the side, allowing space between herself and Cara for him to join.

"Rachael..." He grabbed onto her shoulders with each of her hands, his eyes went cross, barely registering the girl in front of him. He felt her body tense up and searched around in an act of confusion when she maintained a smile on her face. His arms lowered and he faced the two girls.

"Listen, you two need to be staying hidden from here out, do you understand? You cannot leave your homes. You cannot go anywhere alone. You are at risk. Where is Stacy?"

Rachael and Cara exchanged a glance. "Nicholas..." Rachael began easily. "Why don't you sit down for a minute? Catch your breath?"

"No, I do not need to catch my breath. I need to train. I should have been training every moment I was here, every night. I should have been building strength, I should have been researching and praying and doing more..."

Nicholas flung his heavy head into his hands, letting the weight of his thoughts cause it to fall forward. "Stacy and I need to be together...now."

CHAPTER SEVENTY-SEVEN

"Stacy needs space, Nicholas," Rachael told him uneasily.

A light flickered in his mind. "So, she is here?" He said certainly. He looked now—they were not casually sitting on her porch, they were barricading it from him. "Stand aside."

Rachael grimaced, playfully. "Explicit directions not to, Mr. Andrews. But I assure you she is perhaps more aware of the dangers and her need to be aware of everything then even you."

So, she was here and she had told. He felt somewhat reassured. Yet, he did not want Stacy angry with him. They did not have time for anger and frustration. They needed to move.

"It is not that simple. There are a lot of complex parts that her grandfather and I understand readily. Stacy is intelligent, Stacy should have full knowledge, we simply needed to have the conversation quickly to plan and to have her putting emotion into the discussion...."

Rachael had raised her eyebrow more and more as he talked, now the grimace that encompassed her face told him to simply stop talking.

"Fun fact about Americans, Mr. Andrews," Rachael began with a grin. "If you tell them not to do something, their rambunctious ego and inflated sense of pride tell them to do that very thing. Give. Her. Space..."

"You do not understand..." Nicholas repeated, shaking his head back and forth violently.

"That there's an army of crazed Dukhovian soldiers coming to kill her?" Rachael asked in a level voice. "We know. But what will angering her help? Space, young Nicholas. There's plenty of people to protect her."

Plenty of people to protect her.

Nicholas closed his eyes and pictured it...

Her grandparents—strong, fearless, and informed as the Knowledge Spirit.

Her parents—intelligent, reliable, skilled.

Her friends—dedicated, selfless, wise.

Nicholas had not prepared, but they had. This was something they knew would come and he knew they were prone to protect her. He knew that they had to have a plan because not to...well, it was just too arrogant.

He closed his eyes, wrapping his mind around the idea. He was still nervous, he was still a wreck—he needed Stacy on his side now more than ever before.

His legs shook beneath his weight, forcing himself onto the porch. He had collapsed, but he was not weak, he was not leaving—her family had a plan and so would he. They would play their part—and he would play his.

CHAPTER 78

FUEL TO THE FIRE

A purplish hue replaced the cloudless gray of the sky, turning dawn to dusk, orange to white, and fear to pain.

Rachael and Cara had left long ago, after verifying their trust in him, but Nicholas remained seating—waiting and watching. The sound of aircrafts overhead had caused him to stir relentlessly—but nothing happened. Not yet. They were waiting.

What were they waiting for? What were they going to do when they got here? Were they even coming, or was Nicholas just seeing a worst-case scenario?

The realization hit him like a bag of bricks right to the gut—but this time, he had a solution.

Closing his eyes, getting ready to stitch up the seams…

It would not be like connecting to Stacy, he already knew that. He knew that he had tried and failed countless times in Dukhovia, but so much had changed since Dukhovia—he believed in himself, he had hope, he had people that cared for him, he had a family…

A cup of tea stirred mindlessly on a table. The air hung thick with rage, disgust, and uncertainty…

The door to the small, unknown room crept open and a tall figure walked in. The man's body was stiff, but extraordinarily well-decorated in military badges deeming him someone of importance, of value.

"Another plan, sir?"

The man stirring the tea said nothing, only continued to stir until he stopped, two legs planted firmly on the ground.

"Sasha?"

"Patrolling the waters."

An affirming grunt.

Then, as if realizing the man had just appeared, the man shifted emotions, positioning his hand to the seat across from him. "Please." He requested and smiled once the man was seated. "Tell me, have you ever met an American before?"

The man's voice almost shook with fear. "No sir."

He breathed in, a heaviness in his chest. "They are a funny people in that they tend to love what they claim to hate and vice versa. For example, a young woman might reportedly detest tea. In the eyes of the people, she refuses to drink it, degrades it, would even destroy it, yet in the safety and comfort of her home, she will gladly enjoy a cup of tea, cater to it, ensure it is made just so with all the proper instruments.

"Let us consider the opposite. She claims to love tea. She thinks of nothing but, yet when it comes time to drink the tea, to care for the tea, she has no idea how, she has no desire because they have all only been words."

The new man waited for the purpose to The Czar's tale.

"Now imagine that cup of tea is no cup of tea at all. Imagine it is our country."

Silence fell, emptying the bright, sunshine filled space of any feeling at all.

"I see, sir."

"Imagine we get there, we welcome her back to the palace for training."

"The longer we train her, the stronger she will become, and she will be able to stop us. And if we do not truly train her..."

He cut the man off with a raise of his hand. Anger rose once more and the teacup smashed against the window revealing the outside—a bright, moving sky full of clouds high around them.

Nicholas stood to his feet.

The aircraft. They were already on the aircraft. They had no time. No time at all.

He breathed. He knew that what Tom and he had discussed was worst case scenario, he also knew he would do anything necessary to save his heir and protect his country. He sighed, wishing the two could align.

Time drew on with Stacy never coming outside. Her parents entered and left. Her mother had brought him out a bowl of soup and slice of bread. Her father brought him a blanket, a pillow, and an overused invitation to come inside. Nicholas was grateful, but his eyes remained pierced to the sky until several minutes went by without hearing any rotating blades and the moment the patter of light footsteps and the swing of the opening door grasped all of his attention.

"Stacy!" He immediately pulled her in, cradling her in his arms as he breathed her in. His hands pressed against her hair, but he did not truly feel her. He could not hear her breathing, could not smell the lilac body scrub Rachael got her for her birthday...His ears searched the skies for the sound of a fading chopper—nothing was there. But it would be. It would be soon.

Her arms flung protectively around his neck, pulling herself closer. "Nicholas," she whispered, a tear dripped down her face. "I'm so sorry."

"Sh. Promise me you will stop doing that, please?" He held onto either side of her face as he spoke. "It is becoming increasingly dangerous out here. You must allow me to keep you safe."

Stacy nodded her head. "I'm sorry. I didn't mean to scare you, to..." She stopped, but he knew—she did not want him to bring up his old fears. He knew because he felt it—the panic that he would lose the first safe, caring person he had come across in so very long. His stomach ached at the thought.

"I gave you my word that I trusted you would protect me and I just...I want to help Dukhovia...and everything's changing and I can't do it...I'm scared."

Surprisingly, Nicholas chuckled lightly, not releasing his touch on Stacy's warm cheek. "So, the relentless Stacy Matthews has the ability to house fear after all?" He embraced her once more, bringing her ear close to his mouth as he whispered. "Here I was thinking even the devil would run for cover in your presence."

"The theory has yet to be tested," Stacy replied in a condescending voice. Then her eyes narrowed. "Are you going to tell me what you and Tom talked about?"

He smiled. There she was. "Do you want a full history lesson on our constitution, its articles, and the power legislation lacks?"

She grimaced. "Okay, maybe you were right. But tell me next time—I don't like being kept in the dark."

Nicholas's smile melted away. "Of course, you have spent far too much time there. I do not want to be the one that holds the key to someone else's prison. I simply...reacted."

"How you were trained to," she said, knowingly, her eyes following his as she looked out at the sky and then their surroundings. "When will he be here?"

"If they're flying straight here, half a day, I suppose. But they may stop. Plan. Thomas and I will be tracking them every step of the way. And we will be ready." His answers were truthful as he filled her in on what he heard.

"I want to fight," Stacy said, slowly.

Nicholas waited, he knew she was anticipating his reaction, so he breathed, considering their options. "We shall continue to train. If and when it turns into a battle, I will determine if you are ready. These are heavily trained soldiers, Stacy Grace. You do need to serve Dukhovia, but not dead."

Her eyes darted back and forth in a way that made his gut twist, but she nodded her head.

"He won't kill me," she whispered after a long time.

Nicholas's head snapped towards her. "What?"

She shrugged. "He won't. You've told me enough to realize that. If it was as simple as killing me, he would have just come here and done it himself or you would have. But that wasn't your plan, your plan was to bring me *willingly* to Dukhovia."

Nicholas tensed. "I believe you are correct; however, I have learned to never assume anything when it comes to Arkady. As you can see by his ability to manipulate the Spirit Connection, he has a way of getting what he wants. I cannot...Dukhovia cannot afford to subject you to his loopholes, nor his temper.

"Arkady needs you in Dukhovia, yes, and that means waiting for him to come here. Waiting is the best chance we have at trying to reason with him. No matter what happens, he will not hurt you on American soil."

"But he'll shoot me unconscious, bag up my body, and take it back to Dukhovia," Stacy suggested plainly.

Nicholas shook his head. His mouth formed into a thin line as he imagined the image. "No, he will not do anything to an American rashly and not without his entire military alliance waiting on the front lines." Nicholas brought his hand up to his chin, lost in thought. "As you stated, Arkady *wants* you to go to Dukhovia willingly, however, even if we put up a fight, he is aware that the Americans hold technology he has never dreamt of, and they are not bound by any moral laws to refrain from using it. He may put his people in danger, but never himself."

Nicholas huffed, considering his final words. "Once they are here, I will bring you to him. I will allow him to get close enough to feel your Spirit, but nothing more. Then we will disclose to him all your strengths. We will prove to him that an American ruler can be fair and just. We will assure him that the Spirits surely have a stronger path for his family, perhaps guiding you."

"And if it fails?" Stacy asked, her voice skeptical as his mock confidence.

Nicholas swallowed, shuttering at the thought. "If he does not see things our way, he will become violent. You must be nowhere near that Stacy, do you understand? You must listen to me."

Stacy looked at him, unmoving. "Okay," her voice muttered through a thin, pressed line.

"They will fight," Nicholas sighed. "But we will fight ten times harder."

Stacy nodded, sliding her hand into his and grasping on. They managed it. They managed to hold each other without slipping, without breaking at the electricity. The voltage was power now. A weapon to be utilized together—not to separate.

Stacy smiled, imagining this all-powerful, dictator-czar, running frightened just from their very presence, from the feel of the strength of their entwined Spirits, knowing that he could not compromise—but she knew she was banking on a miracle.

CHAPTER 79

AN ERA OF CHANGE

S tacy's eyes flashed open. She was in a pool of sweat and confusion as she
recounted the dream she had just woken up from.

*Rainbows jetting out from the sky around her, people frolicking, hand
in hand, amongst meadows of pink and white daisies, purple lilies, and an array
of colorful tulips. Where a sunflower shot out of the ground, towering over anyone,
there was sure to be a stream connecting it all, giving life to it all, pushing it all
forward...*

She felt comfort, she felt at peace. She could not wait to face a world so in-
depth with this beauty.

*Darkness elevated and encompassed the entire scenery. Shots of orange,
yellow, and red devastated the trees to the north, extinguishing the streams to the
south.*

Stacy shot up in fear. She looked around, panic-stricken.

The dream and its whereabouts made no logical sense to her, so she lay back
down, and shut her eyes, accepting defeat at her inability to decipher the message.

Beauty.

Fire.

Life.

Death.

Nicholas's face.

She closed her eyes, hugged herself, reassured herself, feeling his warmth
around her. Good. Pure. Innocent.

*A waterfall cascaded down from behind a mountain. Stacy walked toward it,
moving closer.*

"What is it?" Stacy felt herself ask out of her control.

*"It is called the River of Life. The falls represent the Spirit of the Water while
each fall is a purpose."*

*"Why water?" She did not understand the seemingly basic questions that she
asked.*

*"Water is said to be the strongest element of life," he replied. "It can be
interrupted by stones and other foreign objects... but it is always flowing." He
walked closer to the fall, right underneath it, and Stacy felt herself go forward too.*

*"All can go through it," he exampled by placing his hand in the stream. "But
it will always push pass." He motioned to the water simply rerouting to go around
his hand. "No matter the strength of the penetrating force." He lifted a huge, flat*

rock, the size of a tree trunk that Stacy imagined he could never lift in real life. He held it beneath the falls. Water still cascaded into the gulf below.

"No other element can be without water, Stacy. The earth needs it for life. It is present in the air. Its molecules present in even the strongest of..."

There was a burst from the other side of the waterfall. A fire detonated from the underside of the falls, sending them flying backward. They stood and were in the same spot, close to the falls.

Together, the two rushed to try and put out the fire. The falls turned into individual people, trying to help stop the fire... but it was too late. The land was untouched, but the falls were gone.

Beauty, existence, life.

Hate, tragedy, despair...

Then the Dukhovian flag melting away. Melting into nothing.

She could not fall back asleep that time. It was only about 4:30 in the morning, but she was wide awake.

She leaned her head against her bed, her thoughts assimilating as she stared at her flag of Dukhovia, thought about the dream, and back again...

Movement. The word popped into her head like a direct call. She could guess and educate herself on what her dreams meant all day long but at the end of that day there was only one clear, concrete next move and the dream had fed it right to her: movement.

CHAPTER 80

...THEY'RE COMING

"Do I want nachos or Cheetos to be my first food of the new year?" Dylan was holding one of each up as the friends gathered around in the Matthews' garage waiting for the ball to drop.

Everyone was laughing and joining in on the fun. Even Cara, despite the date of the dance apparently needing to be pushed back. They had fireworks meant to set off as a huge display when the ball dropped, but they had already blown through all but four of them. They had way too much food and too few eaters. Cody managed to set up his Xbox on the double screen TV, making their game much more graphic.

The party was fully in force for everyone, even Nicholas...when he was engaging and not tapping his foot while leaning against the wall.

Stacy broke away from a game of ping pong with Rachael, Jade, and Andy and dropped down onto his lap.

"You don't seem so happy, sir," she cooed into his ear, pressing her face up against his.

Nicholas's arms wrapped tightly around Stacy. He put his mouth close to her ear. "I do not like waiting." He released his arms and motioned for her to stand up. "I am going to take another walk."

Stacy stood and watched him go. He had been walking the perimeter of the street every half hour. He clenched up every time a firework went off and refused to give up his tension.

Her fear expanded when his deepened, but Nicholas had been telling her that her growth towards the Spirits would be her biggest protector when Arkady arrived, and she was trying to trust in them.

"We'll do a press release next Thursday..."

Stacy overheard Dan talking with Cara about announcing her introduction to the band. Stacy had approached her with the idea after her help the last few days. It was an offer that was always on the table, but Cara was a time and place kind of girl. Everyone was thrilled she finally accepted.

But Stacy was...struggling with the timing. Thursday was almost a week away and everything could be different by then. Everything could be changed. Perhaps that was her plan—if she was out, Cara was her replacement.

She breathed in deeply, taking in the sight of her friends. How happy they all were, how alive. Her lids closed and an image of the garage in a fiery blaze with all her friends lying on the ground passed before her eyes.

CHAPTER EIGHTY

She breathed again. They would be protected. They would not be harmed. *Nothing can happen that isn't meant to be, as long as we do what's right.*

"One minute warning!" Dylan announced, shoving people aside to get his lighter to the fireworks.

Cody, Joey, and Jimmy ran up with them, setting off the last four at once. Perhaps they planned the perfection.

They shot up right on que, going off as the final moments of 2006 came to a close and a new beginning was born.

"Promise me you'll get some sleep tonight?" Stacy asked Nicholas as she wrapped herself around him before saying goodbye.

He shook his head. His eyes darted around the yard, never looking at her. "No, Stacy, you know I cannot do that. You are too important."

Stacy rolled her eyes. "Then how will I survive if my protector diminishes thirty seconds into this imminent battle you are awaiting?"

Nicholas tried to acknowledge her comment with laughter, but it was a halfhearted attempt.

"Hey," Stacy latched onto him, her arms wrapping around his neck as they stood. He immediately grabbed onto her waist. "Let's make this count. Say they do come, say everything we have ends. I want this moment with you."

Nicholas swallowed, his piercing blue eyes transfixed on hers like to leave would end everything. "They will take everything from us."

Stacy shrugged, pushing down her own fear. "Then let's not let them have right now. Be with me. Just be with me."

His heart swelled and he allowed his head to drop into Stacy's shoulders as they began to slowly sway, dancing to a sad and melodious tune, but it was their tune. It was their rhythm. It was their comfort. In that moment, he could fall apart completely—so he did.

They stayed like that for a long time. Until the others had gone and the New Year arrived, bringing with it all the unknown and promises of surprise.

Nicholas stayed the night that night—but he never slept, and Stacy knew it. She heard him creep out the door later that night—every hour—to continue his watches. The next day, he was the same statue of concern.

***

Stacy opened the door and closed it with great difficulty—Nicholas had some sort of makeshift security system to warn him if someone tried to enter the house in the event he fell asleep or was patrolling the other side of the house. Stacy did not bother letting him know they already had an alarm system; doing it his way made him more comfortable.

She did not quite understand the what looked like rope made out of the wood of a tree wrapped around her door—what tree did he even get them from? But she knew the intricate twist would delay an intruder, and her and her parents both knew that if Nicholas deemed it a safety precaution, it was as good as such.

They had not yet told the rest of the family what was going on—and no one really questioned it. Perhaps they knew, perhaps they just assumed Nicholas was a lunatic considering his own colorful past—perhaps they were right.

Time passed by and Nicholas never heard the sounds of the sharp, metal blades beating against wind and gravity to find him. He ran his hand along the back of his neck—there was nothing stopping them from finding him.

Him.

Nicholas never wrote to Arkady. He never attempted to connect with him and thus, never verified Stacy's location. The only way he would find Stacy would be through tracking Nicholas. His staying here was a hindrance. His staying was putting her in direct danger.

Nicholas glanced back into the house, watching Stacy as she watched him back, mirroring his anxious eyes. His chest ached, but he knew he could only delay the inevitable for so long...

But he also meant what he said—Arkady's temper was perhaps worse than even Nicholas's. In his right mind, he would not track and capture Stacy on his own. But if he was not in his right mind, or if he decided to risk his own ruling to 'protect Dukhovia', as he considered it.

Nicholas clenched his teeth wishing so badly he could go back to the start. He imagined himself that day in the library, that day in the woods, boring over maps. If only his gift was time travel, he would give anything to go back and tell his past self to run. Run now. Because she is worthy. Because you making matters worse is only going to make Arkady angrier. Because you are desperately in love with her.

He knew it a long time ago. It was no new realization. But he had allowed himself to think the word, to feel how it felt just to consider, perhaps even whisper. It was comfortable and confident dancing across his lips—but it was also full of fear and pain and remorse. How could he allow himself to love the person he put in danger? How could he deserve the honor? And how could he fall in love with a girl that would inevitably slip away from him?

He twiddled his fingers, blocking out his thoughts, blocking out Stacy's uneven breathing pattern on the other side of the door. Could he be so full of fear that he imagined the entire scenario? Was the aircraft he heard simply an American plane running a test trial?

No. He swore he heard the rickety turn and brutal scraping of metal on metal that Arkady was likely too stubborn to fix. It was *his* plane. The plane that brought him here. Nicholas would recognize it anywhere.

But then, where did it go? Arkady would not be hiding somewhere in America, waiting for the proper moment. He would want to spend as little time as possible in this sorry nation and fly away eternally.

You can protect her and still win. You can win this.

CHAPTER EIGHTY

Ah, Erlik. Hello, old friend.

"Nicholas."

Stacy's voice warmed him the way his mother's voice used to. The simple care in her voice was like a speech telling him it was going to be okay, he was going to be safe, his purpose would be found, the Spirits would forgive him. He could not argue with it, but the convincing in his own head was easy to barter with.

Nicholas grasped onto both her hands; the weight of her Spirit crashed into his like a wave on a ship that would wash to sea. So forceful, so strong. He held her for dear life.

"They aren't coming," she told him softly. "No one is here."

He looked into the sky. The fog pattern that the Dukhovian plane he took left behind was not present, not even a trace. He could go back to his apartment, gather the things necessary to test the air and truly see if they were there—but his instincts told him no.

The air did not smell like the same type of fuel. The blades did not sound the same, not exactly.

He nodded, a faint smile crawling onto his lips. "Maybe you are right. I just need some air."

Stacy laughed. "You've been sitting outside on this stoop for the last four days—air's all you've been getting. I think it's going to your head." She nudged her fist into his hair.

He playfully swatted her hand away. "Time to clear my head, is what I mean," he offered. He looked at her up and down. She seemed much calmer than usual. Even the wrinkles at the end of her sleeves from her pushing them up and down every time she got anxious ceased to be present.

"Will you take a walk with me?" He requested, holding his hand down to her as he stood.

Stacy smiled and gladly accepted.

It had been a month. They both realized this as they walked. A month since his feet first hit American soil, repulsed and reluctant to continue on with his journey.

A month, since the first time their first stand-off in the school courtyard, anger splitting between the two, one at themselves, one at the other.

A month of secrets, hidden knowledge, and self-empowerment rushing together as the two came completely apart from the lives they once knew, to the ones they were meant to fulfill. Nothing felt normal anymore, but everything felt so right. Secrets answered, pasts revealed. Everything they needed to move forward.

"Tell me more about your family," Stacy asked, her pace was even with his, flat. "You know all our deep, dark secrets," She smiled brilliantly. "I feel like I barely know yours."

Nicholas was quiet for a moment, thinking of where to begin, thinking of how grateful he was for the time that came and passed where he had someone to discuss his family life with at all.

"My family has deep, dark secrets too," he disclosed. "That is why I must be the one to restore our family honor. There has been so much time spent discussing our shame, I can scarcely recall a story of glory."

Nicholas took a deep breath, taking in the surroundings. His gaze was off again, scanning the sky to for a hope at a memory of a different time, for a different circumstance, but resonating for the first time with the one he had.

"You will bring the Demitona's, honor, Nicholas, by following your heart. By following your true path and exceeding it the best way you can. You have the opportunity they never did. They will be proud of you for that, not regaining it just because some idiot says so. And making the right choices—regardless of the outcome."

There it is. The peace that filled his heart, the warmth that surged through him as a child prior to age two. When all was right in the world, when he was fulfilling his destiny by the way he lived his life...the way it was supposed to be. Before he was ever told otherwise.

"I know you don't like to hear it," Stacy went on, "but you really are incredibly courageous, Nicholas. And you're a good person. Living in Dukhovia, growing up an heir being trained to not succeed...it all seems difficult enough, but to go it alone... People were meant for companionship, right?"

Nicholas mulled it over in his mind. "Perhaps."

Suddenly, Stacy smiled ruthlessly. "It doesn't matter what he says anymore—Arkady or anyone else in Dukhovia. I'm going to rule someday and when I do, the Demitona's will be given a statue in North Bridge. The bravery of Nicholas the First will be celebrated as a national holiday. And I'll tear up any reminder of the Andrews name."

The two laughed simultaneously. Then, Nicholas picked Stacy up, twirling her in a circular pattern. It was as if an angel was flying before him.

Their path continued until it became much smoother. The sidewalks were completely clear of snow, clearing the path to a beautifully made ice sculpture. One appeared every year, but no one ever knew where from.

This year, it was a swan, its wings spread wide and welcoming. It was not prepared to take flight, it was prepared to take in. The two stopped in front of it, admirably.

"It's hard to believe someone spent so much time out here to make this," Stacy said in awe, her thoughts drifting to the beautiful, thoughtful carvings Nicholas had created. It seemed a lifetime ago. Her hands were shoved into her pockets; Nicholas did the same.

"Maybe we have more heirs in America than we thought," he offered.

CHAPTER EIGHTY

Stacy smiled at the idea. The idea of having more people, of having people all over the world to come to Dukhovia's aid—they were not completely without a chance. "A Spirit gift, maybe," she theorized.

Nicholas smiled. "We have to discover yours."

Stacy grimaced. "The idea of just finding out what you've already taught me has always seemed so impossible. Now something else to find out…"

He did not let her finish, instead, he took her hand and gave it a reassuring squeeze. "We will figure it out together."

She smiled at him, her bright eyes shining with appreciation and acceptance. "What are some other gifts people have? Or options?"

Nicholas shrugged. "Anything, truly. It could be something common but exasperated to near-perfection—an incredible doctor, for example. It all depends which Spirit gives you the gift. The Spirits might be able to guide you, form safe passage for you, or even conjure up forces in order to bring you aid. It all has to deal with what you believe in and if you believe in it strong enough."

Then the world faded from around them, they went from only seeing each other, only noticing each other, to watching their worlds shred apart, ripping and tearing as chaos burned around them.

Nicholas's eyes widened first: pure, frozen horror stuck to his face. His heart felt like it would rage right out his chest.

"We have to go!" His words were erratic and pressured as he latched onto her hand, pulling away. "We have to go; we have to go."

"Nicholas! What's going on?"

He paused, frozen to his spot. Every feature wild with fear. "He's coming. Arkady is coming. Now."

Stacy froze. She could only stare at his hollow, empty face. He had gone white as a ghost. "How? When?"

Nicholas looked like he was about to throw up. His throat wobbled as he spoke. "Any minute," he croaked.

Stacy started looking around herself, frantically.

"They are in a small aircraft—there may even be several," Nicholas said in a hurry.

Stacy nodded. Nicholas kept whipping his head around, but he made her face forward. They ran faster than they ever had, but they were in a field of forest, completely alone, completely isolated from town. They would never make it.

They were tearing through the forest, ripping through branches and pine with no regard to dodge them. Nicholas was skilled at this—but Stacy was struggling.

He looked from her to behind him quickly, seeming to think something over. Then he lunched towards her, grabbing onto her hand. The shock rocked through them stronger than it ever had, but she knew what he was doing—she needed his guidance, his help. She stayed latched onto him, despite the feel of exhilaration, the feeling of power, the feeling that took over nearly all her other senses. Her vision blurred, her hearing became faint, she felt like she was sucked into space, floating, no feeling, no existing...

But she trusted him.

Then Nicholas suddenly stopped, freezing in his place.

"Are we there?" Stacy asked, her vision still blurred.

Nicholas did not answer, instead a voice that sent a chill down her spine and caused her hair to stand on end whispered into her ear.

It was a fear she never knew.

"Oh, we are here."

CHAPTER 81

RUTHLESS EVIL

A tight gasping sound escaped Stacy's lips, bringing tears to her eyes. She held her hair back in an effort to see what was going on, but Nicholas had snatched onto her, holding her back. She was frantic, her head moving around the field before them, searching for the root of the shrill voice that had whispered in her ear moments before—there was no one there.

She stayed in her place, her senses slowly coming back to her. In front of her, about one hundred feet away, circling them in like a pack of wolves, stood what must have been the Dukhovian military's top men.

Her chest ached. Rows and rows of men dressed in pale blue uniforms, some of them yielding a sword, others yielding nothing but looks of stone-cold violence. She made not a sound. Nicholas was frozen as well, but he seemed to be looking around—he was planning. Plotting. She should be doing the same.

The propellers of the still running planes whipped around quickly, causing Nicholas's hair to lash across his forehead, blinding Stacy from his vision for the most terrifyingly long second of his life. A pit in his stomach swelled with a fear he never knew.

"Do not worry, Stacy," he whispered in her ear, pulling her away from their line of vision. "I can handle this. I can protect us."

But Stacy scarcely heard them, instead, her mind was infiltrated with the hollow echo of a deafening coo: *protect the heir, protect them.* Over and over.

The sound of the propellers lightened as they began to shut down, but the gust and thick fog surrounding the area only seemed to increase.

Nicholas pulled Stacy to her feet, slowly backing her up against a tree, too concentrated in fog to be able to see.

"Show no fear," he whispered to her.

And just like that, Nicholas became the war machine he was that first day of class. He was not himself. He was not his gentle, compassionate, safe self. He was in defense-mode, protection mode—he was at risk.

Protect the heir.

Several unsettling moments ticked by until, like clockwork, the engines ceased movement. Silenced filled the eerie park as nothing but the creak of the worn-down machines filled an ear.

Nothing happened. No one moved. It was almost as if they could get up and run, investigate an abandoned mission, or some third option—any third option—which resulted in the same chance of survival.

Stacy stood safely behind the protection of Nicholas. He was trained to take out armies of men—twenty in ten seconds if she recalled properly—these few men would be nothing to him. Yet, the hand that told her to stay behind him was not that confident, was not that prepared, it shook with the uncertainty of the strengths of the twenty men he would be faced with, on top of the single most important and valuable life that he swore to protect—had he ever protected a life other than his own?

Suddenly, an ear wrenching pierce sounded throughout the wooded area. The sound was followed by one and then another. Stacy tried hard to find the root of the noise, but all she could make out was the vague distinction of three or four of the enhanced machines. Others she simply could see nothing of but their outline and the feeling in her gut confirming their existence.

The ground shook beneath their feet. Another harsh crashing echoed into oblivion, a rattling following. The fog had begun to rise. More sounds echoed and filled Stacy's ears: footsteps, whispers, laughter, shuttering…She could see less, she could hear more, her heart beat louder though she cursed it to stay still.

Then, the fog began to clear away. The machines in front of them appeared to be helicopters, but they were sturdier, stronger. They were cased entirely in a freshly painted, light blue metal—christened with a Russian and Dukhovian flag— with not even so much as a window for the pilot to be able to see out of. There was nothing but a few slits on the sides of the aircraft where windows *should* be.

Then, out of the shadows of the trace amounts of fog, eight armed soldiers left the sanctuary of their plane, then another eight from the next. Nicholas held onto Stacy's hand, pulling her even closer to him, if it were even possible.

And then, from the plane in the center, the largest, the sturdiest, came a man poised with a face of belligerence, agitation...and impatience. His neat and pressed uniform set him apart from the other man, they deemed him more important, more worthy. His light blue that much lighter, his badges multiplied compared to theirs. His poise as he rounded towards them—deadly.

Two men walked with him. One that was nearly as decorated as he and a third rather plain looking man. The last man was no solider, nor did he appear to be in command. He was simply—there. Eyes and hair just as dark as the other two. Skin just as tanned. But face seemed just as likely to throw up as Stacy was.

"Well, well, well, Sir Nicholas, this is certainly not how I foresaw our reunion." His voice was like one-thousand icicles to her heart. It was the low rumble of his tone, it was the lax yet pointedness of his words.

"I was not due back yet," Nicholas claimed through barred teeth. His voice was calm, almost steady, but Stacy felt the shudder in his body and she was certain Arkady could detect it.

Arkady cocked his head. "But it does not appear you were prepared to leave. Not from the thoughts I heard, anyway."

Petrified horror-struck Nicholas as understanding flickered on his face. His eyes darted away only for a second when Arkady threw something to the ground and the sound of clattering metal filled their ears.

"A peace offering," Arkady hissed, nodding towards the sword.

"Well then," Arkady said in a venomous tone, clicking his tongue against teeth that were prepared to kill. "Please introduce me to our heir." His hand dipped down at the final word, dripping with pure hatred as dark as the eyes he now lay on Stacy.

"You will not get near her," Nicholas explained and his hand tightened around Stacy's arm. "Only as far as I say or we run."

Arkady maintained his death-like stare on Stacy and though her voice was completely unreachable—she glared right back. Memorizing the pattern of each wrinkle, searching past the eyes of darkness for a sense of humanity, a sense of morality, an answer to how he interpreted his actions to be just from the standpoint of any person, let alone a Dukhovian ruler.

And she was to be that ruler. The one that saved Dukhovia, the one that brought great peace. She would not allow herself to hide. She would not allow herself to be protected. She would be the one calling the shots, she would be the one making calls.

This was her country. She did not deserve to be pushed around by the man destroying it. She stepped right up next to Nicholas. Side by side.

Arkady seemed amused over Nicholas's rules, but either complied or played along out of interest. He inched closer, Nicholas and Stacy slowly and carefully moved their stiff limbs.

"There. Far enough," Nicholas ordered when they were roughly fifteen feet apart.

Stacy's breath was stuck in her chest, threatening to choke her alive. The closeness of the evil before her only exemplified when he was close enough to feel her Spirit—because she could feel his too.

Daunting. Rigid. It did not feel like how she did when she was near or even touching Nicholas. The power that shot through her when hers and Nicholas's hands touched brought visions of light, of beauty, of energy that could save a world. This feeling, this energy—it was rotted and black. She saw images of children lying dead on their door steps. She saw their parents crying over them or them crying over their parents. She saw the devil and felt hell itself.

The demon's lips formed into a sly grin. "A woman, after all."

Nicholas felt Stacy's arm buckle, hot tension rising inside of her. Her face formed into a grimace, but Nicholas spoke before she had a chance to get herself killed. "Correct—and a very excellent one at that. Much of what we thought America to be is true, I fear, however, there are also quite a few exceptions. Stacy

Matthews is one of those exceptions, sir. She is brilliant, she is kind, and her dedication to Dukhovia runs deeper than many of those who walk the land now."

Nicholas's intentional jab at his mentor was not missed by the man, who quickly buried his frustration in exchange for a faux pleasantness.

"Ah, very good, very good," he spoke. "Then she is able to recite our doctrines from memory?"

Nicholas shook his head. "No, sir, not yet. As no heir is able to do so before training, but as Stacy is predicted to be stronger than any other, she will certainly learn quicker than any other. What she does possess are qualities that cannot be taught. A call towards peace, devotion towards our nation, a sense of justice and wisdom, family ties that would impress the Spirit of Ancestry."

"Hm," Arkady said, unmoved. "Unfortunately, Sir Nicholas, I do not believe your lovesick heart will be enough to convince the entire country of Dukhovia. I understand that you have a very difficult past: outcasted by your nation for your family's mistakes, the tragic death of your mother and father..."

And there he was fully. That man with manic, wild anger. A caged lion had erupted with an urge for violence, a sense for destruction, not stopping until defeat rang in.

He pounced. Hands wrapped tightly on Arkady's throat.

"MY PARENT'S DEATHS WERE NOT TRAGIC, THEY WERE MURDERED!"

Stacy saw the air leaving The Czar's lungs, Nicholas's grip getting tighter—and not a single one of those back-up soldiers Arkady brought were doing a thing. Not even the man whom Stacy could guess to be his second in command—the man whose uniform Stacy recognized as that of a sailor. Yes, she recognized the symbol from a blanket she was given as an infant when her and Kevin were rescued. He was an admiral. Her eyes squinted towards the name—Admiral Alexander.

It's a trick. Stacy thought. It had to be. If he attacks the Czar—or worse, kills him—what? They can send him to prison to rot? No confusing ties or who is or is not an heir? Just a murderer.

Another murder. No, no matter who it was, Nicholas did not want to be that person...

With all her might, Stacy charged at The Czar, knocking Nicholas's grip loose.

Then Nicholas saw it and Stacy did too—one of the soldiers from the line had stepped out, a knife held prominently in their hand. And then they charged—directly for Stacy.

"STACY NO!"

Nicholas abandoned the Czar who stood to watch the scene unfold. Nicholas put his arms up, blocking the man. He fell back as not another solider moved to provide aid.

Stacy heard the crunching of bone and both the man's wrists snapped.

Nicholas kicked him to the ground as he howled out in pain. Sending a knee to his stomach, Nicholas had him pinned. He pulled up his arms and twisted the man's neck laying the lifeless body abandoned on the cold, hard ground.

Stacy tried to gasp, but she hardly had a second before the sound of the remaining soldier's feet picked up, like a herd of wild animals running towards Stacy and Nicholas—they attack first. That was the trap. First to kill and they have grounds to attack. She silently cursed Nicholas's temper.

Every man charged in their direction. Nicholas's anger was evident in his eyes as he made the same realization as Stacy, but the minute he caught a glimpse of her, anger was replaced entirely with concern.

"STACY!"

Stacy backed away. Nicholas was by her side in a heartbeat, grabbing her and leading her towards a shelter in the trees.

Two men approached them, but Nicholas simply released Stacy long enough to snap both their necks and carried on.

Stacy wheeled around, counting at a glance. Fifteen soldiers had stepped out of the small, compact aircraft. Fifteen. Of those fifteen, three were gone. Twelve remaining.

Stacy knew that she did not fully understand what was happening, her head ached at the realization, but watching Nicholas ending the lives of these people without an ounce of remorse made it all the worse.

You don't know, she told herself. *You don't.* He very well may have known that these men were not good for Dukhovia. Perhaps if Arkady was corrupted, they were as well. But he had said it was not black and white. He had said that some wanted to remain traditional while others just wanted rid of her. Which were they? Did it really matter? They were still her people.

She dared another look behind her...down to ten, down to eight. They kept approaching and Nicholas would simply maneuver his body in a set of skills that made him look almost invisible, sometimes using the men's confusion against each other. But she also noticed the men were sent in waves of two—never more. Why? Why not gang up on him? He said he could handle so many more than two, why not bring as many as they could pile in?

Trick.

Stacy tried to step in—truthfully. But she never realized how weak she was when she was not simply training with her mother or a friend. She lifted her hand to block and was quickly forced to the ground. Then again and her arm was grabbed and twisted behind her head. She prepared to have her head snapped the same way Nicholas did to so many others—yet suddenly the hand holding her dropped and she fell to the ground freely, scrambling to her feet.

Nicholas's response was pure barbaric detonation.

CHAPTER EIGHTY-ONE

Stacy backed away, breathing heavy. Nicholas was saving her, but yet he was an uncontrollable monster. He threw one man against the next. He brought one to his knees then reached an arm behind him and cracked the skull of another. Then one was getting his face smashed into the ground until it was unrecognizable. Then one lost an arm that became used as a human sword to beat down every person. Then Nicholas took out his real sword and sliced through two men in one, even swipe.

And then they were down to the three. Three men remained and none of them were charging for them.

Nicholas and Stacy had reached the tree. Nicholas forced Stacy in the opening and then stood in front of it, guarding her. She did not fight it. She wanted to help, she wanted to fight, but seeing him, seeing the other men—she knew she needed to better herself.

She closed her eyes attempting to block out the scene, attempting to control her breathing. It was impossible. She could not breathe. She could not breathe. She could not breathe. She did not remember how.

Breathe. Breathe. In and out. Stacy, come on!

"Stacy, look out!"

Four. There were four remaining. She lost count somewhere. Nicholas had abandoned the tree to approach Arkady, but the last man standing now held Stacy. He leapt forward, stabbing the soldier, causing Stacy to smack her head on the ground, rendering her unconscious.

Nicholas made to pick her up, but the final solider had not completely fallen. He was too weak and too far to complete his goal, but he waved his sword as far as it would go, slicing into Nicholas's arm and plunging as far as it would reach into his stomach. Nicholas turned around, driving the sword out of his stomach and into the man's eye. Then he fell to the ground in pain.

Arkady, the Admiral, and the last man approached.

Nicholas looked at them through squinted eyes, trying to remain conscious, trying to catch his breath and stop his bleeding.

"Consider this a warning," Arkady breathed down to him. "You have one week's time. One. Sit and consider what it is you are willing to do for your country. Save it—or watch it slip away and turn into…" His words drifted off as he lay his hand out, exposing the scene of dead bodies. "This."

Nicholas threw up. He lifted his head long enough to see a sea of police cars swarm the area as close as they could, Chief Grayson at the front of the line.

Sirens echoed around the block, as troops from the surrounding cities filed in. Cars were lining up by the dozen, at least six choppers were in the air.

Nicholas's head was falling and he felt himself fading in and out, hearing the sound of a gunshot, then nothing, then several gun shots, then nothing but the roar of starting planes.

He looked up and saw the legs of the fighters rushing to get back on their planes and fly away. Nicholas inched his way towards Stacy, unable to grab any more than her hand before fading completely to black.

"I need an ambulance—NOW."

"St. Mazu's is closest."

"No, Heart of America. Don't send them anywhere other than Heart of America. And don't let a single press member in the hospital."

Stacy heard the voices fading in and out. Her eyes opened as she was loaded onto a stretcher, looking directly into her uncle's worried and agitated eyes.

"Nicholas," she reached out, frantically searching for his hand. She felt cool fingertips find hers.

"Stacy. Sh." He managed.

"What happened?" She pressed.

"I do not know," he answered weakly. He closed his eyes for a few seconds, pressing his fingers to his forehead as the memories filed back in and he realized what they meant.

"All those people," Stacy whimpered. "Nicholas, you killed all those people."

Nicholas shook his head. "No...Only about half of them." He shut his eyes again, then reopened them as if something revolutionary had crossed his mind. "The soldiers..."

Stacy nodded her head.

"I did not recognize any of the soldiers."

Stacy was confused, the pit in her stomach increasing with the confession. "Is that good? His old supporters have left him?"

Nicholas was shaking his head, the best he could. "His army has grown."

CHAPTER 82

GRACE AND PATIENCE

$\mathcal{N}$ icholas…?" Stacy tried sitting up, inching herself up onto her elbows. "Nick!"

"He is fine," the EMT told her, lowering her back down as Nicholas lost consciousness. "You both need rest until we can run the proper tests."

Stacy laid back down and shut her eyes, avoiding the glare of her uncle and the pressing questions they would receive the moment they were no longer in critical condition—a state she was not even sure she was in now.

She did not want to explain alone, nor did she really know what to say anyway. What had happened? Nicholas had said that the Dukhovians feared the weaponry of the Americans, but for every single one of those men to pack up and go without even taking her with them seemed strange.

Stacy! Look out!

Don't bother to run, little girl…

Don't bother to run. She had not. They were clearly outnumbered and Nicholas knew they did not come to negotiate. He knew that they did not stand a chance. Then why were they not both killed on the spot? Was it a game to them? With all she knew of The Czar thus far—the odds were in favor of such.

Willing. They want me to go willingly to Dukhovia. Why?

Soon, she could bear the thought of the fight no longer and her thoughts drifted to a world where her and Nicholas could be together peacefully, where he was healthy, he was safe, and everything around them was pure bliss.

. . .

Stacy awoke to the sound of loud sirens, beeping machines, and voices talking a mile a minute. She felt her body being rolled into a room and Nicholas's turned down an opposite hallway. She remembered yelling his name, she remembered seeing them put something on his chest, scream 'clear' and the jolt that sent Nicholas out of his gurney. She remembered him not responding.

"NO! NO!"

Nurses and doctors rushed to her side to calm her. Her arms flailed in every direction. They were lifting her eyelids to peer into them with a light. They were wheeling her into an MRI room, begging her to remain still.

After the doors closed and she accepted the fact that if she escaped, she would have no idea where to go, she complied. She laid emotionless and silent as they did the tests they wanted to, diagnosed her with a concussion, and discharged her to her uncle in a cold, empty waiting room filled with nothing but burgundy chairs and two coffee machines.

"How are you feeling?" He asked her anxiously.

Stacy shrugged. Honestly…mortified. The events were so traumatic she would not care if she never stepped foot in a hospital ever again. "I need to see Nicholas."

Richard did not respond.

Stacy's heart thud against her chest. "Where is he?!" She yelled.

Richard got up and put his arm around her shoulder. "Sh, Stacy, he's fine. He lost a lot of blood and they punctured his pancreas. It was…strange. His body seemed as if it were trying to heal but the intensity of the wound kept undoing the progress, it made it difficult for doctors to know what to do…"

"Because he's strong. He's like me. He'll heal on his own."

"He'll be out of surgery in a few hours."

"No," Stacy protested, looking around. "I need to be with him. He can't be alone. He needs me."

Richard sighed, shifting calmly. "I understand, kid, really, I do. But let's just let them do all they can first and then if that doesn't work, we'll let the Spirits take over. Fair?"

Agitated, she agreed. Just like she was unable to fight, she was unable to perform surgery if he truly needed it. Useless. That's what she was in this country. Absolutely useless.

Richard had a pager, something different than what he typically carried. It began to buzz in his pocket, distracting him for a moment.

"They're just waiting on the blood transfusion," Richard told her. "He's stable. He's going to be alright."

Stacy refused to believe it until he came walking through those doors. He was too beat up, too hurt to be okay. The image of him being wheeled down the hall, doctors yelling, lights flashing, zoomed through her mind. She needed him. "Where are Tom and Terra?" She demanded. They would let her through.

"They're on their way," Richard explained.

Her eyes widened in horror. "They're not *doing* the surgery? Is that a joke?"

"Tom is on the phone in case they run into anything abnormal and they should be here any moment. Relax."

She settled into a chair, pouting like a child.

"Stacy…What happened out there?"

She looked at him crossed, avoiding eye contact. "I don't really know," she admitted. "That's why I need Nicholas."

Richard no longer pressed her. He let her stare with intense anger at the opening of the waiting room, then eventually off into an uneven, frequently interrupted sleep.

Hours later, as the sun started to close in, engulfing the hospital in the dark of night, a door creaked open and the sound of a crutch clonking down the hall approached.

"Nicholas!" Stacy was up and running to him in a heartbeat.

He gave her a halfhearted smile, limping down the hallway with the help of a nurse.

"I have never seen someone heal so quickly from so many injuries," she said, steadying him next to Stacy. The two exchanged a glance and smirked. "This is a very strong man, with a very thick head. He insists on leaving although, I would rather him remain supervised for a few days at least. Please keep an eye on him."

Stacy nodded and helped Nicholas to sit down.

"He'll be kept a close eye on," Richard promised and the uneasiness in Stacy's stomach confirmed the doubt in her head that Richard had not intended that promise to be made in Nicholas's best interests. Cody probably had him pegged against Nicholas from the start.

Out of the corner of her eye, Stacy's gaze captured the sight of a police cruiser that had just pulled up to the hospital doors. The door opened and closed again only after letting out a large, elder police officer.

Stacy felt herself give Richard a hot look as he started walking in the direction of the officer.

"Nicholas, are you alright?" Stacy fussed, hurrying to sit next to him.

Nicholas grunted in pain on his way down, but was nodding his head. His fingers automatically wrapped themselves around Stacy's as he took his seat.

"I was so worried," she whispered. "What happened back there?"

"They got away," Richard answered for him, returning with the elder cop in tow, waiting with a notepad. "We need to know exactly why they were here."

Stacy looked at Nicholas and squeezed his hand, nodding once.

A siren sounded from outside. Intuition told Stacy to glance, though she only planned to look away again, expecting to see an ambulance or something of relevance to a hospital. Instead, her eyes took in the image of police cruisers circling the building, their officers stepping out with their weapons to surround the building from rooftop to ground.

"Uncle Richey!" Stacy bellowed, jumping to her feet to look out the door. "What do you think you're doing, Nicholas is innocent! He's injured!"

"If injuries equaled innocence, Stacy Grace, our facilities would see a lot less action," Richard noted, not taking his eyes off Nicholas.

"You're not taking him!" Stacy howled. Hot tears poured down her face, stinging the scratches that she just noticed on her chin. "I won't let you!"

Stacy flung her arm forward, reaching for her uncle's taser, gun, handcuffs— whichever came out of his belt the easiest and whichever would prove to be the most useful.

"Stacy, no..."

Nicholas retaliated, reaching his hand up to pull her back. In the next instant, too quick for Stacy's aching mind to grasp, the new officer was pulling both Nicholas's arms back, slamming him against the wall.

"UNCLE RICHEY! STOP IT!"

Nicholas did not fight, he grunted against the wall, shutting his eyes in pain.

"STACY GO WAIT OUTSIDE!" Richard shouted back, walking towards the cop as he handcuffed Nicholas.

"No!" Nicholas yelled.

The other officer began escorting Stacy out of the hospital by the arm.

"NO! She needs protection!"

Richard rounded on Nicholas, turning away from Stacy "What's the threat?"

Nicholas did not answer, it was unclear whether or not he even heard the question. He watched Stacy getting whisked away into a completely defenseless world and tore away from the officer, chasing after her.

"GET HIM! TAKE HIM DOWN, BOOK HIM NOW!" The officer bellowed.

Richard ran as five other officers burst through the doors, tackling Nicholas to the ground. Nicholas tried to break away, but his strength was diminishing quicker than it ever had before.

"If you lock me up, I will be out within the hour," Nicholas breathed. "Listen to me!"

Richard paused, saying and doing nothing. Waiting as the hastened breathing of everyone in the room began to even out.

"Alright, let him up," Richard ordered. The officers pulled him to his feet, dragging him over. "Get my niece."

Nicholas glanced down at his handcuffs and gestured over to the chair. Richard nodded and let him sit.

Stacy reentered, hugging Nicholas tightly. "Oh, Nicholas, I'm so sorry."

Nicholas let his head rest against Stacy's neck, feeling her warmth, her heartbeat, her existence.

"Look, Nicholas, I think you're a good kid and I want to believe that. I've gotten to know you, I've seen your true side. But I have mixed evidence on that and now I find you two at the center of another country on our land..."

"I mean, a logical person would probably assume we were in the wrong place at the wrong time, not that he staged a terrorist attack."

"Unless that logical person had evidence to the contrary," he replied.

So, what evidence? What little bits and pieces had Tom and Terra told? No sooner did she think the questions then did Richard pull a file from his bag—a thick file. "Family history of treason through seditious conspiracy, intent to commit manslaughter, complicit to manslaughter..."

Tom and Terra had not said a word—he requested his file.

Damn paperwork.

But that still begged the question—why? He was the head of law enforcement and they knew Nicholas's mission—did they not believe he would, or maybe could, complete it? Did they decide on their own to not deem him a threat?

Nicholas stretched, he passed his crutch over to Stacy and grabbed the edge of his chair with one hand, the back of the wall with the other, and rose himself back up. "They *are* here because of me," he said simply.

"Go on," Richard questioned.

Nicholas nodded once. "I was sent here by those men to get Stacy."

Richard's face had gone completely blank, confusion engulfing his interrogative mindset. He knew nothing. Not even that she was an heir. "For Stacy? Why?"

The elder cop was now in full force with his pen and paper.

Nicholas explained his story, he explained it even when Richard's face contorted, unsure whether he was supposed to look at him with remorse, fear, or rage.

When Richard finally did speak, his voice was slow and even. "Why didn't they kill you?" He asked, slowly. "How didn't they?"

Nicholas looked down, perhaps ashamed. "It's a game. They need us to act first to stay in good graces with the Spirits. They provoked me and I attacked first. They just came to send a message and they wanted to make sure that message was loud and clear—they still control me." A tear formed in Nicholas's eye, falling to his lap.

Stacy hurried over to him. The tear settling in deeper to the painfully tight feeling in her chest. He finally thought he was away and now here he was, injured again because of this crazed man. This crazed man ruling *her* country. She was seeing red.

"What else did they say?" Richard asked slowly.

Nicholas looked from Stacy to Richard, then, keeping his voice low, revealed the deadline they had given.

The whole time Richard listened with a protective, grace-giving persona.

Then Nicholas clicked his tongue, looking towards Stacy with anticipation before he revealed: "He is stronger than I thought."

They both look at him, perplexed. "He is not just tracking me from my Spirit—he can hear my thoughts even when I don't project them."

Both their faces lit with wild fear, but Stacy, her mind appeared to be going as quick as his as she replayed their conversations.

"I need to practice blocking him," Nicholas breathed when no one else knew what to say. "Detecting and blocking. It's the only way."

Stacy shook her head with confidence. "If he can learn it, we can too. All he did was give us an easier way to anticipate his actions."

Nicholas and Richard beamed at her with pride, then Richard listened to a call on his radio and changed his persona.

"You'll stay with Tom and Terra," he indicated.

Stacy quickly wrapped him in a hug that he automatically returned. "I can't promise more won't come of this. But I can promise you that if I have anything to say about it, you will stay with us— safely."

Nicholas gazed at the man with the same grateful, admirable, yet questioning eyes.

Richard's response was vague and crystal clear. "It's not always black and white, right?"

Nicholas and Richard talked on for a while about ways to track and trap the army. The other police left and Stacy and Nicholas finally breathed.

"Thank you for keeping me safe," Stacy murmured quietly, resting her head on Nicholas's shoulder.

Nicholas looked at her, his hand softly moving through her long, dark hair. "That will always be my pleasure, my darling. Always and forever."

Stacy's heart welled in her chest, she gave him a squeeze, wishing she could get even closer to him.

"I am embarrassed," Nicholas whispered to her. "I am so incredibly sorry you had to witness me...be like that."

Stacy bit her lip, unsure what to say. It was self-defense—right? "Those are our people too, Nicholas. We have to try to get everyone back on our side, not get rid of the ones who disagree with us. There will always be someone who disagrees, we have to be worthy of agreeing with."

Nicholas nodded his head, then turned and looked at her, truly taking her in for the first time. She had been so incredibly brave, yet so incredibly fragile. The combination was deadly. "One week." He repeated.

Stacy looked away.

"If I leave, they will go, Stacy Grace."

Stacy grasped his hand tightly. "Nicholas. We need to make a promise to each other. You haven't just sworn to protect me, we've sworn to stand by each other. Where you go, I go."

"There is no way around it..."

Stacy shook her head. "My place is in Dukhovia. Your place is in Dukhovia. If in one week's time we cannot convince them to leave—we go. We go and we fight for our country. Whether that looks like building up our own army or looking for those who still side with us."

Nicholas nodded his head in slow agreement. "And in the meantime?"

"Training," Stacy answered simply. Then she relaxed, moving her body as close to his as it could go, then folded herself into his strong chest. It was a place of security, a place of trust. "And whatever we want it to be. It's our time. We cannot allow him to take it from us. If we only have so many days left to spend with our friends and family, to enjoy each other—then we seize those moments without a thought to him."

Nicholas smiled a weary smile, whether from disagreement or fatigue, she did not know. Finally, he smiled. "Where you go, I go, my darling."

CHAPTER 83

EVEN THE STARS IN THE SKY STOOD STILL

ours later, Terra came running in from the back of the hospital in lightning bolt fashion, Tom walking behind her.

"Oh! You two, are you alright?" She looked them over head to toe, checking and redressing all Nicholas's wounds with extra care.

"We're okay, Terra."

"I'll just grab his discharge papers. Oh, and I'll want to get all his lab tests," Terra called over to a nurse. "Stacy, your uncle will drive you home."

Stacy nodded. Terra wasted no time, rushing off to get her lab work. Tom and Nicholas waited and then the two helped Nicholas out to their car. In the next few minutes, Stacy and Richard followed.

"You can lay in the back if you're tired," Richard offered.

"I'm not a criminal, I just date them," she smirked.

Richard laughed, though he was worried, they all were.

It was decided that Stacy and her friends were to be kept a very close eye on. No one was allowed to go anywhere alone. Stacy and Nicholas could not be alone together.

Her friends had different responses: some who wanted to know every little thing that happened and how and why…and those who said nothing, who perhaps already expected something to this degree and knew what brought it.

***

"It's not slang, it's called a contraction. You use it to shorten your words. Imagine all the free time you would have to learn how to sword fight, track wolves, and whatever else it is you do."

Nicholas closed his eyes, painfully.

"Now, repeat after me: Can't. 'I can't'."

Nicholas's smile spread from one ear to the next. He grabbed Stacy's hand and kissed it softly. "I *cannot* imagine what my life would be like if I had never met you."

"Slang free, that one's for certain."

Stacy and Nicholas laughed together. They did on most days after class ended and she ran out to Tom's and Terra's to help him. Usually alone, but sometimes with Rachael or with Cara. It had been three days since the incident and he was healing, occasionally having the energy to joke around and talk…

"I brought you soup," Stacy had said the first day, handing him a container with a spoon.

"You made it?" He asked nervously.

"Oh stop, my parents helped me," she assured him.

"That does not help me," Nicholas responded.

"Come on, now, they love you!" Stacy explained opening the soup for him from which he willingly ate. "Now, you'll start to feel dizzy in a few minutes, that'll wear off." They both laughed.

…Other days, he was not up to talking and barely able to stay awake. On those days, Stacy let him rest and read to him or gave him pep talks on how he better be feeling better the day of the dance—which would be the day before their time ran out.

"I do not even know what to wear," he might manage to say.

"That's okay," Stacy said happily. "Tom will be more than happy to help you. Right Tom?"

Tom peeked in the room and raised his eyebrow. "Of course," he said flatly, not at all enthused with the idea of playing dress-up.

No matter the day, Nicholas was always practicing blocking.

***

"Walk, walk, no, no, no eyes closed, eyes closed." Stacy led Nicholas by the hand to Tom and Terra's backyard. It was her turn to plan an extravagant date. She had found the creator of the swan and had him create something truly magnificent. Next, she had set up a telescope and laid out all vegetarian dishes— she had already eaten.

"And voila!"

Nicholas looked around, his eyes taking in the carved ice statue with a sense of pride. It was a soldier, a sword swung over his left side, barring the same marks as Nicholas's.

"My protector," Stacy said with a smile. "Now you can have one too."

Nicholas walked up to it and grinned. "You even had them mimic my loyalty carvings."

"Come again?" She asked.

He laughed. "The marks on my sword. I receive them after moving up a level. For example, we receive one when being accepted into the military, when we become worthy of fighting for one's country, when we show extreme loyalty. It is a nickname of sorts—loyalty carving."

"I love it," Stacy grinned. "This is called a telescope."

"Telescope," Nicholas repeated. "What does it do?"

"Why don't you take a look." She smiled, stepping back for him.

Nicholas eagerly moved forward, looking through. "Is this…" Silence. "This is not…?" Silence again. "Stacy…am I in space?"

He laughed with the joy she hoped to receive, then spent hours looking from books to space and teaching her all he learned. The whole time ringing with hope, with purity, with happiness.

Just as she intended.

CHAPTER 84

IMPENETRABLE

$\mathcal{J}$he night of the dance was warm. It had been four (Probably, right?) days-time since the encounter with Arkady and Nicholas's body had healed tremendously well. He still walked with a limp of pain at times, but Terra had said she was impressed with how well he was healing—and how well he was sleeping.

Still, Nicholas seemed to be more distracted and slow moving, especially the day of the dance. He needed assistance from Terra to dress, but he managed to put on a very formal tux with a lime green tie that matched Stacy's dress perfectly. Terra straightened it for him repeatedly while Tom gave him the "staying safe" talk.

"Why, who knew a Dukhovian assassin could look so kind and innocent when dressed up," Stacy had greeted him with.

Nicholas bowed to her and took her hand, maintaining eye contact with those piercing blues. "It is all but a part of my ploy."

He lifted his arm as high as he could and allowed her to twirl beneath his fingers. Her hands rested delicately against the tops of his aching shoulders.

Terra and Grace took several pictures, Terra pulling Nicholas aside every couple shots to readjust his hair, his tie, and triple checking his wrappings before sending them on their way.

Both got into the car with Grace, who would be dropping them off. Stacy had not yet attempted her driver's license exam, contrary to the rest of her friends who took it on their birthdays and would be driving to the dance that night. At least she still had Cara to be licenseless with.

Grace's truck pulled up to drop the kids off slowly, bidding them a safe and happy night before speeding away.

"Hey!"

Stacy and Nicholas turned to see Rachael and Cody climbing out of his convertible. The flashing shimmer of Rachael's long, yellow gown caught the gaze of several onlookers, many of whom stopped to take pictures, knowing it was a Leighton original.

Cody walked up alongside of her in his light gray tux and matching yellow tie, happy for the first time in a while as he placed his hand proudly on Rachael's bare back, leading her inside.

"You guys look great!" Cara cheered. She was sitting at a table just outside the gymnasium, collecting money before they went inside. Around her were several bowls of chips and cookies that Dylan and Jade were already lingering at, though everyone knew they would have nothing to do with the provided beverages.

"As do you, my vision in pink," Rachael complimented. "Hey, don't forget about coming over tomorrow afternoon! I'll start teaching you all our songs and Dan will think you're an old pro by the time he gets ahold of you."

Cara grinned brilliantly. "Wouldn't miss it!"

Next, Nicholas and Stacy stepped up to her. Nicholas took out his wallet, but Cara stopped him.

"The tickets are donation only," she explained. "Santifini's rule to get the dance approved—it had to be linked to a fundraiser. They go towards the class trip at the end of the year."

Nicholas's eyes met the signs at the front of her table where she had deduced exactly how much money would be needed per student, where they were going, and how much money would be spent towards what.

Tickets: $6 per student.

$200 per student, eagerly awaiting to learn more about our history!

This trip to Washington, D.C. and Virginia will change the lives of you and those around you!

Cost breakdown...

Nicholas extended his hand into his wallet and pulled out six-hundred dollars. "Then, I suppose we better make sure at least some of these students get to attend, shall we?"

Cara smiled and nodded her gratitude.

Miranda and Joey entered together. Miranda's dress was multi-colored and erratic; long in the back and short in the front, the floral pattern was hard to understand where it started and where it began along with if it was even floral.

Andy and one of Dan's best friends, Rob, came in shortly behind them; her pale blue dress short and plain. Andy looked uncomfortable and out of place at the dance, and almost scrutinizing others when they deemed her 'unable to have fun' which typically led to her doing something crazy to prove that she did, in fact, know how to have fun.

Rob was the complete opposite: he was as crazy and rebellious as they came and was all for encouraging her to do whatever she had to do to prove herself.

"Do you know how to dance?" Stacy asked Nicholas uneasily as she led him out onto the dance floor.

"We have danced before," he said, surprised.

Stacy barked with laughter, imagining them slow dancing to one of *The Rockers* songs. "And when the beat is a tad faster?"

Currently, the music playing was some form of hip-hop. Nicholas watched the surrounding students throwing their arms in the air and bending their knees to the ground. Some of them lay their backs down flat, stomachs in the air in some type of painful expression of dance.

"Not quite so senselessly," he replied quickly. He had already grabbed her by the hand and was spinning her faster than ever. He dipped her down and then flung her out, reeling her back into his arms. One of his hands was on her waist, the other just barely in her hand, palms opposing each other. She had her free hand on his shoulder and the two rocked back and forth quickly.

"Nicholas!" She laughed as he picked her up and spun her in the air, her dress a whirl of lime.

The chaperones tended to hover over them the most which was annoying in the beginning, but they soon got used to it and chose to tune out Mr. Garnet from computer science, Mrs. Simms from history, and even Santifini.

Santifini. She had not spoken to him since he returned. She did not feel the need any longer. She had no facts to check, no lies to trace. Her and Nicholas knew everything of each other's worlds and it was going to stay that way, even as they battled for Dukhovia together. Neither of them had told anyone else about their plan to go to Dukhovia—but they would. They would take anyone who wanted to go with them.

Stacy watched Nicholas staring over in his direction and turned her head to meet his gaze. "Don't let him bother you," Stacy encouraged, turning his eyes back to hers and smiling.

Nicholas's mouth twitched into an attempted smile, one Stacy was familiar with when met with the emptiness in his eyes.

Stacy glanced over at Santfini too. "Those things he said, about the innocence of his family…"

Nicholas shook his head, his eyes once again finding Santifini's face. This time, Santifini met his gaze and the exchange of their stone-cold gazes seemed to house some understanding of an unspoken promise.

"Untrue," he mumbled so low Stacy could hardly hear over the roar of the music. "As far as I know. I was told the village was plotting to destroy a spiritual building in St. Karsburg." His eyes flashed away from Santifini and he held onto Stacy. "I do not know who was telling the truth."

"Can we join this party?" Rachael jumped in the arms of the couple, separating them. She took Nicholas's hands into hers as Cody took Stacy's.

"You are an excellent dancer, Mr. Andrews." Rachael complimented. Her eyes were wild with pleasure, her hair such a tousled mess that he strongly doubted she would ever forgive herself if she were aware of its nature. "Join the band?"

Nicholas put his hand on the crossing of her straps in the back, near her neck, not daring to drop to their typical place where her back was exposed. "Seems that invitation has been circulating."

The two both glanced over at Cara, happily laughing with Santifini.

"She's playing suck-up and trying to steal valedictorian right from under my nose," Rachael said in a grim voice.

"So that is why you invited her over to help her practice tomorrow? A well thought out plan," Nicholas joked. Holding a hand in the normal manner, one that was not repulsed by his, was a comfort he did not know he needed.

"Oh, we aren't all so cunning, Nicholas Tyler. A terrorist on our very land and I lead you right to us. I'm beaming with pride."

Nicholas laughed, shaking his head. What an odd group they all were that they were all so confident and comfortable in his presence. What a perfect group.

"How's your concussion?" Cody asked his swaying cousin.

Stacy tilted her head to the side. "I could say the same for you. And your eye? And your arm?" Stacy gestured down. Cody had yet another fight the moment classes returned.

Cody rolled his eyes. "I'm fine. It was a tenth-grade crybaby, you were attacked by an entire army. Hardly the same."

"Made it out alive, though," Stacy said with the same grin she would have used had she not missed their winning championship game.

"Hm." Cody huffed and glanced over at Nicholas, a disgruntled look crossing his face when Rachael threw her head back and laughed uncontrollably.

"He's a good guy!" Stacy bellowed at him, shaking his shoulders. "When are you going to see that?"

Cody eyed him, continuing to dance with his cousin. "Well, let's see, him bringing you into this situation didn't really up his chances at my approval."

"He's trying to keep me safe, Cody," Stacy told him, keeping her eyes down low.

Cody dipped her down. "He was sent here to hurt you."

"But he's not," Stacy objected. "He is not the criminal in any of this. He's a victim. He was always the victim."

Cody's eyes flashed over to Nicholas and Rachael again, lingering on her wrist. "Not always."

Stacy rolled her eyes and threw her arms around her cousin's neck as the song ended, hugging him tightly. "She's stronger than you make her out to be," she whispered to him. "And the sooner you realize that, the sooner you might actually have a chance." Stacy left him with that, smiling as she strode away to meet back up with Rachael and Nicholas, who were already drinking pop with Andy and Miranda.

Stacy smiled as she watched them: the girls drinking casually, and Nicholas; every once in a while, swirling the bubbly, sugar induced substance and then casually dumping small amounts into the fountain behind him.

"Just a couple more songs and we're setting off the fireworks!" Cara cheered, racing up to her friends with Mrs. Simms in tow. "Remember, they were meant to have the effect that the dance was on New Years so picture super nostalgic timing and super romantic sparks in the air!"

The dance seemed to last forever, and Stacy did not mind one bit. The moments her and Nicholas spent dancing seemed to be moments frozen in perfectly safe, still time. They danced nonstop and the feeling of his arms around her body when they swayed made her feel like she was in a parallel universe, completely shielded from any harm.

Sparks did fly that night—and they were from more than just explosives derived from Chinese revolutionary wartimes. They brightened up everything that was going on in this town, within all families. Then the wind blew coolly, but everything else had an opposite reaction.

The fireworks were set up, and everyone was crowding along the lit-up gazebos and candlelit tables, fighting for the most romantic spot.

Cody and Rachael had a table near the front of the fireworks. He kept lifting his hand, inching closer to holding hers and then backing away, inching towards hers and then backing away...All the while she sat perfectly still, staring happily off into the distance, completely unaware.

Stacy took Nicholas's hand and led him farther from the rest of them. Away from the romantic scenery, to the edges of the courtyard where it could be just the two of them, and they continued to sway to the sound of faint music.

"I need to thank you," she said in a hushed voice, her head rest on his chest.

"Whatever for?" He pondered.

She smiled faintly. "You saved my life. Not just from Dukhovian soldiers, but from my mind. I was spiraling before you came—unsure if I would ever find the answers to my growing list of questions. I never thought I'd feel so...confident."

"Nor did I," Nicholas's voice was soft, each syllable like the strum of the perfect cord. "You gave me a reason to want to live, Stacy Grace. You became a light at the end of a very dark tunnel and made me a person worth being. You are and always will be my entire world."

Stacy lifted her head and Nicholas his, the two found themselves locked into each other's eyes, each sinking and falling deeper into each other in every way they could. Then she chuckled, her head returning to its resting place. "You're an idiot," she whispered to him, resting her head on his shoulder as they danced.

He laughed quietly in return. "And why is that?"

Her head rose up, glistening hazel eyes meeting the shimmering blue intensely. "Because you were always a person worth being, Nicholas Demitona. All on your own. You don't have to have it all figured out to be able to live the life you were meant to."

Nicholas nodded his head, letting the emotion that she made him feel consume and overwhelm him, without an attempt at restraint.

"So, thank you," she told him with a gentle squeeze around his aching waist. "For showing me the world I was meant to exist in."

CHAPTER EIGHTY-FOUR

"You do not owe that to me," Nicholas sighed. "You are the strongest heir Dukhovia has ever seen, you would have found your way without me."

Stacy shook her head slowly, her eyes deep as they pieced him together in every way. "Not if you were meant to lead me to it."

Nicholas let that sink in. His heart skipped a beat and his sweaty hands slipped on hers for a minute, securing themselves once more. Palms opposing.

"Nicholas, I have this desire to protect Dukhovia that I could never explain. I didn't know about any war or resistance, but I felt drawn..." Stacy took Nicholas's hand in hers and intertwined their fingers. "Now I feel locked." She closed her fingers, tightening around his.

The whirl of their connection sunk in. No longer was she looking at darkness, but overwhelming blossoms of color, portraying cracks of gray. "I can't escape my fate now. And I refuse to."

Nicholas gulped, realizing for the first time that everything was coming together, that everything about his life, his past, his struggle to the Spirits and his struggle within himself was all for a greater purpose. And that backwards, roundabout journey was to lead him right where he was, right where he was meant to be. Because, without him, without Stacy, the fate of Dukhovia was as bleak as the night sky they now stood inching closer together under...

Nicholas's hand found its way to Stacy's face. He traced along both her cheeks and down her collar bone. The feeling sent a chill down her spine. He ran the back of his hand along her arm, then slowly leaned in close to her. His voice was dry, breaking. Nerves. "I have not said these words in a lifetime, but I love you, Stacy Grace Matthews. I have so much love for you."

Stacy could not help it. Despite how little she looked for it, how much of it she already had, Nicholas's confession was the answer to a prayer. It was as if she was locking in everything he brought her—the knowledge, the peace, herself. "Nicholas Aloyshenka Aleksis Demitona—you have my entire heart."

And then both their hearts leapt, beating twice as fast as they ever had before. Their breathing became unsteady, their limbs weak. Nicholas gulped, parting his lips and moving closer and closer to the soft, supple pair parting for him, inching closer, hesitating, and getting ever so closer...

And then the mouth that had vowed to do everything in her honor, despite his dishonor, reached closer, longing to touch, to taste, to experience the greatest sense of closeness that could be provided, to feel their passion on each other...

"Nicholas..."

"Oh, Stacy..."

CHAPTER 85

DAY SIX

Stacy's lips worked quickly, sweeping over Nicholas's mouth, greedily trapping his tongue. She could not get enough. She ran her hands through his hair as he pushed her against the vibrant tree, pulling her closer and closer.

And then the tree burst into flame and Nicholas right along with it. Flames spilled from the grand oak and licked the sides of the hills, until nothing was left but burnt and withered bones and charred field.

***

Nicholas threw his body violently over his pillow. It had been several nights since he awoke with a nightmare, but tonight was a repeat. He thrashed and screamed a blood curdling sound, convincing Terra completely that The Czar had to be close by.

But he was nowhere to be found and Terra did the same thing she did every night, tucking him back in, rubbing his arm, and singing him Dukhovian lullabies until sleep found him once more.

And it was day six.

CHAPTER 86

SACRIFICE

Stacy thought of the first day she met Nicholas. Two complete strangers living in two different world's that would collide at the perfect moment. Her moment of desperation on a frantic search for answers—who she was, why she was, the meaning of her dream, of her nation. And his final crossroads—right or wrong, the evil concealed with secrets and lies to finally be exposed. A freedom he never knew, but always deserved. Still deserves.

Stacy had lived a life of perfection despite those few moments of desperation. She had friends that would circle the world for her—and perhaps they would. She had family that would set the world aflame to ensure her protection—and perhaps they would.

But it was time for her to do more, to be more. Now that she knew the dream was more than her brain overreacting, now that she knew she had a purpose uniquely structured for her—it was time. And it had to be this way. It had to be her—just her.

Nicholas did not get the same chance she did. He did not get the family, the friends, the chance to find hobbies and make mistakes. It was not fair and it was his turn for fair.

She did not give it long until anyone came after her, but she hoped. She hoped they would hear her truth and understand it to some degree. Perhaps a part of her wished they would follow—but only if all went according to plan. And right now—plan did not have much to it.

But she could not do it. After all they had been through, after their confession last night—she could not make good on her promise. He deserved more, and if she loved him as much as she had claimed, then she had to do this.

So, she had written a letter, perfectly sealed and etched on the outside of the envelope, were words telling him everything he needed to know—*when I go, you stay.* She felt a pit in her stomach as she had sealed the letter, flashes of the night before in her mind as they had breathed in each other's scents for the last time, as they had leaned in for one kiss, and then two or three more…

Where you go, I go, he had whispered to her. She confirmed it back to him. She closed her eyes. Kissing Nicholas was like being on an island watching waves dance across a setting sun. And he deserved a chance for the sun to rise again. For destiny to find him.

She thought of destiny…and of fate. If destiny was their predetermined path, then fate was the driving force of that. And it was a never-ending, ever-changing battle. Because in the life Stacy had lived thus far, everything about safety and love told her to stay right where she was. But the simplicity was never there. The questions to answer, the egos to soothe, the hearts to break to discover her true path, her true destiny—well it was a battle in and of itself.

And then there was Nicholas. If the path to find her destiny was a battle, his was the entire war. Loss, fighting, devastation, murder. Never clear, never knowing. Always lost.

Then she thought of the Dukhovians, of The Czar and his loyal admiral. They made this relationship impossible and their feelings powerless. They altered the course of destiny forever. Nicholas had never wanted any of this to happen. But it had. But it would continue to no matter what because no matter the time that passed, no matter the cloak of eternal happiness she was shielded under when their lips met—they were sitting ducks in every moment.

Waiting would not allow their relationship to flourish. Waiting would not change the fate of either one of them. Waiting was a distraction tactic by the greatest Dukhovian mastermind Stacy would ever come to know.

He never had a choice or anyone there to help him. He was completely alone. The fear in that loneliness made it impossible for her to inform him of her mission. He would only stop her. And leaving him out of this was best regardless.

And so, she walked. And as she walked, she recited everything in her head that she had ever been taught or read regarding Dukhovia.

The Karauth is the oldest and most mystical building in Dukhovia. Said to be the private dwelling of the Moon Spirit while still on Earth, The Karauth is said to make miracles happen by those who seek it out and pray with earnest purpose.

Inside the Karauth existed a number of rumored relics, whose existence dates back to even before the Moon Spirit.

Legend has it, this hammer-shaped weapon was used as a protective tactic against dark and evil forces at the dawn of time. The Moon Spirit was created as a guard of the universe and received these relics from God for safe keeping.

But the answer to her destiny, to saving her country was not in anything she had learned thus far. No. It was not in America at all.

It was something she had to chase after. It was something she had to board the last, sold-out flight to Dukhovia in secrecy in order to learn. It was something that she had to use every skill she had learned from observing Nicholas: to be sneaky, to be alert, to blend, to hide every ounce of realistic and pungent fear…and bury it.

Hood up, eyes down.

And when, at last, she took her seat on the nearly empty flight…

Wow, Tom and Terra need to work on the security of this place.

CHAPTER 87

CHOICE

*N*icholas was quiet when he tip-toed out of the house that next morning. Something in his chest already felt hollow, but he knew that saying goodbye to Tom and Terra would only exemplify it. They were as caring of people as he could ever hope to find, especially in America. He hoped the world learned to be kind to them.

It was funny how nostalgic leaving his life in America now was. He had arrived with a hesitant fear in his pocket, unsure how he felt leaving Dukhovia, unsure what to expect in the most modernized country in the world. But here he found home and it was here his heart burned over leaving.

But it had to be done. Because it was the only way to protect Stacy. He felt a pull at his stomach and bile swell up in his throat at the thought. The thought of leaving her was impossible. But the thought of her or her family getting hurt was even worse. If he failed to perform his duty, Arkady would need to find a new way to convince her to come to America without risking upsetting the Spirits.

He had savored those last few moments with her before he made his decision. The moment when he held her close, his arms securing her as close to him as she could be, feeling her, experiencing her. Then the realization hit and he had whispered into her ear *"Where you go, I go"*. Not a lie, not a broken promise—a chance. A chance to continue to *go*. And she would always be with him.

Nicholas entered the airport with hesitation. He was not sure what he would find, but this was his final destination. For one crucial piece of information he had withheld from everyone—Stacy, the police, Tom and Terra—because he knew in his heart what he would have to do. From the moment he connected to Arkady and perhaps even sooner—he knew. He was meeting Arkady here.

You have one week's time. Though it does not seem you would have any difficulty finding me, I will make it easy on you. We will meet at the airport. That way there is evidence that we have gone. And I hear the owners are such great people.

Nicholas disagreed. Using their airport seemed…well, senseless. They could easily land the plane or refuse to take off. Oh well, Arkady controlled Dukhovia with fear and he likely thought he could America as well. If he could not, Nicholas was not going to be the one to allow him to come to that realization.

"Nicholas!" There it was. His one fear. That he would have a repeat of his very first time in the airport and it would make it all the more difficult, yet all the more obvious that he had to go.

He turned around slowly, opening his arms. "Rachael." He forced a smile, but knew he could never phase the queen of emotions.

"Look!" She lifted her hand, her face contorted as she shifted and shaped whatever emotion she was feeling to push a chair into the table across the room.

He smiled, then considered the irony in how he taught her such a skill when it was the same idea that led him to connect his and Stacy's Spirits—a tool in his pocket all the while, never properly taught.

"Amazing. A little more practice and you will be lifting these planes."

She winked at him. "So, is it date night at the airport or something?"

Nicholas eyed her with confusion, but his heart had already plummeted to his stomach. "What do you mean by that?"

"Stace was here earlier," she said casually, then shrugged.

Nicholas grabbed her shoulders and spun her around, looking into her eyes with force and pressure. He felt as though holding her was the only thing keeping him up. "Rachael," his voice shook as he spoke, the words hardly audible. "How long ago was Stacy here? Where is she now? Did you see her leave?"

"No," Rachael shook her head. Panic was starting to enter her mind, but she continued. "She sometimes comes and pretends to take the flights to Dukhovia then stays on when they get to the connecting flight and comes home. It helps her. I—I didn't think anything of it."

"She is not to be travelling on her own," Nicholas spat through gritted teeth. His voice was becoming hoarse, his entire body shaking. "Especially. On a flight. To Dukhovia."

"I…" Rachael held her head, the pushed in chair fell over.

He honed in now, trying to connect to Arkady—nothing. But he was early. He intended to be early in order to avoid an ambush.

Stacy… He had tested his ability to connect to her—the last few nights. He had travelled further and further testing it out. First to the edge of town and then in a bus. He could reach her as far as an hour out.

He swallowed hard, testing it now—nothing.

Nicholas tore around the airport looking for any sign of Stacy, for any sign of Arkady. A kicked over snowbank, an army of light blue, an empty suitcase, a hot brand…

Nothing. Nothing. Nothing.

They're gone.

He spun back on Rachael. "Rachael, I was supposed to be meeting Arkady here."

"What?!" She shouted, terror taking over every part of her.

CHOICE

"I was going to turn myself in. Stacy did not know and she did not know Arkady would be here."

"Ugh! Why can't you guys just start learning to talk to each other! Come on!" She grabbed his arm, pulling him through a maze of back hallways and blinking boards. They were both flying at top speed, no other sound but the echo of their pounding shoes and their ragged breathing. She stopped when they reached a man with a headset, staring at a screen, repeatedly hitting a button and muttering the same phrase over and over.

"Michael," she said in as gentle a voice as she could in the moment. "We need to connect to Flight 170. It's an emergency."

"I've been trying to connect to that flight for the last twenty minutes," Michael said with worry to his tone. "There's no response. We're sending back up to its last known location."

"What is the last known location?" Nicholas spat, thrusting a paper and pen away from the desk.

Michael gave him the coordinates.

"We need to get to Tom and Terra's," he breathed.

Rachael nodded. "Michael, Stacy is on that flight. I need you to call me and Tom or Terra the first you hear anything, okay?"

They did not wait for his confirmation before running out to the parking lot. "The bus station is closest," Nicholas hollered over the roar of conversation and leaving flights.

Rachael managed a grin. "Bus station? You forget I drive in style now," she said, dangling keys before him.

He tried to laugh back, but whatever sound came out of him hardly sounded amused. "Try to not get a ticket on our maiden voyage." He joked.

The two climbed into her car and took off down the highway at top speed. Nicholas did not care about the pit in his stomach. He did not care about having to vomit out the window three times. He did not even care about Rachael lecturing him the entire ride on communication and being fair. All he could think about was that somewhere far enough away that he could not reach her, the love of his life and savior of his country was potentially dead.

CHAPTER 88

MY COUNTRY, YOUR BLOOD

Stacy sat with her back poised against the comfortable leather seat. She had never ridden in first class before. She thought it was wrong. Anytime she got on a flight, it was to pretend like she was going to Dukhovia and she did not feel like running or hiding from her country called for such luxuries.

But now, this is where she had been ordered to sit and while she did not necessarily see herself taking orders for long, she was complying.

"It was a brave choice you made, turning yourself in," the evil voice drawled as he pushed a tea cup towards her. "I cannot imagine the burden of losing your family and friends all in one day."

She clicked her tongue, looking out the window as she spoke. "Somethings are worth losing everything for."

"So very nostalgic. It is no wonder you had no trouble convincing Sir Nicholas of your uncanny talents."

Stacy's face was void of emotion as she looked the embodiment of sin dead in the eye. "Perhaps it is easier for those who are closer and more obedient to the Spirits to detect another person with such strengths."

"Perhaps," he said nonchalantly, pouring himself more tea.

She could see the anger rise in cheeks, but he refused to give it away. Stacy did not care. Fear still coursed through her every time the plane made an unfamiliar shake or sudden sound, but Nicholas had been so brave around this man all for the sake of his country, she could be too. More to it, her country *needed* her to be strong—and so she would.

Though it was rather difficult. Sitting so close to the person who had so severely hurt the man she loved. The man who burned him, the man who was responsible for all those lashes, for all those welts and scars. The man who murdered the only person whom ever cared for and protected him.

She had to fidget with her hands to keep herself from strangling him where they sat—alone in the front of the plane, surrounded by peaceful, ordinary music and the clattering of plates. Faint scents of desserts wafted through the area every so often, but she saw nothing more than carts lined with tea kettles and hot water.

She assessed everything every moment for a threat—just like Nicholas taught her. Anything that could be used as a weapon, any sudden changes. Rule of thumb, he had said, if it seems suspicious—it is. She gulped. So far, nothing had been all too terrifying. Then again, she was not sure what she had expected when she decided to attempt to connect to Arkady and find him, turning herself in. She certainly did not expect this and she did not expect it to last long.

"I am doing you a favor, you know," he said the words tenderly. She had noticed that he also refused to look at her and she wondered if he was like this with everyone. He only stirred his tea and, every once in a while, glanced out the window or towards the door—so Stacy did too. "Dukhovia would eat you alive."

"Is that so?"

"I know, I know. It is the definition of peace and physical evidence of heaven on Earth. You are not wrong. Dukhovia is all of those things." He shrugged, folding his hands in his lap. "But not for an American. You may think you would not change anything. You may think you honor and respect all our traditions—but there are things that are simply second-nature to you that would upset the balance of our country. Things that you do without even thinking about, without even recognizing. You cannot undo those things, not completely. You will never be able to wash away which you were bred into."

Stacy was quiet for a moment, the fact that he was partially right burning into her reality. "Well," she decided. "Let us hope that the people of Dukhovia are more willing to have a slightly modern ruler with the passion to protect them than a fully traditional ruler that doesn't give two shits if they all die tomorrow."

That had done it. Stacy remained poised as Arkady smashed the table with his fist. The hot tea cup bounced, crashing and cracking to pieces on the table below it. The liquid oozed out from around them, threatening to destroy his perfectly pressed, blue pants.

He pushed himself back and stood to his feet to meet her eyes. It was the first time he looked at her, really looked at her, and the first time he looked directly into her eyes.

She looked back—straightlaced and focused. The action did not seem to please the ruler. Something seemed to snap inside of him as he stared back at her. Then, his mouth curled up into a malicious grin that made her heart skip a beat.

"I believe our people would find it rather hard to believe that the granddaughter of a mass murderer would have any chance at protecting them."

It happened before she could think it through. She had been harboring all of her rage about what Arkady did to Nicholas, her country, her life, and now he had hit her hottest pressure point—her family. He knew it. He meant to do it, but it did not matter. Perhaps Stacy's anger was as erratic and unpredictable as Nicholas's, but she used all the strength her rage gave her, all the skill Nicholas taught her—and punched The Czar right in the face.

Blood gushed from his nose onto his perfectly, pressed uniform. He started to swing back at her, but hit the wall of the airplane, causing blood to rush from his knuckles. He threw his head back and laughed, stopping himself.

Stacy's eyes widened as the blood stopped almost immediately and only moments later his knuckles did the same. She had never seen healing occur so quickly.

"Go ahead," he egged on, his laughter filling the cabin. "Try again!"

She paused a moment, looking at herself as she stood—teeth gritted, in the stance to strike again. But he had set up that family comment on purpose and he wanted him to hit her. He made her come to him at the airport, made Nicohlas hit first—why?

Difficult as it was, she stopped herself. "I don't need to prove myself to someone who clearly already sees me as a threat," she spat.

"Ha! A threat!"

She cocked her head to the side. "You said it yourself—Dukhovia is not yours or mine. Those are *our* people."

CHAPTER 89

ABANDONED

Nicholas and Rachael gave little to no explanation when they arrived at the hospital. They saw the look on Nicohlas's face, the pain in Rachael's eyes, and all Nicholas had to say was "she is gone" and they were boarding a plane to track Flight 170.

The flight bumped and jumped through the air, shooting across the sky like a bullet. It was a small plane, the four barely fit in the compact space, but Terra said it would be best for trying to get close to Stacy if they were still in the air—and that was the difficult thing.

They had no idea why connection had been lost. Michael did not call back with any news. If they had simply cut all tracking, they could be anywhere by now. If they had lost tracking because of a crash, well…

Nicholas could not think about it. He allowed Tom and Terra to utilize the methods they had for tracking the ship while he tuned into The Spirit of both Stacy and Arkady to try to find them. Finally, just as they were passing over a sea that rocked with crashing waves as dark as night, Nicholas's eyes flashed open.

"Here! Here!"

Terra looked around for a place to land, but they were mostly surrounded by jagged rock and the peaks of decaying mountains. "I'll have to keep flying—but I'll search up here while you guys go on foot! Rachael, stay with me."

Everyone was in agreement, Nicholas flying out of the airplane before they even neared the ground.

Together, he and Tom searched all around the barren land, but nothing that looked remotely like it could be Stacy or a plane surfaced, nor were there many places to hide. Nicholas continuously tested his connection and wondered why Stacy was not replying.

Then he froze where he was and a scene played before him—Arkady standing over him on a plane.

The window, he tried to say. *Look out the window.*

She did and Nicholas saw the plane teetering on the edge of one of the cliffs.

"The cliffside!" Nicholas roared the words and lunched forward. Tom asked no questions and was right behind him.

The two expertly dodged pieces of jagged rock, sharp and deadly enough to take one of their lives. Wind whipped viciously at each of their faces, but they were simple obstacles. Nothing stopped them from their goal.

"No!"

Nicholas's breath was knocked out of him as they approached charred remains of Flight 170. Pieces of tattered, worn wing, gleaming with remaining streaks of red. It was destroyed—but it was only a piece of the plane and Nicholas did not know enough about aircrafts to know whether or not the rest of the flight could still be in the air without it.

He looked to Tom for confirmation who was, in fact, looking up into the sky.

No pain.

Losing his grasp on reality, Nicholas began to climb over the cliffside, ripping at the shards of metal on the plane. A physical object. If he had a physical object to hold, it would help him. Tears blinded him as they soaked his face, Nicholas wiped himself clean with a dirt-covered sleeve, only furthering his troubles.

No pain.

What do I do? Erlik, where are you now?

Silence.

"Nicholas, Nicholas, you're hurting yourself..."

No pain.

He would not listen to Tom. He continued to tear at the metal pieces, but did nothing but shred his skin. He did not care when it began to rain around him. He did not care when rusted metal scraped apart his hands and arms. He refused to stop until he found his way to her. Not until he knew she would be safe.

Then he could take her place.

No pain, only purpose.

CHAPTER 90

ESCAPE

$\mathcal{F}$ierce and demanding winds circled the land of decay and ruin. Every attempt at safe haven yielded new and far worse disappointment until those who fought were emptied of their fuel to fight.

Nicholas and Tom had climbed back aboard The Heart of America—the flight Terra now flew. Nicholas came back with armfuls of the shredded metal, emptying them onto the desolate floor, further shrinking the size of their space.

Then, just before taking off, Nicholas's perked up, he heard the whining purr of an engine and spun around, bolting for the edge of the cliff.

"Nicholas!" Rachael and Terra both called after him, but Tom had heard it too and ran to his side.

There, just feet above the water, was the rest of Flight 170, still air-borne, but only just.

"Back on the plane!" Tom declared and the two ran faster than ever before.

Terra had already started the engine and took flight, but Rachael reached down and aided in pulling the two on board.

Nicholas stood at the door of the plane, not taking his eyes off the object below as it dipped and pulled towards its side, seeming to skirt by on the last of its fumes.

"Get me close enough and I can jump onto it," he instructed Tom and Terra.

They exchanged a reluctant glance, but Tom began quickly connecting a parachute to Nicholas and explaining its use. Nicholas was grateful, but hardly listening, his eyes still refusing to look away from the determined, yet doomed plane below.

Terra did as instructed, lowering herself closer and closer.

The wind closer to the dark sea was harsh and below freezing, causing issues with Terra's ability to shift in certain ways, but Nicholas prepared himself. He prepared himself for everything except the discovery that…no. She was alive. She had to be alive....

Ignoring the uneasy feeling as he steadied himself just above Flight 170, he lunged down below.

The feeling was like nothing he ever felt before. Terror and freedom coursed through his veins like the blood that had been there all along. Wind threatened to further blind his eye sight and pieces of loose muck stung his eyes—he would miss. Just narrowly, but he was about to miss the plane.

Strange sounds resonated from the plane below as it began to vibrate and heave, shaking fiercely. Then it stopped, returning to its normal chaotic path and it was his body that seemed out of its own control. Then he shifted, sailing across the air with ease and landing directly onto the plane.

He looked up, meeting Rachael's pleading eyes with gratitude.

He worked quickly, scaling down the plane until he was able to jump in through a cracked window.

"Stacy!"

"Nicholas!"

He found her huddled in the corner of the flight; Arkady's body lay unconscious on the floor.

Easy. Too easy.

"Where are the others?" He roared over the sounds of whistling wind and roaring jets.

"The Admiral is flying the plane and I haven't seen the other man," she shouted back.

Albert. The only one to ever show him an ounce of kindness. Or, kindness in his own way, he supposed. Perhaps the only one to remain neutral, to not attack him, to not harm him. He was no threat.

"Come on."

Nicholas lifted Stacy into his arms, preparing to jump easily into the water only a few feet below. Water. Thank the Spirits it was water.

The Admiral must have heard what was happening, or Albert had outed them after all, because in the moment he readied his body to jump, the plane tilted and shifted, crunching over its own weight and brokenness and began to climb higher into the air. It moaned in protest, but The Admiral pushed it, further, further. Soon they were further from the water than Nicholas felt comfortable jumping, unknowing its depths.

Frantic breaths filled him as his nostrils flared. He looked back at The Heart of America and looked from himself to the parachute.

They could not rely on Rachael's still intermediate skills, but in this moment, it was all they had.

The plane pulled higher, inching closer and closer to being level with the cliffside it had scraped against and lost its pieces. Fifty feet higher, now one-hundred, one-fifty.

But the closer they came to the cliff, the closer Tom and Terra got to them—fifty feet, thirty…

Nicholas could not wait for The Heart of America to get any closer. No matter how little he knew of this type of machinery, he knew that the screeching cry coming from its engine signaled it was soon to die and drop them if they did not do so freely on their own.

ESCAPE

Twenty feet out. Nicholas held Stacy, keeping her body as close to his as possible. She swung, forcing her legs around his waist, her arms up to his neck, and her eyes closed.

"Do you trust me?" Nicholas asked, looking down at her.

She looked back at him as if something reassured her, then nodded, the faintest smile on her lips. "More than anything." Then she bit her lip. "Not so much the physics."

Nicholas smiled and shrugged. "Well, you failed our last physics test." He joked, planting a kiss on the top of her head. "Eyes closed, my love. Ready one…two…three!"

Stacy and Nicholas dropped instantly what felt like one thousand feet, falling faster and faster down. Then he opened the parachute and they began to coast.

Stacy lifted her head looking around at the immaculate view—snow covered mountaintops, turbulent seas, ice cold winds. It was everything an heir could dream.

Then their bodies lunged rigidly forward. Nicholas secured his hold on Stacy and waited. They moved closer to The Heart of America, then closer still. Then the plane itself shifted forward and Nicholas was able to grab onto a piece of metal and pull he and Stacy inside.

CHAPTER 91

WHERE YOU GO, I GO

Stacy did not even have time to scream before feeling the fear whirling around, the speed of her body falling so carelessly, then, as if it were being yanked from her insides towards nothingness, she hit a hard, metal floor.

Stacy uncovered her ears and opened her eyes. They did not have loud crashes in heaven—and she expected the floor to be much more comfortable, least of all warm. Maybe she was reincarnated already. Would she keep her memories?

"Stacy, are you okay?" Nicholas had his arm around her shaking shoulders.

She looked up at him and said nothing. She glanced around. Terra and Tom were in the cockpit of their helicopter, staring with fear and relief in their direction. She had not died. Somehow, *they survived.*

"Oh, Nicholas!" She jumped up, flinging her arms around his neck with everything she had.

"Stacy, my love," Nicholas held her close, running his hands around her back and through her hair, making sure she was truly still alive.

Terra was at both their sides in a second, helping them to their feet. "Oh my, are you children okay?"

Stacy and Nicholas both looked at each other and nodded. Then, Tom was at the wheel of the plane, steering it off course and increasing the speed to the point they all fell backwards.

Then Rachael was at both their feet. "What on *Earth* were you thinking?"

Stacy gulped, looking towards Nicholas. His pleading, puppy-dog eyes trapped her into telling the truth. "I couldn't let you be taken back. I couldn't let you be put in danger. I knew you would likely come after me, but I just…I'm sorry. I guess I didn't think everything through."

"Oh, darling," Nicholas said squeezing her tightly. "Your beauty truly does transcend your entire being."

She blinked through the hard to follow compliment, but smiled, then averted her attention to the front of the plane.

"Tom, what are you doing?" Stacy shouted over the roar of the increased blades.

"Catching up with the plane," he muttered, not tearing his focus from the view in front of him. "How many are there?"

"Just the three of them," Nicholas answered for her.

The plane was back in view. Tom inched closer and closer but then…

CHAPTER NINETY-ONE

Six small, circular objects shot out from the plane. Several of them fell automatically, but the last one inched closer and they could see smoke emitting from it…

"NO!" Tom hurled the plane to the left causing them all to shift and fall on one another. Too late. The bomb had struck the front of their plane and they spiraled down towards the sea below.

Stacy, Rachael, and Nicholas all reached for each other. Terra flung herself over all three kids and then Tom rushed to the back, throwing his arms around everyone.

The plane shot down into the water, submerging completely. Nicholas and Stacy looked at each other and nodded. Each grabbed ahold of their family members and kicked with ease to the surface.

"Come on!" They rushed back into a cave but not before turning to see the red of Flight 170 before them—it had been cast down into the sea as well.

Rachael was shuttering with cold as the five rushed back into the cave to hide. Everything in the plane was soaked, but Tom scrambled to look around for something to build a fire.

"The temperatures are freezing," Terra said, rubbing Rachael's shoulders. "She'll get frostbite soon if we can't get her warm."

Stacy shot a worried glance towards Nicholas. Worried…and guilty. She had put everyone in danger; it was all her fault. She just wanted to help Dukhovia, so desperately wanted to help Dukhovia, but Nicholas had been right—she needed time, she needed to learn. Simply going and expecting everything to work out was not going to happen. Her best friend's life was at risk now—how many other lives would she put at risk if she continued to do things so senselessly? She needed to listen to Nicholas. He was right. He was always right.

Stacy gulped, looking out at the entrance of the cave. Nothing seemed to be moving from the other downed flight. No heads that peaked out, no screams from within.

"Does anyone know where we are?" Stacy asked.

"Near Ellesmere," Terra answered and Stacy quickly realized that she did not know why she bothered to ask.

She looked back at the plane; Nicholas had not torn his eyes from it. Finally, it started to creak and the door pushed open—three men filed out. Tom and Terra looked over, abandoning the fire they had been trying to make.

"Nicholas, take over the fire," Tom said it as an order. "We will take care of them."

Stacy began to protest, but she looked back at Rachael, shuddered, and quickly helped Nicholas. She mimicked everything he did, remembering everything he taught her until a fire sparked. They pushed Rachael as close as they could until her teeth stopped chattering and her bluing color returned to moderately-normal.

"Stacy," Nicholas said as they rubbed sticks. "No matter what happens, I will always be here for you."

Stacy was shaking her head, confused. "I know."

Terra and Tom had approached the men, their heads hung high. "You will leave my family alone. That includes Sir Nicholas."

Arkady busted out into laughter, seemingly uncaring that his two men were covered in blood and hardly conscious. "How very fitting. The great grandson of our greatest traitor brought into another disgraced family."

Stacy and Nicholas both felt their blood boil where they sat.

Tom stepped up, mere inches from Arkady's face. "I'd appreciate you changing your attitude towards my family, Czar." He spat the harsh words through barred teeth.

"No," Arkady hissed back. "I will stick with noting them as the disgrace that they are. The dis...grace." He said the word slowly for emphasis.

"Here's what's going to happen." It was Terra who spoke now, her voice shaking as badly as her hands. "We are going to go home with our family. Once we arrive, we are immediately going to begin an appeal against our granddaughter's banishment and when you deny it, we are going to return home, rejoin the army and take our country back.

"During that time, if you so much as whisper a thought to any of your men about hurting any member of our family, the American military will be pleased to find out that terrorists hijacked one of our planes in Spain in order to enter the country. Do we have an understanding?"

Arkady did not so much as look into Terra's eyes. No, he did not tear his eyes from Tom and Tom did not tear his eyes from Arkady.

Then Arkady swung forward, knocking Tom to the ground.

The fight seemed nearly equal as the men were about the same in age, but Arkady appeared a bit stronger. But in this moment, skill seemed to go entirely out the window and they could have been two school boys fighting over their lunch.

Nicholas came running in, attempting to shield Tom—but he would not put his hands on Arkady.

The Admiral came up from behind, grabbing onto Nicholas and readying to snap his neck.

"NO!" Stacy lunched forward, throwing herself into the battle.

Nicholas, Tom, and Terra both called for her to go back, even Rachael attempted to shout her name.

Terra grabbed her by the arm, bringing her, thrashing and screaming against her hold, back towards the cave.

"Enough!" The Admiral shouted, drawing his sword from his belt.

CHAPTER NINETY-ONE

Nicholas's hand automatically went to his pant leg, but his sword was gone, it had fallen into the sea with the plane. It was no matter, he did not need it…

"NICHOLAS NO!" Tom roared, stopping Nicholas before he could lunge forward.

But he had.

In the same moment, a wave crashed ashore and The Admiral lost his footing. As he stumbled, his sword sliced cleanly through Nicholas's old wound.

Nicholas howled in pain, falling to the ground. Blood spurted out around him in a pool, joining with the sea as it poured and poured.

"NO!" Tom scooped Nicholas into his arms and ran towards the cave. Terra and Rachael were already kicking out the fire, running to the back down the long maze of tunnel. They ran and ran, Tom carrying a howling Nicholas until they found a way to secure themselves behind one of the cave entrances, a stone blocking the path of the three men attacking—but only slightly.

"Tom, what do we do? What do we do?" Terra asked, sobbing as her hands pressed into Nicholas's open wounds. Stacy was next to them, doing anything Terra told her to do to try to cease the sputtering blood.

"Let me think, let me think…" Tom's words were rushed as they left his mouth.

Stacy ran her bloodied hands through Nicholas's hair, trying to comfort him, to ease his unsteady, desperate breathing.

"Please…please…"

"I'm trying, we're trying," she sobbed, looking away as Terra exposed the open the gash. She knew that if the Spirits were not acting to save his life, he would already be gone. She had never gotten this seriously hurt, how much were the Spirits able to do?

"Stacy…"

Terra had forced open Nicholas's closing hands, Stacy immediately pressed her palms into his and let her body run ragged, run on fumes of nothingness, pressing her Spirit into his until she felt him force her away.

"Listen…" He croaked. "We already know," he whispered. "We already planned."

Stacy had fallen to the floor, exhausted from the strain. Cold. "What are you talking about?" Stacy asked slowly.

He reached a shaking hand forward, she met him halfway, their tired and weak bodies connecting at the very tips of their fingers. "I have to go. It is the only way to protect you. It has always been the only way."

"Nicholas, no…What Terra just said. We'll do what Terra just said…we'll do it together…we…not apart…" Stacy tried to argue, but felt herself fading as she did.

"If we stay, he won't give up. He won't back down without a fight. Ever. If I go... he will have a victory and it will buy us time. They are desperate right now. We must give them a piece of a win..."

Stacy looked to her grandparents, desperate and confused, but neither of them argued her case. Neither tried.

"Nicholas..." She felt her heart slipping away, her stomach hollowing out. She could scream, she could cry, she could slaughter the three men herself...But she couldn't. She couldn't do any of those things. She could hardly move.

Stacy's insides were curling. The Dukhovians wanted *her*. Nicholas had already sacrificed his whole life and his entire family because of her, now he was walking into open fire. No, it did not make sense. It simply made no sense.

"We need to give them what they want, my love. But we aren't giving up. We will never give up. I will get to Dukhovia and I will signal to you. I will practice every single day and you will do the same. We will connect to each other and when I have prepared the rebels for your arrival, we will fight for our land. This is just the first step in the process, Stacy Grace. It's just the first step."

She could hardly hear him. She sobbed uncontrollably, Rachael's cold, frail arms holding tight onto her back. "Stacy..."

No. She refused to believe this would be how it would end. So much hope, so much answered just for it all to be ripped away? No. Her mind was a flash of memories, replaying everything he ever said to her, looking for something to save them, to stop him.

"I am so honored to have met the greatest heir Dukhovia has ever known and I am even more honored to love you. Always, my love. Where you go...I go."

"Then I'll go," she sobbed. "I'll go, I'll go."

"Our Spirits are one, Stacy Grace. Our souls. Remember that and you will know that we will never be without each other. You will always be with me."

She tried to protest, but she was so tired, and so weak, and so broken.

"Always with me," he promised. Then he sat up. Blood still dripped from his body and he could hardly stand, but he managed to get to the entrance of the cave just as the last stone blocking them in was knocked away.

She failed.

She failed to protect Nicholas. She failed to protect the heir. The flashes of fire in her dream took over. Taking over the dream, taking over her family, taking over the family she knew and loved.

Stacy held his face; the dried blood caked on so heavily she could hardly feel him. But she held him, she breathed him in. He pushed a loose strand of black hair behind her ear. She shook it free. He laughed a small laugh and kissed her. Fully, closely. The kiss was everything, but it was final. For one more moment they lingered, her soft skin up against his warm lips, then he walked away and the world turned into bitter, icy cold.

CHAPTER 92

GONE

The plane had taken off without so much as an argument. So simple, so quick, yet so permanent. Stacy had lingered for several moments, watching and waiting for the other shoe to drop, for the punchline, for the early April Fools—it never came. The plane did not turn around. It did not come back.

The world did not exist anymore. There was no sunshine, there was no light. Everything that could have been was now nonexistent. Everything that was, was no more.

And none of it made sense. Why did the Spirits even allow any of this to happen? What was the point? For one brief moment, Stacy held all the answers and Dukhovia had a chance. Now…there was nothing. She was back to wondering. Dukhovia so close, yet forever out of reach. The only thing that happened was that Nicholas, the boy horrifically abused his entire life, had a little taste of freedom, a little taste of love, and then he was pulled back to the life he fought like hell to leave. What was the point in that?

They're coming. Protect the heir. Suddenly everything about the dream made sense. It was a warning for them to protect each other from this eminent doom. She had all the warning in the world. She still failed.

Shortly after the badly damaged plane rattled away, likely towards a perfectly fine aircraft on the flatter side of the mountain, the planes attempting to search for The Heart of America arrived. They rushed Rachael to warmth and safety and collected as much information as they could from Tom and Terra—who lied better than they ever had before.

So close. So close to having so much back up. The police had come, several additional flights. Yet he was gone, just like that.

No one tried to change his mind or go after him. Stacy had lost so much energy saving Nicholas that she could hardly move. And then it was too late and she was back and she was home and now…nothing.

And so all that was left—was realization. The realization that she would not go to Dukhovia and save the country that was in a brutal and irrelevant fight. She would not stop the war, or save a single life. And her and Nicholas would never be together. She could hardly even bet on him making it to Dukhovia alive.

But she would wait. Every single day she would wait for that tug on her Spirit telling her Nicholas was knocking and that it was time. As hopeless as she felt, she did keep an ounce of it somewhere in the back of her mind, locked into a drawer and shoved in the corner with a blanket over it. Maybe she would get the signal and they would go to Dukhovia. Maybe.

"Hey, where have you been?" It was Grace's voice that asked the question Stacy thought would send her emotions spiraling out of control. She expected herself to breakdown, expected an endless fit of tears that she was too wild to tame.

Stacy looked up with a blank stare. No emotion came out because there was nothing left to feel, nothing *worth* feeling. She had experienced everything in the last month: happiness, fulfillment, love, purpose...Everything had been extinguished and exhausted.

Grace took in Stacy's rough condition: dirty clothes and tear-stricken face. "Baby girl, what happened?" She jumped up and went over to her daughter, throwing her arms around her.

"He's gone," she mustered up and then came the breakdown...It happened when she was told it was okay when she knew it would not be. When she had to say the words that meant so much more than saying goodbye to a new friend. The words that meant she had lost herself and abandoned Dukhovia once again.

Grace did not say a thing. Her response was silent and comforting. She held Stacy tight and kissed her head. She walked her over into the living room and sat down with her on the couch as she cried and cried...and cried some more.

Terra and Tom called several times. Grace ignored every ring.

The room spun with every passing moment.

Stacy fell silent.

Then, she would close her eyes. Images of the brave and majestic waters flowed down over a lush, green mountainside.

A tear rolled down Stacy's face.

Then, she would close her eyes. And that same mountainside burst into flames, throwing her and Nicholas into a dark oblivion countless times until she was unable to picture the mountainside at all and all she saw was the dark, emptiness of fallen ash.

The same. Everything the same.

CHAPTER 93

A NEW DAWN

Time passed through the night in a haze. Eventually, Stacy's tears dried and she was nothing but a motionless, empty structure of molecules. Everything made matters worse. The ticking of the clock, promising her that time was still moving and that while she sat, Nicholas's end was drawing nearer. If not from his wounds, then from his captors. The setting sun and rising moon, beckoning her to take action, to make a move that was long past permissible.

"Are you hungry?" Grace asked softly. She brushed Stacy's hair out of her eyes as she stared blankly at the TV.

"No."

"You should have something to drink."

Grace handed Stacy the cup of cool, ice water in hesitation.

She waved it away.

At some point, the point where Stacy no longer kept Grace in arms reach, her mother did answer phone calls.

Phone calls from Tom and Terra.

Phone calls from her uncle.

Phone calls from her friends.

Stacy overheard her talking with Terra about how the Dukhovian's did in fact hijack their plane and how security measures should have never let another plane leave their airport. But fear.

Stacy tensed when she heard Terra explain that there was a traitor here in town that allowed them access to the choppers they had in the field. Tensed, but wondered if there was truly much else she could lose.

She was dead to Nicholas. She was dead to Dukhovia and dead to her purpose. Her country.

At half-past nine, a frail knock rapped at the door, followed by the flinging open of the grand oak and the slamming against its hinges. Rachael raced across the foyer, then, catching sight of Stacy, walked slowly into the living room.

"Hi," Stacy managed.

"Hey," Rachel smiled. She sat down near Stacy and pulled her head into her lap, stroking her hair the way Grace had.

Stacy caught sight of the hand she was using and grabbed it. "No more cast."

Rachael frowned. "Yeah, Terra took it off this morning. You should have seen Cody, he was frantic." Rachael laughed, but stopped herself.

"It's okay," Stacy told her. "He loves you, you know. He really does."

Rachael's fingers twitched for a moment in Stacy's hair. A teary smile crossed Rachael's face. "We're just friends," she said in a non-convincing voice. "That's all we'll ever need to be."

Rachael scooched away from Stacy and helped her sit up. "So, what happens next?"

Stacy shrugged. "Nicholas said that as long as The Dukhovians have him, that I'll be safe. That that's all they need. But how does that make sense: the whole point of coming here was for me and they just left me like they realized I was fool's gold."

Rachael could not stop the slight smile at the term Stacy picked up from her one and only passed social studies exam. But, the thickness in her best friend's voice resonated with her more than anything.

"Well, Nicholas said the Shaman's predictions were everchanging, right? Maybe you aren't an heir anymore, maybe you have a different purpose now. And maybe his connections allowed him to see that."

Stacy looked up, shocked. The idea had not occurred to her. "No," she stammered. "It's Dukhovia, it will always be Dukhovia."

Rachael smiled, holding her friend's hand. "I never said whatever this new purpose might be didn't have to do with Dukhovia."

Stacy looked into her eyes, letting their calm become her calm. Then she remembered what she had told Nicholas, that his purpose would not make him miserable. The same was true for herself—if being an heir fulfilled her, then an heir she would be. If not, if being one made her lose her mind, then... The Spirits wouldn't do that.

"Anyway, maybe it's just an interim purpose," Rachael theorized. "While we figure things out."

Stacy nodded her head slowly, up and down, then jolted up. "We?"

Rachael flipped her hair and sneered. "Oh please, I know you don't think we're all about to let you figure out how to save Nicholas and Dukhovia alone." Rachael winked and glanced partially into the foyer where Cody, Dan, Miranda, Jade, Cara, Dylan, Andy, Joey, Jimmy, and Jamie all stood.

"I can put college off for a year," Dan offered, leading the gang into the living room.

Stacy sat up, her heart allowing something comforting and warm to seep inside and expand to her body...joy.

"Do that and I'll never forgive you," Stacy replied, hugging her brother. "Harvard, here you come."

"Actually," he began, scratching the back of his neck. "The University of Bucharest in Romania offered me the ability to do a duel masters/bachelor's degree in computer science and molecular biology while still maintaining leadership over the band."

"You're going to dictate us from abroad?" Stacy asked quietly, envying her brother with a twinkle in her eye.

"I'll be able to do a semester there and a semester here. I'll alternate. Plus, MIT had such great things to say about my externship that Bucharest already promised to put me in one of their top-secret military operations studying the effects of biomolecular growth."

"Hm. Well, we won't tell you just let that slip to a room of eleven other people and you might still have a fighting chance."

Dan and Stacy smiled at each other, conveying words they had not exchanged in quite some time and were long overdue for. It was a message of understanding, of appreciation, of well wishes even in times that seemed utterly wrought.

The rest of her friends burst into laughter and the jokes began.

I wouldn't join the FBI anytime soon, Danny Boy.

Are they gonna be after you now? Should we alert the Witness Protection Program?

No, they're probably in on it too, it's up to us to keep him safe.

Stacy glanced from friend to friend, each face, each strength and personality. It was true, what they had always said… She truly was the luckiest girl in the world. A number of friends surrounded her. A tight knit family that she suddenly understood why her mother took so much pride in. Nothing was promised. Not even family. And everything had to do with timing. It made her stomach weak, but it also gave her hope.

And so maybe. Maybe she could not rule Dukhovia now—but she would someday. She could not save Dukhovia now—but someday the war would end. And she could not help a single Dukhovian, but she could help her friends. She could help Americans. Afterall, that was Dukhovia's goal. To shift the world back to harmony, not just Dukhovia.

CHAPTER 94

SURVIVAL

Stacy tried to consider Rachael's words, to search for a new purpose. But the nights once filled with commands to protect the heir were now filled with her screams when she awoke from visions of Nicholas being beaten brutally to death.

They were filled with pain. They were filled with weakness.

The more time that passed by without hearing from him, the more she was forced to accept the undeniable truth that by this time, he would be dead and long forgotten by anyone on Dukhovian soil...

The less Stacy was reminded of the wondrous land, the more she felt it slipping from her memory. Nothing was around to remind her of it, no one was up for talking about it. They thought it would upset her, they thought it was detrimental to her wellbeing. And it made her feel invisible.

People acted like what they said around her had to be monitored. As if mention of the word "Dukhovia" or anything in the Russian language would send her packing her bags, catching the first flight east. Nothing was normal anymore. Not even the feeling in her stomach that now caused her to fall to her knees in the hallway in agony.

Stacy sat by her flag every day, trying to hold onto the connection she once felt. But, the promise of answers that existed when Nicholas was here now seemed like a distant dream that she would never fall back asleep to. She wore the necklace she previously ridiculed with honor, a visible reminder that she could take Dukhovia with her everywhere she went. But a reminder that did not make the churning of her stomach and the pounding of her head disappear...

...

"Are you ready to practice?" Rachael was at Stacy's bathroom door, a forced smile on her face...the same forced smile everyone used now.

"Hm," Stacy grunted in response, sticking her toothbrush in her mouth. She could hear the strumming of her guitar as Dan tuned it. Rachael's drums were singing a *rap, tap, rap, tap* pattern that used to bring her peace and excitement.

Rachael had to get her out of bed this morning. Stacy had stayed home the last couple days of school and Dan was lenient on letting her sit out of practice for the first few days, but he was not allowing it to happen again. Stacy appreciated that, it made her feel human.

Stacy brushed her teeth weakly. She doubted the attempt was even effective for one aspect of its purpose let alone the entirety. She leaned her head back to gargle, an ache overtaking her arms as she steadied herself against the sink, the cool taste of metal inhabiting her mouth.

Her spit released, taking a portion of blood out with it.

Stacy grabbed a piece of toilet paper and blotted at her gums, heading down to the basement for practice. She was playing a new song for them today and hoping they liked it as they told her to "rework" the last seven of the like.

Ah Ah Ah Ah
Ah Ah Ah AH
Ah Ah AH AH
Ah AH AH AH
I can feel you,
All around me
Life is for me
No one's against me.
Ah da da da da
Da da dee dum
Da da da da
Da da dee dum
Ooo Ooo
Ooo Ooo
Ooo Ooo
Ooo Ooo
I can see it falling to pieces
Mm Mm hm hm Mm hm hm
Mm Mm hm hm Mm Mm hm hm
Life unclear, now
Path stuck on rewind
If life itself is against me
Who is with me?
La dee dee dum
La dee dee do
La dee dee dum
La dee dee doom
Where'd you go?
My shield of protection?
Where did you go?
I cannot feel you.
La Di di di
What's life without you?
La di di di
La do do do
All that's left to do is sur-vive

SURVIVAL

La di la di la di la dum
La di la di la di la dum
All we do these unclear moments
Is survive.
All we do these precious moments
Is survive.
Survive.
All we do these unkind moments
Is survive.
I can see it falling to pieces.
Through this tragedy let's
Disappear.

Stacy dropped her guitar to the ground under the weight of her aching fingers. Her friends gave a mix of confused and understanding looks. Stacy refrained from understanding, but she knew what was happening. She could feel the Spirits leaving her body, abandoning her just like she abandoned Dukhovia, abandoned Nicholas. Time deserved to come to a close for her, it was what she expected. But what she did not know, was that this was only the beginning.

CHAPTER 95

IT'S OVER

Spells of dizziness and jitters of shaking continued to tear down everything that once made Stacy the luckiest girl in the world. Practice and school became harder and harder to get through without having to sit down or request a nap. Her body was trying to fight whatever this was, but her body was not winning.

"You should really go to the hospital," Rachael would tell her. All her friends would tell her.

"And what? Get the utmost pleasure of Mr. and Mrs. Thomas Grayson bickering in my ear about self-help? No thanks."

The truth was she did *want* to go to the doctors on most days. She wanted to give her grandparents the proper chance to look her over. She knew that in a heartbeat they would be able to cure her. They were the greatest doctors and scientists in the world. But she also knew that whatever was going on was likely due to her Spirit. Perhaps because she was so lost, perhaps because a large piece of it, the piece that was Nicholas, was now gone… Whatever the answer was, she could not bear to hear it. And anyway, she was just…so, so tired…

And the pain was just too, too much…

And there was the medicine cabinet with the medicine, which was much closer than the hospital, or even the car for that matter.

***

"Stacy, Stacy, my love, are you feeling better?"

Grace came into the room an hour later. She shook Stacy's shoulder and panic filled her body.

"DAN!" Grace called, throwing her grading book down and putting her arms around Stacy, pulling her up. "DAN!"

Dan came running in. "What is it, mom?"

"Stacy isn't waking up. I'm bringing her to the hospital. Call your grandparents and have them meet us at the door, okay?"

"Su…" Dan stopped, worried by his mother's frantic face. It was now becoming clear what was happening to his sister.

"What?" Grace asked for clarification.

"Uh…nothing," Dan stammered. "Sure."

Grace kissed Dan and ran out of the house, leaving Dan frozen. He could not recall a conversation with his mother that did not consist of some type of slang language and a joke…until now. And since when did he have *grandparents*?

CHAPTER NINETY-FIVE

Minutes later, Grace and Dan were rushing Stacy to the front of the hospital where Tom and Terra were waiting with a gurney. They raced her down the hall, into room after room, running test after test.

Grace took matters into her own hands, collecting a sample of her blood to run her own tests on once Kevin arrived. They arrived at no answers other than Stacy was in a deep, deep sleep.

"How is she?" Cara asked Dan, later that night.

"Not good. Terra and Tom ran some blood tests, but we haven't heard anything. She's been asleep for six hours now."

Grace squeezed Stacy's hand, refusing to leave her side for anything.

Rachael stood silent in the far corner of the room. She was listening intently and trying to understand what was happening, trying to understand how someone who was so healthy and so unbreakable for sixteen years could suddenly be so helpless and broken. And she could not help but suspect it had everything to do with Nicholas.

***

"Dan?" Stacy's head rose up in a confused daze, early that next morning. She was in a hospital room surrounded by a sea of flowers, cards, and her favorite European chocolates. *Rachael.*

"Sweetheart..." Grace jolted up, gripping tightly onto Stacy's hand.

Dan smiled at the sound of his sister's voice. He tapped Kevin's elbow, who sat up immediately and leaned towards Stacy with a smile.

Stacy rubbed her face tiredly and looked at the clocks, but forgot the time she fell asleep to begin with. It seemed she completely forgot how to tell time. She kicked the blanket that was covering her off the edge of the couch and sat up. "How long was I asleep?"

"About fifteen hours," Dan answered hesitantly. He quickly tried to change the subject. "Look, Stacy, everyone stopped by and brought these things for you." He picked up a heart shaped chocolate box from Andy.

Stacy muttered something in Russian annoyed at Dan's decision to always change the subject in bad situations. Dan did not speak the language, so he just remained quiet, but he sensed her frustration.

"What's wrong with me?" She asked.

"We don't know yet," Kevin answered. "But we're going to find out. We won't let anything happen to you."

Stacy sat back. Kevin was making promises. She remembered promises she made and promises that were made to her. All broken. Everything was broken.

"Everything is fine," Dan said hesitantly. He could no longer bring himself to look at her. "You're going to be alright."

A flash of anger shot across Stacy's face as she whipped her neck around. "No Dan, everything is not fine. I AM NOT GOING TO BE ALRIGHT! I'VE NEVER

BEEN SICK A DAY IN MY LIFE AND NOW I'M SICKER THAN EVER! THERE IS NO ONE PROTECTING ME ANYMORE! THERE IS NO BEING ALRIGHT!" She stopped yelling and breathed heavily, tears pulling at her eyes. She grabbed at her throat, gasping for breath. "I'm not going to die, Dan... I am not going to...I'M NOT!" Stacy held her head and tried to calm down, but she had lost control of her body. Her head was swirling at top speed as if on a merry-go-round that had gone off the tracks. So many things were moving together at once that she could not take it...her eyes closed and she fell towards the floor.

"STACY!" Dan reacted quickly, his eyes bulging from his head as he and Kevin caught her in their arms.

Grace was on her feet in a heartbeat, steadying her back to the bed.

Dan's ears tuned out the sound of the uneven beeping of the machine behind him and slammed on his sister's chest with his hands. Kevin pulled him back in a frenzy, Grace screamed for her father.

"Daddy!"

Tom ran into the room, Terra accompanying him.

Stacy's eyes zoomed open only for a second. She reached towards Dan, grasping at her lungs.

"Come on, Stacy, come back! Come back!" Dan cradled her in his arms. "Stacy..."

Terra and Tom glanced at each other. Tom nodded and withdrew a small, glass tube from his pocket. He immediately inserted the clear liquid into one of Stacy's IVs.

"She's stabilizing," a nurse stated.

Dan caught his breath, then, a flashing light outside the window caught his attention. He raced over and looked down. It was only a matter of time before the media caught on to Stacy's illness.

"Mom, what was that?" Grace asked, warily.

Terra did not answer. She furrowed her brows and pursed her lips. "Just a medicine, darling. We'll see if it helps and administer more if needed. We'll send a specialist in momentarily."

Grace gave her a dirty look and flew through the door after her. Why on *Earth* was she being so secretive? Why was she being so *formal*? This was her daughter. *Her* daughter. She had every right to know what was happening.

"Mom, what the hell was that?" Grace shot.

Terra closed her eyes, anticipating the reaction.

"Hello, Dr. Grayson."

Terra turned her direction away from Grace and to the new, tall, dark-skinned gentlemen who just approached her. Terra smiled. "Grace, this is Dr. Fuglemen. Dr. Fuglemen, my daughter, Grace. Grace, Dr. Fuglemen is a highly trained and sought after specialist that we often use in our hospital."

Grace continued to stab her mother with eyes of deceit. "What kind of specialist?" Grace demanded.

Kevin walked out of the room, hearing the uproar.

Terra nodded for everyone to follow her into a conference room where they took their seats around a long, unforgettable table, and stared at a screen showing images of Stacy's body, Stacy's cells, and confirming Stacy's future.

The doctor's discussed what was found and repeated how, not wanting the results to be true, they drew more blood, more marrow, and ran even more tests. They discussed other possibilities, causes, why what they were seeing could not be true…and why what they were seeing had to be the truth.

Grace caught on first, falling into Kevin's chest. Her sobs soaked him instantly. She stood and paced the room a few times before falling back to the floor, reaching for Kevin's hand, hugging his leg…

It did not take everyone else long to figure out what was happening, and their reactions were to be expected: tears, shock, absolute silence…

No one could believe it. How could it have happened? The doctor said they were unsure how this specific illness rooted, but the few ideas they did have did not matter now.

None of it made sense and disagreement still hung in the air, with Tom even refusing to document it as her official diagnosis. But for now- it was true. It was fact, even if it seemed such an impossible question to ask let alone answer. How was it possible? How could Stacy Grace Matthews, the luckiest girl in the world, have cancer?

CHAPTER 96

A WAR TO LIVE

$\mathcal{T}$he doctor and nurse offered a support team to help the family with this grievance. They also suggested they tell Stacy in order for her to be more accepting of the diagnosis and treatment. Grace, however, did not wish to tell her right away. She did not want to tell her until absolutely necessary. She wanted Stacy to hold onto her hope. As did Grace herself, despite knowing the secret could not remain…

June was in full swing now. The summer heat helped keep Stacy warm and she spent a lot of time out in the sun. Today was an important day, however, and she only got to spend so much time outside before being ushered upstairs to change into the new, floral dress her mother had chosen for her.

Stacy put the dress on with ease and, taking an extra moment to sit before making the journey, traveled down the stairs to her brother's room where he was standing in front of the mirror, straightening his tie in his cap and gown. His gold cords and red and black sash were strung around his door knob, anxiously awaiting their placement.

"Wow, look how handsome we are this evening," Stacy complimented in a hoarse voice.

Dan turned around, surprised. "Stacy." He abandoned his tie and ushered his sister over to his bed. "Sit down, you shouldn't be up wandering."

Stacy took his arms and stopped him before he made it all the way over to his bed. "Now, now, you can't give your valedictorian speech looking like you didn't even pass Tie Tying 101. Is that what you'd call it? Tie tying? Ha. Who names these things?"

Dan ceased movement and allowed Stacy to fix his tie and straighten his hair for him. He watched as her shaking hands smoothed his gown out.

"Remember when we were kids and you wanted to be a doctor like Tom and Terra?" Stacy asked, fumbling with the tie.

Dan laughed loudly. "I insisted you needed surgery on your stubbed toe and threatened to tell Uncle Richey if mom and dad didn't take you to the hospital."

"And I vowed to follow in Aunt Terra's footsteps and become a lawyer if the surgery threatened my career as a dancer."

Both laughed at the memory.

"I guess it wasn't my calling," he admitted, sheepishly.

CHAPTER NINETY-SIX

Stacy ignored the comment. "Now look at you. All grown up, knowledgeable about the uses of peroxide and Neosporin and headed off to change science one country at a time."

"I'll come back anytime you need to bandage that toe up," Dan promised.

Stacy smiled. "I'm gonna hold you to that." She extended her arm behind the door and grabbed onto his cords and sash.

She draped his gold cords around his shoulders, trying to move quickly so that he did not notice her shaking body. "Hold on to your wedding invites, ladies and gentlemen, this stud won't stay single long." Stacy laughed.

Dan smiled, this time sitting on his bed himself so that she would follow. She was too smart for that trick.

Stacy pressed her hand against her brother's shoulder for one split, comforting second. "I'm so proud of you, big brother."

Dan nodded, at a loss for words. Stacy patted his shoulder and started heading for the door.

Dan watched her walk. Her *walk*. He could not remember ever seeing her do anything other than a run, hop, or at the very least, a skip. Now she shifted one leg after the other as though she could barely stand the idea of movement.

"Stacy."

She turned around, a smile on her face.

"I just wanted to let you know I love you," he said, in a shaking voice. "And you're the best sister in the world."

Silence fell on the both of them.

"You're going to do great things someday too. You know that, don't you?"

Stacy kept her prim and proper smile plastered on her face and shrugged. "I guess we'll see, won't we?"

The four got into Grace's truck and made the trip to the school. Grace helped Stacy climb onto the second row of the bleachers, which they—unbeknownst to Stacy—reserved for her convenience.

The gymnasium was decorated in celebrative black and red ribbon, packed wall to wall with students who had their whole futures ahead of them. Some knowing their paths, others not, but all having the chance for something...

Dan was at the top of those students, academically. It showed. He was aware that he had an abundance of knowledge, stored and filed away at his very fingertips. The other students knew it as well. They knew where to go when they needed that knowledge just as much as where they needed to go for the newest sports update.

Stacy stood to her feet at the conclusion of Dan's speech, clapping and beaming louder than anyone in the crowd. He was so strong, proud, and focused. He had every right to be.

Dan met Stacy's eyes and winked, giving her a thumbs up. Stacy returned the gesture, then automatically reached up to her head as she felt a dizzy spell come on. She knew she had to sit, but it was too late, she was passed that. The room was spinning, her stomach felt sick.

Stacy felt around for her mother's arm, but could not latch onto it. Stacy's eye stayed glued on Dan, his lips mouthing her name, his vocals expelling it at top volume.

Grace and Kevin both were at Stacy's side, then Tom and Terra were carrying her out.

No...Dan. Dan.

Stacy was not sure if the words were actually leaving her mouth or if she was just thinking them. Everything was moving so fast. Everything was happening so quickly.

"Mom..." She felt the word leave her lips that time, she knew it did. The word was comfort on her lips, it fulfilled her...

"Shh, baby..." Grace held her little girl close, unable to face what might happen next. She was terrified. Sixteen years. Grace had her little girl for sixteen years and she only knew her for fourteen of those. Years of perfection Years of togetherness. Years of perfect, close family bliss.

Stacy felt her body hit the grass, rain trickled down onto her face from the tree tops above her. The school was filing out to watch the scene unfold. Stacy did not even care. If the graduation paused, good. She did not want Dan's graduation to go missed.

"Now."

Stacy heard the word, but did not know what Tom...or Terra...did. Suddenly, air was pulsing through her lungs and she was gasping, sitting up beneath the trees.

"Mom," Stacy cried, falling into her arms.

"Oh, Stacy." Grace held Stacy close, two arms around her, making no plan to ever release her grasp.

Stacy panted in the heat of the summer's day, glancing up, expecting to be looking out at a sea of curious eyes. Instead, it was just her mother. They were no longer at the front of the school, but a grassy patch behind the baseball fields, where the sun refused to shine and the air hung thick with moisture.

"Mom." Stacy's voice was weak. "What's wrong with me?"

Grace wrapped her arm around Stacy's head that lay in her lap and brushed back her hair. The back of Grace's hand felt Stacy's cheek, hot with frustration. She looked out at the grass and took a deep breathe. "You have leukemia, cancer, sweetheart."

"What?" Stacy jolted out of her mother's lap, eyes a dead latch on her identical pair. Her eyes disproved nothing, but confirmed every fear skirting across Stacy's mind, building, fighting for a position to be top priority. "No..."

CHAPTER NINETY-SIX

Stacy jumped to her feet, her mind foggy with the feeling of deceit. "No!" How could they do this? How could the Spirits abandon her this much? They were just done with her, just like that? They barely even gave her the chance to redeem herself before tossing her away.

Stacy grabbed onto a tree branch and snapped it from its trunk. She flung it into another tree, beating each branch, stick, and root that dared expose itself to her tirade.

"HOW COULD THEY! HOW COULD THEY DO THIS TO ME!"

She hurled the massive tree branch across a field of smaller trees, shattering them limb by limb. Sticks and bark fell down around her, scratching at her wrists and legs, destroying the perfect, lilac sundress.

Stacy fell back in tears, but not due to the jabbing pain on her wrists where the shards of tree and stone had pierced her or even from the excruciating pain coming from her stomach. Those were a bee sting compared to what she felt.

How could she be so stupid? To think that she had a chance? She would never rule Dukhovia, she would never even make it there. She had one of the worst diseases known to humanity. There was no cure. Sure, sometimes people got better…but she had her luck. The Spirits were done with her. Now she would truly be abandoning all of Dukhovia. She was abandoning everyone.

No weddings. No births. No being queen, or czar, or figuring out what type of governmental system Dukhovia even had.

It would become decided that she would live her life as it had been to best her ability. She would play the best she could, she would exist with her friends and family the best she could. But nothing would ever come of it. Perhaps that was not so different than her life cancer free.

Gray. It was the only word that came to mind as she tried to process what her life meant to her. It was not black. It was not white.

Her life had been glamour and joy. It had been luck and love. It had been victory.

But it had also been struggle. It had been confusion and chaos. And isolation. It had been a battle. After battle. After battle.

Perhaps that was her new purpose, that was what her life would be. Perhaps that was what life was for everyone: victory and battle, making it through the turmoil that leads to your purpose, your destiny. Maybe, after all, life is just one big war to reach your destiny.

Well, if that was the case, then bring on the war.

About the Author

Sarah Lindsay Peterson was born and raised in Youngstown, OH, where she began writing at a young age. Inspired by life's many trials, Sarah saw writing as an outlet from reality and a means to create a new world. Sarah's hope is that her book's ideals spread, inspiring grace for humanity across the world. A War Through Destiny was first written when Sarah was eleven-years-old in the fifth grade. It is now being published nearly twenty years (and just as many rewrites) later, the summer after Sarah's daughter finished the fifth grade. Originally writing both a prequel to the series and nine other books to follow AWTD, Sarah plans to continue to write until the story of her characters (or friends) is fully told

About the Illustrator

Amanda Huk began her journey as a fantasy artist just a few years ago. Her first painting was inspired by a book, and it will not be her last. Her work creates immersive, thoughtfully crafted worlds that invite viewers to slow down, look closer, and step into something entirely new. With a focus on detail and atmosphere, she brings stories and characters to life through art in the most enchanting way.

About the Illustrator

Elijah Coker designed and created the drawings of Stacy and Nicholas found at the front of this book. Elijah's inspiration to draw came from observing character art by Square Enix for games such as Final Fantasy and Kingdom Hearts. Though AWTD wasn't specifically created as an anime, with little information about the characters, Sarah Lindsay Peterson felt Elijah read her mind and was able to use his unique and incredible skillset in order to put on paper what had, for twenty years prior, only existed in Sarah's mind.